I0784273

Bram Stoker

Occult & Supernatural Tales

OK Publishing 2021

Bram Stoker

The Greatest Occult & Supernatural Tales of Bram Stoker

Including Gothic Horror Classics & Dark Fantasy Collections

Published by

Books

- Advanced Digital Solutions & High-Quality book Formatting -

musaicumbooks@okpublishing.info

2021 OK Publishing

ISBN 978-80-272-7836-7

Contents

Dracula's Guest	13
The Judge's House	21
The Squaw	31
The Secret of the Growing Gold	39
The Gipsy Prophecy	47
The Coming of Abel Behenna	53
The Burial of the Rats	63
A Dream of Red Hands	77
Crooken Sands	83
The Occasion	95
A Lesson in Pets	99
Coggins's Property	105
The Slim Syrens	109
A New Departure in Art	113
Mick the Devil	119
In Fear of Death	123
At Last	129
Chin Music	133
A Deputy Waiter	137
Work'us	143
A Corner in Dwarfs	147
A Criminal Star	151
A Star Trap	157
A Moon-Light Effect	163
Under the Sunset	171
The Rose Prince	175
The Invisible Giant	185
The Shadow Builder	193
How 7 Went Mad	199
Lies and Lilies	207
The Castle of the King	211
The Wondrous Child	219
The Red Stockade	229
The Dualists	237
Bis Dat Qui Non Cito Dat	238
Halcyon Days	239
Rumours of War	240

The Tucket Sounds 241

The First Crusade 242

'Let the Dead Past Bury It's Dead' 244

A Cloud with Golden Lining 245

The Crystal Cup 249

I. The Dream-Birth 250

II. The Feast of Beauty 253

III. The Story of the Moonbeam 256

Buried Treasures 259

Chapter I - The Old Wreck 260

Chapter II - Wind and Tide 263

Chapter III - The Iron Chest 265

Chapter IV - Lost and Found 268

The Chain of Destiny 271

I. A Warning 272

II. More Links 277

III. The Third To-morrow 282

IV. Afterwards 290

Our New House 297

The Man from Shorrox' 303

A Yellow Duster 311

The 'Eroes of the Thames 315

The Way of Peace 319

Greater Love 323

Lord Castleton Explains 331

The Seer 335

CHAPTER I. Second Sight 336

CHAPTER II. Gormala 339

Midnight Tales 343

The Funeral Party 344

The Shakespeare Mystery 345

A Deal With the Devil 346

Dracula's Guest

When we started for our drive the sun was shining brightly on Munich, and the air was full of the joyousness of early summer. Just as we were about to depart, Herr Delbrück (the maître d'hôtel of the Quatre Saisons, where I was staying) came down, bareheaded, to the carriage and, after wishing me a pleasant drive, said to the coachman, still holding his hand on the handle of the carriage door:

'Remember you are back by nightfall. The sky looks bright but there is a shiver in the north wind that says there may be a sudden storm. But I am sure you will not be late.' Here he smiled, and added, 'for you know what night it is.'

Johann answered with an emphatic, 'Ja, mein Herr,' and, touching his hat, drove off quickly. When we had cleared the town, I said, after signalling to him to stop:

'Tell me, Johann, what is tonight?'

He crossed himself, as he answered laconically: 'Walpurgis nacht.' Then he took out his watch, a great, old-fashioned German silver thing as big as a turnip, and looked at it, with his eyebrows gathered together and a little impatient shrug of his shoulders. I realised that this was his way of respectfully protesting against the unnecessary delay, and sank back in the carriage, merely motioning him to proceed. He started off rapidly, as if to make up for lost time. Every now and then the horses seemed to throw up their heads and sniffed the air suspiciously. On such occasions I often looked round in alarm. The road was pretty bleak, for we were traversing a sort of high, wind-swept plateau. As we drove, I saw a road that looked but little used, and which seemed to dip through a little, winding valley. It looked so inviting that, even at the risk of offending him, I called Johann to stop-and when he had pulled up, I told him I would like to drive down that road. He made all sorts of excuses, and frequently crossed himself as he spoke. This somewhat piqued my curiosity, so I asked him various questions. He answered fencingly, and repeatedly looked at his watch in protest. Finally I said:

'Well, Johann, I want to go down this road. I shall not ask you to come unless you like; but tell me why you do not like to go, that is all I ask.' For answer he seemed to throw himself off the box, so quickly did he reach the ground. Then he stretched out his hands appealingly to me, and implored me not to go. There was just enough of English mixed with the German for me to understand the drift of his talk. He seemed always just about to tell me something-the very idea of which evidently frightened him; but each time he pulled himself up, saying, as he crossed himself: 'Walpurgis-Nacht!'

I tried to argue with him, but it was difficult to argue with a man when I did not know his language. The advantage certainly rested with him, for although he began to speak in English, of a very crude and broken kind, he always got excited and broke into his native tongue-and every time he did so, he looked at his watch. Then the horses became restless and sniffed the air. At this he grew very pale, and, looking around in a frightened way, he suddenly jumped forward, took them by the bridles and led them on some twenty feet. I followed, and asked why he had done this. For answer he crossed himself, pointed to the spot we had left and drew his carriage in the direction of the other road, indicating a cross, and said, first in German, then in English: 'Buried him-him what killed themselves.'

I remembered the old custom of burying suicides at cross-roads: 'Ah! I see, a suicide. How interesting!' But for the life of me I could not make out why the horses were frightened.

Whilst we were talking, we heard a sort of sound between a yelp and a bark. It was far away; but the horses got very restless, and it took Johann all his time to quiet them. He was pale, and said, 'It sounds like a wolf-but yet there are no wolves here now.'

'No?' I said, questioning him; 'isn't it long since the wolves were so near the city?'

'Long, long,' he answered, 'in the spring and summer; but with the snow the wolves have been here not so long.'

Whilst he was petting the horses and trying to quiet them, dark clouds drifted rapidly across the sky. The sunshine passed away, and a breath of cold wind seemed to drift past us. It was only a breath, however, and more in the nature of a warning than a fact, for the sun came out brightly again. Johann looked under his lifted hand at the horizon and said:

'The storm of snow, he comes before long time.' Then he looked at his watch again, and, straightway holding his reins firmly-for the horses were still pawing the ground restlessly and shaking their heads-he climbed to his box as though the time had come for proceeding on our journey.

I felt a little obstinate and did not at once get into the carriage.

'Tell me,' I said, 'about this place where the road leads,' and I pointed down.

Again he crossed himself and mumbled a prayer, before he answered, 'It is unholy.'

'What is unholy?' I enquired.

'The village.'

'Then there is a village?'

'No, no. No one lives there hundreds of years.' My curiosity was piqued, 'But you said there was a village.'

'There was.'

'Where is it now?'

Whereupon he burst out into a long story in German and English, so mixed up that I could not quite understand exactly what he said, but roughly I gathered that long ago, hundreds of years, men had died there and been buried in their graves; and sounds were heard under the clay, and when the graves were opened, men and women were found rosy with life, and their mouths red with blood. And so, in haste to save their lives (aye, and their souls! —and here he crossed himself) those who were left fled away to other places, where the living lived, and the dead were dead and not-not something. He was evidently afraid to speak the last words. As he proceeded with his narration, he grew more and more excited. It seemed as if his imagination had got hold of him, and he ended in a perfect paroxysm of fear-white-faced, perspiring, trembling and looking round him, as if expecting that some dreadful presence would manifest itself there in the bright sunshine on the open plain. Finally, in an agony of desperation, he cried:

'Walpurgis nacht!' and pointed to the carriage for me to get in. All my English blood rose at this, and, standing back, I said:

'You are afraid, Johann-you are afraid. Go home; I shall return alone; the walk will do me good.' The carriage door was open. I took from the seat my oak walking-stick —which I always carry on my holiday excursions-and closed the door, pointing back to Munich, and said, 'Go home, Johann-Walpurgis-nacht doesn't concern Englishmen.'

The horses were now more restive than ever, and Johann was trying to hold them in, while excitedly imploring me not to do anything so foolish. I pitied the poor fellow, he was deeply in earnest; but all the same I could not help laughing. His English was quite gone now. In his anxiety he had forgotten that his only means of making me understand was to talk my language, so he jabbered away in his native German. It began to be a little tedious. After giving the direction, 'Home!' I turned to go down the cross-road into the valley.

With a despairing gesture, Johann turned his horses towards Munich. I leaned on my stick and looked after him. He went slowly along the road for a while: then there came over the crest of the hill a man tall and thin. I could see so much in the distance. When he drew near the horses, they began to jump and kick about, then to scream with terror. Johann could not hold them in; they bolted down the road, running away madly. I watched them out of sight, then looked for the stranger, but I found that he, too, was gone.

With a light heart I turned down the side road through the deepening valley to which Johann had objected. There was not the slightest reason, that I could see, for his objection; and I daresay I tramped for a couple of hours without thinking of time or distance, and certainly without seeing a person or a house. So far as the place was concerned, it was desolation itself. But I did not notice this particularly till, on turning a bend in the road, I came upon a scattered fringe of wood; then I recognised that I had been impressed unconsciously by the desolation of the region through which I had passed.

I sat down to rest myself, and began to look around. It struck me that it was considerably colder than it had been at the commencement of my walk —a sort of sighing sound seemed to be around me, with, now and then, high overhead, a sort of muffled roar. Looking upwards I noticed that great thick clouds were drifting rapidly across the sky from North to South at a great height. There were signs of coming storm in some lofty stratum of the air. I was a little chilly, and, thinking that it was the sitting still after the exercise of walking, I resumed my journey.

The ground I passed over was now much more picturesque. There were no striking objects that the eye might single out; but in all there was a charm of beauty. I took little heed of time and it was only when the deepening twilight forced itself upon me that I began to think of how I should find my way home. The brightness of the day had gone. The air was cold, and the drifting of clouds high overhead was more marked. They were accompanied by a sort of far-away rushing sound, through which seemed to come at intervals that mysterious cry which the driver had said came from a wolf. For a while I hesitated. I had said I would see the deserted village, so on I went, and presently came on a wide stretch of open country, shut in by hills all around. Their sides were covered with trees which spread down to the plain, dotting, in clumps, the gentler slopes and hollows which showed here and there. I followed with my eye the winding of the road, and saw that it curved close to one of the densest of these clumps and was lost behind it.

As I looked there came a cold shiver in the air, and the snow began to fall. I thought of the miles and miles of bleak country I had passed, and then hurried on to seek the shelter of the wood in front. Darker and darker grew the sky, and faster and heavier fell the snow, till the earth before and around me was a glistening white carpet the further edge of which was lost in misty vagueness. The road was here but crude, and when on the level its boundaries were not so marked, as when it passed through the cuttings; and in a little while I found that I must have strayed from it, for I missed underfoot the hard surface, and my feet sank deeper in the grass and moss. Then the wind grew stronger and blew with ever increasing force, till I was fain to run before it. The air became icy-cold, and in spite of my exercise I began to suffer. The snow was now falling so thickly and whirling around me in such rapid eddies that I could hardly keep my eyes open. Every now and then the heavens were torn asunder by vivid lightning, and in the flashes I could see ahead of me a great mass of trees, chiefly yew and cypress all heavily coated with snow.

I was soon amongst the shelter of the trees, and there, in comparative silence, I could hear the rush of the wind high overhead. Presently the blackness of the storm had become merged in the darkness of the night. By-and-by the storm seemed to be passing away: it now only came in fierce puffs or blasts. At such moments the weird sound of the wolf appeared to be echoed by many similar sounds around me.

Now and again, through the black mass of drifting cloud, came a straggling ray of moonlight, which lit up the expanse, and showed me that I was at the edge of a dense mass of cypress and yew trees. As the snow had ceased to fall, I walked out from the shelter and began to investigate more closely. It appeared to me that, amongst so many old foundations as I had passed, there might be still standing a house in which, though in ruins, I could find some sort of shelter for a while. As I skirted the edge of the copse, I found that a low wall encircled it, and following this I presently found an opening. Here the cypresses formed an alley leading up to a square mass of some kind of building. Just as I caught sight of this, however, the drifting clouds obscured the moon, and I passed up the path in darkness. The wind must have grown colder, for I felt myself shiver as I walked; but there was hope of shelter, and I groped my way blindly on.

I stopped, for there was a sudden stillness. The storm had passed; and, perhaps in sympathy with nature's silence, my heart seemed to cease to beat. But this was only momentarily; for suddenly the moonlight broke through the clouds, showing me that I was in a graveyard, and that the square object before me was a great massive tomb of marble, as white as the snow that lay on and all around it. With the moonlight there came a fierce sigh of the storm, which appeared to resume its course with a long, low howl, as of many dogs or wolves. I was awed and shocked, and felt the cold perceptibly grow upon me till it seemed to grip me by the heart. Then while the flood of moonlight still fell on the marble tomb, the storm gave further evidence of renewing, as though it was returning on its track. Impelled by some sort of fascination, I approached the sepulchre to see what it was, and why such a thing stood alone in such a place. I walked around it, and read, over the Doric door, in German:

COUNTESS DOLINGEN OF GRATZ

IN STYRIA

SOUGHT AND FOUND DEATH

1801

On the top of the tomb, seemingly driven through the solid marble-for the structure was composed of a few vast blocks of stone-was a great iron spike or stake. On going to the back I saw, graven in great Russian letters:

'The dead travel fast.'

There was something so weird and uncanny about the whole thing that it gave me a turn and made me feel quite faint. I began to wish, for the first time, that I had taken Johann's advice. Here a thought struck me, which came under almost mysterious circumstances and with a terrible shock. This was Walpurgis Night!

Walpurgis Night, when, according to the belief of millions of people, the devil was abroad-when the graves were opened and the dead came forth and walked. When all evil things of earth and air and water held revel. This very place the driver had specially shunned. This was the depopulated village of centuries ago. This was where the suicide lay; and this was the place where I was alone-unmanned, shivering with cold in a shroud of snow with a wild storm gathering again upon me! It took all my philosophy, all the religion I had been taught, all my courage, not to collapse in a paroxysm of fright.

And now a perfect tornado burst upon me. The ground shook as though thousands of horses thundered across it; and this time the storm bore on its icy wings, not snow, but great hailstones which drove with such violence that they might have come from the thongs of Balearic slingers-hailstones that beat down leaf and branch and made the shelter of the cypresses of no more avail than though their stems were standing-corn. At the first I had rushed to the nearest tree; but I was soon fain to leave it and seek the only spot that seemed to afford refuge, the deep Doric doorway of the marble tomb. There, crouching against the massive bronze door, I gained a certain amount of protection from the beating of the hailstones, for now they only drove against me as they ricocheted from the ground and the side of the marble.

As I leaned against the door, it moved slightly and opened inwards. The shelter of even a tomb was welcome in that pitiless tempest, and I was about to enter it when there came a flash of forked-lightning that lit up the whole expanse of the heavens. In the instant, as I am a living man, I saw, as my eyes were turned into the darkness of the tomb, a beautiful woman, with rounded cheeks and red lips, seemingly sleeping on a bier. As the thunder broke overhead, I was grasped as by the hand of a giant and hurled out into the storm. The whole thing was so sudden that, before I could realise the shock, moral as well as physical, I found the hailstones beating me down. At the same time I had a strange, dominating feeling that I was not alone. I looked towards the tomb. Just then there came another blinding flash, which seemed to strike the iron stake that surmounted the tomb and to pour through to the earth, blasting and crumbling the marble, as in a burst of flame. The dead woman rose for a moment of agony, while she was lapped in the flame, and her bitter scream of pain was drowned in the thundercrash. The last thing I heard was this mingling of dreadful sound, as again I was seized in the giant-grasp and dragged away, while the hailstones beat on me, and the air around seemed reverberant with the howling of wolves. The last sight that I remembered was a vague, white, moving mass, as if all the graves around me had sent out the phantoms of their sheeted-dead, and that they were closing in on me through the white cloudiness of the driving hail.

Gradually there came a sort of vague beginning of consciousness; then a sense of weariness that was dreadful. For a time I remembered nothing; but slowly my senses returned. My feet seemed positively racked with pain, yet I could not move them. They seemed to be numbed. There was an icy feeling at the back of my neck and all down my spine, and my ears, like my feet, were dead, yet in torment; but there was in my breast a sense of warmth which was, by comparison, delicious. It was as a nightmare —a physical nightmare, if one may use such an expression; for some heavy weight on my chest made it difficult for me to breathe.

This period of semi-lethargy seemed to remain a long time, and as it faded away I must have slept or swooned. Then came a sort of loathing, like the first stage of sea-sickness, and a wild desire to be free from something —I knew not what. A vast stillness enveloped me, as though all the world were asleep or dead-only broken by the low panting as of some animal close to me. I felt a warm rasping at my throat, then came a consciousness of the awful truth, which chilled me to the heart and sent the blood surging up through my brain. Some great animal was lying on me and now licking my throat. I feared to stir, for some instinct of prudence bade me lie still; but the brute seemed to realise that there was now some change in me, for it raised its head. Through my eyelashes I saw above me the two great flaming eyes of a gigantic wolf. Its sharp white teeth gleamed in the gaping red mouth, and I could feel its hot breath fierce and acrid upon me.

For another spell of time I remembered no more. Then I became conscious of a low growl, followed by a yelp, renewed again and again. Then, seemingly very far away, I heard a 'Holloa! holloa!' as of many voices calling in unison. Cautiously I raised my head and looked in the direction whence the sound came; but the cemetery blocked my view. The wolf still continued to yelp in a strange way, and a red glare began to move round the grove of cypresses, as though following the sound. As the voices drew closer, the wolf yelped faster and louder. I feared to make either sound or motion. Nearer came the red glow, over the white pall which stretched into the darkness around me. Then all at once from beyond the trees there came at a trot a troop of horsemen bearing torches. The wolf rose from my breast and made for the cemetery. I saw one of the horsemen (soldiers by their caps and their long military cloaks) raise his carbine and take aim. A companion knocked up his arm, and I heard the ball whizz over my head. He had evidently taken my body for that of the wolf. Another sighted the animal as it slunk away, and a shot followed. Then, at a gallop, the troop rode forward-some towards me, others following the wolf as it disappeared amongst the snow-clad cypresses.

As they drew nearer I tried to move, but was powerless, although I could see and hear all that went on around me. Two or three of the soldiers jumped from their horses and knelt beside me. One of them raised my head, and placed his hand over my heart.

'Good news, comrades!' he cried. 'His heart still beats!'

Then some brandy was poured down my throat; it put vigour into me, and I was able to open my eyes fully and look around. Lights and shadows were moving among the trees, and I heard men call to one another. They drew together, uttering frightened exclamations; and the lights flashed as the others came pouring out of the cemetery pell-mell, like men possessed. When the further ones came close to us, those who were around me asked them eagerly:

'Well, have you found him?'

The reply rang out hurriedly:

'No! no! Come away quick-quick! This is no place to stay, and on this of all nights!'

'What was it?' was the question, asked in all manner of keys. The answer came variously and all indefinitely as though the men were moved by some common impulse to speak, yet were restrained by some common fear from giving their thoughts.

'It-it-indeed!' gibbered one, whose wits had plainly given out for the moment.

'A wolf-and yet not a wolf!' another put in shudderingly.

'No use trying for him without the sacred bullet,' a third remarked in a more ordinary manner.

'Serve us right for coming out on this night! Truly we have earned our thousand marks!' were the ejaculations of a fourth.

'There was blood on the broken marble,' another said after a pause —'the lightning never brought that there. And for him-is he safe? Look at his throat! See, comrades, the wolf has been lying on him and keeping his blood warm.'

The officer looked at my throat and replied:

'He is all right; the skin is not pierced. What does it all mean? We should never have found him but for the yelping of the wolf.'

'What became of it?' asked the man who was holding up my head, and who seemed the least panic-stricken of the party, for his hands were steady and without tremor. On his sleeve was the chevron of a petty officer.

'It went to its home,' answered the man, whose long face was pallid, and who actually shook with terror as he glanced around him fearfully. 'There are graves enough there in which it may lie. Come, comrades-come quickly! Let us leave this cursed spot.'

The officer raised me to a sitting posture, as he uttered a word of command; then several men placed me upon a horse. He sprang to the saddle behind me, took me in his arms, gave the word to advance; and, turning our faces away from the cypresses, we rode away in swift, military order.

As yet my tongue refused its office, and I was perforce silent. I must have fallen asleep; for the next thing I remembered was finding myself standing up, supported by a soldier on each side of me. It was almost broad daylight, and to the north a red streak of sunlight was reflected, like a path of blood, over the waste of snow. The officer was telling the men to say nothing of what they had seen, except that they found an English stranger, guarded by a large dog.

'Dog! that was no dog,' cut in the man who had exhibited such fear. 'I think I know a wolf when I see one.'

The young officer answered calmly: 'I said a dog.'

'Dog!' reiterated the other ironically. It was evident that his courage was rising with the sun; and, pointing to me, he said, 'Look at his throat. Is that the work of a dog, master?'

Instinctively I raised my hand to my throat, and as I touched it I cried out in pain. The men crowded round to look, some stooping down from their saddles; and again there came the calm voice of the young officer:

'A dog, as I said. If aught else were said we should only be laughed at.'

I was then mounted behind a trooper, and we rode on into the suburbs of Munich. Here we came across a stray carriage, into which I was lifted, and it was driven off to the Quatre Saisons-the young officer accompanying me, whilst a trooper followed with his horse, and the others rode off to their barracks.

When we arrived, Herr Delbrück rushed so quickly down the steps to meet me, that it was apparent he had been watching within. Taking me by both hands he solicitously led me in. The officer saluted me and was turning to withdraw, when I recognised his purpose, and insisted that he should come to my rooms. Over a glass of wine I warmly thanked him and his brave comrades for saving me. He replied simply that he was more than glad, and that Herr Delbrück had at the first taken steps to make all the searching party pleased; at which ambiguous utterance the maître d'hôtel smiled, while the officer pleaded duty and withdrew.

'But Herr Delbrück,' I enquired, 'how and why was it that the soldiers searched for me?'

He shrugged his shoulders, as if in depreciation of his own deed, as he replied:

'I was so fortunate as to obtain leave from the commander of the regiment in which I served, to ask for volunteers.'

'But how did you know I was lost?' I asked.

'The driver came hither with the remains of his carriage, which had been upset when the horses ran away.'

'But surely you would not send a search-party of soldiers merely on this account?'

'Oh, no!' he answered; 'but even before the coachman arrived, I had this telegram from the Boyar whose guest you are,' and he took from his pocket a telegram which he handed to me, and I read:

Bistritz.

> Be careful of my guest-his safety is most precious to me. Should aught happen to him, or if he be missed, spare nothing to find him and ensure his safety. He is English and therefore adventurous. There are often dangers from snow and wolves and night. Lose not a moment if you suspect harm to him. I answer your zeal with my fortune. —*Dracula.*

As I held the telegram in my hand, the room seemed to whirl around me; and, if the attentive maître d'hôtel had not caught me, I think I should have fallen. There was something so strange in all this, something so weird and impossible to imagine, that there grew on me a sense of my being in some way the sport of opposite forces-the mere vague idea of which seemed in a way to paralyse me. I was certainly under some form of mysterious protection. From a distant country had come, in the very nick of time, a message that took me out of the danger of the snow-sleep and the jaws of the wolf.

The Judge's House

When the time for his examination drew near Malcolm Malcolmson made up his mind to go somewhere to read by himself. He feared the attractions of the seaside, and also he feared completely rural isolation, for of old he knew it charms, and so he determined to find some unpretentious little town where there would be nothing to distract him. He refrained from asking suggestions from any of his friends, for he argued that each would recommend some place of which he had knowledge, and where he had already acquaintances. As Malcolmson wished to avoid friends he had no wish to encumber himself with the attention of friends' friends, and so he determined to look out for a place for himself. He packed a portmanteau with some clothes and all the books he required, and then took ticket for the first name on the local time-table which he did not know.

When at the end of three hours' journey he alighted at Benchurch, he felt satisfied that he had so far obliterated his tracks as to be sure of having a peaceful opportunity of pursuing his studies. He went straight to the one inn which the sleepy little place contained, and put up for the night. Benchurch was a market town, and once in three weeks was crowded to excess, but for the remainder of the twenty-one days it was as attractive as a desert. Malcolmson looked around the day after his arrival to try to find quarters more isolated than even so quiet an inn as 'The Good Traveller' afforded. There was only one place which took his fancy, and it certainly satisfied his wildest ideas regarding quiet; in fact, quiet was not the proper word to apply to it-desolation was the only term conveying any suitable idea of its isolation. It was an old rambling, heavy-built house of the Jacobean style, with heavy gables and windows, unusually small, and set higher than was customary in such houses, and was surrounded with a high brick wall massively built. Indeed, on examination, it looked more like a fortified house than an ordinary dwelling. But all these things pleased Malcolmson. 'Here,' he thought, 'is the very spot I have been looking for, and if I can get opportunity of using it I shall be happy.' His joy was increased when he realised beyond doubt that it was not at present inhabited.

From the post-office he got the name of the agent, who was rarely surprised at the application to rent a part of the old house. Mr. Carnford, the local lawyer and agent, was a genial old gentleman, and frankly confessed his delight at anyone being willing to live in the house.

'To tell you the truth,' said he, 'I should be only too happy, on behalf of the owners, to let anyone have the house rent free for a term of years if only to accustom the people here to see it inhabited. It has been so long empty that some kind of absurd prejudice has grown up about it, and this can be best put down by its occupation-if only,' he added with a sly glance at Malcolmson, 'by a scholar like yourself, who wants its quiet for a time.'

Malcolmson thought it needless to ask the agent about the 'absurd prejudice'; he knew he would get more information, if he should require it, on that subject from other quarters. He paid his three months' rent, got a receipt, and the name of an old woman who would probably undertake to 'do' for him, and came away with the keys in his pocket. He then went to the landlady of the inn, who was a cheerful and most kindly person, and asked her advice as to such stores and provisions as he would be likely to require. She threw up her hands in amazement when he told her where he was going to settle himself.

'Not in the Judge's House!' she said, and grew pale as she spoke. He explained the locality of the house, saying that he did not know its name. When he had finished she answered:

'Aye, sure enough-sure enough the very place! It is the Judge's House sure enough.' He asked her to tell him about the place, why so called, and what there was against it. She told him that it was so called locally because it had been many years before-how long she could not say, as she was herself from another part of the country, but she thought it must have been a hundred years or more-the abode of a judge who was held in great terror on account of his harsh sentences and his hostility to prisoners at Assizes. As to what there was against the house itself she could not tell. She had often asked, but no one could inform her; but there was a general feeling that there was *something*, and for her own part she would not take all the money in Drinkwater's Bank and stay in the house an hour by herself. Then she apologised to Malcolmson for her disturbing talk.

'It is too bad of me, sir, and you-and a young gentlemen, too-if you will pardon me saying it, going to live there all alone. If you were my boy-and you'll excuse me for saying it-you wouldn't sleep there a night, not if I had to go there myself and pull the big alarm bell that's on the roof!' The good creature was so manifestly in earnest, and was so kindly in her intentions, that Malcolmson, although amused, was touched. He told her kindly how much he appreciated her interest in him, and added:

'But, my dear Mrs. Witham, indeed you need not be concerned about me! A man who is reading for the Mathematical Tripos has too much to think of to be disturbed by any of these mysterious "somethings", and his work is of too exact and prosaic a kind to allow of his having any corner in his mind for mysteries of any kind. Harmonical Progression, Permutations and Combinations, and Elliptic Functions have sufficient mysteries for me!' Mrs. Witham kindly undertook to see after his commissions, and he went himself to look for the old woman who had been recommended to him. When he returned to the Judge's House with her, after an interval of a couple of hours, he found Mrs. Witham herself waiting with several men and boys carrying parcels, and an upholsterer's man with a bed in a car, for she said, though tables and chairs might be all very well, a bed that hadn't been aired for mayhap fifty years was not proper for young bones to lie on. She was evidently curious to see the inside of the house; and though manifestly so afraid of the 'somethings' that at the slightest sound she clutched on to Malcolmson, whom she never left for a moment, went over the whole place.

After his examination of the house, Malcolmson decided to take up his abode in the great dining-room, which was big enough to serve for all his requirements; and Mrs. Witham, with the aid of the charwoman, Mrs. Dempster, proceeded to arrange matters. When the hampers were brought in and unpacked, Malcolmson saw that with much kind forethought she had sent from her own kitchen sufficient provisions to last for a few days. Before going she expressed all sorts of kind wishes; and at the door turned and said:

'And perhaps, sir, as the room is big and draughty it might be well to have one of those big screens put round your bed at night-though, truth to tell, I would die myself if I were to be so shut in with all kinds of-of "things", that put their heads round the sides, or over the top, and look on me!' The image which she had called up was too much for her nerves, and she fled incontinently.

Mrs. Dempster sniffed in a superior manner as the landlady disappeared, and remarked that for her own part she wasn't afraid of all the bogies in the kingdom.

'I'll tell you what it is, sir,' she said; 'bogies is all kinds and sorts of things-except bogies! Rats and mice, and beetles; and creaky doors, and loose slates, and broken panes, and stiff drawer handles, that stay out when you pull them and then fall down in the middle of the night. Look at the wainscot of the room! It is old-hundreds of years old! Do you think there's no rats and beetles there! And do you imagine, sir, that you won't see none of them? Rats is bogies, I tell you, and bogies is rats; and don't you get to think anything else!'

'Mrs. Dempster,' said Malcolmson gravely, making her a polite bow, 'you know more than a Senior Wrangler! And let me say, that, as a mark of esteem for your indubitable soundness of head and heart, I shall, when I go, give you possession of this house, and let you stay here by yourself for the last two months of my tenancy, for four weeks will serve my purpose.'

'Thank you kindly, sir!' she answered, 'but I couldn't sleep away from home a night. I am in Greenhow's Charity, and if I slept a night away from my rooms I should lose all I have got to live on. The rules is very strict; and there's too many watching for a vacancy for me to run any risks in the matter. Only for that, sir, I'd gladly come here and attend on you altogether during your stay.'

'My good woman,' said Malcolmson hastily, 'I have come here on purpose to obtain solitude; and believe me that I am grateful to the late Greenhow for having so organised his admirable charity-whatever it is-that I am perforce denied the opportunity of suffering from such a form of temptation! Saint Anthony himself could not be more rigid on the point!'

The old woman laughed harshly. 'Ah, you young gentlemen,' she said, 'you don't fear for naught; and belike you'll get all the solitude you want here.' She set to work with her cleaning; and by nightfall, when Malcolmson returned from his walk-he always had one of his books to study as he walked-he found the room swept and tidied, a fire burning in the old hearth, the lamp lit, and the table spread for supper with Mrs. Witham's excellent fare. 'This is comfort, indeed,' he said, as he rubbed his hands.

When he had finished his supper, and lifted the tray to the other end of the great oak dining-table, he got out his books again, put fresh wood on the fire, trimmed his lamp, and set himself down to a spell of real hard work. He went on without pause till about eleven o'clock, when he knocked off for a bit to fix his fire and lamp, and to make himself a cup of tea. He had always been a tea-drinker, and during his college life had sat late at work and had taken tea late. The rest was a great luxury to him, and he enjoyed it with a sense of delicious, voluptuous ease. The renewed fire leaped and sparkled, and threw quaint shadows through the great old room; and as he sipped his hot tea he revelled in the sense of isolation from his kind. Then it was that he began to notice for the first time what a noise the rats were making.

'Surely,' he thought, 'they cannot have been at it all the time I was reading. Had they been, I must have noticed it!' Presently, when the noise increased, he satisfied himself that it was really new. It was evident that at first the rats had been frightened at the presence of a stranger, and the light of fire and lamp; but that as the time went on they had grown bolder and were now disporting themselves as was their wont.

How busy they were! and hark to the strange noises! Up and down behind the old wainscot, over the ceiling and under the floor they raced, and gnawed, and scratched! Malcolmson smiled to himself as he recalled to mind the saying of Mrs. Dempster, 'Bogies is rats, and rats is bogies!' The tea began to have its effect of intellectual and nervous stimulus, he saw with joy another long spell of work to be done before the night was past, and in the sense of security which it gave him, he allowed himself the luxury of a good look round the room. He took his lamp in one hand, and went all around, wondering that so quaint and beautiful an old house had been so long neglected. The carving of the oak on the panels of the wainscot was fine, and on and round the doors and windows it was beautiful and of rare merit. There were some old pictures on the walls, but they were coated so thick with dust and dirt that he could not distinguish any detail of them, though he held his lamp as high as he could over his head. Here and there as he went round he saw some crack or hole blocked for a moment by the face of a rat with its bright eyes glittering in the light, but in an instant it was gone, and a squeak and a scamper followed. The thing that most struck him, however, was the rope of the great alarm bell on the roof, which hung down in a corner of the room on the right-hand side of the fireplace. He pulled up close to the hearth a great high-backed carved oak chair, and sat down to his last cup of tea. When this was done he made up the fire, and went back to his work, sitting at the corner of the table, having the fire to his left. For a little while the rats disturbed him somewhat with their perpetual scampering, but he got accustomed to the noise as one does to the ticking of a clock or to the roar of moving water; and he became so immersed in his work that everything in the world, except the problem which he was trying to solve, passed away from him.

He suddenly looked up, his problem was still unsolved, and there was in the air that sense of the hour before the dawn, which is so dread to doubtful life. The noise of the rats had ceased. Indeed it seemed to him that it must have ceased but lately and that it was the sudden cessation which had disturbed him. The fire had fallen low, but still it threw out a deep red glow. As he looked he started in spite of his *sang froid*.

There on the great high-backed carved oak chair by the right side of the fireplace sat an enormous rat, steadily glaring at him with baleful eyes. He made a motion to it as though to hunt it away, but it did not stir. Then he made the motion of throwing something. Still it did not stir, but showed its great white teeth angrily, and its cruel eyes shone in the lamplight with an added vindictiveness.

Malcolmson felt amazed, and seizing the poker from the hearth ran at it to kill it. Before, however, he could strike it, the rat, with a squeak that sounded like the concentration of hate, jumped upon the floor, and, running up the rope of the alarm bell, disappeared in the darkness beyond the range of the green-shaded lamp. Instantly, strange to say, the noisy scampering of the rats in the wainscot began again.

By this time Malcolmson's mind was quite off the problem; and as a shrill cock-crow outside told him of the approach of morning, he went to bed and to sleep.

He slept so sound that he was not even waked by Mrs. Dempster coming in to make up his room. It was only when she had tidied up the place and got his breakfast ready and tapped on the screen which closed in his bed that he woke. He was a little tired still after his night's hard work, but a strong cup of tea soon freshened him up and, taking his book, he went out for his morning walk, bringing with him a few sandwiches lest he should not care to return till dinner time. He found a quiet walk between high elms some way outside the town, and here he spent the greater part of the day studying his Laplace. On his return he looked in to see Mrs. Witham and to thank her for her kindness. When she saw him coming through the diamond-paned bay window of her sanctum she came out to meet him and asked him in. She looked at him searchingly and shook her head as she said:

'You must not overdo it, sir. You are paler this morning than you should be. Too late hours and too hard work on the brain isn't good for any man! But tell me, sir, how did you pass the night? Well, I hope? But my heart! sir, I was glad when Mrs. Dempster told me this morning that you were all right and sleeping sound when she went in.'

'Oh, I was all right,' he answered smiling, 'the "somethings" didn't worry me, as yet. Only the rats; and they had a circus, I tell you, all over the place. There was one wicked looking old devil that sat up on my own chair by the fire, and wouldn't go till I took the poker to him, and then he ran up the rope of the alarm bell and got to somewhere up the wall or the ceiling —I couldn't see where, it was so dark.'

'Mercy on us,' said Mrs. Witham, 'an old devil, and sitting on a chair by the fireside! Take care, sir! take care! There's many a true word spoken in jest.'

'How do you mean? Pon my word I don't understand.'

'An old devil! The old devil, perhaps. There! sir, you needn't laugh,' for Malcolmson had broken into a hearty peal. 'You young folks thinks it easy to laugh at things that makes older ones shudder. Never mind, sir! never mind! Please God, you'll laugh all the time. It's what I wish you myself!' and the good lady beamed all over in sympathy with his enjoyment, her fears gone for a moment.

'Oh, forgive me!' said Malcolmson presently. 'Don't think me rude; but the idea was too much for me-that the old devil himself was on the chair last night!' And at the thought he laughed again. Then he went home to dinner.

This evening the scampering of the rats began earlier; indeed it had been going on before his arrival, and only ceased whilst his presence by its freshness disturbed them. After dinner he sat by the fire for a while and had a smoke; and then, having cleared his table, began to work as before. Tonight the rats disturbed him more than they had done on the previous night. How they scampered up and down and under and over! How they squeaked, and scratched, and gnawed! How they, getting bolder by degrees, came to the mouths of their holes and to the chinks and cracks and crannies in the wainscoting till their eyes shone like tiny lamps as the firelight rose and fell. But to him, now doubtless accustomed to them, their eyes were not wicked; only their playfulness touched him. Sometimes the boldest of them made sallies out on the floor or along the mouldings of the wainscot. Now and again as they disturbed him Malcolmson made a sound to frighten them, smiting the table with his hand or giving a fierce 'Hsh, hsh,' so that they fled straightway to their holes.

And so the early part of the night wore on; and despite the noise Malcolmson got more and more immersed in his work.

All at once he stopped, as on the previous night, being overcome by a sudden sense of silence. There was not the faintest sound of gnaw, or scratch, or squeak. The silence was as of the grave. He remembered the odd occurrence of the previous night, and instinctively he looked at the chair standing close by the fireside. And then a very odd sensation thrilled through him.

There, on the great old high-backed carved oak chair beside the fireplace sat the same enormous rat, steadily glaring at him with baleful eyes.

Instinctively he took the nearest thing to his hand, a book of logarithms, and flung it at it. The book was badly aimed and the rat did not stir, so again the poker performance of the previous night was repeated; and again the rat, being closely pursued, fled up the rope of the alarm bell. Strangely too, the departure of this rat was instantly followed by the renewal of the noise made by the general rat community. On this occasion, as on the previous one, Malcolmson could not see at what part of the room the rat disappeared, for the green shade of his lamp left the upper part of the room in darkness, and the fire had burned low.

On looking at his watch he found it was close on midnight; and, not sorry for the *divertissement*, he made up his fire and made himself his nightly pot of tea. He had got through a good spell of work, and thought himself entitled to a cigarette; and so he sat on the great oak chair before the fire and enjoyed it. Whilst smoking he began to think that he would like to know where the rat disappeared to, for he had certain ideas for the morrow not entirely disconnected with a rat-trap. Accordingly he lit another lamp and placed it so that it would shine well into the right-hand corner of the wall by the fireplace. Then he got all the books he had with him, and placed them handy to throw at the vermin. Finally he lifted the rope of the alarm bell and placed the end of it on the table, fixing the extreme end under the lamp. As he handled it he could not help noticing how pliable it was, especially for so strong a rope, and one not in use. 'You could hang a man with it,' he thought to himself. When his preparations were made he looked around, and said complacently:

'There now, my friend, I think we shall learn something of you this time!' He began his work again, and though as before somewhat disturbed at first by the noise of the rats, soon lost himself in his propositions and problems.

Again he was called to his immediate surroundings suddenly. This time it might not have been the sudden silence only which took his attention; there was a slight movement of the rope, and the lamp moved. Without stirring, he looked to see if his pile of books was within range, and then cast his eye along the rope. As he looked he saw the great rat drop from the rope on the oak arm-chair and sit there glaring at him. He raised a book in his right hand, and taking careful aim, flung it at the rat. The latter, with a quick movement, sprang aside and dodged the missile. He then took another book, and a third, and flung them one after another at the rat, but each time unsuccessfully. At last, as he stood with a book poised in his hand to throw, the rat squeaked and seemed afraid. This made Malcolmson more than ever eager to strike, and the book flew and struck the rat a resounding blow. It gave a terrified squeak, and turning on his pursuer a look of terrible malevolence, ran up the chair-back and made a great jump to the rope of the alarm bell and ran up it like lightning. The lamp rocked under the sudden strain, but it was a heavy one and did not topple over. Malcolmson kept his eyes on the rat, and saw it by the light of the second lamp leap to a moulding of the wainscot and disappear through a hole in one of the great pictures which hung on the wall, obscured and invisible through its coating of dirt and dust.

'I shall look up my friend's habitation in the morning,' said the student, as he went over to collect his books. 'The third picture from the fireplace; I shall not forget.' He picked up the books one by one, commenting on them as he lifted them. '*Conic Sections* he does not mind, nor *Cycloidal Oscillations*, nor the *Principia*, nor *Quaternions*, nor *Thermodynamics*. Now for the book that fetched him!' Malcolmson took it up and looked at it. As he did so he started, and a sudden pallor overspread his face. He looked round uneasily and shivered slightly, as he murmured to himself:

'The Bible my mother gave me! What an odd coincidence.' He sat down to work again, and the rats in the wainscot renewed their gambols. They did not disturb him, however; somehow their presence gave him a sense of companionship. But he could not attend to his work, and after striving to master the subject on which he was engaged gave it up in despair, and went to bed as the first streak of dawn stole in through the eastern window.

He slept heavily but uneasily, and dreamed much; and when Mrs. Dempster woke him late in the morning he seemed ill at ease, and for a few minutes did not seem to realise exactly where he was. His first request rather surprised the servant.

'Mrs. Dempster, when I am out to-day I wish you would get the steps and dust or wash those pictures-specially that one the third from the fireplace —I want to see what they are.'

Late in the afternoon Malcolmson worked at his books in the shaded walk, and the cheerfulness of the previous day came back to him as the day wore on, and he found that his reading was progressing well. He had worked out to a satisfactory conclusion all the problems which had as yet baffled him, and it was in a state of jubilation that he paid a visit to Mrs. Witham at 'The Good Traveller'. He found a stranger in the cosy sitting-room with the landlady, who was introduced to him as Dr. Thornhill. She was not quite at ease, and this, combined with the doctor's plunging at once into a series of questions, made Malcolmson come to the conclusion that his presence was not an accident, so without preliminary he said:

'Dr. Thornhill, I shall with pleasure answer you any question you may choose to ask me if you will answer me one question first.'

The doctor seemed surprised, but he smiled and answered at once, 'Done! What is it?'

'Did Mrs. Witham ask you to come here and see me and advise me?'

Dr. Thornhill for a moment was taken aback, and Mrs. Witham got fiery red and turned away; but the doctor was a frank and ready man, and he answered at once and openly.

'She did: but she didn't intend you to know it. I suppose it was my clumsy haste that made you suspect. She told me that she did not like the idea of your being in that house all by yourself, and that she thought you took too much strong tea. In fact, she wants me to advise you if possible to give up the tea and the very late hours. I was a keen student in my time, so I suppose I may take the liberty of a college man, and without offence, advise you not quite as a stranger.'

Malcolmson with a bright smile held out his hand. 'Shake! as they say in America,' he said. 'I must thank you for your kindness and Mrs. Witham too, and your kindness deserves a return on my part. I promise to take no more strong tea-no tea at all till you let me-and I shall go to bed tonight at one o'clock at latest. Will that do?'

'Capital,' said the doctor. 'Now tell us all that you noticed in the old house,' and so Malcolmson then and there told in minute detail all that had happened in the last two nights. He was interrupted every now and then by some exclamation from Mrs. Witham, till finally when he told of the episode of the Bible the landlady's pent-up emotions found vent in a shriek; and it was not till a stiff glass of brandy and water had been administered that she grew composed again. Dr. Thornhill listened with a face of growing gravity, and when the narrative was complete and Mrs. Witham had been restored he asked:

'The rat always went up the rope of the alarm bell?'

'Always.'

'I suppose you know,' said the Doctor after a pause, 'what the rope is?'

'No!'

'It is,' said the Doctor slowly, 'the very rope which the hangman used for all the victims of the Judge's judicial rancour!' Here he was interrupted by another scream from Mrs. Witham, and steps had to be taken for her recovery. Malcolmson having looked at his watch, and found that it was close to his dinner hour, had gone home before her complete recovery.

When Mrs. Witham was herself again she almost assailed the Doctor with angry questions as to what he meant by putting such horrible ideas into the poor young man's mind. 'He has quite enough there already to upset him,' she added. Dr. Thornhill replied:

'My dear madam, I had a distinct purpose in it! I wanted to draw his attention to the bell rope, and to fix it there. It may be that he is in a highly overwrought state, and has been studying too much, although I am bound to say that he seems as sound and healthy a young man, mentally and bodily, as ever I saw-but then the rats-and that suggestion of the devil.' The doctor shook his head and went on. 'I would have offered to go and stay the first night with him but that I felt sure it would have been a cause of offence. He may get in the night some strange fright or hallucination; and if he does I want him to pull that rope. All alone as he is it will give us warning, and we may reach him in time to be of service. I shall be sitting up pretty late tonight and shall keep my ears open. Do not be alarmed if Benchurch gets a surprise before morning.'

'Oh, Doctor, what do you mean? What do you mean?'

'I mean this; that possibly-nay, more probably-we shall hear the great alarm bell from the Judge's House tonight,' and the Doctor made about as effective an exit as could be thought of.

When Malcolmson arrived home he found that it was a little after his usual time, and Mrs. Dempster had gone away-the rules of Greenhow's Charity were not to be neglected. He was glad to see that the place was bright and tidy with a cheerful fire and a well-trimmed lamp. The evening was colder than might have been expected in April, and a heavy wind was blowing with such rapidly-increasing strength that there was every promise of a storm during the night. For a few minutes after his entrance the noise of the rats ceased; but so soon as they became accustomed to his presence they began again. He was glad to hear them, for he felt once more the feeling of companionship in their noise, and his mind ran back to the strange fact that they only ceased to manifest themselves when that other-the great rat with the baleful eyes-came upon the scene. The reading-lamp only was lit and its green shade kept the ceiling and the upper part of the room in darkness, so that the cheerful light from the hearth spreading over the floor and shining on the white cloth laid over the end of the table was warm and cheery. Malcolmson sat down to his dinner with a good appetite and a buoyant spirit. After his dinner and a cigarette he sat steadily down to work, determined not to let anything disturb him, for he remembered his promise to the doctor, and made up his mind to make the best of the time at his disposal.

For an hour or so he worked all right, and then his thoughts began to wander from his books. The actual circumstances around him, the calls on his physical attention, and his nervous susceptibility were not to be denied. By this time the wind had become a gale, and the gale a storm. The old house, solid though it was, seemed to shake to its foundations, and the storm roared and raged through its many chimneys and its queer old gables, producing strange, unearthly sounds in the empty rooms and corridors. Even the great alarm bell on the roof must have felt the force of the wind, for the rope rose and fell slightly, as though the bell were moved a little from time to time and the limber rope fell on the oak floor with a hard and hollow sound.

As Malcolmson listened to it he bethought himself of the doctor's words, 'It is the rope which the hangman used for the victims of the Judge's judicial rancour,' and he went over to the corner of the fireplace and took it in his hand to look at it. There seemed a sort of deadly interest in it, and as he stood there he lost himself for a moment in speculation as to who these victims were, and the grim wish of the Judge to have such a ghastly relic ever under his eyes. As he stood there the swaying of the bell on the roof still lifted the rope now and again; but presently there came a new sensation —a sort of tremor in the rope, as though something was moving along it.

Looking up instinctively Malcolmson saw the great rat coming slowly down towards him, glaring at him steadily. He dropped the rope and started back with a muttered curse, and the rat turning ran up the rope again and disappeared, and at the same instant Malcolmson became conscious that the noise of the rats, which had ceased for a while, began again.

All this set him thinking, and it occurred to him that he had not investigated the lair of the rat or looked at the pictures, as he had intended. He lit the other lamp without the shade, and, holding it up went and stood opposite the third picture from the fireplace on the right-hand side where he had seen the rat disappear on the previous night.

At the first glance he started back so suddenly that he almost dropped the lamp, and a deadly pallor overspread his face. His knees shook, and heavy drops of sweat came on his forehead, and he trembled like an aspen. But he was young and plucky, and pulled himself together, and after the pause of a few seconds stepped forward again, raised the lamp, and examined the picture which had been dusted and washed, and now stood out clearly.

It was of a judge dressed in his robes of scarlet and ermine. His face was strong and merciless, evil, crafty, and vindictive, with a sensual mouth, hooked nose of ruddy colour, and shaped like the beak of a bird of prey. The rest of the face was of a cadaverous colour. The eyes were of peculiar brilliance and with a terribly malignant expression. As he looked at them, Malcolmson grew cold, for he saw there the very counterpart of the eyes of the great rat. The lamp almost fell from his hand, he saw the rat with its baleful eyes peering out through the hole in the corner of the picture, and noted the sudden cessation of the noise of the other rats. However, he pulled himself together, and went on with his examination of the picture.

The Judge was seated in a great high-backed carved oak chair, on the right-hand side of a great stone fireplace where, in the corner, a rope hung down from the ceiling, its end lying coiled on the floor. With a feeling of something like horror, Malcolmson recognised the scene of the room as it stood, and gazed around him in an awestruck manner as though he expected to find some strange presence behind him. Then he looked over to the corner of the fireplace-and with a loud cry he let the lamp fall from his hand.

There, in the Judge's arm-chair, with the rope hanging behind, sat the rat with the Judge's baleful eyes, now intensified and with a fiendish leer. Save for the howling of the storm without there was silence.

The fallen lamp recalled Malcolmson to himself. Fortunately it was of metal, and so the oil was not spilt. However, the practical need of attending to it settled at once his nervous apprehensions. When he had turned it out, he wiped his brow and thought for a moment.

'This will not do,' he said to himself. 'If I go on like this I shall become a crazy fool. This must stop! I promised the doctor I would not take tea. Faith, he was pretty right! My nerves must have been getting into a queer state. Funny I did not notice it. I never felt better in my life. However, it is all right now, and I shall not be such a fool again.'

Then he mixed himself a good stiff glass of brandy and water and resolutely sat down to his work.

It was nearly an hour when he looked up from his book, disturbed by the sudden stillness. Without, the wind howled and roared louder than ever, and the rain drove in sheets against the windows, beating like hail on the glass; but within there was no sound whatever save the echo of the wind as it roared in the great chimney, and now and then a hiss as a few raindrops found their way down the chimney in a lull of the storm. The fire had fallen low and had ceased to flame, though it threw out a red glow. Malcolmson listened attentively, and presently heard a thin, squeaking noise, very faint. It came from the corner of the room where the rope hung down, and he thought it was the creaking of the rope on the floor as the swaying of the bell raised and lowered it. Looking up, however, he saw in the dim light the great rat clinging to the rope and gnawing it. The rope was already nearly gnawed through-he could see the lighter colour where the strands were laid bare. As he looked the job was completed, and the severed end of the rope fell clattering on the oaken floor, whilst for an instant the great rat remained like a knob or tassel at the end of the rope, which now began to sway to and fro. Malcolmson felt for a moment another pang of terror as he thought that now the possibility of calling the outer world to his assistance was cut off, but an intense anger took its place, and seizing the book he was reading he hurled it at the rat. The blow was well aimed, but before the missile could reach him the rat dropped off and struck the floor with a soft thud. Malcolmson instantly rushed over towards him, but it darted away and disappeared in the darkness of the shadows of the room. Malcolmson felt that his work was over for the night, and determined then and there to vary the monotony of the proceedings by a hunt for the rat, and took off the green shade of the lamp so as to insure a wider spreading light. As he did so the gloom of the upper part of the room was relieved, and in the new flood of light, great by comparison with the previous darkness, the pictures on the wall stood out boldly. From where he stood, Malcolmson saw right opposite to him the third picture on the wall from the right of the fireplace. He rubbed his eyes in surprise, and then a great fear began to come upon him.

In the centre of the picture was a great irregular patch of brown canvas, as fresh as when it was stretched on the frame. The background was as before, with chair and chimney-corner and rope, but the figure of the Judge had disappeared.

Malcolmson, almost in a chill of horror, turned slowly round, and then he began to shake and tremble like a man in a palsy. His strength seemed to have left him, and he was incapable of action or movement, hardly even of thought. He could only see and hear.

There, on the great high-backed carved oak chair sat the Judge in his robes of scarlet and ermine, with his baleful eyes glaring vindictively, and a smile of triumph on the resolute, cruel mouth, as he lifted with his hands a *black cap*. Malcolmson felt as if the blood was running from his heart, as one does in moments of prolonged suspense. There was a singing in his ears. Without, he could hear the roar and howl of the tempest, and through it, swept on the storm, came the striking of midnight by the great chimes in the market place. He stood for a space of time that seemed to him endless still as a statue, and with wide-open, horror-struck eyes, breathless. As the clock struck, so the smile of triumph on the Judge's face intensified, and at the last stroke of midnight he placed the black cap on his head.

Slowly and deliberately the Judge rose from his chair and picked up the piece of the rope of the alarm bell which lay on the floor, drew it through his hands as if he enjoyed its touch, and then deliberately began to knot one end of it, fashioning it into a noose. This he tightened and tested with his foot, pulling hard at it till he was satisfied and then making a running noose of it, which he held in his hand. Then he began to move along the table on the opposite side to Malcolmson keeping his eyes on him until he had passed him, when with a quick movement he stood in front of the door. Malcolmson then began to feel that he was trapped, and tried to think of what he should do. There was some fascination in the Judge's eyes, which he never took off him, and he had, perforce, to look. He saw the Judge approach-still keeping between him and the door-and raise the noose and throw it towards him as if to entangle him. With a great effort he made a quick movement to one side, and saw the rope fall beside him, and heard it strike the oaken floor. Again the Judge raised the noose and tried to ensnare him, ever keeping his baleful eyes fixed on him, and each time by a mighty effort the student just managed to evade it. So this went on for many times, the Judge seeming never discouraged nor discomposed at failure, but playing as a cat does with a mouse. At last in despair, which had reached its climax, Malcolmson cast a quick glance round him. The lamp seemed to have blazed up, and there was a fairly good light in the room. At the many rat-holes and in the chinks and crannies of the wainscot he saw the rats' eyes; and this aspect, that was purely physical, gave him a gleam of comfort. He looked around and saw that the rope of the great alarm bell was laden with rats. Every inch of it was covered with them, and more and more were pouring through the small circular hole in the ceiling whence it emerged, so that with their weight the bell was beginning to sway.

Hark! it had swayed till the clapper had touched the bell. The sound was but a tiny one, but the bell was only beginning to sway, and it would increase.

At the sound the Judge, who had been keeping his eyes fixed on Malcolmson, looked up, and a scowl of diabolical anger overspread his face. His eyes fairly glowed like hot coals, and he stamped his foot with a sound that seemed to make the house shake. A dreadful peal of thunder broke overhead as he raised the rope again, whilst the rats kept running up and down the rope as though working against time. This time, instead of throwing it, he drew close to his victim, and held open the noose as he approached. As he came closer there seemed something paralysing in his very presence, and Malcolmson stood rigid as a corpse. He felt the Judge's icy fingers touch his throat as he adjusted the rope. The noose tightened-tightened. Then the Judge, taking the rigid form of the student in his arms, carried him over and placed him standing in the oak chair, and stepping up beside him, put his hand up and caught the end of the swaying rope of the alarm bell. As he raised his hand the rats fled squeaking, and disappeared through the hole in the ceiling. Taking the end of the noose which was round Malcolmson's neck he tied it to the hanging-bell rope, and then descending pulled away the chair.

———————————

When the alarm bell of the Judge's House began to sound a crowd soon assembled. Lights and torches of various kinds appeared, and soon a silent crowd was hurrying to the spot. They knocked loudly at the door, but there was no reply. Then they burst in the door, and poured into the great dining-room, the doctor at the head.

There at the end of the rope of the great alarm bell hung the body of the student, and on the face of the Judge in the picture was a malignant smile.

The Squaw

Nurnberg at the time was not so much exploited as it has been since then. Irving had not been playing *Faust*, and the very name of the old town was hardly known to the great bulk of the travelling public. My wife and I being in the second week of our honeymoon, naturally wanted someone else to join our party, so that when the cheery stranger, Elias P. Hutcheson, hailing from Isthmian City, Bleeding Gulch, Maple Tree County, Neb. turned up at the station at Frankfort, and casually remarked that he was going on to see the most all-fired old Methuselah of a town in Yurrup, and that he guessed that so much travelling alone was enough to send an intelligent, active citizen into the melancholy ward of a daft house, we took the pretty broad hint and suggested that we should join forces. We found, on comparing notes afterwards, that we had each intended to speak with some diffidence or hesitation so as not to appear too eager, such not being a good compliment to the success of our married life; but the effect was entirely marred by our both beginning to speak at the same instant-stopping simultaneously and then going on together again. Anyhow, no matter how, it was done; and Elias P. Hutcheson became one of our party. Straightway Amelia and I found the pleasant benefit; instead of quarrelling, as we had been doing, we found that the restraining influence of a third party was such that we now took every opportunity of spooning in odd corners. Amelia declares that ever since she has, as the result of that experience, advised all her friends to take a friend on the honeymoon. Well, we 'did' Nurnberg together, and much enjoyed the racy remarks of our Transatlantic friend, who, from his quaint speech and his wonderful stock of adventures, might have stepped out of a novel. We kept for the last object of interest in the city to be visited the Burg, and on the day appointed for the visit strolled round the outer wall of the city by the eastern side.

The Burg is seated on a rock dominating the town and an immensely deep fosse guards it on the northern side. Nurnberg has been happy in that it was never sacked; had it been it would certainly not be so spick and span perfect as it is at present. The ditch has not been used for centuries, and now its base is spread with tea-gardens and orchards, of which some of the trees are of quite respectable growth. As we wandered round the wall, dawdling in the hot July sunshine, we often paused to admire the views spread before us, and in especial the great plain covered with towns and villages and bounded with a blue line of hills, like a landscape of Claude Lorraine. From this we always turned with new delight to the city itself, with its myriad of quaint old gables and acre-wide red roofs dotted with dormer windows, tier upon tier. A little to our right rose the towers of the Burg, and nearer still, standing grim, the Torture Tower, which was, and is, perhaps, the most interesting place in the city. For centuries the tradition of the Iron Virgin of Nurnberg has been handed down as an instance of the horrors of cruelty of which man is capable; we had long looked forward to seeing it; and here at last was its home.

In one of our pauses we leaned over the wall of the moat and looked down. The garden seemed quite fifty or sixty feet below us, and the sun pouring into it with an intense, moveless heat like that of an oven. Beyond rose the grey, grim wall seemingly of endless height, and losing itself right and left in the angles of bastion and counterscarp. Trees and bushes crowned the wall, and above again towered the lofty houses on whose massive beauty Time has only set the hand of approval. The sun was hot and we were lazy; time was our own, and we lingered, leaning on the wall. Just below us was a pretty sight —a great black cat lying stretched in the sun, whilst round her gambolled prettily a tiny black kitten. The mother would wave her tail for the kitten to play with, or would raise her feet and push away the little one as an encouragement to further play. They were just at the foot of the wall, and Elias P. Hutcheson, in order to help the play, stooped and took from the walk a moderate sized pebble.

'See!' he said, 'I will drop it near the kitten, and they will both wonder where it came from.'

'Oh, be careful,' said my wife; 'you might hit the dear little thing!'

'Not me, ma'am,' said Elias P. 'Why, I'm as tender as a Maine cherry-tree. Lor, bless ye. I wouldn't hurt the poor pooty little critter more'n I'd scalp a baby. An' you may bet your variegated socks on that! See, I'll drop it fur away on the outside so's not to go near her!' Thus saying, he leaned over and held his arm out at full length and dropped the stone. It may be that there is some attractive force which draws lesser matters to greater; or more probably that the wall was not plump but sloped to its base-we not noticing the inclination from above; but the stone fell with a sickening thud that came up to us through the hot air, right on the kitten's head, and shattered out its little brains then and there. The black cat cast a swift upward glance, and we saw her eyes like green fire fixed an instant on Elias P. Hutcheson; and then her attention was given to the kitten, which lay still with just a quiver of her tiny limbs, whilst a thin red stream trickled from a gaping wound. With a muffled cry, such as a human being might give, she bent over the kitten licking its wounds and moaning. Suddenly she seemed to realise that it was dead, and again threw her eyes up at us. I shall never forget the sight, for she looked the perfect incarnation of hate. Her green eyes blazed with lurid fire, and the white, sharp teeth seemed to almost shine through the blood which dabbled her mouth and whiskers. She gnashed her teeth, and her claws stood out stark and at full length on every paw. Then she made a wild rush up the wall as if to reach us, but when the momentum ended fell back, and further added to her horrible appearance for she fell on the kitten, and rose with her black fur smeared with its brains and blood. Amelia turned quite faint, and I had to lift her back from the wall. There was a seat close by in shade of a spreading plane-tree, and here I placed her whilst she composed herself. Then I went back to Hutcheson, who stood without moving, looking down on the angry cat below.

As I joined him, he said:

'Wall, I guess that air the savagest beast I ever see —'cept once when an Apache squaw had an edge on a half-breed what they nicknamed "Splinters" 'cos of the way he fixed up her papoose which he stole on a raid just to show that he appreciated the way they had given his mother the fire torture. She got that kinder look so set on her face that it jest seemed to grow there. She followed Splinters mor'n three year till at last the braves got him and handed him over to her. They did say that no man, white or Injun, had ever been so long a-dying under the tortures of the Apaches. The only time I ever see her smile was when I wiped her out. I kem on the camp just in time to see Splinters pass in his checks, and he wasn't sorry to go either. He was a hard citizen, and though I never could shake with him after that papoose business-for it was bitter bad, and he should have been a white man, for he looked like one —I see he had got paid out in full. Durn me, but I took a piece of his hide from one of his skinnin' posts an' had it made into a pocket-book. It's here now!' and he slapped the breast pocket of his coat.

Whilst he was speaking the cat was continuing her frantic efforts to get up the wall. She would take a run back and then charge up, sometimes reaching an incredible height. She did not seem to mind the heavy fall which she got each time but started with renewed vigour; and at every tumble her appearance became more horrible. Hutcheson was a kind-hearted man-my wife and I had both noticed little acts of kindness to animals as well as to persons-and he seemed concerned at the state of fury to which the cat had wrought herself.

'Wall, now!' he said, 'I du declare that that poor critter seems quite desperate. There! there! poor thing, it was all an accident-though that won't bring back your little one to you. Say! I wouldn't have had such a thing happen for a thousand! Just shows what a clumsy fool of a man can do when he tries to play! Seems I'm too darned slipperhanded to even play with a cat. Say Colonel!' it was a pleasant way he had to bestow titles freely —'I hope your wife don't hold no grudge against me on account of this unpleasantness? Why, I wouldn't have had it occur on no account.'

He came over to Amelia and apologised profusely, and she with her usual kindness of heart hastened to assure him that she quite understood that it was an accident. Then we all went again to the wall and looked over.

The cat missing Hutcheson's face had drawn back across the moat, and was sitting on her haunches as though ready to spring. Indeed, the very instant she saw him she did spring, and with a blind unreasoning fury, which would have been grotesque, only that it was so frightfully real. She did not try to run up the wall, but simply launched herself at him as though hate and fury could lend her wings to pass straight through the great distance between them. Amelia, womanlike, got quite concerned, and said to Elias P. in a warning voice:

'Oh! you must be very careful. That animal would try to kill you if she were here; her eyes look like positive murder.'

He laughed out jovially. 'Excuse me, ma'am,' he said, 'but I can't help laughin'. Fancy a man that has fought grizzlies an' Injuns bein' careful of bein' murdered by a cat!'

When the cat heard him laugh, her whole demeanour seemed to change. She no longer tried to jump or run up the wall, but went quietly over, and sitting again beside the dead kitten began to lick and fondle it as though it were alive.

'See!' said I, 'the effect of a really strong man. Even that animal in the midst of her fury recognises the voice of a master, and bows to him!'

'Like a squaw!' was the only comment of Elias P. Hutcheson, as we moved on our way round the city fosse. Every now and then we looked over the wall and each time saw the cat following us. At first she had kept going back to the dead kitten, and then as the distance grew greater took it in her mouth and so followed. After a while, however, she abandoned this, for we saw her following all alone; she had evidently hidden the body somewhere. Amelia's alarm grew at the cat's persistence, and more than once she repeated her warning; but the American always laughed with amusement, till finally, seeing that she was beginning to be worried, he said:

'I say, ma'am, you needn't be skeered over that cat. I go heeled, I du!' Here he slapped his pistol pocket at the back of his lumbar region. 'Why sooner'n have you worried, I'll shoot the critter, right here, an' risk the police interferin' with a citizen of the United States for carryin' arms contrairy to reg'lations!' As he spoke he looked over the wall, but the cat on seeing him, retreated, with a growl, into a bed of tall flowers, and was hidden. He went on: 'Blest if that ar critter ain't got more sense of what's good for her than most Christians. I guess we've seen the last of her! You bet, she'll go back now to that busted kitten and have a private funeral of it, all to herself!'

Amelia did not like to say more, lest he might, in mistaken kindness to her, fulfil his threat of shooting the cat: and so we went on and crossed the little wooden bridge leading to the gateway whence ran the steep paved roadway between the Burg and the pentagonal Torture Tower. As we crossed the bridge we saw the cat again down below us. When she saw us her fury seemed to return, and she made frantic efforts to get up the steep wall. Hutcheson laughed as he looked down at her, and said:

'Goodbye, old girl. Sorry I injured your feelin's, but you'll get over it in time! So long!' And then we passed through the long, dim archway and came to the gate of the Burg.

When we came out again after our survey of this most beautiful old place which not even the well-intentioned efforts of the Gothic restorers of forty years ago have been able to spoil-though their restoration was then glaring white-we seemed to have quite forgotten the unpleasant episode of the morning. The old lime tree with its great trunk gnarled with the passing of nearly nine centuries, the deep well cut through the heart of the rock by those captives of old, and the lovely view from the city wall whence we heard, spread over almost a full quarter of an hour, the multitudinous chimes of the city, had all helped to wipe out from our minds the incident of the slain kitten.

We were the only visitors who had entered the Torture Tower that morning-so at least said the old custodian-and as we had the place all to ourselves were able to make a minute and more satisfactory survey than would have otherwise been possible. The custodian, looking to us as the sole source of his gains for the day, was willing to meet our wishes in any way. The Torture Tower is truly a grim place, even now when many thousands of visitors have sent a stream of life, and the joy that follows life, into the place; but at the time I mention it wore its grimmest and most gruesome aspect. The dust of ages seemed to have settled on it, and the darkness and the horror of its memories seem to have become sentient in a way that would have satisfied the Pantheistic souls of Philo or Spinoza. The lower chamber where we entered was seemingly, in its normal state, filled with incarnate darkness; even the hot sunlight streaming in through the door seemed to be lost in the vast thickness of the walls, and only showed the masonry rough as when the builder's scaffolding had come down, but coated with dust and marked here and there with patches of dark stain which, if walls could speak, could have given their own dread memories of fear and pain. We were glad to pass up the dusty wooden staircase, the custodian leaving the outer door open to light us somewhat on our way; for to our eyes the one long-wick'd, evil-smelling candle stuck in a sconce on the wall gave an inadequate light. When we came up through the open trap in the corner of the chamber overhead, Amelia held on to me so tightly that I could actually feel her heart beat. I must say for my own part that I was not surprised at her fear, for this room was even more gruesome than that below. Here there was certainly more light, but only just sufficient to realise the horrible surroundings of the place. The builders of the tower had evidently intended that only they who should gain the top should have any of the joys of light and prospect. There, as we had noticed from below, were ranges of windows, albeit of mediaeval smallness, but elsewhere in the tower were only a very few narrow slits such as were habitual in places of mediaeval defence. A few of these only lit the chamber, and these so high up in the wall that from no part could the sky be seen through the thickness of the walls. In racks, and leaning in disorder against the walls, were a number of headsmen's swords, great double-handed weapons with broad blade and keen edge. Hard by were several blocks whereon the necks of the victims had lain, with here and there deep notches where the steel had bitten through the guard of flesh and shored into the wood. Round the chamber, placed in all sorts of irregular ways, were many implements of torture which made one's heart ache to see-chairs full of spikes which gave instant and excruciating pain; chairs and couches with dull knobs whose torture was seemingly less, but which, though slower, were equally efficacious; racks, belts, boots, gloves, collars, all made for compressing at will; steel baskets in which the head could be slowly crushed into a pulp if necessary; watchmen's hooks with long handle and knife that cut at resistance-this a speciality of the old Nurnberg police system; and many, many other devices for man's injury to man. Amelia grew quite pale with the horror of the things, but fortunately did not faint, for being a little overcome she sat down on a torture chair, but jumped up again with a shriek, all tendency to faint gone. We both pretended that it was the injury done to her dress by the dust of the chair, and the rusty spikes which had upset her, and Mr. Hutcheson acquiesced in accepting the explanation with a kind-hearted laugh.

But the central object in the whole of this chamber of horrors was the engine known as the Iron Virgin, which stood near the centre of the room. It was a rudely-shaped figure of a woman, something of the bell order, or, to make a closer comparison, of the figure of Mrs. Noah in the children's Ark, but without that slimness of waist and perfect *rondeur* of hip which marks the aesthetic type of the Noah family. One would hardly have recognised it as intended for a human figure at all had not the founder shaped on the forehead a rude semblance of a woman's face. This machine was coated with rust without, and covered with dust; a rope was fastened to a ring in the front of the figure, about where the waist should have been, and was drawn through a pulley, fastened on the wooden pillar which sustained the flooring above. The custodian pulling this rope showed that a section of the front was hinged like a door at one side; we then saw that the engine was of considerable thickness, leaving just room enough inside for a man to be placed. The door was of equal thickness and of great weight, for it took the custodian all his strength, aided though he was by the contrivance of the pulley, to open it. This weight was partly due to the fact that the door was of manifest purpose hung so as to throw its weight downwards, so that it might shut of its own accord when the strain was released. The inside was honeycombed with rust-nay more, the rust alone that comes through time would hardly have eaten so deep into the iron walls; the rust of the cruel stains was deep indeed! It was only, however, when we came to look at the inside of the door that the diabolical intention was manifest to the full. Here were several long spikes, square and massive, broad at the base and sharp at the points, placed in such a position that when the door should close the upper ones would pierce the eyes of the victim, and the lower ones his heart and vitals. The sight was too much for poor Amelia, and this time she fainted dead off, and I had to carry her down the stairs, and place her on a bench outside till she recovered. That she felt it to the quick was afterwards shown by the fact that my eldest son bears to this day a rude birthmark on his breast, which has, by family consent, been accepted as representing the Nurnberg Virgin.

When we got back to the chamber we found Hutcheson still opposite the Iron Virgin; he had been evidently philosophising, and now gave us the benefit of his thought in the shape of a sort of exordium.

'Wall, I guess I've been learnin' somethin' here while madam has been gettin' over her faint. 'Pears to me that we're a long way behind the times on our side of the big drink. We uster think out on the plains that the Injun could give us points in tryin' to make a man uncomfortable; but I guess your old mediaeval law-and-order party could raise him every time. Splinters was pretty good in his bluff on the squaw, but this here young miss held a straight flush all high on him. The points of them spikes air sharp enough still, though even the edges air eaten out by what uster be on them. It'd be a good thing for our Indian section to get some specimens of this here play-toy to send round to the Reservations jest to knock the stuffin' out of the bucks, and the squaws too, by showing them as how old civilisation lays over them at their best. Guess but I'll get in that box a minute jest to see how it feels!'

'Oh no! no!' said Amelia. 'It is too terrible!'

'Guess, ma'am, nothin's too terrible to the explorin' mind. I've been in some queer places in my time. Spent a night inside a dead horse while a prairie fire swept over me in Montana Territory-an' another time slept inside a dead buffler when the Comanches was on the war path an' I didn't keer to leave my kyard on them. I've been two days in a caved-in tunnel in the Billy Broncho gold mine in New Mexico, an' was one of the four shut up for three parts of a day in the caisson what slid over on her side when we was settin' the foundations of the Buffalo Bridge. I've not funked an odd experience yet, an' I don't propose to begin now!'

We saw that he was set on the experiment, so I said: 'Well, hurry up, old man, and get through it quick!'

'All right, General,' said he, 'but I calculate we ain't quite ready yet. The gentlemen, my predecessors, what stood in that thar canister, didn't volunteer for the office-not much! And I guess there was some ornamental tyin' up before the big stroke was made. I want to go into this thing fair and square, so I must get fixed up proper first. I dare say this old galoot can rise some string and tie me up accordin' to sample?'

This was said interrogatively to the old custodian, but the latter, who understood the drift of his speech, though perhaps not appreciating to the full the niceties of dialect and imagery, shook his head. His protest was, however, only formal and made to be overcome. The American thrust a gold piece into his hand, saying: 'Take it, pard! it's your pot; and don't be skeer'd. This ain't no necktie party that you're asked to assist in!' He produced some thin frayed rope and proceeded to bind our companion with sufficient strictness for the purpose. When the upper part of his body was bound, Hutcheson said:

'Hold on a moment, Judge. Guess I'm too heavy for you to tote into the canister. You jest let me walk in, and then you can wash up regardin' my legs!'

Whilst speaking he had backed himself into the opening which was just enough to hold him. It was a close fit and no mistake. Amelia looked on with fear in her eyes, but she evidently did not like to say anything. Then the custodian completed his task by tying the American's feet together so that he was now absolutely helpless and fixed in his voluntary prison. He seemed to really enjoy it, and the incipient smile which was habitual to his face blossomed into actuality as he said:

'Guess this here Eve was made out of the rib of a dwarf! There ain't much room for a full-grown citizen of the United States to hustle. We uster make our coffins more roomier in Idaho territory. Now, Judge, you jest begin to let this door down, slow, on to me. I want to feel the same pleasure as the other jays had when those spikes began to move toward their eyes!'

'Oh no! no! no!' broke in Amelia hysterically. 'It is too terrible! I can't bear to see it! —I can't! I can't!' But the American was obdurate. 'Say, Colonel,' said he, 'why not take Madame for a little promenade? I wouldn't hurt her feelin's for the world; but now that I am here, havin' kem eight thousand miles, wouldn't it be too hard to give up the very experience I've been pinin' an' pantin' fur? A man can't get to feel like canned goods every time! Me and the Judge here'll fix up this thing in no time, an' then you'll come back, an' we'll all laugh together!'

Once more the resolution that is born of curiosity triumphed, and Amelia stayed holding tight to my arm and shivering whilst the custodian began to slacken slowly inch by inch the rope that held back the iron door. Hutcheson's face was positively radiant as his eyes followed the first movement of the spikes.

'Wall!' he said, 'I guess I've not had enjoyment like this since I left Noo York. Bar a scrap with a French sailor at Wapping-an' that warn't much of a picnic neither —I've not had a show fur real pleasure in this dod-rotted Continent, where there ain't no b'ars nor no Injuns, an' wheer nary man goes heeled. Slow there, Judge! Don't you rush this business! I want a show for my money this game —I du!'

The custodian must have had in him some of the blood of his predecessors in that ghastly tower, for he worked the engine with a deliberate and excruciating slowness which after five minutes, in which the outer edge of the door had not moved half as many inches, began to overcome Amelia. I saw her lips whiten, and felt her hold upon my arm relax. I looked around an instant for a place whereon to lay her, and when I looked at her again found that her eye had become fixed on the side of the Virgin. Following its direction I saw the black cat crouching out of sight. Her green eyes shone like danger lamps in the gloom of the place, and their colour was heightened by the blood which still smeared her coat and reddened her mouth. I cried out:

'The cat! look out for the cat!' for even then she sprang out before the engine. At this moment she looked like a triumphant demon. Her eyes blazed with ferocity, her hair bristled out till she seemed twice her normal size, and her tail lashed about as does a tiger's when the quarry is before it. Elias P. Hutcheson when he saw her was amused, and his eyes positively sparkled with fun as he said:

'Darned if the squaw hain't got on all her war paint! Jest give her a shove off if she comes any of her tricks on me, for I'm so fixed everlastingly by the boss, that durn my skin if I can keep my eyes from her if she wants them! Easy there, Judge! don't you slack that ar rope or I'm euchered!'

At this moment Amelia completed her faint, and I had to clutch hold of her round the waist or she would have fallen to the floor. Whilst attending to her I saw the black cat crouching for a spring, and jumped up to turn the creature out.

But at that instant, with a sort of hellish scream, she hurled herself, not as we expected at Hutcheson, but straight at the face of the custodian. Her claws seemed to be tearing wildly as one sees in the Chinese drawings of the dragon rampant, and as I looked I saw one of them light on the poor man's eye, and actually tear through it and down his cheek, leaving a wide band of red where the blood seemed to spurt from every vein.

With a yell of sheer terror which came quicker than even his sense of pain, the man leaped back, dropping as he did so the rope which held back the iron door. I jumped for it, but was too late, for the cord ran like lightning through the pulley-block, and the heavy mass fell forward from its own weight.

As the door closed I caught a glimpse of our poor companion's face. He seemed frozen with terror. His eyes stared with a horrible anguish as if dazed, and no sound came from his lips.

And then the spikes did their work. Happily the end was quick, for when I wrenched open the door they had pierced so deep that they had locked in the bones of the skull through which they had crushed, and actually tore him-it-out of his iron prison till, bound as he was, he fell at full length with a sickly thud upon the floor, the face turning upward as he fell.

I rushed to my wife, lifted her up and carried her out, for I feared for her very reason if she should wake from her faint to such a scene. I laid her on the bench outside and ran back.

Leaning against the wooden column was the custodian moaning in pain whilst he held his reddening handkerchief to his eyes. And sitting on the head of the poor American was the cat, purring loudly as she licked the blood which trickled through the gashed socket of his eyes.

I think no one will call me cruel because I seized one of the old executioner's swords and shore her in two as she sat.

The Secret of the Growing Gold

When Margaret Delandre went to live at Brent's Rock the whole neighbourhood awoke to the pleasure of an entirely new scandal. Scandals in connection with either the Delandre family or the Brents of Brent's Rock, were not few; and if the secret history of the county had been written in full both names would have been found well represented. It is true that the status of each was so different that they might have belonged to different continents-or to different worlds for the matter of that-for hitherto their orbits had never crossed. The Brents were accorded by the whole section of the country a unique social dominance, and had ever held themselves as high above the yeoman class to which Margaret Delandre belonged, as a blue-blooded Spanish hidalgo out-tops his peasant tenantry.

The Delandres had an ancient record and were proud of it in their way as the Brents were of theirs. But the family had never risen above yeomanry; and although they had been once well-to-do in the good old times of foreign wars and protection, their fortunes had withered under the scorching of the free trade sun and the 'piping times of peace.' They had, as the elder members used to assert, 'stuck to the land', with the result that they had taken root in it, body and soul. In fact, they, having chosen the life of vegetables, had flourished as vegetation does-blossomed and thrived in the good season and suffered in the bad. Their holding, Dander's Croft, seemed to have been worked out, and to be typical of the family which had inhabited it. The latter had declined generation after generation, sending out now and again some abortive shoot of unsatisfied energy in the shape of a soldier or sailor, who had worked his way to the minor grades of the services and had there stopped, cut short either from unheeding gallantry in action or from that destroying cause to men without breeding or youthful care-the recognition of a position above them which they feel unfitted to fill. So, little by little, the family dropped lower and lower, the men brooding and dissatisfied, and drinking themselves into the grave, the women drudging at home, or marrying beneath them-or worse. In process of time all disappeared, leaving only two in the Croft, Wykham Delandre and his sister Margaret. The man and woman seemed to have inherited in masculine and feminine form respectively the evil tendency of their race, sharing in common the principles, though manifesting them in different ways, of sullen passion, voluptuousness and recklessness.

The history of the Brents had been something similar, but showing the causes of decadence in their aristocratic and not their plebeian forms. They, too, had sent their shoots to the wars; but their positions had been different and they had often attained honour-for without flaw they were gallant, and brave deeds were done by them before the selfish dissipation which marked them had sapped their vigour.

The present head of the family-if family it could now be called when one remained of the direct line-was Geoffrey Brent. He was almost a type of worn out race, manifesting in some ways its most brilliant qualities, and in others its utter degradation. He might be fairly compared with some of those antique Italian nobles whom the painters have preserved to us with their courage, their unscrupulousness, their refinement of lust and cruelty-the voluptuary actual with the fiend potential. He was certainly handsome, with that dark, aquiline, commanding beauty which women so generally recognise as dominant. With men he was distant and cold; but such a bearing never deters womankind. The inscrutable laws of sex have so arranged that even a timid woman is not afraid of a fierce and haughty man. And so it was that there was hardly a woman of any kind or degree, who lived within view of Brent's Rock, who did not cherish some form of secret admiration for the handsome wastrel. The category was a wide one, for Brent's Rock rose up steeply from the midst of a level region and for a circuit of a hundred miles it lay on the horizon, with its high old towers and steep roofs cutting the level edge of wood and hamlet, and far-scattered mansions.

So long as Geoffrey Brent confined his dissipations to London and Paris and Vienna-anywhere out of sight and sound of his home-opinion was silent. It is easy to listen to far off echoes unmoved, and we can treat them with disbelief, or scorn, or disdain, or whatever attitude of coldness may suit our purpose. But when the scandal came close home it was another matter; and the feelings of independence and integrity which is in people of every community which is not utterly spoiled, asserted itself and demanded that condemnation should be expressed. Still there was a certain reticence in all, and no more notice was taken of the existing facts than was absolutely necessary. Margaret Delandre bore herself so fearlessly and so openly-she accepted her position as the justified companion of Geoffrey Brent so naturally that people came to believe that she was secretly married to him, and therefore thought it wiser to hold their tongues lest time should justify her and also make her an active enemy.

The one person who, by his interference, could have settled all doubts was debarred by circumstances from interfering in the matter. Wykham Delandre had quarrelled with his sister-or perhaps it was that she had quarrelled with him-and they were on terms not merely of armed neutrality but of bitter hatred. The quarrel had been antecedent to Margaret going to Brent's Rock. She and Wykham had almost come to blows. There had certainly been threats on one side and on the other; and in the end Wykham, overcome with passion, had ordered his sister to leave his house. She had risen straightway, and, without waiting to pack up even her own personal belongings, had walked out of the house. On the threshold she had paused for a moment to hurl a bitter threat at Wykham that he would rue in shame and despair to the last hour of his life his act of that day. Some weeks had since passed; and it was understood in the neighbourhood that Margaret had gone to London, when she suddenly appeared driving out with Geoffrey Brent, and the entire neighbourhood knew before nightfall that she had taken up her abode at the Rock. It was no subject of surprise that Brent had come back unexpectedly, for such was his usual custom. Even his own servants never knew when to expect him, for there was a private door, of which he alone had the key, by which he sometimes entered without anyone in the house being aware of his coming. This was his usual method of appearing after a long absence.

Wykham Delandre was furious at the news. He vowed vengeance-and to keep his mind level with his passion drank deeper than ever. He tried several times to see his sister, but she contemptuously refused to meet him. He tried to have an interview with Brent and was refused by him also. Then he tried to stop him in the road, but without avail, for Geoffrey was not a man to be stopped against his will. Several actual encounters took place between the two men, and many more were threatened and avoided. At last Wykham Delandre settled down to a morose, vengeful acceptance of the situation.

Neither Margaret nor Geoffrey was of a pacific temperament, and it was not long before there began to be quarrels between them. One thing would lead to another, and wine flowed freely at Brent's Rock. Now and again the quarrels would assume a bitter aspect, and threats would be exchanged in uncompromising language that fairly awed the listening servants. But such quarrels generally ended where domestic altercations do, in reconciliation, and in a mutual respect for the fighting qualities proportionate to their manifestation. Fighting for its own sake is found by a certain class of persons, all the world over, to be a matter of absorbing interest, and there is no reason to believe that domestic conditions minimise its potency. Geoffrey and Margaret made occasional absences from Brent's Rock, and on each of these occasions Wykham Delandre also absented himself; but as he generally heard of the absence too late to be of any service, he returned home each time in a more bitter and discontented frame of mind than before.

At last there came a time when the absence from Brent's Rock became longer than before. Only a few days earlier there had been a quarrel, exceeding in bitterness anything which had gone before; but this, too, had been made up, and a trip on the Continent had been mentioned before the servants. After a few days Wykham Delandre also went away, and it was some weeks before he returned. It was noticed that he was full of some new importance-satisfaction, exaltation-they hardly knew how to call it. He went straightway to Brent's Rock, and demanded to see Geoffrey Brent, and on being told that he had not yet returned, said, with a grim decision which the servants noted:

'I shall come again. My news is solid-it can wait!' and turned away. Week after week went by, and month after month; and then there came a rumour, certified later on, that an accident had occurred in the Zermatt valley. Whilst crossing a dangerous pass the carriage containing an English lady and the driver had fallen over a precipice, the gentleman of the party, Mr. Geoffrey Brent, having been fortunately saved as he had been walking up the hill to ease the horses. He gave information, and search was made. The broken rail, the excoriated roadway, the marks where the horses had struggled on the decline before finally pitching over into the torrent-all told the sad tale. It was a wet season, and there had been much snow in the winter, so that the river was swollen beyond its usual volume, and the eddies of the stream were packed with ice. All search was made, and finally the wreck of the carriage and the body of one horse were found in an eddy of the river. Later on the body of the driver was found on the sandy, torrent-swept waste near Täsch; but the body of the lady, like that of the other horse, had quite disappeared, and was-what was left of it by that time-whirling amongst the eddies of the Rhone on its way down to the Lake of Geneva.

Wykham Delandre made all the enquiries possible, but could not find any trace of the missing woman. He found, however, in the books of the various hotels the name of 'Mr. and Mrs. Geoffrey Brent'. And he had a stone erected at Zermatt to his sister's memory, under her married name, and a tablet put up in the church at Bretten, the parish in which both Brent's Rock and Dander's Croft were situated.

There was a lapse of nearly a year, after the excitement of the matter had worn away, and the whole neighbourhood had gone on its accustomed way. Brent was still absent, and Delandre more drunken, more morose, and more revengeful than before.

Then there was a new excitement. Brent's Rock was being made ready for a new mistress. It was officially announced by Geoffrey himself in a letter to the Vicar, that he had been married some months before to an Italian lady, and that they were then on their way home. Then a small army of workmen invaded the house; and hammer and plane sounded, and a general air of size and paint pervaded the atmosphere. One wing of the old house, the south, was entirely re-done; and then the great body of the workmen departed, leaving only materials for the doing of the old hall when Geoffrey Brent should have returned, for he had directed that the decoration was only to be done under his own eyes. He had brought with him accurate drawings of a hall in the house of his bride's father, for he wished to reproduce for her the place to which she had been accustomed. As the moulding had all to be re-done, some scaffolding poles and boards were brought in and laid on one side of the great hall, and also a great wooden tank or box for mixing the lime, which was laid in bags beside it.

When the new mistress of Brent's Rock arrived the bells of the church rang out, and there was a general jubilation. She was a beautiful creature, full of the poetry and fire and passion of the South; and the few English words which she had learned were spoken in such a sweet and pretty broken way that she won the hearts of the people almost as much by the music of her voice as by the melting beauty of her dark eyes.

Geoffrey Brent seemed more happy than he had ever before appeared; but there was a dark, anxious look on his face that was new to those who knew him of old, and he started at times as though at some noise that was unheard by others.

And so months passed and the whisper grew that at last Brent's Rock was to have an heir. Geoffrey was very tender to his wife, and the new bond between them seemed to soften him. He took more interest in his tenants and their needs than he had ever done; and works of charity on his part as well as on his sweet young wife's were not lacking. He seemed to have set all his hopes on the child that was coming, and as he looked deeper into the future the dark shadow that had come over his face seemed to die gradually away.

All the time Wykham Delandre nursed his revenge. Deep in his heart had grown up a purpose of vengeance which only waited an opportunity to crystallise and take a definite shape. His vague idea was somehow centred in the wife of Brent, for he knew that he could strike him best through those he loved, and the coming time seemed to hold in its womb the opportunity for which he longed. One night he sat alone in the living-room of his house. It had once been a handsome room in its way, but time and neglect had done their work and it was now little better than a ruin, without dignity or picturesqueness of any kind. He had been drinking heavily for some time and was more than half stupefied. He thought he heard a noise as of someone at the door and looked up. Then he called half savagely to come in; but there was no response. With a muttered blasphemy he renewed his potations. Presently he forgot all around him, sank into a daze, but suddenly awoke to see standing before him someone or something like a battered, ghostly edition of his sister. For a few moments there came upon him a sort of fear. The woman before him, with distorted features and burning eyes seemed hardly human, and the only thing that seemed a reality of his sister, as she had been, was her wealth of golden hair, and this was now streaked with grey. She eyed her brother with a long, cold stare; and he, too, as he looked and began to realise the actuality of her presence, found the hatred of her which he had had, once again surging up in his heart. All the brooding passion of the past year seemed to find a voice at once as he asked her:

'Why are you here? You're dead and buried.'

'I am here, Wykham Delandre, for no love of you, but because I hate another even more than I do you!' A great passion blazed in her eyes.

'Him?' he asked, in so fierce a whisper that even the woman was for an instant startled till she regained her calm.

'Yes, him!' she answered. 'But make no mistake, my revenge is my own; and I merely use you to help me to it.' Wykham asked suddenly:

'Did he marry you?'

The woman's distorted face broadened out in a ghastly attempt at a smile. It was a hideous mockery, for the broken features and seamed scars took strange shapes and strange colours, and queer lines of white showed out as the straining muscles pressed on the old cicatrices.

'So you would like to know! It would please your pride to feel that your sister was truly married! Well, you shall not know. That was my revenge on you, and I do not mean to change it by a hair's breadth. I have come here tonight simply to let you know that I am alive, so that if any violence be done me where I am going there may be a witness.'

'Where are you going?' demanded her brother.

'That is my affair! and I have not the least intention of letting you know!' Wykham stood up, but the drink was on him and he reeled and fell. As he lay on the floor he announced his intention of following his sister; and with an outburst of splenetic humour told her that he would follow her through the darkness by the light of her hair, and of her beauty. At this she turned on him, and said that there were others beside him that would rue her hair and her beauty too. 'As he will,' she hissed; 'for the hair remains though the beauty be gone. When he withdrew the lynch-pin and sent us over the precipice into the torrent, he had little thought of my beauty. Perhaps his beauty would be scarred like mine were he whirled, as I was, among the rocks of the Visp, and frozen on the ice pack in the drift of the river. But let him beware! His time is coming!' and with a fierce gesture she flung open the door and passed out into the night.

Later on that night, Mrs. Brent, who was but half-asleep, became suddenly awake and spoke to her husband:

'Geoffrey, was not that the click of a lock somewhere below our window?'

But Geoffrey-though she thought that he, too, had started at the noise-seemed sound asleep, and breathed heavily. Again Mrs. Brent dozed; but this time awoke to the fact that her husband had arisen and was partially dressed. He was deadly pale, and when the light of the lamp which he had in his hand fell on his face, she was frightened at the look in his eyes.

'What is it, Geoffrey? What dost thou?' she asked.

'Hush! little one,' he answered, in a strange, hoarse voice. 'Go to sleep. I am restless, and wish to finish some work I left undone.'

'Bring it here, my husband,' she said; 'I am lonely and I fear when thou art away.'

For reply he merely kissed her and went out, closing the door behind him. She lay awake for awhile, and then nature asserted itself, and she slept.

Suddenly she started broad awake with the memory in her ears of a smothered cry from somewhere not far off. She jumped up and ran to the door and listened, but there was no sound. She grew alarmed for her husband, and called out: 'Geoffrey! Geoffrey!'

After a few moments the door of the great hall opened, and Geoffrey appeared at it, but without his lamp.

'Hush!' he said, in a sort of whisper, and his voice was harsh and stern. 'Hush! Get to bed! I am working, and must not be disturbed. Go to sleep, and do not wake the house!'

With a chill in her heart-for the harshness of her husband's voice was new to her-she crept back to bed and lay there trembling, too frightened to cry, and listened to every sound. There was a long pause of silence, and then the sound of some iron implement striking muffled blows! Then there came a clang of a heavy stone falling, followed by a muffled curse. Then a dragging sound, and then more noise of stone on stone. She lay all the while in an agony of fear, and her heart beat dreadfully. She heard a curious sort of scraping sound; and then there was silence. Presently the door opened gently, and Geoffrey appeared. His wife pretended to be asleep; but through her eyelashes she saw him wash from his hands something white that looked like lime.

In the morning he made no allusion to the previous night, and she was afraid to ask any question.

From that day there seemed some shadow over Geoffrey Brent. He neither ate nor slept as he had been accustomed, and his former habit of turning suddenly as though someone were speaking from behind him revived. The old hall seemed to have some kind of fascination for him. He used to go there many times in the day, but grew impatient if anyone, even his wife, entered it. When the builder's foreman came to inquire about continuing his work Geoffrey was out driving; the man went into the hall, and when Geoffrey returned the servant told him of his arrival and where he was. With a frightful oath he pushed the servant aside and hurried up to the old hall. The workman met him almost at the door; and as Geoffrey burst into the room he ran against him. The man apologised:

'Beg pardon, sir, but I was just going out to make some enquiries. I directed twelve sacks of lime to be sent here, but I see there are only ten.'

'Damn the ten sacks and the twelve too!' was the ungracious and incomprehensible rejoinder.

The workman looked surprised, and tried to turn the conversation.

'I see, sir, there is a little matter which our people must have done; but the governor will of course see it set right at his own cost.'

'What do you mean?'

'That 'ere 'arth-stone, sir: Some idiot must have put a scaffold pole on it and cracked it right down the middle, and it's thick enough you'd think to stand hanythink.' Geoffrey was silent for quite a minute, and then said in a constrained voice and with much gentler manner:

'Tell your people that I am not going on with the work in the hall at present. I want to leave it as it is for a while longer.'

'All right sir. I'll send up a few of our chaps to take away these poles and lime bags and tidy the place up a bit.'

'No! No!' said Geoffrey, 'leave them where they are. I shall send and tell you when you are to get on with the work.' So the foreman went away, and his comment to his master was:

'I'd send in the bill, sir, for the work already done. 'Pears to me that money's a little shaky in that quarter.'

Once or twice Delandre tried to stop Brent on the road, and, at last, finding that he could not attain his object rode after the carriage, calling out:

'What has become of my sister, your wife?' Geoffrey lashed his horses into a gallop, and the other, seeing from his white face and from his wife's collapse almost into a faint that his object was attained, rode away with a scowl and a laugh.

That night when Geoffrey went into the hall he passed over to the great fireplace, and all at once started back with a smothered cry. Then with an effort he pulled himself together and went away, returning with a light. He bent down over the broken hearth-stone to see if the moonlight falling through the storied window had in any way deceived him. Then with a groan of anguish he sank to his knees.

There, sure enough, through the crack in the broken stone were protruding a multitude of threads of golden hair just tinged with grey!

He was disturbed by a noise at the door, and looking round, saw his wife standing in the doorway. In the desperation of the moment he took action to prevent discovery, and lighting a match at the lamp, stooped down and burned away the hair that rose through the broken stone. Then rising nonchalantly as he could, he pretended surprise at seeing his wife beside him.

For the next week he lived in an agony; for, whether by accident or design, he could not find himself alone in the hall for any length of time. At each visit the hair had grown afresh through the crack, and he had to watch it carefully lest his terrible secret should be discovered. He tried to find a receptacle for the body of the murdered woman outside the house, but someone always interrupted him; and once, when he was coming out of the private doorway, he was met by his wife, who began to question him about it, and manifested surprise that she should not have before noticed the key which he now reluctantly showed her. Geoffrey dearly and passionately loved his wife, so that any possibility of her discovering his dread secrets, or even of doubting him, filled him with anguish; and after a couple of days had passed, he could not help coming to the conclusion that, at least, she suspected something.

That very evening she came into the hall after her drive and found him there sitting moodily by the deserted fireplace. She spoke to him directly.

'Geoffrey, I have been spoken to by that fellow Delandre, and he says horrible things. He tells to me that a week ago his sister returned to his house, the wreck and ruin of her former self, with only her golden hair as of old, and announced some fell intention. He asked me where she is-and oh, Geoffrey, she is dead, she is dead! So how can she have returned? Oh! I am in dread, and I know not where to turn!'

For answer, Geoffrey burst into a torrent of blasphemy which made her shudder. He cursed Delandre and his sister and all their kind, and in especial he hurled curse after curse on her golden hair.

'Oh, hush! hush!' she said, and was then silent, for she feared her husband when she saw the evil effect of his humour. Geoffrey in the torrent of his anger stood up and moved away from the hearth; but suddenly stopped as he saw a new look of terror in his wife's eyes. He followed their glance, and then he too, shuddered-for there on the broken hearth-stone lay a golden streak as the point of the hair rose though the crack.

'Look, look!' she shrieked. 'Is it some ghost of the dead! Come away-come away!' and seizing her husband by the wrist with the frenzy of madness, she pulled him from the room.

That night she was in a raging fever. The doctor of the district attended her at once, and special aid was telegraphed for to London. Geoffrey was in despair, and in his anguish at the danger of his young wife almost forgot his own crime and its consequences. In the evening the doctor had to leave to attend to others; but he left Geoffrey in charge of his wife. His last words were:

'Remember, you must humour her till I come in the morning, or till some other doctor has her case in hand. What you have to dread is another attack of emotion. See that she is kept warm. Nothing more can be done.'

Late in the evening, when the rest of the household had retired, Geoffrey's wife got up from her bed and called to her husband.

'Come!' she said. 'Come to the old hall! I know where the gold comes from! I want to see it grow!'

Geoffrey would fain have stopped her, but he feared for her life or reason on the one hand, and lest in a paroxysm she should shriek out her terrible suspicion, and seeing that it was useless to try to prevent her, wrapped a warm rug around her and went with her to the old hall. When they entered, she turned and shut the door and locked it.

'We want no strangers amongst us three tonight!' she whispered with a wan smile.

'We three! nay we are but two,' said Geoffrey with a shudder; he feared to say more.

'Sit here,' said his wife as she put out the light. 'Sit here by the hearth and watch the gold growing. The silver moonlight is jealous! See, it steals along the floor towards the gold-our gold!' Geoffrey looked with growing horror, and saw that during the hours that had passed the golden hair had protruded further through the broken hearth-stone. He tried to hide it by placing his feet over the broken place; and his wife, drawing her chair beside him, leant over and laid her head on his shoulder.

'Now do not stir, dear,' she said; 'let us sit still and watch. We shall find the secret of the growing gold!' He passed his arm round her and sat silent; and as the moonlight stole along the floor she sank to sleep.

He feared to wake her; and so sat silent and miserable as the hours stole away.

Before his horror-struck eyes the golden-hair from the broken stone grew and grew; and as it increased, so his heart got colder and colder, till at last he had not power to stir, and sat with eyes full of terror watching his doom.

In the morning when the London doctor came, neither Geoffrey nor his wife could be found. Search was made in all the rooms, but without avail. As a last resource the great door of the old hall was broken open, and those who entered saw a grim and sorry sight.

There by the deserted hearth Geoffrey Brent and his young wife sat cold and white and dead. Her face was peaceful, and her eyes were closed in sleep; but his face was a sight that made all who saw it shudder, for there was on it a look of unutterable horror. The eyes were open and stared glassily at his feet, which were twined with tresses of golden hair, streaked with grey, which came through the broken hearth-stone.

The Gipsy Prophecy

'I really think,' said the Doctor, 'that, at any rate, one of us should go and try whether or not the thing is an imposture.'

'Good!' said Considine. 'After dinner we will take our cigars and stroll over to the camp.'

Accordingly, when the dinner was over, and the *La Tour* finished, Joshua Considine and his friend, Dr Burleigh, went over to the east side of the moor, where the gipsy encampment lay. As they were leaving, Mary Considine, who had walked as far as the end of the garden where it opened into the laneway, called after her husband:

'Mind, Joshua, you are to give them a fair chance, but don't give them any clue to a fortune-and don't you get flirting with any of the gipsy maidens-and take care to keep Gerald out of harm.'

For answer Considine held up his hand, as if taking a stage oath, and whistled the air of the old song, 'The Gipsy Countess.' Gerald joined in the strain, and then, breaking into merry laughter, the two men passed along the laneway to the common, turning now and then to wave their hands to Mary, who leaned over the gate, in the twilight, looking after them.

It was a lovely evening in the summer; the very air was full of rest and quiet happiness, as though an outward type of the peacefulness and joy which made a heaven of the home of the young married folk. Considine's life had not been an eventful one. The only disturbing element which he had ever known was in his wooing of Mary Winston, and the long-continued objection of her ambitious parents, who expected a brilliant match for their only daughter. When Mr. and Mrs. Winston had discovered the attachment of the young barrister, they had tried to keep the young people apart by sending their daughter away for a long round of visits, having made her promise not to correspond with her lover during her absence. Love, however, had stood the test. Neither absence nor neglect seemed to cool the passion of the young man, and jealousy seemed a thing unknown to his sanguine nature; so, after a long period of waiting, the parents had given in, and the young folk were married.

They had been living in the cottage a few months, and were just beginning to feel at home. Gerald Burleigh, Joshua's old college chum, and himself a sometime victim of Mary's beauty, had arrived a week before, to stay with them for as long a time as he could tear himself away from his work in London.

When her husband had quite disappeared Mary went into the house, and, sitting down at the piano, gave an hour to Mendelssohn.

It was but a short walk across the common, and before the cigars required renewing the two men had reached the gipsy camp. The place was as picturesque as gipsy camps-when in villages and when business is good-usually are. There were some few persons round the fire, investing their money in prophecy, and a large number of others, poorer or more parsimonious, who stayed just outside the bounds but near enough to see all that went on.

As the two gentlemen approached, the villagers, who knew Joshua, made way a little, and a pretty, keen-eyed gipsy girl tripped up and asked to tell their fortunes. Joshua held out his hand, but the girl, without seeming to see it, stared at his face in a very odd manner. Gerald nudged him:

'You must cross her hand with silver,' he said. 'It is one of the most important parts of the mystery.' Joshua took from his pocket a half-crown and held it out to her, but, without looking at it, she answered:

'You have to cross the gipsy's hand with gold.'

Gerald laughed. 'You are at a premium as a subject,' he said. Joshua was of the kind of man-the universal kind-who can tolerate being stared at by a pretty girl; so, with some little deliberation, he answered:

'All right; here you are, my pretty girl; but you must give me a real good fortune for it,' and he handed her a half sovereign, which she took, saying:

'It is not for me to give good fortune or bad, but only to read what the Stars have said.' She took his right hand and turned it palm upward; but the instant her eyes met it she dropped it as though it had been red hot, and, with a startled look, glided swiftly away. Lifting the curtain of the large tent, which occupied the centre of the camp, she disappeared within.

'Sold again!' said the cynical Gerald. Joshua stood a little amazed, and not altogether satisfied. They both watched the large tent. In a few moments there emerged from the opening not the young girl, but a stately looking woman of middle age and commanding presence.

The instant she appeared the whole camp seemed to stand still. The clamour of tongues, the laughter and noise of the work were, for a second or two, arrested, and every man or woman who sat, or crouched, or lay, stood up and faced the imperial looking gipsy.

'The Queen, of course,' murmured Gerald. 'We are in luck tonight.' The gipsy Queen threw a searching glance around the camp, and then, without hesitating an instant, came straight over and stood before Joshua.

'Hold out your hand,' she said in a commanding tone.

Again Gerald spoke, *sotto voce*: 'I have not been spoken to in that way since I was at school.'

'Your hand must be crossed with gold.'

'A hundred per cent. at this game,' whispered Gerald, as Joshua laid another half sovereign on his upturned palm.

The gipsy looked at the hand with knitted brows; then suddenly looking up into his face, said:

'Have you a strong will-have you a true heart that can be brave for one you love?'

'I hope so; but I am afraid I have not vanity enough to say "yes".'

'Then I will answer for you; for I read resolution in your face-resolution desperate and determined if need be. You have a wife you love?'

'Yes,' emphatically.

'Then leave her at once-never see her face again. Go from her now, while love is fresh and your heart is free from wicked intent. Go quick-go far, and never see her face again!'

Joshua drew away his hand quickly, and said, 'Thank you!' stiffly but sarcastically, as he began to move away.

'I say!' said Gerald, 'you're not going like that, old man; no use in being indignant with the Stars or their prophet-and, moreover, your sovereign-what of it? At least, hear the matter out.'

'Silence, ribald!' commanded the Queen, 'you know not what you do. Let him go-and go ignorant, if he will not be warned.'

Joshua immediately turned back. 'At all events, we will see this thing out,' he said. 'Now, madam, you have given me advice, but I paid for a fortune.'

'Be warned!' said the gipsy. 'The Stars have been silent for long; let the mystery still wrap them round.'

'My dear madam, I do not get within touch of a mystery every day, and I prefer for my money knowledge rather than ignorance. I can get the latter commodity for nothing when I want any of it.'

Gerald echoed the sentiment. 'As for me I have a large and unsaleable stock on hand.'

The gipsy Queen eyed the two men sternly, and then said: 'As you wish. You have chosen for yourself, and have met warning with scorn, and appeal with levity. On your own heads be the doom!'

'Amen!' said Gerald.

With an imperious gesture the Queen took Joshua's hand again, and began to tell his fortune.

'I see here the flowing of blood; it will flow before long; it is running in my sight. It flows through the broken circle of a severed ring.'

'Go on!' said Joshua, smiling. Gerald was silent.

'Must I speak plainer?'

'Certainly; we commonplace mortals want something definite. The Stars are a long way off, and their words get somewhat dulled in the message.'

The gipsy shuddered, and then spoke impressively. 'This is the hand of a murderer–the murderer of his wife!' She dropped the hand and turned away.

Joshua laughed. 'Do you know,' said he, 'I think if I were you I should prophesy some jurisprudence into my system. For instance, you say "this hand is the hand of a murderer." Well, whatever it may be in the future–or potentially–it is at present not one. You ought to give your prophecy in such terms as "the hand which will be a murderer's", or, rather, "the hand of one who will be the murderer of his wife". The Stars are really not good on technical questions.'

The gipsy made no reply of any kind, but, with drooping head and despondent mien, walked slowly to her tent, and, lifting the curtain, disappeared.

Without speaking the two men turned homewards, and walked across the moor. Presently, after some little hesitation, Gerald spoke.

'Of course, old man, this is all a joke; a ghastly one, but still a joke. But would it not be well to keep it to ourselves?'

'How do you mean?'

'Well, not tell your wife. It might alarm her.'

'Alarm her! My dear Gerald, what are you thinking of? Why, she would not be alarmed or afraid of me if all the gipsies that ever didn't come from Bohemia agreed that I was to murder her, or even to have a hard thought of her, whilst so long as she was saying "Jack Robinson."'

Gerald remonstrated. 'Old fellow, women are superstitious–far more than we men are; and, also they are blessed–or cursed–with a nervous system to which we are strangers. I see too much of it in my work not to realise it. Take my advice and do not let her know, or you will frighten her.'

Joshua's lips unconsciously hardened as he answered: 'My dear fellow, I would not have a secret from my wife. Why, it would be the beginning of a new order of things between us. We have no secrets from each other. If we ever have, then you may begin to look out for something odd between us.'

'Still,' said Gerald, 'at the risk of unwelcome interference, I say again be warned in time.'

'The gipsy's very words,' said Joshua. 'You and she seem quite of one accord. Tell me, old man, is this a put-up thing? You told me of the gipsy camp–did you arrange it all with Her Majesty?' This was said with an air of bantering earnestness. Gerald assured him that he only heard of the camp that morning; but he made fun of every answer of his friend, and, in the process of this raillery, the time passed, and they entered the cottage.

Mary was sitting at the piano but not playing. The dim twilight had waked some very tender feelings in her breast, and her eyes were full of gentle tears. When the men came in she stole over to her husband's side and kissed him. Joshua struck a tragic attitude.

'Mary,' he said in a deep voice, 'before you approach me, listen to the words of Fate. The Stars have spoken and the doom is sealed.'

'What is it, dear? Tell me the fortune, but do not frighten me.'

'Not at all, my dear; but there is a truth which it is well that you should know. Nay, it is necessary so that all your arrangements can be made beforehand, and everything be decently done and in order.'

'Go on, dear; I am listening.'

'Mary Considine, your effigy may yet be seen at Madame Tussaud's. The juris-imprudent Stars have announced their fell tidings that this hand is red with blood–your blood. Mary! Mary! my God!' He sprang forward, but too late to catch her as she fell fainting on the floor.

'I told you,' said Gerald. 'You don't know them as well as I do.'

After a little while Mary recovered from her swoon, but only to fall into strong hysterics, in which she laughed and wept and raved and cried, 'Keep him from me–from me, Joshua, my husband,' and many other words of entreaty and of fear.

Joshua Considine was in a state of mind bordering on agony, and when at last Mary became calm he knelt by her and kissed her feet and hands and hair and called her all the sweet names and said all the tender things his lips could frame. All that night he sat by her bedside and held her hand. Far through the night and up to the early morning she kept waking from sleep and crying out as if in fear, till she was comforted by the consciousness that her husband was watching beside her.

Breakfast was late the next morning, but during it Joshua received a telegram which required him to drive over to Withering, nearly twenty miles. He was loth to go; but Mary would not hear of his remaining, and so before noon he drove off in his dog-cart alone.

When he was gone Mary retired to her room. She did not appear at lunch, but when afternoon tea was served on the lawn under the great weeping willow, she came to join her guest. She was looking quite recovered from her illness of the evening before. After some casual remarks, she said to Gerald: 'Of course it was very silly about last night, but I could not help feeling frightened. Indeed I would feel so still if I let myself think of it. But, after all these people may only imagine things, and I have got a test that can hardly fail to show that the prediction is false-if indeed it be false,' she added sadly.

'What is your plan?' asked Gerald.

'I shall go myself to the gipsy camp, and have my fortune told by the Queen.'

'Capital. May I go with you?'

'Oh, no! That would spoil it. She might know you and guess at me, and suit her utterance accordingly. I shall go alone this afternoon.'

When the afternoon was gone Mary Considine took her way to the gipsy encampment. Gerald went with her as far as the near edge of the common, and returned alone.

Half-an-hour had hardly elapsed when Mary entered the drawing-room, where he lay on a sofa reading. She was ghastly pale and was in a state of extreme excitement. Hardly had she passed over the threshold when she collapsed and sank moaning on the carpet. Gerald rushed to aid her, but by a great effort she controlled herself and motioned him to be silent. He waited, and his ready attention to her wish seemed to be her best help, for, in a few minutes, she had somewhat recovered, and was able to tell him what had passed.

'When I got to the camp,' she said, 'there did not seem to be a soul about, I went into the centre and stood there. Suddenly a tall woman stood beside me. "Something told me I was wanted!" she said. I held out my hand and laid a piece of silver on it. She took from her neck a small golden trinket and laid it there also; and then, seizing the two, threw them into the stream that ran by. Then she took my hand in hers and spoke: "Naught but blood in this guilty place," and turned away. I caught hold of her and asked her to tell me more. After some hesitation, she said: "Alas! alas! I see you lying at your husband's feet, and his hands are red with blood."'

Gerald did not feel at all at ease, and tried to laugh it off. 'Surely,' he said, 'this woman has a craze about murder.'

'Do not laugh,' said Mary, 'I cannot bear it,' and then, as if with a sudden impulse, she left the room.

Not long after Joshua returned, bright and cheery, and as hungry as a hunter after his long drive. His presence cheered his wife, who seemed much brighter, but she did not mention the episode of the visit to the gipsy camp, so Gerald did not mention it either. As if by tacit consent the subject was not alluded to during the evening. But there was a strange, settled look on Mary's face, which Gerald could not but observe.

In the morning Joshua came down to breakfast later than usual. Mary had been up and about the house from an early hour; but as the time drew on she seemed to get a little nervous and now and again threw around an anxious look.

Gerald could not help noticing that none of those at breakfast could get on satisfactorily with their food. It was not altogether that the chops were tough, but that the knives were all so blunt. Being a guest, he, of course, made no sign; but presently saw Joshua draw his thumb across the edge of his knife in an unconscious sort of way. At the action Mary turned pale and almost fainted.

After breakfast they all went out on the lawn. Mary was making up a bouquet, and said to her husband, 'Get me a few of the tea-roses, dear.'

Joshua pulled down a cluster from the front of the house. The stem bent, but was too tough to break. He put his hand in his pocket to get his knife; but in vain. 'Lend me your knife, Gerald,' he said. But Gerald had not got one, so he went into the breakfast room and took one from the table. He came out feeling its edge and grumbling. 'What on earth has happened to all the knives-the edges seem all ground off?' Mary turned away hurriedly and entered the house.

Joshua tried to sever the stalk with the blunt knife as country cooks sever the necks of fowl-as schoolboys cut twine. With a little effort he finished the task. The cluster of roses grew thick, so he determined to gather a great bunch.

He could not find a single sharp knife in the sideboard where the cutlery was kept, so he called Mary, and when she came, told her the state of things. She looked so agitated and so miserable that he could not help knowing the truth, and, as if astounded and hurt, asked her:

'Do you mean to say that *you* have done it?'

She broke in, 'Oh, Joshua, I was so afraid.'

He paused, and a set, white look came over his face. 'Mary!' said he, 'is this all the trust you have in me? I would not have believed it.'

'Oh, Joshua! Joshua!' she cried entreatingly, 'forgive me,' and wept bitterly.

Joshua thought a moment and then said: 'I see how it is. We shall better end this or we shall all go mad.'

He ran into the drawing-room.

'Where are you going?' almost screamed Mary.

Gerald saw what he meant-that he would not be tied to blunt instruments by the force of a superstition, and was not surprised when he saw him come out through the French window, bearing in his hand a large Ghourka knife, which usually lay on the centre table, and which his brother had sent him from Northern India. It was one of those great hunting-knives which worked such havoc, at close quarters with the enemies of the loyal Ghourkas during the mutiny, of great weight but so evenly balanced in the hand as to seem light, and with an edge like a razor. With one of these knives a Ghourka can cut a sheep in two.

When Mary saw him come out of the room with the weapon in his hand she screamed in an agony of fright, and the hysterics of last night were promptly renewed.

Joshua ran toward her, and, seeing her falling, threw down the knife and tried to catch her.

However, he was just a second too late, and the two men cried out in horror simultaneously as they saw her fall upon the naked blade.

When Gerald rushed over he found that in falling her left hand had struck the blade, which lay partly upwards on the grass. Some of the small veins were cut through, and the blood gushed freely from the wound. As he was tying it up he pointed out to Joshua that the wedding ring was severed by the steel.

They carried her fainting to the house. When, after a while, she came out, with her arm in a sling, she was peaceful in her mind and happy. She said to her husband:

'The gipsy was wonderfully near the truth; too near for the real thing ever to occur now, dear.'

Joshua bent over and kissed the wounded hand.

The Coming of Abel Behenna

The little Cornish port of Pencastle was bright in the early April, when the sun had seemingly come to stay after a long and bitter winter. Boldly and blackly the rock stood out against a background of shaded blue, where the sky fading into mist met the far horizon. The sea was of true Cornish hue-sapphire, save where it became deep emerald green in the fathomless depths under the cliffs, where the seal caves opened their grim jaws. On the slopes the grass was parched and brown. The spikes of furze bushes were ashy grey, but the golden yellow of their flowers streamed along the hillside, dipping out in lines as the rock cropped up, and lessening into patches and dots till finally it died away all together where the sea winds swept round the jutting cliffs and cut short the vegetation as though with an ever-working aerial shears. The whole hillside, with its body of brown and flashes of yellow, was just like a colossal yellow-hammer.

The little harbour opened from the sea between towering cliffs, and behind a lonely rock, pierced with many caves and blow-holes through which the sea in storm time sent its thunderous voice, together with a fountain of drifting spume. Hence, it wound westwards in a serpentine course, guarded at its entrance by two little curving piers to left and right. These were roughly built of dark slates placed endways and held together with great beams bound with iron bands. Thence, it flowed up the rocky bed of the stream whose winter torrents had of old cut out its way amongst the hills. This stream was deep at first, with here and there, where it widened, patches of broken rock exposed at low water, full of holes where crabs and lobsters were to be found at the ebb of the tide. From amongst the rocks rose sturdy posts, used for warping in the little coasting vessels which frequented the port. Higher up, the stream still flowed deeply, for the tide ran far inland, but always calmly for all the force of the wildest storm was broken below. Some quarter mile inland the stream was deep at high water, but at low tide there were at each side patches of the same broken rock as lower down, through the chinks of which the sweet water of the natural stream trickled and murmured after the tide had ebbed away. Here, too, rose mooring posts for the fishermen's boats. At either side of the river was a row of cottages down almost on the level of high tide. They were pretty cottages, strongly and snugly built, with trim narrow gardens in front, full of old-fashioned plants, flowering currants, coloured primroses, wallflower, and stonecrop. Over the fronts of many of them climbed clematis and wisteria. The window sides and door posts of all were as white as snow, and the little pathway to each was paved with light coloured stones. At some of the doors were tiny porches, whilst at others were rustic seats cut from tree trunks or from old barrels; in nearly every case the window ledges were filled with boxes or pots of flowers or foliage plants.

Two men lived in cottages exactly opposite each other across the stream. Two men, both young, both good-looking, both prosperous, and who had been companions and rivals from their boyhood. Abel Behenna was dark with the gypsy darkness which the Phœnician mining wanderers left in their track; Eric Sanson-which the local antiquarian said was a corruption of Sagamanson-was fair, with the ruddy hue which marked the path of the wild Norseman. These two seemed to have singled out each other from the very beginning to work and strive together, to fight for each other and to stand back to back in all endeavours. They had now put the coping-stone on their Temple of Unity by falling in love with the same girl. Sarah Trefusis was certainly the prettiest girl in Pencastle, and there was many a young man who would gladly have tried his fortune with her, but that there were two to contend against, and each of these the strongest and most resolute man in the port-except the other. The average young man thought that this was very hard, and on account of it bore no good will to either of the three principals: whilst the average young woman who had, lest worse should befall, to put up with the grumbling of her sweetheart, and the sense of being only second best which it implied, did not either, be sure, regard Sarah with friendly eye. Thus it came, in the course of a year or so, for rustic courtship is a slow process, that the two men and woman found themselves thrown much together. They were all satisfied, so it did not matter, and Sarah, who was vain and something frivolous, took care to have her revenge on both men and women in a quiet way. When a young woman in her 'walking out' can only boast one not-quite-satisfied young man, it is no particular pleasure to her to see her escort cast sheep's eyes at a better-looking girl supported by two devoted swains.

At length there came a time which Sarah dreaded, and which she had tried to keep distant the time when she had to make her choice between the two men. She liked them both, and, indeed, either of them might have satisfied the ideas of even a more exacting girl. But her mind was so constituted that she thought more of what she might lose, than of what she might gain; and whenever she thought she had made up her mind she became instantly assailed with doubts as to the wisdom of her choice. Always the man whom she had presumably lost became endowed afresh with a newer and more bountiful crop of advantages than had ever arisen from the possibility of his acceptance. She promised each man that on her birthday she would give him his answer, and that day, the 11th of April, had now arrived. The promises had been given singly and confidentially, but each was given to a man who was not likely to forget. Early in the morning she found both men hovering round her door. Neither had taken the other into his confidence, and each was simply seeking an early opportunity of getting his answer, and advancing his suit if necessary. Damon, as a rule, does not take Pythias with him when making a proposal; and in the heart of each man his own affairs had a claim far above any requirements of friendship. So, throughout the day, they kept seeing each other out. The position was doubtless somewhat embarrassing to Sarah, and though the satisfaction of her vanity that she should be thus adored was very pleasing, yet there were moments when she was annoyed with both men for being so persistent. Her only consolation at such moments was that she saw, through the elaborate smiles of the other girls when in passing they noticed her door thus doubly guarded, the jealousy which filled their hearts. Sarah's mother was a person of commonplace and sordid ideas, and, seeing all along the state of affairs, her one intention, persistently expressed to her daughter in the plainest words, was to so arrange matters that Sarah should get all that was possible out of both men. With this purpose she had cunningly kept herself as far as possible in the background in the matter of her daughter's wooings, and watched in silence. At first Sarah had been indignant with her for her sordid views; but, as usual, her weak nature gave way before persistence, and she had now got to the stage of acceptance. She was not surprised when her mother whispered to her in the little yard behind the house: —

'Go up the hillside for a while; I want to talk to these two. They're both red-hot for ye, and now's the time to get things fixed!' Sarah began a feeble remonstrance, but her mother cut her short.

'I tell ye, girl, that my mind is made up! Both these men want ye, and only one can have ye, but before ye choose it'll be so arranged that ye'll have all that both have got! Don't argy, child! Go up the hillside, and when ye come back I'll have it fixed —I see a way quite easy!' So Sarah went up the hillside through the narrow paths between the golden furze, and Mrs. Trefusis joined the two men in the living-room of the little house.

She opened the attack with the desperate courage which is in all mothers when they think for their children, howsoever mean the thoughts may be.

'Ye two men, ye're both in love with my Sarah!'

Their bashful silence gave consent to the barefaced proposition. She went on.

'Neither of ye has much!' Again they tacitly acquiesced in the soft impeachment.

'I don't know that either of ye could keep a wife!' Though neither said a word their looks and bearing expressed distinct dissent. Mrs. Trefusis went on:

'But if ye'd put what ye both have together ye'd make a comfortable home for one of ye-and Sarah!' She eyed the men keenly, with her cunning eyes half shut, as she spoke; then satisfied from her scrutiny that the idea was accepted she went on quickly, as if to prevent argument:

'The girl likes ye both, and mayhap it's hard for her to choose. Why don't ye toss up for her? First put your money together-ye've each got a bit put by, I know. Let the lucky man take the lot and trade with it a bit, and then come home and marry her. Neither of ye's afraid, I suppose! And neither of ye'll say that he won't do that much for the girl that ye both say ye love!'

Abel broke the silence:

'It don't seem the square thing to toss for the girl! She wouldn't like it herself, and it doesn't seem-seem respectful like to her —' Eric interrupted. He was conscious that his chance was not so good as Abel's in case Sarah should wish to choose between them:

'Are ye afraid of the hazard?'

'Not me!' said Abel, boldly. Mrs. Trefusis, seeing that her idea was beginning to work, followed up the advantage.

'It is settled that ye put yer money together to make a home for her, whether ye toss for her or leave it for her to choose?'

'Yes,' said Eric quickly, and Abel agreed with equal sturdiness. Mrs. Trefusis' little cunning eyes twinkled. She heard Sarah's step in the yard, and said:

'Well! here she comes, and I leave it to her.' And she went out.

During her brief walk on the hillside Sarah had been trying to make up her mind. She was feeling almost angry with both men for being the cause of her difficulty, and as she came into the room said shortly:

'I want to have a word with you both-come to the Flagstaff Rock, where we can be alone.' She took her hat and went out of the house up the winding path to the steep rock crowned with a high flagstaff, where once the wreckers' fire basket used to burn. This was the rock which formed the northern jaw of the little harbour. There was only room on the path for two abreast, and it marked the state of things pretty well when, by a sort of implied arrangement, Sarah went first, and the two men followed, walking abreast and keeping step. By this time, each man's heart was boiling with jealousy. When they came to the top of the rock, Sarah stood against the flagstaff, and the two young men stood opposite her. She had chosen her position with knowledge and intention, for there was no room for anyone to stand beside her. They were all silent for a while; then Sarah began to laugh and said: —

'I promised the both of you to give you an answer to-day. I've been thinking and thinking and thinking, till I began to get angry with you both for plaguing me so; and even now I don't seem any nearer than ever I was to making up my mind.' Eric said suddenly:

'Let us toss for it, lass!' Sarah showed no indignation whatever at the proposition; her mother's eternal suggestion had schooled her to the acceptance of something of the kind, and her weak nature made it easy to her to grasp at any way out of the difficulty. She stood with downcast eyes idly picking at the sleeve of her dress, seeming to have tacitly acquiesced in the proposal. Both men instinctively realising this pulled each a coin from his pocket, spun it in the air, and dropped his other hand over the palm on which it lay. For a few seconds they remained thus, all silent; then Abel, who was the more thoughtful of the men, spoke:

'Sarah! is this good?' As he spoke he removed the upper hand from the coin and placed the latter back in his pocket. Sarah was nettled.

'Good or bad, it's good enough for me! Take it or leave it as you like,' she said, to which he replied quickly:

'Nay lass! Aught that concerns you is good enow for me. I did but think of you lest you might have pain or disappointment hereafter. If you love Eric better nor me, in God's name say so, and I think I'm man enow to stand aside. Likewise, if I'm the one, don't make us both miserable for life!' Face to face with a difficulty, Sarah's weak nature proclaimed itself; she put her hands before her face and began to cry, saying —

'It was my mother. She keeps telling me!' The silence which followed was broken by Eric, who said hotly to Abel:

'Let the lass alone, can't you? If she wants to choose this way, let her. It's good enough for me-and for you, too! She's said it now, and must abide by it!' Hereupon Sarah turned upon him in sudden fury, and cried:

'Hold your tongue! what is it to you, at any rate?' and she resumed her crying. Eric was so flabbergasted that he had not a word to say, but stood looking particularly foolish, with his mouth open and his hands held out with the coin still between them. All were silent till Sarah, taking her hands from her face laughed hysterically and said:

'As you two can't make up your minds, I'm going home!' and she turned to go.

'Stop,' said Abel, in an authoritative voice. 'Eric, you hold the coin, and I'll cry. Now, before we settle it, let us clearly understand: the man who wins takes all the money that we both have got, brings it to Bristol and ships on a voyage and trades with it. Then he comes back and marries Sarah, and they two keep all, whatever there may be, as the result of the trading. Is this what we understand?'

'Yes,' said Eric.

'I'll marry him on my next birthday,' said Sarah. Having said it the intolerably mercenary spirit of her action seemed to strike her, and impulsively she turned away with a bright blush. Fire seemed to sparkle in the eyes of both men. Said Eric: 'A year so be! The man that wins is to have one year.'

'Toss!' cried Abel, and the coin spun in the air. Eric caught it, and again held it between his outstretched hands.

'Heads!' cried Abel, a pallor sweeping over his face as he spoke. As he leaned forward to look Sarah leaned forward too, and their heads almost touched. He could feel her hair blowing on his cheek, and it thrilled through him like fire. Eric lifted his upper hand; the coin lay with its head up. Abel stepped forward and took Sarah in his arms. With a curse Eric hurled the coin far into the sea. Then he leaned against the flagstaff and scowled at the others with his hands thrust deep into his pockets. Abel whispered wild words of passion and delight into Sarah's ears, and as she listened she began to believe that fortune had rightly interpreted the wishes of her secret heart, and that she loved Abel best.

Presently Abel looked up and caught sight of Eric's face as the last ray of sunset struck it. The red light intensified the natural ruddiness of his complexion, and he looked as though he were steeped in blood. Abel did not mind his scowl, for now that his own heart was at rest he could feel unalloyed pity for his friend. He stepped over meaning to comfort him, and held out his hand, saying:

'It was my chance, old lad. Don't grudge it me. I'll try to make Sarah a happy woman, and you shall be a brother to us both!'

'Brother be damned!' was all the answer Eric made, as he turned away. When he had gone a few steps down the rocky path he turned and came back. Standing before Abel and Sarah, who had their arms round each other, he said:

'You have a year. Make the most of it! And be sure you're in time to claim your wife! Be back to have your banns up in time to be married on the 11th April. If you're not, I tell you I shall have my banns up, and you may get back too late.'

'What do you mean, Eric? You are mad!'

'No more mad than you are, Abel Behenna. You go, that's your chance! I stay, that's mine! I don't mean to let the grass grow under my feet. Sarah cared no more for you than for me five minutes ago, and she may come back to that five minutes after you're gone! You won by a point only-the game may change.'

'The game won't change!' said Abel shortly. 'Sarah, you'll be true to me? You won't marry till I return?'

'For a year!' added Eric, quickly, 'that's the bargain.'

'I promise for the year,' said Sarah. A dark look came over Abel's face, and he was about to speak, but he mastered himself and smiled.

'I mustn't be too hard or get angry tonight! Come, Eric! we played and fought together. I won fairly. I played fairly all the game of our wooing! You know that as well as I do; and now when I am going away, I shall look to my old and true comrade to help me when I am gone!'

'I'll help you none,' said Eric, 'so help me God!'

'It was God helped me,' said Abel simply.

'Then let Him go on helping you,' said Eric angrily. 'The Devil is good enough for me!' and without another word he rushed down the steep path and disappeared behind the rocks.

When he had gone Abel hoped for some tender passage with Sarah, but the first remark she made chilled him.

'How lonely it all seems without Eric!' and this note sounded till he had left her at home—and after.

Early on the next morning Abel heard a noise at his door, and on going out saw Eric walking rapidly away: a small canvas bag full of gold and silver lay on the threshold; on a small slip of paper pinned to it was written:

'Take the money and go. I stay. God for you! The Devil for me! Remember the 11th of April. —ERIC SANSON.' That afternoon Abel went off to Bristol, and a week later sailed on the *Star of the Sea* bound for Pahang. His money-including that which had been Eric's —was on board in the shape of a venture of cheap toys. He had been advised by a shrewd old mariner of Bristol whom he knew, and who knew the ways of the Chersonese, who predicted that every penny invested would be returned with a shilling to boot.

As the year wore on Sarah became more and more disturbed in her mind. Eric was always at hand to make love to her in his own persistent, masterful manner, and to this she did not object. Only one letter came from Abel, to say that his venture had proved successful, and that he had sent some two hundred pounds to the bank at Bristol, and was trading with fifty pounds still remaining in goods for China, whither the *Star of the Sea* was bound and whence she would return to Bristol. He suggested that Eric's share of the venture should be returned to him with his share of the profits. This proposition was treated with anger by Eric, and as simply childish by Sarah's mother.

More than six months had since then elapsed, but no other letter had come, and Eric's hopes which had been dashed down by the letter from Pahang, began to rise again. He perpetually assailed Sarah with an 'if!' If Abel did not return, would she then marry him? If the 11th April went by without Abel being in the port, would she give him over? If Abel had taken his fortune, and married another girl on the head of it, would she marry him, Eric, as soon as the truth were known? And so on in an endless variety of possibilities. The power of the strong will and the determined purpose over the woman's weaker nature became in time manifest. Sarah began to lose her faith in Abel and to regard Eric as a possible husband; and a possible husband is in a woman's eye different to all other men. A new affection for him began to arise in her breast, and the daily familiarities of permitted courtship furthered the growing affection. Sarah began to regard Abel as rather a rock in the road of her life, and had it not been for her mother's constantly reminding her of the good fortune already laid by in the Bristol Bank she would have tried to have shut her eyes altogether to the fact of Abel's existence.

The 11th April was Saturday, so that in order to have the marriage on that day it would be necessary that the banns should be called on Sunday, 22nd March. From the beginning of that month Eric kept perpetually on the subject of Abel's absence, and his outspoken opinion that the latter was either dead or married began to become a reality to the woman's mind. As the first half of the month wore on Eric became more jubilant, and after church on the 15th he took Sarah for a walk to the Flagstaff Rock. There he asserted himself strongly:

'I told Abel, and you too, that if he was not here to put up his banns in time for the eleventh, I would put up mine for the twelfth. Now the time has come when I mean to do it. He hasn't kept his word' —here Sarah struck in out of her weakness and indecision:

'He hasn't broken it yet!' Eric ground his teeth with anger.

'If you mean to stick up for him,' he said, as he smote his hands savagely on the flagstaff, which sent forth a shivering murmur, 'well and good. I'll keep my part of the bargain. On Sunday I shall give notice of the banns, and you can deny them in the church if you will. If Abel is in Pencastle on the eleventh, he can have them cancelled, and his own put up; but till then, I take my course, and woe to anyone who stands in my way!' With that he flung himself down the rocky pathway, and Sarah could not but admire his Viking strength and spirit, as, crossing the hill, he strode away along the cliffs towards Bude.

During the week no news was heard of Abel, and on Saturday Eric gave notice of the banns of marriage between himself and Sarah Trefusis. The clergyman would have remonstrated with him, for although nothing formal had been told to the neighbours, it had been understood since Abel's departure that on his return he was to marry Sarah; but Eric would not discuss the question.

'It is a painful subject, sir,' he said with a firmness which the parson, who was a very young man, could not but be swayed by. 'Surely there is nothing against Sarah or me. Why should there be any bones made about the matter?' The parson said no more, and on the next day he read out the banns for the first time amidst an audible buzz from the congregation. Sarah was present, contrary to custom, and though she blushed furiously enjoyed her triumph over the other girls whose banns had not yet come. Before the week was over she began to make her wedding dress. Eric used to come and look at her at work and the sight thrilled through him. He used to say all sorts of pretty things to her at such times, and there were to both delicious moments of love-making.

The banns were read a second time on the 29th, and Eric's hope grew more and more fixed though there were to him moments of acute despair when he realised that the cup of happiness might be dashed from his lips at any moment, right up to the last. At such times he was full of passion-desperate and remorseless-and he ground his teeth and clenched his hands in a wild way as though some taint of the old Berserker fury of his ancestors still lingered in his blood. On the Thursday of that week he looked in on Sarah and found her, amid a flood of sunshine, putting finishing touches to her white wedding gown. His own heart was full of gaiety, and the sight of the woman who was so soon to be his own so occupied, filled him with a joy unspeakable, and he felt faint with languorous ecstasy. Bending over he kissed Sarah on the mouth, and then whispered in her rosy ear —

'Your wedding dress, Sarah! And for me!' As he drew back to admire her she looked up saucily, and said to him —

'Perhaps not for you. There is more than a week yet for Abel!' and then cried out in dismay, for with a wild gesture and a fierce oath Eric dashed out of the house, banging the door behind him. The incident disturbed Sarah more than she could have thought possible, for it awoke all her fears and doubts and indecision afresh. She cried a little, and put by her dress, and to soothe herself went out to sit for a while on the summit of the Flagstaff Rock. When she arrived she found there a little group anxiously discussing the weather. The sea was calm and the sun bright, but across the sea were strange lines of darkness and light, and close in to shore the rocks were fringed with foam, which spread out in great white curves and circles as the currents drifted. The wind had backed, and came in sharp, cold puffs. The blow-hole, which ran under the Flagstaff Rock, from the rocky bay without to the harbour within, was booming at intervals, and the seagulls were screaming ceaselessly as they wheeled about the entrance of the port.

'It looks bad,' she heard an old fisherman say to the coastguard. 'I seen it just like this once before, when the East Indiaman *Coromandel* went to pieces in Dizzard Bay!' Sarah did not wait to hear more. She was of a timid nature where danger was concerned, and could not bear to hear of wrecks and disasters. She went home and resumed the completion of her dress, secretly determined to appease Eric when she should meet him with a sweet apology-and to take the earliest opportunity of being even with him after her marriage. The old fisherman's weather prophecy was justified. That night at dusk a wild storm came on. The sea rose and lashed the western coasts from Skye to Scilly and left a tale of disaster everywhere. The sailors and fishermen of Pencastle all turned out on the rocks and cliffs and watched eagerly. Presently, by a flash of lightning, a 'ketch' was seen drifting under only a jib about half-a-mile outside the port. All eyes and all glasses were concentrated on her, waiting for the next flash, and when it came a chorus went up that it was the *Lovely Alice*, trading between Bristol and Penzance, and touching at all the little ports between. 'God help them!' said the harbour-master, 'for nothing in this world can save them when they are between Bude and Tintagel and the wind on shore!' The coastguards exerted themselves, and, aided by brave hearts and willing hands, they brought the rocket apparatus up on the summit of the Flagstaff Rock. Then they burned blue lights so that those on board might see the harbour opening in case they could make any effort to reach it. They worked gallantly enough on board; but no skill or strength of man could avail. Before many minutes were over the *Lovely Alice* rushed to her doom on the great island rock that guarded the mouth of the port. The screams of those on board were faintly borne on the tempest as they flung themselves into the sea in a last chance for life. The blue lights were kept burning, and eager eyes peered into the depths of the waters in case any face could be seen; and ropes were held ready to fling out in aid. But never a face was seen, and the willing arms rested idle. Eric was there amongst his fellows. His old Icelandic origin was never more apparent than in that wild hour. He took a rope, and shouted in the ear of the harbour-master:

'I shall go down on the rock over the seal cave. The tide is running up, and someone may drift in there!'

'Keep back, man!' came the answer. 'Are you mad? One slip on that rock and you are lost: and no man could keep his feet in the dark on such a place in such a tempest!'

'Not a bit,' came the reply. 'You remember how Abel Behenna saved me there on a night like this when my boat went on the Gull Rock. He dragged me up from the deep water in the seal cave, and now someone may drift in there again as I did,' and he was gone into the darkness. The projecting rock hid the light on the Flagstaff Rock, but he knew his way too well to miss it. His boldness and sureness of foot standing to him, he shortly stood on the great round-topped rock cut away beneath by the action of the waves over the entrance of the seal cave, where the water was fathomless. There he stood in comparative safety, for the concave shape of the rock beat back the waves with their own force, and though the water below him seemed to boil like a seething cauldron, just beyond the spot there was a space of almost calm. The rock, too, seemed here to shut off the sound of the gale, and he listened as well as watched. As he stood there ready, with his coil of rope poised to throw, he thought he heard below him, just beyond the whirl of the water, a faint, despairing cry. He echoed it with a shout that rang into the night. Then he waited for the flash of lightning, and as it passed flung his rope out into the darkness where he had seen a face rising through the swirl of the foam. The rope was caught, for he felt a pull on it, and he shouted again in his mighty voice:

'Tie it round your waist, and I shall pull you up.' Then when he felt that it was fast he moved along the rock to the far side of the sea cave, where the deep water was something stiller, and where he could get foothold secure enough to drag the rescued man on the overhanging rock. He began to pull, and shortly he knew from the rope taken in that the man he was now rescuing must soon be close to the top of the rock. He steadied himself for a moment, and drew a long breath, that he might at the next effort complete the rescue. He had just bent his back to the work when a flash of lightning revealed to each other the two men-the rescuer and the rescued.

Eric Sanson and Abel Behenna were face to face-and none knew of the meeting save themselves; and God.

On the instant a wave of passion swept through Eric's heart. All his hopes were shattered, and with the hatred of Cain his eyes looked out. He saw in the instant of recognition the joy in Abel's face that his was the hand to succour him, and this intensified his hate. Whilst the passion was on him he started back, and the rope ran out between his hands. His moment of hate was followed by an impulse of his better manhood, but it was too late.

Before he could recover himself, Abel encumbered with the rope that should have aided him, was plunged with a despairing cry back into the darkness of the devouring sea.

Then, feeling all the madness and the doom of Cain upon him, Eric rushed back over the rocks, heedless of the danger and eager only for one thing-to be amongst other people whose living noises would shut out that last cry which seemed to ring still in his ears. When he regained the Flagstaff Rock the men surrounded him, and through the fury of the storm he heard the harbour-master say: —

'We feared you were lost when we heard a cry! How white you are! Where is your rope? Was there anyone drifted in?'

'No one,' he shouted in answer, for he felt that he could never explain that he had let his old comrade slip back into the sea, and at the very place and under the very circumstances in which that comrade had saved his own life. He hoped by one bold lie to set the matter at rest for ever. There was no one to bear witness-and if he should have to carry that still white face in his eyes and that despairing cry in his ears for evermore-at least none should know of it. 'No one,' he cried, more loudly still. 'I slipped on the rock, and the rope fell into the sea!' So saying he left them, and, rushing down the steep path, gained his own cottage and locked himself within.

The remainder of that night he passed lying on his bed-dressed and motionless-staring upwards, and seeming to see through the darkness a pale face gleaming wet in the lightning, with its glad recognition turning to ghastly despair, and to hear a cry which never ceased to echo in his soul.

In the morning the storm was over and all was smiling again, except that the sea was still boisterous with its unspent fury. Great pieces of wreck drifted into the port, and the sea around the island rock was strewn with others. Two bodies also drifted into the harbour-one the master of the wrecked ketch, the other a strange seaman whom no one knew.

Sarah saw nothing of Eric till the evening, and then he only looked in for a minute. He did not come into the house, but simply put his head in through the open window.

'Well, Sarah,' he called out in a loud voice, though to her it did not ring truly, 'is the wedding dress done? Sunday week, mind! Sunday week!'

Sarah was glad to have the reconciliation so easy; but, womanlike, when she saw the storm was over and her own fears groundless, she at once repeated the cause of offence.

'Sunday so be it,' she said without looking up, 'if Abel isn't there on Saturday!' Then she looked up saucily, though her heart was full of fear of another outburst on the part of her impetuous lover. But the window was empty; Eric had taken himself off, and with a pout she resumed her work. She saw Eric no more till Sunday afternoon, after the banns had been called the third time, when he came up to her before all the people with an air of proprietorship which half-pleased and half-annoyed her.

'Not yet, mister!' she said, pushing him away, as the other girls giggled. 'Wait till Sunday next, if you please-the day after Saturday!' she added, looking at him saucily. The girls giggled again, and the young men guffawed. They thought it was the snub that touched him so that he became as white as a sheet as he turned away. But Sarah, who knew more than they did, laughed, for she saw triumph through the spasm of pain that overspread his face.

The week passed uneventfully; however, as Saturday drew nigh Sarah had occasional moments of anxiety, and as to Eric he went about at night-time like a man possessed. He restrained himself when others were by, but now and again he went down amongst the rocks and caves and shouted aloud. This seemed to relieve him somewhat, and he was better able to restrain himself for some time after. All Saturday he stayed in his own house and never left it. As he was to be married on the morrow, the neighbours thought it was shyness on his part, and did not trouble or notice him. Only once was he disturbed, and that was when the chief boatman came to him and sat down, and after a pause said:

'Eric, I was over in Bristol yesterday. I was in the ropemaker's getting a coil to replace the one you lost the night of the storm, and there I saw Michael Heavens of this place, who is a salesman there. He told me that Abel Behenna had come home the week ere last on the *Star of the Sea* from Canton, and that he had lodged a sight of money in the Bristol Bank in the name of Sarah Behenna. He told Michael so himself-and that he had taken passage on the *Lovely Alice* to Pencastle. 'Bear up, man,' for Eric had with a groan dropped his head on his knees, with his face between his hands. 'He was your old comrade, I know, but you couldn't help him. He must have gone down with the rest that awful night. I thought I'd better tell you, lest it might come some other way, and you might keep Sarah Trefusis from being frightened. They were good friends once, and women take these things to heart. It would not do to let her be pained with such a thing on her wedding day!' Then he rose and went away, leaving Eric still sitting disconsolately with his head on his knees.

'Poor fellow!' murmured the chief boatman to himself; 'he takes it to heart. Well, well! right enough! They were true comrades once, and Abel saved him!'

The afternoon of that day, when the children had left school, they strayed as usual on half-holidays along' the quay and the paths by the cliffs. Presently some of them came running in a state of great excitement to the harbour, where a few men were unloading a coal ketch, and a great many were superintending the operation. One of the children called out:

'There is a porpoise in the harbour mouth! We saw it come through the blow-hole! It had a long tail, and was deep under the water!'

'It was no porpoise,' said another; 'it was a seal; but it had a long tail! It came out of the seal cave!' The other children bore various testimony, but on two points they were unanimous-it, whatever 'it' was, had come through the blow-hole deep under the water, and had a long, thin tail —a tail so long that they could not see the end of it. There was much unmerciful chaffing of the children by the men on this point, but as it was evident that they had seen something, quite a number of persons, young and old, male and female, went along the high paths on either side of the harbour mouth to catch a glimpse of this new addition to the fauna of the sea, a long-tailed porpoise or seal. The tide was now coming in. There was a slight breeze, and the surface of the water was rippled so that it was only at moments that anyone could see clearly into the deep water. After a spell of watching a woman called out that she saw something moving up the channel, just below where she was standing. There was a stampede to the spot, but by the time the crowd had gathered the breeze had freshened, and it was impossible to see with any distinctness below the surface of the water. On being questioned the woman described what she had seen, but in such an incoherent way that the whole thing was put down as an effect of imagination; had it not been for the children's report she would not have been credited at all. Her semi-hysterical statement that what she saw was 'like a pig with the entrails out' was only thought anything of by an old coastguard, who shook his head but did not make any remark. For the remainder of the daylight this man was seen always on the bank, looking into the water, but always with disappointment manifest on his face.

Eric arose early on the next morning-he had not slept all night, and it was a relief to him to move about in the light. He shaved himself with a hand that did not tremble, and dressed himself in his wedding clothes. There was a haggard look on his face, and he seemed as though he had grown years older in the last few days. Still there was a wild, uneasy light of triumph in his eyes, and he kept murmuring to himself over and over again:

'This is my wedding-day! Abel cannot claim her now-living or dead! —living or dead! Living or dead!' He sat in his arm-chair, waiting with an uncanny quietness for the church hour to arrive. When the bell began to ring he arose and passed out of his house, closing the door behind him. He looked at the river and saw the tide had just turned. In the church he sat with Sarah and her mother, holding Sarah's hand tightly in his all the time, as though he feared to lose her. When the service was over they stood up together, and were married in the presence of the entire congregation; for no one left the church. Both made the responses clearly-Eric's being even on the defiant side. When the wedding was over Sarah took her husband's arm, and they walked away together, the boys and younger girls being cuffed by their elders into a decorous behaviour, for they would fain have followed close behind their heels.

The way from the church led down to the back of Eric's cottage, a narrow passage being between it and that of his next neighbour. When the bridal couple had passed through this the remainder of the congregation, who had followed them at a little distance, were startled by a long, shrill scream from the bride. They rushed through the passage and found her on the bank with wild eyes, pointing to the river bed opposite Eric Sanson's door.

The falling tide had deposited there the body of Abel Behenna stark upon the broken rocks. The rope trailing from its waist had been twisted by the current round the mooring post, and had held it back whilst the tide had ebbed away from it. The right elbow had fallen in a chink in the rock, leaving the hand outstretched toward Sarah, with the open palm upward as though it were extended to receive hers, the pale drooping fingers open to the clasp.

All that happened afterwards was never quite known to Sarah Sanson. Whenever she would try to recollect there would become a buzzing in her ears and a dimness in her eyes, and all would pass away. The only thing that she could remember of it all—and this she never forgot—was Eric's breathing heavily, with his face whiter than that of the dead man, as he muttered under his breath:

'Devil's help! Devil's faith! Devil's price!'

The Burial of the Rats

Leaving Paris by the Orleans road, cross the Enceinte, and, turning to the right, you find yourself in a somewhat wild and not at all savoury district. Right and left, before and behind, on every side rise great heaps of dust and waste accumulated by the process of time.

Paris has its night as well as its day life, and the sojourner who enters his hotel in the Rue de Rivoli or the Rue St. Honore late at night or leaves it early in the morning, can guess, in coming near Montrouge-if he has not done so already-the purpose of those great waggons that look like boilers on wheels which he finds halting everywhere as he passes.

Every city has its peculiar institutions created out of its own needs; and one of the most notable institutions of Paris is its rag-picking population. In the early morning-and Parisian life commences at an early hour-may be seen in most streets standing on the pathway opposite every court and alley and between every few houses, as still in some American cities, even in parts of New York, large wooden boxes into which the domestics or tenement-holders empty the accumulated dust of the past day. Round these boxes gather and pass on, when the work is done, to fresh fields of labour and pastures new, squalid hungry-looking men and women, the implements of whose craft consist of a coarse bag or basket slung over the shoulder and a little rake with which they turn over and probe and examine in the minutest manner the dustbins. They pick up and deposit in their baskets, by aid of their rakes, whatever they may find, with the same facility as a Chinaman uses his chopsticks.

Paris is a city of centralisation-and centralisation and classification are closely allied. In the early times, when centralisation is becoming a fact, its forerunner is classification. All things which are similar or analogous become grouped together, and from the grouping of groups rises one whole or central point. We see radiating many long arms with innumerable tentaculae, and in the centre rises a gigantic head with a comprehensive brain and keen eyes to look on every side and ears sensitive to hear-and a voracious mouth to swallow.

Other cities resemble all the birds and beasts and fishes whose appetites and digestions are normal. Paris alone is the analogical apotheosis of the octopus. Product of centralisation carried to an *ad absurdum*, it fairly represents the devil fish; and in no respects is the resemblance more curious than in the similarity of the digestive apparatus.

Those intelligent tourists who, having surrendered their individuality into the hands of Messrs. Cook or Gaze, 'do' Paris in three days, are often puzzled to know how it is that the dinner which in London would cost about six shillings, can be had for three francs in a café in the Palais Royal. They need have no more wonder if they will but consider the classification which is a theoretic speciality of Parisian life, and adopt all round the fact from which the chiffonier has his genesis.

The Paris of 1850 was not like the Paris of to-day, and those who see the Paris of Napoleon and Baron Hausseman can hardly realise the existence of the state of things forty-five years ago.

Amongst other things, however, which have not changed are those districts where the waste is gathered. Dust is dust all the world over, in every age, and the family likeness of dust-heaps is perfect. The traveller, therefore, who visits the environs of Montrouge can go go back in fancy without difficulty to the year 1850.

In this year I was making a prolonged stay in Paris. I was very much in love with a young lady who, though she returned my passion, so far yielded to the wishes of her parents that she had promised not to see me or to correspond with me for a year. I, too, had been compelled to accede to these conditions under a vague hope of parental approval. During the term of probation I had promised to remain out of the country and not to write to my dear one until the expiration of the year.

Naturally the time went heavily with me. There was not one of my own family or circle who could tell me of Alice, and none of her own folk had, I am sorry to say, sufficient generosity to send me even an occasional word of comfort regarding her health and well-being. I spent six months wandering about Europe, but as I could find no satisfactory distraction in travel, I determined to come to Paris, where, at least, I would be within easy hail of London in case any good fortune should call me thither before the appointed time. That 'hope deferred maketh the heart sick' was never better exemplified than in my case, for in addition to the perpetual longing to see the face I loved there was always with me a harrowing anxiety lest some accident should prevent me showing Alice in due time that I had, throughout the long period of probation, been faithful to her trust and my own love. Thus, every adventure which I undertook had a fierce pleasure of its own, for it was fraught with possible consequences greater than it would have ordinarily borne.

Like all travellers I exhausted the places of most interest in the first month of my stay, and was driven in the second month to look for amusement whithersoever I might. Having made sundry journeys to the better-known suburbs, I began to see that there was a *terra incognita*, in so far as the guide book was concerned, in the social wilderness lying between these attractive points. Accordingly I began to systematise my researches, and each day took up the thread of my exploration at the place where I had on the previous day dropped it.

In the process of time my wanderings led me near Montrouge, and I saw that hereabouts lay the Ultima Thule of social exploration —a country as little known as that round the source of the White Nile. And so I determined to investigate philosophically the chiffonier-his habitat, his life, and his means of life.

The job was an unsavoury one, difficult of accomplishment, and with little hope of adequate reward. However, despite reason, obstinacy prevailed, and I entered into my new investigation with a keener energy than I could have summoned to aid me in any investigation leading to any end, valuable or worthy.

One day, late in a fine afternoon, toward the end of September, I entered the holy of holies of the city of dust. The place was evidently the recognised abode of a number of chiffoniers, for some sort of arrangement was manifested in the formation of the dust heaps near the road. I passed amongst these heaps, which stood like orderly sentries, determined to penetrate further and trace dust to its ultimate location.

As I passed along I saw behind the dust heaps a few forms that flitted to and fro, evidently watching with interest the advent of any stranger to such a place. The district was like a small Switzerland, and as I went forward my tortuous course shut out the path behind me.

Presently I got into what seemed a small city or community of chiffoniers. There were a number of shanties or huts, such as may be met with in the remote parts of the Bog of Allan-rude places with wattled walls, plastered with mud and roofs of rude thatch made from stable refuse-such places as one would not like to enter for any consideration, and which even in water-colour could only look picturesque if judiciously treated. In the midst of these huts was one of the strangest adaptations —I cannot say habitations —I had ever seen. An immense old wardrobe, the colossal remnant of some boudoir of Charles VII, or Henry II, had been converted into a dwelling-house. The double doors lay open, so that the entire ménage was open to public view. In the open half of the wardrobe was a common sitting-room of some four feet by six, in which sat, smoking their pipes round a charcoal brazier, no fewer than six old soldiers of the First Republic, with their uniforms torn and worn threadbare. Evidently they were of the *mauvais sujet* class; their bleary eyes and limp jaws told plainly of a common love of absinthe; and their eyes had that haggard, worn look of slumbering ferocity which follows hard in the wake of drink. The other side stood as of old, with its shelves intact, save that they were cut to half their depth, and in each shelf of which there were six, was a bed made with rags and straw. The half-dozen of worthies who inhabited this structure looked at me curiously as I passed; and when I looked back after going a little way I saw their heads together in a whispered conference. I did not like the look of this at all, for the place was very lonely, and the men looked very, very villainous. However, I did not see any cause for fear, and went on my way, penetrating further and further into the Sahara. The way was tortuous to a degree, and from going round in a series of semi-circles, as one goes in skating with the Dutch roll, I got rather confused with regard to the points of the compass.

When I had penetrated a little way I saw, as I turned the corner of a half-made heap, sitting on a heap of straw an old soldier with threadbare coat.

'Hallo!' said I to myself; 'the First Republic is well represented here in its soldiery.'

As I passed him the old man never even looked up at me, but gazed on the ground with stolid persistency. Again I remarked to myself: 'See what a life of rude warfare can do! This old man's curiosity is a thing of the past.'

When I had gone a few steps, however, I looked back suddenly, and saw that curiosity was not dead, for the veteran had raised his head and was regarding me with a very queer expression. He seemed to me to look very like one of the six worthies in the press. When he saw me looking he dropped his head; and without thinking further of him I went on my way, satisfied that there was a strange likeness between these old warriors.

Presently I met another old soldier in a similar manner. He, too, did not notice me whilst I was passing.

By this time it was getting late in the afternoon, and I began to think of retracing my steps. Accordingly I turned to go back, but could see a number of tracks leading between different mounds and could not ascertain which of them I should take. In my perplexity I wanted to see someone of whom to ask the way, but could see no one. I determined to go on a few mounds further and so try to see someone-not a veteran.

I gained my object, for after going a couple of hundred yards I saw before me a single shanty such as I had seen before-with, however, the difference that this was not one for living in, but merely a roof with three walls open in front. From the evidences which the neighbourhood exhibited I took it to be a place for sorting. Within it was an old woman wrinkled and bent with age; I approached her to ask the way.

She rose as I came close and I asked her my way. She immediately commenced a conversation; and it occurred to me that here in the very centre of the Kingdom of Dust was the place to gather details of the history of Parisian rag-picking —particularly as I could do so from the lips of one who looked like the oldest inhabitant.

I began my inquiries, and the old woman gave me most interesting answers she had been one of the ceteuces who sat daily before the guillotine and had taken an active part among the women who signalised themselves by their violence in the revolution. While we were talking she said suddenly: 'But m'sieur must be tired standing,' and dusted a rickety old stool for me to sit down. I hardly liked to do so for many reasons; but the poor old woman was so civil that I did not like to run the risk of hurting her by refusing, and moreover the conversation of one who had been at the taking of the Bastille was so interesting that I sat down and so our conversation went on.

While we were talking an old man-older and more bent and wrinkled even than the woman-appeared from behind the shanty. 'Here is Pierre,' said she. 'M'sieur can hear stories now if he wishes, for Pierre was in everything, from the Bastille to Waterloo.' The old man took another stool at my request and we plunged into a sea of revolutionary reminiscences. This old man, albeit clothed like a scarecrow, was like any one of the six veterans.

I was now sitting in the centre of the low hut with the woman on my left hand and the man on my right, each of them being somewhat in front of me. The place was full of all sorts of curious objects of lumber, and of many things that I wished far away. In one corner was a heap of rags which seemed to move from the number of vermin it contained, and in the other a heap of bones whose odour was something shocking. Every now and then, glancing at the heaps, I could see the gleaming eyes of some of the rats which infested the place. These loathsome objects were bad enough, but what looked even more dreadful was an old butcher's axe with an iron handle stained with clots of blood leaning up against the wall on the right hand side. Still, these things did not give me much concern. The talk of the two old people was so fascinating that I stayed on and on, till the evening came and the dust heaps threw dark shadows over the vales between them.

After a time I began to grow uneasy. I could not tell how or why, but somehow I did not feel satisfied. Uneasiness is an instinct and means warning. The psychic faculties are often the sentries of the intellect, and when they sound alarm the reason begins to act, although perhaps not consciously.

This was so with me. I began to bethink me where I was and by what surrounded, and to wonder how I should fare in case I should be attacked; and then the thought suddenly burst upon me, although without any overt cause, that I was in danger. Prudence whispered: 'Be still and make no sign,' and so I was still and made no sign, for I knew that four cunning eyes were on me. 'Four eyes-if not more.' My God, what a horrible thought! The whole shanty might be surrounded on three sides with villains! I might be in the midst of a band of such desperadoes as only half a century of periodic revolution can produce.

With a sense of danger my intellect and observation quickened, and I grew more watchful than was my wont. I noticed that the old woman's eyes were constantly wandering towards my hands. I looked at them too, and saw the cause-my rings. On my left little finger I had a large signet and on the right a good diamond.

I thought that if there was any danger my first care was to avert suspicion. Accordingly I began to work the conversation round to rag-picking —to the drains-of the things found there; and so by easy stages to jewels. Then, seizing a favourable opportunity, I asked the old woman if she knew anything of such things. She answered that she did, a little. I held out my right hand, and, showing her the diamond, asked her what she thought of that. She answered that her eyes were bad, and stooped over my hand. I said as nonchalantly as I could: 'Pardon me! You will see better thus!' and taking it off handed it to her. An unholy light came into her withered old face, as she touched it. She stole one glance at me swift and keen as a flash of lightning.

She bent over the ring for a moment, her face quite concealed as though examining it. The old man looked straight out of the front of the shanty before him, at the same time fumbling in his pockets and producing a screw of tobacco in a paper and a pipe, which he proceeded to fill. I took advantage of the pause and the momentary rest from the searching eyes on my face to look carefully round the place, now dim and shadowy in the gloaming. There still lay all the heaps of varied reeking foulness; there the terrible blood-stained axe leaning against the wall in the right hand corner, and everywhere, despite the gloom, the baleful glitter of the eyes of the rats. I could see them even through some of the chinks of the boards at the back low down close to the ground. But stay! these latter eyes seemed more than usually large and bright and baleful!

For an instant my heart stood still, and I felt in that whirling condition of mind in which one feels a sort of spiritual drunkenness, and as though the body is only maintained erect in that there is no time for it to fall before recovery. Then, in another second, I was calm-coldly calm, with all my energies in full vigour, with a self-control which I felt to be perfect and with all my feeling and instincts alert.

Now I knew the full extent of my danger: I was watched and surrounded by desperate people! I could not even guess at how many of them were lying there on the ground behind the shanty, waiting for the moment to strike. I knew that I was big and strong, and they knew it, too. They knew also, as I did, that I was an Englishman and would make a fight for it; and so we waited. I had, I felt, gained an advantage in the last few seconds, for I knew my danger and understood the situation. Now, I thought, is the test of my courage-the enduring test: the fighting test may come later!

The old woman raised her head and said to me in a satisfied kind of way:

'A very fine ring, indeed —a beautiful ring! Oh, me! I once had such rings, plenty of them, and bracelets and earrings! Oh! for in those fine days I led the town a dance! But they've forgotten me now! They've forgotten me! They? Why they never heard of me! Perhaps their grandfathers remember me, some of them!' and she laughed a harsh, croaking laugh. And then I am bound to say that she astonished me, for she handed me back the ring with a certain suggestion of old-fashioned grace which was not without its pathos.

The old man eyed her with a sort of sudden ferocity, half rising from his stool, and said to me suddenly and hoarsely:

'Let me see!'

I was about to hand the ring when the old woman said:

'No! no, do not give it to Pierre! Pierre is eccentric. He loses things; and such a pretty ring!'

'Cat!' said the old man, savagely. Suddenly the old woman said, rather more loudly than was necessary:

'Wait! I shall tell you something about a ring.' There was something in the sound of her voice that jarred upon me. Perhaps it was my hyper-sensitiveness, wrought up as I was to such a pitch of nervous excitement, but I seemed to think that she was not addressing me. As I stole a glance round the place I saw the eyes of the rats in the bone heaps, but missed the eyes along the back. But even as I looked I saw them again appear. The old woman's 'Wait!' had given me a respite from attack, and the men had sunk back to their reclining posture.

'I once lost a ring —a beautiful diamond hoop that had belonged to a queen, and which was given to me by a farmer of the taxes, who afterwards cut his throat because I sent him away. I thought it must have been stolen, and taxed my people; but I could get no trace. The police came and suggested that it had found its way to the drain. We descended —I in my fine clothes, for I would not trust them with my beautiful ring! I know more of the drains since then, and of rats, too! but I shall never forget the horror of that place-alive with blazing eyes, a wall of them just outside the light of our torches. Well, we got beneath my house. We searched the outlet of the drain, and there in the filth found my ring, and we came out.

'But we found something else also before we came! As we were coming toward the opening a lot of sewer rats-human ones this time-came towards us. They told the police that one of their number had gone into the drain, but had not returned. He had gone in only shortly before we had, and, if lost, could hardly be far off. They asked help to seek him, so we turned back. They tried to prevent me going, but I insisted. It was a new excitement, and had I not recovered my ring? Not far did we go till we came on something. There was but little water, and the bottom of the drain was raised with brick, rubbish, and much matter of the kind. He had made a fight for it, even when his torch had gone out. But they were too many for him! They had not been long about it! The bones were still warm; but they were picked clean. They had even eaten their own dead ones and there were bones of rats as well as of the man. They took it cool enough those other-the human ones-and joked of their comrade when they found him dead, though they would have helped him living. Bah! what matters it-life or death?'

'And had you no fear?' I asked her.

'Fear!' she said with a laugh. 'Me have fear? Ask Pierre! But I was younger then, and, as I came through that horrible drain with its wall of greedy eyes, always moving with the circle of the light from the torches, I did not feel easy. I kept on before the men, though! It is a way I have! I never let the men get it before me. All I want is a chance and a means! And they ate him up-took every trace away except the bones; and no one knew it, nor no sound of him was ever heard!' Here she broke into a chuckling fit of the ghastliest merriment which it was ever my lot to hear and see. A great poetess describes her heroine singing: 'Oh! to see or hear her singing! Scarce I know which is the divinest.'

And I can apply the same idea to the old crone-in all save the divinity, for I scarce could tell which was the most hellish-the harsh, malicious, satisfied, cruel laugh, or the leering grin, and the horrible square opening of the mouth like a tragic mask, and the yellow gleam of the few discoloured teeth in the shapeless gums. In that laugh and with that grin and the chuckling satisfaction I knew as well as if it had been spoken to me in words of thunder that my murder was settled, and the murderers only bided the proper time for its accomplishment. I could read between the lines of her gruesome story the commands to her accomplices. 'Wait,' she seemed to say, 'bide your time. I shall strike the first blow. Find the weapon for me, and I shall make the opportunity! He shall not escape! Keep him quiet, and then no one will be wiser. There will be no outcry, and the rats will do their work!'

It was growing darker and darker; the night was coming. I stole a glance round the shanty, still all the same! The bloody axe in the corner, the heaps of filth, and the eyes on the bone heaps and in the crannies of the floor.

Pierre had been still ostensibly filling his pipe; he now struck a light and began to puff away at it. The old woman said:

'Dear heart, how dark it is! Pierre, like a good lad, light the lamp!'

Pierre got up and with the lighted match in his hand touched the wick of a lamp which hung at one side of the entrance to the shanty, and which had a reflector that threw the light all over the place. It was evidently that which was used for their sorting at night.

'Not that, stupid! Not that! the lantern!' she called out to him.

He immediately blew it out, saying: 'All right, mother I'll find it,' and he hustled about the left corner of the room-the old woman saying through the darkness:

'The lantern! the lantern! Oh! That is the light that is most useful to us poor folks. The lantern was the friend of the revolution! It is the friend of the chiffonier! It helps us when all else fails.'

Hardly had she said the word when there was a kind of creaking of the whole place, and something was steadily dragged over the roof.

Again I seemed to read between the lines of her words. I knew the lesson of the lantern.

'One of you get on the roof with a noose and strangle him as he passes out if we fail within.'

As I looked out of the opening I saw the loop of a rope outlined black against the lurid sky. I was now, indeed, beset!

Pierre was not long in finding the lantern. I kept my eyes fixed through the darkness on the old woman. Pierre struck his light, and by its flash I saw the old woman raise from the ground beside her where it had mysteriously appeared, and then hide in the folds of her gown, a long sharp knife or dagger. It seemed to be like a butcher's sharpening iron fined to a keen point.

The lantern was lit.

'Bring it here, Pierre,' she said. 'Place it in the doorway where we can see it. See how nice it is! It shuts out the darkness from us; it is just right!'

Just right for her and her purposes! It threw all its light on my face, leaving in gloom the faces of both Pierre and the woman, who sat outside of me on each side.

I felt that the time of action was approaching, but I knew now that the first signal and movement would come from the woman, and so watched her.

I was all unarmed, but I had made up my mind what to do. At the first movement I would seize the butcher's axe in the right-hand corner and fight my way out. At least, I would die hard. I stole a glance round to fix its exact locality so that I could not fail to seize it at the first effort, for then, if ever, time and accuracy would be precious.

Good God! It was gone! All the horror of the situation burst upon me; but the bitterest thought of all was that if the issue of the terrible position should be against me Alice would infallibly suffer. Either she would believe me false-and any lover, or any one who has ever been one, can imagine the bitterness of the thought-or else she would go on loving long after I had been lost to her and to the world, so that her life would be broken and embittered, shattered with disappointment and despair. The very magnitude of the pain braced me up and nerved me to bear the dread scrutiny of the plotters.

I think I did not betray myself. The old woman was watching me as a cat does a mouse; she had her right hand hidden in the folds of her gown, clutching, I knew, that long, cruel-looking dagger. Had she seen any disappointment in my face she would, I felt, have known that the moment had come, and would have sprung on me like a tigress, certain of taking me unprepared.

I looked out into the night, and there I saw new cause for danger. Before and around the hut were at a little distance some shadowy forms; they were quite still, but I knew that they were all alert and on guard. Small chance for me now in that direction.

Again I stole a glance round the place. In moments of great excitement and of great danger, which is excitement, the mind works very quickly, and the keenness of the faculties which depend on the mind grows in proportion. I now felt this. In an instant I took in the whole situation. I saw that the axe had been taken through a small hole made in one of the rotten boards. How rotten they must be to allow of such a thing being done without a particle of noise.

The hut was a regular murder-trap, and was guarded all around. A garroter lay on the roof ready to entangle me with his noose if I should escape the dagger of the old hag. In front the way was guarded by I know not how many watchers. And at the back was a row of desperate men —I had seen their eyes still through the crack in the boards of the floor, when last I looked-as they lay prone waiting for the signal to start erect. If it was to be ever, now for it!

As nonchalantly as I could I turned slightly on my stool so as to get my right leg well under me. Then with a sudden jump, turning my head, and guarding it with my hands, and with the fighting instinct of the knights of old, I breathed my lady's name, and hurled myself against the back wall of the hut.

Watchful as they were, the suddenness of my movement surprised both Pierre and the old woman. As I crashed through the rotten timbers I saw the old woman rise with a leap like a tiger and heard her low gasp of baffled rage. My feet lit on something that moved, and as I jumped away I knew that I had stepped on the back of one of the row of men lying on their faces outside the hut. I was torn with nails and splinters, but otherwise unhurt. Breathless I rushed up the mound in front of me, hearing as I went the dull crash of the shanty as it collapsed into a mass.

It was a nightmare climb. The mound, though but low, was awfully steep, and with each step I took the mass of dust and cinders tore down with me and gave way under my feet. The dust rose and choked me; it was sickening, fœtid, awful; but my climb was, I felt, for life or death, and I struggled on. The seconds seemed hours; but the few moments I had in starting, combined with my youth and strength, gave me a great advantage, and, though several forms struggled after me in deadly silence which was more dreadful than any sound, I easily reached the top. Since then I have climbed the cone of Vesuvius, and as I struggled up that dreary steep amid the sulphurous fumes the memory of that awful night at Montrouge came back to me so vividly that I almost grew faint.

The mound was one of the tallest in the region of dust, and as I struggled to the top, panting for breath and with my heart beating like a sledge-hammer, I saw away to my left the dull red gleam of the sky, and nearer still the flashing of lights. Thank God! I knew where I was now and where lay the road to Paris!

For two or three seconds I paused and looked back. My pursuers were still well behind me, but struggling up resolutely, and in deadly silence. Beyond, the shanty was a wreck —a mass of timber and moving forms. I could see it well, for flames were already bursting out; the rags and straw had evidently caught fire from the lantern. Still silence there! Not a sound! These old wretches could die game, anyhow.

I had no time for more than a passing glance, for as I cast an eye round the mound preparatory to making my descent I saw several dark forms rushing round on either side to cut me off on my way. It was now a race for life. They were trying to head me on my way to Paris, and with the instinct of the moment I dashed down to the right-hand side. I was just in time, for, though I came as it seemed to me down the steep in a few steps, the wary old men who were watching me turned back, and one, as I rushed by into the opening between the two mounds in front, almost struck me a blow with that terrible butcher's axe. There could surely not be two such weapons about!

Then began a really horrible chase. I easily ran ahead of the old men, and even when some younger ones and a few women joined in the hunt I easily distanced them. But I did not know the way, and I could not even guide myself by the light in the sky, for I was running away from it. I had heard that, unless of conscious purpose, hunted men turn always to the left, and so I found it now; and so, I suppose, knew also my pursuers, who were more animals than men, and with cunning or instinct had found out such secrets for themselves: for on finishing a quick spurt, after which I intended to take a moment's breathing space, I suddenly saw ahead of me two or three forms swiftly passing behind a mound to the right.

I was in the spider's web now indeed! But with the thought of this new danger came the resource of the hunted, and so I darted down the next turning to the right. I continued in this direction for some hundred yards, and then, making a turn to the left again, felt certain that I had, at any rate, avoided the danger of being surrounded.

But not of pursuit, for on came the rabble after me, steady, dogged, relentless, and still in grim silence.

In the greater darkness the mounds seemed now to be somewhat smaller than before, although-for the night was closing-they looked bigger in proportion. I was now well ahead of my pursuers, so I made a dart up the mound in front.

Oh joy of joys! I was close to the edge of this inferno of dustheaps. Away behind me the red light of Paris was in the sky, and towering up behind rose the heights of Montmarte —a dim light, with here and there brilliant points like stars.

Restored to vigour in a moment, I ran over the few remaining mounds of decreasing size, and found myself on the level land beyond. Even then, however, the prospect was not inviting. All before me was dark and dismal, and I had evidently come on one of those dank, low-lying waste places which are found here and there in the neighbourhood of great cities. Places of waste and desolation, where the space is required for the ultimate agglomeration of all that is noxious, and the ground is so poor as to create no desire of occupancy even in the lowest squatter. With eyes accustomed to the gloom of the evening, and away now from the shadows of those dreadful dustheaps, I could see much more easily than I could a little while ago. It might have been, of course, that the glare in the sky of the lights of Paris, though the city was some miles away, was reflected here. Howsoever it was, I saw well enough to take bearings for certainly some little distance around me.

In front was a bleak, flat waste that seemed almost dead level, with here and there the dark shimmering of stagnant pools. Seemingly far off on the right, amid a small cluster of scattered lights, rose a dark mass of Fort Montrouge, and away to the left in the dim distance, pointed with stray gleams from cottage windows, the lights in the sky showed the locality of Bicêtre. A moment's thought decided me to take to the right and try to reach Montrouge. There at least would be some sort of safety, and I might possibly long before come on some of the cross roads which I knew. Somewhere, not far off, must lie the strategic road made to connect the outlying chain of forts circling the city.

Then I looked back. Coming over the mounds, and outlined black against the glare of the Parisian horizon, I saw several moving figures, and still a way to the right several more deploying out between me and my destination. They evidently meant to cut me off in this direction, and so my choice became constricted; it lay now between going straight ahead or turning to the left. Stooping to the ground, so as to get the advantage of the horizon as a line of sight, I looked carefully in this direction, but could detect no sign of my enemies. I argued that as they had not guarded or were not trying to guard that point, there was evidently danger to me there already. So I made up my mind to go straight on before me.

It was not an inviting prospect, and as I went on the reality grew worse. The ground became soft and oozy, and now and again gave way beneath me in a sickening kind of way. I seemed somehow to be going down, for I saw round me places seemingly more elevated than where I was, and this in a place which from a little way back seemed dead level. I looked around, but could see none of my pursuers. This was strange, for all along these birds of the night had followed me through the darkness as well as though it was broad daylight. How I blamed myself for coming out in my light-coloured tourist suit of tweed. The silence, and my not being able to see my enemies, whilst I felt that they were watching me, grew appalling, and in the hope of some one not of this ghastly crew hearing me I raised my voice and shouted several times. There was not the slightest response; not even an echo rewarded my efforts.

For a while I stood stock still and kept my eyes in one direction. On one of the rising places around me I saw something dark move along, then another, and another. This was to my left, and seemingly moving to head me off.

I thought that again I might with my skill as a runner elude my enemies at this game, and so with all my speed darted forward.

Splash!

My feet had given way in a mass of slimy rubbish, and I had fallen headlong into a reeking, stagnant pool. The water and the mud in which my arms sank up to the elbows was filthy and nauseous beyond description, and in the suddenness of my fall I had actually swallowed some of the filthy stuff, which nearly choked me, and made me gasp for breath. Never shall I forget the moments during which I stood trying to recover myself almost fainting from the fœtid odour of the filthy pool, whose white mist rose ghostlike around. Worst of all, with the acute despair of the hunted animal when he sees the pursuing pack closing on him, I saw before my eyes whilst I stood helpless the dark forms of my pursuers moving swiftly to surround me.

It is curious how our minds work on odd matters even when the energies of thought are seemingly concentrated on some terrible and pressing need. I was in momentary peril of my life: my safety depended on my action, and my choice of alternatives coming now with almost every step I took, and yet I could not but think of the strange dogged persistency of these old men. Their silent resolution, their steadfast, grim, persistency even in such a cause commanded, as well as fear, even a measure of respect. What must they have been in the vigour of their youth. I could understand now that whirlwind rush on the bridge of Arcola, that scornful exclamation of the Old Guard at Waterloo! Unconscious cerebration has its own pleasures, even at such moments; but fortunately it does not in any way clash with the thought from which action springs.

I realised at a glance that so far I was defeated in my object, my enemies as yet had won. They had succeeded in surrounding me on three sides, and were bent on driving me off to the left-hand, where there was already some danger for me, for they had left no guard. I accepted the alternative-it was a case of Hobson's choice and run. I had to keep the lower ground, for my pursuers were on the higher places. However, though the ooze and broken ground impeded me my youth and training made me able to hold my ground, and by keeping a diagonal line I not only kept them from gaining on me but even began to distance them. This gave me new heart and strength, and by this time habitual training was beginning to tell and my second wind had come. Before me the ground rose slightly. I rushed up the slope and found before me a waste of watery slime, with a low dyke or bank looking black and grim beyond. I felt that if I could but reach that dyke in safety I could there, with solid ground under my feet and some kind of path to guide me, find with comparative ease a way out of my troubles. After a glance right and left and seeing no one near, I kept my eyes for a few minutes to their rightful work of aiding my feet whilst I crossed the swamp. It was rough, hard work, but there was little danger, merely toil; and a short time took me to the dyke. I rushed up the slope exulting; but here again I met a new shock. On either side of me rose a number of crouching figures. From right and left they rushed at me. Each body held a rope.

The cordon was nearly complete. I could pass on neither side, and the end was near.

There was only one chance, and I took it. I hurled myself across the dyke, and escaping out of the very clutches of my foes threw myself into the stream.

At any other time I should have thought that water foul and filthy, but now it was as welcome as the most crystal stream to the parched traveller. It was a highway of safety!

My pursuers rushed after me. Had only one of them held the rope it would have been all up with me, for he could have entangled me before I had time to swim a stroke; but the many hands holding it embarrassed and delayed them, and when the rope struck the water I heard the splash well behind me. A few minutes' hard swimming took me across the stream. Refreshed with the immersion and encouraged by the escape, I climbed the dyke in comparative gaiety of spirits.

From the top I looked back. Through the darkness I saw my assailants scattering up and down along the dyke. The pursuit was evidently not ended, and again I had to choose my course. Beyond the dyke where I stood was a wild, swampy space very similar to that which I had crossed. I determined to shun such a place, and thought for a moment whether I would take up or down the dyke. I thought I heard a sound-the muffled sound of oars, so I listened, and then shouted.

No response; but the sound ceased. My enemies had evidently got a boat of some kind. As they were on the up side of me I took the down path and began to run. As I passed to the left of where I had entered the water I heard several splashes, soft and stealthy, like the sound a rat makes as he plunges into the stream, but vastly greater; and as I looked I saw the dark sheen of the water broken by the ripples of several advancing heads. Some of my enemies were swimming the stream also.

And now behind me, up the stream, the silence was broken by the quick rattle and creak of oars; my enemies were in hot pursuit. I put my best leg foremost and ran on. After a break of a couple of minutes I looked back, and by a gleam of light through the ragged clouds I saw several dark forms climbing the bank behind me. The wind had now begun to rise, and the water beside me was ruffled and beginning to break in tiny waves on the bank. I had to keep my eyes pretty well on the ground before me, lest I should stumble, for I knew that to stumble was death. After a few minutes I looked back behind me. On the dyke were only a few dark figures, but crossing the waste, swampy ground were many more. What new danger this portended I did not know-could only guess. Then as I ran it seemed to me that my track kept ever sloping away to the right. I looked up ahead and saw that the river was much wider than before, and that the dyke on which I stood fell quite away, and beyond it was another stream on whose near bank I saw some of the dark forms now across the marsh. I was on an island of some kind.

My situation was now indeed terrible, for my enemies had hemmed me in on every side. Behind came the quickening roll of the oars, as though my pursuers knew that the end was close. Around me on every side was desolation; there was not a roof or light, as far as I could see. Far off to the right rose some dark mass, but what it was I knew not. For a moment I paused to think what I should do, not for more, for my pursuers were drawing closer. Then my mind was made up. I slipped down the bank and took to the water. I struck out straight ahead so as to gain the current by clearing the backwater of the island, for such I presume it was, when I had passed into the stream. I waited till a cloud came driving across the moon and leaving all in darkness. Then I took off my hat and laid it softly on the water floating with the stream, and a second after dived to the right and struck out under water with all my might. I was, I suppose, half a minute under water, and when I rose came up as softly as I could, and turning, looked back. There went my light brown hat floating merrily away. Close behind it came a rickety old boat, driven furiously by a pair of oars. The moon was still partly obscured by the drifting clouds, but in the partial light I could see a man in the bows holding aloft ready to strike what appeared to me to be that same dreadful pole-axe which I had before escaped. As I looked the boat drew closer, closer, and the man struck savagely. The hat disappeared. The man fell forward, almost out of the boat. His comrades dragged him in but without the axe, and then as I turned with all my energies bent on reaching the further bank, I heard the fierce whirr of the muttered 'Sacre!' which marked the anger of my baffled pursuers.

That was the first sound I had heard from human lips during all this dreadful chase, and full as it was of menace and danger to me it was a welcome sound for it broke that awful silence which shrouded and appalled me. It was as though an overt sign that my opponents were men and not ghosts, and that with them I had, at least, the chance of a man, though but one against many.

But now that the spell of silence was broken the sounds came thick and fast. From boat to shore and back from shore to boat came quick question and answer, all in the fiercest whispers. I looked back —a fatal thing to do-for in the instant someone caught sight of my face, which showed white on the dark water, and shouted. Hands pointed to me, and in a moment or two the boat was under weigh, and following hard after me. I had but a little way to go, but quicker and quicker came the boat after me. A few more strokes and I would be on the shore, but I felt the oncoming of the boat, and expected each second to feel the crash of an oar or other weapon on my head. Had I not seen that dreadful axe disappear in the water I do not think that I could have won the shore. I heard the muttered curses of those not rowing and the laboured breath of the rowers. With one supreme effort for life or liberty I touched the bank and sprang up it. There was not a single second to spare, for hard behind me the boat grounded and several dark forms sprang after me. I gained the top of the dyke, and keeping to the left ran on again. The boat put off and followed down the stream. Seeing this I feared danger in this direction, and quickly turning, ran down the dyke on the other side, and after passing a short stretch of marshy ground gained a wild, open flat country and sped on.

Still behind me came on my relentless pursuers. Far away, below me, I saw the same dark mass as before, but now grown closer and greater. My heart gave a great thrill of delight, for I knew that it must be the fortress of Bicêtre, and with new courage I ran on. I had heard that between each and all of the protecting forts of Paris there are strategic ways, deep sunk roads where soldiers marching should be sheltered from an enemy. I knew that if I could gain this road I would be safe, but in the darkness I could not see any sign of it, so, in blind hope of striking it, I ran on.

Presently I came to the edge of a deep cut, and found that down below me ran a road guarded on each side by a ditch of water fenced on either side by a straight, high wall.

Getting fainter and dizzier, I ran on; the ground got more broken-more and more still, till I staggered and fell, and rose again, and ran on in the blind anguish of the hunted. Again the thought of Alice nerved me. I would not be lost and wreck her life: I would fight and struggle for life to the bitter end. With a great effort I caught the top of the wall. As, scrambling like a catamount, I drew myself up, I actually felt a hand touch the sole of my foot. I was now on a sort of causeway, and before me I saw a dim light. Blind and dizzy, I ran on, staggered, and fell, rising, covered with dust and blood.

'Halt la!'

The words sounded like a voice from heaven. A blaze of light seemed to enwrap me, and I shouted with joy.

'Qui va la?' The rattle of musketry, the flash of steel before my eyes. Instinctively I stopped, though close behind me came a rush of my pursuers.

Another word or two, and out from a gateway poured, as it seemed to me, a tide of red and blue, as the guard turned out. All around seemed blazing with light, and the flash of steel, the clink and rattle of arms, and the loud, harsh voices of command. As I fell forward, utterly exhausted, a soldier caught me. I looked back in dreadful expectation, and saw the mass of dark forms disappearing into the night. Then I must have fainted. When I recovered my senses I was in the guard room. They gave me brandy, and after a while I was able to tell them something of what had passed. Then a commissary of police appeared, apparently out of the empty air, as is the way of the Parisian police officer. He listened attentively, and then had a moment's consultation with the officer in command. Apparently they were agreed, for they asked me if I were ready now to come with them.

'Where to?' I asked, rising to go.

'Back to the dust heaps. We shall, perhaps, catch them yet!'

'I shall try!' said I.

He eyed me for a moment keenly, and said suddenly:

'Would you like to wait a while or till tomorrow, young Englishman?' This touched me to the quick, as, perhaps, he intended, and I jumped to my feet.

'Come now!' I said; 'now! now! An Englishman is always ready for his duty!'

The commissary was a good fellow, as well as a shrewd one; he slapped my shoulder kindly. 'Brave garçon!' he said. 'Forgive me, but I knew what would do you most good. The guard is ready. Come!'

And so, passing right through the guard room, and through a long vaulted passage, we were out into the night. A few of the men in front had powerful lanterns. Through courtyards and down a sloping way we passed out through a low archway to a sunken road, the same that I had seen in my flight. The order was given to get at the double, and with a quick, springing stride, half run, half walk, the soldiers went swiftly along. I felt my strength renewed again-such is the difference between hunter and hunted. A very short distance took us to a low-lying pontoon bridge across the stream, and evidently very little higher up than I had struck it. Some effort had evidently been made to damage it, for the ropes had all been cut, and one of the chains had been broken. I heard the officer say to the commissary:

'We are just in time! A few more minutes, and they would have destroyed the bridge. Forward, quicker still!' and on we went. Again we reached a pontoon on the winding stream; as we came up we heard the hollow boom of the metal drums as the efforts to destroy the bridge was again renewed. A word of command was given, and several men raised their rifles.

'Fire!' A volley rang out. There was a muffled cry, and the dark forms dispersed. But the evil was done, and we saw the far end of the pontoon swing into the stream. This was a serious delay, and it was nearly an hour before we had renewed ropes and restored the bridge sufficiently to allow us to cross.

We renewed the chase. Quicker, quicker we went towards the dust heaps.

After a time we came to a place that I knew. There were the remains of a fire —a few smouldering wood ashes still cast a red glow, but the bulk of the ashes were cold. I knew the site of the hut and the hill behind it up which I had rushed, and in the flickering glow the eyes of the rats still shone with a sort of phosphorescence. The commissary spoke a word to the officer, and he cried:

'Halt!'

The soldiers were ordered to spread around and watch, and then we commenced to examine the ruins. The commissary himself began to lift away the charred boards and rubbish. These the soldiers took and piled together. Presently he started back, then bent down and rising beckoned me.

'See!' he said.

It was a gruesome sight. There lay a skeleton face downwards, a woman by the lines-an old woman by the coarse fibre of the bone. Between the ribs rose a long spike-like dagger made from a butcher's sharpening knife, its keen point buried in the spine.

'You will observe,' said the commissary to the officer and to me as he took out his note book, 'that the woman must have fallen on her dagger. The rats are many here-see their eyes glistening among that heap of bones-and you will also notice' —I shuddered as he placed his hand on the skeleton —'that but little time was lost by them, for the bones are scarcely cold!'

There was no other sign of any one near, living or dead; and so deploying again into line the soldiers passed on. Presently we came to the hut made of the old wardrobe. We approached. In five of the six compartments was an old man sleeping-sleeping so soundly that even the glare of the lanterns did not wake them. Old and grim and grizzled they looked, with their gaunt, wrinkled, bronzed faces and their white moustaches.

The officer called out harshly and loudly a word of command, and in an instant each one of them was on his feet before us and standing at 'attention!'

'What do you here?'

'We sleep,' was the answer.

'Where are the other chiffoniers?' asked the commissary.

'Gone to work.'

'And you?'

'We are on guard!'

'Peste!' laughed the officer grimly, as he looked at the old men one after the other in the face and added with cool deliberate cruelty: 'Asleep on duty! Is this the manner of the Old Guard? No wonder, then, a Waterloo!'

By the gleam of the lantern I saw the grim old faces grow deadly pale, and almost shuddered at the look in the eyes of the old men as the laugh of the soldiers echoed the grim pleasantry of the officer.

I felt in that moment that I was in some measure avenged.

For a moment they looked as if they would throw themselves on the taunter, but years of their life had schooled them and they remained still.

'You are but five,' said the commissary; 'where is the sixth?' The answer came with a grim chuckle.

'He is there!' and the speaker pointed to the bottom of the wardrobe. 'He died last night. You won't find much of him. The burial of the rats is quick!'

The commissary stooped and looked in. Then he turned to the officer and said calmly:

'We may as well go back. No trace here now; nothing to prove that man was the one wounded by your soldiers' bullets! Probably they murdered him to cover up the trace. See!' again he stooped and placed his hands on the skeleton. 'The rats work quickly and they are many. These bones are warm!'

I shuddered, and so did many more of those around me.

'Form!' said the officer, and so in marching order, with the lanterns swinging in front and the manacled veterans in the midst, with steady tramp we took ourselves out of the dustheaps and turned backward to the fortress of Bicêtre.

My year of probation has long since ended, and Alice is my wife. But when I look back upon that trying twelvemonth one of the most vivid incidents that memory recalls is that associated with my visit to the City of Dust.

A Dream of Red Hands

The first opinion given to me regarding Jacob Settle was a simple descriptive statement, 'He's a down-in-the-mouth chap': but I found that it embodied the thoughts and ideas of all his fellow-workmen. There was in the phrase a certain easy tolerance, an absence of positive feeling of any kind, rather than any complete opinion, which marked pretty accurately the man's place in public esteem. Still, there was some dissimilarity between this and his appearance which unconsciously set me thinking, and by degrees, as I saw more of the place and the workmen, I came to have a special interest in him. He was, I found, for ever doing kindnesses, not involving money expenses beyond his humble means, but in the manifold ways of forethought and forbearance and self-repression which are of the truer charities of life. Women and children trusted him implicitly, though, strangely enough, he rather shunned them, except when anyone was sick, and then he made his appearance to help if he could, timidly and awkwardly. He led a very solitary life, keeping house by himself in a tiny cottage, or rather hut, of one room, far on the edge of the moorland. His existence seemed so sad and solitary that I wished to cheer it up, and for the purpose took the occasion when we had both been sitting up with a child, injured by me through accident, to offer to lend him books. He gladly accepted, and as we parted in the grey of the dawn I felt that something of mutual confidence had been established between us.

The books were always most carefully and punctually returned, and in time Jacob Settle and I became quite friends. Once or twice as I crossed the moorland on Sundays I looked in on him; but on such occasions he was shy and ill at ease so that I felt diffident about calling to see him. He would never under any circumstances come into my own lodgings.

One Sunday afternoon, I was coming back from a long walk beyond the moor, and as I passed Settle's cottage stopped at the door to say 'How do you do?' to him. As the door was shut, I thought that he was out, and merely knocked for form's sake, or through habit, not expecting to get any answer. To my surprise, I heard a feeble voice from within, though what was said I could not hear. I entered at once, and found Jacob lying half-dressed upon his bed. He was as pale as death, and the sweat was simply rolling off his face. His hands were unconsciously gripping the bedclothes as a drowning man holds on to whatever he may grasp. As I came in he half arose, with a wild, hunted look in his eyes, which were wide open and staring, as though something of horror had come before him; but when he recognised me he sank back on the couch with a smothered sob of relief and closed his eyes. I stood by him for a while, quite a minute or two, while he gasped. Then he opened his eyes and looked at me, but with such a despairing, woeful expression that, as I am a living man, I would have rather seen that frozen look of horror. I sat down beside him and asked after his health. For a while he would not answer me except to say that he was not ill; but then, after scrutinising me closely, he half arose on his elbow and said:

'I thank you kindly, sir, but I'm simply telling you the truth. I am not ill, as men call it, though God knows whether there be not worse sicknesses than doctors know of. I'll tell you, as you are so kind, but I trust that you won't even mention such a thing to a living soul, for it might work me more and greater woe. I am suffering from a bad dream.'

'A bad dream!' I said, hoping to cheer him; 'but dreams pass away with the light-even with waking.' There I stopped, for before he spoke I saw the answer in his desolate look round the little place.

'No! no! that's all well for people that live in comfort and with those they love around them. It is a thousand times worse for those who live alone and have to do so. What cheer is there for me, waking here in the silence of the night, with the wide moor around me full of voices and full of faces that make my waking a worse dream than my sleep? Ah, young sir, you have no past that can send its legions to people the darkness and the empty space, and I pray the good God that you may never have!' As he spoke, there was such an almost irresistible gravity of conviction in his manner that I abandoned my remonstrance about his solitary life. I felt that I was in the presence of some secret influence which I could not fathom. To my relief, for I knew not what to say, he went on:

'Two nights past have I dreamed it. It was hard enough the first night, but I came through it. Last night the expectation was in itself almost worse than the dream-until the dream came, and then it swept away every remembrance of lesser pain. I stayed awake till just before the dawn, and then it came again, and ever since I have been in such an agony as I am sure the dying feel, and with it all the dread of tonight.' Before he had got to the end of the sentence my mind was made up, and I felt that I could speak to him more cheerfully.

'Try and get to sleep early tonight-in fact, before the evening has passed away. The sleep will refresh you, and I promise you there will not be any bad dreams after tonight.' He shook his head hopelessly, so I sat a little longer and then left him.

When I got home I made my arrangements for the night, for I had made up my mind to share Jacob Settle's lonely vigil in his cottage on the moor. I judged that if he got to sleep before sunset he would wake well before midnight, and so, just as the bells of the city were striking eleven, I stood opposite his door armed with a bag, in which were my supper, an extra large flask, a couple of candles, and a book. The moonlight was bright, and flooded the whole moor, till it was almost as light as day; but ever and anon black clouds drove across the sky, and made a darkness which by comparison seemed almost tangible. I opened the door softly, and entered without waking Jacob, who lay asleep with his white face upward. He was still, and again bathed in sweat. I tried to imagine what visions were passing before those closed eyes which could bring with them the misery and woe which were stamped on the face, but fancy failed me, and I waited for the awakening. It came suddenly, and in a fashion which touched me to the quick, for the hollow groan that broke from the man's white lips as he half arose and sank back was manifestly the realisation or completion of some train of thought which had gone before.

'If this be dreaming,' said I to myself, 'then it must be based on some very terrible reality. What can have been that unhappy fact that he spoke of?'

While I thus spoke, he realised that I was with him. It struck me as strange that he had no period of that doubt as to whether dream or reality surrounded him which commonly marks an expected environment of waking men. With a positive cry of joy, he seized my hand and held it in his two wet, trembling hands, as a frightened child clings on to someone whom it loves. I tried to soothe him:

'There, there! it is all right. I have come to stay with you tonight, and together we will try to fight this evil dream.' He let go my hand suddenly, and sank back on his bed and covered his eyes with his hands.

'Fight it? —the evil dream! Ah! no, sir, no! No mortal power can fight that dream, for it comes from God-and is burned in here;' and he beat upon his forehead. Then he went on:

'It is the same dream, ever the same, and yet it grows in its power to torture me every time it comes.'

'What is the dream?' I asked, thinking that the speaking of it might give him some relief, but he shrank away from me, and after a long pause said:

'No, I had better not tell it. It may not come again.'

There was manifestly something to conceal from me-something that lay behind the dream, so I answered:

'All right. I hope you have seen the last of it. But if it should come again, you will tell me, will you not? I ask, not out of curiosity, but because I think it may relieve you to speak.' He answered with what I thought was almost an undue amount of solemnity:

'If it comes again, I shall tell you all.'

Then I tried to get his mind away from the subject to more mundane things, so I produced supper, and made him share it with me, including the contents of the flask. After a little he braced up, and when I lit my cigar, having given him another, we smoked a full hour, and talked of many things. Little by little the comfort of his body stole over his mind, and I could see sleep laying her gentle hands on his eyelids. He felt it, too, and told me that now he felt all right, and I might safely leave him; but I told him that, right or wrong, I was going to see in the daylight. So I lit my other candle, and began to read as he fell asleep.

By degrees I got interested in my book, so interested that presently I was startled by its dropping out of my hands. I looked and saw that Jacob was still asleep, and I was rejoiced to see that there was on his face a look of unwonted happiness, while his lips seemed to move with unspoken words. Then I turned to my work again, and again woke, but this time to feel chilled to my very marrow by hearing the voice from the bed beside me:

'Not with those red hands! Never! never!' On looking at him, I found that he was still asleep. He woke, however, in an instant, and did not seem surprised to see me; there was again that strange apathy as to his surroundings. Then I said:

'Settle, tell me your dream. You may speak freely, for I shall hold your confidence sacred. While we both live I shall never mention what you may choose to tell me.'

He replied:

'I said I would; but I had better tell you first what goes before the dream, that you may understand. I was a schoolmaster when I was a very young man; it was only a parish school in a little village in the West Country. No need to mention any names. Better not. I was engaged to be married to a young girl whom I loved and almost reverenced. It was the old story. While we were waiting for the time when we could afford to set up house together, another man came along. He was nearly as young as I was, and handsome, and a gentleman, with all a gentleman's attractive ways for a woman of our class. He would go fishing, and she would meet him while I was at my work in school. I reasoned with her and implored her to give him up. I offered to get married at once and go away and begin the world in a strange country; but she would not listen to anything I could say, and I could see that she was infatuated with him. Then I took it on myself to meet the man and ask him to deal well with the girl, for I thought he might mean honestly by her, so that there might be no talk or chance of talk on the part of others. I went where I should meet him with none by, and we met!' Here Jacob Settle had to pause, for something seemed to rise in his throat, and he almost gasped for breath. Then he went on:

'Sir, as God is above us, there was no selfish thought in my heart that day, I loved my pretty Mabel too well to be content with a part of her love, and I had thought of my own unhappiness too often not to have come to realise that, whatever might come to her, my hope was gone. He was insolent to me-you, sir, who are a gentleman, cannot know, perhaps, how galling can be the insolence of one who is above you in station-but I bore with that. I implored him to deal well with the girl, for what might be only a pastime of an idle hour with him might be the breaking of her heart. For I never had a thought of her truth, or that the worst of harm could come to her-it was only the unhappiness to her heart I feared. But when I asked him when he intended to marry her his laughter galled me so that I lost my temper and told him that I would not stand by and see her life made unhappy. Then he grew angry too, and in his anger said such cruel things of her that then and there I swore he should not live to do her harm. God knows how it came about, for in such moments of passion it is hard to remember the steps from a word to a blow, but I found myself standing over his dead body, with my hands crimson with the blood that welled from his torn throat. We were alone and he was a stranger, with none of his kin to seek for him and murder does not always out-not all at once. His bones may be whitening still, for all I know, in the pool of the river where I left him. No one suspected his absence, or why it was, except my poor Mabel, and she dared not speak. But it was all in vain, for when I came back again after an absence of months-for I could not live in the place —I learned that her shame had come and that she had died in it. Hitherto I had been borne up by the thought that my ill deed had saved her future, but now, when I learned that I had been too late, and that my poor love was smirched with that man's sin, I fled away with the sense of my useless guilt upon me more heavily than I could bear. Ah! sir, you that have not done such a sin don't know what it is to carry it with you. You may think that custom makes it easy to you, but it is not so. It grows and grows with every hour, till it becomes intolerable, and with it growing, too, the feeling that you must for ever stand outside Heaven. You don't know what that means, and I pray God that you never may. Ordinary men, to whom all things are possible, don't often, if ever, think of Heaven. It is a name, and nothing more, and they are content to wait and let things be, but to those who are doomed to be shut out for ever you cannot think what it means, you cannot guess or measure the terrible endless longing to see the gates opened, and to be able to join the white figures within.

'And this brings me to my dream. It seemed that the portal was before me, with great gates of massive steel with bars of the thickness of a mast, rising to the very clouds, and so close that between them was just a glimpse of a crystal grotto, on whose shining walls were figured many white-clad forms with faces radiant with joy. When I stood before the gate my heart and my soul were so full of rapture and longing that I forgot. And there stood at the gate two mighty angels with sweeping wings, and, oh! so stern of countenance. They held each in one hand a flaming sword, and in the other the latchet, which moved to and fro at their lightest touch. Nearer were figures all draped in black, with heads covered so that only the eyes were seen, and they handed to each who came white garments such as the angels wear. A low murmur came that told that all should put on their own robes, and without soil, or the angels would not pass them in, but would smite them down with the flaming swords. I was eager to don my own garment, and hurriedly threw it over me and stepped swiftly to the gate; but it moved not, and the angels, loosing the latchet, pointed to my dress, I looked down, and was aghast, for the whole robe was smeared with blood. My hands were red; they glittered with the blood that dripped from them as on that day by the river bank. And then the angels raised their flaming swords to smite me down, and the horror was complete —I awoke. Again, and again, and again, that awful dream comes to me. I never learn from the experience, I never remember, but at the beginning the hope is ever there to make the end more appalling; and I know that the dream does not come out of the common darkness where the dreams abide, but that it is sent from God as a punishment! Never, never shall I be able to pass the gate, for the soil on the angel garments must ever come from these bloody hands!'

I listened as in a spell as Jacob Settle spoke. There was something so far away in the tone of his voice-something so dreamy and mystic in the eyes that looked as if through me at some spirit beyond-something so lofty in his very diction and in such marked contrast to his workworn clothes and his poor surroundings that I wondered if the whole thing were not a dream.

We were both silent for a long time. I kept looking at the man before me in growing wonderment. Now that his confession had been made, his soul, which had been crushed to the very earth, seemed to leap back again to uprightness with some resilient force. I suppose I ought to have been horrified with his story, but, strange to say, I was not. It certainly is not pleasant to be made the recipient of the confidence of a murderer, but this poor fellow seemed to have had, not only so much provocation, but so much self-denying purpose in his deed of blood that I did not feel called upon to pass judgment upon him. My purpose was to comfort, so I spoke out with what calmness I could, for my heart was beating fast and heavily:

'You need not despair, Jacob Settle. God is very good, and His mercy is great. Live on and work on in the hope that some day you may feel that you have atoned for the past.' Here I paused, for I could see that deep, natural sleep this time, was creeping upon him. 'Go to sleep,' I said; 'I shall watch with you here and we shall have no more evil dreams tonight.'

He made an effort to pull himself together, and answered:

'I don't know how to thank you for your goodness to me this night, but I think you had best leave me now. I'll try and sleep this out; I feel a weight off my mind since I have told you all. If there's anything of the man left in me, I must try and fight out life alone.'

'I'll go tonight, as you wish it,' I said; 'but take my advice, and do not live in such a solitary way. Go among men and women; live among them. Share their joys and sorrows, and it will help you to forget. This solitude will make you melancholy mad.'

'I will!' he answered, half unconsciously, for sleep was overmastering him.

I turned to go, and he looked after me. When I had touched the latch I dropped it, and, coming back to the bed, held out my hand. He grasped it with both his as he rose to a sitting posture, and I said my goodnight, trying to cheer him:

'Heart, man, heart! There is work in the world for you to do, Jacob Settle. You can wear those white robes yet and pass through that gate of steel!'

Then I left him.

A week after I found his cottage deserted, and on asking at the works was told that he had 'gone north', no one exactly knew whither.

Two years afterwards, I was staying for a few days with my friend Dr. Munro in Glasgow. He was a busy man, and could not spare much time for going about with me, so I spent my days in excursions to the Trossachs and Loch Katrine and down the Clyde. On the second last evening of my stay I came back somewhat later than I had arranged, but found that my host was late too. The maid told me that he had been sent for to the hospital —a case of accident at the gas-works, and the dinner was postponed an hour; so telling her I would stroll down to find her master and walk back with him, I went out. At the hospital I found him washing his hands preparatory to starting for home. Casually, I asked him what his case was.

'Oh, the usual thing! A rotten rope and men's lives of no account. Two men were working in a gasometer, when the rope that held their scaffolding broke. It must have occurred just before the dinner hour, for no one noticed their absence till the men had returned. There was about seven feet of water in the gasometer, so they had a hard fight for it, poor fellows. However, one of them was alive, just alive, but we have had a hard job to pull him through. It seems that he owes his life to his mate, for I have never heard of greater heroism. They swam together while their strength lasted, but at the end they were so done up that even the lights above, and the men slung with ropes, coming down to help them, could not keep them up. But one of them stood on the bottom and held up his comrade over his head, and those few breaths made all the difference between life and death. They were a shocking sight when they were taken out, for that water is like a purple dye with the gas and the tar. The man upstairs looked as if he had been washed in blood. Ugh!'

'And the other?'

'Oh, he's worse still. But he must have been a very noble fellow. That struggle under the water must have been fearful; one can see that by the way the blood has been drawn from the extremities. It makes the idea of the *Stigmata* possible to look at him. Resolution like this could, you would think, do anything in the world. Ay! it might almost unbar the gates of Heaven. Look here, old man, it is not a very pleasant sight, especially just before dinner, but you are a writer, and this is an odd case. Here is something you would not like to miss, for in all human probability you will never see anything like it again.' While he was speaking he had brought me into the mortuary of the hospital.

On the bier lay a body covered with a white sheet, which was wrapped close round it.

'Looks like a chrysalis, don't it? I say, Jack, if there be anything in the old myth that a soul is typified by a butterfly, well, then the one that this chrysalis sent forth was a very noble specimen and took all the sunlight on its wings. See here!' He uncovered the face. Horrible, indeed, it looked, as though stained with blood. But I knew him at once, Jacob Settle! My friend pulled the winding sheet further down.

The hands were crossed on the purple breast as they had been reverently placed by some tender-hearted person. As I saw them my heart throbbed with a great exultation, for the memory of his harrowing dream rushed across my mind. There was no stain now on those poor, brave hands, for they were blanched white as snow.

And somehow as I looked I felt that the evil dream was all over. That noble soul had won a way through the gate at last. The white robe had now no stain from the hands that had put it on.

Crooken Sands

Mr Arthur Fernlee Markam, who took what was known as the Red House above the Mains of Crooken, was a London merchant, and being essentially a cockney, thought it necessary when he went for the summer holidays to Scotland to provide an entire rig-out as a Highland chieftain, as manifested in chromolithographs and on the music-hall stage. He had once seen in the Empire the Great Prince —'The Bounder King' —bring down the house by appearing as 'The MacSlogan of that Ilk,' and singing the celebrated Scotch song, 'There's naething like haggis to mak a mon dry!' and he had ever since preserved in his mind a faithful image of the picturesque and warlike appearance which he presented. Indeed, if the true inwardness of Mr. Markam's mind on the subject of his selection of Aberdeenshire as a summer resort were known, it would be found that in the foreground of the holiday locality which his fancy painted stalked the many hued figure of the MacSlogan of that Ilk. However, be this as it may, a very kind fortune-certainly so far as external beauty was concerned-led him to the choice of Crooken Bay. It is a lovely spot, between Aberdeen and Peterhead, just under the rock-bound headland whence the long, dangerous reefs known as The Spurs run out into the North Sea. Between this and the 'Mains of Crooken' —a village sheltered by the northern cliffs-lies the deep bay, backed with a multitude of bent-grown dunes where the rabbits are to be found in thousands. Thus at either end of the bay is a rocky promontory, and when the dawn or the sunset falls on the rocks of red syenite the effect is very lovely. The bay itself is floored with level sand and the tide runs far out, leaving a smooth waste of hard sand on which are dotted here and there the stake nets and bag nets of the salmon fishers. At one end of the bay there is a little group or cluster of rocks whose heads are raised something above high water, except when in rough weather the waves come over them green. At low tide they are exposed down to sand level; and here is perhaps the only little bit of dangerous sand on this part of the eastern coast. Between the rocks, which are apart about some fifty feet, is a small quicksand, which, like the Goodwins, is dangerous only with the incoming tide. It extends outwards till it is lost in the sea, and inwards till it fades away in the hard sand of the upper beach. On the slope of the hill which rises beyond the dunes, midway between the Spurs and the Port of Crooken, is the Red House. It rises from the midst of a clump of fir-trees which protect it on three sides, leaving the whole sea front open. A trim old-fashioned garden stretches down to the roadway, on crossing which a grassy path, which can be used for light vehicles, threads a way to the shore, winding amongst the sand hills.

When the Markam family arrived at the Red House after their thirty-six hours of pitching on the Aberdeen steamer *Ban Righ* from Blackwall, with the subsequent train to Yellon and drive of a dozen miles, they all agreed that they had never seen a more delightful spot. The general satisfaction was more marked as at that very time none of the family were, for several reasons, inclined to find favourable anything or any place over the Scottish border. Though the family was a large one, the prosperity of the business allowed them all sorts of personal luxuries, amongst which was a wide latitude in the way of dress. The frequency of the Markam girls' new frocks was a source of envy to their bosom friends and of joy to themselves.

Arthur Fernlee Markam had not taken his family into his confidence regarding his new costume. He was not quite certain that he should be free from ridicule, or at least from sarcasm, and as he was sensitive on the subject, he thought it better to be actually in the suitable environment before he allowed the full splendour to burst upon them. He had taken some pains, to insure the completeness of the Highland costume. For the purpose he had paid many visits to 'The Scotch All-Wool Tartan Clothing Mart' which had been lately established in Copthall-court by the Messrs. MacCallum More and Roderick MacDhu. He had anxious consultations with the head of the firm-MacCallum as he called himself, resenting any such additions as 'Mr.' or 'Esquire.' The known stock of buckles, buttons, straps, brooches and ornaments of all kinds were examined in critical detail; and at last an eagle's feather of sufficiently magnificent proportions was discovered, and the equipment was complete. It was only when he saw the finished costume, with the vivid hues of the tartan seemingly modified into comparative sobriety by the multitude of silver fittings, the cairngorm brooches, the philibeg, dirk and sporran that he was fully and absolutely satisfied with his choice. At first he had thought of the Royal Stuart dress tartan, but abandoned it on the MacCallum pointing out that if he should happen to be in the neighbourhood of Balmoral it might lead to complications. The MacCallum, who, by the way, spoke with a remarkable cockney accent, suggested other plaids in turn; but now that the other question of accuracy had been raised, Mr. Markam foresaw difficulties if he should by chance find himself in the locality of the clan whose colours he had usurped. The MacCallum at last undertook to have, at Markam's expense, a special pattern woven which would not be exactly the same as any existing tartan, though partaking of the characteristics of many. It was based on the Royal Stuart, but contained suggestions as to simplicity of pattern from the Macalister and Ogilvie clans, and as to neutrality of colour from the clans of Buchanan, Macbeth, Chief of Macintosh and Macleod. When the specimen had been shown to Markam he had feared somewhat lest it should strike the eye of his domestic circle as gaudy; but as Roderick MacDhu fell into perfect ecstasies over its beauty he did not make any objection to the completion of the piece. He thought, and wisely, that if a genuine Scotchman like MacDhu liked it, it must be right-especially as the junior partner was a man very much of his own build and appearance. When the MacCallum was receiving his cheque-which, by the way, was a pretty stiff one-he remarked:

'I've taken the liberty of having some more of the stuff woven in case you or any of your friends should want it.' Markam was gratified, and told him that he should be only too happy if the beautiful stuff which they had originated between them should become a favourite, as he had no doubt it would in time. He might make and sell as much as he would.

Markam tried the dress on in his office one evening after the clerks had all gone home. He was pleased, though a little frightened, at the result. The MacCallum had done his work thoroughly, and there was nothing omitted that could add to the martial dignity of the wearer.

'I shall not, of course, take the claymore and the pistols with me on ordinary occasions,' said Markam to himself as he began to undress. He determined that he would wear the dress for the first time on landing in Scotland, and accordingly on the morning when the *Ban Righ* was hanging off the Girdle Ness lighthouse, waiting for the tide to enter the port of Aberdeen, he emerged from his cabin in all the gaudy splendour of his new costume. The first comment he heard was from one of his own sons, who did not recognise him at first.

'Here's a guy! Great Scott! It's the governor!' And the boy fled forthwith and tried to bury his laughter under a cushion in the saloon. Markam was a good sailor and had not suffered from the pitching of the boat, so that his naturally rubicund face was even more rosy by the conscious blush which suffused his cheeks when he had found himself at once the cynosure of all eyes. He could have wished that he had not been so bold for he knew from the cold that there was a big bare spot under one side of his jauntily worn Glengarry cap. However, he faced the group of strangers boldly. He was not, outwardly, upset even when some of the comments reached his ears.

'He's off his bloomin' chump,' said a cockney in a suit of exaggerated plaid.

'There's flies on him,' said a tall thin Yankee, pale with sea-sickness, who was on his way to take up his residence for a time as close as he could get to the gates of Balmoral.

'Happy thought! Let us fill our mulls; now's the chance!' said a young Oxford man on his way home to Inverness. But presently Mr. Markam heard the voice of his eldest daughter.

'Where is he? Where is he?' and she came tearing along the deck with her hat blowing behind her. Her face showed signs of agitation, for her mother had just been telling her of her father's condition; but when she saw him she instantly burst into laughter so violent that it ended in a fit of hysterics. Something of the same kind happened to each of the other children. When they had all had their turn Mr. Markam went to his cabin and sent his wife's maid to tell each member of the family that he wanted to see them at once. They all made their appearance, suppressing their feelings as well as they could. He said to them very quietly:

'My dears, don't I provide you all with ample allowances?'

'Yes, father!' they all answered gravely, 'no one could be more generous!'

'Don't I let you dress as you please?'

'Yes, father!'—this a little sheepishly.

'Then, my dears, don't you think it would be nicer and kinder of you not to try and make me feel uncomfortable, even if I do assume a dress which is ridiculous in your eyes, though quite common enough in the country where we are about to sojourn?' There was no answer except that which appeared in their hanging heads. He was a good father and they all knew it. He was quite satisfied and went on:

'There, now, run away and enjoy yourselves! We shan't have another word about it.' Then he went on deck again and stood bravely the fire of ridicule which he recognised around him, though nothing more was said within his hearing.

The astonishment and the amusement which his get-up occasioned on the *Ban Righ* was, however, nothing to that which it created in Aberdeen. The boys and loafers, and women with babies, who waited at the landing shed, followed *en masse* as the Markam party took their way to the railway station; even the porters with their old-fashioned knots and their new-fashioned barrows, who await the traveller at the foot of the gang-plank, followed in wondering delight. Fortunately the Peterhead train was just about to start, so that the martyrdom was not unnecessarily prolonged. In the carriage the glorious Highland costume was unseen, and as there were but few persons at the station at Yellon, all went well there. When, however, the carriage drew near the Mains of Crooken and the fisher folk had run to their doors to see who it was that was passing, the excitement exceeded all bounds. The children with one impulse waved their bonnets and ran shouting behind the carriage; the men forsook their nets and their baiting and followed; the women clutched their babies, and followed also. The horses were tired after their long journey to Yellon and back, and the hill was steep, so that there was ample time for the crowd to gather and even to pass on ahead.

Mrs. Markam and the elder girls would have liked to make some protest or to do something to relieve their feelings of chagrin at the ridicule which they saw on all faces, but there was a look of fixed determination on the face of the seeming Highlander which awed them a little, and they were silent. It might have been that the eagle's feather, even when arising above the bald head, the cairngorm brooch even on the fat shoulder, and the claymore, dirk and pistols, even when belted round the extensive paunch and protruding from the stocking on the sturdy calf, fulfilled their existence as symbols of martial and terrifying import! When the party arrived at the gate of the Red House there awaited them a crowd of Crooken inhabitants, hatless and respectfully silent; the remainder of the population was painfully toiling up the hill. The silence was broken by only one sound, that of a man with a deep voice.

'Man! but he's forgotten the pipes!'

The servants had arrived some days before, and all things were in readiness. In the glow consequent on a good lunch after a hard journey all the disagreeables of travel and all the chagrin consequent on the adoption of the obnoxious costume were forgotten.

That afternoon Markam, still clad in full array, walked through the Mains of Crooken. He was all alone, for, strange to say, his wife and both daughters had sick headaches, and were, as he was told, lying down to rest after the fatigue of the journey. His eldest son, who claimed to be a young man, had gone out by himself to explore the surroundings of the place, and one of the boys could not be found. The other boy, on being told that his father had sent for him to come for a walk, had managed-by accident, of course-to fall into the water butt, and had to be dried and rigged out afresh. His clothes not having been as yet unpacked this was of course impossible without delay.

Mr. Markam was not quite satisfied with his walk. He could not meet any of his neighbours. It was not that there were not enough people about, for every house and cottage seemed to be full; but the people when in the open were either in their doorways some distance behind him, or on the roadway a long distance in front. As he passed he could see the tops of heads and the whites of eyes in the windows or round the corners of doors. The only interview which he had was anything but a pleasant one. This was with an odd sort of old man who was hardly ever heard to speak except to join in the 'Amens' in the meeting-house. His sole occupation seemed to be to wait at the window of the post-office from eight o'clock in the morning till the arrival of the mail at one, when he carried the letter-bag to a neighbouring baronial castle. The remainder of his day was spent on a seat in a draughty part of the port, where the offal of the fish, the refuse of the bait, and the house rubbish was thrown, and where the ducks were accustomed to hold high revel.

When Saft Tammie beheld him coming he raised his eyes, which were generally fixed on the nothing which lay on the roadway opposite his seat, and, seeming dazzled as if by a burst of sunshine, rubbed them and shaded them with his hand. Then he started up and raised his hand aloft in a denunciatory manner as he spoke: —

'"Vanity of vanities, saith the preacher. All is vanity." Mon, be warned in time! "Behold the lilies of the field, they toil not, neither do they spin, yet Solomon in all his glory was not arrayed like one of these." Mon! Mon! Thy vanity is as the quicksand which swallows up all which comes within its spell. Beware vanity! Beware the quicksand, which yawneth for thee, and which will swallow thee up! See thyself! Learn thine own vanity! Meet thyself face to face, and then in that moment thou shalt learn the fatal force of thy vanity. Learn it, know it, and repent ere the quicksand swallow thee!' Then without another word he went back to his seat and sat there immovable and expressionless as before.

Markam could not but feel a little upset by this tirade. Only that it was spoken by a seeming madman, he would have put it down to some eccentric exhibition of Scottish humour or impudence; but the gravity of the message-for it seemed nothing else-made such a reading impossible. He was, however, determined not to give in to ridicule, and although he had not yet seen anything in Scotland to remind him even of a kilt, he determined to wear his Highland dress. When he returned home, in less than half-an-hour, he found that every member of the family was, despite the headaches, out taking a walk. He took the opportunity afforded by their absence of locking himself in his dressing-room, took off the Highland dress, and, putting on a suit of flannels, lit a cigar and had a snooze. He was awakened by the noise of the family coming in, and at once donning his dress made his appearance in the drawing-room for tea.

He did not go out again that afternoon; but after dinner he put on his dress again-he had, of course dressed for dinner as usual-and went by himself for a walk on the sea-shore. He had by this time come to the conclusion that he would get by degrees accustomed to the Highland dress before making it his ordinary wear. The moon was up and he easily followed the path through the sand-hills, and shortly struck the shore. The tide was out and the beach firm as a rock, so he strolled southwards to nearly the end of the bay. Here he was attracted by two isolated rocks some little way out from the edge of the dunes, so he strolled towards them. When he reached the nearest one he climbed it, and, sitting there elevated some fifteen or twenty feet over the waste of sand, enjoyed the lovely, peaceful prospect. The moon was rising behind the headland of Pennyfold, and its light was just touching the top of the furthermost rock of the Spurs some three-quarters of a mile out; the rest of the rocks were in dark shadow. As the moon rose over the headland, the rocks of the Spurs and then the beach by degrees became flooded with light.

For a good while Mr. Markam sat and looked at the rising moon and the growing area of light which followed its rise. Then he turned and faced eastwards and sat with his chin in his hand looking seawards, and revelling in the peace and beauty and freedom of the scene. The roar of London-the darkness and the strife and weariness of London life-seemed to have passed quite away, and he lived at the moment a freer and higher life. He looked at the glistening water as it stole its way over the flat waste of sand, coming closer and closer insensibly-the tide had turned. Presently he heard a distant shouting along the beach very far off.

'The fishermen calling to each other,' he said to himself and looked around. As he did so he got a horrible shock, for though just then a cloud sailed across the moon he saw, in spite of the sudden darkness around him, his own image. For an instant, on the top of the opposite rock he could see the bald back of the head and the Glengarry cap with the immense eagle's feather. As he staggered back his foot slipped, and he began to slide down towards the sand between the two rocks. He took no concern as to falling, for the sand was really only a few feet below him, and his mind was occupied with the figure or simulacrum of himself, which had already disappeared. As the easiest way of reaching *terra firma* he prepared to jump the remainder of the distance. All this had taken but a second, but the brain works quickly, and even as he gathered himself for the spring he saw the sand below him lying so marbly level shake and shiver in an odd way. A sudden fear overcame him; his knees failed, and instead of jumping he slid miserably down the rock, scratching his bare legs as he went. His feet touched the sand-went through it like water-and he was down below his knees before he realised that he was in a quicksand. Wildly he grasped at the rock to keep himself from sinking further, and fortunately there was a jutting spur or edge which he was able to grasp instinctively. To this he clung in grim desperation. He tried to shout, but his breath would not come, till after a great effort his voice rang out. Again he shouted, and it seemed as if the sound of his own voice gave him new courage, for he was able to hold on to the rock for a longer time than he thought possible-though he held on only in blind desperation. He was, however, beginning to find his grasp weakening, when, joy of joys! his shout was answered by a rough voice from just above him.

'God be thankit, I'm nae too late!' and a fisherman with great thigh-boots came hurriedly climbing over the rock. In an instant he recognised the gravity of the danger, and with a cheering 'Haud fast, mon! I'm comin'!' scrambled down till he found a firm foothold. Then with one strong hand holding the rock above, he leaned down, and catching Markam's wrist, called out to him, 'Haud to me, mon! Haud to me wi' ither hond!'

Then he lent his great strength, and with a steady, sturdy pull, dragged him out of the hungry quicksand and placed him safe upon the rock. Hardly giving him time to draw breath, he pulled and pushed him-never letting him go for an instant-over the rock into the firm sand beyond it, and finally deposited him, still shaking from the magnitude of his danger, high upon the beach. Then he began to speak:

'Mon! but I was just in time. If I had no laucht at yon foolish lads and begun to rin at the first you'd a bin sinkin' doon to the bowels o' the airth be the noo! Wully Beagrie thocht you was a ghaist, and Tom MacPhail swore ye was only like a goblin on a puddick-steel! "Na!" said I. "Yon's but the daft Englishman-the loony that had escapit frae the waxwarks." I was thinkin' that bein' strange and silly-if not a whole-made feel-ye'd no ken the ways o' the quicksan'! I shouted till warn ye, and then ran to drag ye aff, if need be. But God be thankit, be ye fule or only half-daft wi' yer vanity, that I was no that late!' and he reverently lifted his cap as he spoke.

Mr. Markam was deeply touched and thankful for his escape from a horrible death; but the sting of the charge of vanity thus made once more against him came through his humility. He was about to reply angrily, when suddenly a great awe fell upon him as he remembered the warning words of the half-crazy letter-carrier: 'Meet thyself face to face, and repent ere the quicksand shall swallow thee!'

Here, too, he remembered the image of himself that he had seen and the sudden danger from the deadly quicksand that had followed. He was silent a full minute, and then said:

'My good fellow, I owe you my life!'

The answer came with reverence from the hardy fisherman, 'Na! Na! Ye owe that to God; but, as for me, I'm only too glad till be the humble instrument o' His mercy.'

'But you will let me thank you,' said Mr. Markam, taking both the great hands of his deliverer in his and holding them tight. 'My heart is too full as yet, and my nerves are too much shaken to let me say much; but, believe me, I am very, very grateful!' It was quite evident that the poor old fellow was deeply touched, for the tears were running down his cheeks.

The fisherman said, with a rough but true courtesy:

'Ay, sir! thank me and ye will-if it'll do yer poor heart good. An' I'm thinking that if it were me I'd be thankful too. But, sir, as for me I need no thanks. I am glad, so I am!'

That Arthur Fernlee Markam was really thankful and grateful was shown practically later on. Within a week's time there sailed into Port Crooken the finest fishing smack that had ever been seen in the harbour of Peterhead. She was fully found with sails and gear of all kinds, and with nets of the best. Her master and men went away by the coach, after having left with the salmon-fisher's wife the papers which made her over to him.

As Mr. Markam and the salmon-fisher walked together along the shore the former asked his companion not to mention the fact that he had been in such imminent danger, for that it would only distress his dear wife and children. He said that he would warn them all of the quicksand, and for that purpose he, then and there, asked questions about it till he felt that his information on the subject was complete. Before they parted he asked his companion if he had happened to see a second figure, dressed like himself on the other rock as he had approached to succour him.

'Na! Na!' came the answer, 'there is nae sic another fule in these parts. Nor has there been since the time o' Jamie Fleeman-him that was fule to the Laird o' Udny. Why, mon! sic a heathenish dress as ye have on till ye has nae been seen in these pairts within the memory o' mon. An' I'm thinkin' that sic a dress never was for sittin' on the cauld rock, as ye done beyont. Mon! but do ye no fear the rheumatism or the lumbagy wi' floppin' doon on to the cauld stanes wi' yer bare flesh? I was thinking that it was daft ye waur when I see ye the mornin' doon be the port, but it's fule or eediot ye maun be for the like o' thot!' Mr. Markam did not care to argue the point, and as they were now close to his own home he asked the salmon-fisher to have a glass of whisky-which he did-and they parted for the night. He took good care to warn all his family of the quicksand, telling them that he had himself been in some danger from it.

All that night he never slept. He heard the hours strike one after the other; but try how he would he could not get to sleep. Over and over again he went through the horrible episode of the quicksand, from the time that Saft Tammie had broken his habitual silence to preach to him of the sin of vanity and to warn him. The question kept ever arising in his mind: 'Am I then so vain as to be in the ranks of the foolish?' and the answer ever came in the words of the crazy prophet: '"Vanity of vanities! All is vanity." Meet thyself face to face, and repent ere the quicksand shall swallow thee!' Somehow a feeling of doom began to shape itself in his mind that he would yet perish in that same quicksand, for there he had already met himself face to face.

In the grey of the morning he dozed off, but it was evident that he continued the subject in his dreams, for he was fully awakened by his wife, who said:

'Do sleep quietly! That blessed Highland suit has got on your brain. Don't talk in your sleep, if you can help it!' He was somehow conscious of a glad feeling, as if some terrible weight had been lifted from him, but he did not know any cause of it. He asked his wife what he had said in his sleep, and she answered:

'You said it often enough, goodness knows, for one to remember it —"Not face to face! I saw the eagle plume over the bald head! There is hope yet! Not face to face!" Go to sleep! Do!' And then he did go to sleep, for he seemed to realise that the prophecy of the crazy man had not yet been fulfilled. He had not met himself face to face-as yet at all events.

He was awakened early by a maid who came to tell him that there was a fisherman at the door who wanted to see him. He dressed himself as quickly as he could-for he was not yet expert with the Highland dress-and hurried down, not wishing to keep the salmon-fisher waiting. He was surprised and not altogether pleased to find that his visitor was none other than Saft Tammie, who at once opened fire on him:

'I maun gang awa' t' the post; but I thocht that I would waste an hour on ye, and ca' roond just to see if ye waur still that fou wi' vanity as on the nicht gane by. An I see that ye've no learned the lesson. Well! the time is comin', sure eneucht! However I have all the time i' the marnins to my ain sel', so I'll aye look roond jist till see how ye gang yer ain gait to the quicksan', and then to the de'il! I'm aff till ma wark the noo!' And he went straightway, leaving Mr. Markam considerably vexed, for the maids within earshot were vainly trying to conceal their giggles. He had fairly made up his mind to wear on that day ordinary clothes, but the visit of Saft Tammie reversed his decision. He would show them all that he was not a coward, and he would go on as he had begun-come what might. When he came to breakfast in full martial panoply the children, one and all, held down their heads and the backs of their necks became very red indeed. As, however, none of them laughed-except Titus, the youngest boy, who was seized with a fit of hysterical choking and was promptly banished from the room-he could not reprove them, but began to break his egg with a sternly determined air. It was unfortunate that as his wife was handing him a cup of tea one of the buttons of his sleeve caught in the lace of her morning wrapper, with the result that the hot tea was spilt over his bare knees. Not unnaturally, he made use of a swear word, whereupon his wife, somewhat nettled, spoke out:

'Well, Arthur, if you will make such an idiot of yourself with that ridiculous costume what else can you expect? You are not accustomed to it-and you never will be!' In answer he began an indignant speech with: 'Madam!' but he got no further, for now that the subject was broached, Mrs. Markam intended to have her say out. It was not a pleasant say, and, truth to tell, it was not said in a pleasant manner. A wife's manner seldom is pleasant when she undertakes to tell what she considers 'truths' to her husband. The result was that Arthur Fernlee Markam undertook, then and there, that during his stay in Scotland he would wear no other costume than the one she abused. Woman-like his wife had the last word-given in this case with tears:

'Very well, Arthur! Of course you will do as you choose. Make me as ridiculous as you can, and spoil the poor girls' chances in life. Young men don't seem to care, as a general rule, for an idiot father-in-law! But I must warn you that your vanity will some day get a rude shock-if indeed you are not before then in an asylum or dead!'

It was manifest after a few days that Mr. Markam would have to take the major part of his outdoor exercise by himself. The girls now and again took a walk with him, chiefly in the early morning or late at night, or on a wet day when there would be no one about; they professed to be willing to go out at all times, but somehow something always seemed to occur to prevent it. The boys could never be found at all on such occasions, and as to Mrs. Markam she sternly refused to go out with him on any consideration so long as he should continue to make a fool of himself. On the Sunday he dressed himself in his habitual broadcloth, for he rightly felt that church was not a place for angry feelings; but on Monday morning he resumed his Highland garb. By this time he would have given a good deal if he had never thought of the dress, but his British obstinacy was strong, and he would not give in. Saft Tammie called at his house every morning, and, not being able to see him nor to have any message taken to him, used to call back in the afternoon when the letter-bag had been delivered and watched for his going out. On such occasions he never failed to warn him against his vanity in the same words which he had used at the first. Before many days were over Mr. Markam had come to look upon him as little short of a scourge.

By the time the week was out the enforced partial solitude, the constant chagrin, and the never-ending brooding which was thus engendered, began to make Mr. Markam quite ill. He was too proud to take any of his family into his confidence since they had in his view treated him very badly. Then he did not sleep well at night, and when he did sleep he had constantly bad dreams. Merely to assure himself that his pluck was not failing him he made it a practice to visit the quicksand at least once every day; he hardly ever failed to go there the last thing at night. It was perhaps this habit that wrought the quicksand with its terrible experience so perpetually into his dreams. More and more vivid these became, till on waking at times he could hardly realise that he had not been actually in the flesh to visit the fatal spot. He sometimes thought that he might have been walking in his sleep.

One night his dream was so vivid that when he awoke he could not believe that it had only been a dream. He shut his eyes again and again, but each time the vision, if it was a vision, or the reality, if it was a reality, would rise before him. The moon was shining full and yellow over the quicksand as he approached it; he could see the expanse of light shaken and disturbed and full of black shadows as the liquid sand quivered and trembled and wrinkled and eddied as was its wont between its pauses of marble calm. As he drew close to it another figure came towards it from the opposite side with equal footsteps. He saw that it was his own figure, his very self, and in silent terror, compelled by what force he knew not, he advanced-charmed as the bird is by the snake, mesmerised or hypnotised-to meet this other self. As he felt the yielding sand closing over him he awoke in the agony of death, trembling with fear, and, strange to say, with the silly man's prophecy seeming to sound in his ears: '"Vanity of vanities! All is vanity!" See thyself and repent ere the quicksand swallow thee!'

So convinced was he that this was no dream that he arose, early as it was, and dressing himself without disturbing his wife took his way to the shore. His heart fell when he came across a series of footsteps on the sands, which he at once recognised as his own. There was the same wide heel, the same square toe; he had no doubt now that he had actually been there, and half horrified, and half in a state of dreamy stupor, he followed the footsteps, and found them lost in the edge of the yielding quicksand. This gave him a terrible shock, for there were no return steps marked on the sand, and he felt that there was some dread mystery which he could not penetrate, and the penetration of which would, he feared, undo him.

In this state of affairs he took two wrong courses. Firstly he kept his trouble to himself, and, as none of his family had any clue to it, every innocent word or expression which they used supplied fuel to the consuming fire of his imagination. Secondly he began to read books professing to bear upon the mysteries of dreaming and of mental phenomena generally, with the result that every wild imagination of every crank or half-crazy philosopher became a living germ of unrest in the fertilising soil of his disordered brain. Thus negatively and positively all things began to work to a common end. Not the least of his disturbing causes was Saft Tammie, who had now become at certain times of the day a fixture at his gate. After a while, being interested in the previous state of this individual, he made inquiries regarding his past with the following result.

Saft Tammie was popularly believed to be the son of a laird in one of the counties round the Firth of Forth. He had been partially educated for the ministry, but for some cause which no one ever knew threw up his prospects suddenly, and, going to Peterhead in its days of whaling prosperity, had there taken service on a whaler. Here off and on he had remained for some years, getting gradually more and more silent in his habits, till finally his shipmates protested against so taciturn a mate, and he had found service amongst the fishing smacks of the northern fleet. He had worked for many years at the fishing with always the reputation of being 'a wee bit daft,' till at length he had gradually settled down at Crooken, where the laird, doubtless knowing something of his family history, had given him a job which practically made him a pensioner. The minister who gave the information finished thus: —

'It is a very strange thing, but the man seems to have some odd kind of gift. Whether it be that "second sight" which we Scotch people are so prone to believe in, or some other occult form of knowledge, I know not, but nothing of a disastrous tendency ever occurs in this place but the men with whom he lives are able to quote after the event some saying of his which certainly appears to have foretold it. He gets uneasy or excited-wakes up, in fact-when death is in the air!'

This did not in any way tend to lessen Mr. Markam's concern, but on the contrary seemed to impress the prophecy more deeply on his mind. Of all the books which he had read on his new subject of study none interested him so much as a German one *Die Döppleganger*, by Dr. Heinrich von Aschenberg, formerly of Bonn. Here he learned for the first time of cases where men had led a double existence-each nature being quite apart from the other-the body being always a reality with one spirit, and a simulacrum with the other. Needless to say that Mr. Markam realised this theory as exactly suiting his own case. The glimpse which he had of his own back the night of his escape from the quicksand-his own footmarks disappearing into the quicksand with no return steps visible-the prophecy of Saft Tammie about his meeting himself and perishing in the quicksand-all lent aid to the conviction that he was in his own person an instance of the döppleganger. Being then conscious of a double life he took steps to prove its existence to his own satisfaction. To this end on one night before going to bed he wrote his name in chalk on the soles of his shoes. That night he dreamed of the quicksand, and of his visiting it-dreamed so vividly that on walking in the grey of the dawn he could not believe that he had not been there. Arising, without disturbing his wife, he sought his shoes.

The chalk signatures were undisturbed! He dressed himself and stole out softly. This time the tide was in, so he crossed the dunes and struck the shore on the further side of the quicksand. There, oh, horror of horrors! he saw his own footprints dying into the abyss!

He went home a desperately sad man. It seemed incredible that he, an elderly commercial man, who had passed a long and uneventful life in the pursuit of business in the midst of roaring, practical London, should thus find himself enmeshed in mystery and horror, and that he should discover that he had two existences. He could not speak of his trouble even to his own wife, for well he knew that she would at once require the fullest particulars of that other life-the one which she did not know; and that she would at the start not only imagine but charge him with all manner of infidelities on the head of it. And so his brooding grew deeper and deeper still. One evening-the tide then going out and the moon being at the full-he was sitting waiting for dinner when the maid announced that Saft Tammie was making a disturbance outside because he would not be let in to see him. He was very indignant, but did not like the maid to think that he had any fear on the subject, and so told her to bring him in. Tammie entered, walking more briskly than ever with his head up and a look of vigorous decision in the eyes that were so generally cast down. As soon as he entered he said:

'I have come to see ye once again-once again; and there ye sit, still just like a cockatoo on a pairch. Weel, mon, I forgie ye! Mind ye that, I forgie ye!' And without a word more he turned and walked out of the house, leaving the master in speechless indignation.

After dinner he determined to pay another visit to the quicksand-he would not allow even to himself that he was afraid to go. And so, about nine o'clock, in full array, he marched to the beach, and passing over the sands sat on the skirt of the nearer rock. The full moon was behind him and its light lit up the bay so that its fringe of foam, the dark outline of the headland, and the stakes of the salmon-nets were all emphasised. In the brilliant yellow glow the lights in the windows of Port Crooken and in those of the distant castle of the laird trembled like stars through the sky. For a long time he sat and drank in the beauty of the scene, and his soul seemed to feel a peace that it had not known for many days. All the pettiness and annoyance and silly fears of the past weeks seemed blotted out, and a new holy calm took the vacant place. In this sweet and solemn mood he reviewed his late action calmly, and felt ashamed of himself for his vanity and for the obstinacy which had followed it. And then and there he made up his mind that the present would be the last time he would wear the costume which had estranged him from those whom he loved, and which had caused him so many hours and days of chagrin, vexation, and pain.

But almost as soon as he arrived at this conclusion another voice seemed to speak within him and mockingly to ask him if he should ever get the chance to wear the suit again-that it was too late-he had chosen his course and must now abide the issue.

'It is not too late,' came the quick answer of his better self; and full of the thought, he rose up to go home and divest himself of the now hateful costume right away. He paused for one look at the beautiful scene. The light lay pale and mellow, softening every outline of rock and tree and house-top, and deepening the shadows into velvety-black, and lighting, as with a pale flame, the incoming tide, that now crept fringe-like across the flat waste of sand. Then he left the rock and stepped out for the shore.

But as he did so a frightful spasm of horror shook him, and for an instant the blood rushing to his head shut out all the light of the full moon. Once more he saw that fatal image of himself moving beyond the quicksand from the opposite rock to the shore. The shock was all the greater for the contrast with the spell of peace which he had just enjoyed; and, almost paralysed in every sense, he stood and watched the fatal vision and the wrinkly, crawling quicksand that seemed to writhe and yearn for something that lay between. There could be no mistake this time, for though the moon behind threw the face into shadow he could see there the same shaven cheeks as his own, and the small stubby moustache of a few weeks' growth. The light shone on the brilliant tartan, and on the eagle's plume. Even the bald space at one side of the Glengarry cap glistened, as did the cairngorm brooch on the shoulder and the tops of the silver buttons. As he looked he felt his feet slightly sinking, for he was still near the edge of the belt of quicksand, and he stepped back. As he did so the other figure stepped forward, so that the space between them was preserved.

So the two stood facing each other, as though in some weird fascination; and in the rushing of the blood through his brain Markam seemed to hear the words of the prophecy: 'See thyself face to face, and repent ere the quicksand swallow thee.' He did stand face to face with himself, he had repented-and now he was sinking in the quicksand! The warning and prophecy were coming true.

Above him the seagulls screamed, circling round the fringe of the incoming tide, and the sound being entirely mortal recalled him to himself. On the instant he stepped back a few quick steps, for as yet only his feet were merged in the soft sand. As he did so the other figure stepped forward, and coming within the deadly grip of the quicksand began to sink. It seemed to Markam that he was looking at himself going down to his doom, and on the instant the anguish of his soul found vent in a terrible cry. There was at the same instant a terrible cry from the other figure, and as Markam threw up his hands the figure did the same. With horror-struck eyes he saw him sink deeper into the quicksand; and then, impelled by what power he knew not, he advanced again towards the sand to meet his fate. But as his more forward foot began to sink he heard again the cries of the seagulls which seemed to restore his benumbed faculties. With a mighty effort he drew his foot out of the sand which seemed to clutch it, leaving his shoe behind, and then in sheer terror he turned and ran from the place, never stopping till his breath and strength failed him, and he sank half swooning on the grassy path through the sandhills.

Arthur Markam made up his mind not to tell his family of his terrible adventure-until at least such time as he should be complete master of himself. Now that the fatal double-his other self-had been engulfed in the quicksand he felt something like his old peace of mind.

That night he slept soundly and did not dream at all; and in the morning was quite his old self. It really seemed as though his newer and worser self had disappeared for ever; and strangely enough Saft Tammie was absent from his post that morning and never appeared there again, but sat in his old place watching nothing, as of old, with lack-lustre eye. In accordance with his resolution he did not wear his Highland suit again, but one evening tied it up in a bundle, claymore, dirk and philibeg and all, and bringing it secretly with him threw it into the quicksand. With a feeling of intense pleasure he saw it sucked below the sand, which closed above it into marble smoothness. Then he went home and announced cheerily to his family assembled for evening prayers:

'Well! my dears, you will be glad to hear that I have abandoned my idea of wearing the Highland dress. I see now what a vain old fool I was and how ridiculous I made myself! You shall never see it again!'

'Where is it, father?' asked one of the girls, wishing to say something so that such a self-sacrificing announcement as her father's should not be passed in absolute silence. His answer was so sweetly given that the girl rose from her seat and came and kissed him. It was:

'In the quicksand, my dear! and I hope that my worser self is buried there along with it-for ever.'

The remainder of the summer was passed at Crooken with delight by all the family, and on his return to town Mr. Markam had almost forgotten the whole of the incident of the quicksand, and all touching on it, when one day he got a letter from the MacCallum More which caused him much thought, though he said nothing of it to his family, and left it, for certain reasons, unanswered. It ran as follows: —

'The MacCallum More and Roderick MacDhu.
'The Scotch All-Wool Tartan Clothing Mart.
Copthall Court, E.C.,
30th September, 1892.

'Dear Sir, —I trust you will pardon the liberty which I take in writing to you, but I am desirous of making an inquiry, and I am informed that you have been sojourning during the summer in Aberdeenshire (Scotland, N.B.). My partner, Mr. Roderick MacDhu-as he appears for business reasons on our bill-heads and in our advertisements, his real name being Emmanuel Moses Marks of London-went early last month to Scotland (N.B.) for a tour, but as I have only once heard from him, shortly after his departure, I am anxious lest any misfortune may have befallen him. As I have been unable to obtain any news of him on making all inquiries in my power, I venture to appeal to you. His letter was written in deep dejection of spirit, and mentioned that he feared a judgment had come upon him for wishing to appear as a Scotchman on Scottish soil, as he had one moonlight night shortly after his arrival seen his 'wraith'. He evidently alluded to the fact that before his departure he had procured for himself a Highland costume similar to that which we had the honour to supply to you, with which, as perhaps you will remember, he was much struck. He may, however, never have worn it, as he was, to my own knowledge, diffident about putting it on, and even went so far as to tell me that he would at first only venture to wear it late at night or very early in the morning, and then only in remote places, until such time as he should get accustomed to it. Unfortunately he did not advise me of his route so that I am in complete ignorance of his whereabouts; and I venture to ask if you may have seen or heard of a Highland costume similar to your own having been seen anywhere in the neighbourhood in which I am told you have recently purchased the estate which you temporarily occupied. I shall not expect an answer to this letter unless you can give me some information regarding my friend and partner, so pray do not trouble to reply unless there be cause. I am encouraged to think that he may have been in your neighbourhood as, though his letter is not dated, the envelope is marked with the postmark of "Yellon" which I find is in Aberdeenshire, and not far from the Mains of Crooken.

'I have the honour to be, dear sir,

'Yours very respectfully,

'Joshua Sheeny Cohen Benjamin
'(The MacCallum More.)'

The Occasion

For a little while the train seemed to stumble along amongst the snowdrifts. Every now and again there would be a sudden access of speed as a drift was cleared, just as in a saw-mill the 'buzz' saw rushes round at accelerated speed as the log is cleaved, or as a screw 'races' when the wave falls away. Then would follow an ominous slowing down as the next snowdrift was encountered. The Manager, pulling up the blind and peering out on the waste of snow, remarked:

'Nice cheerful night this; special nice place to be snowed up. So far as I can see, there isn't a house between the North Sea and the Grampians. There! we've done it at last! Stuck for good this time!' - for the slow movement of the train stopped altogether. The rest of the Company waited in anxious expectancy, and it was with a general sigh of relief that they saw the door on the sheltered side of the saloon open under the vigorous jerk of the Guard: anything was better than the state of uncertainty to which they had been reduced by the slow, spasmodic process of the last two hours. The Guard shook the rough mass of snow from him as he came in and closed the door.

'Very sorry to tell you, Ladies and Gentlemen, that we've come to a stop at last. We've been fighting the snow ever since we left Aberdeen, and the driver had hopes we might win on as far as Perth. But these drifts are one too many for us. Here we are till daylight unless we can get some place nigh at hand for ye to shelter.' The practical mind of the Manager at once grasped a possibility.

'Why not go back to Aberdeen? We have cleared the road so far, and we should be able to run back over it now.' The Guard shook his head.

'That mecht do by ordinar'; but with a wind like this and such a snowfall as I've never seen the like of, we wouldn't be able to run a mile. But, anyhow, the Stoker has gone out to prospect; and we'll soon know what to expect.'

'Tell the Driver to come here,' said the Manager. 'I should like to know exactly how we stand as to possibilities.' As the door opened for his passing out, the keen blast of icy air which rushed in sent a shiver through the whole Company. They were all too miserable and too anxious to say anything, so the silence was unbroken till the Guard returned with the Engine-Driver, the latter muffled, his black, oily clothes additionally shiny with the running of the melted snow.

'Where are we?' asked the Manager.

'Just about ten miles from anywhere, so far as I can make out. The snow falls so fast that you cannot see ten feet ahead, and the Stoker has come back, unable to get twenty yards away from the train.'

'Then I suppose there is no help for us till the storm ceases?'

'None!'

'And we have to pass the night on the train without any sort of comfort that you can give us?'

'That's so.' A groan from all followed the words. The Manager went on:

'Then we must do what we can to keep warm at least. We must make a fire here.' The Guard struck in sharply:

'Mak' a fire in the Company's carriage, and burn the whole timing up to a cender? Ye'll no mak' a fire here!' He spoke decisively. The Manager answered with equal decision:

'Who will prevent us?'

'I will.'

'Indeed! How will you do it?'

'By the authority of the Great North line which I represent. So tak' ye formal notice that I forbid any fire in the carriage.' He paused, self-satisfied.

The Manager, taking his writing-pad from his pocket, wrote a few words. Then he said suavely:

'You understand I call on you as the representative of the Company to fulfil the Company's contract and leave us in London.'

'Ye know verra weel that I canna' do it.'

'So you admit that, relying, I presume, on the common law of force majeure to relieve you?'

'Aye!'

'Then read this paper; you see it is a formal notice. Now if you rely on force majeure, so do we; and we have a good deal more force majeure than you have! So here we'll make a fire, and, if need be, we'll fight your crowd in the doing of it. Brooke, you go to the workmen's carriage and tell them to come here.'

The Call Boy departed on his errand, and the Manager, seeing that the Guard had caved in, went on more genially:

'We'll not do any harm, as you shall soon see; but, anyhow, we don't mean to die like rats in a trap. Fire we must have, but we'll so arrange it that there will not be any harm done. All our people will come in here, and your men can come also and share the warmth when we get it.'

'Aye! when ye get it,' murmured the Engine-Driver. The Manager smiled. 'You will see!' he observed. 'I shall stage-manage this. You may look on and get a wrinkle for other snow-up-pings.'

At this moment the door was torn open, and in rushed the half-dozen workmen, carpenters and property men, headed by the Master Machinist and the Property Master. The rear was brought up by the Baggage Master. The feet of all were clogged heavily with snow. The Manager spoke up just in time to prevent blows:

'Be quiet, men! We are snowed up, and will have to make ourselves comfortable as well as we can. We must make a fire here. Ruggles' - this to the Property Master - 'can you get out any of the things from the vans?'

'Quite easy, sir! We're not loaded too full, and there is a clear way up the car.'

'And you, Hempitch?' - this to the Master Machinist.

'Same, sir. We're not full either.'

'Very well! We must first make a fire in this carriage -' Here the guard broke in:

'Ye'll no mak' a fire here - except ower ma deid body.'

'Hush, man!' said the Manager, holding up his hand. 'You'll see it will be all right. Just wait a while, and you will be satisfied; and then we shan't have to knock you on the head or tie you up. Now, Hempitch, you get out the thunder and lay it here on the floor on the lee side of the car opposite this window; you will see, Guard, that the iron sheet will protect the floor. You, Ruggles, get a good lump of modelling clay from Pygmalion and make a rim all round to keep in the ashes. Then, Hempitch, have half-a-dozen iron braces and lay them on billets or a couple of stage boxes. On this platform put down one of the fireplaces - any one will do. Then, Ruggles, you will put a Louis XI chimney over it, with a fire backing behind, and make an asbestos fire-cloth into a chimney leading out of the window; you can seal it up with clay. The Engine-Driver here will bring us some live coals from his engine, and one of the carpenters can take his saw and cut down a piece of the fence that I saw outside made of old sleepers.'

The railway servants were intelligent men, and recognised the safety and comfort of the plan; so they went to the engine to get the live coals. When the workmen were bringing the coal, the Manager said to the Baggage Master:

'You had better bring in a couple of baskets of the furs from Michael Strogoff; they will help to make us comfortable. And now, ladies and gentlemen, you had better produce your provisions. I see you have all hampers for the journey to London, and we can have supper. I have myself a big jar of Highland whiskey and we shall have as jolly a time as we can.'

All was bustle, and though for a while the saloon was deathly cold whilst the various things ordered were being brought in, the extempory fireplace was so quickly organised and the fire burned so well that warmth and comfort were soon realised. The Engine-Driver brought one or two appliances from his own store, notably a flat kettle, which, filled with melted snow, was soon hissing on the fire. The Property Master produced crockery from his professional stores; and supper began amidst the utmost comfort and good humour.

When it was done, punch and tea were made and handed round, and pipes and cigars were lit. The Company, wrapped in furs, gathered as closely as they could get round the fire.

After a while the general buzz of conversation began to subside, and desultory remarks now and then marked the transition to absolute silence. This was after a while broken by the Manager with a sudden eruption of speech which seemed to awake the drowsy faculties of his companions.

A Lesson in Pets

'Once before, I spent some time with the Company in a saloon which was not altogether ideal.

'Oh, do tell us about it,' said the Leading Lady. 'We have hours at least to spend here, and it will help to pass the time.'

'Hear! hear!' came from the rest of the Company, who at least always seemed to like to hear the Manager speak. The Manager rose and bowed with his hand on his heart as though before the curtain, sat down again, and began:

'It was a good many years ago - about ten, I should think - when I had out the No 1 Company of "Revelations of Society". Some of you will remember the piece. It had a long run both in town and country.'

'I know it well,' said the Heavy Father. 'When I was a Leading Juvenile I played Geoffroi D'Almontiere, the French villain, in the Smalls in old George Bucknill's Company, with Evangeline Destrude as Lady Margaret Skeffington. A ripping good piece it was, too. I often wonder that someone doesn't revive it. It's worth a dozen of these namby-pamby - rot-gut-problem -'

'Hush! hush!' came the universal interruption, and the growing indignation of the speaker calmed down. The Manager went on:

'That time we had an eruption of dogs.'

'Of what's?'

'How?'

'Of dogs?'

'How that time?'

'Oh, do explain!' from the Company. The Manager resumed:

'Of dogs, and other things. But I had better begin at the beginning. On the previous tour I had out "The Lesson of the Cross", and as we were out to rake in all the goody-goodies, I thought it best to have an ostensibly moral tone about the whole outfit. So I picked them out on purpose for family reasons. There were with us none but married folk, and no matter how old and ugly the women were, I knew they'd pass muster with the outside crowd that we were catering for. But I did not quite expect what would happen. Every one of them brought children. I wouldn't have minded so much if they had brought the bigger ones that could have gone on to swell the crowds. I'd have paid their fares for them, too. But they only took babies and little kiddies that needed someone to look after them all the time. The number of young nursemaids and slips of girls from the workhouse and institutions that we had with us you wouldn't credit. When I got down to the station and saw the train that the Inspector pointed out as my special, I could not believe my eyes. There was hardly a window that hadn't a baby being held out of it, and the platform was full of old women and children all crowing, laughing, and crying and snapping their fingers and wiping their eyes and waving pocket-handkerchiefs. Somehow the crowd outside had tumbled to it, and it being Sunday afternoon, they kept pouring in and guying the whole outfit. I could do nothing then but get into my own compartment and pull down the blind, and pray that we might get away on time.

'When we got to Manchester, where we opened, there was the usual Sunday crowd to see the actors. When we came sliding round the curve of the Exchange I looked out, and saw with pleasure the public anxiety to catch the first glimpse of the celebrated "Lesson of the Cross" Company, as they had it well displayed on our bills. But I saw run along all the faces in the line, just as you see a breeze sweep over a cornfield, a look of wonder; and then a white flash as the teeth of every man, woman, and child became open with a grin. I looked back, and there again was that infernal row of babies being dandled in front of the windows. The crowd began to cheer; I waited till they closed round the babies, and then I bolted for my hotel.

'It was the same thing over and over again all through that tour. Every place at which we arrived or from which we went away had the same crowd; and we went and came in howls of laughter. I wouldn't have minded so much if it did us any good; but somehow it only disappointed a lot of people who came to the play to see the crowd of babies, and wanted their money back when they found they weren't on. I spoke to some of the Company quietly as to whether they couldn't manage to send some of the young 'uns home; but they all told me that domestic arrangements were complete, and that they couldn't change them. The only fun I had was with one young couple who I knew were only just married. They had with them a little girl about three years old, whom they had dressed up as a boy. When I remonstrated with them they frankly told me that as all the others had children with them they thought it would look too conspicuous without, and so they had hired the child from a poor relation, and were responsible for it for the tour. This made me laugh, and I could say no more.

'Then there was another drawback from all the children; there wasn't an infant epidemic within a hundred miles of us that some of them didn't get - measles, whooping-cough, chicken-pock, mumps, ringworm - the whole lot of them, till the train not only looked like a creche, but smelt like a baby-farm and a hospital in one. Why, if you will believe me, during the year that I toured that blessed Company - and we had a mighty prosperous time of it, take it for all in all - the entire railway system of England was strewn with feeding-bottles and rusks.'

'Oh, Mr Benville Nonplusser, how can you?' remonstrated the First Old Woman. The Manager went on:

'Just before the end of the tour I got all the Company together, and told them that never again would I allow a baby to be taken on any tour of mine; at all events, in my special trains. And that resolution I've kept from that day to this.

'Well, the next tour we went on was very different. It was, as I said, with the "Revelations of Society", and, of course, the cast was quite different. We wanted to get a sort of toney, upper-crust effect; so I got a lot of society amateurs to walk on. The big parts were, of course, done by good people, but all the small ones were done by swells. It wasn't altogether a pleasant time, for there was no end to the jealousies. The society amateurs were, as usual, more theatrical than the theatricals; the airs that some of them gave themselves would make you laugh. This put up the backs of our own crowd - and they got their shirts out, I can tell you. At first I tried to keep the peace, for these swell supers were mighty good and just what we wanted in the play; but after a bit it got to a regular division of camps, and I found that whatever I did must be wrong. Whateverone got or did they all wanted, and nothing was allowed to pass that gave even a momentary advantage or distinction to any of the crowd. By-and-by I began to have to put my foot down, but every time I did so there was a kick somewhere; so I had to be careful lest I should have no one at all to play the piece.

'I seemed never to be able to get an hour's rest from some of the jealousies that were constantly springing up. If I could have managed to forestall any of them it would have been easy enough, but the worst of it all was that they were perpetually breaking out in a new place; and it was only when it was too late to do anything to prevent a row that I came to know the cause of the one then on.

'Having forbidden babies on the former tour, I did not think it was necessary to forbid anything else; and the consequence was that I suddenly found that we had broken out in an eruption of Pets. My Leading Lady then, Miss Flora Montressor, who had been with me on seven tours and was an established favourite all over the Provinces, had a little toy wheaten terrier that she had taken with her everywhere since ever she had been with me. Often other members had asked my Acting Manager if they too might bring dogs; but he had always put them off, telling them that the railway people didn't allow it, and that it would be better not to press the matter, as Miss Montressor from her position was a privileged person. This had always been enough with the regular Company, but the new lot had all of them got pets of some kind, and after the first journey, when their attention had been called to the irregularity, they simply produced dog-tickets, and said they would pay for them themselves. That was enough for the other lot, and before the next journey came there wasn't a soul in the whole crowd but had a pet of some kind. Of course, they were mostly dogs - and a queer lot they were, from the tiniest kind of toy up to the biggest sort of mastiff. The railway people weren't ready for them – it would have taken a new kind of van for them all – and I wasn't ready for them either; so I said nothing then. The following Sunday I got them all together, and told them that after that journey I was afraid I could not permit the thing to go on. The station was then like a dog-show, and I could hardly hear myself speak for the barking and yelping and howling. There were mastiffs and St Bernards, and collies and poodles and terriers and bull-dogs and Skyes, and King Charleys and dachshunds and turnspits – every kind of odd illustration of the family of the canine world. One man had got a cat with a silver collar, and led it by a string; another had a tame frog; and several had squirrels, white mice, rabbits, rats, a canary in a cage, and a tame duck. Our Second Low Comedy Merchant had got a young pig, but it got away at the station, and he hadn't time to follow it up. When I spoke to the Company they were silent, and they all held up their dog-tickets – all except Miss Flora Montressor, who said quietly:

"'You gave me leave years ago to bring my little dog."

'Well, I saw that nothing could be done then except with the kind of row that I didn't want. So I went to my own compartment to think the matter over.

'I soon came to the conclusion that an object-lesson of some kind was required; and then a bright idea struck me:

"'I should get a pet myself."

'We were then bound for Liverpool, and early in the week I slipped down to my old friend Ross, the animal importer, to consult with him. In my early days I had had to do with a circus, and I thought that on this occasion I might turn my knowledge to account. He was out, so I asked one of the men if he could recommend me some sort of pet that wouldn't be pleasant for a nervous person to travel with. He wasn't a humorous man, and at once suggested a tiger. "We have a lovely full-grown one," he said, "just in from Bombay. He's as savage as they make 'em. We have to keep him in a place by himself, for when we put him 'in a room with any of the others, he terrifies them so that they are like to quit in a body."

'I thought this cure might be too drastic, and I didn't want to close my tour in a cemetery or a gaol, so I suggested something milder. He tried me with pumas, leopards, crocodiles, wolves, bears, gorillas, and even with a young elephant; but none of them seemed as if it would suit. Just then Ross himself came in, and took me off to see something new.

"'Just come in," he said; "three ton of boa-constrictor from Surinam. The finest lot I've ever come across." When I looked at them, although my early training had somewhat accustomed me tosuch matters, I felt a little uneasy. There they lay in cases like melonbeds, with nothing over them but a glass frame, with not even a hasp to hold it down. A great slimy, many-coloured mass all folded about and coiled up and down and round and round; – except for a head sticking out here and there one would have thought that it was all one big reptile. Ross saw me move a little, so he said, toreassure me:

"'You needn't be skeered. This weather they're half torpid. It's pretty cold now, and even if the heat were to get at them they wouldn't wake up." I didn't like them, all the same, for whenever one of them would give a gulp, swallowing whatever food he was on at the moment – a rat or a rabbit or what not – the whole mass would stir and heave and writhe a little. I thought how nice a lot of them would look amongst my crowd; so there and then I agreed with Ross to hire a lot of them for the next journey. One of his men was to come down with my workmen to Carlisle, whither we were bound, to take them back again.

'I arranged with the railway company to have for that journey one of their large excursion saloons, so that all the members of the Company would have to travel together instead of going into separate compartments grouped in parties. When they gathered at the station none of them were satisfied. There was, however, no overt grumbling. I had casually mentioned, and the word had gone round, that I was coming with them myself, and had prepared a treat for them. That they evidently expected something in the way of a picnic was manifested by the frequent inquiries of some of them from the porters and the Baggage Master as to whether my personal luggage had arrived. I had carefully arranged with Ross's people that my contribution was not to be brought till the last moment, and I had privately tipped the Guard and asked him to be ready for an immediate start after its arrival. The special train had been scheduled for a quick run, and was not to stop between Liverpool and Carlisle.

'As the starting time drew near, the Company took their places as they had secured them in the saloon, the first comers getting to the furthest ends. The carriage became by a sort of natural selection divided into two camps. The dogs belonging to either side were in the centre. When "all aboard" had been called out by my Acting Manager after his usual custom, the last of the Company took their places. Then a heavy truck came quickly along the platform, surrounded by several men. It contained two great boxes with unfastened lids, and as there were many hands available these were quickly lifted into the saloon. One was placed opposite the door on the off-side of the carriage, and the other put just inside the door of entry, which it blocked.

'Then the door was slammed and locked; the Guard's whistle sounded, and we were off.

'I needn't tell you that all this time the dogs were barking and howling for all they were worth, and some of them were only held back by their owners from flying at each other. The cat had taken refuge on a hat-rack, and stood growling, with her tail thickened and lashing about. The frog sat complacently in its box beside its master, and the rats and mice were nowhere to be seen in their cages. When the baskets came in some of the dogs cowered down and shivered, whilst others barked fiercely and could hardly be held back. I got out my Sunday paper and began to read quietly, awaiting developments.

'For a while the angry dogs kept up their clamour, and one of them, the mastiff, became almost unmanageable. His master called out to me:

'"I can't hold him much longer. There must be something in that box that upsets him."

'"Indeed!" I said, and went on reading. Then one or two of the Company began to get alarmed; one of them came over and looked curiously at the box, bent close and sniffed suspiciously, and drew back. This whetted the curiosity of others, and several more came around and bent down and sniffed. Then they began to whisper amongst themselves, and one of them asked me point-blank:

'"Mr Benville Nonplusser, what is in that box?"

'"Only some pets of mine," I answered, without looking up from my paper.

'"Very nasty pets, whatever they are," she answered tartly. "They smell very nasty." To which I replied:

'"We all have our fancies, my dear. You have yours and I have mine; and since all you belonging to this Company have your pets with you, I have determined to establish some of mine. You'll doubtless grow to like them in time. In fact, you'd better begin, for they are likely to be with you every journey henceforth."

'"May we look?" asked one of the young men. I nodded acquiescence, and as he stooped to lift the lid the rest gathered round – all except the man with the mastiff, who had his hands full with that clamorous beast. The young man raised the lid, and as he saw what was within, threw it back as he recoiled, so that it fell over, leaving the whole interior exposed. Then the crowd drew back with a shudder, and some of the women began to scream. I was afraid that they might attract attention, as we were then nearing a station, so I said quietly:

'"You had better be as quiet as you can. Nothing irritates serpents so much as noise. They think it is their opportunity for seeking prey!" This bold statement seemed to be verified by the fact that some of the boa-constrictors sleepily raised their heads with a faint hissing. Whereupon the crowd simply tumbled over each other in their efforts to reach the further corners of the saloon. By this time the man with the mastiff was becoming exhausted by his struggling with the powerful animal. As I wished to push home my lesson, I said:

'"You had better keep those dogs quiet. If you don't, I shall not answer for the consequences. If that mastiff manages to attack the serpents, as he is trying to, they will spring out and fight, and then –" I was silent, for at such a point silence is the true eloquence. The fear of all was manifested by their blanched faces and trembling forms.

'"I'm afraid I can't hold him any longer!" gasped out the man.

"'Then,' said I, 'some of your companions who have dogs also should try to help you. If not, it will be too late!' So several others came, and by the aid of their rug-straps they managed to tie the brute securely to a leg of the bench. Seeing that they were nearly all half-paralysed with fright, I lifted the lid to the top of the box again; at which they seemed to breathe more freely. When they saw me actually sitting on the box, something like a far-off smile began to glow on the countenances of some of them. I kept urging them to keep the animals quiet; and as this was a never-ceasing work, they had something to occupy them.

'I was a little nervous myself at first, and had any of the boa-constrictors knocked his head against the lid of the box I should have made a jump away. However, as they remained absolutely tranquil, my own courage grew.

'And so some hours passed, with occasional episodes, such as when some one of the many pets would make a disturbance. The singing of the canary, for instance, was resisted with angry curses. But the vials of the wrath of all were emptied forth at its owner when the hitherto silent duck began its homely song, "Quack, quack!"

"'Will you keep that blasted brute quiet?" came an angry whisper from the worn-out owner of the mastiff. Upon which a good many of those on whom time had had a quieting effect smiled.

'When my watch told me that we were within a short distance of Carlisle, I stood upon the box and made a little speech:

"'Ladies and Gentlemen, I trust that the episode of to-day, unpleasant though it may have been, will not be ultimately without beneficial effect. You have learned that each one of you owes something to the general good, and that the selfish pursuance of your own pleasure in small ways has sooner or later to be accounted for. When I remonstrated with each of you as to this animal business, you chose to take your own way, and even went so far as to reconcile your personal and sectional jealousies in order to unite against me. I therefore thought that I would bring the difficulty home to you in a striking way! Have I done so?"

'For a while there was silence; and then a smile and a faint affirmative answer here and there, so I went on:

"'Now I hope you will all take it in as good part as I have taken all that went before. Anyhow, my mind is made up. Pets shall be included with babies in the Index Expurgatorius of our tour. In the meantime, for the remainder of this tour, if anyone else brings pets, so shall I; and I think you know that I know how to choose my own. Anyone objecting to this can cancel the engagement right here. Has anyone got anything to say?" Some shrugged their shoulders, but all were silent; and I knew that my victory was complete. As I was stepping down, however, I caught Miss Montressor's eye as tearfully she looked at me and then at her little dog, so I added:

"'This does not apply to Miss Montressor, who years ago had permission to take her dog. I shall certainly not deprive her of that privilege now."

'And not a soul objected.'

'Next!' said the Acting Manager, Mr Wragge, who, being by the needs of his calling a pushful person, usually took such prominent responsibilities as were unallotted or unattached, and who in the present instance had become by a sort of natural selection, manifested by tacit consent of the Company, Master of the Ceremonies.

There was dead silence, for the seance was as yet so young that no one seemed to wish to be put forward. The keen-eyed MC recognised the situation at a glance, and, turning to the Leading Lady on the Manager's left, said:

'You'll have to go on next, Miss Venables. The turn will travel with the wine - if we had any for it to travel with.' The hint was not lost on the First Low Comedian, who promptly unscrewed the top of his flask and gallantly pushed it, together with a tumbler and the water-bottle, in front of the blushing girl. 'Here is the wine,' he said; 'vin du pays.' She made a gentle motion of protest, but the Manager poured a small portion of whiskey in the glass, together with a fair supply of water. She acknowledged the courtesy with a pretty little bow, and then turned an appealing eye round the Company. 'I will with pleasure do what I can for the public good,' she said, 'but I am really and truly at a loss to know what to tell. My life has not yet been a very adventurous one, and I don't know anything worth telling that has ever happened to myself.'

One of the Young Gentlemen, who secretly admired her from afar, blurted out:

'I know something which would interest us all.'

'What is that?' asked the MC quickly. The Young Man blushed and stammered as he answered, looking apprehensively at the object of his devotion, who gazed at him inquiringly with bent brows:

'It was some joke - something - I don't know what it was - that they had in the "Her Grace the Blanchisseuse" Company just before I joined them. Someone had sworn them all to secrecy, so no one would tell me why it was that they always spoke of Miss Venables as "Coggins's Property."'

The girl laughed merrily. 'Oh, I did that. It was too funny altogether. I didn't mind it myself; but there was another; poor Coggins, who was an excellent fellow, took to heart so much the perpetual chaff of the Company that he sent in his resignation. I knew that he had a wife and family, and would not leave a good situation unless he was really hurt; so I made a personal request to everyone, and they all promised not to tell how the name came to be. But I am not bound, so if you like I will tell you; for the thing is all over long ago, and Coggins is a prosperous builder in the Midlands'

'Hear! hear!' came from all, for their expectations were aroused. So the Leading Lady began:

Coggins's Property

'When I was in "Her Grace the Blanchisseuse", I had just gone on the stage and played a lot of little parts of a line or two. Sometimes I was a body without a voice, and sometimes a voice without a body!'

'Vox et praeterea nihil,' murmured another Young Man, who had been to a public school.

'Amongst the voice parts was one which was supposed to come from a queen who was in bed in a room off the salon which was represented in the scene. The edge of the bed was dimly seen, and I had to put out a hand with a letter and speak two lines. My attendant took the letter, the door was shut - and that was all. Of course, I had not to dress for the part, except that I put on a little silk and lace jacket, and one sleeve as of a nightdress, so I used to come on from the side just before my cue and slip into, or, rather, on to the bed. Then a property man came with a quilt embroidered with the Imperial Arms, which he threw over me, tucking in the edge nearest the audience. The man originally appointed to this work was Coggins, and as he had a great deal of work to do - for it was a "property" play - he only got to me in time to do his work and clear out before the door opened and my attendant came in. Coggins was an excellent fellow, grave, civil, punctual, sober, and as steady and stolid as a rock. The scene was a silent one, and what appeared to be my room was almost in the dark. The effect to the audience was to see through the lighted salon this dim sleeping chamber; to see a white hand with a letter emerge from the bed curtains, and to hear a drowsy voice as of one newly roused from sleep. There was no opportunity of speaking a word, and no need for it. Coggins knew his work thoroughly, and the stage manager and his assistants insisted on the most rigorous silence. After a few nights, when I found Coggins so attentive in his work, I said "goodnight" when I passed him at the stage-door, and gave him a shilling. He seemed somewhat surprised, but doffed his cap with the utmost respect. Henceforward we always saluted each other, each in our own way; and he had an occasional shilling, which he always received with a measure of surprise. In other portions of his nightly work and mine I often came in contact with, or rather in juxtaposition to, Coggins; but he never seemed to show the same delicate nicety which he exhibited towards me in his manipulations of my tucking-up in "Her Grace the Blanchisseuse". The piece, as you know, had a long run in London, and then the original Company went round the "Greats" for a whole season. Of course, the Manager took with him all the people who worked in London who were necessary, and amongst them came the excellent and stolid Coggins.

'After months of work done under all possible conditions, we all came to know our cues so well that we were able to cut the time pretty fine; we often turned up at our places only at the moment of our cues. My own part was essentially favourable for this, and I am afraid I began to cut it a little too fine; for I got to arriving at my place just a second or two before Coggins made his appearance with the Imperial quilt.

'At last one night, in the Grand at Leeds - you know what a huge theatre it is, and how puzzling to get on the right floor - I went just across the line of safety. I was chatting in the dressing-room with Birdie Squeers, when the call-boy came tearing along the passage shouting: "Miss Venables, Miss Venables. You're late! Hurry up, or there will be a stage wait!" I jumped for the door and tore along the passage, and got to the back of the stage just in time to meet the stolid Coggins with his stolidity for once destroyed. He had the Imperial quilt as usual folded over one arm, but he was gesticulating wildly with the other. "'Ere!" he called in a fierce whisper to a group of the other workmen. "Who the 'ell has took my Property?"

'"Yer property!" said one of the others. "Garn! ye juggins. Hain't ye got it on yer arm?"

'"This! This is all right," he answered. "That ain't what I mean. Wot I want is wot I covers up with this."

'"Well, and ain't the bed there? You keep your hair on, and don't be makin' a hass of yerself." I heard no more, for I slipped by and got on to the bed from the back. Coggins had evidently made up his mind that his particular work should not be neglected. He was not responsible for the figure in the bed, but only for putting on the quilt; and on the quilt should go. His look of blank amazement when he found that the quilt did not lie flat as on his first effort amused me. I heard him murmur to himself:

"'A trick, is it? Puttin' the Property back like that. I'll talk to them when the Act's over." Coggins was a sturdy fellow, and I had heard him spoken of as a bruiser, so I thought I would see for myself the result of his chagrin. I suppose it was a little cruel of me, but I felt a certain sort of chagrin myself. I was a newcomer to the stage, and I had hitherto felt a sort of interest in Coggins. His tender, nightly devotion to his work, of which I was at least the central figure, had to me its own romantic side. He was of the masses, and I had come of the classes, but he was a man and I a woman, and a man's devotion is always sweet - to a woman. I had often taken to heart Claude Melnotte's romantic assumption of Pauline's reply to his suit:

"That which the Queen of Navarre gave to the poor Troubadour:

"Show me the oracle that can tell nations I am beautiful."

'But it had begun to dawn upon me that my friend and humble admirer, Coggins, had no interest in me at all. My part in the play came to an end before the close of the scene, and so when the doors were closed I slipped from my place as usual; I did not, however, go to my dressing-room as was my habit, but waited to see what Coggins would do. In his usual course he came and removed his quilt; and again there was a look of annoyed amazement on his face when he found that it lay flat on the bed. Again he murmured:

"'So they've took the Property away again, have they? We'll seeabout it presently." When he had removed the Imperial quilt two other men came, and as usual lifted away the bed, the Empress's bedroom being opened no more during the play. As there was no more to be done till the play was over, I went to the stage-door, ostensibly to ask if there were any letters for me, but in reality because the workmen usually assembled there when not wanted on the stage, and it was here that I expected the denouement. Several of the carpenters and property men were smoking outside the stage-door, and to them presently came Coggins, thoroughly militant in manner.

"'Now, you chaps," he said, "there's somethin' I want to know; an' I mean to 'ave it, stryte 'ere! Which of you's 'avin' a lark with me?"

"'Wot jer' mean?" said one of the others with equal truculence. He was a local man, and certainly looked like a fighter. "Wot are ye givin' us?"

'Coggins, recognising an antagonist worthy of consideration, replied as calmly as he could:

"'Wot I want to know is 'oo's a plyin' tricks with my Property?"

"'What property, Coggins?" asked one of his own pals.

"'Yer know as well as I do; the one wot I covers up on the bed with that quilt." There was a roar of laughter from the men, and a hail of chaff began to rain on him.

"'Oh! if that's your property, Coggins, I wonder what your missis will say when she hears it!"

"'Why, that ain't no property; it's a gal."

"'Well, boys, when the divorce is asked for we can prove that there weren't nothin' 'atween 'em. When old Jeune 'ears that he didn't know the differ between a property and a gal, he'll up and say, "Not guilty. The prisoner leaves the Court without the slightest stain on his character."

'Coggins grew very pale and perplexed-looking, and in a changed voice he asked:

"'Boys, is this all a cod or what?"

"'Not a bit of a cod," said one. "Do ye mean to say that you didn't know that what you tucked up every night was one of the young ladies?"

"'No!" he answered hotly. "'Ow could I know it? I never come on except just in time to put on the quilt and tuck it up. It was nearly dark, and it never said nothin'! An' 'ow the 'ell was I to know the bally thing was alive!" This was said with such an air of sincerity that it broke me all up, and I burst into laughter. Coggins turned angrily round, but, seeing me, took off his cap with his usual salute.

"'That's yer Property, Coggins!" said one of the men; and Coggins was speechless.

'Of course, he was unmercifully chaffed, and so was I. Various members of the Company used to come up to me on all sorts of occasions, and, after gazing into my eyes and touching me, would say in a surprised way:

'"Why, the bally thing's alive!"

'Coggins appeared to have a rough time of it with some of the others. For weeks he never had less than one black eye, and not only were most of our own men in a similar condition, but we left behind us wherever we went quite a crop of contusions. I knew it was no use my saying anything on my own account, for you might as well ask the wind to leave the thrashing-floor alone as for a parcel of friends to drop a good subject of chaff; but after a while I had to take pity on poor Coggins, for he sent in his resignation. I knew he had a wife and family, and that as his situation was a good one he would not leave it unless hard pressed. So I spoke to him about it. I think that his explanation had, if possible, more unconscious humour in it than his mistake. But there was pathos, too, and Coggins showed himself to be, according to his lights, a true gentleman.

'"There's two things, Miss, that I can't get away from. My missis is a good ole sort, and takes care of the kids beautiful. But she believes that there ain't in the world only one Coggins - I'm him; and as I 'ave to be away so much on tour she gets to thinkin' that there's other wimmin as foolish as herself. That makes her a bit jealous; an' if she was to 'ear that I was every night a-tuckin' up a beautiful young lady - savin' your presence - in a bed, she would give me Johnny-up-the-orchard. An' besides, Miss - I hope you'll forgive me, but I want to do the right thing if I can - I've not give up carpenterin' and took to the styge without learnin' somethin' of the ways of the quality. I was in the Dook o' York's Theatre when they had a ply what showed as how in high society if a man gets a girl into any trouble, no matter how innocent, but so as how she's chaffed by her pals, he's got to marry her to put it right. An', ye see, Miss, as how bein' married already I couldn't do the right thing ... so I've resigned, and must look for another shop."

''Ow would a dead byby suit you to hear on?' asked the Sewing Woman, with an interrogative glance round the company. 'I know of one that was simply 'arrowing.' The ensuing silence was expressive.

No one said a word; all looked at the fire meditatively. The Second Low Comedian sighed. In a half-reflective, half-apologetic way she went on, as if thinking aloud rather than speaking:

'Not that I know overmuch of bybies, anyhow, never havin' 'ad none of my own, though that's partly due that I was never married. Any'ow, I never 'ad the chances of some - married or onmarried.'

The Wardrobe Mistress, known in the Company as 'Ma,' here felt it incumbent on her, as the ostensible matron of the party, to say something on such a theme:

'Well, bybies is interesting things, alive or dead. But I don't know whether they're the cause of most noise alive or dyin' or dead. Seems to me that we've got to have it out either in screaming or sobbing or mourning, whatever you do. So, my dears, it's just as well to take things as they come, and make the best of them.'

'You may bet your immortal on that!' said the Second Low Comedian. 'Ma's head is level!' With the instinct of the profession, they all applauded the 'point,' and Ma beamed round her. Applause given to herself was a rare commodity with her.

'All right! then we'll drive on,' said the bustling MC. 'You choose your own topic, Mrs Wrigglesworth - or, rather, Miss Wrigglesworth, as I should say after your recent confession of spinsterhood.' The Sewing Woman coughed, cleared her throat, and made those other preparations usual to the inexperienced speaker. In the pause the Tragedian's deep voice resounded:

'Dead babies are always cheerful. I love them on the walls of the Academy. The Christy Minstrels' deepest bass as he trills his carol, "Cradle's Empty; Baby's Gone", fills me with delight. On such a night as this, surrounded as we are by the profound manifestations of Nature's feller forces, the theme is not uncongenial. Methinks the very snow-wreaths with which the driving tempest smites the windows of our prison-house are the beatings of dead baby fingers as they clamour to lay ice-cold touches on our hearts.' The Company, especially the women, shuddered, and the comments were varied.

'Lor'!' said the Wardrobe Mistress.

'Bones!' - the slang name of the Tragedian - 'never beat that in his nach. He'll be wanting to have a play written round it,' said the Low Comedian. The Tragedian glared and breathed hard, but said nothing. He contented himself with swallowing at a gulp the remainder of his whiskey-punch.

'Refill the Death Goblet!' said the Second Low Comedian in a sepulchral voice. 'Here, Dandy' - this to the Leading Juvenile - 'pass the whiskey.'

The servile desire to please, habitual to her, animated the Sewing Woman to proceed on her task:

'Well, Mr Benville Nonplusser,' she began, 'and Lydies and Gentlemen, which I 'opes you'll not expect too much from me in the litery way. Now, if it was a-sewin' on of buttons - no matter wherever placed! An' many a queer tale I could tell you of them if I could remember 'em, and the lydies wouldn't object - though blushes is becomin' to 'em, the dears! Or if I could do summat with a needle and thread, even in a 'urry in the dark and the styge a-waitin' of -' She was interrupted by the Low Comedian, who said insinuatingly:

'Go on, my dear. This ain't the time nor place for one to object to anything. The ladies' blushes will do them good, and will make us all feel young again. Besides' - here he winked round at the Company - 'the humour, conscious or unconscious,, offf the various situations with which your episodical narrative must be tinged will give an added force to the gruesomeness which is attendant on the defunct homunculus.'

'You are too bad, Mr Parmentire,' whispered the Singing Chambermaid to him. 'If she makes us blush you will be responsible.'

'I accept the responsibility!' he answered gallantly to her, adding sotto voce to the Prompter: 'And I won't need any cut-throat insurance at Lloyd's to protect me against that hazard.' The Sewing Woman went on:

'Well, as to the dead byby, which it makes me cry only to think of it, and its poor young mother growin' colder and colder in spite of 'ot poultices -'

Her voice was beginning to assume that nasal tone which with a woman of her class is at once a prelude to and a cause of tears. So the Manager promptly interrupted:

'We're simply in raptures about that baby; but as an introduction to the story, couldn't you give us some personal reminiscence? The baby, you see, couldn't be your own, and therefore it can only be a matter of hearsay -'

'Lor' bless you're 'eart, sir, but I ain't 'ad anythink to reminisce.'

'Well, anything you've seen or heard in the theatre. Come now, you've been a long time in the business; did you never see anything heroic happen?'

'As 'ow, sir, 'eroes not bein' much in my way?'

'Well, for instance, have you never seen a situation saved by promptness, or resource, or daring, or by the endurance of pain -'

'Oh, yes, sir. I seen them things all in one, but it wasn't anythink to do with the dead byby.'

'Well, just tell us first how it was, and how resource and readiness and the endurance of pain saved the situation.'

As the Manager spoke he glanced around the Company with a meaning look; so she proceeded:

The Slim Syrens

'The first show what I ever went out with was Mr Sloper's Company for the Society Gal, what was called "The Syrens." You see, when the play was first done, society 'ad long wysts and thin 'ips and no bust to speak of, and the lydies what plyed in it original was chose according. My! but they was a skinny lot - reg'lar bags o' bones; if ye'd a biled down the lot for stock you'd no need to 'ave skimmed it. W'y, the tights they wore! - Speakin' of legs as yards of pump-water ain't in it; theirs looked as you might 'ave rolled 'em up on a spool. And as to their chestys - why, you might 'ave put 'em through the mangle and none ever the wuss - except the mangle from jerkiness, where it might 'ave well expected to take it a bit india-rubbery. But the ply 'ad so long a run that the fashion got changed, and the swells began to like 'em thick. So the gals got changed, too; some of 'em makin' up with 'eavy fleshings an' them shove-up corsets, what'd take a pinch out of your - your stummick an' swell out your throat with it, till they come into line with the fashion. Lor', the things I've seen the girls do to make theirselves look bulkier than what nature made 'em! Any'ow, when they 'ad run the fust companies twice round the Greats, Mr Sloper thought as 'ow 'e'd go one better on the fashion. "Ketch the risin' tide" was ever 'is mortar! So the company engyged for "The New Edition Society Gal" was corkers! They used to say in the wardrobe as 'ow there was a twenty-stun standard, and no one would be engyged that couldn't pass the butcher. Of course, the wardrobe of the theayter or the travelling shows was no use for "The Slim Syrens" - for that's what they came to be kown as. We 'ad to 'ave a lot of tights made a purpose, and when they come 'ome the young man 'as brought 'em laughed that much that he cried, and he wanted to stay an' see 'em put on, till I 'unted 'im out. I never see such tights in all my time. They was wove that bias everywhere as I felt my 'eart sink when I thought of 'ow we was to take up ladders in 'em; for fat girls does a deal more in that wy than slim ones - let alone the 'arder pullin' to drag 'em on. But the tights wasn't the wust. You remember, Mrs Solomon, as 'ow there's a scene when Society goes in for to restore Wat-ho, and the 'ole bilin' dresses theirselves as shepherds. Mr Sloper didn't want to spend no more money than he could 'elp; so down he goes to Morris Angel's, tykin' me and Mrs Beilby, that was wardrobe mistress to the Slim Syrens, with 'im. Well, ole Morris Angel trots out all the satin britches as 'e 'ad in stock. Of course, the most of 'em was no use to our little lot, but we managed to pick out a few that was likely for lydies what runs large. These did for some of the crowd, and, of course, the principals got theirs made to order. They wasn't so much fuller than Angel's lot, arter all; for our lydies, though bulky, liked good fits, and sure enough at the dress rehearsal most of them looked as if they had been melted and poured in. Mr Sloper and the styge manager and some of the syndicate gentlemen what came to see the rehearsal had no end of fun, and the things they said, and the jokes they made, and the way that the girls run after 'em and 'ammered of 'em playful, as girls does, 'd made you laugh to have seen it. And talk of blushin'! Well, there! The most particular of the lot, and him what didn't like the laughin' and the jokin', was Mr Santander, that was going to take out the Company as manager - him what they called "Smack" Santander in the green room. There was one girl what was his ladyfriend as he had put into the lead, though the other girls said as 'ow she 'ad no rights to be shoved on that way. But, there! Gals is mostly like that when another gal gets took up and 'elped on. Why, the things what I've 'eard and seen just because a girl was put into the front row! When she was bein' dressed, which it was in the wardrobe, because Mr Santander was that particular that Miss Amontillado should be dressed careful, well do I remember the remark as Mrs Beilby made: "Well, Miss," says she, "there's no denyin' of that you are very fine and large!" Which was gospel truth, and no concealin' of it either in the wardrobe or on the styge, an' most of all in the orchestra, where the gentlemen never left for their whiskey-and-soda, or their beer or cards or what not, or a smoke, till she 'ad gone to 'er dressin'-room, which most of 'em got new glasses - them what didn't use opery-glasses. Well, when dress rehearsal was over, Mr Sloper 'e tried to be very serious, and, says he, "Lydies, you must try and be careful; remember that you carry weight!" - which that hended 'is speech for 'im, for he choked with laughter till the syndicate gentleman come and slapped 'im on the back, and then laughed, too, fit to bust.

'When we was startin' the season Mr Santander sent for me and spoke to me about Miss Amontillado, and told me that it was as much as my plyce was worth if anything went wrong with 'er. I told 'im as 'ow I'd do my best, and I took Miss Amontillado aside, and, ses I, "Miss, it's temptin' providence it is," says I, "for a fine, strapping young lydy as you in britches like them," I says. "You do kick about that free," I says; "and satin is only satin at the best, and though the stryn is usual on it in the right direction up and down, there's the stryn on yours all round. What if I was you I wouldn't take no chances," I says. Well, she laughed, and says she, "Well, you dear old geeser" - for she was a young lydy as was alwys kind and affable to her inferiors - "and what would you do if you was me?" "Well, miss," I says, "if I was as gifted as you is, I'd have them made on webbin' what'd 'old, and wouldn't show if the wust come to the wust." She only laughed, and gave me sixpence, and, says she, "You're a good ole sort, Sniffles" - for that's what some of the young ones called me - "and I'll tell Smack how well you look after me. Then perhaps he'll raise your screw.

'Both Mr Santander and Miss Amontillado was anxious about the first night, and there was bets in the dressin'-room as to how she'd come off in 'er 'igh-kickin' act. You'll remember, Mrs Solomon, 'ow the ply goes, as 'ow to the surprise of all, the young Society gal as didn't do nothin' more nor a skirt-dance, sudden ups and tykes the kyke from all the perfeshionals. When Miss Amontillado was dressed for the act in her shepherd dress, I says to her, "Now miss," I says, "do be keerful"; and Mr Santander 'e says, "'Ear! 'ear!" 'e says. "Oh, I'm all right," she says. "Look 'ere, Smack," and she ups and does a split as made my 'eart jump, it was that sudden, and up on her 'eels agin afore you could say Jack Robinson!

'Well, just then I 'eard the Call-Boy a-comin' down the passidge 'ollerin', "Miss Amontillado! Miss Amontillado!" "'Ere!" she says; and as he came into the room she puts 'er 'ands over 'er 'ead and does a sal-lam that low that 'er back 'air nigh swept the floor. And lo and behold! as she bent I 'ears a 'ideous crack; and there was 'er back up and down in two 'alves as you'd 'ave put a sweepin' brush atween.

'"Now you've done it, Miss," I says; and there was she laughin' and cryin' all in a moment, for it weren't no joke to 'er to 'ave her big scene queered like that the fust time as she done it. And there was Mr Santander a-tearin' at 'is 'air - which there wasn't none too much of it - and 'im a-bullyin' of 'er dreadful, and sayin' as 'ow 'e'd cancel 'er engygement - which 'e weren't no gentleman, that 'e weren't. And all the time the Call-Boy yellin' out, "Miss Amontillado, there'll be a styge wyte!" and 'im fit to bust laughin'. Impident young monkey! I knew as 'ow if anything was to be done it must be done quick, so I whips out a big sailmaker's needle what we sewed canvas with and the tapes on the stair-treads, an' a lot of waxend twine as I kep' for fixin' reefs in the ballet shoes; for it wasn't no child's play as to them britches with a fine gal like that, and them so tight. I tried to get a holt of the two sides of the tear to bring 'em together; but, lor' bless you! the reef was that wide I couldn't get 'em close any'ow. The dresser that was in with me, she tried to 'elp; but it weren't no use. And then Mr Santander 'e kem and 'ad a try, but it weren't no go. Then I tykes the Call-Boy by the 'air of 'is 'ead and mykes 'im ketch 'old too, 'im bein' a bicyclist and 'is fingers that 'ard. Then the gas-man came to 'elp with two sets of pinchers; but all we could do we couldn't make them sides of that split meet.

'We was all in despair and the time goin' by; we could 'ear the 'ootin' in front at the wayt, and the styge-manager kem tearin' along, yellin' and cursin' and shoutin' out, "What in 'ell is wrong? Where is the bally girl? Why don't she 'urry up?"

'At that very moment a hinspiration came to me. It was a hinspiration an' nothink else, for there was that there poor gal's success at styke, much less 'er situation. "'Ere," say I, "my dear, just you lie down on the sofy on yer fyce, with yer bust on the cushing and yer toes out with yer 'eels in the air." She sor in a flash what I were up to, and chucked 'erself on the sofy, and the Call-Boy shoved a bolster under 'er instep. My! but she bent up double that'ard that I 'eard the webbin' of the abominable belt as she wore go crack.

'But, lydies and gents, the situation was saved; the roos was a pernounced success. Them two distant hedges kem together like twins a-kissin', and afore you could say "Boo!" I 'ad my needle and was a-sewin' of 'em up that firm. I was in such a 'urry that some of the stitches took in the skin as well as the satin. But she was a plucky gal, and tho' she 'owled, she didn't wriggle away. There wasn't no time to cut the thread, and as soon as the last stitch was in she jumps up, tearin' the stitches through her skin, and bounds out on the styge with the needle 'anging' be'ind. Mind you, 'er blood was up, and she landed on to the styge like a good 'un.

'The roar that come from the Johnnies when they see 'er was good to 'ear!

'But this is nothin' to do with what I was goin' to tell you about that story of the dead byby -'

'Oh! blow the dead baby,' said the Second Low Comedian. 'Put it in a bottle and keep it on the shelf till called for. After an act of living valour like what you've told us, we don't want anything dead.'

'Next!' said the MC, in the pause that ensued.

The Low Comedian being next in order had been gradually becoming more ill at ease as his own time approached; it was manifest that in the armoury of his craft was no weapon suited to deal with a necessity of extempore narration. Some of those on whom he was accustomed to sharpen his wits knew, either instinctively or by experience, of this weakness, and commenced to redress or avenge whatever they might have suffered at his hands. They began by encouragement, outwardly genuine and hearty, but with an underlying note of irony which could not fail to wound a spirit sensitive on the point of its own importance:

'Buck up, old man.'

'Drive on, Gags.'

'Have a drink first. You're always funnier afterwards.'

'What do you mean by that?' asked the indignant Low Comedian, fiercely. 'What do you mean by "afterwards"? Do you mean when I'm drunk, or have had too much, or what?'

'Only a joke!' said the Prompter, in a deprecatory way, for his was the unhappy remark. The Heavy Father who was usually one of his butts struck in:

'He probably meant that you were funnier in your intention after the opportunity of being funny had existed as a fact.' The Low Comedian did not see his way to a fitting reply, so he replied to the arrow with a stone:

'Indeed! If I was you, old man, I would try Irish! It's sometimes hard to understand you through Scotch!'

'Time!' cried out the MC, anxious to prevent what looked like the beginning of a quarrel. The bottle, or I should say the Tribune, rests with Mr Parmentire.' The Low Comedian looked at the fire reflectively for a few seconds; then he passed his hand through his hair, and after glaring all round the Company, began:

'I suppose you know, Ladies and Gentlemen, that there is a current idea that a Low Comedian must be always humorous.' He was interrupted by the Tragedian, who, prefacing his remark with a Mephistophelean Ha-ha-ha! said:

'If there is, it is a mistake; or, at best, an exploded idea. Surely, humour is the last quality to be expected from a Comedian, let alone a Low Comedian. But, of course, I may be prejudiced; I never took much stock of the horse-collar myself'

'Si-lence! Si-lence!' said the watchful MC in the manner of a Court crier, whilst the Leading Juvenile whispered to the Prompter:

'Bones got in at him for the dead baby fingers that time.' The Low Comedian went on:

'Well, if humour in private life is expected, it's not always to be had, as Bones has very properly implied in his best knock-down-and-drag-out manner, however we may deceive the public by our arts and utterances in public.

A New Departure in Art

'I remember once being called on to be humorous under circumstances which made me feel that fun was as difficult to catch as a bat with a fishing rod.' With the cultivated instinct of listeners, which all actors must be able to pretend to be, the Company gave simultaneously that movement of eagerness which implies a strained attention. The perfection and simultaneity of the movement was art, but the spirit of truth lay behind it, for all felt whatever was coming was real. The Low Comedian, with the trained instinct of an actor, felt that his audience was with him - en rapport - and allowed himself a thought more breadth in his manner as he proceeded:

'I was playing "Con" in The Shaughraun for want of a better, having been put into the part because I could manage a kind of brogue. We had a wretched Company, and we went to wretched places, places nearly bad enough to do us justice. At last we found ourselves in a little town on the west side of the Bog of Allen. It was hopeless business, for the people were poor; the room we played in was an awful hole, and the shebeen which they called a hotel where we all stayed was a holy terror. The dirt on the floor had caked, and felt like sand under your feet. As to the beds -'

'Oh, don't, Mr Parmentire; it's too dreadful!' said the Leading Lady, shuddering. So he went on:

'Anyhow, the audience - what there was of them - were fine. They weren't used to play-acting, and I think most of them took what they saw as reality - certainly while the curtain was up. We played three nights; the second night when I came out a big-made young man came up to me and said:

'"Kin I have a wurrd wid ye, sorr?"

'"Begob! but ye may," said I, in as near a brogue as I could get to his. "Twinty av ye loike!"

'"Then whisper me," said he, and, taking me by the arm, he led me across the street where we were alone. "What is it?" I asked.

'"I seen ye, sorr, at the wake to-night. Begorra, but it was an illigant toime. Shure the fun iv that would have done good to a rale corpse, much less to his frinds. I wondher now wud ye care to do a neighbourly act?" He said this with considerable diffidence. There was something genial and winning in his way, as there is generally with Irishmen; so I said as heartily as I could that I hoped I would, and asked him how I could do it. His face brightened as he answered:

'"Well, there's a wake to-night, a rale wake, yer ann'r, at Kenagh beyant and the widdy is in a most dishtressful state intirely. Now, av yer ann'r as is used to the divarshins iv wakes would come, shure it might help to cheer her up. It's only a rough place, surr, an' the byes an' the girrls is all there is; but there's lashins iv whiskey an' tobaccy, an' wan iv the quality like yer ann'r will be mighty welkim."

'That did it! For a man who took me for one of the quality I would have done anything! I tell you, you have to be mucking about for a spell in such places as we had been, and treated with the contempt which used to be the actor's meed in his private life in such places in my young days, to appreciate fully the help such a thing was to one's self-esteem. I told my pals that I was going to a local party, for I didn't want to disturb my new dignity all at once, and went off with my friend. We went on a donkey cart without springs. Such a cart, and such a road! There was a bundle of straw to sit on, so I was comfortable enough; except when the jolting through an unusually deep rut banged me about more than was consistent with physical self-restraint. At last we stopped where a small house stood back some hundred yards from the road. The light was coming through the little windows and the open door, that seemed quite bright through the inky blackness of the night. I separated myself from the straw as well as I could, and got down. A small boy appeared out of the darkness, like an attendant demon, and took away the donkey and cart. It seemed to fade into space, for, as it disappeared through a gap in the hedge, the wheels ceased to sound upon the soft turf. My friend said:

'"Stiddy, surr! the boreen is a bit rough!" He was right; it was! I stumbled towards the house through what seemed the bed of a small watercourse floored with peculiarly uneven boulders. When we got near the house, the light from within told more on the darkness, and as we came close to the projecting porch, the white oblong of the open doorway to the right became darkened as a figure came out to meet us - an elderly woman with grey hair and a white cap and a black dress. She curtsied when she saw my dress, and said with a certain air of distinction that most Irish-women have in their moments of reserve, and which all good women have in their grief:

'"Welkim, yer ann'r. I thank ye kindly for pathernisin' this house iv woe!"

'"God save all here!" said my cicerone as he removed his caubeen.

'I repeated the salutation, feeling a little bit chokey about the throat as I followed the woman into the house.

'The room was a good-sized one, for it was no peasant's hut I was in, but a substantial farm-house. Seated about it were some thirty or forty people of both sexes, old and young. Nearly all the men were smoking, some short cutty pipes as black as your hat, others long churchwardens, which manifestly came from a batch which lay on a table beside a substantial roll of "Limerick twist." The tobacco was strong, and so were the lungs of the smokers, so the room was in a sort of thick haze, which swayed about in visible wreaths whenever a passing gust drove in through the open door. There was a huge fire of turf on the hearth, over which hung a great black kettle puffing steam like a locomotive. The air was fragrant with whiskey punch, of which some great jugs were scattered about. The guests drank from all kinds of vessels of glass, crockery, tin, and wood, each of which seemed pro bono publico, for they were attacked at times by those nearest with the utmost impartiality. As there was manifestly not seating room for so many people, a good many of the women, old as well as young, sat on the men's knees in the most matter-of-fact way and with the utmost decorum.

'My cicerone, who was on all sides saluted as "Dan," took a pipe from the table and filled it. One of the girls, shifting from her living stool, took a blazing turf from the fire with the tongs, and held it to him as a light. He then helped himself to punch from the nearest vessel, looking round the room and repeating the salutation: "God save all here!"

'The widow herself pressed me into an armchair, vacated for the purpose by a powerful-looking young man who had been sitting with a girl on each knee. She then handed me a steaming jorum of punch in one of the few glass tumblers which she had wiped with the corner of her apron before filling it. She also gave me a pipe and tobacco, and brought me herself a sod of turf with which to light it when filled. This was the evident courtesy to a stranger, which, through all her grief, was a duty not to be overlooked.

'Nearly all those present seemed cheerful; some of them laughed, and I could not but feel that the instinct and purpose of the occasion was to counteract in some way the gloom and grief which were centred round the black coffin which rested on two chairs in the centre of the room. I could not myself but feel moved and solemn as I looked at it. The lid was laid on loosely, slightly drawn down so as to show the dead face which lay, still and waxen, within. A crucifix of black wood with the Figure in white lay on the coffin lid, together with some loose flowers, amongst which a bunch of arum lilies stood out in their white beauty.

'I think I really needed the punch to brace me up, for there was something so touching in the whole affair - the deep-felt grief held back with so stern a purpose, the sympathy of so many friends, all giving what comfort they could with their presence, combating the chill of death with the warmth of living and loving hearts - that it almost broke me up. It was evident that they had had some music, for a flute lay on the table, and a set of bagpipes stood in a corner. I sat quiet and waited, for I feared that, in my ignorance, I might jar on some feeling of those afflicted, either by some sin of commission, or of omission. I felt a little uncomfortable occupying a chair all to myself when every other seat in the place did double or treble duty; and I found myself beginning to speculate whether some of the girls would come and sit on my knee. But they didn't.'

'Showed their good taste!' said the Tragedian with a saturnine smile as he reapplied himself to his toddy.

'That's just it, Bones!' answered the Low Comedian sharply, 'showed their good taste! Remember that these weren't the pothouse rabble that you are accustomed to. They were decent, respectable folk, who could be familiar enough with one another without any ill thought of their neighbours or themselves, but they wouldn't lower themselves by a like familiarity with strangers, especially when they had any mistaken idea that their guest belonged to the quality.'

'Anyhow, they showed their good taste, whether according to Bones's idea or mine, and so I sat in solitary grandeur, and was by degrees fetched up to the level of the acceptance of fact by the whiskey punch. The restraint of the presence of a stranger wore away shortly, and I listened with interest to some of the music, quaint old airs with a lilt in them, and always an underlying note of pathos. This was especially manifest in the bagpipes, for the Irish bagpipes so far differs from the Scotch that it produces a softness of tone impossible to the other. You do not know, perhaps, that the Irish pipes have half-notes, whilst the Scotch have only full ones.'

Here a sort of modified snort was heard in the immediate neighbourhood of the Musical Director, and a remark was made, sotto voce, in which the words 'grandmother' and 'eggs' were distinguishable. The Low Comedian turned a swift glance in the direction, but said nothing, and, after a pause, went on:

'Presently Dan got up and said:

'"Widdy, this gintleman here is the funniest wan that iver I seen. Maybe now ye wouldn't mind av he was to give us a taste iv what he can do?"

'The Widow gravely nodded as she replied: "Shure, an' av his ann'r will pathernise us so far, we'll all be grateful to him. What like kind iv fun, Dan, does his ann'r consave?" I felt my heart sink. You know I'm not bashful.'

'You're not! not by a jugful!' interrupted the Tragedian. The Low Comedian smiled. He understood, from the low 'h-s-s-s-h' that ran through the saloon that the audience were with him, so he reserved his repartee, and went on:

'Not as a general rule, but there is a time for everything, and here, in the very presence of death, perpetually emphasised to me by the light of the candles which surrounded the coffin, flickering through the smoke, levity seemed out of place. Dan's chuckle of laughter as he began to speak almost disgusted me:

'"Oh, byes, but he's the funny man entirely. I seen him to-night play-actin', an' I thought I'd laugh the buttons from aff iv me britches."

'"What did he do, Dan?" asked one of the girls.

'"Begob, but he reprisinted a corpse. 'Twas the most comical thing I iver seen." He was interrupted by a violent sobbing from the widow, who, throwing her apron over her head, sat down beside the coffin, one hand leaning over till it touched the marble cheek and rocked herself to and fro in floods of tears. All her self-restraint seemed broken down in an instant. Some of the younger women sympathetically burst into tears; and the scene became almost in a moment one of unmitigated grief.

'But the very purpose for which the wake is ordained is to combat grief and its more potent manifestation. The stronger and more experienced spirits in the room looked at each other, and prompt action was taken. One old man put his arm round the widow, and with a fair use of force, raised her to her feet and led her back to her seat by the chimney corner, where she rocked herself to and fro for a little, but in silence. Each "boy" who had a crying girl on his knee, put his arms round her and began to kiss and pet and comfort her, and the crying soon ceased. The old man who had attended to the widow said, in a half-apologetic way:

'"Don't mind her, neighbours! Shure, 'tis the ways iv weemen when their hearts is sore. It's hard, it is, for the poor souls to bear up all the time, an' yez mustn't be hard on thim when they're bruk down. It's different wid us min!" There was an iron resolution in the man's bearing, and a break in his voice which showed me that he was one of those whose self-control was accomplished with effort. "Who is he?" I asked from the man sitting next me.

"'Shure, an' he's the brother iv the corpse, surr!" came the answer. The apologetic words were received with a series of sympathetic nods and shakings of the head and muttered words of acquiescence:

"'Thrue for ye!"

"'Begob, but that's so!"

"'Weemin is only weemin, afther all!"

"'The poor crathur; God be aisy wid her in her sorra!" In the midst of this, Dan went on just as if nothing had happened. That he was right in his endeavour was shown by the brighter look on the faces of all as he resumed:

"'Twas the funniest thing I iver seen! He was the corp himself, and him not dead at all. Tear an ages! but that was a quare wake intirely. Wid the corpse drinkin' the keener's punch whiniver she nodded her head." Here the keener, sitting on a low stool on the side of the coffin away from the fire, hearing through her somnolence the implied slight to her function, woke on the instant, and, with a half-angry look at the speaker, said: "Keeners doesn't sleep - not till the words is said over the grave." Then, as if to show that she herself was wide awake, she raised a keene which, beginning low and sad, rose and rose in pitch and volume till the rafters seemed to buzz and ring with the mournful sound. Thenceforth, and throughout the remainder of the night, she keened at intervals, generally choosing such times as the interruption of the current proceedings would bring into prominence the importance of her lugubrious office. No one, however, considered her professional labours as an interruption, but went on just as if nothing were occurring. It was embarrassing at first, but after awhile no more interrupted one than the ticking of a clock or the whistling of the wind, or the rush and clash of waves. Dan proceeded:

"'Thin he tuk the shnuff, an' threw it in the faces iv the polis."

"'An' what did he do that for, wastin' it on the likes iv them?" asked a fierce-looking old woman.

"'To make them incapable, for shure!"

"'Make them incapable! Wid shnuff! Wid shnuff!" she said with fine scorn. "Musha, but that's not the way I'd make the polis incapable - more'n they are already. It's wid a blackthorn on their skulls, an' plenty iv it at that!" There was a slight pause, which was broken by an old woman, who said in a conversational way:

"'Who'd a thought, now, that there was that comicality in a wake? Musha, but I've been attindin' them for half a hundhred years, an' I niver seen a funny wan yet."

'Dan at once championed his own choice.

"'Maybe, acushla, that was because this gintleman wasn't the corpse on the occasion. Av he had a-been like I seen him the night, it's houldin' in yer stummick wid laughin' ye'd be!"

"'Corpses does be ginerally sarious enough!" remarked an old man. "I'm thinkin' it's grateful we'd be to wan what'd give us divarshion iv any kind." Dan didn't seem to like these interruptions. There was something of the spirit of the impresario in him, and he manifestly wished to exploit what he considered his funny-man addition to the entertainment, so he began to explain:

'"Musha! but won't yez undhershtand that this wasn't a real corp, but a man what was only purtendin' to be wan. It was play-actin' and his ann'r is the funniest man I ivver seen."'

'Limited opportunities have very dreadful effects!' murmured the Tragedian; but no one took any notice. The Low Comedian proceeded:

'Dan turned to me and says he: "Wudn't yer ann'r do somethin' funny?"

"'Good God!" I said, "I couldn't be funny in the presence of the dead - it wouldn't be respectful!"

"'Put that out iv yer mind, surr," said the brother of the corpse; "shure, all these frinds an' neighbours is here out iv respect, an yet they does what they can to cheer up the poor widdy woman that has but little to comfort her in her sorra. It's well, so it is, to help her to forgit!" This was so manifestly true that I bowed to the occasion, and said that I would do what I could to amuse them. I would just take a minute to think of something, if they would pardon me. With true Irish delicacy they began to talk to each other, ostensibly letting me alone as

I wished. Dan smiled round with the consciousness that his efforts were about to be crowned with success, and remarked for the general good:

"'Begob, there was wan quare thing, at the wake I'm tellin' yez iv - all the girrls on the flure wint wan afther th'other an' kissed the corpse!" There was a murmur of incredulous astonishment from all, and many whisperings and strugglings between the girls and the men who held them on their knees.

"'That wouldn't do you, Katty!" remarked one young man to the girl beside him, but her retort came pat, "It'd be a good custom for you, avick, for the only chance you'd iver get in yer life is whin ye're dead." Then there was a pinch unseen, and a most manifest smack on the man's face which would have given a less hardy person a headache for a day. It was evident that conversation was being made on my account, for the next remarks kept on the subject of me and my work.

"'Begob! but play-actin' is a mighty curious thing intirely!" said a man. "I seen some iv it wanst at a fair in Limerick. Shure, they was bins that was play-actin',44 an' cute enough they wor."

"'I seen a man wan time at Ballinasloe Heifer Fair turnin' music out iv a box, an' him wid a monkey dhressed up like a gineral!"

"'An' I seen dogs what would climb up a laddher an' purtend to be dead, an' would jump as high as yer head through a hoop. I wonder, surr," this to me, "if ye would jump a bit through a hoop. Mind ye, it's a mighty divartin' thing to luk at, an' would do the widdy a power iv good."

'I really could not stand this; it was too damned humiliating - our Art compared with the antics of a hen, a monkey, and a dog, as if we were all comrades of equality. But it was all meant in so kindly a way that I made up my mind to sing a comic song. I gave them "Are you there, Moriarty!" for all I was worth. Artistically, it was a success, though, the subject being a glorification of police, was, I felt after I had begun, deplorably inappropriate. They were a splendid audience, and after I had begun to entertain them, I felt I could depend on them thoroughly, so played with the thing, and did it as well as I could. But at first it was dreadful to stand up there looking down on the dead man in his coffin, and facing the widow with her swollen eyes, with the crucifix and the flowers and the death-lights right under me to try to be comic. It was the ghastliest thing I ever knew, or that I ever shall know. I felt at first like a fiend and a cad and a villain and a scoffer, all in one. In fact, I may say that in that awful moment I realised what it must be to be a tragedian! It was only when I saw the apron slowly drawn from the face of the widow, and her poor, worn eyes brightening up perceptibly through her tears, that I began to understand how salutary was the purpose of the wake. Finally, I gave them "Shamus O'Brien" as a recitation, and that went like wildfire. So we passed right into the dawn, when the grey came stealing in through the narrow windows and the open door, and making the guttering candles look dissolute; when the men were nodding their heads, and the girls were, many of them, fast asleep in their arms with their heads on the frieze-clad shoulders, and their ruddy lips open in sleep. Well, anyhow, I was mighty tired when I came away to drive into Fenagh in the donkey cart and the straw, but felt the effort was not wasted when the whole band of friends - they were real friends now - came down the boreen to see me off, and the poor widow looked gratefully at me as she waved her hand from the open door with the first red of the coming dawn falling full upon her with a sort of promise of hope.'

When the applause had subsided, the Manager stood up and said:

'Ladies and gentlemen, before we go any further I want to see one thing done - to see two very good friends of mine shake hands. Two very good fellows; two leaders and representatives of the great branches of the art that we all love, and whose exercise is our vocation, Tragedy and Comedy. Not that I know such a thing is necessary, for in the close companionship which our work necessitates we can chaff one another without mercy. But there are some strangers here, these gentlemen' - here he pointed to the railway men - 'who are our guests; and I should not like them to think that the girding at each other with passages of humour and satire which has been going on between the accomplished representatives of the buskin and the sock was other than in perfect good fellowship.'

Both men saw the necessity of the case, and each standing up held out a hand.

'Gags, old boy, here's your good health and your family's, and may they live long and prosper,' said the Tragedian.

'Bones, my old pal,' said the Low Comedian, 'here's a nail in your coffin and no hair on your head; and when I regard those hyacinthine locks of yours and see the strength and symmetry of the form of which all your comrades are so proud, I think that is tantamount to the farthest-off manifestation of ill that I can imagine.' The men, who were really old and tried friends, though they had eternal passages of arms, shook hands cordially. The MC grasped the fact that the situation was complete.

'Next!' he said, indicating the Prompter with the hand which did not contain the hot grog. So the Prompter began:

I suppose I must confine myself to some personal experience, and that connected with the theatre. It is a pity I am so limited; as if I were free to speak of the adventures of my youth by flood and field, "I could a tale unfold" that would "freeze your young blood and make each particular hair to stand on end like quills upon the fretful porcupine."'

'Talking about floods, what was that about a flood of which you were speaking to Gags the other night? It seemed mighty interesting to both of you.' This from the Heavy Father.

'Oh, that,' answered the Prompter, with a short laugh. 'That wasn't half bad; but it wasn't what you'd call a story; and though I was there, anything that happened was not strictly personal to me. Mr Hupple was there too. He can tell you more about it than I can, for I only knew about going through the flood and what the conductor said; but he heard the confessions.'

'Never mind about him now,' said the MC. 'We shall come to him presently.'

'Tell us about your part, anyhow.' This suggestion came from the Manager. So the Prompter took it as a command - or as a stage direction, at any rate. Bending low, he said:

'Whatever you wish, Mr Benville Nonplusser, must be done.'

Mick the Devil

'It was when I was with the Windsor Theatre Company in America in the 'eighties. I was then Second Lead. Things change, alas! Well, we had been North and East and West, and were entering on the last quarter of an eight months' tour when we got to New Orleans. There had been an unusually dry fall, and the rivers were down to the lowest known for years. The earth was all baked and cracked; the trees were burned up with drought, and the grass and undergrowth were as brown as December bracken. The Mississippi was so low that the levees were visible down below the piles, and the water that went swirling by looked as thick as pea-soup. We were playing a three weeks' engagement, before, during, and after Mardi Gras; and as we had been doing two months of one-night stands, we were all glad to have the spell of rest in one place. No one can imagine, till they try it, what a wearisome business it is changing camps every day or every few days. Sometimes you get so dazed with it all that when you wake up in the morning you can't remember where you are - even though you had not been up with the boys the night before.

'Just before Mardi Gras the weather changed. There came for two days a close, damp heat, which was the most terrible thing I ever experienced. It was impossible to keep dry, and I was in nightly fear that the whole paint would wash away from everyone. It was just a miracle how moustaches stuck on; and as for the flush of youth and beauty on the girls' cheeks! - well, "there is a Providence that shapes our ends, rough hew them how we will." Then the rain came down. Great Scott! what rain, both as regards quality and quantity! It seemed as if the sky was full of angels emptying buckets. The ground was so hard that at first the rain didn't sink into it, but ran off into the streams and the river. You know what a place New Orleans is! It has its head just above water, when the level is low; but when the Mississippi rises, the levees fill up and the river rushes on high over the city level. We didn't mind the rain, though it spoiled the show in the streets, for it cooled the air, and that was much.

'I certainly never saw anything uglier than the streets of New Orleans. Theoretically, the place is delightful, and if I were only to give you bare facts I should mislead you altogether. What would you think, for instance, of streets by each side of which run streams of water whose gurgling is always in your ears as you walk? Sounds nice, don't it? But then the whole place is clay, and the water is muddy with it; the streams in the streets are full of dirty water, with refuse of all kinds tumbling lazily along. If you dig a foot deep in any street you find water; that is why the gas-pipes are in the air, and why the dead are buried above ground in stucco-covered vaults like bakers' ovens. Well, the rain kept on, and the Mississippi rose till it was up to the top of the levees, and we in New Orleans began to wonder when the city would be flooded out. One day, when I saw the base of the banks beginning to cave in, I felt glad that we were leaving the neighbourhood that night. We were bound for Memphis, and our train was scheduled to leave at one o'clock in the morning. Before turning in, I met the Sectional Engineer tramping up and down and chewing the end of his cigar in a frightful fashion, and we got into conversation. I saw he was anxious, and asked him the cause. He told me in confidence - "in my clothes," he called it - that there had been a "wash-out" in the Valley section of the line, on which it had been arranged that we should travel; and so we would have to go round another way. As I was going on the journey, I was naturally anxious, too, and began to pump him, pretending that I was not at all afraid. He tumbled to it, and explained the trouble to me:

'"You see, I am afraid of Bayou Pierre. There's a spongy gap a couple of miles wide, with a trestle bridge across it over which you have to pass. At the best of times I am anxious about that trestle, for the ground is so bad that anything might happen at any time. But now, with a fortnight's rain and the Mississippi up the levees and the bottoms flooded all over the country, that blessed place will be like an estuary of the sea. The bridge isn't built for weather like this, and the flood is sure to be well over it. A train running on it will have to take chance whether it is there at all; and if any of it is gone - swept away or caved in - well, God help the train! That's all I can say, for everyone in it will die like a rat in a trap!"

'This was distinctly comforting to one of the travellers! I did not know exactly what to do or say, so I just managed to gasp out a question without giving myself away:

'"How long will it take us to get to Bayou Pierre?"

'"Well, say that you start about three o'clock, you will be there about noon or a little before it!" I said good-night and went into the train, determined to wake up pretty early and be ready to have some business in some local town about ten.

I didn't sleep very well, and the grey dawn was edging its way under the dark blind of my sleeping berth when I dropped off. I had plenty of disturbing dreams. The last I remember was that a great crocodile came out of a raging flood, snapped me up in its mouth, and began whirling me along at an inconceivably rapid rate. For a while I tried to make up my mind what I would do. There was no denying the pace at which we were going; I could distinctly hear the whirring of the wheels.

'Then, with a gasp, I remembered that crocodiles don't use wheels, and I jumped out of my berth faster even than I usually did when the nigger porter put his black hand over my face or pulled my toes. We seemed to be going at a terrific pace. The carriage rocked to and fro, and I had to hold on, or I should have been vthrown about as in a cabin at sea in a storm. I looked out of the window and saw palm and cypress and great swathes of hanging Florida moss on the live-oaks as we whirled by. It was evident we were not going to stop soon. I looked at my watch; it was close to eleven o'clock. I ran back and hammered at the door of the drawing-room of the car where our manager made himself comfortable. He called out "Come in"; I evidently astonished him when I burst in in my pyjamas and a violent state of excitement. "Well, Mr Gallimant, what is it?" he asked shortly, as he stood up. "Do you know," I said, "that we are going to cross a flooded creek on a trestle bridge under water, and that it may be washed away?"

'"No," he said, quite coolly, "I don't! Who has been filling you up with fool-talk?"

'"The engineer of the line told me last night," I answered, unthinkingly.

'"Told you last night!" he said sarcastically. "Then why did you not let me know before? Oh, I see; you wanted to get off in time yourself and let the rest of us meet the danger. You needn't deny it; I see it in your face. Then let me tell you that if you had got off and stayed behind, you'd have found your berth full when you caught us up. See?" I saw pretty well that there was no sympathy to be had from him, so I ran through the train looking for the conductor, whom I found in the observation-room on the last car. Several of the Company, seeing my excitement, took it for granted that something was wrong, and followed me. When we burst in on the conductor, who was making an entry in his book, he looked up and said:

'"Well, what's wrong with you all?"

'"Here, you, stop the train!" I cried. "We want to get out before we're drowned!"

'"Oh, indeed!" he said coolly. "And how do you know you're going to be drowned?"

'"Because," I said, in a heat, "we are going to run over Bayou Pierre on the trestle bridge, and it's under water. Who knows that part of it mayn't be washed away or have collapsed?" He actually smiled at me.

'"Now, do you know," he said, "that shows great knowledge, both topographical and prob-lematical, on your part! And so you want to get out? Well, you can't. Tell you why? Mick Devlin was put on to drive this train because he's the daringest driver on the whole fit-out. 'Mick the Devil' they call him. And Mick is letting her go now for all she is worth. Listen to that; she's going seventy, clean. Mick knows his part of the job, and I guess you've all got to keep your hair on and sit tight while Mick has his hand on the throttle."'

'Here's luck to Mick!' said the driver of the engine, in a hearty voice.

'Hush, h-s-s-h!' said the rest, for they were getting interested in the story. The Prompter went on:

'"Why does he want to go so fast?" I said.

"'Now you're beginning to talk!" he answered; "and as you know so much, I'll tell you more. Mick knows what he's about; what he doesn't know about engines and bridges and floods isn't much worth knowin'. See? We've got to go across Bayou Pierre to-day; and belike we'll be the last to cross it before the floods go down. You know some of the dangers, but you don't know as much as Mick. Someone has been fillin' you up with bogey talk, and you've taken it not only for Gospel, but for all the Gospel there is. The Sectional Engineer is a permanent-way man, and he looks on his work from the standpoint of statical force. But, you see, Mick's special province is dynamics. He knows all the dangers that there Engineer ladled into you; and he takes his chances on them blindfold, for he can do nothing. If there is a wash-out or a collapse anywhere, it's kingdom-come for us all, anyhow. But then there's other dangers that Mick knows, and I know; mayhap the Sectional Engineer knows them, too, though he didn't talk of them, for they don't belong to his trade."

"'What are the other dangers?" I gasped out with what appearance of nonchalance I could muster, for the doorway was crowded with a lot of deadly-white faces. The conductor actually smiled as he replied:

"'I guess I'd better explain" - here he actually laughed - "though I daresay some of ye think it's pretty tiresome listening to a dissertation on coming dangers whilst a mad Irishman is whirling you all to perdition. Well, be it so! Your own boss made a contract. The railway company agreed to it; and Mick and me undertook to carry it out. Our Yard-Master said we was to put you down in Nashville, flood or no flood; and so we shall, the will of God alone objectin'. An' what the will of God is we'll try to find out for sure. You see, this flood has been out nigh on a week. Floods in a big place like Bayou Pierre don't, as a rule, run strong enough to wash clean away like a sea or a big river does. But it can weaken. It eddies everlastingly round the bases of piles, and it softens the mortar between the bricks of the piers. There's a lot of them in this bridge we're coming to, for though you'll hardly believe it when you see it, it's only a flat valley, except in floods, with streams running through it here and there. When pierwork or brickwork is demoralised and weakened that way, though it will stand all right till it gets a shock, it will suddenly go all to bits if it gets jarred. You know what that means. Each pier holds a piece of a bridge; and if it goes, down goes the whole thing. Now, have any of you ever thought of the weight, the deadweight, of a train? Such a one as ours will weigh, engine and tender and brake and goods and passengers and all, more than half a million pounds. Put that suddenly on the top of one of these tottering piles or weakened piers, and what'll happen? Why, the darned thing will slide, or warp, or twist, or crumble away, or grind together; and this, mind you, without a steady force of water to wash away every fragment of mortar as it is disturbed. So as we travel over them we're helping to make the wash-outs and collapses that the Sectional Engineer fears."

'He paused, and through the beating of my own heart and the throbbing of the pulses in my own head I could hear a sort of sobbing groan from the womenkind - they were far too frightened to scream. Without was the whirring rush of the wheels and the panting of the engine taxed to its utmost with our terrific speed. The Conductor looked keenly into the faces of all before he went on:

"'Now, Mick knows all about this, and he also knows the way to minimise the risk. Why, he's doin' it now; that is why he's goin' at our present pace! Mick's workin' this job bald-headed!"

"'Why?" The question was gasped out by one of the ladies, her eyes as round as a bird's with fright. The Conductor nodded approval.

"'Now, that's good! I like to see people that's reasonable and don't quite let their fears master them. Well, ma'am, I'll tell you why. A pier can't fall all in a second; it takes time to break up anything that it has taken time to put together, even if it has to be hoisted with dynamite. Now, our pressure is great, but it doesn't last long. The quicker we go, the shorter it lasts; so that when things are real bad - so near a collapse that it only wants a finishing touch - we can be up and over before the crash comes. I've seen Mick take a train through three feet of water in a flood on one of the Pan Handle branches, and felt the last car pull up the slope of the girders of a bridge as the pier collapsed behind us. Don't you be skeered, any of you! Mick's the right man in the right place; an' if you're goin' to get through to-day he's the man to take you. If not, we're well out of it compared with him! Drownin' is an easy death, they say; but if the engine goes down head first, as she will if there be aught wrong, there's steam enough in the boilers and heat enough to cook him and his mate while they're drownin'!

"'Well, s'long! I'm goin' up to the baggage-car in front to be near Mick. We've worked together too long to be parted at the last, if it should come. There she goes! we're into Bayou Pierre now, and so long as we're on the trestle, all any of you can do is to say your prayers and confess your sins. After that - well, I don't think I'd worry much about it as yet!"

'He passed on his way, leaving behind him a sense of gallant manhood that made me ashamed of being afraid.

'The speed had manifestly diminished, although we still went at a considerable rate; there was a queer sound, a sort of hissing scream as the water was churned by our rushing wheels.

'I stepped out on the rear platform and looked around. In front of me, as I stood, the shore we had left receded farther and farther at every instant. The dwarf palms became a stunted mass, and the clumps of cypress and live-oak seemed to dwindle away into shrubs. Around us was a waste of water flowing swiftly under our feet; a great frothy yellow tide, with here and there floating masses of debris - logs, hay, dead cattle, and drift of every imaginable kind. On either side it was the same. Leaning out over the rail I could just see the far shore, a dim line on the horizon. We were driving through the flood at a great pace and our engine sent before us, as does the prow of a steamer, a wave whose flanks fell ever back on us as we swept along. Now and again we could feel a sort of shiver or a sudden shock, as though something had loosened or given way under us. But somehow we ran along all right; and as the shore we had passed grew dimmer, and as the far shore grew closer, our spirits rose and the fear fell away from us.

'It was with glad hearts that we felt the solid ground under us and heard the old roar of the wheels again. The squealing of the brakes was like music as we drew up on the track a little later on.

'The engine seemed to pant like an animal which has gone through hard stress; and her master, Mick the Devil, looking gay and easy and debonnair, raised his cap in answering salute as we all tumbled out and raised three cheers for him in true Anglo-Saxon fashion.'

'Now, Mr Hupple,' said the MC, 'as we learned from Gallimant that you were on the train crossing Bayou Pierre, and that you heard the confessions, perhaps you will tell us something of what happened?' There came a chorus of entreaty from all, amongst which the voices of the ladies were the most eager. Confessions - of other people - are always interesting. The Second Low Comedian had a hint of the duty before him, and seemed quite prepared. He began at once:

In Fear of Death

'Our little lot comprised the major part of the Company. None of them had talked to the Sectional Engineer, and so were not prepared to save their own skins by bolting without ever giving a hint to their pals. I never knew the full measure of our friend's bravery before!'

'Time!' said the MC, warningly. He nodded cheerfully and went on:

'It was only when we were actually in the water that any of them began to concern themselves. Indeed, at first no one seemed to mind, for we had often before made a dash over a flooded stream. But when the speed slackened and the rush of the wheels in the water made a new sort of sound, they all ran to the windows and looked out. Some of the festive spirits thought it a good opportunity to frighten the girls, and put up a joke on the more timid of the men. It didn't seem a difficult job so far as some of them were concerned, for the surprise was rapidly becoming terror. Everything seemed to lend itself to the presiding influence; the yellow water seeming to go two ways at once as it flowed past us and as we crossed its course; the horrible churning of our wheels which seemed to come up from under us through the now opened windows; the snorting and panting of the engine; the looks of fear and horror growing on the blanching faces around; all seemed to culminate towards hysteria. The most larky of the men was young Gatacre, who was understudy for Huntley Vavasseur, then our Leading Juvenile. He pretended to be terribly afraid, and cowered down and hid his face and groaned, all the time winking at some of us. But presently, as the waste of water grew wider and wider, his glances out of the window became more anxious, and I could see his lips grow white. All at once he became ghastly pale, and, throwing up his hands, broke out into a positive wail of terror, and began to pray in a most grovelling manner - there is no other way to describe it. To some of us it was revolting, and we should have liked to kick him; but its effect on the girls was dreadful. All the hysteria of panic which had been coming on broke out at once, and within half a minute the place was like the Stool-of-Repentance corner at a Revival Meeting.

'I am glad to say that, with these exceptions, they were in the main brave and sensible people, who kept their own heads and tried to make, for very shame's sake, their friends keep theirs. It seems to me that really good women are never finer than when they are helping a weak sister. I mean really helping when it isn't altogether pleasant work. I don't count it help to a woman, lashing out wastefully with other people's Eau de Cologne, and ostentatiously loosening her stays, and then turning to the menkind who are looking on helplessly, with a "phew!" as if they knew what was wrong with her all the time. We all know how our women help each other, for we are all comrades, and the girls are the best of us. But on this occasion the womenkind were a bit panicky, and even those who kept their heads and tried to shield the others from the effects of their hysterical abandon, were pale and rocky themselves, and kept one eye on the yellow flood running away under us.

'I certainly never did hear such a giving away as in the confessions of some of them, and I tell you that it wasn't pleasant to listen to. It made some of us men angry and humiliated to think that we could be so helpless. We took some of the girls and tried to actually shake them back into reason, but, Lord bless you! it wasn't the least use. The more we shook them, the more we shook out of them things which were better left unsaid. It almost seemed as if confession was a pebbly sort of thing that could be jerked out of one, like corn out of a nose-bag. The whole thing was so infernally sudden that one had no time to think. One moment we were all composed and jolly, and the next there were these poor women babbling out the most distressing and heartrending things, and we quite unable to stop them. The funny thing, as it seemed to me now, was that it never occurred to any of us to shove off and leave them alone! Anyhow, we didn't go, at all events till the fat was in the fire. Fortunately, the poor girls didn't have much to confess that seemed very wrong to most of us. There were one or two nasty and painful things, of course, but we all shut our memories, and from that day to this it never made any difference in any way that I could ever see - except in one case, where a wife told an old story to her husband. I can see the scene now. The terror in her grey eyes, the frown in his pale face, all the whiter by contrast with his hair. "Sun and Shade," we used to call them.'

He broke off suddenly, paused a moment, and then resumed:

'But that was their own business, and though it never seemed to come right, none of us ever said a word about it.'

'Did none of the men confess anything?' asked the Singing Chambermaid. There was in the tone of her voice that underlying note of militant defiance which is always evident when the subject of woman in the abstract is mentioned in mixed company. The Second Low Comedian smiled as he replied:

'Certainly, my dear! I thought you understood that I was speaking of the young ladies of both sexes. You remember that the first, in fact the one to set them off, was an alleged Man.'

'Well, these things, you see, made the painful side of the incident, for it is not pleasant to hear people say things which you know they will grieve for bitterly afterwards. But there was another side, which was both interesting and amusing: the way in which the varieties of character came out in the confessions, and the manner of their coming. If we hadn't known already - I speak for myself - we should have been able to differentiate the weaknesses of the various parties, and to have got a knowledge of the class of things which they fondly hoped they had kept hidden. I suppose it is such times that reveal us to ourselves, or would do so if we had grace to avail ourselves of our opportunities. Anyhow, the dominant note of each personality was struck in so marked a way that the scene became a sort of character-garden with living flowers!'

When the applause which followed his poetic 'tag' had ceased, there was a chorus of indignant disappointment:

'Is that all?'

'Why stop just as it was getting interesting?'

'Just fancy, with material like that, to fade out in vague generalities!'

'Can't you tell us some more of the things they said?'

'What's the use of telling us of confessions when you keep it dark what they were.'

'Was there anything so very compromising, to you or to anybody else, that you should hesitate?'

'That's just it,' said the Second Low Comedian with a grin. 'If there was anything compromising, I would tell it with pleasure, especially, I need not say, if it concerned myself. But of all the confessions that were ever written or spoken, I suppose there never were any as little compromising as on this occasion. With the one exception that I have spoken of, and on which all our lips are sealed, there was nothing which would injure the character of a sergeant in the Archangelic police force. Of course, I except the young man who began the racket. There was not one of those who "confessed" who did not compromise himself or herself. But the subjects were so odd! I didn't know there were so many sinless wickednesses in the whole range of evil!'

'What on earth do you mean?' said the Leading Lady with the wide open eyes of stage amazement. 'Do give us some examples, so that we may be able to follow you.'

'Ah! I thought that was what you wanted!' he answered with a wink. 'You would like to hear the confessions, good or bad, or, rather, bad or worse, and judge for yourself as to their barometric wickedness. All right! I will tell you all I remember.

'There was our Leading Lady, I mention no names, who had been on the stage, to my own knowledge, twenty-eight years, and she was in the Second Lead when I met her first at Halifax in Wibster's Folly, which was a popular stock piece on the Yorkshire Circuit. She confessed to having deceived, not only the public, but her friends, even her dear friends of the Company, and would like to put herself right with them all and have their forgiveness ere she died. Her sin was one of vanity, for she had deceived them as to her age. She had acknowledged to twenty-nine; but now in her last hour, with the death drops on her brow, and the chill of the raging flood already striking into her very soul, she would confess. They knew how hard it was for a woman to be true when dealing with her age; women at least would understand her; she would confess that she was really thirty-three. Then she sank down on her knees, in a picturesque position, which she had often told her friends she made famous in East Lynne, and held up her hands and implored their forgiveness. Do you know that nearly all those present were so touched by her extraordinary self-sacrifice in that trying moment, that they turned away and hid their faces in their hands. I could myself see the shoulders of some of them shake with emotion.

'Well, her example was infectious; she was hardly on her knees when our Juvenile Lead took up the running. With a heart-breaking bitter sob, such as adorned his performance in Azrael the Prodigal, he held his hands aloft with the fingers interlaced, and, looking up to the gallery - I mean the roof, or the sky, or whatever he saw above him with either his outer or his inner eye - he mourned his malingering in the way of pride. He had been filled with ungodly pride, when during his very first engagement, having been promoted through sheer merit - having swept, if he might say so, upward like a rocket through the minor ranks of the profession, he had emerged in sober splendour amongst the loftier altitudes. Oh, even that fact had not bounded his excesses of pride. That evil quality, which, like jealousy, "mocks the meat it feeds on," had grown with the enlarging successes which seemed to whirl upon him like giant snowflakes from the Empyrean. When the Mid-Mudland Anti-Baptist Scrutiniser had spoken of him as "the rising histrionic genius who was destined to lift from the shrouded face of Melpomene the seemingly ineradicable shadow which the artistic incompetence of a re-puritanised age had thrown upon it," he had felt elated with the thought that on his shoulder rested the weight of the banner of art, which it would be his duty, as well as his pride, to carry amongst the Nations, and unfurl even before the eyes of their Kings. Ah! but that was not his worst sin, for with the years that had carried the greatness of his stormy youth into the splendour of his prime young manhood, had grown an ever-increasing pride in what he knew from the adoring looks of women and their passionate expressions of endearment - both written and verbal - was the divine gift of physical beauty in perfection. In which gift was included the voice at once sweet and powerful which evoked that enthusiastic tribute from the Bootle Local Government Questioner, wherein occurred the remarkable passage: "It is rare, if not unique, to find in the tones of a human voice, centred in no matter how perfect a physical entourage, at once the subtlety of the lyre, the great epigrammatic precision of the ophicleide, and the resonant doom-sounding thunder of the clarion and the bassoon." So, too, was included a bearing of grace and nobility which "recalled" as the Midland humoristic organ, The Pushful Joe, remarked, "the worth of the youthful emperor Gluteus Maximus." Oh! these things were indeed sources of a pride, which was at best a weakness of poor humanity. Still, it should be held in check, and this in proportion to its natural strength. "Mea culpa! Mea culpa!" he said in the tones with which he used to thrill the house in Don Alzavar the Penitent, or the Monk of Madrid. He went on further, for pride seemed to have no limit, but essayed, when fixed in daring and lofty natures, to scale the very bastions of Olympus. He was proud - oh, so proud that in this dread moment, when he stood hand-in-hand with his fellow-brother, Death, he could see its earthly littleness. It was when depicting the roles in which he had won his greatest fame, he had, with the best and purest intention, he assured us, dared the blue ribbon of histrionic achievement in essaying the part of Hamlet in the Ladbroke Hall. He had found his justification of Metropolitan endeavour in the striking words of the Westbourne Grove and Neighbouring Parishes' Chronicle of Striking Events: "The triumph of our youngest 'Hamlet' is as marked as his many successes in less ambitious walks of histrionic renown!"'

He was interrupted by our First Low Comedy Merchant, who said:

'Time! old man. There are others who want a chance of public confession whilst Death still stares us in the face.' He was followed by our Heavy Man, who added:

'It's a good idea, as well as a new one, to confess your Notices. Anyhow, it makes a variety from having to pretend to read them every time you strike a man for a drink.' The Leading Juvenile glared at his interrupters, in the manner which he was used to assume as Geoffrey Plantagenet in The Baffled Usurper. He was about to loose the vials of his wrath upon them when our First Singing Chambermaid, who had been furtively preparing for her effort by letting down her back hair, flung herself upon her knees with a piercing shriek, and, holding up her hands invocatively after the manner of The Maiden's Prayer, cried out, interrupting herself all the while with muttered sobs of choking anguish:

"'Oh, ye Powers, to whom is given the priceless guardianship of Maiden life, look down in forgiving pity upon the delinquencies of one who, though without evil purpose, but in the guilelessness of her innocent youth, and with the surpassing cruelty of the young and thoughtless, hath borne hard upon the passionate but honourable love of Dukes and Marquises! Peccavi! Peccavi!! Peccavi!!!" with which final utterance she fell fainting upon her face, and struggled convulsively, till, seeing that no one flew to her assistance, she lay still a moment, and then ignominiously rose to her feet and retired, outwardly sobbing and inwardly scowling, to her section.

'Hardly, however, had she spoken her tag when two aspirants for confessional honours sought to "catch the speaker's eye." One of them was the Understudy of the last confessor, the other the First Old Woman. They were something of an age and appearance, each being on the shady side of something, and stout in proportion. They both had deep voices, and as neither would at first give way, their confessions were decidedly clamorous and tangled, but full of divine possibilities of remorse. They both had flung themselves on their knees, right and left, like the kneeling figures beside an Elizabethan tomb. We all stood by, with admiring sympathy manifested in our choking inspirations and on our broadening smiles. It was a pretty fair struggle. The First Old Woman was fighting for her position, and that is a strong stimulus to effort; the other was endeavouring to win a new height in her Olympian ambition, and that is also a strong aid to endeavour. They both talked so loud and so fast that none of us could follow a word that either of them said. But neither would give way, till our Tragedian, beginning to despair of an opening for his confession, drew a deep breath and let us have it after the manner of his celebrated impersonation of the title-role of Manfred in the Alpine storm, in which you will remember that he has to speak against the thunder, the bassoon, the wind, and the rain - not to mention the avalanches, though he generally makes a break for them to pass. The women held out as long as they could, and finally, feeling worsted by the Tragedian's thunder, they joined against the common enemy, and shrieked hysterically in unison as long as their breath held out. Our Tragedian's confession was immense. I wish I could remember it word for word as he gave it, with long dwelling on his pet words, and crashing out his own particular consonants. We were all silent, for we wanted to remember, for after use, what he said. Being a Tragedian, he began, of course, with Jove:

"'Thou Mighty One who sittest on the cloud-capped heights of Olympus, and regardest the spectral figure of the mighty Hyster seated in his shadowy cart, deign to hear the murmurings of a heart whose mightiest utterances have embodied the noblest language of the chiefest bards. Listen, O son of Saturn! O husband of Juno! O father of Thalia and Melpomene! O brother of Neptune and Pluto! O lover of Leda and Semele and Danae and of all the galaxy of celestial beauties who crowned with love the many-sided proclivities of Thou, most multitudinous-hearted God! Hear the sad wail of one who has devoted himself to the Art of Roscius! Listen to the voice that has been wont to speak in thundrous tones to the ears of a wondering world, now stilled to the plaintive utterance of deepening regret. Hear me mourn the lost opportunities of a not-unsuccessful life! When I think that I have had at my foot the ball of success, and in my sublime indifference spurned it from me as a thing of little worth, well knowing that in all the years genius such as mine must ever command the plaudits of an enraptured world, what can I say or how announce the magnitude, or even the name, of my sin? Hear me then, O mighty Jove..."

'Just then the dull threshing and swishing of the submerged wheels changed to the normal roar and resonance, as we left the trestle bridge and swept into the cutting beyond. The first one to speak was the Prompter, who said:

"'Your attack was a little slow, Mr Montressor. It's a bit hard that the curtain has to drop before the invocation is properly begun!"

There was a pause, chiefly utilised for the consumption of heeltaps and the replenishment of drinking vessels. It was broken by the voice of one of the Young Men who sat at some distance from the fire and quite away from the Prompter – a Young Man who wore his hair long and had literary ambitions. He spoke of himself sometimes as 'a Man of Letters as well as a Player.'

'How small the world is! Do you know that out of that very episode that Mr Hupple has just spoken of came a strange circumstance? If I were next on the list I could give it as a fitting corollary.'

'Corolly or no corolly,' the Sewing Woman was heard to murmur, the punch having had some effect in creating a certain drowsiness which fell on her like a robe. 'Corolly or no corolly, it ain't in it with the Dead Byby I was a-tellin' ye of.'

The MC stopped the threatened reminiscence by shaking her by the shoulder. 'Wake up, dear lady,' he said, 'and learn of the smallness of the world. I think we may take it,' he added, looking round, 'that in such an exceptional case we may break the rule and ask Bloze to go on next.' 'Bloze' was the nickname of Mr Horatio Sparbrook (stage name) given to him for an attempt he had once made to introduce realism into the part of Gaspard in The Lady of Lyons in replying to Claude's entreaty to pardon the blows which he had received in his service: 'Bloze! Melnotte, Bloze! Bloze!' instead of the traditional 'Balows! Melnotte, Balows! Balows!' Without further preface Mr Sparbrook began:

'Mr Hupple mentioned that in that memorable journey across the flooded Bayou Pierre a certain confession was made. May I ask if that was done in your hearing?' Considerable curiosity was manifested, and the faces of all were turned towards the Second Low Comedian, awaiting his reply. After a pause it came with a certain reluctance:

'Yes, more than one of us did hear the confession. No one seemed to mind it at the time; but there was a painful result. There were few words, but they meant much. We didn't ever see them speaking to each other after that, but when that tour ended they both resigned, and I never saw either of them again. Someone told me that they had both given up the stage! I'd like to know how you came to know of it. There was a sort of understanding amongst those of us who saw the scene and heard what was said that we wouldn't ever speak of it. I've never done so from that time to this.'

'Was he a tall, well-featured man, with clustering grey hair?'

'It was black then; as black as Bones's! I beg your pardon, old man' – this to the Tragedian. The Young Man continued:

'And was she handsome and somewhat aquiline? A fine woman with a presence, and thick white hair, and grey eyes like stars?'

'She had beautiful grey eyes as big and bright as lamps, but her hair was golden. They were the handsomest young couple I think I ever saw; and up to that time I believe they simply doted on each other. I tell you it was a grief to us all what happened that journey.' The Young Man said very gravely:

'If we knew everything, as the Almighty knows it, perhaps we should regret some things more than we do, and others less. I only guessed that Bayou Pierre was the scene of that confession; the other end of the story comes from across the world.' There was a shiver of expectation from all. Here was a good story that seemed to have a living interest. A stillness, as marked as that of the falling snow without, reigned in the car.

At Last

'When I was young - I'm not very old yet, but I was very young then, and it all seems long ago - I made an ass of myself. It wasn't very bad, not criminal; but I was pretty well ashamed of it, for my people were of high rank and held a great position in the county. When I came back I was afraid to tell the girl I was engaged to. She was a clever girl, and she knew by a sort of instinct that there was something, and asked me what it was. I denied that there was anything. That did for me, for I knew she was clean grit, and that she would have the truth or nothing, and as I didn't want to tell her I was a liar as well as an ass, I shoved for Australia. What I did there doesn't concern you much, and it was pretty tame, anyhow. I only mention this that you may understand something later. I had been a medical student, and liked the work so well that I have had a sneaking fondness for everything connected with it ever since. On the ship I went out on was a nurse, who was going out as an assistant matron to one of the Melbourne hospitals. She was a young woman, but with white hair; and she used to come down to the steerage - where I was - and try to be of service. I had become a kind of volunteer help to the doctor, who recognised that I had been a gentleman - you are not much of a gentleman in a steerage, I can tell you - and made things a little comfortable for me in several ways. By being about with him I met the nurse, and we became very good friends. She was very sympathetic, and knew pretty well that I was sore-hearted about something; and with the natural sweet helpfulness of a woman - God bless 'em! - soon got to know my secret. One night - I shall never forget it, a heavy, still night with the moon a blaze of gold over the silent sea - we sat out late, right over the screw, which ground away beneath us but disturbed us no more than the ticking of a clock. The mystery of the place, and the hunger for sympathy which always gnawed at my soul, got the better of me, and I opened my heart as I have never done before or since. When I stopped I saw that her great eyes were gleaming out over the sea, and the tears were rolling down her cheeks. She turned to me and took my hand between both of hers and said:

'"Oh! why didn't you tell her all? She would have forgiven all - everything, and would have loved you better for it all your life long. It is the concealment that hurts! Noble natures feel it most. I know, I know it too well, out of the bitterness of my broken heart!" I saw here a sorrow far greater than my own, and tried to comfort her. It seemed a relief to her, as it had been to me, to speak of her trouble, and I encouraged her confidence. She told me that in her youth she had run away with a man whom she thought she loved; they were married at a registry, but after a while she found out that he was married already. She wanted to leave him then at once, but he terrorised her, threatening to kill her if she tried to leave him. So she had perforce to remain with him till, happily, he met with a fatal accident and she was free. Then her baby was born dead, and she found herself alone.'

Here there was an interruption on the part of the Sewing Woman, who remarked sotto voce:

'He's a-tykin' of my Dead Byby, too!'

'Hush! hush!' said the MC. And the Young Man went on:

'She changed her name, and after trying work of several kinds, found her way on the stage. There she fell in love, in real love, with a man she honoured; and when she found that he loved her too, she was afraid to tell him the dark chapter of her life lest she should lose him. She thought that as it was all past, and as no trace remained, no one need ever know. She was married and was ideally happy, and, after a couple of years, which had brought them a daughter, towards the end of a certain tour was on her way home where she would see her little baby daughter again, when in a time of great peril, when everyone round her was making confession of all they had ever done wrong, she was drawn into the hysterical whirlpool, and told her husband all that had been. He seemed cut to the heart, but said very little - not a word of reproach. Then she, too, felt constrained to silence, and a barrier seemed to grow up between them, so that when they reached England - home was a name only, and not a reality - they did not seem able to speak freely; and it became apparent to both that nothing remained but to separate. He had wished to take the child, and when the subject was mooted, said he wanted to take her far away where she would never know what had been. "Oh, I loved him so," she wailed, "that I felt that all I could give him was my child. The baby when she grew up would never know her mother's shame. It was a bitter atonement for my deceit; but it was all I could do. Perhaps God will account it to me and my child and the husband that I love, and somehow turn it to usefulness in His good time."

'Well, I comforted her as well as I could, though there was not much comfort to her in the world, poor soul, separated from her husband, whom she still loved, and from their child. We became fast friends, and we often wrote to each other; and in all my wanderings I kept her informed of my whereabouts.

'I went up-country herding,' and after a weary, weary time on

'The bitter road the younger son must tread
Ere he win to hearth and saddle of his own,
Mid the riot of the shearers in the shed
In the silence of the herder's hut alone,'

I found my way to a lonely place on the edge of a creek. It was a lovely spot, and the man who owned it had evidently given time and care to its beautifying, for all the natural trees and flowers were used to the best advantage, and it was a delight to see growing with the added luxuriance of a new soil all the home flowers as well. My employer, Mr Macrae, was a crank in some ways, but he was a gentleman, and he made my life a very different one from what it had been in my stock-keeping apprenticeship. He, too, soon recognised that I had been a gentleman, and took me into the house instead of letting me camp outside in a rough shed, as is the usual thing with hired hands. Oh! the comfort and luxury of being in a real house with real bedding and real food, after a bunk and damper of your own making. Mr Macrae was very kindly, but stern on certain points. He simply idolised his little daughter, a bright, pretty child with golden hair and big grey eyes that I seemed, when I saw them, to have known all my life. The sun seemed to the father to rise and set in the child; but even to her he could be stern, even cruel, to an extent I never saw equalled. One night after dinner the little thing was nestling up to him and playing with him in her usual coaxing way. He asked her some little question, and she fenced with the answer. This seemed all at once to make him stern, and he asked some more questions with a fierce gravity which frightened the child. She attempted playfulness as a weapon against wrath, as a woman does; but the father would have none of it. He brushed it aside and continued his inquisition. It was quite apparent to me that the child had little or nothing to conceal, but she was frightened, and in her fear yielded to the weakness of the woman within her and lied. It was a harmless little lie at worst, one rather of not telling the truth than of speaking falsely; but it seemed to inflame the father to a white heat. His eyes glowed with the intensity of his anger. He mastered himself, however, and his cold anger was infinitely worse than his hot. He took the child very tenderly in his arms and said:

'"Little one, you know that I love you?"

'"Yes, daddy!" came the pretty voice, in a flood of tears.

'"And you know I wouldn't hurt you but for your good, darling?"

'"Yes, daddy! But, oh, daddy, daddy, don't hurt me! - don't hurt me!"

'"I must, my little one, I must! You will have to remember all your life what it is to lie; that fire on earth or in hell is the liar's portion. And it is better that you learn it now than suffer it hereafter and make others suffer!" He bent down towards the fire, holding her hand in his; her pitiful little struggles were as nothing in his powerful grasp. Seeing me instinctively draw near, for I thought to protect the child, he motioned me back gravely.

'"Do not interfere. It is necessary that my child learn a little lesson to save her a harder one later on."

'With an iron determination, and with lips set and growing white as snow, he put for a moment the rosy fingers of the child on the hot bar of the grate. Despite her shriek of pain, he held it there quite a second or two, and then drew her back almost fainting. The child loved and trusted him in spite of the cruel act, and clung to him, sobbing as if her little heart would break. He held her close to him, and then disengaged her arm very gently from his neck. He stepped closer to the fire, and saying to her: "See, little one, you have no pain that is not mine!" thrust his own right hand down into the very heart of the glowing fire. He held it there a few seconds without a quiver, whilst fine child shrieked and flew to him and dragged the hand away.

"'Oh, daddy, daddy, daddy!" she wailed, "and I have by my lying made you suffer this!" As I am a living man, I saw a glad light flash into his eyes, though the pain he suffered must have been excruciating. With his other hand he stroked the child's golden locks as he said:

"'It was worth pain, my little one, that you should learn so great a truth."

'I could not but be silent in face of such a splendid heroism, and offered to use such medical knowledge as I possessed on his behalf. He accepted cheerfully, and when I had got oil and lint he made me dress the child's burn before allowing me to attend to his own. It was a bad burn, and I was in real fear that it might have an ill ending. He made light of it, however, and tried to keep up the child's spirits. I tried to help him, and she went to bed less unhappy than I expected. Macrae's strength and constitution stood to him, and, though the hand was badly scarred, he fully recovered its use.

'That night he was so feverish that I insisted on sitting up with him. I was able to give him some ease, and he was grateful for it. He talked with me more freely than he had ever done. He insisted on going several times to see how the child slept. He came back after one of these visits with his eyes wet, and as he lay down on his bed said softly:

"'Poor little mite! God forgive me if I was wrong; but I thought it best!" Then turning to me, he went on:

"'I suppose you thought me not merely brutal, but fiendish. But if you knew how deeply for her own future happiness I value truth, you would perhaps be tolerant with me. It was a lie that ruined her mother's life and my own; and I would guard her against such an evil. Her mother and I loved each other, and there seemed no flaw in our lives; but once when in danger of death as we were rushing through a seething flood, she confessed to me that the innocence which had charmed me at the first was but an acted lie; that she had loved another man before she had seen me, and had lived with him guiltily. But, there! that page of my life is closed for ever." He said no more, and, of course, I never referred to the subject again. It struck me afterwards as strange that two people whom I had met had each suffered from a similar cause - as I myself had suffered - but it never struck me to connect them.

'After that night we became better friends, for we seemed to understand each other. I grew to love the child almost as much as if she had been my own daughter. During all that time I worked hard, and had few distractions; but I promised myself a treat when I should go over to Warrow, the nearest town beyond the Creek, for I had heard from Nurse Dora that she had become matron of the hospital there. The time which I had promised myself for my holiday was at hand, when little Dora fell ill of a fever. The white woman who was with us got it at the same time, and Macrae and I had to do the nursing ourselves. The floods were out, and the Creels was like a sea; the natives, seeing a fever in the house, ran away. It was a quick fever, though a low one, and in a few days the woman died. The child got worse and worse, and her moaning was pitiful to hear. The father used to sit hour after hour with his head in his hands and groan. One evening I heard him say that if we had a woman to nurse her she might be saved; and this gave me an idea. I said nothing except that I was going out for a bit, for my mind was made up that I would try to fetch my friend the matron. I took my mare, Wild Meg, and swam the flooded Creek; and early in the morning, riding for all I was worth, fetched up at Warrow. I went to the hospital and asked for the matron. When she came my heart leaped, and something within me seemed to cry out. It was as though two ends of an electric current were come together. Little Dora's fever-wasted face, as I had seen it the night before on the pillow, was reproduced in the pale lineaments of her who stood before me. I understood it all now. The man with the story; the woman with the story; the child parted from the mother; the mother who lied! Heaven had sent at the moment me, who, coming across the world, held in his hand the two ends of this chain of destiny. I told her of the child who was ill, dying; she wept, but said her duty held her to her post. Then I described the child and the solitary man, and a quick light leaped to her eyes. Hope had dawned in that withered heart! She said not a word, but with a gesture to me to wait, disappeared behind the hospital. In a minute she reappeared, leading by the bridle a magnificent roan horse.

'"Come!" she said, and sprang to the saddle.

'We rode all day without a word. Late in the afternoon we struck the creek, just as a thunderstorm came on, which in a moment lashed the flood into a raging torrent. But nothing daunted her. She rode boldly into the water, I following, and together we battled the watery element. Through danger and toil we won the further shore, though our two gallant steeds fell dead within sight of the house. We hurried in, she leading, I following. When she stood in the doorway Macrae rose to his feet with a wild cry:

"Dora, Dora, my darling, come at last! Now the child must live!" Then he fell fainting on the floor.'

Mr Sparbrook paused and looked round. Some of the womenkind were wiping their eyes, and sniffed, their bosoms heaving. Some office men said 'Hear! hear!' feebly. The only audible remark was the comment of the Wardrobe Mistress:

'Mr Bloze is a-goin' of it this evening. He'll be a-puttin' of it into a ply. Him in Australiar! W'y, I've known 'im since 'e was a nipper, which 'is mother 'ad a puddin' shop at Ipswich close along of the theyatre, an' 'e never was hout of England in 'is life!'

'You're next on the list,' said the MC to the Second Heavies, Mr Hemans, who was sipping his hot grog with a preternaturally solemn look and manner.

'I know it, alas! I pity you all; but duty must be done. I suppose it is not necessary that I wander into the fields of romance?' - this with a covert look at the last story-teller.

'You give us fact, old man!' said the MC. 'After the heroics, a little sordid realism won't come amiss. If you could manage to tell us something funny we should all be grateful.'

'Anything in the shape of a Dead Byby?' he asked, with his face for one instant illumined by a humorous twinkle in his eye.

'Lydies and gents, not forgettin' of you, Mr Benville Nonplusser, sir, whenever ye likes I'm ready to go on with the 'arrowin' tyle of the Dead Byby what I eluded to before if - 'She was cut short by the Second Heavies, who had no intention of being 'queered' at the start by this species of realism:

'No dead babies in mine, thank you; but I was going to tell you of a somewhat humorous episode of a live baby - I may say a very-much-alive baby, '

'Hear! hear!' 'Silence!' 'Hus-s-sh!'

'Next!' said the MC to the Second Heavies, who was ready to begin:

'Some of you may perhaps know that I was not always an actor! That I am not one even now,' he added quickly, seeing the Tragedian take his pipe from his lips preparatory to making a caustic comment. 'Having had aspirations towards the stage, and in especial towards high tragedy, I naturally became a commercial traveller, for I thought that self-possession and sheer, unadulterated, unmitigated impudence were the qualities which I ought to cultivate most assiduously!'

'Look here,' said the Tragedian, half rising from his seat. Seeing, however, no sympathy in the faces of the Company, he sat down again and smoked hard. The Second Heavies went on:

'From that I graduated into the undertaking business, for I soon saw that lugubriousness was a still more important item of stock-in-trade if my ambition was ever to be materialised. It was strange, however, that in neither branch of tragic art did I succeed. The clients considered me as a "drummer" too solemn, and suspected a levity of manner superimposed upon a lugubriety of appearance. I found the greater centres of civilisation slow to compete for my mature efforts. So, crossing the seas, I gradually drifted towards the Setting Sun, earning for a time a precarious livelihood by drumming in the neighbourhood of the Black Mountains a new "Curative Compound" calculated to obviate equally the ravages of sunstroke or frost-bite.

Chin Music

'One night we were journeying in the west of the Rockies over a road bed which threatened to jerk out our teeth with every loosely-laid sleeper on the line.

'Travelling in that part of the world, certainly in the days I speak of, was pretty hard. The travellers were mostly men, all over-worked, all over-anxious, and intolerant of anything which hindered their work or interfered with the measure of their repose. In night journeys the berths in the sleeping cars were made up early, and as all the night trains were sleeping cars, the only thing to be done was to turn in at once and try and sleep away the time. As most of us were tired out with the day's work, the arrangement suited everybody.

'The weather was harsh; sneezing and coughing was the order of the day. This made the people in the sleeper, all men, irritable: all the more that as most of them were contributing to the general chorus of sounds coming muffled through quilts and curtains, it was impossible to single out any special offender for general execration. After a while, however, the change of posture from standing or sitting to lying down began to have some kind of soothing effect, and new sounds of occasional snoring began to vary the monotony of irritation. Presently the train stopped at a way station; then ensued a prolonged spell of shunting backwards and forwards with the uncertainty of jerkiness which is so peculiarly disturbing to imperfect sleep; and then two newcomers entered the sleeper, a man and a baby. The baby was young, quite young enough to be defiantly ignorant and intolerant of all rules and regulations regarding the common good. It played for its own hand alone, and as it was extremely angry and gifted with exceptionally powerful lungs, the fact of its presence and its emotional condition, even though the latter afforded a mystery as to its cause, were immediately apparent. The snoring ceased, and its place was taken by muttered grunts and growls; the coughing seemed to increase with the renewed irritation, and everywhere was the rustling of ill-at-ease and impotent humanity. Curtains were pulled angrily aside, the rings shrieking viciously on the brass rods, and faces with bent brows and gleaming eyes and hardening mouths glared savagely at the intruder on our quiet, for so we now had tardily come to consider by comparison him and it. The newcomer did not seem to take the least notice of anything, but went on in a stolid way trying to quiet the child, shifting it from one arm to the other, dandling it up and down, and rocking it sideways.

'I took considerable amusement, myself, from the annoyance of my fellow-passengers. I had no cold myself, and so had been worried by their discomforting sounds; besides, I had come to the car from a dinner with clients, where the wine of the country had circulated with quite sufficient freedom. When a man has a large family - I regret to say that at that time my first wife was nursing her seventh - he acquires a certain indifference to infantile querulousness. As a matter of fact, he does not feel sympathy with the child at all, his pity being reserved for other people.

'All babies are malignant; the natural wickedness of man, as elaborated at the primeval curse, seems to find an unadulterated effect in their expressions of feeling.

'I confess that the sight of a child crying, and especially crying angrily - unless, of course, it disturbs me in anything I may be doing - affords me a pleasure which is at once philosophi-cal,humorous, contemplative, reminiscent and speculative.'

'Oh, Mr Hemans, how horrid you are to say such things!' said the Leading Lady. 'You know you don't think anything of the kind. There's no one who loves little children better than you do, or who is so considerate to them!' He made no reply, but only held up a hand in protest, smiling sweetly as he resumed:

'This baby was a peculiarly fine specimen of its class. It seemed to have no compunction whatever, no parental respect, no natural affection, no mitigation in the natural virulence of its rancour. It screamed, it roared, it squalled, it bellowed. The root ideas of profanity, of obscenity, of blasphemy were mingled in its tone. It beat with clenched fist its father's face, it clawed at his eyes with twitching fingers, it used its head as an engine with which to buffet him. It kicked, it struggled, it wriggled, it writhed, it twisted itself into serpentine convolutions, till every now and then, what with its vocal and muscular exertions, it threatened to get black in the face. All the time the stolid father simply tried to keep it quiet with eternal changes of posture and with whispered words, "There, now, pet!" "Hush! lie still, little one." "Rest, dear one, rest!" He was a big, lanky, patient-looking, angular man with great rough hands and enormous feet, which he shifted about as he spoke; so that man and child together seemed eternally restless.

'The thing appeared to have a sort of fascination for most of the men in the car. The curtains of a lot of berths were opened, and a lot of heads appeared, all scowling. I chuckled softly to myself, and tried to conceal my merriment, lest I should spoil the fun. No one said anything for a long time, till at last one wild-eyed, swarthy, long-bearded individual, who somehow looked like a Mormon Elder, said:

"'Say, mister! What kind of howling-piece is it you have got there? Have none of you boys got a gun?"

'There came from the bunks a regular chorus of acquiescence: "The durned thing had ought to be killed!"

"'Beats prairie dogs in full moon!"

"'When I woke up with it howlin', thought I had got 'em again."

"'Never mind, boys, it may be a blessin' in disguise. Somethin' bad is comin' to us on this trip, an' arter this 'twill be easy work to die!"

'The man spoke up:

"'I'm sorry, gentlemen, if she incommodes you!" The words were so manifestly inadequate that there was a roar of laughter which seemed to shake the car. West of the Mississippi things are, or at any rate they used to be, a bit rough, and ideas followed suit. Laughter, when it came, was rough and coarse, and on this occasion even the lanky man seemed to feel it. He only tried to hold the child closer to him, as if to shield it from the hail of ironical chaff which followed.

"'Incommode us! Oh, not at all. It's the most soothing concourse of sweet sounds I ever heard."

"'Bully for baby syrups!"

"'Pray, don't let us disturb the concert with our sleeping."

"'Jerk us out a little more chin-music!"

"'There's no place like home with a baby in it."

'Just opposite where the man moved restlessly with the child was the bunk of a young giant whom I had noticed turning in earlier in the evening. He had not seemed to have noticed the disturbance, but now his curtains were thrust aside fiercely and he appeared, lifting himself on one elbow, and he asked in an angry tone:

"'Say you, where's its mother, anyhow?" The man replied in a low, weary tone, without looking round:

"'She's in the baggage-car, sir - in her coffin!"

'Well, you could have heard the silence that came over all the men. The baby's screaming and the rush, and roar, and rattle of the train seemed unnatural breakers of the profound stillness. In an instant the young man, clad only in his under-flannels, was out on the floor and close to the man.

"'Say, stranger," he said, "if I'd knowed that, I'd a bit my tongue out afore I'd 'a spoke! An' now I look at you, my poor fellow, I see you're most wore out! Here, give me the child, and you turn into my bunk an' rest. No! you needn't be afeered" - for he saw the father shrink away a little and hold the child closer. "I'm one of a big family, an' I've nursed the baby often. Give her over! I'll take care of her, an' I'll talk to the conductor, and we'll see that you're called when the time comes." He put out his great hands and lifted the little one, the father resigning her to his care without a word. He held her in one arm whilst with the other he helped the newcomer into his empty berth.

'Strange to say, the child made no more struggle. It may have been that the young blood or the young flesh gave something of the warmth and softness of the mother's breast which it missed, or that the fresh, young nerves soothed where the worn nerves of the sorrowing man had only irritated; but, with a peaceful sigh, the little one leaned over, let its head fall on the young man's shoulder, and seemingly in an instant was fast asleep.

'And all night long, up and down, up and down, in his stockinged feet, softly marched the flannel-clad young giant, with the baby asleep on his breast, whilst in his bunk the tired, sorrow-stricken father slept - and forgot.'

There was a long pause, with here and there a sniffle, whilst down the faces of many the tears trickled. The first to speak was the Leading Lady. Her face was as a masque of tender feeling, and the yearning of her voice went straight to every heart:

'That mother's body may have been far distant from where her baby and her husband slept, but somehow I think that her soul was not very far away.'

Again there was a long pause, broken by the Low Comedian:

'So that's what you call a funny story! A pretty bally funny story it is, to make us feel like this. Look at me!' His eyes were all blurred with crying. The next remark was made by the Sewing-Woman, a question asked with much anxiety:

'Did the Byby die, sir?'

And then everyone else in the saloon burst into a roar of laughter; the pent-up feelings of all had found a vent. The Second Heavies looked around with a complacent smile on his solemn face as he remarked:

'If it wasn't funny, what in thunder are you all laughing at?'

'I think you are next, my dear,' said the MC to the Singing Chambermaid.

'Oh, I do wish someone would go on for me,' she protested with a pretty embarrassment, or what was an excellent assumption of the same. 'I do feel so bashful!'

'That being a condition antecedent to soubrette success!' interrupted the Tragedian. She smiled at him with a helpless little simper, and went on:

'Couldn't you give my understudy a chance?'

'Not me!' answered the latter quickly, 'I don't mind winging a part when there's an accident; but you had your part in good time, and now, if you're not letter-perfect, you must do your own fluffing!'

'Quite right, too!' said the Prompter, who was not, as a rule, attached to understudies. The Manager nodded approval, so the Singing Chambermaid, with an appealing look round the Company, went on:

A Deputy Waiter

'When I began my career, I was ambitious to shine upon the lyric stage - no, sir! not in Shaftesbury Avenue.' The interpolation was in answer to the Tragedian's again removing his pipe from his lips, preparatory to some effort of biting sarcasm. I intended Grand Opera, the whole big thing. I didn't take much stock of Comedy in those days. Indeed, I thought Comedy was vulgar!' Here there was an approving grunt from the Tragedian. Without turning to him she went on:

'As vulgar as tragedy was ridiculous! You needn't laugh, boys and girls - that was when I was young - very young; I know better about both things now.

'Well, they said at the Conservatoire in Paris that I might succeed if a something-or-other happened to my throat, and that in such case I would be a star, for my voice would be abnormally high. However, the something-or-other didn't come off, and I had to look for success in a different way. I didn't know at that time that I had latent those gifts of Comedy and humour which have since then lifted me to my present height in my career. This is all nothing, however; it is only to explain how I came to be an intimate friend of the great cantatrice, Helda, who was a class-fellow of my own. She went up like a rocket, if you like; and the stick never fell till it fell into her grave! In all her success she never forgot me, and whenever she knew I was in the same town, or near it, she always had me to come and stay with her. It was sometimes a nice change for me, too, for things were up-and-down with me. She was a good creature, and was able to take, in a lordly sort of way, all the honours that were showered upon her. But they must have oppressed her now and again; for when I would come to her she would love to pretend that I was the great star, and would make me sit opposite her at dinner, or at supper after the play, when we were alone, all hung over with the magnificent jewels that Kings and Queens had given her. I liked it all at first, but after a few years, when the hollowness of the world had been burned into me, I began to feel it in my inmost heart as a bitter sort of mockery. Of course, I wouldn't have let her know my feeling for the world, for it would have cut her to the quick; so there was never any change, and the old girlish game went on to the end.

'It was when I was with her in Chicago that I had an adventure of an odd kind. Some of you may have heard of it?'

She looked round interrogatively; the silence was broken by the voice of the Tragedian:

'They've forgotten it, my dear, those who haven't become doddery since then!'

'Bones, when you counter, even a woman, you shouldn't hit below the belt!' said one of the young men, who had been at Oxford. The Tragedian glared at him, the appalling impudence of the youngster, who looked angry, and seemed to mean what he said, being unprecedented. A Young Man to put a Tragedian to rights! Of all the -! He felt, however, that he was in the wrong, and remained silent, waiting. The Singing Chambermaid looked saucily round her; but there was a tremble in the curl of her lips, and a furtive dimness as of unshed tears in her eyes. The blow had told. She went on:

'It is long ago; there is no denying that! But it seems to me all as clear as if it were yesterday! There was I, all alone, in Helda's flat. It was in the Annexe, where there are suites of rooms with an outer door on the corridor with a regular latch-key. Helda was singing in Fidelio, and her maids were with her. I had stayed at home, because I was "under the weather," to use an Americanism, and I wasn't in The Fatal Legacy, which our company was giving that night at McVicker's. I was lying back in a comfortable chair, half dozing, when I heard the door open with a latch-key. I didn't turn round, for there was a special waiter who attended each suite, and I thought he had come to ask if I wished for coffee, as he usually did about that time when we were at home. It seemed as if at the same time the housemaid had gone in to make up the bedrooms. He did not speak to me as usual, so I said sleepily:

'"Fritz." There was no answer.

"'I think, Fritz,' I said, 'I would like a cup of tea to-night, instead of coffee.' He still said nothing, so I looked round, and saw that it was a strange waiter. 'Oh,' I said, 'I thought it was Fritz. Where is he?' The man answered me with perfect politeness:

"'He has gone out, madam! This is his night off, but I am to take his place.'

"'Then,' I said, 'will you kindly bring my tea as soon as you can. I have a headache, and it may do it good.' I sank back in my chair again. I did not hear him go out, so I looked round and said: 'Do pray make haste,' for his waiting irritated me. He had not stirred, but stood there looking at me fixedly. I began to feel a bit frightened, for there was, I thought, a wild look in his eyes as of a man hunted or desperate. In Helda's room I heard the rustle of the chambermaids at their work. I rose quickly and went towards the door, intending to join them and then get somebody else sent up instead of the new waiter, who was, I had by this time settled in my mind, mad. Just, however, as my hand was on the door-knob, a voice behind me, thin and keen, said in a fierce whisper:

"'Stop!' I turned round and looked straight into the muzzle of a revolver pointed at my head. For an instant I was too paralysed to scream out, and then I felt that the only way to deal with a madman was to be calm and cool. Let me tell you, however, that being calm and cool under certain conditions is no easy task. I would just then have given my year's salary to have been able to have appeared hot and flustered. The voice came again:

"'Sit there! His hand pointed to the piano stool. I sat down. Again came the voice:

"'I know you; you are a Singing Chambermaid! Sing!'

'In the midst of all my trouble it was some comfort to find my professional abilities recognised, even by a lunatic. When I looked at him to ask what I should sing, I saw his eyes roll horribly. I thought it better not to ask questions, so I started at once my great song, 'George's Kiss is not like Daddy's,' which I had rendered famous in the Farce-Comedy, From the West. At first he did not seem to like it. Some of you may have heard it - of course, in your extreme youth' - this with a reproachful look at the Tragedian. 'It begins wonderingly, and then works up and up with each verse. It is a song that has to be acted, and in those days I used to finish the refrain with a high note, a sort of suggestion of sudden surprise as one gives at an unexpected pinch. The 'Inter-ocean' called it 'Miss Pescod's yelp.' The boys in the gallery used to take it up, and the latter verses were always chorused by the audience.

'My lunatic friend had evidently not heard the song, though I had been singing it three times a week in Chicago for a whole month, so I guessed that, as he knew me as an actress, he must have seen me in some other town. He entered into the spirit of the thing, however, and when he heard the end of the first verse his face relaxed, and he cried, 'Hear! Hear!' Thenceforward he made me sing the refrain of every verse over several times, and joined in the chorus himself. He seemed to be satisfied with my complaisance, for though he held the revolver in his hand, he did not keep it pointed at me.

'In the middle of one of the verses the door from the bedroom opened very slightly and so softly that, had I not seen it, I should not have known; the maids were evidently listening. This was my chance; I called out imperatively and sharply:

"'Come in!'

'The door was instantly shut - so quickly that this time it sounded loudly; at the same instant the muzzle of the revolver rose and covered me.

"'Silence!' came the fierce whisper. 'This treat is for me alone! It is deah to someone if it be shared!' I tried to go on singing, but the sudden terror was too much for me. I put my hands to my forehead to steady myself. At that instant I heard the lintel of the outer door click; the maids had evidently gone.

'I looked up at the waiter. He was grinning with a savage delight; and as I was now quite powerless, I sank to the floor. He said, with his eyes rolling:

"'Mine alone! All for me now! All the entrancing delight of music from a Master voice! Then he pointed the revolver at me, saying:

"'Get up, Singing Chambermaid! Sing! Sing to me! Sing for your life!'

'It is astonishing what a restorative a revolver, properly used, can be. I don't know but that when I have a theatre of my own I won't present one to my Stage Manager. It would be a prompt and admirable help!'

'Hear! Hear!' said the Stage Manager enthusiastically. She resumed:

'Well, I got up quickly and went on with the song just where I had left off. It didn't do to have any fooling around under the circumstances. I sang for all I was worth, and the lunatic joined in the chorus with a gleeful zest which was bewildering. I would like to have scratched him!

'When he had encored the whole song twice, I began to get tired. It was no joke to me; and if it hadn't seemed really a matter of life and death, I couldn't have gone on. When I made a protest, he scowled at me, and his hand rose with the revolver. After a moment's thought he said:

'"You can have five minutes' rest from singing, but you must go on playing."

'I began to play. I thought some merry tune might soothe him, and I started into a Scotch reel. The effect was so far good that he began to snap his fingers and to keep time with his feet. All the time my brain was working, and it flashed across me that if I could move him thus to my will with music, I might be able to devise some means to rid myself of him. There was so much of hope in the thought that it almost overcame me, and I began to laugh. The instant my hands stopped, his moved, and the revolver rose again.

'"Play up, or you're lost!" came the peremptory whisper.

'Nature is nature, and necessity is necessity, and I suppose that hysterics is the result of the struggle between them. Anyhow, I kept playing away at the reel, and all the time rolling on the piano stool with laughing. Presently I was recalled by a peremptory word:

'"Time!" I looked round; the revolver still covered me. He went on:

'"The five minutes is up! Singing Chambermaid, do your work! Follow your vocation! Exercise your calling! Practise your art! Sing!"

'"What shall I sing?" I asked in desperation. His face wore a sardonic smile as he replied:

'"Sing the same song again. You will have time to think of something else whilst you are singing it!"

'I began the song again. I used to think it very funny, and full of a sort of quaint plaintiveness, but now it seemed only a mass of distressing rubbish - false sentiment, indelicate, inane. From that hour I could never sing it without a nauseating sense of humiliation.'

'Hear! Hear!' said the Tragedian, but drew back under the fierce 'Hsh' of the Company. The Singing Chambermaid looked at him reproachfully, and went on:

'Presently my lunatic waiter drew close to me, and whispered:

'"Don't stop! If you pause a moment you are a dead woman. Here is Fritz; I hear his footsteps." He must have had wonderful ears, I thought; but that is the way of madness. "When he opens the door, tell him that you are practising some songs, and don't want to be disturbed. Remember, I am watching you! If you even falter, your life and his are forfeit! I am desperate! The music is mine alone, and alone I will have it!" He withdrew to the bedroom, leaving the door slightly open. He could not be seen from the outer door, but he could see me. And I could see him, with his revolver pointed at my head, and a set, vindictive, threatening scowl upon his evil face. I knew that he would kill me if I did not do as he wished, so when Fritz opened the door, I called to him as complacently as I could - there is some use in stage training:

'I am practising, Fritz, and do not wish to be disturbed. I shall want nothing till Madame comes in.'

'"Goot!" said the pleasant Fritz, and he at once withdrew.

'Then my mad friend came out from the room, and said, showing his teeth with a grim smile:

'"You showed your nerve and your wisdom, Singing Chambermaid; now sing!"

'Well, I sang, and sang, and sang all the songs I could think of, till I grew so weary that I could hardly sit erect; and my brain began to reel. The maniac then began to grow more desperate. As I grew fainter he levelled his pistol at me and forced me to go on from very fear of death.

His face began to twitch, his eyes to roll horribly, and his mouth to work convulsively as he called, in a fierce whisper:

'"Go on. Sing! Sing! Faster! Faster! Faster!"

'He made me go faster and faster still, beating time with the revolver, till my breath began to go. I held on in mortal fear till even sheer terror could no longer uphold me. The last thing I saw as I fell senseless from the stool was his scowling face and the bobbing muzzle of the revolver as he called, "Faster! Faster!"

'The next thing I remember is hearing Helda's voice, seemingly coming from a great distance. I recognised the tone before I heard the words, but things grew clearer and clearer, and at last I knew that it was her hands which held my head up. Then I heard distinctly the words she said:

'"Oh, don't bother! What does it matter? I would rather see her her dear self than all the jewels in Christendom!" Then came a gruff, strong voice:

'"But, look here, ma'am. Time is everything now! We can't begin till we get some kind of clue. Do you just tell us what you know; we'll do the rest.' She answered impatiently:

'"I really know nothing, except what I've told you already. I came in after the Opera, and found her here in a dead faint. Perhaps, when she regains her consciousness, she will be able to tell us something." Then came the strong voice again:

'"And you, Fritz Darmstetter, have you no more to say than this: 'I came several times during the evening, and heard her singing, generally the same song over and over again. Something about George and Daddy. When, at last, I opened the door, she told me to go away, as she was practising, and did not want to be disturbed. She would not want anything till Madame came"?'

'"Dat is so!" Here I seemed to become awake. I opened my eyes, and when I saw my dear Helda close to me, I clung to her and implored her to protect me. She promised me that she would. Then, somewhat reassured, I looked round and saw myself surrounded with a crowd. At one side was a row of gigantic policemen, with a still more gigantic inspector standing in front of them; on the other side were a lot of the hotel servants, male and female, and Helda's maids, who were wringing their hands. One of the policemen carried Helda's Russia-leather jewel-case with the lid wrenched off. When the Inspector saw my eyes open he stooped and, with a sweep of his arm, lifted me to my feet.

'"Now," he said in a commanding voice, "now, young lady, tell me what you know!"

'I suppose we women know a man's voice when we hear it, and we, or our mothers before us, have learned to obey, so I spoke out instinctively:

'"The lunatic came in and pointed a revolver at me, and made me sing all the evening till I fell down with fatigue!"

'"What was he like, miss?" asked the giant Inspector in an imperative voice.

'"He was thin," I answered. "He had dark whiskers and a shaven upper lip, and his eyes rolled!" Then I proceeded to tell him all I knew of the lunatic's strange proceedings.

'As I spoke, there came a queer sort of grin on the faces of the policemen; the Inspector seemed to voice their sentiments as he said:

'"Well, ma'am, this case is pretty clever. Guess its Dimeshow Pete this time. The old man has fooled us all. He seems to have been tarnation clever over it! That was a cute scheme of his to make the young woman sing over and over again the same song with the high note, like as she was practising, whilst his confederates got off with the swag. Guess they're off on the Lake Shore special hours ago, and he's gone on the Flyer, and has jumped at Lake. Pete's a peach! He's been too many for us this time, but I reckon we'll chalk it up to him agin the time comes!"'

For some little time the eyes of the Company had been gradually focussing the Tragedian, who was next in order. He had himself shown to experienced eyes a certain uneasiness, though he tried with all the wile of his craft to disguise it in a mantle of degage self-possession.

When the last speaker had completely finished - this, his auditory being actors, being when the applause had entirely ceased and the opportunity for encore or recall had come and gone - the MC spoke:

'Now, Mr Dovercourt, we hope for the honour of hearing from you!' There was an immediate chorus from all the Company, the Manager being bland - not exactly patronising, but striking an exact mean between condescension and respect - whilst the rest all down the line with an ever-growing serious attention which began with the Low Comedian's companionable deference and ended with the Sewing Woman's self-abasement.

The latter, who through effluxion of time which had put her own literary effort in historical perspective, and influxion of the cup that cheers, felt herself in a halo of imaginative glory, added her tearful request:

'And if I might make so hold, Mr Wragge, seein' as 'ow I may now claim to be myself a sister hartis, though in a numble wy, I would wenture to arsk if you could tell us out of tragic lore some instance of anythink which isn't about a dead byby, which the same belongs to my spear, an'' - this said with an air of vicious determination - 'I means to 'old to my rights, though I be a numble woman what knows her plyce for all the -'

Her eloquence was cut short by the MC, who said, with a stern determination which reached her intelligence through her somewhat clouded faculties:

'That will do, Mrs Wrigglesworth! When your turn comes again we'll call on you, never fear. In the meantime, you must not interrupt anyone else; more especially one whom we all respect and admire so much as we do our Tragedian, the glory of our Company, the pride of our calling, the perfected excellence of our Art. Mr Dovercourt, here is your very good health! Ladies and gentlemen all! in the good old fashion: Hip, Hip, Hurrah!'

The toast was drunk standing, and with a manifest respect on the part of all, which was a really effective tribute to his branch of his Art. Growl as they may, the companions of the Tragedian have always a secret respect, if not for the Man, at least for the Artist.

The Tragedian began:

Work'us

'As my friend Parmentire said earlier in this symposium, the humour is not always to its - ah! professional exponent, the Comedian. It may somewhat mitigate the gloom in which the enactment of my special roles in the greater passions for which opportunity has been given to me - and others - yes, to others - by the Master, Shakespeare, and the galaxy of dramatic, poetic talent which has carried down to our day the torch of tragic thought, if I, in this hour of social communion when, if I may be allowed the expression, the buskin is unlaced and the sock is - ah! somewhat eased, relate to you a somewhat humorous episode of my "hot youth," when, like our dear Prince Hal, I occasionally made the welkin ring in its darker hours before the dawn.

'Looking back over the vista of time, those hours of revelry seem to have left a less effaceable mark on memory than does the whirlwind of jealous passion, or even the soft dalliance of the hours of love.'

'Oh, Mr Dovercourt!' said the Second Lady, putting up her fingers to screen a modest blush. The Tragedian, pleased, went on:

'It is, perhaps, the contrast between my hours within what I may call my art-workshop and those without its pale - what a great writer has called the "irony of things" - which makes my memory cling to little trivial absurdities of days long gone; whilst the same memory has lost sight of many an hour of paramount triumph, snatched from eager humanity even before the very thrones of the Kings of the Earth. Ah, me! those halcyon days which are gone for aye! But "sit still my soul" and "break my heart, for I must hold my tongue." Well, it was when I was in the stock at Wigan, when Hulliford Greenlow controlled the theatrical destinies of that home of the black diamond. A few of us choice spirits were used as a habit to assemble nightly when our work at the theatre was over. Our rendezvous was at the hotel, or rather I should say the public-house, known as "The Merry Maiden." It was in reality but a drinking house; but there were a few bedrooms which were now and again occupied by some overcome reveller. The place, however, had so bad a reputation in the eyes of the police that no one would willingly remain in it after the withdrawal of the extraneous company, unless quite overcome by his libations to Bacchus. Naturally our conversation, if at times pronounced, was bright; and naturally, too, there were at times jokes, both practical and - and - ah - verbal, consonant with the various dispositions of the nightly frequenters of the house. There were a few choice spirits who were outsiders to our habitual galaxy, and efforts were often made by others to penetrate our charmed circle. We were, however, conservative in our tendencies. We cared for none of the guests who were not good company; and the landlord, a genial soul but thoroughly equipped with business instincts, did not care for any company which was devoid of surplus cash. Naturally the more choice spirits amongst us had at times periods of - ah - petrifaction, when, in fact, the ghost had not walked; and at such times we were wont to reap in a practical shape the harvest of which the seed-time had been a certain toleration extended to repetition on the part of some of our eclectic community, and the exercise of some of our histrionic talents in enacting the part of listeners.

'One night we had a strange experience in the shape of a fresh guest. He was a very young man, a weakling and somewhat deformed. In fact, our genial host called our attention at first to his - ah - eccentricity by the humorous way in which he addressed him as "my lord," it being our custom in those days to designate as a nobleman anyone whom Dame Nature had in a malevolent moment inflicted with a curvature of the spine. The youth was ill at ease, but he was so manifestly ambitious to share our revelry, and he was so eager in his appreciation of our merry quips and cranks - the flashing by-play of our intellectual swords - that we decided tacitly to allow him to remain amongst us. Our humorous but business-like host took care that the new-comer's expenditure on the goods of his trade was commensurate with his enjoyment. On further visits of this young nobleman he so harassed him into needless expenditure - an expenditure manifestly ill according to his means, for his garments were poor and worn - that one or two of our duller spirits interfered, and chid our host into a more decorous observance of the economic proprieties. The youth would join us at irregular periods, but seldom a week passed that he did not make his appearance. After a little his shyness wore away, and now and again he ventured to make a remark, generally of an abstruse kind and necessitating for its full understanding an intimate acquaintance with the classics. By this time, too, we had come to know something of the youth's personal surroundings. He was the son of a man who had been a teacher in a school, but who had been killed at a fire whilst he was helping at a rescue. His widow, being penniless, had, of course, to go to the Union, where the boy was brought up. Being a cripple and unable to play or work with other boys, he had been allowed to take advantage of the school, and had read all the books he could get and had taught himself some of the dead languages. When these facts had come to our knowledge, some of our community were not well pleased that he should have come amongst us. There is, Ladies and Gentlemen, a very natural prejudice against the workhouse taint, and some of the high-spirited members of our little coterie resented it. Ourgenial host was one of the most indignant. He was, though himself a man of humble origin, one of very fine feelings, and he said it hurt him, and it hurt his house, to be tainted with any workhouse scum - such was the humorous way in which he expressed himself. "To think," said he, "of his damned impudence, comin' 'ere to my 'ouse - my 'otel - a-spendin' of money while 'is hold mother is a-livin' in the workus, kep' by rates paid by you an' me. I'll let 'im know what I thinks before I've done with 'im." The man who had told us the story set the landlord right upon one point; the old lady was not living in the Union, nor had been for some time. So soon as her son had begun to earn money, which he did, it was said, by writing for papers and magazines, he had taken her out, and they lived together in a tiny house some distance outside the town, where rent was cheap.

'Well, we were discussing the affair, when "lo! and behold you" -'

'My hown words! 'E's a-stealin' of 'em from me!' came from the Sewing Woman, with a snort. 'H-ss-sh!' went round the company.The Tragedian glared, and went on:

'When lo! and behold you, who should come in but the very hunchback himself in a new suit of clothes. We all tried to look as if there was nothing strange; but do what we would, the conversation from that moment on kept about nothing else than the workhouse. Our genial host did not say a word, from which I gathered that he had some deep design. At first the young man coloured up and flushed something painful to see; but presently he went over to the bar and gave an order sotto voce. Then he came back amongst us,and, standing up, said something like this:

'"Gentlemen, I want you all to drink a bowl of punch with me. To-night is a red-letter night with me, and I want you all, good fellows that you are, to let me speak my gratitude to you. For you have done for me more than you perhaps know. You let me come amongst you and share all your fun, and get inspiration from your brilliancy. I feel most keenly all you have just been saying about the workhouse. No one knows better than I know how true it all is. But I owe it something; I owe it much. It sheltered my mother in her trouble, and it sheltered me in my youth. It gave me education, and made thus for me possibilities which I might not otherwise have had. And, indeed, I am grateful to it. But the life there is a barren one at best, and there is little light through its dull, sad shade. I wanted a contrast to this shade of my youth, and I heard someone speak of you fellows and your brighter evenings here. I was earning but little money, but the schooling which my mother and I had gone through made our wants but few, and I was able to save each week the necessary sum to pay my footing here. My dear mother wished it. She used to sit up for me till I returned whenever I came here; and before we went to bed I told her of you all and most of the clever things I had heard. Then out of all your brightness, and with the contrast to what I knew already, I found I could begin the play I had longed to write. You gave me material! You gave me inspiration! You gave me hope! And I wish you could know the depth of gratitude in my heart. My play is to be rehearsed tomorrow at the Crown Theatre in London, and I am to be there to help. I got some little money only yesterday for a story, and you see me in the first good suit of clothes I ever had. I tell you all these things because you have been so good to me that I want you to feel, one and all, how much I owe you. This shirt I wear, my mother made herself and washed and ironed for me; and it touched me when I was coming out to-night when she brought it to me and said: 'My boy, I can't be with you, but I want you to feel that I am near you. Every stitch in this is put in with love and hope, and you must feel it, whether you think of it or not.' It was she who counselled me to come here to-night to thank you all, my good friends; to close worthily the door on the old life, and bring, if I may, into the new life some of the good feeling that you have so freely given me in the old." He appeared moved, and the tears were in his eyes. We all drank his punch, of course; and as it was his punch we had, of course, to drink his health. Then, if you please, our genial host got up and said that he was going to stand a bowl of punch too, so that we might bid our young friend adieu. So we drank his punch also. Then he came and whispered to me to order another bowl of punch. "I'll pay for it. See that his Lordship drinks plenty; I mean to be even with Work'us!" So the whisper went round the jovial spirits that our young friend was to have a skinful. And he had. He was not accustomed to such freedom of liquor, and after the first few glasses it wasn't hard to persuade him to drink more. He was always reminding us that he had to catch the train for London at 8.15, and he kept showing us his ticket.

'Then we put him to bed in a room of "The Merry Maiden." We all helped. But before we went away we took the gloss off that new suit of clothes. I daresay we were a bit rougher than was necessary; but it was so excruciatingly funny to think of when he would wake with a headache and find his new clothes torn and burned in holes, and stabbed with a penknife, and blotched with ink and candle-grease. Finally we put the shirt up the chimney and dragged it about the floor a bit till it was a real picture. As we came away our genial host observed with a laugh: "'Lord Work'us' will find it like old times when he sees his clothes."

'Well, our little joke wasn't quite complete after all. We had, of course, intended that he should miss his train; but it seems that early in the morning his mother came looking for him, and learned from a servant that he was there. Our genial host was still asleep, so there was no one to prevent her entering. I believe she just got him to the train in time. He hadn't a coin about him after he had paid for his bowl of punch.

'I heard from one of the Company at the Crown that he arrived in a terrible state. He was well plucked enough, I will say that for him; and he would have gone on with his work looking like a scarecrow, only that by some evil chance Grandison, the Manager, saw him in time and took him away to his own room and let him wash and rigged him up.

'Anyhow, he never came back to Wigan. And now look at thejustice of things! Here's this workhouse upstart with a fortune. They say he has over a hundred thousand pounds, his wife and his mother drive about in carriages; whilst men of genius like myself have to pig it in hovels with the riffraff of the stage. Pah!'

He drowned the depth of his indignant emotion in his drink.

For a time no one spoke; the men smoked, the women looked down at nothing on their laps. The first sound heard was from the Engine-Driver:

'That's a funny story - a really funny story! I won't say what I think, because this is Christmas-time, and the gent who told it is an old one with one foot in the grave. I'm from Wigan, I am. So you can fancy how nice it is for me to hear a story like that. I know where "The Merry Maiden" is, and I know, too, the sort of reputation that the "genial host" bears. Bless him! I'll look in there when I'm next at home, and see if we can't fix up another joke of some kind!'

Later on he was heard to say in private conversation with the MC:

'Look here, mister, you're a man of the world. Tell me, how do the beaks look nowadays on scrappin' in the Midlands? What do they consider a fair fine where there has been a holy shindy and some hound has been wiped the floor with?'

'You are next, Murphy,' said the MC, looking at the Super-Master, and at the same time handing a glass of steaming whisky punch. 'Don't be afraid of this. 'Tis John Jamieson.'

'I'm a timarious man be nature,' he answered as he began to sip the punch as a preliminary, 'but whin I'm dhragged into publicity like this I'm tuk be the short hairs, so ye'll pardon me,

I thrust, Ladies and Gents all, av I thransgress in me shortcomin's.' Being an Irishman, he was regarded by the Company as a humorist, and felt that he had to keep up that perilous reputation - just as he had to strain himself now and again to achieve a sufficient brogue.

'I suppose 't would be betther for me to shtay on dhry land an' to give an expayrence iv me own, rather than to be afther gettin' into difficulties be puttin' out to say what I don't know in the way of shtories an' consates. Illi robur et aes triplex circa pectus erat. Yous'll remimber!' He had been brought up at a hedge school, and always advanced the preposterous statement that he had been 'at College.'

'All right, Murphy. What you will, but hurry up! This isn't Monday trunks, but Sunday hand-bags!' The professional simile was received with laughter and applause by the actors; but Murphy, who was a shrewd fellow, knew too much to waste his opportunity on quips and cranks, so went on at once.

A Corner in Dwarfs

'I was Super-Master at the Lane Theatre when the "Stage Children's Act" was passed. I had to make it up a bit, for it was part iv me wurrk t' engage the kids as well as the exthras, an' it was a rare job that year, I can tell ye. Ould Gustavus had quarrelled the year before with Madam Laffan, the dancin' misthress, iv Old Street, who used to take all the East-end childher, an' Mrs Purefoy had made her fortune and retired, so there was no one west with a stock of trained kids. The Act, you remimber, was pushed through be the faddists, an' became law before anyone could wink. Then the throuble began. The parents what usually kem beggin' an' prayin' to have their kids took on began to trate even me haughty, an' t' ask for conthracts. They wanted double an' tribble pay. They thought they had a right to sell their childher's services, and that the new law couldn't touch them. So ould Gustavus held off in turn, when, lo and behold! you –'

'He's stealin' my words too!' murmured the Sewing Woman under her breath. She didn't dare to speak out loud for fear of offending him. Murphy was a kindly creature, and often showed her small kindnesses.

'– the beaks shut down on the whole thing, and wouldn't allow any childher at all to be engaged. We was all at our wits' end thin. We had for Pantomime that Christmas Cinderella. It was to be all done be childher, an' the scenery an' props an' costumes was all made. As time wint on I began to get anxious. Childher want a lot of tachin' an' dhrillin', and av ye have to take 'em in the raw 'tis no light job. There ginerally is a lot of such about, and in usual circumstances – unless you have lift it too late – there does be plinty of the wans that have been on before, and have only to be freshened up and taught the business iv the new play. Av coorse, every thayatre has its own lists of thim what comes to be re-engaged – I think it only just to say that I'm not the only first-class Super-Master in the business! So by-an'-by, whin the Governor asked me how many kids I had engaged, I had to say to him:

'"Sorra a wan! Don't you remimber ye towld me not to engage a bally one – an' bally ind to me!" Ould Gustavus was a man what niver got angry or swore or stamped about like some; but he had the nasty tongue on him that was a dale sight worse. So, sez he:

'"Oh, indade! Then, Mr Murphy, let me point out this to ye. If I've no supers an' no extras an' no childher, I don't seem to know that I have any use for a Super-Master – you undhershtand?"

'"I do!" sez I, an' wint out fit to hould. Whin I was shmokin' outside the stage-door, the call-boy kem yellin' out:

'"Ye're wanted be the Guvernor, Murphy, at wanst."

'Whin I kem in he says to me quite gintly – so gintly that I began to suspect he was up to some devilment:

'"Be the way, Murphy, in makin' any engagements, I want ye to put in yer own name as employer. It may be a good thing, ye know, for ye personally, an' 'twill make no differ to me."

'While he was shpakin' I seen at a glance what he was up to – I think that quick. "Oh-ho!" sez I to meself, "that's the game, is it? 'Tis to be me what employs them! An' thin, whin the polis does be comin' along undher the new Act, 'tis the employer that has to be run in!..."

'"May I have some forrms, surr?" I sez.

'"Certainly – as many as ye like. Take this ordher to Miles's an' get them to print ye a set." While he was shpakin', he tore out a forrm from th' ordher book, and handed it to me wid a conthract forrm which he had althered. "Tell them to print it like that – I have althered the name."

'"Thin, surr," I sez, "'tis me as employs them. I suppose I can do what I like in that way?"

'"Certainly, certainly," he sez. "You have a free hand in the matter. I shall make a contract with you when I want them."

'"An' their pay, sir?" I sez.

'"Oh, that is all right. You don't have to pay thim till work begins, ye know."

'"That's thrue!" sez I, an' wid that I wint out.

I got me forrms from the printer next day - hundhreds, thousands iv them - an' set to worrk. I had a game av me own on, an' I tuk not a sowl in me confidence. I knew 'twas no use gettin' childher at all, for whin the time'd come, the magisthrates wouldn't let thim wurrk at all, at all. So I luk'd round an' picked out all the small young weemen I could find that was nice an' shlim.

'My! but wasn't there a lot iv them. I had no idea that London was so full iv shlim young undher-sized weemen. I suppose I used to like big girrls best, and plazed me eye whin I selected them. But there was I now engagin' the shmall wans be the score, be the hundhred, an' just whisperin' a word to aich iv thim to hould their tongues about their engagement, lest others'd crowd in an' kape thim out.

'Thin I laid out some iv me own savin's in fares to all the big cities where they had pan-tomimes, an' I chose in the same way hundhreds iv shlim, short girls ivrywhere.

'Thin, whin I got back to London, I engaged, in Gustavus's name this time, a lot of kids for Misther Gustavus - rale childher this time. I had had a "force majeure" clause put in the conthract forrm in ordher to purtect him.

'Ould Gustavus made his conthract wid me, agreein' to pay me for aich iv the childher a shillin' a week more than usual. That was more than what I had agreed with their parents for; so in case there was no objections wid the polis they'd be betther off than usual. So that was all right.

'We began rehearsin' all right. An' wint on at it for two weeks: whin lo an' behold ye -'

'My words again!' murmured the aggrieved Sewing Woman.

'- down came the polis with a summons for ould Gustavus for contravenin' the Act be usin' on the stage the labour iv childher undher sixteen. He wint off to Bow Street quite cocky, takin' me with him. For defince he said, in the first place, he wasn't employin' labour at all, for his theatre wasn't even open. An' in the second he wasn't the employer at all. It was me. But the magistrate shut him up short. He said he'd have him know that that was a quibble, as it was within his knowledge that I was in his employment on his staff, and that as I was his agent the legal maxim facit per alium facit per se came in.

'"He's not me agent!" he says out loud. "An' look here, Murphy, I discharge ye on the shpot!"

'"That's enough," sez the magistrate. "Your dischargin' the man is a proof that he was yer agent up to that moment. Now the way you shtand is this. As this man Murphy was your agent, the childher were engaged be you; an' if y' allow them to appear in public you will go to prison. I accept the statement that they've not as yet been employed, as I understand that rehearsal is rather an unpaid preparation for employment than employment itself. I shall there-fore discharge you to-day - or rather I shall postpone the hearing till afther Christmas. And, by the way, since you discharged this man summarily, you are, I take it, liable for a week's wages. You had betther pay him at once if you are wise! If not, an action will lie against you, and the proof will come from the Coort!"

'When we were in the street he sez to me:

'"Well?"

'"It looks like the end, surr, though it's only the beginning'."

'"Of course, Murphy, I'll keep you on," he sez.

'"Thank ye, surr," sez I, "but I'm makin' other arrangements."

'"How do ye mane?" sez he.

'"I mane this, surr," sez I, "that ye've planted me for yer own purposes, an' now I intind that what grows out iv me plantin' is me own."

'"I don't undhershtand," sez he, "yit!"

'"Ye will by an' by," sez I. "Look here, Misther Gustavus, for yer own nefayrious purposes ye tould me t' engage a lot iv childher for the pantomime, an' ye tould me t' ingage them in me own name. That was so that whin the polis'd come at ye ye might say, as ye done just now to the beak, that it wasn't you at all, but me. Now it was ayther you or me what engaged them be conthract. If 'twas you ye had to shtand the racket, or would have done if the sayson had begun - which it hadn't; an' ye'd have th' advantage, too. But ye said it wasn't you whin ye thought the polis had got ye, an' ye wanted to have me run in for it. So that's off. But if 'twas me what engaged thim, thin 'tis me what'll git the benefit. See? Moreover, ye discharrged me in the Coort, an' the beak himself said ye'd have to pay me me salary for a week. So now I'm free av ye, wid the kay iv the shtreet in me hand. But I've got the conthracts what I've made wid a lot iv people in all kinds iv places. These are me own prawperty, an' I'm goin' to use thim in me own way. The only conthracts what is made in your name is wid the childher for yer own pantomime, an' thim ye has to shtand be. I might have tould his worship that they wor your conthracts, but I thought as ye swore at the beginnin' that they worn't I'd hould them over in case ye should git obstreperous later on.

'"So now ye're in the soup. Ye won't be let play the childher what ye engaged. An' I can tell ye now that ye won't be allowed any childhers at all, at all. But I've got meself in me own employment a number iv likely young weemen iv shmall patthern what'll be able to play in shpite iv all the polis in the counthry. So av ye're wishful to git what ye want, Misther Gustavus, it's me that ye'll have t'apply to. I hould the whole shtock. There is no use yer kickin'. I can prove me bona fides all along the line. 'Tis you what'll figure out as the bloated capitalist what deceived the poor honest workin' man - that's me - what thrusted him. What made nefayrious conthracts wid poor innocent childhers what'll have a hungry Christmas. An' what perjured hisself in a courthouse, which can be proved be the beak hisself an' some iv yer conthracts ye made wid the childher. Not be me, av coorse, for didn't ye swear that I was not in yer sarvice. But anyhow ye have got a force majeure clause in. That'll not look well, will it? As if 'twas I what put it in, whin I haven't the same clause even for me own purtection in me own conthracts."

'"So, Misther Gustavus, ye'd betther be quick in engagin' some iv me throup iv dancers. I'll only charge double for sich iv thim what is took from me by me first pathron."

'Well, th' ould man was in a clift shtick, an' knew it. So he made me come back wid him to his office, an' then an' there made an iron-clad conthract wid me for the sarvices iv more'n a hundhred iv me dwarfs. "Mind ye," I had said to him, "ye can have as many as iver ye want at the price av ye take tham at wanst. But if ye lave it over to take more later in case ye find ye've not enough, ye'll have to come in line wid the rest av the managers. No man can come in on the ground floor a second time!"

'It all kem off well. As soon as the rehearsals began the polis woke up an' got shpry all over the counthry. The managers was all run in. Like ould Gustavus they couldn't be punished bekase they hadn't done nothin' wrong, as yet. But they tuk fright, as was intended, an' gave undhertakins not to employ any childher at all while th' Act run. An' so they all had to come, in the long run, to me what had cornered all the dwarfs. Mind ye, I was careful not to use that word, for if they'd any iv them heard it, they'd have riz up an' flew away like a flock iv pigeons does, all about nothin'.

'Then the fun began. Shmall weemin is more up in themselves than big wans. So the shtage managers an' bally masters what was in the habit of drillin' childher in the pantomime sayson soon found out the differ. Some iv them thried to thrate the little weemin - "beautiful childher" is what I called them, so they thought I was a very nice man, an' we got on well with aich other, an' I had no quarrellin' wid them - as if they was kids, an' ordhered them about somethin' crool. They soon found out the mishtake. Wan iv them - Cuthbert Kinsey it was, of the Royal at Queenhythe - gave wan iv them a slap on th' ear. But she could scrap a bit, so she could; she was a sturdy, plucky little party what could whip her weight in wild cats, as the Yankees say. She just put up her dooks an' wint for him. She gave him wan on the bread-basket an' another on the boko what made him go into the claret business sthraight. So for that sayson he kep his hooks down. My! but there was scrappin' in some theyatres, for the budlets wouldn't shtand no guff. An' whin the bally masters an' shtage managers found they was weemin an' tried to make love to them things was worse. Moreover, they tuk breaches iv promise whiniver the chap had any oof at all. I'm tellin' ye the carnage among bachelors in theyatres that year was frightful. I was a bachelor meself in thim days, so I have cause enough to know it!'

'Was that when and how you met your wife, Mr Roscoe?' asked the Second Old Woman, a big-built woman with a temper of her own.

The rest of the Company smiled, for it was an open secret that Mrs Roscoe, who had once been wardrobe mistress, had been required to leave the Company on account of her success in a face-slapping episode wherein the Second Old Woman had fared badly. The Super Master, who, both as one occupying a post on the managerial staff and also as an Irishman from whom a large measure of courtesy to women was expected, kept strict guard on his temper except when quelling a riot or pleasantry amongst his own crowd, answered sweetly:

'Yes, ma'am. I am proud to say it was. I bless the day.'

'She is not here, I notice,' said the Second Old Woman, with asuavity equal to his own. 'May I ask you why that is?'

'Certainly, ma'am.' he replied heartily. 'She is away on a long tour in America with a first-class Company.'

'Oh! And she is Wardrobe - as an assistant, I suppose?'

'No, ma'am,' he replied sadly. 'I regret to say she has gone down in the world.'

'I see. A Dresser, then?'

'No, ma'am. Lower still; she is First Old Woman. But then I should say that it is a Company so good that the Old Women are played by young and pretty ones. Not by real has-beens or never-wases, as is usually the case!' The ready laugh of the younger members of the Company showed that the shot had told. The Second Old Woman's anger flamed out in her face as she said still - by a great effort - suavely:

'I hope she is now respectable?'

'Keeps, ma'am! - keeps, not "is"! She is and has always been respectable. And is always a quiet, tender-hearted woman. Except, of course, when she has to chastise insolence - as you very well know.'

The Second Old Woman contented herself by glaring, as she realised from the universal titter that the laugh was against her. The Super Master swallowed his consolation - steaming hot though it was.

The MC turned to the next on the line, The Advance Agent, an alert-looking man of middle age.

'I hope you will give us something next, Alphage. It is so seldom that we have the honour of seeing you whilst we are on the road that we should look on it as the lost opportunity of our lives if we do not hear some story or reminiscence of your own life.'

'All right, old man. I'll do what I can. You won't mind, I hope, Ladies and Gentlemen, if it is a bit dull. But the fact is that I've been so much in the habit of inventing lies about my stars that plain fact comes to be prosaic. Anyhow, it may be a change for me; I'm tired of finding out new virtues of my employers or ringing the changes on the old ones.

A Criminal Star

'Of course, you all remember Wolseley Gartside -'

'Rather!' This was from the Tragedian. 'I remember when he took that name. Indeed, I was not pleased with him about it; it clashed with the name I had taken myself - or, rather - ahem! - which my sponsors took for me at my christening. I consoled myself with the reflection that Wolseley was a later name historically than Wellesley.' The Advance Agent went on:

'Gartside, like many others who have risen from the ranks - the ranks of his profession - was, well, a wee, tiny bit over-sensitive in matters of public esteem. In fact, he did not like to be neglected -'

Here the Second Heavies interrupted with a rapidity and acerbity which left an impression that indignation was founded on aggrievement:

' "Over-sensitive in matters of public esteem!" I like that. He had got the swelled head bad, if that be what you mean. He wanted the earth, he did! The way he hustled other people off the posters was indecent! And the size of type he clamoured for was an inducement to blindness and an affront to the common sense of an educated community.' The Advance Agent went on calmly:

'- did not like to be neglected. This was all bad enough when he was engaged by someone else; but when he was out on his own with nothing to check him except the reports of his treasurer, he became a holy terror. There wasn't any crowding of names off the bill then; there were simply no names at all. Names of other people, I mean; his name was all right so long as the paper was up to the biggest stands, and the types were the largest to be had in the town. Later on he went even further and had all his printing done in London or New York from types cut special.' The Second Heavies cut in again:

'No! Mr Wolseley Gartside didn't mean to get neglected so long as there was a public Press to be influenced or a hoarding to be covered.'

'Exactly!' said the Advance Agent drily. He was beginning to fear that his pitch would be queered by the outpouring of the grievances of the Second Heavies. The professional instinct of the audience made for peace. They were all trained to listen. Mr Alphage seized the opportunity, and went on:

'When he was arranging his first American tour he wanted to get someone who, as a persona grata, could command the Press; who understood human nature to the core; who had the instinct of a diplomatist, the experience of a field-marshall, the tact of an Attorney-General; the -'

'All right, old man. We know you took him in tow.'

'Thank you, Bones! I understand. Gartside was a tragedian, too, and of course wanted the whole stage. They're all the same.'

'Well, of all the -' began Dovercourt; but there he stopped. There was a readiness of repartee about the Advance Agent that disturbed his self-serenity.

'So I took him in tow, as Bones calls it. I thought my work was piloting. But Bones knows; he, too, belongs to the hungry, egotist lot who have to be dragged into publicity - like Wolseley Gartside!

'Well, before I started out, which he insisted should be a full week ahead of him, he began to teach me my business. At first I pointed out to him that the whole mechanism of advance publicity wasn't wrong because he hadn't done it. But he took me up short, and expressed his opinions pretty freely, I admit. He gave me quite a dissertation on publicity, telling me that to hit the public you must tell them plenty. They wanted to know all about a man; they didn't care much whether it was good or bad; but on the whole they preferred bad. Then he went on to give me what he called my instructions. That I was to have paragraphs about him every day. "Make me out," he said, "a sort of Don Juan, with a fierce, revengeful nature. A man from whose hate no man is safe; no woman from his love. Never mind moral character. The public don't want it - nor no more do I. Say whatever you please about me so long as you make people talk. Now I don't want argument with you. Do you just carry out my instructions, and all will be well. But if you don't, you'll get the order of the chuck." I didn't want to argue with him. To begin with, a man like that isn't worth argument - especially about instructions. Instructions! Just fancy an Advance Agent who knows his business being instructed by a Star that he has got to boom, and to whose vanity - no, sensitiveness - he has to minister. Why, compared with even a duffer at my work the biggest and brightest star in the theatrical firmament don't know enough to come in out of the rain! I was very angry with him, I admit; but in a flash there came to me out of his own very instructions an idea which put anger out of my mind. The top dog isn't angry - though he may bite! "Very well, Mr Wolseley Gartside," said I to myself, said I, "I'll carry out your instructions with exactness. They're yours, not mine; so if anything comes out wrong you are the responsible party." Before I went to bed I wrote out a mem of my "instructions."

'"The public want to know everything about a man. Tell them plenty - all they want. They don't care whether it's good or bad. On the whole, they prefer bad. Give them paragraphs every day. Make me a Don Juan, fierce, revengeful, passionate. No man safe from my hate; no woman from my love. Don't aim at moral character; the public don't want it; no more do I. Say whatever you please about me so long as you make people talk. Make things lively before I come!"

'I headed this "Instructions to Montague Phase Alphage, Advance Agent to Wolseley Gartside, Esquire." In the morning I brought it to him and asked him to sign and date it, as I wished to carry out his instructions to the full, and to take for myself advantage of his wisdom and his splendid initiative power. He signed it, looking very pleased. The sort of smirk that tragedians use when they're feeling good.

'The next day I started out on my travels. The tour was to begin with a week of one-night stands. Wolseley Gartside had insisted on making out the tour himself, and, of course, he knew better than anybody - everybody else. You know what that means, Wragge. I certainly covered the ground for him that week. I simply lived in trains, and I wore out the stairs of all the offices of what they called newspapers. Do you know, I think there must be a special angelic squad told off to look after advance agents. And if there is, my chap must have had what they call a hellova time. It's a direct mercy that I didn't develop acute DT in letting the penny-a-liners of that group of one-horse towns have the time of their lives. They tumbled to it quick that they would not have to write any themselves, for, of course, I did all that myself. It was best that way, anyhow, for not one of them could have written a decent par to save his soul.

'I filled them all up with Wolseley Gartside; and they filled up as much space as the editorial staff could spare from ads. Generally I paid for the printing, too - though who benefited by it I don't know. I thought Gartside would darken the air when he got my bill; but I did him well - in quantity, at all events. But the quality was good, too; just what the old man liked. I not only painted him as a man of transcendent genius and as an artist that had no peer in past or present, but gave him such a character as a libertine that the local Don Juans began over their drink to talk of reviving lynching, and the womenkind exhausted the dry goods stores for new frocks and fal-lals of all kinds. Why, they tell me that the demand for toupees and false fronts and extensions was such that the New York wholesale hair houses sent down a whole flock of drummers. The back-numbers were going to have a turn at him as well as the girls and the frisky matrons! I gave him out as having the courage of a lion and the heart of a fiend; the skill at cards of a prestidigitateur; the style and daring in the hunt of Buffalo Bill; the learning of an Erasmus; the voice of a De Reske; the strength of Milo - it was before Sandow's time. I finished it all off with a hypnotic gift which was unique; which from the stage could rule audiences, and in the smoking-room or the boudoir could make man or woman his obedient slave. I got most of the newspapers to take up hypnotism as a theme of controversy, and wrote lots of letters on the subject, under various names, which opened people's eyes as to the power of that mysterious craft - or quality, whichever it is - and the consequent danger attendant on their daily lives. I suppose I needn't say that the whole controversy everywhere circled round

Gartside and his wonderful powers. I tell you that by the Sunday afternoon when my Star came along with his crowd in his special, with his private car at the tail of it, and him on the rear platform, the women of Patricia City, where he opened, were in a flutter. They didn't know whether it was hope or fear. Knowing the sex as I do, I am inclined to think it was hope. To tame and subdue a dragon of voluptuous impurity is the dearest wish of a good woman's heart!'

'Oh, really, Mr Phase Alphage ...' said the First Old Woman, raising an index finger of remonstrance.

'True, dear lady, true. It is trite as a record, as well as solemn as a truth.'

'Aye, it is truth, indeed. Sad truth!' murmured the Tragedian, in a thunderous bass. 'The experiences of my own hot youth have proven it to the full. 'Twas not gifts of mind or body, all-compelling though these be, nor the fascinations of our glamorous calling. Rather would I call it the maelstrom of passion which the Apple of Eden begot in the breast of woman.'

'Rather a mixed metaphor that!' said the young man from Oxford, who seemed to have taken on himself the task of keeping the Tragedian to order. 'But we understand what you mean. Drive on, Alphage.'

'I was fifty miles on my road when the day of opening came; but I ran back - that came out of my own pocket, too! - to see Gartside and hear what he thought of the way I had exploited him. I boarded his train down the line, and came on with him. He was both jubilant and effusive, and said my work in advance was the best he had ever had. "Go on, my boy, go on, and follow it up. You are on the right tack!" were the last words he said to me. I dropped off at the depot, and got on the outward train, for I didn't want to get pitched into by him when he should find the excitement was less than he expected. I do believe he thought there would be in waiting a murderous crowd, with a rope, intent on a neck-tie party, with a few regiments of State troops to counteract them.

'When I got into the next town the Press was full of what had been said at Patricia City, and wanted me to go at least one better, or they couldn't use my stuff at all. That would be checkmate to me as Advance Agent, so I was in a real difficulty. I couldn't increase the praise of my Star, so the only thing was to go down. I made up my mind to go deeper and deeper into crime. There was no help for it. I knew well that each other town in that group would want its own increase of pressure, and so arranged my plans in the back of my head. I should have to distribute the steps of the downward grade amongst five different towns; so I laid out my work and began to get my copy ready. I never went to bed at all that night, but spent it writing advance matter in shorthand. In the morning I got a smart typewriter and dictated to her from my stenographic script. I sent off that for Tuesday by mail, and got the rest ready to post when the hour should arrive. I had to be careful not to send matter long enough in advance for the comparison of towns, or of different papers in the same town.

'Early on Tuesday morning I got to Hustleville - that was the second town of the tour - and from that moment matters began to hum. All the papers were full, not only of my own matter, but of comments on it. In addition, nearly every one had a leader in which they cut the Tragedian to pieces. The Banner of Freedom wanted to make out his coming to be nothing short of an international outrage.

'"It makes little," it said, "for the comity of nations that an ostensibly friendly country like England should be allowed to dump down on our shores a cargo of criminal decadents like the man Wolseley Gartside and his crowd of hooligans. His being left at large so long as seems to have been the case says little for either the morals or the sanity of the people who have permitted his existence. He is a smirch on the fair face of cosmic law, a living germ of intellectual disease, a cancerous growth even in the parasitic calling which he follows; an outrage to man and morals, to fair living, to development of God's creatures - nay, even to God Himself! The people of this State have not in the past lacked courage or energy to terminate swiftly, by the exercise of rough justice in the open courts of natural law, the opportunities of offenders against public good. We have heard of a human pendulum swinging on a giant bough of one of our noble forest trees; there are recollections in the minds of those of our pioneers who happily survive of worthless miscreants riding on rails clad in unpretentious costumes of feathers and tar. It is up to the heroic souls who founded Hustleville to break the long silence of their well-won repose, and, for protection of the city they have won from forest depths, and for the defence of their kin, to raise voice and hand for woman's honour and man's unshrinking nobility! A hint on such a subject should be sufficient. Verbum sapientice sufficit. We have done."

'This reached Gartside after breakfast, and he at once wired me:

"'Go on; it is well. Banner has struck right note. Shall be ere long living heart of international cyclone!"

'I went on the same afternoon to Comstock, which was next on our route. I had, of course, sent on plenty of advance matter, and the editors had written me gratefully about it. But when I called at the Whoop - which was, I understood, the popular paper - I was received in a manner which was decidedly chilly. I am not, as a rule, lacking in diffidence...'

'Distinctly an understatement, my dear sir,' said the Tragedian, with challenge to battle in his eye. You really wrong yourself by putting it in that negative way!' He glared in return, but went on, calmly:

'...but I admit I was a little nonplussed - no pun intended, Governor' - this to the Manager. 'So I asked the editor if I had hurt or affronted him in any way to cause his greeting to be so different from his written words. He hum'd and haw'd, and finally admitted that he was chagrined that the Comstock Whoop had not been treated as well as the Hustleville Banner of Freedom.

"'How?" I asked. "I sent you twenty per cent more advance copy."

"'Aye. The quantity was all right; but there were none of the spicy details which worked up the dormant conscience of even a one-horse town like Hustleville. Now, I suppose you know that we young towns can't live on the past. Has-been isn't a good diet for growing youth. Moreover, we're all living on one another's backs, with the nails dug in. What we want in the Whoop is anti-soothing syrup; and nothing else is any use to us. So get a move on you and let us have it. We want stronger meat than Hustleville."

"'But there's nothing stronger. To say more wouldn't be true."

'The editor seemed as if struck blind. He raised his hands as if expostulating with the powers of the air, as he said:

"'True! Do I live to hear the Advance Agent of a Troupe speak of truth ... Now, look here, Mister. It's no use talking ethics with you. For either I'm drunk - which would be early in the day for me - or else you've got some sort of freshness on you that I don't understand. And I may tell you for your edification that we don't much care for freshness here. Comstock is a town where we perspire quick; and there's plenty of space in the forest for developing our cem-e-tary. When I got your first letter I told my boys to hold back because this was your funeral, and ye was up in the etiquette. But the boys wasn't altogether pleased. They are good boys, and could knock sparks out of Ananias in making a story. See! So you'd better get to work. You know your man and they don't; so your story is apt to seem more lifelike. I'll want the copy here by seven. Then, the quicker ye quit the better."

'There was nothing for it but to carry out Wolseley Gartside's instructions. It was wife-beating this time that swelled his reputation. I didn't mean to be knocked out by the boys of the Whoop, nor to afford an opportunity for exemplifying the sudorific rapidity of Comstock - no, nor to take a part in de-veloping the cem-e-tary either; so the story of WG's experiences as a defendant in the police-court of Abingchester, in the Peak of Derbyshire - that was well out of the way of public prints - was given in full detail, together with a description of the Lord Chancellor who condemned him, and an exciting account of his escape, riddled with bullets, from the county gaol. The editor read it with a beaming face, and said when he had done:

"'That's the biggest scoop we ever had. Here, I'll give you a straight tip which will put money in your pocket if you get out your copy right smart. There is every indication that when the play is over to-morrow night there will be an adjournment of citizens to the forest, and that one of the oaks will bear a new sort of acorn. One with a bloated body; but a rotten heart. See?"

'I did see; and I sent an urgent letter to WG by the driver of the mail train, telling him frankly where his instructions were likely to lead him.

'He was wise for once, and altered his route. This wasn't a case for vanity, but for skin. So there wasn't any new kind of acorn found on the forest round Comstock, though the search party was all ready.

'Now, Mr Hempitch,' said the MC, 'you're next.' So he began at once.

'All right, sir. Mr Alphage's story of a Star reminds me of a Star of another kind which is more in my line of business.

A Star Trap

"When I was apprenticed to theatrical carpentering my master was John Haliday, who was Master Machinist - we called men in his post 'Master Carpenter' in those days - of the old Victoria Theatre, Hulme. It wasn't called Hulme; but that name will do. It would only stir up painful memories if I were to give the real name. I daresay some of you - not the Ladies (this with a gallant bow all round) - will remember the case of a Harlequin as was killed in an accident in the pantomime. We needn't mention names; Mortimer will do for a name to call him by - Henry Mortimer. The cause of it was never found out. But I knew it; and I've kept silence for so long that I may speak now without hurting anyone. They're all dead long ago that was interested in the death of Henry Mortimer or the man who wrought that death."

"Any of you who know of the case will remember what a handsome, dapper, well-built man Mortimer was. To my own mind he was the handsomest man I ever saw."

The Tragedian's low, grumbling whisper, "That's a large order," sounded a warning note. Hempitch, however, did not seem to hear it, but went on:

"Of course, I was only a boy then, and I hadn't seen any of you gentlemen - Yer very good health, Mr Wellesley Dovercourt, sir, and cettera. I needn't tell you, Ladies, how well a harlequin's dress sets off a nice slim figure. No wonder that in these days of suffragettes, women wants to be harlequins as well as columbines. Though I hope they won't make the columbine a man's part!"

"Mortimer was the nimblest chap at the traps I ever see. He was so sure of hisself that he would have extra weight put on so that when the counter weights fell he'd shoot up five or six feet higher than anyone else could even try to. Moreover, he had a way of drawing up his legs when in the air - the way a frog does when he is swimming - that made his jump look ever so much higher."

"I think the girls were all in love with him, the way they used to stand in the wings when the time was comin' for his entrance. That wouldn't have mattered much, for girls are always falling in love with some man or other, but it made trouble, as it always does when the married ones take the same start. There were several of these that were always after him, more shame for them, with husbands of their own. That was dangerous enough, and hard to stand for a man who might mean to be decent in any way. But the real trial - and the real trouble, too - was none other than the young wife of my own master, and she was more than flesh and blood could stand. She had come into the panto, the season before, as a high-kicker - and she could! She could kick higher than girls that was more than a foot taller than her; for she was a wee bit of a thing and as pretty as pie; a gold-haired, blue-eyed, slim thing with much the figure of a boy, except for. . . and they saved her from any mistaken idea of that kind. Jack Haliday went crazy over her, and when the notice was up, and there was no young spark with plenty of oof coming along to do the proper thing by her, she married him. It was, when they was joined, what you Ladies call a marriage of convenience; but after a bit they two got on very well, and we all thought she was beginning to like the old man - for Jack was old enough to be her father, with a bit to spare. In the summer, when the house was closed, he took her to the Isle of Man; and when they came back he made no secret of it that he'd had the happiest time of his life. She looked quite happy, too, and treated him affectionate; and we all began to think that that marriage had not been a failure at any rate."

"Things began to change, however, when the panto, rehearsals began next year. Old Jack began to look unhappy, and didn't take no interest in his work. Loo - that was Mrs Haliday's name - didn't seem over fond of him now, and was generally impatient when he was by. Nobody said anything about this, however, to us men; but the married women smiled and nodded their heads and whispered that perhaps there were reasons. One day on the stage, when the harlequinade rehearsal was beginning, someone mentioned as how perhaps Mrs Haliday wouldn't be dancing that year, and they smiled as if they was all in the secret. Then Mrs Jack ups and gives them Johnny-up-the-orchard for not minding their own business and telling a pack of lies, and such like as you Ladies like to express in your own ways when you get your back hair down. The rest of us tried to soothe her all we could, and she went off home."

"It wasn't long after that that she and Henry Mortimer left together after rehearsal was over, he saying he'd leave her at home. She didn't make no objections - I told you he was a very handsome man."

"Well, from that on she never seemed to take her eyes from him during every rehearsal, right up to the night of the last rehearsal, which, of course, was full dress - 'Everybody and Everything.'"

"Jack Haliday never seemed to notice anything that was going on, like the rest of them did. True, his time was taken up with his own work, for I'm telling you that a Master Machinist hasn't got no loose time on his hands at the first dress rehearsal of a panto. And, of course, none of the company ever said a word or gave a look that would call his attention to it. Men and women are queer beings. They will be blind and deaf whilst danger is being run; and it's only after the scandal is beyond repair that they begin to talk - just the very time when most of all they should be silent."

"I saw all that went on, but I didn't understand it. I liked Mortimer myself and admired him - like I did Mrs Haliday, too - and I thought he was a very fine fellow. I was only a boy, you know, and Haliday's apprentice, so naturally I wasn't looking for any trouble I could help, even if I'd seen it coming. It was when I looked back afterwards at the whole thing that I began to comprehend; so you will all understand now, I hope, that what I tell you is the result of much knowledge of what I saw and heard and was told of afterwards - all morticed and clamped up by thinking."

"The panto, had been on about three weeks when one Saturday, between the shows, I heard two of our company talking. Both of them was among the extra girls that both sang and danced and had to make theirselves useful. I don't think either of them was better than she should be; they went out to too many champagne suppers with young men that had money to burn. That part doesn't matter in this affair - except that they was naturally enough jealous of women who was married - which was what they was aiming at - and what lived straighter than they did. Women of that kind like to see a good woman tumble down; it seems to make them all more even. Now real bad girls what have gone under altogether will try to save a decent one from following their road. That is, so long as they're young; for a bad one what is long in the tooth is the limit. They'll help anyone down hill - so long as they get anything out of it."

"Well - no offence, you Ladies, as has growed up! - these two girls was enjoyin' themselves over Mrs Haliday and the mash she had set up on Mortimer. They didn't see that I was sitting on a stage box behind a built-out piece of the Prologue of the panto., which was set ready for night. They were both in love with Mortimer, who wouldn't look at either of them, so they was miaw'n cruel, like cats on the tiles. Says one:"

"'The Old Man seems worse than blind; he won't see.'"

"'Don't you be too sure of that,' says the other. 'He don't mean to take no chances. I think you must be blind, too, Kissie.' That was her name - on the bills anyhow, Kissie Mountpelier. 'Don't he make a point of taking her home hisself every night after the play. You should know, for you're in the hall yourself waiting for your young man till he comes from his club.'"

"'Wot-ho, you bally geeser,' says the other - which her language was mostly coarse - 'don't you know there's two ends to everything? The Old Man looks to one end only!' Then they began to snigger and whisper; and presently the other one says:"

"'Then he thinks harm can be only done when work is over!'"

"'Jest so,' she answers. 'Her and him knows that the old man has to be down long before the risin' of the rag; but she doesn't come in till the Vision of Venus dance after half time; and he not till the harlequinade!'"

"Then I quit. I didn't want to hear any more of that sort."

"All that week things went on as usual. Poor old Haliday wasn't well. He looked worried and had a devil of a temper. I had reason to know that, for what worried him was his work. He was always a hard worker, and the panto. season was a terror with him. He didn't ever seem to mind anything else outside his work. I thought at the time that that was how those two chattering girls made up their slanderous story; for, after all, a slander, no matter how false it may be, must have some sort of beginning. Something that seems, if there isn't something that is! But no matter how busy he might be, old Jack always made time to leave the wife at home."

"As the week went on he got more and more pale; and I began to think he was in for some sickness. He generally remained in the theatre between the shows on Saturday; that is, he didn't go home, but took a high tea in the coffee shop close to the theatre, so as to be handy in case there might be a hitch anywhere in the preparation for night. On that Saturday he went out as usual when the first scene was set, and the men were getting ready the packs for the rest of the scenes. By and bye there was some trouble - the usual Saturday kind - and I went off to tell him. When I went into the coffee shop I couldn't see him. I thought it best not to ask or to seem to take any notice, so I came back to the theatre, and heard that the trouble had settled itself as usual, by the men who had been quarrelling going off to have another drink. I hustled up those who remained, and we got things smoothed out in time for them all to have their tea. Then I had my own. I was just then beginning to feel the responsibility of my business, so I wasn't long over my food, but came back to look things over and see that all was right, especially the trap, for that was a thing Jack Haliday was most particular about. He would overlook a fault for anything else; but if it was along of a trap, the man had to go. He always told the men that that wasn't ordinary work; it was life or death."

"I had just got through my inspection when I saw old Jack coming in from the hall. There was no one about at that hour, and the stage was dark. But dark as it was I could see that the old man was ghastly pale. I didn't speak, for I wasn't near enough, and as he was moving very silently behind the scenes I thought that perhaps he wouldn't like anyone to notice that he had been away. I thought the best thing I could do would be to clear out of the way, so I went back and had another cup of tea."

"I came away a little before the men, who had nothing to think of except to be in their places when Haliday's whistle sounded. I went to report myself to my master, who was in his own little glass-partitioned den at the back of the carpenter's shop. He was there bent over his own bench, and was filing away at something so intently that he did not seem to hear me; so I cleared out. I tell you, Ladies and Gents., that from an apprentice point of view it is not wise to be too obtrusive when your master is attending to some private matter of his own!"

"When the 'get-ready' time came and the lights went up, there was Haliday as usual at his post. He looked very white and ill - so ill that the stage manager, when he came in, said to him that if he liked to go home and rest he would see that all his work would be attended to. He thanked him, and said that he thought he would be able to stay. 'I do feel a little weak and ill, sir,' he said. 'I felt just now for a few moments as if I was going to faint. But that's gone by already, and I'm sure I shall be able to get through the work before us all right.'"

"Then the doors was opened, and the Saturday night audience came rushing and tumbling in. The Victoria was a great Saturday night house. No matter what other nights might be, that was sure to be good. They used to say in the perfesh that the Victoria lived on it, and that the management was on holiday for the rest of the week. The actors knew it, and no matter how slack they might be from Monday to Friday they was all taut and trim then. There was no walking through and no fluffing on Saturday nights - or else they'd have had the bird."

"Mortimer was one of the most particular of the lot in this way. He never was slack at any time - indeed, slackness is not a harlequin's fault, for if there's slackness there's no harlequin, that's all. But Mortimer always put on an extra bit on the Saturday night. When he jumped up through the star trap he always went then a couple of feet higher. To do this we had always to put on a lot more weight. This he always saw to himself; for, mind you, it's no joke being driven up through the trap as if you was shot out of a gun. The points of the star had to be kept free, and the hinges at their bases must be well oiled, or else there can be a disaster at any time. Moreover, 'tis the duty of someone appointed for the purpose to see that all is clear upon the stage. I remember hearing that once at New York, many years ago now, a harlequin was killed by a 'grip' - as the Yankees call a carpenter - what outsiders here call a scene-shifter - walking over the trap just as the stroke had been given to let go the counter-weights. It wasn't much satisfaction to the widow to know that the 'grip' was killed too."

"That night Mrs Haliday looked prettier than ever, and kicked even higher than I had ever seen her do. Then, when she got dressed for home, she came as usual and stood in the wings for the beginning of the harlequinade. Old Jack came across the stage and stood beside her; I saw him from the back follow up the sliding ground-row that closed in on the Realms of Delight. I couldn't help noticing that he still looked ghastly pale. He kept turning his eyes on the star trap. Seeing this, I naturally looked at it too, for I feared lest something might have gone wrong. I had seen that it was in good order, and that the joints were properly oiled when the stage was set for the evening show, and as it wasn't used all night for anything else I was reassured. Indeed, I thought I could see it shine a bit as the limelight caught the brass hinges. There was a spot light just above it on the bridge, which was intended to make a good show of harlequin and his big jump. The people used to howl with delight as he came rushing up through the trap and when in the air drew up his legs and spread them wide for an instant and then straightened them again as he came down - only bending his knees just as he touched the stage."

"When the signal was given the counter-weight worked properly. I knew, for the sound of it at that part was all right."

"But something was wrong. The trap didn't work smooth, and open at once as the harlequin's head touched it. There was a shock and a tearing sound, and the pieces of the star seemed torn about, and some of them were thrown about the stage. And in the middle of them came the coloured and spangled figure that we knew."

"But somehow it didn't come up in the usual way. It was erect enough, but there was not the usual elasticity. The legs never moved; and when it went up a fair height - though nothing like usual - it seemed to topple over and fall on the stage on its side. The audience shrieked, and the people in the wings - actors and staff all the same - closed in, some of them in their stage clothes, others dressed for going home. But the man in the spangles lay quite still."

"The loudest shriek of all was from Mrs Haliday; and she was the first to reach the spot where he - it - lay. Old Jack was close behind her, and caught her as she fell. I had just time to see that, for I made it my business to look after the pieces of the trap; there was plenty of people to look after the corpse. And the pit was by now crossing the orchestra and climbing up on the stage."

"I managed to get the bits together before the rush came. I noticed that there were deep scratches on some of them, but I didn't have time for more than a glance. I put a stage box over the hole lest anyone should put a foot through it. Such would mean a broken leg at least; and if one fell through, it might mean worse. Amongst other things I found a queer-looking piece of flat steel with some bent points on it. I knew it didn't belong to the trap; but it came from somewhere, so I put it in my pocket."

"By this time there was a crowd where Mortimer's body lay. That he was stone dead nobody could doubt. The very attitude was enough. He was all straggled about in queer positions; one of the legs was doubled under him with the toes sticking out in the wrong way. But let that suffice! It doesn't do to go into details of a dead body...I wish someone would give me a drop of punch."

"There was another crowd round Mrs Haliday, who was lying a little on one side nearer the wings where her husband had carried her and laid her down. She, too, looked like a corpse; for she was as white as one and as still, and looked as cold. Old Jack was kneeling beside her, chafing her hands. He was evidently frightened about her, for he, too, was deathly white. However, he kept his head, and called his men round him. He left his wife in care of Mrs Homcroft, the Wardrobe Mistress, who had by this time hurried down. She was a capable woman, and knew how to act promptly. She got one of the men to lift Mrs Haliday and carry her up to the wardrobe. I heard afterwards that when she got her there she turned out all the rest of them that followed up - the women as well as the men - and looked after her herself."

"I put the pieces of the broken trap on the top of the stage box, and told one of our chaps to mind them, and see that no one touched them, as they might be wanted. By this time the police who had been on duty in front had come round, and as they had at once telephoned to headquarters, more police kept coming in all the time. One of them took charge of the place where the broken trap was; and when he heard who put the box and the broken pieces there, sent for me. More of them took the body away to the property room, which was a large room with benches in it, and which could be locked up. Two of them stood at the door, and wouldn't let anyone go in without permission."

"The man who was in charge of the trap asked me if I had seen the accident. When I said I had, he asked me to describe it. I don't think he had much opinion of my powers of description, for he soon dropped that part of his questioning. Then he asked me to point out where I found the bits of the broken trap. I simply said:"

"'Lord bless you, sir, I couldn't tell. They was scattered all over the place. I had to pick them up between people's feet as they were rushing in from all sides.'"

"'All right, my boy,' he said, in quite a kindly way, for a policeman, 'I don't think they'll want to worry you. There are lots of men and women, I am told, who were standing by and saw the whole thing. They will be all subpoenaed.' I was a small-made lad in those days - I ain't a giant now! - and I suppose he thought it was no use having children for witnesses when they had plenty of grown-ups. Then he said something about me and an idiot asylum that was not kind - no, nor wise either, for I dried up and did not say another word."

"Gradually the public was got rid of. Some strolled off by degrees, going off to have a glass before the pubs closed, and talk it all over. The rest us and the police ballooned out. Then, when the police had taken charge of everything and put in men to stay all night, the coroner's officer came and took off the body to the city mortuary, where the police doctor made a post mortem. I was allowed to go home. I did so - and gladly - when I had seen the place settling down. Mr Haliday took his wife home in a four-wheeler. It was perhaps just as well, for Mrs Homcroft and some other kindly souls had poured so much whisky and brandy and rum and gin and beer and peppermint into her that I don't believe she could have walked if she had tried."

"When I was undressing myself something scratched my leg as I was taking off my trousers. I found it was the piece of flat steel which I had picked up on the stage. It was in the shape of a star fish, but the spikes of it were short. Some of the points were turned down, the rest were pulled out straight again. I stood with it in my hand wondering where it had come from and what it was for, but I couldn't remember anything in the whole theatre that it could have belonged to. I looked at it closely again, and saw that the edges were all filed and quite bright. But that did not help me, so I put it on the table and thought I would take it with me in the morning; perhaps one of the chaps might know. I turned out the gas and went to bed - and to sleep."

"I must have begun to dream at once, and it was, naturally enough, all about the terrible thing that had occurred. But, like all dreams, it was a bit mixed. They were all mixed. Mortimer with his spangles flying up the trap, it breaking, and the pieces scattering round. Old Jack Haliday looking on at one side of the stage with his wife beside him - he as pale as death, and she looking prettier than ever. And then Mortimer coming down all crooked and falling on the stage, Mrs Haliday shrieking, and her and Jack running forward, and me picking up the pieces of the broken trap from between people's legs, and finding the steel star with the bent points."

"I woke in a cold sweat, saying to myself as I sat up in bed in the dark:"

"'That's it!'"

"And then my head began to reel about so that I lay down again and began to think it all over. And it all seemed clear enough then. It was Mr Haliday who made that star and put it over the star trap where the points joined! That was what Jack Haliday was filing at when I saw him at his bench; and he had done it because Mortimer and his wife had been making love to each other. Those girls were right, after all. Of course, the steel points had prevented the trap opening, and when Mortimer was driven up against it his neck was broken."

"But then came the horrible thought that if Jack did it, it was murder, and he would be hung. And, after all, it was his wife that the harlequin had made love to - and old Jack loved her very much indeed himself and had been good to her - and she was his wife. And that bit of steel would hang him if it should be known. But no one but me - and whoever made it, and put it on the trap - even knew of its existence - and Mr Haliday was my master - and the man was dead - and he was a villain!"

"I was living then at Quarry Place; and in the old quarry was a pond so deep that the boys used to say that far down the water was boiling hot, it was so near Hell."

"I softly opened the window, and, there in the dark, threw the bit of steel as far as I could into the quarry."

"No one ever knew, for I have never spoken a word of it till this very minute. I was not called at the inquest. Everyone was in a hurry; the coroner and the jury and the police. Our governor was in a hurry too, because we wanted to go on as usual at night; and too much talk of the tragedy would hurt business. So nothing was known; and all went on as usual. Except that after that Mrs Haliday didn't stand in the wings during the harlequinade, and she was as loving to her old husband as a woman can be. It was him she used to watch now; and always with a sort of respectful adoration. She knew, though no one else did, except her husband - and me."

When he finished there was a big spell of silence. The company had all been listening intently, so that there was no change except the cessation of Hempitch's voice. The eyes of all were now fixed on Mr Wellesley Dovercourt. It was the role of the Tragedian to deal with such an occasion. He was quite alive to the privileges of his status, and spoke at once:

"H'm! Very excellent indeed! You will have to join the ranks of our profession, Mr Master Machinist - the lower ranks, of course. A very thrilling narrative yours, and distinctly true. There may be some errors of detail, such as that Mrs Haliday never flirted again. I . . . I knew John Haliday under, of course, his real name. But I shall preserve the secret you so judiciously suppressed. A very worthy person. He was stage carpenter at the Duke's Theatre, Bolton, where I first dared histrionic triumphs in the year - ah H'm! I saw quite a good deal of Mrs Haliday at that time. And you are wrong about her. Quite wrong! She was a most attractive little woman - very!"

The Wardrobe Mistress here whispered to the Second Old Woman:

"Well, ma'am, they all seem agoin' of it tonight. I think they must have ketched the infection from Mr Bloze. There isn't a bally word of truth in all Hempitch has said. I was there when the accident occurred - for it was an accident when Jim Bungnose, the clown, was killed. For he was a clown, not a 'arlequin; an' there wasn't no lovemakin' with Mrs 'Aliday. God 'elp the woman as would try to make love to Jim; which she was the Strong Woman in a Circus, and could put up her dooks like a man. Moreover, there wasn't no Mrs 'Aliday. The carpenter at Grimsby, where it is he means, was Tom Elrington, as he was my first 'usband. And as to Mr Dovercourt rememberin'! He's a cure, he is; an' the Limit!"

The effect of the Master Machinist's story was so depressing that the M.C. tried to hurry things on; any change of sentiment would, he thought, be and advantage. So he bustled along:

"Now, Mr Turner Smith, you are the next on the roster. It is a pity we have not an easel and a canvas and paint box here, or even some cartridge pager and charcoal, so that you might give us a touch of your art - what I may call a plastic diversion of the current of narrative genius which has been enlivening the snowy waste around us." The artistic audience applauded this flight of metaphor - all except the young man from Oxford, who contented himself by saying loudly, "Pip-pip!" He had heard something like it before at the Union. The Scene Painter saw coming danger, for the Tragedian had put down his pipe and was clearing his throat; so he at once began:

A Moon-Light Effect

'I'm afraid I cannot give any narrative of a humorous or touching nature. My life has been, as is necessary for the art I follow, an unexciting one. Perhaps it has been just as well; for art requires a measure of calmness if not of isolation for its higher manifestations. Perfection was never achieved amid the silent tumult of conflicting thoughts.'

'Pip-pip' came again from the young man from Oxford. The Tragedian started to his feet - in his momentary passion he forgot to be slow.

'I protest against this unseemly interruption. This intrusion into the privacy of our artistic life of hooligans without soul: this importation to the inner heart of refinement, of the coarser vulgarisms of the world of decadent ineptitude. And when, in addition, the perpetrators of this ignoble infamy seem to be ignorant of the very elemental basis of the respect due to recognised personal supremacy in a glorious art and an honoured calling. Bah! Never mind, Turner Smith. I suppose all the fine arts are to be assailed in turns. Your time will come, however. You can, later, turn this painful episode to professional advantage. I understand that you are doing the scenery of the panto at Poole; why not take for the subject of your opening scene, the gloomy one, The Home of the Hooligan. The audience will show at once their detestation of that offensive class. Doubtless the Costumier will rise to the occasion, and show a peculiarly offensive fiend with a marvel of ill manners. The Musical Conductor, too, can enhance the satirical effect by introducing into his score as a motif the Pip-pip whereby the Hooligan proclaims himself.' Then the Tragedian retired into himself with a victorious air. In the constrained silence that followed the Wardrobe Mistress was heard to whisper to the Sewing Woman:

'Mister Wellesley Dovercourt giv it him in the neck that time. It'll be a lesson to Cattle what he won't forget.' Cattle was the nickname of the young man from Oxford, given to him soon after his joining the company. The occasion had been his writing his name in a landlady's 'book' and putting after it, Oxon. This was looked on by his comrades not as cheek but as bad spelling. The Scene Painter saw his chance to continue, and so resumed his narrative:

'I was Scenic Artist at one time to old Schoolbred, the impresario. It was a special engagement, and just suited me, for at that time I had undertaken a lot of work of various kinds, and was looking about for a painting room. Schoolbred had then a long lease of the Queen's Opera House, which had, as some of you may remember, a magnificent atelier. Old Schoolbred paid me a good salary - that is, he promised it, for he never paid any one if he could help it. I daresay he suspected that I mistrusted him, for he also put it in the agreement that I was to have full use of the painting-room for my own purposes from the time of my signing until I should start at his work. It was then that my solicitor did a wise thing. He, too, knew from old experience that there was sure to be some trouble with Schoolbred, and insisted that I should have a lease of the painting rooms. "Otherwise," he said, "your own property is not safe. If he goes bankrupt the creditors will seize all of yours that is on the premises." When I objected he said:

'"Surely it is all the same to you. You will give him each week a quittance for salary, and he will give you one for rent. It is as broad as it is long; and you wouldn't touch money anyhow." As he found all materials and paid wages I was on velvet, for I should have no expenses. All I risked was my time; and against that I had the use of the finest frames in London. Schoolbred's work was only touching up the old scenes belonging to the Opera House and painting the new opera by Magnoli, Il Campador. My assistant, whom he paid, could do most of the re-painting, and as I knew that his work did not come on till September I had nearly six months rent free, and my time my own.

'When I had moved in my traps I got to work at once. It took me half a day going over the scenery book with Grimshaw, who was then the Stage Carpenter, and off and on a couple of days more examining the scenes before we could get to work. The scenery was old-fashioned - nearly all flats; hardly a cloth, let alone a cut-cloth, in the lot. Heavy old framed stuff that wouldn't fold; and as much messy old timber about it as would furnish a ship-yard. Old Schoolbred had ordered the scenes to be made workable, so that when the time should come of bringing the operas on the road they should be all ready. There would, I saw, be a fine old job for Grimshaw to cut and hinge that mass of scenes so that they would double up for transport. However, Grimshaw was a good man, and work was no terror to him. He got his coat off, and once he was started with his own men I couldn't overtake him. Schoolbred was in a hurry to have the work done - in such a hurry that he didn't even grumble when I had to get a second assistant and two more labourers. Mind you, that meant a lot to him, for weekly wages means ready money; and out-of-pocket expenses have to be paid every Saturday. There were seventeen operas, so that it was no slouch of a job to get them all into moving trim. But there is, I must say, this about a carpenter's job that when the "production" is simplified it means saving labour afterwards. But the more scenes there are - not built scenes, but flats and cloths, wings and borders - to keep in order for nightly use and travel, and the taking to and from the storage, the more the poor scenic artist gets it in the neck.

'However, when we had once got started and I had explained to my assistants what I wanted and roughed out sketches to guide them I was able to get a bit of my own work in hand. I had a whole batch of such at the time. As you know, it was just when I was starting on my own, and every scene that was done was just so much in my pocket. I tell you I worked hard to get a bit ahead and give myself room, so that I wouldn't have to be always pulling the devil by the tail. We all worked day and night; as old Schoolbred didn't grumble at overtime the men were content to do twenty-four hours in the day. Our work has long waits; and as the labourers have to be on hand whenever they are wanted they did themselves well in the way of sleep. At first they had old sacks and such like to lie on; but presently they got luxurious, and nothing would do them but ticking and fresh hay and army blankets to cover them. I didn't mind. Indeed, I never even let on that I noticed.

After all, the men had to rest some time, and when they slept in the theatre it saved them their lodging. As you know, we scenic artists sometimes have our food cooked for us in the paint room in busy times, so that these men lived pretty well free. Naturally, I charged all expenses, as old Schoolbred was in such a hurry that ordinary rules didn't count. He was glad to get the work done so quickly at any cost.

'I had on the frames then a set of scenes for Manfred, which Wilbur Winston had commissioned. I had knocked off the other work quickly in order to be free for this. For this was a production that would make me. The scene of the Thunderstorm in the Alps would put me at the very top. That I held back, for I was anxious to make a great thing of it. It was my first job for Winston, and I wanted him to be pleased. Moreover, he had a great following, and a fine scene at the British was talked about everywhere. There was a lot of built stuff in it and paperwork, so that by the time it was done it bulked up pretty big. It was still in hand when the opera season began. Winston wasn't ready for it, so he asked me to keep it till he should rehearse. Of course, I had to meet his wishes, but happily there was loads of room at the Queen's, even after we had arranged the operas separately so that we could deal with them as they came along. So there wasn't any trouble about that.

'At first the season seemed to promise well enough; but after a night or two business fell off, and Schoolbred was at his wits' end. He was already over head and ears in debt, and this time he was only given credit in the hope that those he owed to would get a bit back. They certainly treated him very well, I will say that. They gave him every possible chance; but when the creditors saw that so far from things getting better they were going from bad to worse, a meeting was held.

'At the meeting steps were taken, and very soon after Schoolbred was in process of being made a bankrupt. A Receiver was appointed by the Court, and took formal possession. Everyone in the theatre was upset about it - except me. I had my lease, and felt like a cock on his own dunghill.

'I found out, however, after a bit that it wasn't all sunshine even with a lease. As an employe I could get salary, if there was any to get; but the liquidator cut down expenses, and, along with the rest, I was discharged. But as a lessor I was held to my lease and had to pay my rent. Long before this, as I said, old Schoolbred's work was finished, and I was working at my own contracts. I could not grumble much as my rent was small, and though I had had practically no salary in the past I had had the use of the atelier. So I paid up regularly, and was glad to be able to work. There was a little nuisance in one way; as the whole Opera house was in charge of the Receiver, and as my lease was only of a little bit of it I had to get a special permit to take out any of my scenes as they were done. I didn't want to make unnecessary trouble for myself, so I never made a bother, but asked formally whenever I wanted a permit. The Receiver was a good enough fellow, and was very civil to me. We became quite friends. Schoolbred kept on working the show with the sanction of the liquidator. He had good assets, remember, and his engagements of star singers were fine.

'One day I came across him in a violent rage. When I asked him what had upset him he could hardly speak at first. At last when he got calmer he said:

"'It's enough to drive a man mad. Here I've been spending money like water to increase the taste for opera; and now, when I've a company that's simply gorgeous and things ought to hum along this Royal death happens and knocks me right out. And the worst of it is it is all old debts except the landlord, and he's the worst of the bunch. Here have I been and restored this old rat's nest of his that had been so long empty that there's not a foot of timber in it that hasn't got the dry-rot. And now he goes and helps to make me a bankrupt - just as if that'll do him any good!"

"'But,' I said, "surely that hasn't made you so violently angry this morning?"

"'Indirectly it has!"

"'How is that?" I asked.

'I have just got an offer from America - a magnificent offer - one that would make any man-ager get up and dance for joy. A fortune, sir, a fortune - a gigantic fortune. Every big town in the United States and Canada and Mexico and South America, where they're all crazy for opera, to follow."

"'But surely," I said, "that is a thing to be glad about, not angry. Why on earth should you stamp about with rage just because unexpectedly fortune has been put within your grasp?"

"'That is just the flaming aggravation of it all."

"'I'm afraid I don't understand," I said.

"'Oh, you don't understand, don't you?" he said, with a bitterness of sarcasm in his tones which showed that the wildness of his rage had passed. "Then I had better explain to you. What is the use of putting fortune in my grasp - and then not letting me grasp it?"

"'It may be very silly of me, Mr Schoolbred," I said, "but still I don't understand."

"'How can I take the golden opportunity when I can't get away from here? Haven't we got bailiffs in the place! Isn't there an Official Receiver! How am I to get to America when these won't let a thing leave the Opera House? You can't play Grand Opera without scenery and properties and costumes, stupid! Here we are with sixteen operas - the best and most popular of them, all ready for the road - and yet we can't get even started. They are all rehearsed and perfect in every detail. I have every one of the artists on two years' engagements at English salary, but to play where and when I please. If I could get to America any time within the next two months there is nothing that could stand between me and success. There's no opposition whatever, and they couldn't get up one in the time. Moreover, I have all the popular artists - every one of them. Aye, and they would have to help me for a month at the beginning on half salaries or no salaries at all, and pay their own personals in addition. For they're in a cleft stick. They are engaged to me, so they can't play with anyone else; and if I don't play them they can't play at all. And yet here I am - here are we all - hung up for want of the sticks and rags. It's cruel! It's wicked! It's vile! If I could only get away out of this."

'Whilst he was talking a thought had come to me that made me very uneasy. How would all this affect me? Since I had been allowed to take out some of my own work that was urgent, things had got worse. Then disaster had been only threatening; now it had come. How would it be if they were to seize my things as well as old Schoolbred's! Then it flashed across me how wise had been the provision of the lease, for now they couldn't take my goods. Old Schoolbred had been watching my face narrowly; now he said, suddenly:

"'But I can't get away. None of us can get away. They have formal possession of everything in the house - and they'll bally well take care to hold very tight so that they can seize everything when the time comes."

"'They can't seize my things!" I said. He rubbed his hands in delight.

"'That is so; you have a lease. I am glad of that." He thought awhile, and his face fell. For a moment there was a gleam, but it faded as quickly as it had come, and there was on him a look of hopeless sadness. It was in his voice, too, when he spoke next:

"'That Receiver is a leery fellow - a sly, cold-blooded, heartless villain! There won't be much consideration for either you or me in the long run. I say, Turner Smith, a word of caution in your ear: Don't you trust him, and if you can help it don't ask any favours from him. Later on it may be all right; but at present he has to think of himself."

"'How do you mean?" said I.

"'He has to hold down his own job. He may be willing enough to help you; but his first duty is to the Court that employs him."

'Two or three days afterwards he came up to my room and said he had a commission to give me, and explained that he was going to make a new departure in opera.

'I am going to show them a realistic up-to-date opera; in fact, an old-fashioned Adelphi drama - except that it will be all sung. It is to be called For the Love of an Actress. The scenes will be all theatre interiors except the third act, which is to be the wicked Billionaire's palace in Park Lane. The Soprano is, of course, the heroine, and is the daughter of the Scenic Artist. She loves with mutual affection the Tenor, who is the unacknowledged son of the Billionaire by a secret marriage. The Billionaire (Bass, of course), who is a widower, wants to marry her, but she refuses. Then he gets mad and carries her off. The Tenor breaks into the Park Lane palace, and there is a great trio, which is ended by the King and all his nobles, who are coming to dine, arriving unexpectedly early. Of course, they are all in their robes as they are dining with a Billionaire. The King happens to have in his pocket the marriage certificate of the Billionaire's first wife, and also of the birth of her son. So then and there he holds a meeting of the House of Lords, and they find the Billionaire guilty. The Headsman is called in, and he is going to be executed when the Soprano in a passionate prayer appeals to the King to save him. 'Spare, oh spare, Most Gracious Ruler, the grandsire of my unborn child!' So the Billionaire makes over his money to his son, whom the King creates a Duke, and all ends happily. How does that strike you, my boy? Eh?"

"'Well, as you ask me," I said, "I think it the balliest rot I ever heard in my life!" He slapped me on the shoulder with quite a merry air, as he explained:

"'Right, my boy, right as rain. Rot is no name for it! That's why I'm so hopeful about it. We'll play it with grim seriousness, and there won't be a scene that isn't prickly with the most outrageous breaches of convenance. All London will rush to see it and laugh their very souls out. The music is fine, full of melody - just the thing for empty-headed smart society that wants to be amused. We're going to be on the pig's back, I can tell you, my boy." He then proceeded to make me a very handsome offer for painting the scenes. He said he had worked it out on a generous basis, because he wouldn't be able to pay me till the opera was out. That was reasonable enough, so I agreed. Then he told me that for the first act we couldn't do better than reproduce the painting room exactly as it stood. "It looks business, you know. All the appliances for scene painting ready with the painter at work - a fine bit of realism. That will fetch the public in itself. The Tenor will make up like you - Willie Larkom will arrange all that. And as it will be good to show the public what an expensive thing an opera is, you, or rather he, will have twelve assistants who will all be made up like the best known members of the Royal Academy. Of course, they are chorus, and will sing a song with a queer catch in the refrain - a discord like the creaking of a windlass." At the door he turned and said:

'"By the way - two things: not a word of this to a soul. The surprise will be half the battle, and I want to get it out quick, so you must get the first act done as soon as ever you can. As this is to be a reproduction of your own atelier, and the painting is in your own hands, there is no need for a model. You can start at once. In order to save time, I have had the flats primed and ready - full stage, my boy, and new canvas framed in folding panels for travelling - and not a wrinkle in the lot. And please note, I want that scene - it is where the lovers meet - to be brilliant moonlight. You must have a practical moon - a big one - shining in through the glass roof. I want to show a new moonlight effect."

'I slipped into my work, and three days afterwards I was almost ready. I kept my doors locked, and not a soul was in the secret except old Schoolbred and myself, and, of course, my own people; but I could trust them.

'It was too bad that I had a delay; but I suppose it could not be helped. It turned out that Wilbur Winston had fixed the date for Manfred, and wanted to get in the Thunderstorm Scene at once, so that he could start the lighting rehearsals. He had decided four days before, but had not announced it, except to a few friends, till he was ready to take rehearsals in hand. I arranged with him that the stuff should be brought into the British on the following Saturday night after the play was over. I got the police permit, which was necessary, for there was a devil of a lot of stuff and huge stuff too. Some of the built pieces were over forty feet long. There was one panorama cloth, which was to go round nearly the whole of the three sides of the stage. This would have to travel on two timber carts roped together head and tail. I was to come early on Sunday and see to its being put together on the British stage, and Winston would begin the lighting with a full staff that night. Rehearsals were to follow from Monday.

'Old Schoolbred was most helpful in arranging things. He certainly could hustle when he put his back into it! He undertook to arrange and look after the carting. I told him how many carts I should require, and the kind. He had a carting contract with the London Haulage Company based on men and horses and hours, so I knew he couldn't best me about the price. It was necessary to keep an eye on the old man, for he was the shiftiest old rascal I ever came across. I told my assistant to look after him, and he undertook to see the stuff safely out. I had, of course, arranged with the Receiver that the scenery should be allowed to come out. He was very nice about it, and I had his written permit in due form. He had not been a bit like what old Schoolbred said of him. I know now even better how false the old trickster was.

'Schoolbred had asked me to set the new scene on the stage - well up, so that it should not be in the way of rehearsals on Saturday after the day-men had gone home. We did not play on that night, so it was easy to arrange. I got my own men and a few that the Governor sent in; the regular day-men of the Opera House were away for the afternoon. The Governor had fixed the day for the "outing" of the theatre staff and employees, and they were having a big dinner up in Islington. The old man provided dinner for them "very handsomely," as they said. It was conventional lighting - plain gas, and all overhead, just as we used in the painting room. Old Schoolbred came and saw it set himself. We didn't want any fuss, so there was no one there except those actually at work. He was very complimentary about my work. He said he couldn't have believed that anyone could have made the dull old painting room so luxurious. "If I had thought you could have done that with it I'm blessed if I would have rented it to you at the money!" he said, in a burst of candour unusual to him.

'"But you asked me to specially," I answered. "Don't you remember you said that you wanted it to look like a miracle of artistic luxury. I took some pains, I can tell you, to paint in all that fine old furniture. Dagmar let me take some drawings in his place; he said he'd be blessed if he'd let his things come here -"

'"Oh, I ain't complaining," he answered. "In fact, I intended to furnish the place up a bit myself, so as I thought I would have some practical safes and things I went to his place and got them - paid him for them too; he wouldn't let them come without. When he told me in confidence which pieces you had taken as models, I purchased them. They are in my own room at the present moment. I'll send them down here to-morrow, so as to be ready for rehearsals."

'There was only one disagreeable incident that day, and strangely enough it came from an unexpected quarter. The men in possession got shirty because they had not been asked to the beano. It was an outrageous position for them to take, when their only duty was to be on and not off the premises. But men in their position can give a lot of trouble by simply doing nothing; and everyone who has had the misfortune of having them in the house knows that it is well to keep them in good humour. I was a bit anxious myself, for, after all, they were the servants of the Court, and they might ruin me by wilfully making some mistake about my permit, and I couldn't get it put right till Monday. If Winston didn't get his Thunderstorm Scene on the Saturday night he might get shirty in his turn and repudiate the whole transaction - then where should I be?'

'In the soup, my boy; in the soup!' said the Low Comedian.

'H-s-s-h!' said the Company in chorus; they wanted to hear what happened.

'However, Schoolbred soothed them with the promise of a dinner for themselves. On the Saturday night I saw the men in possession just sitting down to dinner. The old man had certainly done them well. He had a dinner sent in for them from the Old Red Post Restaurant - soup and fish, and an entree, and joints and sweets and savoury and cheese and dessert and coffee. Moreover, there was champagne up to the masthead, and liqueurs, and brandy and whisky and cigars after. It was all laid out at once, and they looked as if they were enjoying the very sight. Said I to myself: "There won't be any trouble with these fellows about my permit. This banquet of Heliogabalus will make them blind. Moreover, they will be blind in another form before very long. It'll take them till to-morrow afternoon to sleep this off!"

'My assistant, Rooke, was there to see our work off, so I went home to have a good sleep. I knew there would be no time for sleep or rest when Winston began to rehearse his great scene.

'On Sunday, just as I had got my scene set up in the British ready for Winston to see it Rooke came in looking very excited, and took me on one side:

'"Oh, that infernal scoundrel!" he began. He was so excited that I found it difficult to get him to begin. However, he started at last:

'"That old scoundrel Schoolbred! What do you think that he did! It turns out that he made a contract for America - the one he told you was offered him - undertaking to stage sixteen full operas. He had them all ready, as you know; but his trouble was to get them off, for they were in the hands of the Court, with men in possession to watch them. Well, he evidently fixed last night to get off. He had a big Atlantic steamer, the Rockefeller, ready in the docks, and put the whole company, staff and chorus and all, aboard last evening. Then at midnight he had a train of carts ready - there must have been a hundred of them - and on the head of getting out our one scene he carted off the whole lot out of the Opera House. They didn't begin that work, of course, till after our job, for I was there and might have been dangerous. Of course, I left when our own stuff went. In fact, I came on the last cart, and saw it all brought into the British. That yarn about the new opera was all bunkum. The new scene, too, was only a blind to keep our lot quiet and disarm suspicion. The moon was his joke. He had the sofas put in as he said he would, and had the bailiffs carried in and laid on them. They may be there yet for all I know. It would take a whole day to make them conscious. But the job seemed to the police and others continuous - they had the order of the Receiver and the police permit, and there was nothing seemingly out of order. When once the carts got off it was no one's business to enquire where they were going to. So that is how the old rascal shot the moon. He is off on blue water by this time with his whole outfit, and will come back with a fortune. The landlord won't grumble, because Schoolbred must pay his rent, or else they will attach him for stealing their scenery. Nor will the Receiver either, for he is in for a fat job for at least a year to come, nothing to do, and sure of being paid. Even the men in possession whom he diddled will have to be kept here, and they will have an easy time. I daresay they will expect to have every day a blow-out such as they had last night. But they won't get it. They don't know Schoolbred. He is all very generous when he wants anything, but he don't give something for nothing."

'But he did - for once. Before he came back from America he sent me the receipt from the Receiver of my rent for the whole time. He had paid it himself.'

Just then there was a distant noise which came drifting down on the wind. All started to their feet. There was the shrill sound of a whistle. Presently there was a loud knock at the side door of the saloon, and the door was dragged open, to the accompaniment of drifting snow and piercingly cold wind. Two railway men came in, shutting with difficulty the door behind them. One of them shouted out:

'It's a' richt! A snow-ploo wi' twa engines has been sent on frae Dundee. A rotary that has bored a road through the drifts. We're firin' up fast, and ye'll a' sleep in yer beds the nicht - somewhere. An' A'm thinkin' we could dae wi' some o' yer Johnny Walker - hot.'

Under the Sunset

Far, far away, there is a beautiful Country which no human eye has ever seen in waking hours. Under the Sunset it lies, where the distant horizon bounds the day, and where the clouds, splendid with light and colour, give a promise of the glory and beauty which encompass it.

Sometimes it is given to us to see it in dreams.

Now and again come, softly, Angels who fan with their great white wings the aching brows, and place cool hands upon the sleeping eyes. Then soars away the spirit of the sleeper. Up from the dimness and murkiness of the night season it springs. Away through the purple clouds it sails. It hies through the vast expanse of light and air. Through the deep blue of heaven's vault it flies; and sweeping over the far-off horizon, rests in the fair Land Under the Sunset.

This Country is like our own Country in many ways. It has men and women, kings and queens, rich and poor; it has houses, and trees, and fields, and birds, and flowers. There is day there and night also; and heat and cold, and sickness and health. The hearts of men and women, and boys and girls, beat as they do here. There are the same sorrows and the same joys; and the same hopes and the same fears.

If a child from that Country was beside a child here you could not tell the difference between them, save that the clothes alone are different. They talk the same language as we do ourselves. They do not know that they are different from us; and we do not know that we are different from them. When they come to us in their dreams we do not know they are strangers; and when we go to their Country in our dreams we seem to be at home. Perhaps this is because good people's homes are in their hearts; and wheresoever they may be they have peace.

The Country Under the Sunset was for long ages a wondrous and pleasant Land. Nothing there was which was not beautiful and sweet and pleasant. It was only when sin came that things there began to lose their perfect beauty. Even now it is a wondrous and pleasant land.

As the sun is strong there, by the sides of every road are planted great trees which spread out their thick branches. So the travellers have shelter as they pass. The milestones are fountains of sweet cold water, so clear and bright that when the wayfarer comes to one he sits down on the carved stone seat beside it and gives a sigh of relief, for he knows that there is rest.

When it is sunset here, it is the middle of the day there. The clouds gather and shade the Land from the great heat. Then for a little while everything goes to sleep.

This sweet, peaceful hour is called the Rest Time.

When it comes the birds stop their singling, and lie close under the wide eaves of the houses, or in the branches of the trees where they join the stems. The fishes stop darting about in the water, and lie close under the stones, with their fins and tails as still as if they were dead. The sheep and the cattle lie under the trees. The men and women get into hammocks slung between trees or under the verandahs of their houses. Then, when the sun has ceased to glare so fiercely and the clouds have melted away, the living things all wake up.

The only living things that are not asleep in the Rest Time are the dogs. They lie quite quiet, only half asleep, with one eye open and one ear cocked; keeping watch all the time. Then if any stranger comes during the hour of Rest, the dogs rise up and look at him, softly, without barking, lest they should disturb anyone. They know if the new comer is harmless; and if it be so they lie down again, and the stranger lies down too till the Rest Time is over.

But if the dogs think that the stranger is come to do any harm, they bark loudly and growl. The cows begin to low and the sheep to bleat, and the birds to chirp and sing their loudest notes, but without any music in them; and even the fishes begin to dart about and splash the water. The men awake and jump out of their hammocks, and seize their weapons. Then it is an evil time for the intruder. Straightway he is brought into the Court and tried, and if found guilty sentenced, and either put into prison or banished.

Then the men go back to their hammocks, and all living things retire again till the Rest Time is over.

It is the same in the night as in the Rest Time, if an intruder comes to do harm. In the night only the dogs are awake, and the sick people and their nurses.

No one can leave the Country Under the Sunset except in one direction. Those who go there in dreams, or who come in dreams to our world, come and go they know not how; but if an inhabitant tries to leave it, he cannot except by one way. If he tries any other way he goes on and on, turning without knowing it, till he comes to the one place where only he can depart.

This place is called the Portal, and there the Angels keep guard.

Exactly in the middle of the Country is the palace of the King, and the roads stretch away from it on every side. When the King stands on the top of the tower, which rises to a great height from the middle of his palace, he can look along the roads, which are all quite straight.

They seem to become narrower and narrower as they get further, till at last they are lost altogether in the mere distance.

Round the King's palace are gathered the houses of the great nobles, each being close in proportion to the rank of its owner. Outside these again come the houses of the lesser nobles; and then those of all the other people, getting smaller and smaller as they get further.

Every house, big and little, stands in the middle of a garden, which has a fountain and a stream of water in it, and big trees, and beds of beautiful flowers.

Farther off, away towards the Portal, the country gets wilder and wilder. Beyond this there are dense forests and great mountains full of deep caverns, as dark as night. Here wild animals and all cruel things have their home.

Then come bogs and fens and deep shaky morasses, and thick jungles. Then all becomes so wild that the road gets lost altogether.

In the wild places beyond this no man knows what dwells. Some say that the Giants who still exist, live there, and that all poisonous plants there grow. They say that there is a wicked wind there that brings out the seeds of all evil things and scatters them over the earth. Some there are who say that the same wicked wind brings out also the Diseases and Plagues that there exist. Others say that Famine lives there in the marshes, and that he stalks out when men are wicked – so wicked that the Spirits who guard the land are weeping so bitterly that they do not see him pass.

It is whispered that Death has his kingdom in the Solitudes beyond the marshes, and lives in a castle so awful to look at that no one has ever seen it and lived to tell what it is like. Also it is told that all the evil things that live in the marshes are the disobedient Children of Death who have left their home and cannot find their way back again.

But no man knows where the Castle of King Death is. All men and women, boys and girls, and even little wee children should so live that when they have to enter the Castle and see the grim King, they may not fear to behold his face.

For long, Death and his Children stayed without the Portal and all within was joy.

But there came a time when all was changed. The hearts of men grew cold and hard with pride in their prosperity, and they heeded not the lessons which they had been taught. Then when within there was coldness and indifference and disdain, the Angels on guard saw in the terrors that stood without, the means of punishment and the lesson which could do good.

The good lessons came – as good things very often do – after pain and trial, and they taught much. The story of their coming has a lesson for the wise.

At the Portal two Angels for ever kept watch and guard. These angels were so great and so watchful, and were always so steadfast in their guardianship, that there was only one name for them both. Either or both of them would, if spoken to, have been called by the whole name. One of them knew as much as the other did about anything which could have anything known about it. This was not so strange, for they both knew everything. Their name was Fid-Def.

Fid-Def stood on guard at the Portal. Beside them was a Child-Angel, fairer than the light of the sun. The outline of its beautiful form was so soft that it ever seemed to be melting into the air; it seemed a holy living light.

It did not stand as the other Angels did, but floated up and down and all around. Sometimes it was but a tiny speck, and then it would suddenly, without seeming to be making any change, be bigger than the great Guardian Spirits that were the same for ever.

Fid-Def loved the Child-Angel, and as it rose now and again, they spread their great white wings, and it would sometimes stand on them. Its own beautiful soft wings would gently fan their faces as they turned to speak.

But the Child-Angel never went over the threshold. It looked out into the wilderness beyond; but it never put even the tip of its wing over the Portal.

It was asking questions of Fid-Def, and seemed to want to know what was without, and how all there differed from all within.

The questions and the answers of the Angels were not like our questions and answers, for no speech was needed. The moment a thought occurred of wanting to know anything, the question was asked and the answer given. But still the question was given by the Child-Angel and answered by Fid-Def; and if we knew the no-language that the Angels were not-speaking we would have heard thus. Fid-Def was talking to Fid-Def:

"Is not Chiaro beautiful?"

"He is very beautiful. He will be a new power in the Land."

Here Chiaro, who was standing with one foot on the plume of Fid-Def's wing, said:

"Tell me, Fid-Def, what are those dreadful-looking Beings beyond the Portal?"

Fid-Def answered:

"They are Children of King Death. That dreadfullest one of all, enwrapt in gloom, is Skooro, an Evil Spirit."

"How horrible they look!"

"Very horrible, dear Chiaro; and these Children of Death want to pass through the Portal and enter the Land."

Chiaro, at the terrible news, soared up aloft, and got so big that the whole of the Country Under the Sunset was made bright. Soon, however, he grew smaller and smaller till he was only a speck, like the coloured ray seen in a dark room when the sun comes in through a chink. He asked of the Angels of the Portal:

"Tell me, Fid-Def, why do the Children of Death want to get in?"

"Because, dear Child, they are wicked, and wish to corrupt the hearts of the dwellers in the Land."

"But tell me, Fid-Def, can they get in? Surely, if the All-Father says, No! they must stay ever without the Land."

After a pause came the answer of the Angels of the Portal:

"The All-Father is wiser than even the Angels can conceive. He overthroweth the wicked with their own devices, and he trappeth the hunter in his own snare. The Children of Death when they enter - as they are about to do - shall do much good in the Land, which they wish to harm. For lo! the hearts of the people are corrupt. They have forgotten the lessons which they have been taught. They do not know how thankful they should be for their happy lot, for of sorrow they wot not. Some pain or grief or sadness must be to them, that so they may see the error of their ways."

As they spoke, the Angels wept in sorrow for the misdeeds of the people and the pain they must endure.

The Child-Angel answered in awe:

"Then this most horrible Being, too, is to enter the Land. Woe! woe!"

"Dear Child," said the Guardian Spirits, as the Child-Angel crept into their bosoms, "on you devolves a great duty. The Children of Death are about to enter. To you has been entrusted the watching of this dread Being, Skooro. Wheresoever he goeth, there must you be also; and so naught of harm can happen - save only what is intended and allowed."

The Child-Angel, awed by the greatness of the trust, resolved that his duty should be well done. Fid-Def went on:

"You must know, dear Child, that without darkness is no fear of the unseen; and not even the darkness of night can fright if there be light within the soul. To the good and pure there is no fear either of the evil things of the earth or of the Powers that are unseen. To you is trusted to guard the pure and true. Skooro will encompass them with his gloom; but to you is given to steal into their hearts and by your own glorious light to make the gloom of the Child of Death unseen and unknown."

"But from evil-doers - from the wicked, and the ungrateful, and the unforgiving, and the impure, and the untrue you will keep afar off; and so when they look for you to comfort them - as they must ever - they will not see you. They will see only the gloom which your far-off light will make seem darker still, for the shadow will be in their very souls."

"But oh, Child, our Father is kind beyond belief. He orders that should any that are evil repent, you will on the instant fly to them, and comfort them, and help them, and cheer them, and drive the shadow afar off. Should they only pretend to repent, meaning to be again wicked when the danger is past; or should they only act from fear, then will you hide your brightness so that the gloom may grow darker still over them. Now, dear Chiaro, become unseen. The time approaches when the Child of Death is to be allowed to enter the Land. He will try to steal in, and we shall let him, for we must work unseen and unknown, that we may do our duty."

Then the Child-Angel faded slowly away, so that no eye - not even the eye of Fid-Def - could see him; and the Guardian Spirits stood as ever beside the Portal.

The Rest Time came; and all was quiet in the Land.

When the Children of Death afar off in the marshes saw that nothing was stirring, save that the Angels stood as ever on guard, they determined to make another effort to gain entrance to the Land.

Accordingly they resolved themselves into many parts. Each part took a different form, but all together they moved on towards the Portal. Thus the Children of Death drew a-nigh the threshold of the Land.

On the wings of a passing bird they came; on a cloud that drifted slowly in the sky; in the snakes that crawled on the earth - in the worms, and mice, and moles that crept under it; in the fishes that swam and the insects that flew. By earth and water and air they came.

So without let or hindrance; and in many ways, the Children of Death entered the country Under the Sunset; and from that hour all in that fair Land was changed.

Not all at once did the Children of Death make themselves known. One by one the bolder spirits amongst them, stalking with fell footsteps through the Land, filled all hearts with terror as they came.

However, each and all of them left a lesson for good in the hearts of the dwellers in the Land.

The Rose Prince

A long, long time ago - so long ago that if one tries to think ever so far back, it is farther than that again - King Mago reigned in the Country Under the Sunset.

He was an old king, and his white beard had grown so long that it almost touched the ground; and all his reign had been passed in trying to make his people happy.

He had one son, of whom he was very fond. This son, Prince Zaphir, was well worthy of all his father's fondness, for he was as good as can be.

He was still only a boy, and he had never seen his beautiful sweet-faced mother, who had died when he was only a baby. It often made him very sad that he had no mother, when he thought other boys had tender mothers, at whose knees they learned to pray, and who came and kissed them in their beds at night. He felt that it was strange that many of the poor people in his father's dominions had mothers, whilst he, the prince, had none. When he thought thus it made him very humble; for he knew that neither power, nor riches, nor youth, nor beauty will save any one from the doom of all mortals, and that the only beautiful thing in the world whose beauty lasts for ever is a pure, fair soul. He always remembered, however, that if he had no mother he had a father who loved him very dearly, and so was comforted and content.

He used to muse much on many things; and often even in the bright rest-time, when all the people slept, he would go out into the wood, close to the palace, and think and think on all that was beautiful and true, whilst his faithful dog Gomus would crouch at his feet and sometimes wag his tail, as much as to say -

"Here I am, prince; I am not asleep either."

Prince Zaphir was so good and so kind that he never hurt any living thing. If he saw a worm crawling over the road before him he would step over it carefully lest it should be injured. If he saw a fly fallen in the water he would lift it tenderly out and send it forth again, free of wing, into the glorious bright air: so kind was he that all the animals that had once seen him knew him again, and when he went to his favourite seat in the wood there would arise a glad hum from all the living things. Those bright insects, whose colours change hour by hour, would put on their brightest colours, and bask about in the gleams of sunlight that came slanting down between the benches of the trees. The noisy insects put on their mufflers so that they would not disturb him; and the little birds resting on the trees would open their round bright eyes, and come out and blink and wink in the light, and pipe little joyous songs of welcome with all their sweetest notes.

So is it ever with tender, loving people; the living things that have voices as sweet as man's or woman's, and who have languages of their own, although we cannot understand them, all talk to them in joyous notes and bid them welcome in their own pretty ways.

King Mago was proud of his brave, good, handsome boy, and liked him to dress beautifully; and all the people loved to see his bright face and his gay clothing. The King made the great merchants search far and near till they got the largest and finest feather that had ever been seen. This feather he had put in the front of a beautiful cap, the colour of a ruby, and fastened with a brooch made of a great diamond. He gave this cap to Zaphir on his birthday.

As Prince Zaphir walked through the streets, the people saw the great white plume nodding from far away. All were glad when they saw it, and ran to their windows and doors and stood bowing and smiling and waving their hands as their beautiful prince went by. Zaphir always bowed and smiled in return; and he loved his people and gloried in the love that they had for him.

In the Court of King Mago was a companion for Zaphir whom he loved very much. This was the Princess Bluebell. She was the daughter of another king who had been wrongfully deprived of his dominion by a cruel and treacherous enemy, and who had come to King Mago to ask for help and had died in his Court after living there for many, many years. But King Mago had taken his little orphan daughter and had her brought up as his own child.

A great vengeance had come upon the wicked usurper. The Giants had come upon his dominions and had slain him and all his family, and had killed all the people in the land, and had even destroyed all the animals, except those wild ones that were like the Giants themselves. Then the houses began to tumble down from age and decay, and the beautiful gardens to become wild and neglected; and so when after many long years the Giants grew tired and went back to their home in the wilderness, the country that Princess Bluebell owned was such a vast desolation that no one going into it would know that people had ever dwelt there.

Princess Bluebell was very young and very, very beautiful. She, like Prince Zaphir, had never known a mother's love, for her mother, too, had died whilst she was young. She loved King Mago very much, but she loved Prince Zaphir more than all the rest of the world. They had always been companions, and there was not a thought of his heart that she did not know almost before it came there. Prince Zaphir loved her too, more dearly than words can tell, and for her sake he would have done anything, no matter how full of danger. He hoped when he was a man and she a woman that she would marry him, and that they would help King Mago to rule his kingdom justly and wisely, and that there would be no pain or want in the whole country, if they could help it.

King Mago had two little thrones made, and when he sat in state on his great throne the two children sat one on each side of him, and learned how to be King and Queen.

Princess Bluebell had a robe of ermine like a Queen's, and a little sceptre and a little crown, and Prince Zaphir had a sword as bright as a flash of lightning, and it hung in a golden scabbard.

Behind the King's throne the courtiers used to gather; and there were many of these who were great and good, and there were others who were only vain and self-seeking.

There was Phlosbos, the Prime Minister, an old, old man with a long beard like white silk, and he carried a white wand with a gold ring on it.

There was Janisar, the Captain of the Guard, with fierce moustachios and a suit of heavy armour.

Then there was Tufto, an old courtier, a silly old man who did nothing but hang about the great nobles and pay them deference, and every one, high and low, despised him much. He was fat, and had no hair on all his face or head, not even eyebrows, and he looked – oh! so funny, with his big bald head quite white and smooth.

There was Sartorius, a foolish young courtier, who thought that dress was the most important thing in the world; and who accordingly dressed in the finest clothes he could possibly get. But people only smiled at him and sometimes laughed, for there is no honour due to fine clothes, but only to what is in the man himself who wears them. Sartorius always tried to push himself into the front place everywhere, in order to show off his fine clothes; and he thought that because the other courtiers did not try to push him aside in the same way, they acknowledged his right to be first. It was not so, however; they only despised him and would not do what he did.

There was also Skarkrou, who was just the opposite to Sartorius, and who thought – or pretended to think – that untidiness was a good thing; and was as proud or prouder of his rags than Sartorius was of his fine clothes. He too was despised, for he was vain, and his vanity made him ridiculous.

Then there was Gabbleander, who did nothing but talk from morning till night; and who would have talked from night till morning if he could have got any one to listen to him. He too was laughed at, for people cannot always talk sense if they talk much. The foolish things are remembered, but the wise ones are forgotten; and so these talkers of too many things come to be considered foolish.

But no one must think that all the Court of the good King Mago were like these people. No! there were many, many good, and great, and noble, and brave men; but such is life in every country, even the Country Under the Sunset, that there are fools as well as wise men, and cowards as well as brave men, and mean men as well as good men.

Children who wish to become good and great men or good and noble women, should try to know well all the people whom they meet. Thus they will find that there is no one who has not much of good; and when they see some great folly, or some meanness, or some cowardice, or some fault or weakness in another person, they should examine themselves carefully. Then they will see that, perhaps, they too have some of the same fault in themselves - although perhaps it does not come out in the same way - and then they must try to conquer that fault. So they will become more and more good as they grow up; and others will examine them, and when these find they have not the faults, they will love and honour them.

Well, one day King Mago sat on his throne in his robes and his crown, and holding his sceptre in his hand.

At his right hand sat Princess Bluebell, with her robe and crown and sceptre, and with her little dog Smg beside her.

This dog was a great favourite. At first it was called Sumog, because Zaphir's dog was Gomus, and this was the name spelled backwards. But then it was called Smg because this was a name that could not he shouted out, but could only be spoken in a whisper. Bluebell had no need for more than this, for Smg was never far away, but always stayed close to his mistress and watched her.

At the King's left sat Prince Zaphir, on his little throne, with his bright sword and his mighty feather.

Mago was making laws for the good of his people. Round him were gathered all the courtiers, and many people stood in the hall and many more in the street without.

Suddenly there was a loud sound heard - the cracking of a whip and the blowing of a horn - and it came nearer and nearer, and the people in the street began to murmur. Loud cries arose, the King stopped to listen, and the people turned their heads to see who was coming. The crowd opened, and a messenger booted and spurred and covered with dust, rushed into the hall and knelt on one knee before the King, and held out a paper which King Mago took and read eagerly. The people waited in silence to hear the news.

The King was deeply moved, but he knew his people were anxious, so he spoke to them, standing up as he did so: -

"My people, a grievous peril has come upon our Land. We learn from this despatch from the province of Sub-Tegmine, that a terrible Giant has come out of the marshes beyond No-Man's-Land, and is devastating the country. But be not in fear, my people, for to-night many soldiers shall go forth with their arms, and by sunset to-morrow the Giant will have fallen, we trust."

The people bowed their heads with murmured thanks, and all went quietly away to their homes.

That night a body of picked soldiers went out with brave hearts to fight the Giant, and the people cheered them on their way.

All next day and next night the people as well as the King were very anxious; and the second morning they expected news that the Giant was overthrown.

But no news came till nightfall; and then one weary man, covered with dust and blood, and wounded unto death, crawled into the town.

The people made way for him, and he came before the throne and bent low and said -

"Alas! King, I have to tell you that your soldiers have been slain - all save myself. The Giant triumphs and advances towards the city."

Having said so, the pain of his wounds grew so great that he cried out several times and fell down; and when they lifted him up he was dead.

At the sad news which he told a low wail arose from the people. The widows of the slain soldiers cried loudly a little cry, and came and threw themselves before the King's throne, and raised their hands on high and said -

"Oh, King! Oh, King!" and they could say no more with weeping.

Then the King's heart was very, very sore, and he tried to comfort them, but his best comfort was in his tears - for the tears of friends help to make trouble light; and he spoke to the people and said -

"Alas! our soldiers were too few. To-night we will send an army, and perchance the Giant will fall."

That night a gallant army, with many great engines of war and with flags flying and bands playing, went forth against the Giant.

At the head of the army rode Janisar, the captain, with his armour of steel inlaid with gold shining in the glow of the sunset. The scarlet and white trappings of his great black charger looked splendid. At his side, for some distance on his way, rode Prince Zaphir on his white palfrey.

The people all gathered to wish the army success on their departure; and a lot of foolish people who believed in luck threw old shoes after them. One of these shoes struck Sartorius, who was as usual pushing into the front to show himself off, and blackened his eye, and the black of the shoe came off on his new dress and spoiled it. Another shoe – a heavy one with an iron heel – struck Tufto, who was talking to Janisar – on the top of his bald head, and cut it, and then all the people laughed.

Just fancy how a man is despised when people laugh when he is hurt. Old Tufto danced about and got quite angry, and then the people laughed all the more; for nothing is funnier than when a person is so angry that he loses all self-control.

All the people cheered as the army went off. Even the poor widows of the slain soldiers cheered; and the men going away looked at them and resolved that they would conquer or die, like brave soldiers doing their duty.

Princess Bluebell went with King Mago to the top of the tower of the palace, and together they watched the soldiers as they marched away. The king went in soon, but Bluebell stayed on, looking at the helmets glittering and flashing in the sunset till the sun sank down over the horizon.

Just then Prince Zaphir, who had returned, joined her. Then in the twilight on the top of the tower, with many thousand eager, anxious hearts beating in the city below them, and with the beautiful sky overhead, the two children knelt down and prayed for the success of the army on the morrow.

There was no sleep in the city that night.

Next day the people were filled with anxiety; and as the day wore on and there was no news they grew more anxious still.

Towards the evening they heard the sound of a great tumult far away. They knew that a battle was on; and so they waited and waited for news.

They did not go to bed that night at all; but all through the city watch-fires were lighted and everyone stayed awake waiting for the news.

But no news came.

Then the fear became so great that the faces of men and women grew as white as snow, and their hearts as cold. For a long, long time they were silent, for no man dared to speak.

At last one of the widows of the slain soldiers rose up and said –

"I shall arise and go down to the battle-field, and see how fares it there; and shall bring back the news to quiet your poor beating hearts."

Then many men rose and said –

"No! it must not be. We shall go. It were shame to our City if a woman went where men could not. We shall go."

But she answered them with a sad smile –

"Alas! I have no fear of death since my brave husband was killed. I do not wish to live. You must defend the city, I shall go."

Straightway she walked out of the city in the chill grey dawn towards the battle-field. As she moved away and faded in the distance, she seemed to the anxious people like a phantom of Hope passing away from them.

The sun rose and grew bright in the heavens till the rest time came; but men heeded it not, watching and waiting ever.

Presently they saw afar off the figure of a woman running. They ran to meet her and found it was the widow. She came amongst them and cried –

"Woe! woe! Alas! for our army is scattered; our mighty ones are fallen in the pride of their strength. The Giant triumphs, and I fear me all is lost."

There came a great wail from the people; and a hush fell on them, so great was their fear.

Then the King assembled all his Court and people, and took counsel what was best to be done. Many seemed to think that a new army should go forth of all those who were willing to die, if need be, for the good of the Country; but there was much perplexity.

Whilst they were discussing, Prince Zaphir sat silent on his little throne; and his eyes more than once filled with tears at the thought of the sufferings of his beloved people. Now he arose and stood before the throne.

There was silence till he should speak.

As the Prince stood, cap in hand, before the King, there was in his face a look of such high resolve that those who saw it could not help having a new hope. The Prince spoke –

"Oh, King, Father, before you decide further, hear me. It is right that if there be danger in the Land, the first to meet it is the Prince whom the people trust. If there is pain to be felt, who should feel it before him? If death is to come to any, surely it should first strike over his corpse. King, Father, pause but one day. Let me go to-morrow against the Giant. This widow hath told you that now he sleeps after his combat. Tomorrow I shall meet him in fight. If I fall, then will be time to risk the lives of your people; and if it should be that he falls, then all is well."

King Mago knew that the Prince had spoken well; and although it grieved him to see his beloved son running into such danger, he did not try to stop him, but said:

"Oh, son, worthy to be a king, thou hast well spoken! Be it even as thou wilt."

Then the people left the Hall, and King Mago and Bluebell kissed Zaphir. Bluebell said to him:

"Zaphir, you have done right," and she looked at him proudly.

Presently the prince went to bed, that he might sleep, and so be strong for the morrow.

All that night the smiths and armourers and the craftsmen of jewels worked hard and fast. Till daylight the furnaces glowed and the anvils rang; and all hands cunning at artifice plied hard.

In the morning they brought into the Hall, and laid before the throne as a present for Prince Zaphir, a suit of armour such as never before had been seen.

It was wrought of steel and gold, and was all in scales. Each scale was like a different leaf; and it was all burnished and bright as the sun. Between the leaves were jewels, and many more jewels were fastened on them like drops of dew. Thus the armour shone in the light till it dazzled the eyes of whosoever saw it – for the cunning armourers meant that when the Prince fought, his enemy might be half blinded with the glare and so miss his blows.

The helmet was like to a flower, and the Prince's crest was wrought upon it, and the feather and the big diamond in his cap were fastened in front.

When the Prince was equipped, he looked so noble and brave that the people cried out with shouts that he must conquer; and they had new and great hopes.

Then his father, the King, blessed him, and Princess Bluebell kissed him and cried a few tears and gave him a lovely rose, which he fastened on his helmet.

Amid shouting of the people, Prince Zaphir went out to fight the Giant.

His dog, Gomus, wanted to go, but he could not be taken. So Gomus was shut up and howled, for he knew that his dear master was in danger and wanted to be with him.

When Prince Zaphir was gone, Princess Bluebell went to the top of the tower and looked after him till he got so far away that she could no longer see the flashing of his beautiful armour in the sunlight. At first, when she was saying good bye to Zaphir – and she knew that it might be good bye for ever – she did not shed a tear, lest she should pain her beloved Prince, for she knew that he was going into battle, and would need all his bravery and all his firmness. So the last look Zaphir saw on his Bluebell's face was a loving, hopeful, trustful smile. Thus he went into the battle strengthened by the thought that her heart went with him, and that, although her body was far away, her spirit was close to him.

When he was gone, really gone, far away out of sight, and she stood on the top of the tower alone, Bluebell shed many tears; and the great fear of her heart that Zaphir might be killed made her sad unto death. She thought that it might be that he would be killed by the wicked Giant who had already slain two armies, and that then she would never see him again - never see the love in his dear, true eyes - never hear the tones of his tender, sweet voice - never feel the beating of his great, generous heart again.

And so she wept, oh! so bitterly. But as she wept the thought came to her that life does not lie in the power of men, or even of giants; and so she dried her tears, and knelt down and prayed with an humble heart, and rose up comforted, as people always do when they pray earnestly.

Then she went down to the great hall; but King Mago was not there. She looked for him to comfort him, for she knew that his heart must be bleeding for his son in danger.

She found him in his chamber, and he, too, was praying. She knelt beside him, and they put their arms round each other - the old King and the orphan child - and they prayed together; and so they both got comfort.

Together they waited, and waited patiently, for the return of their beloved one. All the city waited too; and neither by day nor night was there sleep in the Country Under the Sunset, for all were waiting for the return of the Prince.

When Zaphir left the city, he went on and on in the direction of the Giant, till the sun grew bright in the heavens, so bright that his golden armour glowed like fire; and then he walked under the shelter of the trees, and he did not pause even in the rest-time, but went ever onward.

Towards evening he heard and saw strange things.

Far off the ground seemed to shake, and a dull rumbling arose of rocks being levelled, and forests being broken down. These were the sounds of the Giant's footsteps, as he came onwards to the city. But Prince Zaphir, although the sounds were very terrible, had no fear, and went bravely onward. Then he began to meet many living things, which swept by him at full speed - for they were the swiftest of their kind, and so had run from the Giant faster than the rest.

On they came, in hundreds and thousands, their numbers getting more and more as the time wore on, and as the Prince and the Giant drew nearer.

There were all the beasts of the field, and all the fowls of the air, and all the insects that fly and crawl. Lions and tigers, and horses and sheep, and mice and cats and rats, and cocks and hens, and foxes and geese and turkeys, all were mixed together, big and little, and all were so frightened at the Giant that they forgot to be afraid of one another. Thus there ran together, cats and mice, wolves and lambs, foxes and geese; and the weak ones did not fear, nor did the strong ones wish to harm.

As they came on, however, all the living things seemed to know that Prince Zaphir was braver than they were, and made room for him to pass. The weakest things, and those most afraid, did not go further in their flight, but tried to get as near the Prince as possible; and many followed him back towards the Giant rather than not be near him.

Further on, in a little while, he met all the old animals that could not come so fast as the rest, and all the poor wounded living things, and all those that were slow of pace. These, too, did not try to go further, for they knew that they were safer near a brave man than in helpless flight.

Then Prince Zaphir saw something, still far off, that looked like a mighty mountain.

It was moving towards him, and his heart beat high, partly with the thought of his coming battle, and partly with hope.

The Giant came closer and closer. His footsteps crushed the rocks, and with his mighty club he swept the forests from his path.

The living things behind Prince Zaphir quailed with fear, and hid their faces in the dust. Some animals, like some foolish people, think that if they do not see anything that they do not want to see, that therefore it ceases to exist.

It is very silly of them.

Then, as the Giant drew near, Prince Zaphir felt that the hour of battle had come.

When he was face to face with a foe more mighty than aught he had ever seen, Zaphir felt as he never felt before. It was not that he was afraid of the Giant, for he felt so brave that, for the good of his people, he could gladly have died then the most painful death. It was that he realized how small a thing he was in the great world.

He saw more clearly than he had ever seen that he was only a speck - a mere atom - in the great living world; and in one moment he knew that if the victory came to him it was not because his arm was strong or his heart brave, but that because it was willed by the One that rules the universe.

Then, in his humility, Prince Zaphir prayed for strength. He doffed his splendid armour, which shone like a sun on earth, he took off the splendid helmet, and he laid by the flashing sword; and they lay in a lifeless heap beside him.

It was a fair sight, that young boy kneeling by the discarded armour. The glittering heap lay all beautiful, glowing in the bright sunset with millions of coloured flashes, till it looked like even unto a living thing. Yet it was sad, and poor, and pitiful beside the boy. There he knelt paying humbly, with his deep earnest eyes lit by the truth and trust that lay in his clean heart and pure soul.

The glittering armour looked like the work of man's hands - as it was, and the work of the hands of good true men; but the beautiful boy kneeling in trust and faith was the work of the hands of God.

As he prayed, Prince Zaphir saw all his life in the past, from the day he could first remember till even then as he was, face to face with the Giant. There was not an unworthy thought that he had ever had, not a cross word he had ever spoken, not an angry look that had ever given another pain, that did not come back to his mind. It grieved him much that there were so many; for they crowded on so thick and fast that he was amazed at their very number.

It is ever thus that the things which we do wrong - although they may seem little at the time, and though from the hardness of our hearts we pass them lightly by - come back to us with bitterness, when danger makes us think how little we have done to deserve help, and how much to deserve punishment.

Prince Zaphir's heart was purified by repentance for all wrongs done in the past, and by high resolves to be good in the future; and when his humble prayer was finished, he rose up, and he felt in his arms a strength that he wot not of. He knew that it was not his own strength, but that he was the humble instrument of saving his beloved people; and in his heart he was very thankful.

The Giant saw presently the glitter of the golden armour, and knew that another enemy had come anigh him.

He gave a great roar of rage and anger, that sounded like the echo of a thunder-clap. On the distant hills it echoed, and it rolled through the far-off valleys, and sunk into mutterings and low growlings, as of wild beasts, in the caves and the mountain fastnesses.

With such sound the Giant ever began his fighting, that so he might terrify his enemies; but the brave heart of the Prince shook not with fear. He became braver than ever as he heard the sound; for he knew that there was the more need for courage, lest his people, and even the King his father, and Bluebell, should fall into the power of the Giant.

Whilst amongst the rocks and forests the footsteps of the Giant crashed, and whilst there uprose around his feet the dust of the desolation which he made, Prince Zaphir gathered from the brook some round pebbles.

He fitted one in the sling which he carried.

As he lifted his arm to whirl the sling round his head, the Giant saw him, and laughed, and pointed in scorn at him with his great hands, which were more savage than tiger's claws. The laugh which the Giant thundered forth was so terrible - so harsh and grim and dreadful, that the living things that had raised their timid eyes to watch the fray buried their heads in the dust again, and quaked with fear.

But even as he laughed his enemy to scorn, the Giant's doom was spoken.

Round Prince Zaphir's head swung the sling, and the whistling pebble flew. It struck the Giant fair in the temple; and even with the scornful laughter on his lips, and with his outstretched hand pointing in derision, he fell prone.

As he fell he gave a single cry, but a cry so loud that it rolled away over the hills and valleys like a peal of thunder. At the sound the living things cowered again, and sagged with fear.

Afar off the people in the City heard the mighty sound; but they knew not what it meant.

As the Giant's great body fell prone, the earth trembled with the shock for many a mile around; and as his great club dropped from his hand, it laid many tall trees of the forest low.

Then Prince Zaphir fell on his knees and prayed with fervent thankfulness for his victory.

Quickly he arose, and, as he knew of the bitter anxiety of the King and people, he never stopped to gather up his armour, but fled fast to the City to bring the joyful tidings.

The night had now fallen and the way was dark; but Prince Zaphir had trust, and he went onward into the darkness with a brave and hopeful heart.

Soon the living things that were noble came around him in their gratitude; and all they that could followed him closely. Many noble animals there were, - lions and tigers and bears, as well as tamer beasts; and their great fiery eyes seemed like lamps, and helped him on his way.

However, as they drew near to the City the wild animals began to stop, for though they trusted Zaphir they feared other men. They growled a low growl of regret and stopped; and Prince Zaphir went on alone.

All night long the city had been awake. In the court King Mago and Princess Bluebell waited and watched together hand in hand. The people in the streets sat around their watch-fires, and they only dared to talk in whispers.

So the long night wore away.

At last the eastern sky began to pale; and then a streak of red fire shot up over the horizon; and the sun rose in his glory; and it was day. The people, when they saw the light and heard the fresh singing of the birds, had hope; and they looked anxiously for the coming of the Prince.

Neither King Mago nor Princess Bluebell dared to go aloft to the tower, but waited patiently in the hall; and their faces were pale as death.

The watchmen of the city and those who joined them looked down the long roadway, expecting ever and anon to see Prince Zaphir's golden armour shining in the bright morning light, and his great white plume, that they knew so well, nodding in the breeze. They knew that they could see it afar off, and so they only glanced nowand again into the distance.

Suddenly there was a shout from all the people - and then a sudden stillness.

They rose to their feet, and with one accord waited for the news.

For oh, joy! there among them - shorn of his bright armour and his nodding plume, but hale - stood their beloved Prince.

VICTORY was in his look.

He smiled on them, raising his hands as if blessing; and pointed to the King's palace, as though to say:

"Our king! his is the right to hear the earliest tidings."

He passed into the hall, all the people following him.

When King Mago and Princess Bluebell heard the shout and felt the stillness that followed, their hearts began to beat, and they waited in great dread.

Princess Bluebell shuddered and cried a little, and drew closer to the King, and leaned her face on his breast.

As she leaned with her face hidden, she felt the King start. She looked up quickly, and there - oh, joy of joys! - was her own beloved Zaphir entering the hall, with all the people following him.

The King stepped down from his throne and took him in his arms, and kissed him; and Bluebell, too, put her arms round him, and kissed him on the mouth.

Prince Zaphir spoke and said:

"Oh King my Father, and oh People! - God has been good to us, and His arm has given us the victory. Lo, the Giant has fallen in the pride of his strength!"

Then such a shout went up from the people that the roof rang again; and the noise went out over the City on the wings of the wind. The glad multitude shouted again and again, till the sound rolled in waves over the whole Dominion, and Under the Sunset that hour there was naught but joy. The King called Zaphir his Brave Son; and Princess Bluebell kissed him again, and called him her Hero.

At that very time, far away in the forest, the Giant lay fallen in the pride of his strength - the foulest thing in all the land - and over his dead body ran the foxes and the stoats. The snakes crawled around his body; and thither, too, crept all the meaner living things that had fled from him when he lived.

From afar off gathered the vultures for their prey.

Close to the slain Giant, shining in the light, lay the golden armour. The great white plume rose from the helmet and even now nodded in the breeze.

When the people came out to see the dead Giant, they found that rank weeds had grown up already where his blood had fallen, but that round the armour that the Prince had doffed had grown a ring of lovely flowers. Fairest of all was a rose tree in bloom, for the rose that Princess Bluebell had given him had taken root, and had blossomed afresh and made a crown of living roses round the helmet and lay against the stem of the plume.

Then the people took reverently home the golden armour; but Prince Zaphir said that not such armour, but a true heart was the best protection, and that he would not dare to put it on again.

So they hung it up in the Cathedral amongst the grand old flags and the helmets of the old knights, as a memorial of the victory over the Giant.

Prince Zaphir took from the helmet the feather that the King his father had given him of old and he wore it again in his cap. The rose that had blossomed was planted in the centre of the palace garden; and it grew so great that many people could sit under it, and be sheltered from the sun by its wealth of flowers.

When Prince Zaphir's birthday came, the people had made in secret a great preparation.

When he rose in the morning to go to the Cathedral, the whole people had assembled and lined the way on every side. Each person, old and young, held one rose. Those who had many roses brought them for those who had none; and each person had only one that all might be equal in the sight of the Prince whom they loved. They had taken off all the thorns from the stems that the Prince's feet might not be hurt. As he passed they threw their roses in the way, till all the long street was a mass of flowers.

As the Prince went by, they stooped and gathered up the roses that his feet had touched; and they treasured them very dearly.

At each birthday of the Prince they did the same for all their lives long. When Zaphir and Bluebell were married, they strewed their path with roses in the same way, for the people loved them much.

Long and happily lived THE ROSE PRINCE - for so they called him - and his beautiful wife Princess Bluebell.

When in the fulness of time King Mago died - as all men must - they ruled as King and Queen. They ruled well and unselfishly, ever denying themselves and striving to make others good and happy.

They were blessed with peace.

The Invisible Giant

Time goes on in the Country Under the Sunset much as it does here.

Many years passed away; and they wrought much change. And now we find a time when the people that lived in good King Mago's time would hardly have known their beautiful Land if they had seen it again.

It had sadly changed indeed. No longer was there the same love or the same reverence towards the king-no longer was there perfect peace. People had become more selfish and more greedy, and had tried to grasp all they could for themselves. There were some very rich and there were many poor. Most of the beautiful gardens were laid waste. Houses had grown up close round the palace; and in some of these dwelt many persons who could only afford to pay for part of a house.

All the beautiful Country was sadly changed, and changed was the life of the dwellers in it. The people had almost forgotten Prince Zaphir, who was dead many, many years ago; and no more roses were spread on the pathways. Those who lived now in the Country Under the Sunset laughed at the idea of more Giants, and they did not fear them because they did not see them. Some of them said,

"Tush! what can there be to fear? Even if there over were giants there are none now."

And so the people sang and danced and feasted as before, and thought only of themselves. The Spirits that guarded the Land were very, very sad. Their great white shadowy wings drooped as they stood at their posts at the Portals of the Land. They hid their faces, and their eyes were dim with continuous weeping, so that they heeded not if any evil thing went by them. They tried to make the people think of their evil-doing; but they could not leave their posts, and the people heard their moaning in the night season and said,

"Listen to the sighing of the breeze; how sweet it is!"

So is it ever with us also, that when we hear the wind sighing and moaning and sobbing round our houses in the lonely nights, we do not think our Angels may be sorrowing for our misdeeds, but only that there is a storm coming. The Angels wept evermore, and they felt the sorrow of dumbness-for though they could speak, those they spoke to would not hear.

Whilst the people laughed at the idea of Giants, there was one old man who shook his head, and made answer to them, when he heard them, and said:

"Death has many children, and there are Giants in the marshes still. You may not see them, perhaps-but they are there, and the only bulwark of safety is in a land of patient, faithful hearts."

The name of this good old man was Knoal, and he lived in a house built of great blocks of stone, in the middle of a wild place far from the city.

In the city there were many great old houses, storey upon storey high; and in these houses lived many poor people. The higher you went up the great steep stairs the poorer were the people that lived there, so that in the garrets were some so poor that when the morning came they did not know whether they should have anything to eat the whole long day. This was very, very sad, and gentle children would have wept if they had seen their pain.

In one of these garrets there lived all alone a little maiden called Zaya. She was an orphan, for her father had died many years before, and her poor mother, who had toiled long and wearily for her dear little daughter-her only child-had died also not long since.

Poor little Zaya had wept so bitterly when she saw her dear mother lying dead, and she had been so sad and sorry for a long time, that she quite forgot that she had no means of living. However, the poor people who lived in the house had given her part of their own food, so that she did not starve.

Then after awhile she had tried to work for herself and earn her own living. Her mother had taught her to make flowers out of paper; so that she made a lot of flowers, and when she had a full basket she took them into the street and sold them. She made flowers of many kinds, roses and lilies, and violets, and snowdrops, and primroses, and mignonette, and many beautiful sweet flowers that only grow in the Country Under the Sunset. Some of them she could make without any pattern, but others she could not, so when she wanted a pattern she took her basket of paper and scissors, and paste, and brushes, and all the things she used, and went into the garden which a kind lady owned, where there grew many beautiful flowers. There she sat down and worked away, looking at the flowers she wanted.

Sometimes she was very sad, and her tears fell thick and fast as she thought of her dear dead mother. Often she seemed to feel that her mother was looking down at her, and to see her tender smile in the sunshine on the water; then her heart was glad, and she sang so sweetly that the birds came around her and stopped their own singing to listen to her.

She and the birds grew great friends, and sometimes when she had sung a song they would all cry out together, as they sat round her in a ring, in a few notes that seemed to say quite plainly:

"Sing to us again. Sing to us again."

So she would sing again. Then she would ask them to sing, and they would sing till there was quite a concert. After a while the birds knew her so well that they would come into her room, and they even built their nests there, and they followed her wherever she went. The people used to say:

"Look at the girl with the birds; she must be half a bird herself, for see how the birds know and love her." From so many people coming to say things like this, some silly people actually believed that she was partly a bird, and they shook their heads when wise people laughed at them, and said:

"Indeed she must be; listen to her singing; her voice is sweeter even than the birds."

So a nickname was applied to her, and naughty boys called it after her in the street, and the nickname was "Big Bird". But Zaya did not mind the name; and although often naughty boys said it to her, meaning to cause her pain, she did not dislike it, but the contrary, for she so gloried in the love and trust of her little sweet-voiced pets that she wished to be thought like them.

Indeed it would be well for some naughty little boys and girls if they were as good and harmless as the little birds that work all day long for their helpless baby birds, building nests and bringing food, and sitting so patiently hatching their little speckled eggs.

One evening Zaya sat alone in her garret very sad and lonely. It was a lovely summer's evening, and she sat in the window looking out over the city. She could see over the many streets towards the great cathedral whose spire towered aloft into the sky higher by far even than the great tower of the king's palace. There was hardly a breath of wind, and the smoke went up straight from the chimneys, getting further and fainter till it was lost altogether.

Zaya was very sad. For the first time for many days her birds were all away from her at once, and she did not know where they had gone. It seemed to her as if they had deserted her, and she was so lonely, poor little maid, that she wept bitter tears. She was thinking of the story which long ago her dead mother had told her, how Prince Zaphir had slain the Giant, and she wondered what the prince was like, and thought how happy the people must have been when Zaphir and Bluebell were king and queen. Then she wondered if there were any hungry children in those good days, and if, indeed, as the people said, there were no more Giants. So she went on with her work before the open window.

Presently she looked up from her work and gazed across the city. There she saw a terrible thing-something so terrible that she gave a low cry of fear and wonder, and leaned out of the window, shading her eyes with her hands to see more clearly.

In the sky beyond the city she saw a vast shadowy Form with its arms raised. It was shrouded in a great misty robe that covered it, fading away into air so that she could only see the face and the grim, spectral hands.

The Form was so mighty that the city below it seemed like a child's toy. It was still far off the city.

The little maid's heart seemed to stand still with fear as she thought to herself, "The Giants, then, are not dead. This is another of them."

Quickly she ran down the high stairs and out into the street. There she saw some people, and cried to them,

"Look! look! the Giant, the Giant!" and pointed towards the Form which she still saw moving onwards to the city.

The people looked up, but they could not see anything, and they laughed and said,

"The child is mad."

Then poor little Zaya was more than ever frightened, and ran down the street crying out still,

"Look, look! the Giant, the Giant!" But no one heeded her, and all said, "The child is mad," and they went on their own ways.

Then the naughty boys came around her and cried out,

"Big Bird has lost her mates. She sees a bigger bird in the sky, and she wants it." And they made rhymes about her, and sang them as they danced round.

Zaya ran away from them; and she hurried right through the city, and out into the country beyond it, for she still saw the great Form before her in the air.

As she went on, and got nearer and nearer to the Giant, it grew a little darker. She could see only the clouds; but still there was visible the form of a Giant hanging dimly in the air.

A cold mist closed around her as the Giant appeared to come onwards towards her. Then she thought of all the poor people in the city, and she hoped that the Giant would spare them, and she knelt down before him and lifted up her hands appealingly, and cried aloud:

"Oh, great Giant! spare them, spare them!"

But the Giant moved onwards still as though he never heard. She cried aloud all the more,

"Oh, great Giant! spare them, spare them!" And she bowed her head and wept, and the Giant still, though very slowly, moved onward towards the city.

There was an old man not far off standing at the door of a small house built of great stones, but the little maid saw him not. His face wore a look of fear and wonder, and when he saw the child kneel and raise her hands, he drew nigh and listened to her voice. When he heard her say, "Oh, great Giant!" he murmured to himself,

"It is then even as I feared. There are more Giants, and truly this is another." He looked upwards, but he saw nothing, and he murmured again,

"I see not, yet this child can see; and yet I feared, for something told me that there was danger. Truly knowledge is blinder than innocence."

The little maid, still not knowing there was any human being near her, cried out again, with a great cry of anguish:

"Oh, do not, do not, great Giant, do them harm. If someone must suffer, let it be me. Take me, I am willing to die, but spare them. Spare them, great Giant and do with me even as thou wilt." But the giant heeded not.

And Knoal-for he was the old man-felt his eyes fill with tears, and he said to himself,

"Oh, noble child, how brave she is, she would sacrifice herself!" And coming closer to her, he put his hand upon her head.

Zaya, who was again bowing her head, started and looked round when she felt the touch. However, when she saw that it was Knoal, she was comforted, for she knew how wise and good he was, and felt that if any person could help her, he could. So she clung to him, and hid her face in his breast; and he stroked her hair and comforted her. But still he could see nothing.

The cold mist swept by, and when Zaya looked up, she saw that the Giant had passed by, and was moving onward to the city.

"Come with me, my child," said the old man; and the two arose, and went into the dwelling built of great stones.

When Zaya entered, she started, for lo! the inside was as a Tomb. The old man felt her shudder, for he still held her close to him, and he said,

"Weep not, little one, and fear not. This place reminds me and all who enter it, that to the tomb we must all come at the last. Fear it not, for it has grown to be a cheerful home to me."

Then the little maid was comforted, and began to examine all around her more closely. She saw all sorts of curious instruments, and many strange and many common herbs and simples hung to dry in bunches on the walls. The old man watched her in silence till her fear was gone, and then he said:

"My child, saw you the features of the Giant as he passed?"

She answered, "Yes."

"Can you describe his face and form to me?" he asked again.

Whereupon she began to tell him all that she had seen. How the Giant was so great that all the sky seemed filled. How the great arms were outspread, veiled in his robe, till far away the shroud was lost in air. How the face was as that of a strong man, pitiless, yet without malice; and that the eyes were blind.

The old man shuddered as he heard, for he knew that the Giant was a very terrible one; and his heart wept for the doomed city where so many would perish in the midst of their sin.

They determined to go forth and warn again the doomed people; and making no delay, the old man and the little maid hurried towards the city.

As they left the small house, Zaya saw the Giant before them, moving towards the city. They hurried on; and when they had passed through the cold mist, Zaya looked back and saw the Giant behind them.

Presently they came to the city.

It was a strange sight to see that old man and that little maid flying to tell people of the terrible Plague that was coming upon them. The old man's long white beard and hair and the child's golden locks were swept behind them in the wind, so quick they came. The faces of both were white as death. Behind them, seen only to the eyes of the pure-hearted little maid when she looked back, came ever onward at slow pace the spectral Giant that hung a dark shadow in the evening air.

But those in the city never saw the Giant; and when the old man and the little maid warned them, still they heeded not, but scoffed and jeered at them, and said,

"Tush! there are no Giants now"; and they went on their way, laughing and jeering.

Then the old man came and stood on a raised place amongst them, on the lowest step of the great fountain with the little maid by his side, and he spake thus:

"Oh, people, dwellers in this Land, be warned in time. This pure-hearted child, round whose sweet innocence even the little birds that fear men and women gather in peace, has this night seen in the sky the form of a Giant that advances ever onward menacingly to our city. Believe, oh, believe; and be warned, whilst ye may. To myself even as to you the sky is a blank; and yet see that I believe. For listen to me: all unknowing that another Giant had invaded our land, I sat pensive in my dwelling; and, without cause or motive, there came into my heart a sudden fear for the safety of our city. I arose and looked north and south and east and west, and on high and below, but never a sign of danger could I see. So I said to myself,

'Mine eyes are dim with a hundred years of watching and waiting, and so I cannot see.' And yet, oh people, dwellers in this land, though that century has dimmed mine outer eyes, still it has quickened mine inner eyes-the eyes of my soul. Again I went forth, and lo! this little maid knelt and implored a Giant, unseen by me, to spare the city; but he heard her not, or, if he heard, answered her not, and she fell prone. So hither we come to warn you. Yonder, says the maid, he passes onward to the city. Oh, be warned; be warned in time."

Still the people heeded not; but they scoffed and jeered the more, and said,

"Lo, the maid and the old man both are mad"; and they passed onwards to their homes-to dancing and feasting as before.

Then the naughty boys came and mocked them, and said that Zaya had lost her birds, and gone mad; and they made songs, and sang them as they danced round.

Zaya was so sorely grieved for the poor people that she heeded not the cruel boys. Seeing that she did not heed them, some of them got still more rude and wicked; they went a little way off, and threw things at them, and mocked them all the more.

Then, sad of heart, the old man arose, and took the little maid by the hand, and brought her away into the wilderness; and lodged her with him in the house built with great stones. That night Zaya slept with the sweet smell of the drying herbs all around her; and the old man held her hand that she might have no fear.

In the morning Zaya arose betimes, and awoke the old man, who had fallen asleep in his chair.

She went to the doorway and looked out, and then a thrill of gladness came upon her heart; for outside the door, as though waiting to see her, sat all her little birds, and many, many more. When the birds saw the little maid they sang a few loud joyous notes, and flew about foolishly for very joy-some of them fluttering their wings and looking so funny that she could not help laughing a little.

When Knoal and Zaya had eaten their frugal breakfast and given to their little feathered friends, they set out with sorrowful hearts to visit the city, and to try once more to warn the people. The birds flew around them as they went, and to cheer them sang as joyously as they could, although their little hearts were heavy.

As they walked they saw before them the great shadowy Giant; and he had now advanced to the very confines of the city.

Once again they warned the people, and great crowds came around them, but only mocked them more than ever; and naughty boys threw stones and sticks at the little birds and killed some of them. Poor Zaya wept bitterly, and Knoal's heart was very sad. After a time, when they had moved from the fountain, Zaya looked up and started with joyous surprise, for the great shadowy Giant was nowhere to be seen. She cried out in joy, and the people laughed and said,

"Cunning child! she sees that we will not believe her, and she pretends that the Giant has gone."

They surrounded her, jeering, and some of them said,

"Let us put her under the fountain and duck her, as a lesson to liars who would frighten us." Then they approached her with menaces. She clung close to Knoal, who had looked terribly grave when she had said she did not see the Giant any longer, and who was now as if in a dream, thinking. But at her touch he seemed to wake up; and he spoke sternly to the people, and rebuked them. But they cried out on him also, and said that as he had aided Zaya in her lie he should be ducked also, and they advanced to lay hands on them both.

The hand of one who was a ringleader was already outstretched, when he gave a low cry, and pressed his hand to his side; and, whilst the others turned to look at him in wonder, he cried out in great pain, and screamed horribly. Even whilst the people looked, his face grew blacker and blacker, and he fell down before them, and writhed a while in pain, and then died.

All the people screamed out in terror, and ran away, crying aloud:

"The Giant! the Giant! he is indeed amongst us!" They feared all the more that they could not see him.

But before they could leave the market-place, in the centre of which was the fountain, many fell dead and their corpses lay.

There in the centre knelt the old man and the little maid, praying; and the birds sat perched around the fountain, mute and still, and there was no sound heard save the cries of the people far off. Then their wailing sounded louder and louder, for the Giant-Plague-was amongst and around them, and there was no escaping, for it was now too late to fly.

Alas! in the Country Under the Sunset there was much weeping that day; and when the night came there was little sleep, for there was fear in some hearts and pain in others. None were still except the dead, who lay stark about the city, so still and lifeless that even the cold light of the moon and the shadows of the drifting clouds moving over them could not make them seem as though they lived.

And for many a long day there was pain and grief and death in the Country Under the Sunset.

Knoal and Zaya did all they could to help the poor people, but it was hard indeed to aid them, for the unseen Giant was amongst them, wandering through the city to and fro, so that none could tell where he would lay his ice-cold hand.

Some people fled away out of the city; but it was little use, for go how they would and fly never so fast they were still within the grasp of the unseen Giant. Ever and anon he turned their warm hearts to ice with his breath and his touch, and they fell dead.

Some, like those within the city, were spared, and of these some perished of hunger, and the rest crept sadly back to the city and lived or died amongst their friends. And it was all, oh! so sad, for there was nothing but grief and fear and weeping from morn till night.

Now, see how Zaya's little bird friends helped her in her need.

They seemed to see the coming of the Giant when no one-not even the little maid herself-could see anything, and they managed to tell her when there was danger just as well as though they could talk.

At first Knoal and she went home every evening to the house built of great stones to sleep, and came again to the city in the morning, and stayed with the poor sick people, comforting them and feeding them, and giving them medicine which Knoal, from his great wisdom, knew would do them good. Thus they saved many precious human lives, and those who were rescued were very thankful, and henceforth ever after lived holier and more unselfish lives.

After a few days, however, they found that the poor sick people needed help even more at night than in the day, and so they came and lived in the city altogether, helping the stricken folk day and night.

At the earliest dawn Zaya would go forth to breathe the morning air; and there, just waked from sleep, would be her feathered friends waiting for her. They sang glad songs of joy, and came and perched on her shoulders and her head, and kissed her. Then, if she went to go towards any place where, during the night, the Plague had laid his deadly hand, they would flutter before her, and try to impede her, and scream out in their own tongue,

"Go back! go back!"

They pecked of her bread and drank of her cup before she touched them; and when there was danger-for the cold hand of the Giant was placed everywhere-they would cry,

"No, no!" and she would not touch the food, or let anyone else do so. Often it happened that, even whilst it pecked at the bread or drank of the cup, a poor little bird would fall down and flutter its wings and die; but all they that died, did so with a chirp of joy, looking at their little mistress, for whom they had gladly perished. Whenever the little birds found that the bread and the cup were pure and free from danger, they would look up at Zaya jauntily, and flap their wings and try to crow, and seemed so saucy that the poor sad little maiden would smile.

There was one old bird that always took a second, and often a great many pecks at the bread when it was good, so that he got quite a hearty meal; and sometimes he would go on feeding till Zaya would Shake her finger at him and say,

"Greedy!" and he would hop away as if he had done nothing.

There was one other dear little bird-a robin, with a breast as red as the sunset-that loved Zaya more than one can think. When he tried the food and found that it was safe to eat, he would take a tiny piece in his bill, and fly up and put it in her mouth.

Every little bird that drank from Zaya's cup and found it good raised its head to say grace; and ever since then the little birds do the same, and they never forget to say their grace-as some thankless children do.

Thus Knoal and Zaya lived, although many around them died, and the Giant still remained in the city. So many people died that one began to wonder that so many were left; for it was only when the town began to get thinned that people thought of the vast numbers that had lived in it.

Poor little Zaya had got so pale and thin that she looked a shadow, and Knoal's form was bent more with the sufferings of a few weeks than it had been by his century of age. But although the two were weary and worn, they still kept on their good work of aiding the sick.

Many of the little birds were dead.

One morning the old man was very weak-so weak that he could hardly stand. Zaya got frightened about him, and said,

"Are you ill, father?" for she always called him father now.

He answered her in a voice alas! hoarse and low, but very, very tender:

"My child, I fear the end is coming: take me home, that there I may die."

At his words Zaya gave a low cry and fell on her knees beside him, and buried her head in his bosom and wept bitterly, whilst she hugged him close. But she had little time for weeping, for the old man struggled up to his feet, and, seeing that he wanted aid, she dried her tears and helped him.

The old man took his staff, and with Zaya helping to support him, got as far as the fountain in the midst of the market-place; and there, on the lowest step, he sank down as though exhausted. Zaya felt him grow cold as ice, and she knew that the chilly hand of the Giant had been laid upon him.

Then, without knowing why, she looked up to where she had last seen the Giant as Knoal and she had stood beside the fountain. And lo! as she looked, holding Knoal's hand, she saw the shadowy form of the terrible Giant who had been so long invisible growing more and more clearly out of the clouds.

His face was stern as ever, and his eyes were still blind.

Zaya cried to the Giant, still holding Knoal tightly by the hand:

"Not him, not him! Oh, mighty Giant! not him! not him!" and she bowed her head and wept.

There was such. anguish in her hart that to the blind eyes of the shadowy Giant came tears that fell like dew on the forehead of the old man. Knoal spake to Zaya:

"Grieve not, my child. I am glad that you see the Giant again, for I have hope that he will leave our city free from woe. I am the last victim, and I gladly die."

Then Zaya knelt to the Giant, and said:

"Spare him! oh! spare him and take me! but spare him! spare him!"

The old man raised himself upon his elbow as he lay, and spake to her:

"Grieve not, my little one, and repine not. Sooth I know that you would gladly give your life for mine. But we must give for the good of others that which is dearer to us than our lives. Bless you, my little one, and be good. Farewell! farewell!"

As he spake the last word he grew cold as death, and his spirit passed away.

Zaya knelt down and prayed; and when she looked up she saw the shadowy Giant moving away.

The Giant turned as he passed on, and Zaya saw that his blind eyes looked towards her as though he were trying to see. He raised the great shadowy arms, draped still in his shroud of mist, as though blessing her; and she thought that the wind that came by her moaning bore the echo of the words:

"Innocence and devotion save the land."

Presently she saw far off the great shadowy Giant Plague moving away to the border of the Land, and passing between the Guardian Spirits out through the Portal into the deserts beyond-for ever.

The Shadow Builder

The lonely Shadow Builder watches ever in his lonely abode.

The walls are of cloud, and round and through them, changing ever as they come, pass the dim shades of all the things that have been.

This endless, shadowy, wheeling, moving circle is called The PROCESSION OF THE DEAD PAST. In it everything is just as it has been in the great world. There is no change in any part; for each moment, as it passes, sends its shade into this dim Procession. Here there are moving people and events - cares - thoughts - follies - crimes - joys - sorrows - places - scenes - hopes and fears, and all that make the sum of life with all its lights and shadows. Every picture in nature where shadow dwells - and that is every one - has here its dim phantom. Here are all pictures that are most fair and most sad to see - the passing gloom over a sunny cornfield when with the breeze comes the dark sway of the full ears as they bend and rise; the ripple on the glassy surface of a summer sea; the dark expanse that lies beyond and without the broad track of moonlight on the water; the lacework of glare and gloom that flickers over the road as one passes in autumn when the moonlight is falling through the naked branches of overhanging trees; the cool, restful shade under the thick trees in summer timewhen the sun is flaming down on the haymaker at work; the dark clouds that flit across the moon, hiding her light, which leaps out again hollowly and coldly; the gloom of violet and black that rises on the horizon when rain is near in summer time; the dark recesses and gloomy caverns where the waterfall hurls itself shrieking into the pool below, - all these shadow pictures, and a thousand others that come by night and day, circle in the Procession among the things that have been.

Here, too, every act that any human being does, every thought - good and bad - every wish, every hope - everything that is secret - is pictured, and becomes a lasting record which cannot be blotted out; for at any time the Shadow Builder may summon with his special hand any one - sleeping or waking - to behold what is pictured of the Dead Past, in the dim, mysterious distance which encompasses his lonely abode.

In this ever-moving Procession of the Dead Past there is but one place where the circling phantoms are not, and where the cloudy walls are lost. There is here a great blackness, dense and deep, and full of gloom, and behind which lies the great real world without.

This blackness is called THE GATE OF DREAD.

The Procession afar off takes from it its course, and when passing on its way it circles again towards the darkness, the shadowy phantoms melt again into the mysterious gloom.

Sometimes the Shadow Builder passes through the vapoury walls of his abode and mingles in the ranks of the Procession; and sometimes a figure summoned by the wave of his spectral hand, with silent footfall stalks out of the mist and pauses beside him. Sometimes from a sleeping body the Shadow Builder summons a dreaming soul; thenfor a time the quick and the dead stand face to face, and men call it a dream of the Past. When this happens, friend meets friend or foe meets foe; and over the soul of the dreamer comes a happy memory long vanished, or the troubled agony of remorse. But no spectre passes through the misty wall, save to the Shadow Builder alone; and no human being - even in a dream - can enter the dimness where the Procession moves along.

So lives the lonely Shadow Builder amid his gloom; and his habitation is peopled by a spectral past.

His only people are of the past; for though he creates shadows they dwell not with him. His children go out at once to their homes in the big world, and he knows them no more till, in the fulness of time, they join the Precession of the Dead Past, and reach, in turn, the misty walls of his home.

For the Shadow Builder there is not night nor day, nor season of the year; but for ever round his lonely dwelling passes the silent Procession of the Dead Past.

Sometimes he sits and muses with eyes fixed and staring, and seeing nothing; and then out at sea there is a cloudless calm or the black gloom of night. Towards the far north or south for long months together he never looks, and then the stillness of the arctic night reigns alone. When the dreamy eyes again become conscious, the hard silence softens into the sounds of life and light.

Sometimes, with set frown on his face and a hard look in the eyes, which flash and gleam dark lightnings, the Shadow Builder sways resolute to his task, and round the world the shadows troop thick and fast. Over the sea sweeps the blackness of the tempest; the dim lights flicker in the cots away upon the lonely moors; and even in the palaces of kings dark shadows pass and fly and glide over all things - yea, through the hearts of the kings themselves - for the Shadow Builder is then dread to look upon.

Now and again, with long whiles between, the Shadow Builder as he completes his task lingers over the work as though he loves it. His heart yearns to the children of his will; and he fain would keep even one shadow to be a companion to him in his loneliness. But the voice of the Great Present is ever ringing in his ears at such times, enjoining him to haste. The giant voice booms out,

"Onwards, onwards."

Whilst the words ring in the ears of the Shadow Builder the completed shadow fades from beneath his hands, and passing unseen through the Gate of Dread, mingles in the great world without, in which it is to play its part. When, in the fulness of time, this shadow comes into the ranks of the Procession of the Dead Past, the Shadow Builder knows it and remembers it; but in his dead heart there is no gleam of loving remembrance, for he can only love the Present, that slips ever from his grasp.

And oh! it is a lonely life which the Shadow Builder lives; and in the weird, sad, solemn, mysterious, silent gloom which encompasses him, he toils on ever at his lonely task.

But sometimes too the Shadow Builder has his joys. Baby shadows spring up, and sunny pictures, alight with sweetness and love, glide from under his touch, and are gone.

Before the Shadow Builder at his task lies a space wherein is neither light nor darkness, neither joy nor gloom. Whatsoever touches it fades away as sand heaps melt before the incoming tide, or like words writ on water. In it all things lose their being and become part of the great Is-Not; and this terrible line of mystery is called THE THRESHOLD. Whatsoever passes into it disappears; and whatsoever emerges from it is complete as it comes and passes into the great world as a thing to run its course. Before the Threshold the Shadow Builder himself is as naught; and in its absorbing might there is that which he cannot sway or rule.

When at his task he summons; and out of the impalpable nothingness of the Threshold there comes the object of his will. Sometimes the shadow bursts full and freshly and is suddenly lost in the gloom of the Gate of Dread; and sometimes it grows softly and faintly, getting fuller as it comes, and so melts away into the gloom.

The lonely Shadow Builder is working in his lonely abode; around him, beyond the vapoury walls, pressing onward as ever, is the circling Procession of the Dead Past. Storm and calm have each been summoned from the Threshold, and have gone; and now in this calm, wistful moment the Shadow Builder pauses at his task, and wishes and wishes till, to his lonely longing wistfulness, the nothingness of THE THRESHOLD sends an answer.

Forth from it grows the shadow of a Baby's foot, stepping with tottering gait out towards the world; then follows the little round body and the big head, and the Baby shadow moves onwards, swaying and balancing with uncertain step. Swift behind it come the Mother's hands stretched out in loving helpfulness, lest it should fall. One step - two - it totters, and is falling; but the Mother's arms are swift, and the gentle hands bear it firmly up. The Child turns and toddles again into its Mother's arms.

Again it strives to walk; and again the Mother's watchful hands are ready. This time it needs not the help; but when the race is over, the shadow Child turns again lovingly to its Mother's breast.

Once again it strives, and it walks boldly and firmly; but the Mother's hands quiver as they hang by her side, whilst a tear sweeps down the cheek, although that cheek is gladdened by a smile.

The Baby shadow turns, and goes a little way off. Then over the misty Nothing on which the shadows fall, flits the flickering shadow of a tiny hand waving; and onward, with firm tread, the shadow of the little feet moves out into the misty gloom of the Gate of Dread, and passes away.

But the Mother's shadow moves not. The hands are pressed to the heart, the loving face is upturned in prayer, and down the cheeks roll great tears. Then her head bows lower as the little feet pass beyond her ken; and lower and lower bends the weeping Mother till she lies prone. Even as he looks, the Shadow Builder sees the shadows fade away, away, and the terrible nothingness of the Threshold only is there.

Then presently in the Procession of the Dead Past circle round the misty walls the shadows that had been - the Mother and the Child.

Now from out the Threshold steps a Youth with brave and buoyant tread; and as on the misty veil his shadow falls, the dress and bearing proclaim him a sailor lad. Close to this shadow comes another - the Mother's. Older and thinner she is, as if with watching, but still the same. The old loving hands array prettily the knotted kerchief hanging loosely on the open throat; and the Boy's hands reach out, take the Mother's face between them, and draw it forward for a kiss. The Mother's arms fly round her Son, and in a close embrace they cling.

The Mother kisses her Boy again and again; and together they stand, as though to part were impossible.

Suddenly the Boy turns as though he heard a call. The Mother clings closer. He seems to remonstrate tenderly; but the loving arms hold tighter, till with gentle force he tears himself away. The Mother takes a step forward, and holds out the thin hands trembling in an agony of grief. The Boy stops; to one knee he bends, then, dashing away his tears, he waves his cap, and hurries on, while once again the Mother sinks to her knees, and weeps.

And so, slowly, once again, the shadows of the Mother and the Child grown greater in the fulness of time, pass out through the Gate of Dread, and circle among the phantoms in the Procession of the Dead Past - the Mother following hard upon the speeding footsteps of her Son.

In the long pause that follows, whilst the Shadow Builder watches, all seems changed. Out from the Threshold comes a mist, such as hangs sometimes over the surface of a tropic sea.

By little and little the mist rolls away, and forth advances, black and great, the prow of a mighty vessel. The shadows of the great sails lie faintly in the cool depths of the sea, as the sails flap idly in the breezeless air. Over the bulwark lean listless figures waiting for a wind to come. The mist on the sea melts slowly away; and by the dark shadows of men sheltering from the sunny glare and fanning themselves with their broad sailor hats, it is plain that the heat is terrible.

Now from far off, behind the ship, comes up over the horizon a black cloud no bigger than a man's hand, but sweeping on with terrible speed. Also, from far away, before her course, rises the edge of a coral reef, scarcely seen above the glassy water, but darkling the depths below.

Those on board see neither of these things, for they shelter under their awnings, and sigh for cool breezes.

Quicker and quicker comes the dark cloud, sweeping faster and faster, and growing blacker and blacker and vaster and vaster as it comes.

Then those on board seem to know the danger. Hurried shadows fly along the decks; up the shadows of the ladders hurry shadows of men. The flapping of the great sails ceases as one by one the willing hands draw them in.

But quicker than the hands of men can work sweeps the tempest.

Onwards it rushes, and terrible things come close behind; black darkness - towering waves that break in fury and fly aloft - the spume of the sea swept heavenwards - the great clouds wheeling in fury; - and in the centre of these flying, whirling, maddening shadows, rocks the shadow of the ship.

As the black darkness of the heavens encompasses all, the rush of shadowy storm sweeps through the Gate of Dread.

As he waits and looks and sees the cyclone whirling amongst the shadows in the Procession of the Dead Past, the Shadow Builder, even in his dead heart, feels a weight of pain for the brave Sailor Boy tossed on the deep, and the anxious Mother sitting lonely at home.

Again from the Threshold passes a shadow, growing deeper as it comes, but very, very faint at first; for here the sun is strong, and there is but little room for shadows on the bare rock which seems to rise from the glare and the glitter of the sea deeps round.

On the lonely rock a Sailor Boy stands; thin and gaunt he is, and his clothing is but a few rags. Sheltering his eyes with his hand, he looks out to sea, where, afar off, the cloudless sky sinks to meet the burning sea; but no speck over the horizon - no distant glitter of a white sail - gives him a ray of hope.

Long, long he peers, till, wearied out, he sits down on the rock and bows his head as if in despair for a time. As the sea falls, he gathers from the rock the shellfish which has come during the tide.

So the day wears on, and the night comes; and in the tropic sky the stars hang like lamps.

In the cool silence of the night the forlorn Sailor Boy rests - sleeps, and dreams. His dreams are of home - of loving arms stretched out to meet him - of banquets spread - of green fields and waving branches, and the sheltering happiness of his mother's love. For in his sleep the Shadow Builder summons his dreaming soul, and shows him all these blessings passing ceaselessly in the Procession of the Dead Past, and so comforts him lest he should despair and die.

Thus wear on many weary days; and the sailor-boy lingers on the lonely rock.

Afar off he can just see a hill that seems to rise over the Water. One morning when the blackening sky and the sultry air promise a storm, the distant mountain seems nearer; and he thinks that he will try to reach it by swimming.

Whilst he is thus resolving, the storm rushes up over the horizon and sweeps him from the lonely rock. He swims with a bold heart; but just as his strength is done, he is cast by the fury of the storm on a beach of soft sand. The storm passes on its way and the waves leave him high and dry. He goes inland, where, in a cave in the rock, he finds shelter, and sinks to sleep.

The Shadow Builder, as he sees all this happen in the shadows on the clouds, and land, and sea, rejoices in his dead heart that the lonely mother perhaps will not wait in vain.

So time wears on, and many, many weary days pass. The Boy becomes a young Man, living in the lonely island; his beard has grown, and he is clothed in a dress of leaves. All day long, save when he is not working to get food to eat, he watches from the mountain top for a ship to come. As he stands looking out over the sea, the sun casts his shadow down the hillside, so that at evening, as it sinks low in the waters, the shadow of the lonely Sailor grows longer and longer, till at the last it makes a dark streak down the hill side, even to the water's edge.

The lonely Man's heart grows heavier and heavier as he waits and watches, whilst the weary time passes and the countless days and nights come and go.

Time comes when he begins to get feebler and feebler. At last he grows sick to death, and lingers long a-dying.

Then these shadows pass away.

Out from the Threshold grows the shadow of an old woman, thin and worn, sitting in a lonely cottage on a jutting cliff. In the window a lamp burns in the night time to welcome the Lost One should he ever return, and to guide him to his Mother's home. By the lamp the Mother watches, till, wearied out, she sinks to sleep.

As she sleeps the Shadow Builder summons her sleeping soul with the wave of his spectral hand.

She stands beside him in the lonely abode, whilst round them through the misty walls passes onward the Procession of the Dead Past.

As she looks, the Shadow Builder lifts his spectral hand to point to the vision of her Son.

But the Mother's eyes are quicker than even the spectral hand that evokes all the shadows of the rushing storm, and ere the hand is raised she sees her Son among the Shadows of the Past. The Mother's heart is filled with unspeakable joy, as she sees him alive and hale, although a prisoner amongst the tropic seas.

But alas! she knows not that in the dim Procession pass only the things that have been; and that although in the past the lonely Sailor lived, in the present - even at the moment - he may be dying or dead.

The Mother stretches out her arms to her Boy; but even as she does, her sleeping soul loses sight of the dim Procession and vanishes from the Shadow Builder's lonely abode. For when she knows that her Boy is alive, there follows a great pain that he is lonely and waits and watches for help; and the quick heart of the Mother is overcome with grief, and she wakes with a bitter cry.

Then as she rises and looks past the dying lamp out into the dawn, the Mother feels that she has seen a vision of her son in sleep, and that he lives and waits for help; and her heart glows with a great resolve.

Quickly then from the Threshold float many shadows. -

A lonely Mother speeding with flying feet to a distant city.

Grave men refusing, but not unkindly, a kneeling woman making an appeal with uplifted hands.

Hard men spurning a praying Mother from their doors.

A wild rabble of bad and thoughtless boys and girls hounding through the streets a hurrying woman.

A shadow of pain on a Mother's heart.

The upcoming of a black cloud of despair, but which hangs far off - for it cannot advance into the bright sunlight of the Mother's resolve.

Weary days with their own myriad shadows.

Lonely nights - black want - cold - hunger and pain; and through all these darkening shadows the swift moving shadow of the Mother's flying feet.

A long long line of such pictures come ever anigh in the Procession, till the dead heart of the Shadow Builder grows icy, and his burning eyes look out savagely on all who give pain and trial to the Mother's faithful heart.

And so all these shadows float out into a black mist, and are lost in the gloom of the Gate of Dread.

Another shadow grows out of the mist. -

An Old Man sits in his armchair. The firelight flickering throws his image, quaintly dancing, on the wall of the room. He is old, for the great shoulders are bowed, and the grand strong face is lined with years. There is another shadow in the room; it is the Mother's - she is standing by the table, and is telling her story; her thin hands point away where in the distance she knows her Son is a prisoner in the lonely seas.

The Old Man rises; the enthusiasm of the Mother's heart has touched him, and back to his memory rush the old love and energy and valour of his youth. The great hand rises, closes, and strikes the table with a mighty blow, as though declaring a binding promise. The Mother sinks to her knees, - she seizes the great hand and kisses it, and stands erect.

Other men come in - they receive orders - they hurry out.

Then come many shadows whose movement and swiftness and firm purpose mean life and hope.

At sunset, when the masts make long shadows on the harbour water, a big ship moves out on her journey to the tropic seas. Men's shadows quickly flit up and down the rigging and along the decks.

As the shadows wheel round the capstan bar the anchor rises; and into the sunset passes the great vessel.

In the bow, like a figure of Hope, stands the Mother, gazing with eager eyes on the far-off horizon.

Then this shadow fades.

A great ship sweeps along with white sails swelling to the breeze; at the bow stands the Mother, gazing ever out into the distance before her.

Storms come and the ship flies before the blast; but she swerves not, for the Mother, with outstretched hand, points the way, and the helmsman swaying beside his wheel obeys the hand.

So this shadow also passes.

The shadows of days and nights come on in quick succession; and the Mother seeks ever for her Son.

So the records of the prosperous journey melt into a faint, dim, misty shadow through which one figure alone stands clear - the watching Mother at the vessel's prow.

Now from the Threshold grow the shadows of the mountain island and of the ship drawing nigh. In the prow the Mother kneels, looking out and pointing. A boat is lowered. Men spring on board with eager feet; but before them all is the Mother. The boat nears the island; the water shallows, and on the hot white beach the men spring to land.

But in the boat's prow still the Mother sits. In her long anxious hours of agony she has seen in her dreams her Son standing afar off and watching; she has seen him wave his arms with a great joy as the ship rises over the horizon's edge; she has seen him standing on the beach waiting; she has seen him rushing through the surf so that the first thing that the lonely Sailor Boy should touch would be his Mother's loving hands.

But alas! for her dreams. No figure with joyous waving arms stands on the summit of the mountain - no eager figure stands at the water's edge or dashes to meet her through the surf. Her heart grows cold and chill with fear.

Has she indeed come too late?

The men leave the boat, comforting her as they go with shakings of the hand and kindly touches upon the shoulder. She motions them to haste and remains kneeling.

The time goes on. The men ascend the mountain; they search, but they find not the lost Sailor Boy, and with slow, halting feet they return to the boat.

The Mother hears them coming afar and rises to meet them. They hang their heads. The Mother's arms go up, tossed aloft in the anguish of despair, and she sinks swooning in the boat.

The Shadow Builder in an instant summons her spirit from her senseless clay, and points to a figure passing, without movement, in the Procession of the Dead Past.

Then quicker than light the Mother's soul flies back full of new-found joy.

She rises from the boat - she springs to land. The men follow wondering.

She rushes along the shore with flying feet; the sailors come close behind.

She stops opposite the entrance to a cave obscured with trailing brambles. Here, without turning, she motions to the men to wait. They pause and she passes within.

For a few moments grim darkness pours from the threshold; and then one sad, sad vision grows and passes. -

A dim, dark cave - a worn man lying prone, and a Mother in anguish bending over the cold clay. On the icy breast she lays her hand; but alas! she cannot feel the beat of the heart she loves.

With a wild, heart-stricken gesture, she flings herself upon the body of her Son and holds it close, close - as though the clasp of a Mother were stronger than the grasp of Death.

The dead heart of the Shadow Builder is alive with pain as he turns away from the sad picture, and with anxious eyes looks where from behind the Gate of Dread, the Mother and Child must come to join the ever-swelling ranks of the Procession of the Dead Past.

Slowly, slowly comes the shadow of the clay cold Mariner passing on.

But swifter than light come the Mother's flying feet. The arms so strong with love are stretched out - the thin hands grasp the passing shadow of her Son and tear him back beyond the Gate of Dread - to life - and liberty - and love.

The lonely Shadow Builder knows now that the Mother's arms are stronger than the grasp of Death.

How 7 Went Mad

On the bank of the river that flows through the Land there stands a beautiful palace, where one of the great men dwells.

The bank rises steep from the rushing water; and the great trees growing on the slope rise so high that their branches wave level with the palace turrets. It is a beautiful spot, where the grass is crisp and short and close like velvet, and as green as emerald. There the daisies shine like stars that have fallen, and lie scattered over the sward.

Many children have lived and grown to be men and women in the old palace, and they have had many pets. Amongst their pets have been many birds - for birds of all kinds love the place. In one corner is a spot which is called the Birds' Burying Ground. Here all the pets are laid when they die; and the grass grows greenly here, and many flowers spring up among the monuments.

One of the boys that had here dwelt had once, as a pet, a raven. He found the bird, whose leg had been wounded, and took it home and nursed it till it grew well again; but the poor thing was lame.

Tineboy was the youth's name; and the bird was called Mr. Daw. As you may imagine, the raven loved the boy and never left him. There was a cage for it in his bedroom, and there the bird went every night to roost when the sun went down. Birds go to bed quite regularly of their own accord; and if you wished to punish a bird you would make him get up. Birds are not like boys and girls. Just fancy punishing boys or girls by not letting them go to bed at sunset, or by preventing them getting up very early in the morning.

Well, when morning came this bird would get up and stretch himself, and wink his eyes, and give a good shake all over, and then feel quite awake and ready to begin the day.

A bird has a much easier time of it in getting up than a boy or a girl. Soap cannot get into its eye; or the comb will not stick in knots of hair, and its shoe-laces never get into black knots. This is because it does not use soap, or combs, or shoe-laces; if it did, perhaps it also would suffer.

When Mr. Daw had quite finished his own dressing, he would hop on the bed and try and wake his master and make him get up; but of the two to wake him was the easier task. When the boy went to school the bird would fly along the road beside him, and would sit near on a tree till school was over, and then would follow him home again in the same way.

Tineboy was very fond of Mr. Daw and he used sometimes to try to make him come into the schoolroom during school-hours. But the bird was very wise, and would not.

One day Tineboy was at his sums, and instead of attending to what he was doing, he kept trying to make Mr. Daw come in. The sum was "multiply 117,649 by 7." Tineboy and Mr. Daw kept looking at one another. Tineboy made signals to the bird to come in. Mr. Daw, however, would not stir; he sat outside in the shade, for the day was very hot, and put his head on one side and looked in knowingly.

"Come in, Mr. Daw," said Tineboy, "and help me to do this sum." Mr. Daw only croaked.

"Seven times nine are seventy-seven, seven times nine are seventy-nine - no ninety-seven. Oh, I don't know - I wish number 7 had never been invented," said Tineboy.

"Croak;" said Mr. Daw.

The day was very hot and Tineboy was very sleepy. He thought that perhaps he would be able to do the sum better if he rested a little while, just to think; and so he put his head down on the table. He was not quite comfortable, for his forehead was on the 7, at least he thought it was; so he shifted it till it hung right down over the edge of the desk. Then, after a while, somehow, very queer things began to happen.

The Teacher was just going to tell them a story.

The scholars had all settled themselves down to listen; the Raven sat on the sill of the open window, put his head on one side, closed one eye - the eye nearest the school-room - so that they might think him asleep, and listened away harder than any of them.

The pupils were all happy - all except three.   One because his leg went to sleep; another because she had her pocket full of curds and wanted to eat them, and couldn't without being found out, and the curds were melting away; and the third, who was awfully sleepy, and awfully anxious to hear the story, and couldn't do either because of the other.

The schoolmaster then began his story.

HOW POOR 7 WENT MAD

"The Alphabet Doctor - "

Here he was interrupted by Tineboy, who said -

"What is an Alphabet Doctor?"

"An Alphabet Doctor," said the schoolmaster, "is the doctor who attends to the sicknesses and diseases of the letters of the Alphabet."

"How have Alphabets diseases and sicknesses?" asked Tineboy.

"Oh, they have plenty. Do you never make a crooked o or a capital A with a lame leg, or a T that is not straight in its back?"

There was a chorus from all the class, "He does. He does often." Ruffin, the biggest boy, said after all the others, "Very often. In fact always."

"Very well, then there must be some one to put them straight again, must there not?"

None of the children could say that there was not. Tineboy alone was heard to mutter to himself, "I don't believe it."

The schoolmaster began again -

"The Alphabet Doctor was sitting down to his tea. He was very tired, for he had been out attending cases all day."

Tineboy again interrupted, "What cases?"

"I can tell you. He had to put in an i which had been omitted, and to alter the leg of an R which had been twisted into a B.

"Well, just as he was beginning his tea a hurried knock came to the door. He went to the door, opened it, and a groom rushed into the room, breathless with running, and said -

"'Oh, Doctor, do come quick; there is a frightful calamity down at our place.'"

"'What is our place?' said the doctor."

"'Oh, you know. The Number Stables.'"

"What are the Number Stables?" said Tineboy, again interrupting.

"The Number Stables," said the Teacher, "are the stables where the numbers are kept."

"Why are they kept in stables?" said Tineboy.

"Because they go so fast."

"How do they go fast?"

"You take a sum and work it and you will see at once. Or look at your multiplication table; it starts with twice one are two, and before you get down the page you are at twelve times twelve. Is that not fast going?"

"Well, they have to keep the numbers in sables, or else they would run away altogether and never be heard of again. At the end of the day they all come home and change their shoes, and get tied up and have their supper."

"The Groom from the Number Stables was very impatient."

"'What is wrong?'   said the Doctor."

"'Oh, poor 7, sir.'"

"'What of him?'"

"'He is mortal bad. We don't think he'll ever get through it.'"

"'Through what?' said the Doctor."

"'Come and see,' said the Groom."

"The Doctor hurried away, taking the lantern with him, for the night was dark, and soon got to the Stables."

"As he got close there was a very curious sound heard - a sound of gasping and choking, and yelling and coughing, and laughing, and a wild, unearthly screech all in one."

"'Oh, do come quick!' said the Groom."

"When the Doctor entered the stables there was poor No. 7 with all the neighbours round him, and he was in a very bad way. He was foaming at the mouth and apparently quite mad. The Nurse from the Grammar Village was holding him by the hand, trying to bleed him. All the neighbours were wringing either their hands or their necks, or were helping to hold him. The Footsmith, - the man," explained the teacher, seeing from the look on Tineboy's face that he was going to ask a question, "the man who puts the feet on the letters and numbers to make them able to stand upright without wearing out,- was holding down the poor demented nuummbeer."

"The Nurse, trying to quiet him, said:"

"'There now, there now, deary - don't go and make a noise. Here comes the good Alphabet Doctor, who will make you unmad.'"

"'I won't be made unmad,' said 7, loudly."

"'But, my good sir,' said the Doctor, 'this cannot go on. You surely are not mad enough to insist on being mad?'"

"'Yes, I am,' said 7, loudly."

"'Then,' said the Doctor blandly, 'if you are mad enough to insist on being mad, we must try to cure your madness or being mad, and then you will be unmad enough to wish to be unmad, and we will cure that too.'"

"I don't understand that," said Tineboy.

"Hush!" said the class.

"The Doctor took out his stethoscope, and his telescope, and his microscope, and his horoscope, and began to use them on poor mad 7."

"First he put the stethoscope to the sole of his foot, and began to talk into it."

"'That is not the way to use that,' said the Nurse; 'you ought to put it to his chest and listen to it.'"

"'Not at all, my dear madam,' said the bland Doctor, 'that is the way with sane people; but, of course, when one is insane, the fact of the disease necessitates an opposite method of treatment.' Then he took the telescope and looked at him to see how near he was, and the microscope to look how small; and then he drew his horoscope."

"Why did he draw it?" said Tineboy.

"Because, my dear child," said the Teacher, "do you not see that by right a horoscope is cast; but as the poor man was mad the horoscope had to be drawn."

"What is a horrorscope?" said Tineboy.

"It is not horrorscope, my child; it is horoscope - a very different thing."

"Well, what is horoscope?"

"Look in your dictionary, my dear child," said the Teacher.

"Well, when the doctor had used all the instruments, he said, 'I use all these in order to find the scope of the disease. I shall now proceed to find the cause. In the first instance, I shall interrogate the patient.'"

"'Now, my good sir, why do you insist on being mad?'"

"'Because I choose.'"

"'Oh, my dear sir, that is not a polite answer. Why do you choose?'"

"'I can't say why,' said 7 'unless I make a speech.'"

"'Well, make a speech.'"

"'I can't speak till I am set free; how can I make a speech with all these people holding me?'"

"'We are afraid to let you go,' said the Nurse, 'you will run away.'"

"'I will not.'"

"'You promise that?' said the doctor."

"'I promise,' said 7."

"'Let him go,' said the Doctor, and accordingly they put a piece of carpet under him, and the Footsmith sat on his head, the way they do when horses fall down in the street. Then they all got clear away, and the Footsmith got away too; and after a long struggle 7 got to his feet."

"'Now make the speech,' said the Doctor."

"'I can't begin,' said 7, 'till I get a glass of water on a table. Who ever heard of any one making a speech without a glass of water!'"

"So they brought a glass of water."

"'Ladies and Gentlemen - ' began 7, and then stopped."

"'What are you waiting for?' said the Doctor."

"'For the applause, of course,' said 7. 'Who ever heard of a speech without applause?'"

"They all applauded."

"'I am mad,' said 7, 'because I choose to be mad; and I never shall, will, might, could, should, would, or ought to be anything but mad. The treatment that I get is enough to make me mad.'"

"'Dear me, dear me!' said the Doctor. 'What treatment?'"

"'Morning, noon, and night am I treated worse than any slave. There is not in the whole range of learning any one thing that has so much to bear as I have. I work hard all the time. I never grumble. I am often a multiple; often a multiplicand. I am willing to bear my share of being a result, but I cannot stand the treatment I get. I am wrong added, wrong divided, wrong subtracted, and wrong multiplied. Other numbers are not treated as I am; and, besides, they are not orphans like me.'"

"'Orphans?' asked the Doctor; 'what do you mean?'"

"'I mean that the other numbers have lots of relations. But I have neither kith nor kin except old Number 1, and he does not count for much; and, besides, I am only his great-great-great-great-grandson.'"

"'How do you mean?' asked the Doctor."

"'Oh, he is an old chap that is there all the time. He has all his children round him, and I only come six generations down.'"

"'Humph!' said the doctor."

"Number 2,' went on 7, 'never gets into any trouble, and 4, 6, and 8 are his cousins. Number 3 is close to 6 and 9. No. 5 is half a decimal and he never gets into trouble. But as for me, I am miserable, ill-treated, and alone.' Here poor 7 began to cry, and bending down his head sobbed bitterly."

When the Teacher got thus far there was an Interruption, for here little Tineboy began to cry too.

"Why are you crying?" said Ruffin, the bully boy.

"I am not crying," said Tineboy, and he cried away faster than ever.

The Teacher went on with the story.

"The Alphabet Doctor tried to cheer poor 7."

"'Hear, hear!' said he."

"7 stopped crying and looked at him. 'No,' said he, 'you should say "speak, speak," it is I that should say "hear, hear."'"

"'Certainly,' said the Doctor, 'you would say that if you were sane; but then, you see, you are not sane, and being mad you say what you should not say.'"

"'That is false,' said 7."

"'I understand,' said the Doctor, 'but do not stop to argue the point. If you were sane you would say "that is true," but you do say "that is false," meaning that you agree with me.'"

"7 looked pleased at being so understood."

"'No,' said he - meaning 'yes.'"

"'Then,' continued the Doctor, 'if you say "speak, speak," when a sane man would say "hear, hear," of course, I should say "hear, hear," when I mean "speak, speak," because I am talking to a madman.'"

"'No, no,' said 7 - meaning, 'yes, yes.'"

"'Go on with your speech,' said the Doctor."

"'No 7 took out his handkerchief and wept.'"

"'Ladies and Gentlemen,' he went on, 'once more I must plead the cause of the poor ill-used number - that is me - this orphan number - this number without kin - '"

Here Tineboy interrupted the Teacher, "How had he no skin?"

"Kin, my child. Kin, not skin," said the Teacher.

"What is the difference between kin and skin?" asked Tineboy.

"There will be but a small difference," said the Teacher, "between this cane and your skin if you interrupt." So Tineboy was quiet.

"Well," said the teacher, "poor 7 went on - 'I implore your pity for this forlorn number. Oh, you boys and girls, think of a poor desolate number, who has no home, no friends, no father, mother, brother, sister, uncle, aunt, nephew, niece, son, daughter, or cousin, and is desolate and alone.'"

Tineboy here set up a terrible howl.

"What are you crying for?" said the Teacher.

"I want poor old 7 to be more happy. I will give him some of my lunch and a share of my bed."

The Teacher turned to the Monitor.

"Tineboy is a good child," he said, "let him for the next week learn 7 times 0 up, and perhaps that will comfort him."

The Raven, sitting in the window, winked his eye to himself and hopped about with a suppressed merry croak, shook his wings, and seemed hugging himself and laughing. Then he hopped softly away, and stole up and hid on the top of the book-case.

The Schoolmaster went on with his story.

"Well, children, after a while poor 7 got better and promised that he would get unmad. Before the Doctor went home again all the Alphabet and Number Children came and shook poor Number 7's hand, and promised that they would be more kind to him in future."

"Now, children, what do you think of the story?"

They all said that they liked it, that it was beautiful, and that they too would try to be more kind to poor 7 for the future. At last Ruffin the bully boy said:

"I don't believe it. And if it is true I wish he had died; we would be better without him."

"Would we?" asked the teacher, "how?"

"Because we would not be troubled with him," said Ruffin.

As he said it there was a sort of queer croak heard from the Raven, but nobody minded, except Tineboy, who said: -

"Mr. Daw, you and I love poor 7, at all events."

The Raven hated Ruffin because he always threw stones at him, and he had tried to pull the feathers out of his tail, and when Ruffin spoke, his croak seemed to mean, "Just you wait." When no one was looking Mr. Daw stole up and hid in the rafters.

Then presently school broke up, and Tineboy went home; but he was not able to find Mr. Daw. He thought he was lost, and was very miserable, and went to bed crying.

In the meantime, when the school was locked up empty, Mr. Daw came down from the rafters very, very quietly - hobbled over to the door, and putting his head down, listened; then he flew and scrambled up on the handle of the door, and looked out through the keyhole. There was nothing to see and nothing to hear.

Then he got up on the Master's desk, flapped his wings, and began to crow like a cock, only very softly, for fear he should be heard.

Presently he went over all the room, flying up to the big sheets of multiplication table, and turning over the pages of the books with his claws, and picking up SOMETHING with his sharp beak.

One would hardly believe it, but he was stealing all the Number Sevens in the place; he picked the Seven off the clock, rubbed it off the slates, and brushed it with his wings off the blackboard.

Mr. Daw knew that if once you can get the whole of any number out of a schoolroom no one else can use it without asking your leave.

Whilst he was picking out all the Sevens he was swelling out very much; and when he had got them all he was exactly Seven times his natural size.

He was not able to do this all at once. It took him the whole night, and when he got back to his corner in the rafters it was nearly time for school to open.

He was now so big that he was only just able to squeeze into the corner and no more.

The school time came, but there was no Master, and there were no Scholars. A whole hour passed; and then the Master came, and the Ushers, and all the Boys and Girls.

When they were all in the Master said –

"You are all very late."

"Please, sir, we could not help it," they all answered together.

"Why could you not help it?"

They all answered at once –

"I wasn't called in time."

"What time are you called at every morning?"

They all seemed about to speak, but all were silent.

"Why don't you answer?" asked the Teacher.

They made motions will their mouths like speaking, but no one said anything.

The Raven up in his corner croaked a quiet laugh all to himself.

"Why don't you answer?" asked the Teacher again. "If I have not my question answered at once, I shall keep you all in."

"Please, sir, we can't," said one.

"Why not?"

"Because" –

Here Tineboy interrupted, "Why were you so late Sir?"

"Well, my boy, I am sorry to say I was late; but the fact is, my servant did not knock at my door at the usual hour."

"What hour, sir?" asked Tineboy.

The Teacher seemed as if he was going to speak, but stopped.

"This is very queer," he said, after a long pause.

Ruffin said, in a sort of swaggering way, "We are not late at all. You are here and we are here – that is all."

"No, it is not all," said the Teacher. "Ten is the hour, and it is now eleven – we have lost an hour."

"How have we lost it?" asked one of the Scholars.

"Well, that is what puzzles me. We must only wait a little and see."

Here Tineboy said suddenly, "Perhaps some one stole it!"

"Stole what?" said the scholars.

"I don't know," said Tineboy.

They all laughed.

"You need not laugh, something is stolen; look at my lesson!" said Tineboy, and he held up the book. Here is what they saw –

```
- 1 are    -
- 2  " 14
- 3  " 21
- 4  " 28
- 5  " 35
- 6  " 42
- -  " 49
- 8  " 56
```

- 9 ” 63
-   10 ” -0

All the Scholars crowded round Tineboy to look at the book. Ruffin did not, for he was looking at the school clock.

"The clock has lost something," said he, and sure enough it did not look all right.

The Teacher looked up - for he was leaning with his head on his desk, groaning.

"What is wrong with it?" he asked.

"Something is missing."

"There is a number out; there are only eleven figures," said the Teacher.

"No, no," said the Scholars.

"Count them out, Ruffin," said the Master.

"1 2 3 4 5 6 8 9 10 11 12."

"Quite right," said the Teacher, "you see there are twelve. No there are not - yes there are - no - yes - no, yes - what is it all about?" and he looked round the room, and then leaned his head on the desk again and groaned.

In the meantime the Raven had crept along the rafters till he had got over the Teacher's desk; and then he got a good heavy Seven and dropped it right on the little bald spot on the top of the Teacher's head. It bounded off the head and fell on the desk before him. The instant the Teacher saw it he knew what was wanting all the time. He covered over the Seven with a piece of blotting Paper. He then called up Ruffin.

"Ruffin, you told me that something was missing - are you sure?"

"Yes, of course."

"Very well. Do you remember that you said yesterday, that you wished a certain Number had died in a madhouse?"

"Yes, I do; and I wish it still."

"Well, that Number has been stolen by some one during the night."

"Hurrah!" said Ruffin, and he threw his book up to the ceiling. It hit poor Mr. Daw, who had another Seven in his beak ready to drop it, and knocked the Seven down. It fell into Tineboy's cap, which he held in his hand. He took it out, and stooped and petted it.

"Poor 7," said Tineboy.

"Give me the Number," said Ruffin.

"I shan't. It belongs to me."

"Then I'll make you," said Ruffin; and he caught hold of Tineboy - even before the Master's face.

"Let me go. I'll not give you my poor Seven," said Tineboy, and he began to scream and cry.

"Ruffin, stand out," said the Master.

Ruffin did so.

"Seven times seven?" asked the Master.

Ruffin did not answer. He could not, for he had not got a Seven.

"I know," said Tineboy.

"Oh, yes," said Ruffin, with a sneer; "he knows because he has a Number."

"Forty-nine," said Tineboy.

"Right," said the Master; "go up, Tineboy."

So Tineboy went up to the top of the class, and Ruffin went down.

"Seven times forty-nine?" asked the Master.

They were all silent.

"Come, answer!" said the Master.

"What is it, yourself?" said Tineboy.

"Well, my boy, I am sorry to say I cannot say. Dear me, it is very queer," and the Master put down his head on the desk again, and groaned louder than ever.

Just then Mr. Daw took another seven and dropped it down on the floor before Tineboy.

"Three hundred and forty-three," said Tineboy, quickly; for he could answer as he had another Seven.

The Teacher looked up and laughed loudly.

"Hurrah, hurrah!" said he.

When the third Seven fell the Raven began to swell.

He got seven times as big as he was, so that he began to lift the slates off the roof.

The Scholars all looked up; Ruffin had his mouth open, and Mr. Daw, anxious to get rid of the Sevens, dropped one into it.

"Two thousand three hundred and one," Ruffin spluttered out.

Mr. Daw dropped another Seven into his mouth, and he spluttered out again worse than ever, "Sixteen thousand eight hundred and seven."

The Raven began hurling Sevens at him as fast as he could; and each time he threw one he grew smaller and smaller, till he got to just his natural size.

Ruffin kept spluttering out and gasping numbers as hard as ever he could, till he grew black in the face and fell down in a fit just as he had come to "Seventy-nine thousand seven hundred and ninety-two billion, two hundred and sixty-six thousand two hundred and ninety-seven million six hundred and twelve thousand and one."

Suddenly Tineboy woke up, and found that he had been dreaming with his head down.

Lies and Lilies

Claribel lived in peace and happiness with her father and mother, from the time she was a little baby till when, at ten years old, she went to school.

Her parents were good, kind people, who loved truth and tried ever to walk in the paths of the just. They taught Claribel all good things, and her mother, Fridolina, used to bring her when every day she went to visit and comfort the sick.

When Claribel went to school, she was even happier, for not only had she her home as it was ever, but there were many new friends also who were of her own age and whom she came to know and love. The school-mistress was very good and very nice and very old, with beautiful white hair and a sweet gentle face that never looked hard or stern, except when some one told a lie. Then the smile would fade from her face; and it was like the change in the sky when the sun has gone down, and she would look grave, and cry silently. If the child who had been wicked came and confessed the fault and promised never never to tell a lie again, the smile would come back like sunshine. But if the child persisted in the lie her face would look stern, and afterwards the stern look would be in the memory of the liar, even when she was not there.

Every day she told all the children of the beauty of Truth and how a lie was so black and terrible a thing. She would also tell them stories from the Great Book; and one that she loved, and that they loved too, was of the Beautiful City where the good people shall live hereafter.

The children never tired of hearing of that City, like a jasper stone clear as crystal, with its twelve gates with names written thereon, and they used to ask the Mistress questions about the Angel who measured the City with a golden reed. Always towards the end of the story, the Mistresse's voice would become very grave, and a hush would steal over the children and they would draw closer together in awe as she told them that outside that beautiful city were for ever condemned to stand "whosoever loveth and maketh a lie."

Then the good Mistress would tell them what a terrible thing it would be to stand there without, and lose all the beauty and eternal glory that lay within. And all for a fault which no human being need ever commit - for telling a lie. People are not very much angry even when a fault has been done, when the truth is told at once; but if a fault is made worse by a lie then everyone is justly angry. If men and women, even fathers and mothers who love their little children very tenderly, are angry, how much more will God be angry against whom the sin of a lie is made.

Claribel loved this story and often cried as she thought of the poor people who will have to stand without the Beautiful City for ever, but she never thought that she would tell a lie herself. Indeed, she never did till temptation came. When people think themselves very good they are in danger of sin, for if we are not ever on the watch against evil we surely do some wrong thing; and as Claribel feared no evil, she was easily led into sin.

The children were all at their sums. A few of them knew their arithmetic and got out their answers and proved them; but some could not get out the answer right, and others stuck and could not get out any answer at all. A couple of naughty ones did not even try to get out the answers, but drew pictures on their slates and wrote their names. Claribel tried to do her sum, but she could not remember 9 times 7, and instead of beginning at "twice one are two" and going on up, she grew idle and lazy and gave up the sum and drew the beginnings of pictures and gave them up too. She looked up at the window thinking of something to draw and saw on the lower panes coloured flowers painted there so as to prevent the children looking at the people outside during lesson time. Claribel fixed on one of these flowers, a lily, and began to draw it.

Skooro saw her looking up and began his evil work. In order to help her to do what she ought not to do he took the shape of a lily and lay on the slate very faintly, so that she had only to draw round his edges and then there was a lily drawn. Now it is not a wrong thing to draw a lily, and if Claribel had drawn it well at a proper time she would have got praise; but a good thing may become a bad thing if it is wrongly done - and so it was with Claribel's lily.

Presently the Mistress asked for the slates. When Claribel brought hers up she knew that she had done wrong and was sorry; but she was only sorry because she was afraid of being punished. When the Mistress asked for the answer she hung down her head and said she could not get it.

"Did you try?" asked the Mistress.

"Yes," she answered, feeling that she had tried for a while.

"Did you idle?" she was asked, "Did you do anything but your sum?" Then she knew that she would get into trouble for idling if she told it; and so forgetting all about the Jasper City and those who are doomed to stand without its beautiful gates, she answered that she had done nothing else but sums. The mistress took her word - for she had always been truthful - and said :

"You were puzzled, I suppose, dear child; let me help you," and she kindly showed her how to work the sum.

As she was going back to her seat, Claribel hung her head, for she knew that she had told a lie, and although it need now never he found out, she was sorrowful, and felt as if she were standing outside the shining City. Even then if she had rushed up to the mistress and said:

"I have done wrong; but I will be a better child again," all would have been well; but she did not, and every minute that passed made such a thing harder to do.

Soon after school was over, and Claribel went sadly home. She did not care to play, for she had told a lie, and her heart was heavy.

When bed-time came she lay down weary, but could not sleep; and she cried very bitterly, for she could not pray. She was sorry that she had told a lie, and she thought it rather hard that her sorrow was not enough to make her happy again; but her conscience said -

"Will you confess to-morrow?" But she thought that it would not be necessary, for the sin was over and she had not done harm to anyone. But all the time she knew that she was wrong. Had the mistress spoken of this, she would have said -

"It is ever thus, dear children. A sin cannot be wiped away till the shame comes first; for without the shame and the acknowledgment of guilt the heart cannot be cleansed from the sin."

At last Claribel sobbed herself to sleep.

Then when she slept, the Child Angel stole into the room and passed over her eyelids, so that even in her sleep she saw the beautiful light, and she thought of the City like a jasper stone, clear as crystal, with its twelve gates with names written thereon. She dreamed that she saw the Angel with the golden reed measuring the city, and Claribel was so happy that she forgot all about her sin. The Child Angel knew all her thoughts, and he grew less and less till his light all died away; and to Claribel in her dream all seemed to grow dark, and she knew that she was standing without the gate of the Beautiful City. The Angel, who held the measuring reed of gold, stood on the battlements of the city, and in a terrible voice said -

"Claribel, stand thou without; thou makest and lovest a lie."

"Oh, no," said Claribel, "I do not love it."

"Then why not confess thy fault?"

Claribel was silent; but she would not confess her sin, for her heart was hard, and the Angel lifted the golden reed, and lo! it blossomed a beautiful lily. Then the Angel said -

"The lilies grow only for the pure, who live within the city; thou must stand without among the liars."

Claribel saw the jasper walls before her towering up and up, and she knew that they were an eternal barrier to her, and that she must ever stand without the Beautiful City; and in the anguish and horror she felt how deep was her sin, and longed to confess it.

Skooro saw that she was repenting, for he, too, could see into her thoughts, and with the darkness of his presence he tried to blot out the whole dream of the Beautiful City.

But the Child Angel crept into her heart and made it light, and the seed of repentance grew and blossomed.

Claribel woke early, and rose and went and told her mistress of her sin, and was happy once more.

All her life long she loved the lilies; for she thought of her lie and of her repentance for it, and that the lilies grow within the Jasper City, which is for the pure alone.

The Castle of the King

When they told the poor Poet that the One he loved best was lying sick in the shadow of danger, he was nigh distraught.

For weeks past he had been alone; she, his Wife, having gone afar to her old home to see an aged grandsire ere he died.

The Poet's heart had for some days been oppressed with a strange sorrow. He did not know the cause of it; he only knew with the deep sympathy which is the poet's gift, that the One he loved was sick. Anxiously had he awaited tidings. When the news came, the shock, although he expected a sad message, was too much for him, and he became nigh distraught.

In his sadness and anxiety he went out into the garden which long years he had cultured for Her. There, amongst the bright flowers, where the old statues stood softly white against the hedges of yew, he lay down in the long uncut summer grass, and wept with his head buried low.

He thought of all the past-of how he had won his Wife and how they loved each other; and to him it seemed a sad and cruel thing that she was afar and in danger, and he not near to comfort her or even to share her pain.

Many many thoughts came back to him, telling the story of the weary years whose gloom and solitude he had forgotten in the brightness of his lovely home.-

How in youth they twain had met and in a moment loved. How his poverty and her greatness had kept them apart. How he had struggled and toiled in the steep and rugged road to fame and fortune.

How all through the weary years he had striven with the single idea of winning such a place in the history of his time, that he should be able to come and to her say, "I love you," and to her proud relations, "I am worthy, for I too have become great."

How amid all this dreaming of a happy time which might come, he had kept silent as to his love. How he had never seen her or heard her voice, or even known her habitation, lest, knowing, he should fail in the purpose of his life.

How time-as it ever does to those who work with honesty and singleness of purpose-crowned the labours and the patience of his life.

How the world had come to know his name and reverence and love it as of one who had helped the weak and weary by his example; who had purified the thoughts of all who listened to his words; and who had swept away baseness before the grandeur and simpleness of his noble thoughts.

How success had followed in the wake of fame.

How at length even to his heart, timorous with the doubt of love, had been borne the thought that he had at last achieved the greatness which justified him in seeking the hand of her he loved.

How he had come back to his native place, and there found her still free.

How when he had dared to tell her of his love she had whispered to him that she, too, had waited all the years, for that she knew that he would come to claim her at the end.

How she had come with him as his bride into the home which he had been making for her all these years. How, there, they had lived happily; and had dared to look into the long years to come for joy and content without a bar.

How he thought that even then, when though somewhat enfeebled in strength by the ceaseless toil of years and the care of hoping, he might look to the happy time to come.

But, alas! for hope; for who knoweth what a day may bring forth? Only a little while ago his Dear One had left him hale, departing in the cause of duty; and now she lay sick and he not nigh to help her.

All the sunshine of his life seemed passing away. All the long years of waiting and the patient continuance in well-doing which had crowned their years with love, seemed as but a passing dream, and was all in vain-all, all in vain.

Now with the shadow hovering over his Beloved One, the cloud seemed to be above and around them, and to hold in its dim recesses the doom of them both.

"Why, oh why," asked the poor Poet to the viewless air, "did love come to us? Why came peace and joy and happiness, if the darkening wings of peril shadow the air around her, and leave me to weep alone?"

Thus he moaned, and raved, and wept; and the bitter hours went by him in his solitude.

As he lay in the garden with his face buried in the long grass, they came to him and told him with weeping, that tidings-sad, indeed-had come.

As they spoke he lifted his poor head and gazed at them; and they saw in the great, dark, tender eyes that now he was quite distraught. He smiled at them sadly, as though not quite understanding the import of their words. As tenderly as they could they tried to tell him that the One he loved best was dead.

They said:-

"She has walked in the Valley of the Shadow;" but he seemed to understand them not.

They whispered,

"She has heard the Music of the Spheres," but still he comprehended not.

Then they spoke to him sorrowfully and said:

"She now abides in the Castle of the King."

He looked at them eagerly, as if to ask:

"What castle? What king?"

They bowed their heads; and as they turned away weeping they murmured to him softly-

"The Castle of the King of Death."

He spake no word; so they turned their weeping faces to him again. They found that he had risen and stood with a set purpose on his face. Then he said sweetly:

"I go to find her, that where she abideth, I too may there abide."

They said to him:

"You cannot go. Beyond the Portal she is, and in the Land of Death."

Set purpose shone in the Poet's earnest, loving eyes as he answered them for the last time:

"Where she has gone, there go I too. Through the Valley of the Shadow shall I wend my way. In these ears also shall ring the Music of the Spheres. I shall seek, and I shall find my Beloved in the Halls of the Castle of the King. I shall clasp her close-even before the dread face of the King of Death."

As they heard these words they bowed their heads again and wept, and said:

"Alas! alas!"

The poet turned and left them; and passed away. They fain would have followed; but he motioned them that they should not stir. So, alone, in his grief he went.

As he passed on he turned and waved his hand to them in farewell. Then for a while with uplifted hand he stood, and turned him slowly all around.

Suddenly his outstretched hand stopped and pointed. His friends looking with him saw, where, away beyond the Portal, the idle wilderness spread. There in the midst of desolation the mist from the marshes hung like a pall of gloom on the far off horizon.

As the Poet pointed there was a gleam of happiness-very very faint it was-in his poor sad eyes, distraught with loss, as if afar he beheld some sign or hope of the Lost One.

Swiftly and sadly the Poet fared on through the burning day.

The Rest Time came; but on he journeyed. He paused not for shade or rest. Never, even for an instant did he stop to cool his parched lips with an icy draught from the crystal springs.

The weary wayfarers resting in the cool shadows beside the fountains raised their tired heads and looked at him with sleepy eyes as he hurried. He heeded them not; but went ever onward with set purpose in his eyes, as though some gleam of hope bursting through the mists of the distant marshes urged him on.

So he fared on through all the burning day, and all the silent night. In the earliest dawn, when the promise of the still unrisen sun quickened the eastern sky into a pale light, he drew anigh the Portal. The horizon stood out blackly in the cold morning light.

There, as ever, stood the Angels who kept watch and ward, and oh, wondrous! although invisible to human eyes, they were seen of him.

As he drew nigh they gazed at him pityingly and swept their great wings out wide, as if to shelter him. He spake; and from his troubled heart the sad words came sweetly through the pale lips:

"Say, Ye who guard the Land, has my Beloved One passed hither on the journey to the Valley of the Shadow, to hear the Music of the Spheres, and to abide in the Castle of the King?"

The Angels at the Portal bowed their heads in token of assent; and they turned and looked outward from the Land to where, far off in the idle wilderness, the dank mists crept from the lifeless bosom of the marsh.

They knew well that the poor lonely Poet was in quest of his Beloved One; so they hindered him not, neither urged they him to stay. They pitied him much for that much he loved.

They parted wide, that through the Portal he might pass without let.

So, the Poet went onwards into the idle desert to look for his Beloved One in the Castle of the King.

For a time he went through gardens whose beauty was riper than the gardens of the Land. The sweetness of all things stole on the senses like the odours from the Isles of the Blest.

The subtlety of the King of Death, who rules in the Realms of Evil, is great. He has ordered that the way beyond the Portal be made full of charm. Thus those straying from the paths ordained for good see around them such beauty that in its joy the gloom and cruelty and guilt of the desert are forgotten.

But as the Poet passed onwards the beauty began to fade away.

The fair gardens looked as gardens do when the hand of care is taken off, and when the weeds in their hideous luxuriance choke, as they spring up, the choicer life of the flowers.

From cool alleys under spreading branches, and from crisp sward which touched as soft as velvet the Wanderer's aching feet, the way became a rugged stony path, full open to the burning glare. The flowers began to lose their odour, and to dwarf to stunted growth. Tall hemlocks rose on every side, infecting the air with their noisome odour.

Great fungi grew in the dark hollows where the pools of dank water lay. Tall trees, with branches like skeletons, rose-trees which had no leaves, and under whose shadow to pause were to die.

Then huge rocks barred the way. These were only passed by narrow, winding passages, over-hung by the ponderous cliffs above, which ever threatened to fall and engulph the Sojourner.

Here the night began to fall; and the dim mist rising from the far-off marshes, took weird shapes of gloom. In the distant fastnesses of the mountains the wild beasts began to roar in their cavern lairs. The air became hideous with the fell sounds of the night season.

But the poor Poet heeded not ill sights or sounds of dread. Onward he went ever-unthinking of the terrors of the night. To him there was no dread of darkness-no fear of death-no consciousness of horror. He sought his Beloved One in the Castle of the King; and in that eager quest all natural terrors were forgot.

So fared he onward through the livelong night. Up the steep defiles he trod. Through the shadows of the huge rocks he passed unscathed. The wild animals came around him roaring fiercely-their great eyes flaming like fiery stars through the blackness of the night.

From the high rocks great pythons crawled and hung to seize their prey. From the crevices of the mountain steeps, and from cavernous rifts in the rocky way poisonous serpents glided and rose to strike.

But close though the noxious things came, they all refrained to attack; for they knew that the lonely Sojourner was bound for the Castle of their King.

Onward still, onward he went-unceasing-pausing not in his course-but pressing ever forward in his quest.

When daylight broke at last, the sun rose on a sorry sight. There toiling on the rocky way, the poor lonely Poet went ever onwards, unheeding of cold or hunger or pain.

His feet were bare, and his footsteps on the rock-strewn way were marked by blood. Around and behind him, and afar off keeping equal pace on the summits of the rocky ridges, came the wild beasts that looked on him as their prey, but that refrained from touching him because he sought the Castle of their King.

In the air wheeled the obscene birds who follow ever on the track of the dying and the lost. Hovered the bare-necked vultures with eager eyes, and hungry beaks. Their great wings flapped lazily in the idle air as they followed in the Wanderer's track. The vulture are a patient folk, and they await the falling of the prey.

From the cavernous recesses in the black mountain gorges crept, with silent speed, the serpents that there lurk. Came the python, with his colossal folds and endless coils, whence looked forth cunningly the small flat head. Came the boa and all his tribe, which seize their prey by force and crush it with the dread strictness of their embrace. Came the hooded snakes and all those which with their venom destroy their prey. Here, too, came those serpents most terrible of all to their quarry-which fascinate with eyes of weird magic and by the slow gracefulness of their approach.

Here came or lay in wait, subtle snakes, which take the colour of herb, or leaf, or dead branch, or slimy pool, amongst which they lurk, and so strike their prey unsuspecting.

Great serpents there were, nimble of body, which hang from rock or branch. These gripping tight to their distant hold, strike downward with the rapidity of light as they hurl their whip-like bodies from afar upon their prey.

Thus came forth all these noxious things to meet the Questing Man, and to assail him. But when they knew he was bound for the dread Castle of their King, and saw how he went onward without fear, they abstained from attack.

The deadly python and the boa towering aloft, with colossal folds, were passive, and for the nonce, became as stone. The hooded serpents drew in again their venomous fangs. The mild, deep earnest eyes of the fascinating snake became lurid with baffled spleen, as he felt his power to charm was without avail. In its deadly descent the hanging snake arrested its course, and hung a limp line from rock or branch.

Many followed the Wanderer onwards into the desert wilds, waiting and hoping for a chance to destroy.

Many other perils also were there for the poor Wanderer in the desert idleness. As he went onward the rocky way got steeper and darker. Lurid fogs and deadly chill mists arose.

Then in this path along the trackless wilderness were strange and terrible things.

Mandrakes-half plant, half man-shrieked at him with despairing cry, as, helpless for evil, they stretched out their ghastly arms in vain.

Giant thorns arose in the path; they pierced his suffering feet and tore his flesh as onward he trod. He felt the pain, but he heeded it not.

In all the long, terrible journey he had but one idea other than his eager search for his Beloved One. He thought that the children of men might learn much from the journey towards the Castle of the King, which began so fair, amidst the odorous gardens and under the cool shadow of the spreading trees. In his heart the Poet spake to the multitude of the children of men; and from his lips the words flowed like music, for he sang of the Golden Gate which the Angels call TRUTH.

"Pass not the Portal of the Sunset Land!
Pause where the Angels at their vigil stand.
Be warned! and press not though the gates lie wide,
But rest securely on the hither side.

Though odorous gardens and cool ways invite,
Beyond are darkest valleys of the night.
Rest! Rest contented.-Pause whilst undefiled,
Nor seek the horrors of the desert wild."

Thus treading down all obstacles with his bleeding feet, passed ever onwards, the poor distraught Poet, to seek his Beloved One in the Castle of the King.

Even as onward he went the life that is of the animals seemed to die away behind him. The jackals and the more cowardly savage animals slunk away. The lions and tigers, and bears, and wolves, and all the braver of the fierce beasts of prey which followed on his track even after the others had stopped, now began to halt in their career.

They growled low and then roared loudly with uplifted heads; the bristles of their mouths quivered with passion, and the great white teeth champed angrily together in baffled rage. They went on a little further; and stopped again roaring and growling as before. Then one by one they ceased, and the poor Poet went on alone.

In the air the vultures wheeled and screamed, pausing and halting in their flight, as did the savage beasts. These too ceased at length to follow in air the Wanderer in his onward course.

Longest of all kept up the snakes. With many a writhe and stealthy onward glide, they followed hard upon the footsteps of the Questing Man. In the blood marks of his feet upon the flinty rocks they found a joy and hope, and they followed ever.

But time came when the awful aspect of the places where the Poet passed checked even the serpents in their track-the gloomy defiles whence issue the poisonous winds that sweep with desolation even the dens of the beasts of prey-the sterile fastnesses which march upon the valleys of desolation. Here even the stealthy serpents paused in their course; and they too fell away. They glided back, smiling with deadliest rancour, to their obscene clefts.

Then came places where plants and verdure began to cease. The very weeds became more and more stunted and inane. Farther on they declined into the sterility of lifeless rock. Then the most noxious herbs that grew in ghastly shapes of gloom and terror lost even the power to harm, which outlives their living growth. Dwarfed and stunted even of evil, they were compact of the dead rock. Here even the deadly Upas tree could strike no root into the pestiferous earth.

Then came places where, in the entrance to the Valley of the Shadow, even solid things lost their substance, and melted in the dank and cold mists which swept along.

As he passed, the distraught Poet could feel not solid earth under his bleeding feet. On shadows he walked, and amid them, onward through the Valley of the Shadow to seek his Beloved One in the Castle of the King.

The Valley of the Shadow seemed of endless expanse. Circled by the teeming mist, no eye could pierce to where rose the great mountains between which the Valley lay.

Yet they stood there-Mount Despair on the one hand, and the Hill of Fear upon the other.

Hitherto the poor bewildered brain of the Poet had taken no note of all the dangers, and horrors, and pains which surrounded him-save only for the lesson which they taught. But now, lost as he was in the shrouding vapour of the Valley of the Shadow, he could not but think of the terrors of the way. He was surrounded by grisly phantoms that ever and anon arose silent in the mist, and were lost again before he could catch to the full their dread import.

Then there flashed across his soul a terrible thought-

Could it be possible that hither his Beloved One had travelled? Had there come to her the pains which shook his own form with agony? Was it indeed necessary that she should have been appalled by all these surrounding horrors?

At the thought of her, his Beloved One, suffering such pain and dread, he gave forth one bitter cry that rang through the solitude-that cleft the vapour of the Valley, and echoed in the caverns of the mountains of Despair and Fear.

The wild cry prolonged with the agony of the Poet's soul rang through the Valley, till the shadows that peopled it woke for the moment into life-in-death. They flitted dimly along, now melting away and anon springing again into life-till all the Valley of the Shadow was for once peopled with quickened ghosts.

Oh, in that hour there was agony to the poor distraught Poet's soul.

But presently there came a calm. When the rush of his first agony passed, the Poet knew that to the Dead came not the horrors of the journey that he undertook. To the Quick alone is the horror of the passage to the Castle of the King. With the thought came to him such peace that even there-in the dark Valley of the Shadow-stole soft music that sounded in the desert gloom like the Music of the Spheres.

Then the poor Poet remembered what they had told him; that his Beloved One had walked through the Valley of the Shadow, that she had known the Music of the Spheres, and that she abode in the Castle of the King. So he thought that as he was now in the Valley of the Shadow, and as he heard the Music of the Spheres, that soon he should see the Castle of the King where his Beloved One abode. Thus he went on in hope.

But alas! that very hope was a new pain that ere this he wot not of.

Hitherto he had gone on blindly, recking not of where he went or what came a-nigh him, so long as he pressed onward on his quest; but now the darkness and the peril of the way had new terrors, for he thought of how they might arrest his course. Such thoughts made the way long indeed, for the moments seemed an age with hoping. Eagerly he sought for the end to come, when, beyond the Valley of the Shadow through which he fared, he should see rising the turrets of the Castle of the King.

Despair seemed to grow upon him; and as it grew there rang out, ever louder, the Music of the Spheres.

Onward, ever onward, hurried in mad haste the poor distraught Poet. The dim shadows that peopled the mist shrank back as he passed, extending towards him warning hands with long gloomy fingers of deadly cold. In the bitter silence of the moment, they seemed to say:

"Go back! Go back!"

Louder and louder rang now the Music of the Spheres. Faster and faster in mad, feverish haste rushed the Poet, amid the shrinking Shadows of the gloomy valley. The peopling shadows as they faded away before him, seemed to wail in sorrowful warning:

"Go back! Go back!"

Still in his ears rang ever the swelling tumult of the music.

Faster and faster he rushed onward; till, at last, wearied nature gave way and he fell prone to earth, senseless, bleeding, and alone.

After a time-how long he could not even guess-he awoke from his swoon.

For awhile he could not think where he was; and his scattered senses could not help him.

All was gloom and cold and sadness. A solitude reigned around him, more deadly than aught he had ever dreamt of. No breeze was in the air; no movement of a passing cloud. No voice or stir of living thing in earth, or water, or air. No rustle of leaf or sway of branch-all was silent, dead, and deserted. Amid the eternal hills of gloom around, lay the valley devoid of aught that lived or grew.

The sweeping mists with their multitude of peopling shadows had gone by. The fearsome terrors of the desert even were not there. The Poet, as he gazed around him, in his utter loneliness, longed for the sweep of the storm or the roar of the avalanche to break the dread horror of the silent gloom.

Then the Poet knew that through the Valley of the Shadow had he come; that scared and maddened though he had been, he had heard the Music of the Spheres. He thought that now hard by the desolate Kingdom of Death he trod.

He gazed all around him, fearing lest he should see anywhere the dread Castle of the King, where his Beloved One abode; and he groaned as the fear of his heart found voice:

"Not here! oh not here, amid this awful solitude."

Then amid the silence around, upon distant hills his words echoed:

"Not here! oh not here," till with the echoing and re-echoing rock, the idle wilderness was peopled with voices.

Suddenly the echo voices ceased.

From the lurid sky broke the terrible sound of the thunder peal. Along the distant skies it rolled. Far away over the endless ring of the grey horizon it swept-going and returning-pealing-swelling-dying away. It traversed the aether, muttering now in ominous sound as of threats, and anon crashing with the voice of dread command.

In its roar came a sound as of a word:

"Onward."

To his knees the Poet sank and welcomed with tears of joy the sound of the thunder. It swept away as a Power from Above the silent desolation of the wilderness. It told him that in and above the Valley of the Shadow rolled the mighty tones of Heaven's command.

Then the Poet rose to his feet, and with new heart went onwards into the wilderness.

As he went the roll of the thunder died away, and again the silence of desolation reigned alone.

So time wore on; but never came rest to the weary feet. Onwards, still onwards he went, with but one memory to cheer him-the echo of the thunder roll in his ears, as it pealed out in the Valley of Desolation:

"Onward! Onward!"

Now the road became less and less rocky, as on his way he passed. The great cliffs sank and dwindled away, and the ooze of the fens crept upward to the mountain's feet.

At length the hills and hollows of the mountain fastnesses disappeared. The Wanderer took his way amid mere trackless wastes, where was nothing but quaking marsh and slime.

On, on he wandered; stumbling blindly with weary feet on the endless road.

Over his soul crept ever closer the blackness of despair. Whilst amid the mountain gorges he had been wandering, some small cheer came from the hope that at any moment some turn in the path might show him his journey's end. Some entry from a dark defile might expose to him, looming great in the distance-or even anigh him-the dread Castle of the King. But now with the flat desolation of the silent marsh around him, he knew that the Castle could not exist without his seeing it.

He stood for awhile erect, and turned him slowly round, so that the complete circuit of the horizon was swept by his eager eyes. Alas! never a sight did he see. Nought was there but the black line of the horizon, where the sad earth lay against the level sky. All, all was compact of a silent gloom.

Still on he tottered. His breath came fast and laboured. His weary limbs quivered as they bore him feebly up. His strength-his life-was ebbing fast.

On, on, he hurried, ever on, with one idea desperately fixed in his poor distraught mind-that in the Castle of the King he should find his Beloved One.

He stumbled and fell. There was no obstacle to arrest his feet; only from his own weakness he declined.

Quickly he arose and went onward with flying feet. He dreaded that should he fall he might not be able to arise again.

Again he fell. Again he rose and went on his way desperately, with blind purpose.

So for a while went he onwards, stumbling and falling; but arising ever and pausing not on his way. His quest he followed, of his Beloved One abiding in the Castle of the King.

At last so weak he grew that when he sank he was unable to rise again.

Feebler and feebler he grew as he lay prone; and over his eager eyes came the film of death.

But even then came comfort; for he knew that his race was run, and that soon he would meet his Beloved One in the Halls of the Castle of the King.

To the wilderness his thoughts he spoke. His voice came forth with a feeble sound, like the moaning before a storm of the wind as it passes through reeds in the grey autumn:

"A little longer. Soon I shall meet her in the Halls of the King; and we shall part no more. For this it is worth to pass through the Valley of the Shadow and to listen to the Music of the Spheres with their painful hope. What boots it though the Castle be afar? Quickly speed the feet of the dead. To the fleeting spirit all distance is but a span. I fear not now to see the Castle of the King; for there, within its chiefest Hall, soon shall I meet my Beloved-to part no more."

Even as he spoke he felt that the end was nigh.

Forth from the marsh before him crept a still, spreading mist. It rose silently, higher-higher-enveloping the wilderness for far around. It took deeper and darker shades as it arose. It was as though the Spirit of Gloom were hid within, and grew mightier with the spreading vapour.

To the eyes of the dying Poet the creeping mist was as a shadowy castle. Arose the tall turrets and the frowning keep. The gateway with its cavernous recesses and its beetling towers took shape as a skull. The distant battlements towered aloft into the silent air. From the very ground whereon the stricken Poet lay, grew, dim and dark, a vast causeway leading into the gloom of the Castle gate.

The dying Poet raised his head and looked. His fast failing eyes, quickened by the love and hope of his spirit, pierced through the dark walls of the keep and the gloomy terrors of the gateway.

There, within the great Hall where the grim King of Terrors himself holds his court, he saw her whom he sought. She was standing in the ranks of those who wait in patience for their Beloved to follow them into the Land of Death.

The Poet knew that he had but a little while to wait, and he was patient-stricken though he lay, amongst the Eternal Solitudes.

Afar off, beyond the distant horizon, came a faint light as of the dawn of a coming day.

As it grew brighter the Castle stood out more and more clearly; till in the quickening dawn it stood revealed in all its cold expanse.

The dying Poet knew that the end was at hand. With a last effort he raised himself to his feet, that standing erect and bold, as is the right of manhood, he might so meet face to face the grim King of Death before the eyes of his Beloved One.

The distant sun of the coming day rose over the horizon's edge.

A ray of light shot upward.

As it struck the summit of the Castle keep the Poet's Spirit in an instant of time swept along the causeway. Through the ghostly portal of the Castle it swept, and met with joy the kindred Spirit that it loved before the very face of the King of Death.

Quicker then than the lightning's flash the whole Castle melted into nothingness; and the sun of the coming day shone calmly down upon the Eternal Solitudes.

In the Land within the Portal rose the sun of the coming day. It shone calmly and brightly on a fair garden, where, among the long summer grass lay the Poet, colder than the marble statues around him.

The Wondrous Child

Far away on the edge of a great creek, that stretched inland from the endless sea, there lay a peaceful village.

Here the husbandmen led a happy, prosperous life. They rose early, so that in the cool grey morn they heard the lark, all invisible in the height of the dawn, singing the morning hymn that he never forgets.

As sunset came stealing on, they returned to their homes, glad of the rest that nightfall brought to them.

In the autumn, when the harvesting was to be done, they worked late, as they were able to do; for at that time the kind Sun and his wife the Moon have a compact that they will help those who work at the harvest. So the sun stays up a little longer, and the moon gets out of her bed in the horizon a little earlier, and thus there is always light to work by.

The red, broad, full-faced moon that looks down on the husbandmen at work is called the Harvest Moon.

The Lord of the Manor of this peaceful village was a very good, kind man, that helped the poor always. At meal-time the door of his mansion stood open; and all who were hungry could enter if they chose, and take seats at the table, and be welcome guests.

This Lord of the Manor had three children, Sibold and May, and one little Baby Boy just come home who had no name as yet.

Sibold had just reached his eighth birthday, and May was within two months of her sixth. They were very fond of each other - as brother and sister should be - and had all their plays together. May thought that Sibold was very big and strong, and whatever he wished to do she always agreed to.

Sibold loved finding things and exploring; and at different times the two children had been over all the domain of their father.

They had certain secret haunts that nobody knew of except themselves. Some of these were very queer, delightful places.

One was in the centre of a hollow Oak tree, where so many squirrels lived that the branches were quite like the streets of a town, with their going to and fro.

Another place was the top of a rock, which was only reached by a narrow path between high bushes of ivy. Here there was a sort of great chair made in the rock, which just held the two; and here they often brought their lunch, and sat half the day looking out over the tree tops to where, far away in the distance, the white edge of the horizon lay on the glittering sea.

Then they would tell each other what they thought about, and what they would like to do, and what they would try to do when they grew up.

There was also another place, which was their favourite of all.

It was under a great Weeping Willow. This was a mighty tree, many hundreds of years old, which towered aloft above the other trees which dotted the sward. The long branches fell downwards so thickly, that even in winter, when the leaves held fallen and the benches were bare, one could hardly see into the hollow that lay within.

When the new spring clothes came home, the whole tree, from its high top even to the mossy ground from which it rose, was a mass of solid green; and it was difficult to get within even if one knew the way.

In one place one of the trailing branches had, a long time ago, been broken in a great storm, winch had laid low many forest trees; but the branches which hung next to this sent forth new green shoots to fill the empty space, and so the opening was covered with thin twigs instead of strong branches.

In summer the leaves covered all with a mass of green; but those who knew the opening could push the twigs aside, and so enter into the bower.

It was a most beautiful bower. No matter how strong the sun glared without, it was within cool and pleasant. From the ground even up to the top, till the very roof where the dark branches meeting made a black mass, all was a delicate green, for the light without came through the leaves softly and gently.

Sibold and May thought that so the sea must look to the Mermaids, who sing and comb their long hair with golden combs down in the cool depths of the ocean.

In the sward around this great tree were many beds of beautiful flowers. Asters, with their wide faces of many colours, staring up straight at the sun without ever winking, and round and over which flitted the gorgeous butterflies, with their wings like rainbows or peacocks or sunsets, or aught that is most beautiful. Sweet Mignonette, where the bees hovered with grateful hum. Pansies, with their delicate big faces trembling on their slender stalks. Tulips, opening their mouths to the sun and the rain; for the Tulip is a greedy flower, that opens his mouth till at last he opens it so wide that his head falls all to pieces and he dies. Hyacinths, with their many bells clustered on one stalk - like a big family party. Great Sunflowers, whose drooping faces shone like children of the parent Sun himself.

There were also great Poppies, with spreading, careless leaves, thick juicy stalks, and grand scarlet flowers, which rise and droop just as they please, and look so free and careless and independent.

Both Sibold and May loved these Poppies, and went every day to look at them. In the beds in the mossy sward, from which the great Willow rose, they grew to an enormous size; so high that when Sibold and May stood hand in hand beside the bed, the great Poppies towered over them till Sibold, standing on tiptoe, could not reach the scarlet flowers.

One day after breakfast, Sibold and May took their lunch with them, and went out to spend the day together wandering about among the woods, for it was a holiday with them. A little tiny Boy brother had arrived in the house, and everybody was busy getting things for him. The children had just seen him for an instant.

Hand in hand Sibold and May went round all their favourite spots. They looked at the cave in the Oak tree, and said "How do you do?" to all the squirrels that lived in the tree, and told them of the new Baby that had come home. Then they went to the rock, and sat together in the seat, and looked away over the sea.

There they sat for a while in the hot sunlight, and talked together of the dear little baby brother that they had seen. They wondered where he came from, and they made up a plan that they would look and look till they found a baby too. Sibold said that he must have come over the sea, and been laid in the parsley-bed by the Angels, so that nurse might find him there and bring him to comfort their poor sick mother. Then they wondered how they would be able to get away over the sea, and they planned that some day Sibold's boat would be made bigger, and they would get into it and sail away over the sea, and search for another little baby all for themselves.

After a while they got tired of sitting in the hot sun; so they left the place, and, hand in hand, wandered on till they came to the level sward where the great Willow tree rose, and where the beds of flowers made the air seem full of colours and perfume.

Hand in hand they walked on, looking at the butterflies, and the bees, and the birds, and the beautiful flowers.

In one bed they found a new flower had come out. Sibold knew it, and told May it was a Tiger-lily; she was afraid to go near it till he told her it could not hurt her, as it was only a flower.

As they went on Sibold picked some flowers from every bed, and gave them to his sister; when they were going away from the Tiger-lily he pulled the flower, and as May was afraid to carry it, he took it himself.

At last they came to the great bed of Poppies. The flowers looked so bright and cool for all their flaming colour, and so careless, that May and Sibold both together thought that they would like to take a lot with them into the Willow Bower; for they were going to eat their lunch there, and they wished the place to be as gay and pretty as possible.

But first they went back to the Oak tree to gather a lot of leaves, for Sibold suggested that they would make the new baby brother the King of the Feast, and that they would make for him a crown of oak. As he would not be there himself, they would put the crown where they could see it well.

When they got to the Oak tree May called out,

"Oh look, Sibold, look, look!"

Sibold looked, and saw that on nearly every branch were a whole lot of squirrels sitting two and two, with their bushy tails over their backs, eating nuts as hard as ever they could.

When the squirrels saw them they were not frightened, for the children had never done them any harm. They gave a sort of queer croak all together, and a funny little skip. Sibold and May began to laugh, but they did not like to disturb them, so they gathered as many oak leaves as they wanted, and went back to the Poppy bed.

"Now, Sibold, dear," said May, "we must get lots of Poppies, for the dear Ba is very very fond of them."

"How do you know?" said Sibold.

"Because he ought to be," she answered. "You and I are, and he is our brother, so of course he is."

So Sibold pulled a lot of the Poppies, and some he took with many of the cool green leaves attached, till they had each an armful of them. Then they gathered up all the other flowers, and entered the Willow Bower to eat their lunch. Sibold went to the spring that rose in the garden, and that ran through it down to the sea. There he filled his cap with water, and brought it back as steadily as he could, so as not to spill much; and returned to the bower. May held open the leafy branches as he came, and when he passed in she let them fall again. As the leafy curtain hung all round them, the two children were alone in the Willow Bower.

Then they set to work to deck their leafy tent with the flowers. They twisted them round the hanging branches, and made a wreath, which they put round the trunk of the tree. Everywhere they put the Poppies as high as they could reach, and then Sibold held up May while she stuck the Tiger-lily in a cleft in the tree-trunk above all the other flowers.

Then the children sat down to their lunch. They were very tired and very hungry, and they enjoyed the rest and the food very much. There was only one thing which they wanted, and that was the new little Baby Brother, so that they might make him the king of the feast.

When lunch was finished, they felt very tired, so they lay down together with their heads on each other's shoulders and their arms twined; and there they went to sleep with the scarlet Poppies nodding all round them.

After a time they were not asleep. It did not seem to be any later in the day, but to be the early morning. Neither of them felt the least sleepy or tired; on the contrary they both wanted to go on a longer expedition than ever.

"Come down to the creek," said Sibold, "and let us get out my boat."

May arose, and they opened the leafy door and went out. They went down to the creek; and there they found Sibold's boat with all its white sails set.

"Let us get in," said Sibold.

"Why?" asked May.

"Because then we can have a sail," he answered.

"But it will not hold us; it is too small," said May, who was rather afraid to go sailing, but did not like to say so.

"Let us try," said her brother. He took hold of the cord that tied the boat to the bank, and drew it in. The line seemed very long, and Sibold appeared to be pulling it in for a great while. However, the boat came in at last. As it drew nearer, it got bigger and bigger, till when it touched the bank, they saw that it was just large enough to hold them both.

"Come, let us get in," said Sibold.

Somehow May did not feel afraid now. She got into the boat and found that in it there were silken cushions of the colour of the Poppy flowers. Then Sibold got in, and pulled away the rope that tied the boat to shore. He sat in the stern, and held the tiller in his hand; May sat on a cushion in the bottom of the boat, and held on to the sides.

The white sails swelled out with a gentle breeze, and they began to move away from the shore; the tiny waves rippled from the bow of the boat. May heard the lap, lap, lap, as they touched the prow, and then fell away.

The sun shone very brightly. The water was as blue as the sky, and so clear that the children could see down into its depths, where the fishes were darting about. There, too, the plants and trees that grow under the water were opening and closing their branches; and the leaves were moving about as those of land trees do when the wind is blowing.

For a little while the boat went straight away from land till they lost sight of the tall Willow tree which rose above the others. Then it seemed to come near to the shore again, and moved on, always so close that the children could see all that was there very plainly.

The shore was very varied; and each moment showed something new and beautiful –

Now it was a jutting rock all covered with trailing plants whose flowers almost touched the water.

Now it was a beach, where the white sand glittered and glistened in the light, and where the waves made a pleasant humming sound as they ran up the shore and down again – as if playing at "touch" with themselves.

Now dark trees with dense foliage overhung the water; but through their gloom shone bright patches far away as the sun streamed down, through some opening, into the glade.

Again there were places where grass as green as emerald sloped right down to the water's edge, and where the Cowslips and Buttercups that grew on the marge as they leant over almost kissed the little waves that rose to meet them.

Then there were places where great trees of Lilac made the air sweet for far around with the breath of their clusters of pink and white blossom, and where the laburnums seemed to shower endless streams of gold from the wealth of flowers which hung from their twisted green branches.

There were also great Palm-trees with their wide leaves making a cool shadow on the earth beneath. Great Cocoa-nut trees up whose stems troops of monkeys kept running to gather the cocoa-nuts which they pulled and threw down below. Aloes with great stalks laden with flowers of purple and gold – for this was the hundredth year when alone the Aloe blooms.

There were Poppies as large as trees; and Lilies whose flowers were bigger than tents.

The children liked all these places, but presently they come to a spot where there was a patch of emerald grass shaded over with giant trees. Around rose or hung or clustered every flower that grows. Tall Sugar-canes sprang from the edge of a tiny stream which ran over a bed of bright stones like jewels. Palms reared their lofty heads, and plants with great leaves rose and made shadows even in the shade. Close by was a crystal spring which bubbled into the tiny stream whence the Sugar-canes rose.

When they saw this place both the children cried out, "Oh, how beautiful! Let us stop here."

The boat seemed to understand their wishes, for without the helm even being touched, it turned and drifted in gently to the shore.

Sibold got out and lifted May to land. He intended to moor the boat; but the moment May got out all the sails folded themselves of their own accord, the anchor jumped overboard, and before it was possible to do anything the boat was anchored close to the shore.

Sibold and May took each other's hands, and they went round the place together, looking at everything.

Presently May said, in a whisper:

"Oh, Sibold, this place is so nice, I wonder if there is any Parsley here."

"Why do you want Parsley?" he asked.

"Because if there was a nice bed of Parsley we might be able to find a Baby – And oh, Sibold, I do so want a Baby."

"Very well then, let us look," said her brother. "There seems to be every kind of plant here; and if there is every kind of plant, you know there must be Parsley." For Sibold was very logical.

So the two children went all round the grassy dell searching; and presently, sure enough, under the spreading leaves of a Citron they found a great bed of Parsley - bigger Parsley than they had ever seen before.

Sibold was quite pleased with it, and said, "This is something like Parsley. Do you know, May, it always puzzled me how a Baby who is so much bigger than the Parsley can be hidden by it; and it must be hidden in it, for I often go out to look in the bed at home, and I never can find one, although nurse always finds one whenever she looks. But she does not look nearly often enough. I know if I was as lucky as she is, I would be always looking."

May found the longing to find a baby grow so strong upon her that she said again:

"Oh, Sibold, I do so long for a Baby; I hope we will find one."

As she spoke there was a queer kind of sound heard - a sort of very, very soft laugh - like a smile set to music.

May was surprised, and, for a moment, did not think of doing anything; she merely pointed, and said:

"Look, look!"

Sibold ran forward, and lifted up the leaf of an enormous Parsley plant; and there - oh, joy of joys! - was lying the dearest little Baby Boy that ever was seen.

May knelt down beside him, and lifted him up, and began to rock him, and sing "Hush a bye, baby," whilst Sibold looked on complacently. However, after a while he got impatient, and said:

"Look here, you know, I found that Baby; he belongs to me."

"Oh, please," said May, "I heard him first. He is mine."

"He is mine," said Sibold; "He is mine," said May; and both began to get a little angry.

Suddenly they heard a low groan - a sort of sound like as if a tune had a toothache. Both children looked down in alarm, and saw that the poor Baby was dead.

They were both horrorstruck, and began to cry; and both asked the other to forgive them, and promised that never, never again they would be angry. When they had done this, the Child opened its eyes, looked at them gravely, and said:

"Now never quarrel or be angry. If you get angry again, either of you, I shall be dead, aye, and buried too, before you can say 'trapsticks.'"

"Indeed, Ba," said May, "I shall never, never be angry again. At least, I shall try not to be."

Said Sibold:

"I assure you, sir, that under no provocation, resulting from whatever concatenation of circumstances, shall I be guilty of the malfaisance of anger."

"How pretty he speaks," said May; and the Baby nodded his head to him familiarly, as much as to say:

"All right, old man, we understand each other."

Then for a while they were all quite quiet. Presently the Baby turned its blue eyes up to May, and said:

"Please, little mother, will you sing to me?"

"What would you like, Ba?" said May.

"Oh, any little trifle; something pathetic," he answered.

"Any particular style?" asked May.

"No, thank you; anything that comes handy. I prefer something simple - some little elementary trifle, as, for instance, any little tune beginning with a chromatic scale in consecutive fifths and octaves, pianissimo - rallentando - excellerando - crescendo - up to an inharmonic change on the dominant of the diminished flat ninth."

"Oh, please, Ba," said May, very humbly, "I do not know anything about that yet. I am only in scales, and, if you please, I do not know what it is all about."

"Look, and you will see," said the Child, and he took a piece of stick and wrote some music on the sand.

"I do not know yet," said May.

Just then a small yellowish-brown animal appeared in the glade chasing a rat. When it came opposite them it suddenly went off like the sound of a pistol.

"Do you know now?" asked the Child.

"No, dear Ba, but it does not matter," she answered.

"Very well, dear," said the Child, kissing her, "anything you please, only let it come straight from your loving little heart;" and he kissed her again.

Then May sang something very sweet and pretty – so sweet and pretty that it made her cry, and Sibold also, and the Baby. She did not know the words, and she did not know the tune, and she had only a vague sort of idea what it was all about; but it was very, very pretty. All the time she was singing she kept nursing the baby, and he put his dear little fat arms round her neck, and loved her very much.

When she was done singing, the Child said:

"Chlap, Chlap, Chlap, M-chlap!"

"What does he mean?" she asked Sibold, in distress, for she saw that the Baby wanted something.

Just then a beautiful Cow put its head over the bushes, and said, "Moo-oo-oo." The Beautiful Child clapped his hands; so did May, who said:

"Oh, I know now. He wants to be fed."

The Cow walked in without being invited; and Sibold said:

"I suppose, May, I had better milk him."

"Please do, dear," said May; and she began cuddling the Baby again, and kissing, and nursing him, and telling him that he would soon be fed now.

Whilst she was thus engaged, she was sitting with her back to Sibold; but the Baby was looking on at the milking operation, with his blue eyes dancing with glee. All at once he began to laugh, so much that May looked round to see what he was laughing at. There was Sibold trying to milk the Cow by pulling its tail.

The Cow did not seem to mind him, but went on grazing.

"Chay, Lady," said Sibold. The Cow began to frisk about.

"Oh, I say," said Sibold, "do hurry up now, and give us some milk; the Ba wants some."

The Cow answered him:

"The dear Ba must not want for aught."

May thought it very strange that the Cow could talk; but as Sibold did not seem to think it strange, she held her tongue.

Sibold began to argue with the Cow: "But really now, Mister Cow, if he must not want for anything, why do you make him want?"

The Cow answered: "Don't blame me. It is your own fault. Try some other way;" and it began to laugh as hard as it could.

Its laugh was very funny, very loud at first, but gradually getting more and more like the Child's laugh, till May could not tell one from the other. Then the Cow stopped laughing, but the Child went on.

"What are you laughing at, Ba?" May asked, for she did not remember to know anything about milking, any more than Sibold. She thought this very funny, for she knew that she had often seen the cows milked at home.

The Baby spoke, "That is not the way to milk a cow."

Then Sibold began to work the Cow's tail up and down like the handle of a pump; but the Baby laughed more than ever.

All at once, without knowing how it came to pass, she felt herself pouring milk out of a watering-pot all over the Baby, who lay on the ground, with Sibold holding down its head. The Baby was crowing and laughing like mad; and when the watering-pot was all emptied, he said:

"Thank you both so much. I never enjoyed dinner so much in my life."

"This is a very queer dear Ba!" said May, in a whisper.

"Very," said Sibold.

Whilst they were talking there came a dreadful sound among the trees, very very far away at first, but getting nearer and nearer every moment. It was like cats who were trying to imitate thunder. The noise came booming through the trees.

"Meiau-u-boom-r-p-s-s. Yarkhow-iau-p-s-s."

May was very much frightened. So also was Sibold, but he would not say so; he felt that he had to protect his little Sister and the Baby, so he got between them and the place the sound came from. May hugged the Child close, and said to him, "Do not fear, dear Ba. We will not let it touch you."

"What is 'it?'" said the Baby.

"I do not know, Ba," she answered. "I wish I did. There it comes now;" for just at that moment a great angry Tiger bounded over the tops of the highest trees, and stood glaring at them out of its great green flaming eyes.

May looked on this terrible thing with her eyes distended with terror; but still she clasped the Baby closer and closer. She kept looking at the Tiger, and saw that he was eyeing not her nor Sibold, but the Baby. This made her more frightened than ever, and she clasped him closer. As she looked, however, she saw that the Tiger's eyes got less and less angry every moment, till at last they were as gentle and tame as those of her own favourite tabby.

Then the Tiger began to purr. The purring was like a cat's purr, but so loud that it sounded like drums. However, she did not mind it, for although loud it seemed as if it meant to be gentle and caressing. Then the Tiger came close, and crouched before the Wondrous Child, and licked his little fat hands with its great rough red tongue, but very gently. The Baby laughed, and patted the Tiger's great nose, and pulled the long bristling whiskers, and said:

"Gee, gee."

The Tiger went on behaving most funnily. It lay down on its back, and rolled over and over, and then stood up and purred louder than ever. Its great tail rose straight into the air, with the top moving about and knocking to and fro a great bunch of grapes that hung down from the tree above. It seemed overwhelmed with joy, and came and crouched again before the Child, and purred round him in the greatest state of happiness. Finally it lay down, smiling and purring, and watching over the Child as if on guard.

Presently there came from the distance another terrible Sound. It was like a great Giant hissing; and was louder than steam, and more multitudinous than a flock of geese. There was also the sound of breaking branches, of the crushing of the undergrowth; and there was a terrible dragging noise like nothing else they had ever heard.

Again Sibold stood out between the sound and May, who once more held the Baby to protect him from harm.

The Tiger rose and arched his back like an angry cat, and got ready to spring on whatsoever should come.

Then there appeared over the tops of the trees the head of an enormous Serpent, with small eyes that shone like sparks of fire, and two great open jaws. These jaws were so big that it really seemed as if the beast's whole head opened in two; and between them appeared a great forked tongue which seemed to spit venom. Behind this monstrous head appeared enormous coils of the Serpent's body moving endlessly. The Tiger growled as if about to spring; but suddenly the Serpent lowered its head submissively. It was gazing at the Wondrous Child; and May looking, also saw that the wee Baby was pointing down as if commanding the Serpent to his feet. Then the Tiger, with a low growl and afterwards a contented purr, went back to its place to watch and guard; the great Serpent came gently and coiled itself in the glade, and it also seemed as if keeping watch and guard over the Wondrous Child.

Again there came another terrible sound. This time it was in the air. Great wings seemed to flap louder than thunder; and from far away the air was darkened by a mighty Bird of Prey that made a shadow over the land with its outspread wings.

As the Bird of Prey swooped down, the Tiger rose again and arched his back as though about to spring to meet it, and the Serpent raised his mighty coils and opened his great jaws as if about to strike.

But when the Bird saw the Child it too became less fierce, and hung in mid air with its head drooped as though making submission. Presently the Serpent coiled itself and lay as before, the Tiger went back to watch and guard, and the Bird of Prey alit in the glade and watched and guarded too.

May and Sibold began to look with wonder on the Beautiful Boy, before whom these monsters made obeisance; but they could not see anything strange.

Again there was another terrible sound - this time out to sea - a rushing and swishing as if some giant thing was lashing the water.

Looking round, the children saw two monsters coming. These were a Shark and a Crocodile. They rose out of the sea and came up on land. The Shark was jumping along, with its tail beating about and its triple rows of great teeth grinding together. The Crocodile was crawling along with its big feet and short bent legs; and its terrible mouth was opening and shutting, snapping its big teeth together.

When these two got near, the Tiger and the Serpent and the Bird of Prey all rose to guard the Child; but when the new comers saw the Baby, they too made submission, and they also kept watch and guard - the Crocodile crawling on the beach, and the Shark moving up and down in the water - just like sentries.

Again May and Sibold looked at the Beautiful Child and wondered.

Once more there was a terrible noise, more awful than had yet been.

The earth seemed to shake, and a deep rumbling sound came from far below. Then, a little way off, a mountain suddenly rose; its top opened, and forth burst, with a sound louder than a storm, fire and smoke. Great volumes of black vapour rose and hung, a dark cloud, overhead. Red-hot stones of enormous size were shot aloft and fell again into the crater, and were lost. Down the sides of the mountain rolled torrents of burning lava, and springs of fiercely-boiling water burst forth on every side.

Sibold and May were more frightened than ever, and May clasped the dear Baby closer to her breast.

The thunder of the burning mountain grew louder and louder, the fiery lava poured thick and fast, and from the crater rose the head of a fiery Dragon, with eyes like burning coals and teeth like tongues of flame.

Then the Tiger and the Serpent and the Bird of Prey, and the Crocodile and the Shark, all prepared to defend the Wondrous Child.

But when the fiery Dragon saw the Boy it, too, was quelled; and it crawled humbly out from the burning crater.

Then the fiery mountain sunk again into the earth, the burning lava disappeared; and the Dragon remained with the others to watch and guard.

Sibold and May were more amazed than ever, and looked at the Baby more curiously still. Suddenly May said to her brother:

"Sibold, I want to whisper you something."

Sibold bent his head, and she whispered very softly into his ear:

"I think the Ba is an Angel!"

Sibold looked at him in awe as he answered:

"I think so, too, dear. What are we to do?"

"I do not know," said May; "I hope he will not be angry with us for calling him 'Ba.'"

"I hope not," said Sibold.

May thought for a moment, and then her face lit up with a glad smile as she said:

"He will not be angry, Sibold. You know we entertained him unawares."

"Quite true," said Sibold.

Whilst they were talking, all sorts of animals and birds and fishes were coming into the glade, walking arm in arm, as well as they could - for none of them had arms. A Lion and a Lamb came first, and these two bowed to the Child, and then went and lay down together. Then came a Fox and a Goose; and then a Hawk and a Pigeon; and then a Wolf and another Lamb; then a Dog and a Cat; and then another Cat and a Mouse; and then another Fox and a Stork; and a Hare and a Tortoise; and a Pike and a Trout; and a Sparrow and a Worm; and many, many others, till all the glade was full of living things all at peace with one another.

They all sat round the glade in pairs, and they all looked at the Wondrous Child.

May whispered again to Sibold:

"I think if he is an Angel we ought to be very respectful to him."

Sibold nodded, slowing that he agreed with her; so she cuddled up the Baby closer and said:

"Please, Mister Ba, do not they all look nice and pretty sitting around like that?"

The Beautiful Child smiled sweetly as he answered:

"Beautiful and sweet they look."

May said again:

"I wish they would always be like that, and never fight nor disagree at all, dear Ba. Oh! I beg your pardon. I mean, Mister Ba."

The Child asked her:

"Why do you beg my pardon?"

"Because I called you Ba, instead of Mister Ba."

The Boy asked again:

"Why should you call me Mister Ba?"

May did not like to say, "Because you are an Angel," as she would like to have said, so she cuddled the Child closer and whispered into his little pink ear:

"You know."

The Child put his little arms round her neck and kissed her, and said, very low and very sweetly, words that all her life long she never forgot:

"I do know. Be always loving and sweet, dear child, and even the Angels will know your thoughts and will listen to your words."

May felt very happy. She looked at Sibold, who bent over and kissed her, and called her "sweet little sister;" and all the animals in pairs, and all the terrible ones on guard, said all together like a cheer:

"Right!"

Then they stopped and made all together each of the noises in turn that any of them used to show they were happy. First they all purred, and then they all crowed, and then cackled, and squeaked, and flapped their wings and wagged their tails.

"Oh, how pretty!" said May again, "look, dear Ba!" She was just going to say Mister when the Child held up its finger, so she only said "Ba."

The Child smiled and said:

"Right, you must call me only Ba."

Again all the animals said together like a shout:

"Right, you must say only Ba," and then they all went through the same ways of showing their joy as before.

May said to the Child - and somehow her voice seemed very, very loud although she did not mean it, but only to whisper.

"Oh, dear Ba, I do so wish they would always continue happy and at peace like this. Is there no way of doing it?"

The Beautiful Child opened its mouth to speak, and all the living things put up their claws, or their wings, or their fins to their ears, to listen attentively.

He spake, and his words seemed full of sound but very soft, like the echo of distant thunder coming over far waters on the wings of music.

"Know, dear children, and know ye all that list - there shall be peace on earth between all living things when the children of men are for one hour in perfect love and harmony with each other. Strive, oh! strive, each and all of you, that it may be so."

As he spoke there came over all a solemn hush, and they were very still.

Then the Wondrous Child seemed to float out of May's arms and to move down toward the sea. All the living things instantly hurried to make a great double line between which he passed.

May and Sibold followed him hand in hand. He waited for them at the marge of the sea and then kissed them both.

Whilst he was kissing them, the boat came close to shore; the anchor climbed on board; the white sails ran aloft, and a fresh breeze began to blow towards home.

The Wondrous Child moved on to the prow, and there rested. Sibold and May went on board, and took their old place; and after kissing their hands to all the living things - who were by this time dancing all together in the glade - they kept their eyes fixed on the Beautiful Boy.

As they sat hand in hand, the boat moved along gently, but very swiftly. The shore, with its many beautiful places, seemed gliding into a dim mist as they swept along.

Presently they saw their own creek, and the great Willow towering over all the other trees on shore.

The boat came to land. The Wondrous Child, floating in the air, moved onward towards the Willow Bower.

Sibold and May followed.

He entered the Bower; they came close after.

As the leafy curtain fell behind them, the figure of the Wondrous Child got dimmer and dimmer; till at last, looking at them lovingly, and waving his tiny hands, as if blessing them, he seemed to melt away into the air.

Sibold and May sat for a long time, hand in hand, thinking. Then both feeling sleepy, they put their arms round each other, and lay down to rest.

In this position they again fell asleep, with the Poppies all around them.

The Red Stockade

We was on the southern part of the China station, when the "George Ranger" was ordered to the Straits of Malacca, to put down the pirates that had been showing themselves of late. It was in the forties, when ships was ships, not iron-kettles full of wheels, and other devilments, and there was a chance of hand-to-hand fighting - not being blown up in an iron cellar by you don't know who. Ships was ships in them days!

There had been a lot of throat-cutting and scuttling, for them devils stopped at nothing. Some of us had been through the straits before, when we was in the "Polly Phemus," seventy-four, going to the China station, and although we had never come to quarters with the Malays, we had seen some of their work, and knew what kind they was. So, when we had left Singapore in the "George Ranger," for that was our saucy, little thirty-eight-gun frigate, - the place wasn't in them days what it is now, - many and many 's the yarn was told in the fo'c'sle, and on the watches, of what the yellow devils could do, and had done. Some of us took it one way, and some another, but all, save a few, wanted to get into hand-grips with the pirates, for all their kreeses, and their stinkpots, and the devil's engines what they used. There was some that didn't mind cold steel of an ordinary kind, and would have faced cutlasses and boarding-pikes, any day, for a holiday, but that didn't like the idea of those knives like crooked flames, and that sliced a man in two, and hacked through the bowels of him. Naturally, we didn't take much stock of this kind; and many's the joke we had on them, and some of them cruel enough jokes, too.

You may be sure there was good stories, with plenty of cutting, and blood, and tortures in them, told in their watches, and nigh the whole ship's crew was busy, day and night, remembering and inventing things that'd make them gasp and grow white. I think that, somehow, the captain and the officers must have known what was goin' on, for there came tales from the ward-room that was worse nor any of ours. The midshipmen used to delight in them, like the ship's boys did, and one of them, that had a kreese, used to bring it out when he could, and show how the pirates used it when they cut the hearts out of men and women, and ripped them up to the chins. It was a bit cruel, at times, on them poor, white-livered chaps, - a man can't help his liver, I suppose, - but, anyhow, there's no place for them in a warship, for they're apt to do more harm by living where there's men of all sorts, than they can do by dying. So there wasn't any mercy for them, and the captain was worse on them than any. Captain Wynyard was him that commanded the corvette "Sentinel" on the China station, and was promoted to the "George Ranger" for cutting up a fleet of junks that was hammering at the "Rajah," from Canton, racing for Southampton with the first of the season's tea. He was a man, if you like, a bulldog full of hellfire, when he was on for fighting; he wouldn't have a white liver at any price. "God hates a coward," he said once, "and under Her Britannic Majesty I'm here to carry out God's will. Trice him up, and give him a dozen!" At least, that's the story they tell of him when he was round Shanghai, and one of his men had held back when the time came for boarding a fire-junk that was coming down the tide. And with that he went in, and steered her off with his own hands.

Well, the captain knew what work there was before us, and that it weren't no time for kid gloves and hair-oil, much less a bokey in your buttonhole and a top-hat, and he didn't mean that there should be any funk on his ship. So you take your davy that it wasn't his fault if things was made too pleasant aboard for men what feared fallin' into the clutches of the Malays.

Now and then he went out of his way to be nasty over such folk, and, boy or man, he never checked his tongue on a hard word when any one's face was pale before him. There was one old chap on board that we called "Old Land's End," for he came from that part, and that had a boy of his on the "Billy Ruffian," when he sailed on her, and after got lost, one night, in cutting out a Greek sloop at Navarino, in 1827. We used to chaff him when there was trouble with any of the boys, for he used to say that his boy might have been in that trouble, too. And now, when the chaff was on about bein' afeered of the Malay's, we used to rub it into the old man; but he would flame up, and answer us that his boy died in his duty, and that he couldn't be afeered of nought.

One night there was a row on among the midshipmen, for they said that one of them, Tempest by name, owned up to being afraid of being kreesed. He was a rare bright little chap of about thirteen, that was always in fun and trouble of some kind; but he was soft-hearted, and sometimes the other lads would tease him. He would own up truthfully to anything he thought, or felt, and now they had drawn him to own something that none of them would - no matter how true it might be. Well, they had a rare fight, for the boy was never backward with his fists, and by accident it came to the notice of the captain. He insisted on being told what it was all about, and when young Tempest spoke out, and told him, he stamped on the deck, and called out:

"I'll have no cowards in this ship," and was going on, when the boy cut in:

"I'm no coward, sir; I'm a gentleman!"

"Did you say you were afraid? Answer me - yes, or no?"

"Yes, sir, I did, and it was true! I said I feared the Malay kreeses; but I did not mean to shirk them, for all that. Henry of Navarre was afraid, but, all the same, he - "

"Henry of Navarre be damned," shouted the captain, "and you, too! You said you were afraid, and that, let me tell you, is what we call a coward in the Queen's navy. And if you are one, you can, at least, have the grace to keep it to yourself! No answer to me! To the masthead for the remainder of the day! I want my crew to know what to avoid, and to know it when they see it!" and he walked away, while the lad, without a word, ran up the maintop.

Some way, the men didn't say much about this. The only one that said anything to the point was Old Land's End, and says he:

"That may be a coward, but I'd chance it that he was a boy of mine."

As we went up the straits and got the sun on us, and the damp heat of that kettle of a place, - Lor' bless ye! ye steam there, all day and all night like a copper at the galley, - we began to look around for the pirates, and there wasn't a man that got drowsy on the watch. We coasted along as we went up north, and took a look into the creeks and rivers as we went. It was up these that the Malays hid themselves; for the fevers and such that swept off their betters like flies, didn't seem to have any effect on them. There was pretty bad bits, I tell you, up some of them rivers through the mango groves, where the marshes spread away, mile after mile, as far as you could see, and where every thing that is noxious, both beast, and bird, and fish, and crawling thing, and insect, and tree, and bush, and flower, and creeper, is most at home.

But the pirate ships kept ahead of us; or, if they came south again, passed us by in the night, and so we ran up till about the middle of the peninsula, where the worst of the piracies had happened. There we got up as well as we could to look like a ship in distress; and, sure enough, we deceived the beggars, for two of them came out one early dawn and began to attack us. They was ugly looking craft, too - long, low hull and lateen - sails, and a double crew twice told in every one of them.

But if the crafts was ugly the men was worse, for uglier devils I never saw. Swarthy, yellow chaps, some of them, and some with shaven crowns and white eyeballs, and others as black as your shoe, with one or two white men, more shame, among them, but all carrying kreeses as long as your arm, and pistols in their belts.

They didn't get much change from us, I tell you. We let them get close, and then gave them a broadside that swept their decks like a hail-storm; but we was unlucky that we didn't grapple them, for they managed to shift off and ran for it. Our boats was out quick, but we daren't follow them where they ran into a wide creek, with mango swamps on each side as far as the eye could reach. The boat came back after a bit and reported that they had run up the river which was deep enough but with a winding channel between great mud-banks, where alligators lay in hundreds. There seemed some sort of fort where the river narrowed, and the pirates ran in behind it and disappeared up the bend of the river.

Then the preparations began. We knew that we had got two craft, at any rate, caged in the river, and there was every chance that we had found their lair. Our captain wasn't one that let things go asleep, and by daylight the next morning we was ready for an attack. The pinnace and four other boats started out under the first lieutenant to prospect, and the rest that was left on board waited, as well as they could, till we came back.

That was an awful day. I was in the second boat, and we all kept well together when we began to get into the narrows of the mouth of the river. When we started, we went in a couple of hours after the flood-tide, and so all we saw when the light came seemed fresh and watery. But as the tide ran out, and the big black mud-banks began to show their heads above everywhere, it wasn't nice, I can tell you. It was hardly possible for us to tell the channels, for everywhere the tide raced quick, and it was only when the boat began to touch the black slime that you knew that you was on a bank. Twice our boat was almost caught this way, but by good luck we pulled and pushed off in time into the ebbing tide; and hardly a boat but touched somewhere. One that was a bit out from the rest of us got stuck at last in a nasty cut between two mud-banks, and as the water ran away the boat turned over on the slope, despite all hercrew could do, and we saw the poor fellows thrown out into the slime. More than one of them began to swim toward us, but behind each came a rush of something dark, and though we shouted and made what noise we could, and fired many shots, the alligators was too close, and with shriek after shriek they went down to the bottom of the filth and slime. Oh, man! it was a dreadful sight, and none the better that it was new to nigh all of us. How it would have taken us if we had time to think about it, I hardly know, but I doubt that more than a few would have grown cold over it; but just then there flew amongst us a hail of small shot from a fleet of boats that had stolen down on us. They drove out from behind a big mud-bank that rose steeper than the others and that seemed solider, too, for the gravel of it showed, as the scour of the tide washed the mud away. We was not sorry, I tell you, to have men to fight with, instead of alligators and mud-banks, in an ebbing tide, in a strange tropical river.

We gave chase at once, and the pinnace fired the twelve-pounder which she carried in the bows, in among the huddle of the boats, and the yells arose as the rush of the alligators turned to where the Malay heads bobbed up and down in the drift of the tide. Then the pirates turned and ran, and we after them as hard as we could pull, till round a sharp bend of the river we came to a narrow place, where one side was steep for a bit and then tailed away to a wilderness of marsh, worse than we had seen. The other side was crowned by a sort of fort, built on the top of a high bank, but guarded by a stockade and a mud-bank which lay at its base. From this there came a rain of bullets, and we saw some guns turned toward us. We was hardly strong enough to attack such a position without reconnoitring, and so we drew away; but not quite quick enough, for before we could get out of range of their guns a round shot carried away the whole of the starboard oars of one of our boats.

It was a dreary pull to the ship, and the tide was agin us, for we all got thinking of what we had to tell, - one boat and crew lost entirely, and a set of oars shot away, - and no work done.

The captain was furious; and, in the ward-room, and in the fo'c'sle that night, there was nothing that wasn't flavored with anger and curses. Even the boys, of all sorts, from the cabin-boys to the midshipmen, was wanting to get at the Malays. However, sharp was the order; and by daylight three boats was up at the stockaded fort, making an accurate survey. I was again in one of the boats; and, in spite of what the captain had said to make us all so angry, - and he had a tongue like vitriol, I tell you, - we all felt pretty down and cold when we got again amongst those terrible mud-banks and saw the slime that shone on them bubble up, when the gray of the morning let us see anything

We found that the fort was one that we would have to take if we wanted to follow the pirates up the river, for it barred the way without a chance. There was a gut of the river between the two great ridges of gravel, and this was the only channel where there was a chance of passing. But it had been staked on both sides, so that only the center was left free. Why, from the fort they could have stoned any one in the boats passing there, only that there wasn't any stone, that we could see, in their whole blasted country!

When we got back, with two cases of sunstroke among us, and reported, the captain ordered preparations for an attack on the fort, and the next morning the ball began. It was ugly work. We got close up to the fort, but, as the tide ran out, we had to sheer away somewhat so as not to get stranded. The whole place swarmed with those grinning devils. They evidently had some way of getting to and from their boats behind the stockade. They did not fire a shot at us, - not at first, - and that was the most aggravating thing that you can imagine. They seemed to know something that we did not, and they only just waited. As the tide sank lower and lower, and the mud-banks grew steeper, and the sun on them began to fizzle, a steam arose that nigh turned our stomachs. Why, the sight of them alone would make your heart sink!

The slime shimmered in all kinds of colors, like the water when there's tarring work on hand, and the whole place seemed alive with all that was horrible. The alligators kept off the boats and the banks close to us, but the thick water was full of eels and water-snakes, and the mud was alive with water-worms and leeches, and horrible, gaudy-colored crabs. The very air was filled with pests, - flies of all kinds, and a sort of big-striped insect that they call the "tiger mosquito," which comes out in the daytime and bites you like red-hot pincers. It was bad enough, I tell you, for us men with hair on our faces, but some of the boys got very white and pale, and they was all pretty silent for a while. All at once the crowd of Malays behind the stockade began to roll their eyes and wave their kreeses and to shout. We knew that there was some cause for it, but couldn't make it out, and this exasperated us more than ever. Then the captain sings out to us to attack the stockade; so out we all jumped into the mud. We knew it couldn't be very deep just there, on account of the gravel beneath. We was knee-deep in a moment, but we struggled, and slipped, and fell over each other; and, when we got to the top of that bank, we was the queerest, filthiest-looking crowd you ever see. But the mud hadn't took the heart out of us, and the Malays, with their necks craned over the stockade, and with the nearest thing to a laugh or a smile that the devil lets them have, drew back and fell, one on another, when they heard our cheer.

Between them and us there was a bit of a dip where the water had been running in the ebb-tide, but which seemed now as dry as the rest, and the foremost of our men charged down the slope, and then we knew why they had kept silent and waited! We was in a regular trap. The first ranks disappeared at once in the mud and ooze in the hollow, and those next were up to their armpits before they could stop. Then those Malay devils opened on us, and while we tried to pull our chaps out, they mowed us down with every kind of small arm they had - and they had a queer assortment, I tell you.

It was all we could do to get back over the slope and to the boats again, - what was left of us, - and, as we hadn't hands enough left even to row with full strength, we had to make for the ship as fast as we could, for their boats began to pass out in a cloud through the narrow by the stockade. But before we went we saw them dragging the live and dead out of the mud with hooks on the end of long bamboos; and there was terrible shrieks from some poor fellows when the kreeses gashed through them. We daren't wait; but we saw enough to make us swear revenge. When we saw them devils stick the bleeding heads of our comrades on the spikes of the stockade, there was nigh a mutiny because the captain wouldn't let us go back and have another try for it. He was cool enough now; and those of us that knew him and understood what was in his mind, when the smile on him showed the white teeth in the corners of his mouth, felt that it was no good day's work that the pirates had done for themselves.

When we got back to the ship and told our tale, it wasn't long till the men was all on fire; and nigh every man took a turn with the grindstone at his cutlass, till they was all like razors. The captain mustered every one on board, and detailed every man to his work in the boats, ready for the next time; and we knew that, by daylight, we were to have another slap at the pirates. We got six-pounders and twelve-pounders in most of the boats, for we was to give them a dose of big shot before we came to close quarters.

When we got up near the stockade, the tide had turned, and we thought it better to wait till dawn, for it was bad work among the mud-banks at the ebb in the dark. So we hung on a while, and then when the sky began to lighten, we made for the fort. When we got nigh enough to see it, there wasn't a man of us who didn't want to have some bloody revenge, for there, on the spikes of the stockade, were the heads of all the poor fellows that we had lost the day before, with a cloud of mosquitoes and flies already beginning to buzz around them in the dawn. But beyond that again, they had painted the outside of the stockade with blood, so that the whole place was a crimson mass. You could smell it as the sun came up!

Well, that day was a hard one. We opened fire with our guns, and the Malays returned it, with all they had got. A fleet of boats came out from beyond the fort, and for a while we had to turn our attention to these. The small guns served us well, and we made a rare havoc among the boats, for our shot went crashing through them, and quite a half of them were sunk. The water was full of bobbing heads; but the tide carried them away from us, and their cries and shrieks came from beyond the fort and then died away. The other boats recognized their danger, and turned and ran in through the narrow, and let us alone for hours after. Then we went at the fort again. We turned our guns at the piles of the stockade, and, of course, every shot told, - but their fire was at too close quarters, and with their rifles and matchlocks, and the rest, they picked us off too fast, and we had to sheer off where our heavy metal could tell without our being within their range. Before we sheered off, we could see that the hole we had knocked in the stockade was only in the outer work, and that the real fort was within. We had to go down the river, as we couldn't go far enough across without danger from the banks, and this only gave us a side view, and, do what we would, we couldn't make an impression, - at least any that we could see.

That was a long and awful day! The sun was blazing on us like a furnace, and we was nigh mad with heat, and flies, and drouth, and anger. It was that hot that if you touched metal it fairly burned you. When the tide was near the flood, the captain ordered up the boats in the wide water now opposite the fort; and there, for a while, we got a fair chance, till, when the ebb began, we should have to sheer off again. By this time our shot was nearly run out, and we thought that we should have to give over; but all at once came order to prepare for attack, and in a few minutes we was working for dear life across the river, straight for the stockade. The men set up a cheer, and the pirates showed over the top of the stockade and waved their kreeses, and more than one of them sliced off pieces of the heads on the spikes, and jeered at us, as much as to say that they would do the same for us in our turn! When we got close up, every one of them had disappeared, and there was a silence of the grave. We knew that there was something up, but what the move was we could not tell, till from behind the fort came rushing again a fleet of boats. We turned on them, and, like we did before, we made mincemeat of them. This time the tide made for us, and the bobbing heads went by us in dozens. Now and then there was a wild yell, as an alligator pulled some one down into the mud. This went on for a little, and we had beaten them off enough to be able to get our grappling - irons ready for climbing the stockade, when the second lieutenant, who was in the outer boat, called out:

"Back with the boats! Back, quick, the tide is falling!" and with one impulse we began to shove off. Then, in an instant, the place became alive again with the Malays, and they began firing on us so quickly that before we could get out into the whirl of tide there was many a dead man in our boats.

There was no use trying to do any more that day, and after we had done what could be done for the wounded, and patched up our boats, for there was plenty of shot-holes to plug, we pulled back to the ship. The alligators had had a good day, and as we went along, and the mud-banks grew higher and higher with the falling of the tide, we could see them lie out lazily, as if they had been gorged. Aye! And there was enough left for the ground-sharks out in the offing; for the men on board told us that every while on the ebb something would go along, bobbing up and down in the swell, till presently there would be a swift ripple of a fin, and then there was no more pirate.

Well! when we got aboard, the rest was mighty anxious to know what had been done; and when we began, with the heads on spikes of the red stockade, the men ground their teeth, and Old Land's End up, and says he:

"The Red Stockade! We'll not forget the name! It'll be our turn next, and then we'll paint it inside this time." And so it was that we came to know the place by that name. That night the captain was like a man that would do murder. His face was like steel, and his eyes was as red as flames. He didn't seem to have a thought for any one; and everything he did was as hard as though his heart were brass. He ordered all that was needful to be done for the wounded, but he added to the doctor: "And, mind you, get them well as soon as you can. We're too shorthanded already!"

Up to now, we all had known him treat men as men, but now he only thought of us as machines for fighting! True enough, he thought the same of himself. Twice that very night he cut up rough in a new way. Of course, the men was talking of the attack, and there was lots of brag and chaff, for all they was so grim earnest, and some of the old fooling went on about blood and tortures. The captain came on deck, and as he walked along, he saw one of the men that didn't like the kreeses, and he didn't evidently like the looks of him, for he turned on his heel and said savagely:

"Send the doctor here!" So the doctor came, and the captain he says to him, cold as ice, and as polite as you please:

"Dr. Fairbrother, there is a sick man here! look at his pale face. Something wrong with his liver, I suppose. It's the only thing that makes a seaman's face white when there's fighting ahead. Take him down to sick bay, and do something for him. I'd like to cut the accursed white liver out of him altogether!" and with that he went down to his cabin.

Well if we was hot for fighting before, we was boiling after that, and we all came to know that the next attack on the Red Stockade would be the last, one way or the other! We had to wait two more days before that could come off, for the boats and tackle had to be made ready, and there wasn't going to be any mistakes made this time.

It was just after midnight when we began to get ready. Every man was to his post. The moon was up, and it was lighter nor a London day, and the captain stood by and saw every man to his place, and nothing escaped him. By and by, as No. 6 boat was filling, and before the officer in charge of it got in, came the midshipman, young Tempest, and when the captain saw him he called him up and hissed out before all the crew:

"Why are you so white? What's wrong with you, anyway? Is your liver out of order, too?"

True enough, the boy was white, but at the flaming insult the blood rushed to his face and we could see it red in the starlight. Then in another moment it passed away and left him paler than ever, and he said with a gentle voice, though standing as straight as a ramrod:

"I can't help the blood in my face, sir. If I'm a coward because I'm pale, perhaps you are right. But I shall do my duty all the same!" and with that he pulled himself up, touched his cap, and went down into the boat.

Old Land's End was behind me in the boat with him, number five to my six, and he whispered to me through his shut teeth:

"Too rough that! He might have thought a bit that he's only a child. And he came all the same, even if he was afeer'd!"

We stole away with muffled oars, and dropped silently into the river on the floodtide. If any man had had any doubts as to whether we was in earnest at other times, he had none then, anyhow. It was a pretty grim time, I tell you, for the most of us felt that whether we won or not this time, there would be many empty hammocks that night in the "George Ranger;" but we meant to win even if we went into the maws of the sharks and crocodiles for it. When we came up close on the flood we lost no time but went slap at the fort. At first, of course, we had crawled up the river in silence, and I think that we took the beggars by surprise, for we was there before the time they expected us. Howsomever, they turned out quick enough and there was soon music on both sides of the stockade. We didn't want to take any chance on the mud-banks this time, so we ran in close under the stockade at once and hooked on. We found that they had repaired the breach we had made the last time. They fought like devils, for they knew that we could beat them hand to hand, if we could once get in, and they sent round the boats to take us on the flank, as they had done each time before. But this time we wasn't to be drawn away from our attack, and we let our boats outside tackle them, while we minded our own business closer home.

It was a long fight and a bloody one. They was sheltered inside, and they knew that time was with them, for when the tide should have fallen, if we hadn't got in we should have our old trouble with the mud-banks all over again. But we knew it, too, and we didn't lose no time. Still, men is only men, after all, and we couldn't fly up over a stockade out of a boat, and them as did get up was sliced about dreadful, - they are handy workmen with their kreeses, and no doubt! We was so hot on the job we had on hand that we never took no note of time at all, and all at once we found the boat fixed tight under us.

The tide had fallen and left us on the bank under the Red Stockade, and the best half of the boats was cut off from us. We had some thirty men left, and we knew we had to fight whether we liked it or not. It didn't much matter, anyhow, for we was game to go through with it. The captain, when he seen the state of things, gave his orders to take the boats out into mid-stream, and shell and shot the fort, whilst we was to do what we could to get in. It was no use trying to bridge over the slobs, for the masts of an old seventy-four wouldn't have done it. We was in a tight place, then, I can tell you, between two fires, for the guns in the boats couldn't fire high enough to clear us every time, without going over the fort altogether, and more than one of our own shots did some of us a harm. The cutter came into the game, and began sending the war-rockets from the tubes. The pirates didn't like that, I tell you, and more betoken, no more did we, for we got as much of them as they did, till the captain saw the harm to us, and bade them cease. But he knew his business, and he kept all the fire of the guns on the one side of the stockade, till he knocked a hole that we could get in by. When this was done, the Malays left the outer wall and went within the fort proper. This gave us some protection, since they couldn't fire right down on us, and our guns kept the boats away that would have taken us from the riverside. But it was hot work, and we began dropping away with stray shots, and with the stinkpots and hand-grenades that they kept hurling over the stockade on to us.

So the time came when we found that we must make a dash for the fort, or get picked out, one by one, where we stood. By this time some of our boats was making for the opening, and there seemed less life behind the stockade; some of them was up to some move, and was sheering off to make up some other devilment. Still, they had their guns in the fort, and there was danger to our boats if they tried to cross the opening between the piles. One did, and went down with a hole in her within a minute. So we made a burst inside the stockade, and found ourselves in a narrow place between the two walls of piles. Anyhow, the place was drier, and we felt a relief in getting out of up to our knees in steaming mud. There was no time to lose, and the second lieutenant, Webster by name, told us to try to scale the stockade in front.

It wasn't high, but it was slimy below and greasy above, and do what we would, we couldn't get no nigher. A shot from a pistol wiped out the lieutenant, and for a moment we thought we was without a leader. Young Tempest was with us, silent all the time, with his face as white as a ghost, though he done his best, like the rest of us. Suddenly he called out:

"Here, lads! take and throw me in. I'm light enough to do it, and I know that when I'm in you'll all follow."

Ne'er a man stirred. Then the lad stamped his foot and called again, and I remember his young, high voice now:

"Seamen to your duty! I command here!"

At the word we all stood at attention, just as if we was at quarters. Then Jack Pring, that we called the Giant, for he was six feet four and as strong as a bullock, spoke out:

"It's no duty, sir, to fling an officer into hell!" The lad looked at him and nodded.

"Volunteers for dangerous duty!" he called, and every man of the crowd stepped out.

"All right, boys!" says he. "Now take me up and throw me in. We'll get down that flag, anyhow," and he pointed to the black flag that the pirates flew on the flagstaff in the fort. Then he took the small flag of the float and put it on his breast, and says he: "This'll suit better."

"Won't I do, sir?" said Jack, and the lad laughed a laugh that rang again.

"Oh, my eye!" says he, has any one got a crane to hoist in the Giant?" The lad told us to catch hold of him, and when Jack hesitated, says he:

"We've always been friends, Jack, and I want you to be one of the last to touch me!" So Jack laid hold of him by one side, and Old Land's End stepped out and took him by the other. The rest of us was, by this time, kicking off our shoes and pulling off our shirts, and getting our knives open in our teeth. The two men gave a great heave together and they sent the boy clean over the top of the stockade. We heard across the river a cheer from our boats, as we began to scramble. There was a pause within the fort for a few seconds, and then we saw the lad swarm up the bamboo flagstaff that swayed under him, and tear down the black flag. He pulled our own flag from his breast and hung it over the top of the post. And he waved his hand and cheered, and the cheer was echoed in thunder across the river. And then a shot fetched him down, and with a wild yell they all went for him, while the cheering from the boats came like a storm.

We never knew quite how we got over that stockade. To this day I can't even imagine how we done it! But when we leaped down, we saw something lying at the foot of the flagstaff all red, - and the kreeses was red, too! The devils had done their work! But it was their last, for we came at them with our cutlasses, - there was never a sound from the lips of any of us, - and we drove them like a hail-storm beats down standing corn! We didn't leave a living thing within the Red Stockade that day, and we wouldn't if there had been a million there!

It was a while before we heard the shouting again, for the boats was coming up the river, now that the fort was ours, and the men had other work for their breath than cheering.

Between us, we made a rare clearance of the pirates' nest that day. We destroyed every boat on the river, and the two ships that we was looking for, and one other that was careened. We tore down and burned every house, and jetty, and stockade in the place, and there was no quarter for them we caught. Some of them got away by a path they knew through the swamp where we couldn't follow them. The sun was getting low when we pulled back to the ship. It would have been a merry enough home-coming, despite our losses, - all but for one thing, and that was covered up with a Union Jack in the captain's own boat. Poor lad! when they lifted him on deck, and the men came round to look at him, his face was pale enough now, and, one and all, we felt that it was to make amends, as the captain stooped over and kissed him on the forehead.

"We'll bury him to-morrow," he said, "but in blue water, as becomes a gallant seaman."

At the dawn, next day, he lay on a grating, sewn in his hammock, with the shot at his feet, and the whole crew was mustered, and the chaplain read the service for the dead. Then he spoke a bit about him, - how he had done his duty, and was an example to all, - and he said how all loved and honored him. Then the men told off for the duty stood ready to slip the grating and let the gallant boy go plunging down to join the other heroes under the sea; but Old Land's End stepped out and touched his cap to the captain, and asked if he might say a word.

"Say on, my man!" said the captain, and he stood, with his cocked hat in his hand, whilst Old Land's End spoke:

"Mates! ye've heerd what the chaplain said. The boy done his duty, and died like the brave gentleman he was! And we wish he was here now. But, for all that, we can't be sorry for him, or for what he done, though it cost him his life. I had a lad once of my own, and I hoped for him what I never wanted for myself, - that he would win fame and honor, and become an admiral of the fleet, as others have done before. But, so help me God! I'd rather see him lying under the flag as we see that brave boy lie now, and know why he was there, than I'd see him in his epaulettes on the quarter-deck of the flagship! He died for his Queen and country, and for the honor of the flag! And what more would you have him do!"

The Dualists

There was joy in the house of Bubb.

For ten long years had Ephraim and Sophonisba Bubb mourned in vain the loneliness of their life. Unavailingly had they gazed into the emporia of baby-linen, and fixed their searching glances on the basket-makers' warehouses where the cradles hung in tempting rows. In vain had they prayed, and sighed, and groaned, and wished, and waited, and wept, but never had even a ray of hope been held out by the family physician.

But now at last the wished-for moment had arrived. Month after month had flown by on leaden wings, and the destined days had slowly measured their course. The months had become weeks; the weeks had dwindled down to days; the days had been attenuated to hours; the hours had lapsed into minutes, the minutes had slowly died away, and but seconds remained.

Ephraim Bubb sat cowering on the stairs, and tried with high-strung ears to catch the strain of blissful music from the lips of his first-born. There was silence in the house--silence as of the deadly calm before the cyclone. Ah! Ephraim Bubb, little thinkest thou that another moment may for ever destroy the peaceful, happy course of thy life, and open to thy too-craving eyes the portals of that wondrous land where childhood reigns supreme, and where the tyrant infant with the wave of his tiny hand and the imperious treble of his tiny voice sentences his parent o the deadly vault beneath the castle moat. As the thought strikes thee thou becomest pale. How thou tremblest as thou findest thyself upon the brink of the abyss! Wouldst that thou could recall the past!

But hark! the die is cast for good or ill. The long years of praying and hoping have found an end at last. From the chamber within comes a sharp cry, which shortly after is repeated. Ah!

Ephraim, that cry is the feeble effort of childish lips as yet unused to the rough, worldly form of speech to frame the word 'father'. In the glow of thy transport all doubts are forgotten; and when the doctor cometh forth as the harbinger of joy he findeth thee radiant with new-found delight.

'My dear sir, allow me to congratulate you--to offer twofold felicitations. Mr Bubb, sir, you are the father of twins!'

Halcyon Days

The twins were the finest children that ever were seen--so at least said the cognoscenti, and the parents were not slow to believe. The nurse's opinion was in itself a proof.

It was not, ma'am, that they was fine for twins, but they was fine for singles, and she had ought to know, for she had nussed a many in her time, both twins and singles. All they wanted was to have their dear little legs cut off and little wings on their dear little shoulders, for to be put one on each side of a white marble tombstone, cut beautiful, sacred to the relic of Ephraim Bubb, that they might, sir, if so be that missus was to survive the father of two such lovely twins--although she would make bold to say, and no offence intended, that a handsome gentleman, though a trifle or two older than his good lady, though for the matter of that she heerd that gentlemen was never too old at all, and for her own part she liked them the better for it: not like bits of boys that didn't know their own minds--that a gentleman what was the father of two such 'eavenly twins (God bless them!) couldn't be called anything but a boy; though for the matter of that she never knowed in her experience--which it was much--of a boy as had such twins, or any twins at all so much for the matter of that. The twins were the idols of their parents, and at the same time their pleasure and their pain. Did Zerubbabel cough, Ephraim would start from his balmy slumbers with an agonized cry of consternation, for visions of innumerable twins black in the face from croup haunted his nightly pillow. Did Zacariah rail at ethereal expansion, Sophonisba with pallid hue and dishevelled locks would fly to the cradle of her offspring. Did pins torture or strings afflict, or flannel or flies tickle, or light dazzle, or darkness affright, or hunger or thirst assail the synchronous productions, the household of Bubb would be roused from quiet slumbers or the current of its manifold workings changed.

The twin's grew apace; were weaned; teethed; and at length arrived at the stage of three years! They grew in beauty side by side, They filled one home, etc.

Rumours of War

Harry Merford and Tommy Santon lived in the same range of villas as Ephraim Bubb. Harry's parents had taken up their abode in no. 25, no. 27 was happy in the perpetual sunshine of Tommy's smiles, and between these two residences Ephraim Bubb reared his blossoms, the number of his mansion being 26. Harry and Tommy had been accustomed from the earliest times to meet each other daily. Their primal method of communication had been by the house-tops, till their respective sires had been obliged to pay compensation to Bubb for damages to his roof and dormer windows; and from that time they had been forbidden by the home authorities to meet, whilst their mutual neighbour had taken the precaution of having his garden walls pebble-dashed and topped with broken glass to prevent their incursions. Harry and Tommy, however, being gifted with daring souls, lofty, ambitious, impetuous natures, and strong seats to their trousers, defied the rugged walls of Bubb and continued to meet in secret.

Compared with these two youths, Castor and Pollux, Damon and Pythias, Eloisa and Abelard are but tame examples of duality or constancy and friendship. All the poets from Hyginus to Schiller might sing of noble deeds and desperate dangers held as naught for friendship's sake, but they would have been mute had they but known of the mutual affection of Harry and Tommy. Day by day, and often night by night, would these two brave the perils of nurse, and father, and mother, of whip and imprisonment, and hunger and thirst, and solitude and darkness to meet together. What they discussed in secret none other knew. What deeds of darkness were perpetrated in their symposia none could tell. Alone they met, alone they remained, and alone they departed to their several abodes. There was in the garden of Bubb a summer-house overgrown with trailing plants, and surrounded by young poplars which the fond father had planted on his children's natal day, and whose rapid growth he had proudly watched. These trees quite obscured the summer-house, and here Harry and Tommy, knowing after a careful observation that none ever entered the place, held their conclaves. Time after time they met in full security and followed their customary pursuit of pleasure. Let us raise the mysterious veil and see what was the great Unknown at whose shrine they bent the knee..Harry and Tommy had each been given as a Christmas box a new knife; and for a long time--nearly a year--these knives, similar in size and pattern, were their chief delights. With them they cut and hacked in their respective homes all things which would not be likely to be noticed; for the young gentlemen were wary and had no wish that their moments of pleasure should be atoned for by moments of pain. The insides of drawers, and desks, and boxes, the underparts of tables and chairs, the backs of pictures frames, even the floors, where corners of the carpets could surreptitiously be turned up, all bore marks of their craftsmanship; and to compare notes on these artistic triumphs was a source of joy. At length, however, a critical time came, some new field of action should be opened up, for the old appetites were sated, and the old joys had begun to pall. It was absolutely necessary that the existing schemes of destruction should be enlarged; and yet this could hardly be done without a terrible risk of discovery, for the limits of safety had long since been reached and passed. But, be the risk great or small, some new ground should be broken--some new joy found, for the old earth was barren, and the craving for pleasure was growing fiercer with each successive day.

The crisis had come: who could tell the issue?

The Tucket Sounds

They met in the arbour, determined to discuss this grave question. The heart of each was big with revolution, the head of each was full of scheme and strategy, and the pocket of each was full of sweet-stuff, the sweeter for being stolen. After having dispatched the sweets, the conspirators proceeded to explain their respective views with regard to the enlargement of their artistic operations. Tommy unfolded with much pride a scheme which he had in contemplation of cutting a series of holes in the sounding board of the piano, so as to destroy its musical properties. Harry was in no wise behindhand in his ideas of reform. He had conceived the project of cutting the canvas at the back of his great-grandfather's portrait, which his father held in high regard among his lares and penates, so that in time when the picture should be moved the skin of paint would be broken, the head fall bodily out from the frame.

At this point of the council a brilliant thought occurred to Tommy. 'Why should not the enjoyment be doubled, and the musical instruments and family pictures of both establishments be sacrificed on the altar of pleasure?' This was agreed to nem. con.; and then the meeting adjourned for dinner. When they next met it was evident that there was a screw loose some-where--that there was 'something rotten in the state of Denmark'. After a little fencing on both sides, it came out that all the schemes of domestic reform had been foiled by maternal vigilance, and that so sharp had been the reprimand consequent on a partial discovery of the schemes that they would have to be abandoned--till such time, at least, as increased physical strength would allow the reformers to laugh to scorn parental threats and injunctions.

Sadly the two forlorn youths took out their knives and regarded them; sadly, sadly they thought, as erst did Othello, of all the fair chances of honour and triumph and glory gone for ever. They compared knives with almost the fondness of doting parents. There they were--so equal in size and strength and beauty--dimmed by no corrosive rust, tarnished by no stain, and with unbroken edges of the keenness of Saladin's sword.

So like were the knives that but for the initials scratched in the handles neither boy could have been sure which was his own. After a little while they began mutually to brag of the superior excellence of their respective weapons. Tommy insisted that his was the sharper, Harry asserted that his was the stronger of the two. Hotter and hotter grew the war of words. The tempers of Harry and Tommy got inflamed, and their boyish bosoms glowed with manly thoughts of daring and hate. But there was abroad in that hour a spirit of a bygone age--one that penetrated even to that dim arbour in the grove of Bubb. The world-old scheme of ordeal was whispered by the spirit in the ear of each, and suddenly the tumult was allayed. With one impulse the boys suggested that they should test the quality of their knives by the ordeal of the Hack.

No sooner said than done. Harry held out his knife edge uppermost; and Tommy, grasping his firmly by the handle, brought down the edge of the blade crosswise on Harry's. The process was then reversed, and Harry became in turn the aggressor. Then they paused and eagerly looked for the result. It was not hard to see; in each knife were two great dents of equal depth; and so it was necessary to renew the contest, and seek a further proof.

What needs it to relate seriatim the details of that direful strife? The sun had long since gone down, and the moon with fair, smiling face had long risen over the roof of Bubb, when, wearied and jaded, Harry and Tommy sought their respective homes. Alas! the splendour of the knives was gone for ever. Ichabod!--Ichabod! the glory had departed and naught remained but two useless wrecks, with keen edges destroyed, and now like unto nothing save the serried hills of Spain.

But though they mourned for their fondly cherished weapons, the hearts of the boys were glad; for the bygone day had opened to their gaze a prospect of pleasure as boundless as the limits of the world.

The First Crusade

From that day a new era dawned in the lives of Harry and Tommy. So long as the resources of the parental establishments could hold out so long would their new amusement continue. Subtly they obtained surreptitious possession of articles of family cutlery not in general use, and brought them one by one to their rendezvous. These came fair and spotless from the sanctity of the butler's pantry. Alas! they returned not as they came.

But in course of time the stock of available cutlery became exhausted, and again the inventive faculties of the youths were called into requisition. They reasoned thus: 'The knife game, it is true, is played out, but the excitement of the hack is not to be dispensed with. Let us carry, then, this great idea into new worlds; let us still live in the sunshine of pleasure; let us continue to hack, but with objects other than knives.'

It was done. Not knives now engaged the attention of the ambitious youths. Spoons and forks were daily flattened and beaten out of shape; pepper castor met pepper castor in combat, and both were borne dying from the field; candlesticks met in fray to part no more on this side of the grave; even epergnes were used as weapons in the crusade of hack.

At last all the resources of the butler's pantry became exhausted, and then began a system of miscellaneous destruction that proved in a little time ruinous to the furniture of the respective homes of Harry and Tommy. Mrs Santon and Mrs Merford began to notice that the wear and tear in their households became excessive. Day after day some new domestic calamity seemed to have occurred. Today a valuable edition of some book whose luxurious binding made it an object for public display would appear to have suffered some dire misfortune, for the edges were frayed and broken and the back loose if not altogether displaced; tomorrow the same awful fate would seem to have followed some miniature frame; the day following the legs of some chair or spider-table would show signs of extraordinary hardship. Even in the nursery the sounds of lamentation were heard..It was a thing of daily occurrence for the little girls to state that when going to bed at night they had laid their dear dollies in their beds with tender care, but that when again seeking them in the period of recess they had found them with all their beauty gone, with legs and arms amputated and faces beaten from all semblance of human form.

Then articles of crockery began to be missed. The thief could in no case be discovered, and the wages of the servants, from constant stoppages, began to be nominal rather than real. Mrs Merford and Mrs Santon mourned their losses, but Harry and Tommy gloated day after day over their spoils, which lay in an ever-increasing heap in the hidden grove of Bubb. To such an extent had the fondness of the hack now grown that with both youths it was an infatuation--a madness--a frenzy.

At length one awful day arrived. The butlers of the houses of Merford and Santon, harassed by constant losses and complaints, and finding that their breakage account was in excess of their wages, determined to seek some sphere of occupation where, if they did not meet with a suitable reward or recognition of their services, they would, at least, not lose whatever fortune and reputation they had already acquired. Accordingly, before rendering up their keys and the goods entrusted to their charge, they proceeded to take a preliminary stock of their own accounts, to make sure of their accredited accuracy. Dire indeed was their distress when they knew to the full the havoc which had been wrought; terrible their anguish of the present, bitter their thoughts of the future. Their hearts, bowed down with weight of woe, failed them quite; reeled the strong brains that had erst overcome foes of deadlier spirit than grief; and fell their stalwart forms prone on the floors of their respective sancta sanctorum.

Late in the day when their services were required they were sought for in bower and hail, and at length discovered where they lay.

But alas for justice! They were accused of being drunk and for having, whilst in that degraded condition, deliberately injured all the property on which they could lay hands. Were not the evidences of their guilt patent to all in the hecatombs of the destroyed? Then they were charged with all the evils wrought in the houses, and on their indignant denial Harry and Tommy, each in his own home, according to their concerted scheme of action, stepped forward and relieved their minds of the deadly weight that had for long in secret borne them down. The story of each ran that time after time he had seen the butler, when he thought that nobody was looking, knocking knives together in the pantry, chairs and books and pictures in the drawing-room and study, dolls in the nursery, and plates in the kitchen. Then, indeed, was the master of each household stern and uncompromising in his demands for justice. Each butler was committed to the charge of myrmidons of the law under the double charge of drunkenness and wilful destruction of property.

Softly and sweetly slept Harry and Tommy in their little beds that night. Angels seemed to whisper to them, for they smiled as though lost in pleasant dreams. The rewards given by proud and grateful parents lay in their pockets, and in their hearts the happy consciousness of having done their duty.

Truly sweet should be the slumbers of the just...

It might be supposed that now the operations of Harry and Tommy would be obliged to be abandoned. Not so, however. The minds of these youths were of no common order, nor were their souls of such weak nature as to yield at the first summons of necessity. Like Nelson, they knew not fear; like Napoleon, they held 'impossible' to be the adjective of fools; and they revelled in the glorious truth that in the lexicon of youth is no such word as 'fail'. Therefore on the day following the éclaircissement of the butlers' misdeeds, they met in the arbour to plan a new campaign. In the hour when all seemed blackest to them, and when the narrowing walls of possibility hedged them in on every side, thus ran the deliberations of these dauntless youths:

'We have played out the meaner things that are inanimate and inert; why not then trench on the domains of life? The dead have lapsed into the regions of the forgotten past--let the living look to themselves.'

That night they met when all households had retired to balmy sleep, and naught but the amorous wailings of nocturnal cats told of the existence of life and sentience. Each bore into the arbour in his arms a pet rabbit and a piece of sticking-plaster. Then, in the peaceful, quiet moonlight, commenced a work of mystery, blood, and gloom. The proceedings began by the fixing of a piece of sticking-plaster over the mouth of each rabbit to prevent it making a noise, if so inclined. Then Tommy held up his rabbit by its scutty tail, and it hung wriggling, a white mass in the moonlight. Slowly Harry raised his rabbit holding it in the same manner, and when level with his head brought it down on Tommy's client.

But the chances had been miscalculated. The boys held firmly to the tails, but the chief portions of the rabbits fell to earth. Ere the doomed beasts could escape, however, the operators had pounced upon them, and this time holding them by the hind legs renewed the trial.

Deep into the night the game was kept up, and the eastern sky began to show signs of approaching day as each boy bore triumphantly the dead corse of his favourite bunny and placed it within its sometime hutch.

Next night the same game was renewed with a new rabbit on each side, and for more than a week--so long as the hutches supplied the wherewithal--the battle was sustained. True that there were sad hearts and red eyes in the juveniles of Santon and Merford as one by one the beloved pets were found dead, but Harry and Tommy, with the hearts of heroes steeled to suffering and deaf to the pitiful cries of childhood, still fought the good fight on to the bitter end.

When the supply of rabbits was exhausted, other munition was not wanting, and for some days the war was continued with white mice, dormice, hedgehogs, guinea pigs, pigeons, lambs, canaries, parakeets, linnets, squirrels, parrots, marmots, poodles, ravens, tortoises, terriers, and cats. Of these, as might be expected, the most difficult to manipulate were the terriers and the cats, and of these two classes the proportion of the difficulties in the way of terrier-hacking was, when compared with those of cat-hacking, about that which the simple lac of the British pharmacopoeia bears to water in the compound which dairymen palm off upon a too-confiding public as milk. More than once when engaged in the rapturous delights of cat-hacking had Harry and Tommy wished that the silent tomb could open its ponderous and massy jaws and engulf them, for the feline victims were not patient in their death agonies, and often broke the bonds in which the security of the artists rested, and turned fiercely on their executioners.

At last, however, all the animals available were sacrificed; but the passion for hacking still remained. How was it all to end?

A Cloud with Golden Lining

Tommy and Harry sat in the arbour dejected and disconsolate. They wept like two Alexanders because there were no more worlds to conquer. At last the conviction had been forced upon them that the resources available for hacking were exhausted. That very morning they had had a desperate battle, and their attire showed the ravages of direful war. Their hats were battered into shapeless masses, their shoes were soleless and heel-less and had the uppers broken, the ends of their braces, their sleeves, and their trousers were frayed, and had they indulged in the manly luxury of coat-tails these too would have gone.

Truly, hacking had become an absorbing passion with them. Long and fiercely had they been swept onwards on the wings of the demon of strife, and powerless at the best of times had been the promptings of good; but now, heated with combat, maddened by the equal success of arms, and with the lust for victory still unsated, they longed more fiercely than ever for some new pleasure: like tigers that have tasted blood they thirsted for a larger and more potent libation.

As they sat, with their souls in a tumult of desire and despair, some evil genius guided into the garden the twin blossoms of the tree of Bubb. Hand in hand Zacariah and Zerubbabel advanced from the back door; they had escaped from their nurses, and with the exploring instinct of humanity, advanced boldly into the great world--the terra incognita, the ultima Thule of the paternal domain.

In the course of time they approached the hedge of poplars, from behind which the anxious eyes of Harry and Tommy looked for their approach, for the boys knew that where the twins were the nurses were accustomed to be gathered together, and they feared discovery if their retreat should be cut off.

It was a touching sight, these lovely babes, alike in form, feature, size, expression, and dress; in fact, so like each other that one 'might not have told either from which'. When the startling similarity was recognized by Harry and Tommy, each suddenly turned, and, grasping the other by the shoulder, spoke in a keen whisper: 'Hack! They are exactly equal! This is the very apotheosis of our art!'

With excited faces and trembling hands they laid their plans to lure the unsuspecting babes within the precincts of their charnel house, and they were so successful in their efforts that in a little time the twins had toddled behind the hedge and were lost to the sight of the parental mansion.

Harry and Tommy were not famed for gentleness within the immediate precincts of their respective homes, but it would have delighted the heart of any philanthropist to see the kindly manner in which they arranged for the pleasures of the helpless babes. With smiling faces and playful words and gentle wiles they led them within the arbour, and then, under pretence of giving them some of those sudden jumps in which infants rejoice, they raised them from the ground. Tommy held Zacariah across his arm with his baby moon-face smiling up at the cob-webs on the arbour roof, and Harry, with a mighty effort, raised the cherubic Zerubbabel aloft.

Each nerved himself for a great endeavour, Harry to give, Tommy to endure a shock, and then the form of Zerubbabel was seen whirling through the air round Harry's glowing and determined face. There was a sickening crash and the arm of Tommy yielded visibly.

The pasty face of Zerubbabel had fallen fair on that of Zacariah, for Tommy and Harry were by this time artists of too great experience to miss so simple a mark. The putty-like noses collapsed, the putty-like cheeks became for a moment flattened, and when in an instant more they parted, the faces of both were dabbled in gore. Immediately the firmament was rent with a series of such yells as might have awakened the dead. Forthwith from the house of Bubb came the echoes in parental cries and footsteps. As the sounds of scurrying feet rang through the mansion, Harry cried to Tommy: 'They will be on us soon. Let us cut to the roof of the stable and draw up the ladder.'

Tommy answered by a nod, and the two boys, regardless of consequences, and bearing each a twin, ascended to the roof of the stable by means of a ladder which usually stood against the wall, and which they pulled up after them.

As Ephraim Bubb issued from his house in pursuit of his lost darlings, the sight which met his gaze froze his very soul. There, on the coping of the stable roof, stood Harry and Tommy renewing their game. They seemed like two young demons forging some diabolical implement, for each in turn the twins were lifted high in air and let fall with stunning force on the supine form of its fellow. How Ephraim felt none but a tender and imaginative father can conceive. It would be enough to wring the heart of even a callous parent to see his children, the darlings of his old age--his own beloved twins--being sacrificed to the brutal pleasure of unregenerate youths, without being made unconsciously and helplessly guilty of the crime of fratricide.

Loudly did Ephraim and also Sophonisba, who, with dishevelled locks, had now appeared upon the scene, bewail their unhappy lot and shriek in vain for aid; but by rare ill-chance no eyes save their own saw the work of butchery or heard the shrieks of anguish and despair. Wildly did Ephraim, mounting on the shoulders of his spouse, strive, but in vain, to scale the stable wall.

Baffled in every effort, he rushed into the house and appeared in a moment bearing in his hands a double-barrelled gun, into which he poured the contents of a shot pouch as he ran. He came anigh the stable and hailed the murderous youths: 'Drop them twins and come down here or I'll shoot you like a brace of dogs.'

'Never!' exclaimed the heroic two with one impulse, and continued their awful pastime with a zest tenfold as they knew that the agonized eyes of parents wept at the cause of their joy.

'Then die!' shrieked Ephraim, as he fired both barrels, right--left, at the hackers.

But, alas! love for his darlings shook the hand that never shook before. As the smoke cleared off and Ephraim recovered from the kick of his gun, he heard a loud twofold laugh of triumph and saw Harry and Tommy, all unhurt, waving in the air the trunks of the twins-the fond father had blown the heads completely off his own offspring.

Tommy and Harry shrieked aloud in glee, and after playing catch with the bodies for some time, seen only by the agonized eyes of the infanticide and his wife, flung them high in the air.

Ephraim leaped forward to catch what had once been Zacariah, and Sophonisba grabbed wildly for the loved remains of her Zerubbabel.

But the weight of the bodies and the height from which they fell were not reckoned by either parent, and from being ignorant of a simple dynamical formula each tried to effect an object which calm, common sense, united with scientific knowledge, would have told them was impossible. The masses fell, and Ephraim and Sophonisba were stricken dead by the falling twins, who were thus posthumously guilty of the crime of parricide.

An intelligent coroner's jury found the parents guilty of the crimes of infanticide and suicide, on the evidence of Harry and Tommy, who swore, reluctantly, that the inhuman monsters, maddened by drink, had killed their offspring by shooting them into the air out of a cannon--since stolen--whence like curses they had fallen on their own heads; and that then they had slain themselves suis manibus with their own hands..Accordingly Ephraim and Sophonisba were denied the solace of Christian burial, and were committed to the earth with 'maimed rites', and had stakes driven through their middles to pin them down in their unhallowed graves till the crack of doom.

Harry and Tommy were each rewarded with national honours and were knighted, even at their tender years.

Fortune seemed to smile upon them all the long after-years, and they lived to a ripe old age, hale of body, and respected and beloved of all.

Often in the golden summer eves, when all nature seemed at rest, when the oldest cask was opened and the largest lamp was lit, when the chestnuts glowed in the embers and the kid turned on the spit, when their great-grandchildren pretended to mend fictional armour and to trim an imaginary helmet's plume, when the shuttles of the good wives of their grandchildren went flashing each through its proper loom, with shouting and with laughter they were accustomed to tell the tale of THE DUALITISTS; OR, THE DEATH DOOM OF THE DOUBLE BORN.

THE END

The Crystal Cup

I. The Dream-Birth

The blue waters touch the walls of the palace; I can hear their soft, lapping wash against the marble whenever I listen. Far out at sea I can see the waves glancing in the sunlight, ever-smiling, ever-glancing, ever-sunny. Happy waves!-happy in your gladness, thrice happy that ye are free!

I rise from my work and spring up the wall till I reach the embrasure. I grasp the corner of the stonework and draw myself up till I crouch in the wide window. Sea, sea, out away as far as my vision extends. There I gaze till my eyes grow dim; and in the dimness of my eyes my spirit finds its sight. My soul flies on the wings of memory away beyond the blue, smiling sea-away beyond the glancing waves and the gleaming sails, to the land I call my home. As the minutes roll by, my actual eyesight seems to be restored, and I look round me in my old birth-house. The rude simplicity of the dwelling comes back to me as something new. There I see my old books and manuscripts and pictures, and there, away on their old shelves, high up above the door, I see my first rude efforts in art.

How poor they seem to me now! And yet, were I free, I would not give the smallest of them for all I now possess. Possess? How I dream.

The dream calls me back to waking life. I spring down from my window-seat and work away frantically, for every line I draw on paper, every new form that springs on the plaster, brings me nearer freedom. I will make a vase whose beauty will put to shame the glorious works of Greece in her golden prime! Surely a love like mine and a hope like mine must in time make some form of beauty spring to life! When He beholds it he will exclaim with rapture, and will order my instant freedom. I can forget my hate, and the deep debt of revenge which I owe him when I think of liberty-even from his hands. Ah! then on the wings of the morning shall I fly beyond the sea to my home-her home-and clasp her to my arms, never more to be separated!

But, oh Spirit of Day! if she should be-No, no, I cannot think of it, or I shall go mad. Oh Time, Time! maker and destroyer of men's fortunes, why hasten so fast for others whilst thou laggest so slowly for me? Even now my home may have become desolate, and she-my bride of an hour-may sleep calmly in the cold earth. Oh this suspense will drive me mad! Work, work! Freedom is before me; Aurora is the reward of my labour!

So I rush to my work; but to my brain and hand, heated alike, no fire or no strength descends. Half mad with despair, I beat myself against the walls of my prison, and then climb into the embrasure, and once more gaze upon the ocean, but find there no hope. And so I stay till night, casting its pall of blackness over nature, puts the possibility of effort away from me for yet another day.

So my days go on, and grow to weeks and months. So will they grow to years, should life so long remain an unwelcome guest within me; for what is man without hope? and is not hope nigh dead within this weary breast?

***

Last night, in my dreams, there came, like an inspiration from the Day-Spirit, a design for my vase.

All day my yearning for freedom-for Aurora, or news of her-had increased tenfold, and my heart and brain were on fire. Madly I beat myself, like a caged bird, against my prison-bars. Madly I leaped to my window-seat, and gazed with bursting eyeballs out on the free, open sea. And there I sat till my passion had worn itself out; and then I slept, and dreamed of thee, Aurora-of thee and freedom. In my ears I heard again the old song we used to sing together, when as children we wandered on the beach; when, as lovers, we saw the sun sink in the ocean, and I would see its glory doubled as it shone in thine eyes, and was mellowed against thy cheek; and when, as my bride, you clung to me as my arms went round you on that desert tongue of land whence rushed that band of sea-robbers that tore me away. Oh! how my heart curses those men-not men, but fiends! But one solitary gleam of joy remains from that dread encounter,-that my struggle stayed those hell-hounds, and that, ere I was stricken down, this right hand sent one of them to his home. My spirit rises as I think of that blow that saved thee from a life worse than death. With the thought I feel my cheeks burning, and my forehead swelling with mighty veins. My eyes burn, and I rush wildly round my prison-house, 'Oh! for one of my enemies, that I might dash out his brains against these marble walls, and trample his heart out as he lay before me!' These walls would spare him not. They are pitiless, alas! I know too well. 'Oh, cruel mockery of kindness, to make a palace a prison, and to taunt a captive's aching heart with forms of beauty and sculptured marble!' Wondrous, indeed, are these sculptured walls! Men call them passing fair; but oh, Aurora! with thy beauty ever before my eyes, what form that men call lovely can be fair to me? Like him who gazes sun-wards, and then sees no light on earth, from the glory that dyes his iris, so thy beauty or its memory has turned the fairest things of earth to blackness and deformity.

In my dream last night, when in my ears came softly, like music stealing across the waters from afar, the old song we used to sing together, then to my brain, like a ray of light, came an idea whose grandeur for a moment struck me dumb. Before my eyes grew a vase of such beauty that I knew my hope was born to life, and that the Great Spirit had placed my foot on the ladder that leads from this my palace-dungeon to freedom and to thee. Today I have got a block of crystal-for only in such pellucid substance can I body forth my dream-and have commenced my work.

I found at first that my hand had lost its cunning, and I was beginning to despair, when, like the memory of a dream, there came back in my ears the strains of the old song. I sang it softly to myself, and as I did so I grew calmer; but oh! how differently the song sounded to me when thy voice, Aurora, rose not in unison with my own! But what avails pining? To work! To work! Every touch of my chisel will bring me nearer thee.

***

My vase is daily growing nearer to completion. I sing as I work, and my constant song is the one I love so well. I can hear the echo of my voice in the vase; and as I end, the wailing song note is prolonged in sweet, sad music in the crystal cup. I listen, ear down, and sometimes I weep as I listen, so sadly comes the echo to my song. Imperfect though it be, my voice makes sweet music, and its echo in the cup guides my hand towards perfection as I work.

Would that thy voice rose and fell with mine, Aurora, and then the world would behold a vase of such beauty as never before woke up the slumbering fires of mans love for what is fair; for if I do such work in sadness, imperfect as I am in my solitude and sorrow, what would I do in joy, perfect when with thee? I know that my work is good as an artist, and I feel that it is as a man; and the cup itself, as it daily grows in beauty, gives back a clearer echo. Oh! if I worked in joy how gladly would it give back our voices!

Then would we hear an echo and music such as mortals seldom hear; but now the echo, like my song, seems imperfect. I grow daily weaker; but still I work on-work with my whole soul-for am I not working for freedom and for thee?

***

My work is nearly done. Day by day, hour by hour, the vase grows more finished. Ever clearer comes the echo whilst I sing; ever softer, ever more sad and heart-rending comes the echo of the wail at the end of the song. Day by day I grow weaker and weaker; still I work on with all my soul. At night the thought comes to me, whilst I think of thee, that I will never see thee more-that I breathe out my life into the crystal cup, and that it will last there when I am gone.

So beautiful has it become, so much do I love it, that I could gladly die to be maker of such a work, were it not for thee-for my love for thee, and my hope of thee, and my fear for thee, and my anguish for thy grief when thou knowest I am gone.

***

251

My work requires but few more touches. My life is slowly ebbing away, and I feel that with my last touch my life will pass out for ever into the cup. Till that touch is given I must not die-I will not die. My hate has passed away. So great are my wrongs that revenge of mine would be too small a compensation for my woe. I leave revenge to a juster and a mightier than I. Thee, oh Aurora, I will await in the land of flowers, where thou and I will wander, never more to part, never more! Ah, never more! Farewell, Aurora-Aurora-Aurora!

II. The Feast of Beauty

The Feast of Beauty approaches rapidly, yet hardly so fast as my royal master wishes. He seems to have no other thought than to have this feast greater and better than any ever held before. Five summers ago his Feast of Beauty was nobler than all held in his sires reign together; yet scarcely was it over, and the rewards given to the victors, when he conceived the giant project whose success is to be tested when the moon reaches her full. It was boldly chosen and boldly done; chosen and done as boldly as the project of a monarch should be. But still I cannot think that it will end well. This yearning after completeness must be unsatisfied in the end-this desire that makes a monarch fling his kingly justice to the winds, and strive to reach his Mecca over a desert of blighted hopes and lost lives. But hush! I must not dare to think ill of my master or his deeds; and besides, walls have ears. I must leave alone these dangerous topics, and confine my thoughts within proper bounds.

The moon is waxing quickly, and with its fulness comes the Feast of Beauty, whose success as a whole rests almost solely on my watchfulness and care; for if the ruler of the feast should fail in his duty, who could fill the void? Let me see what arts are represented, and what works compete. All the arts will have trophies: poetry in its various forms, and prose-writing; sculpture with carving in various metals, and glass, and wood, and ivory, and engraving gems, and setting jewels; painting on canvas, and glass, and wood, and stone and metal; music, vocal and instrumental; and dancing. If that woman will but sing, we will have a real triumph of music; but she appears sickly too. All our best artists either get ill or die, although we promise them freedom or rewards or both if they succeed.

Surely never yet was a Feast of Beauty so fair or so richly dowered as this which the full moon shall behold and hear; but ah! the crowning glory of the feast will be the crystal cup. Never yet have these eyes beheld such a form of beauty, such a wondrous mingling of substance and light. Surely some magic power must have helped to draw such loveliness from a cold block of crystal. I must be careful that no harm happens the vase. To-day when I touched it, it gave forth such a ringing sound that my heart jumped with fear lest it should sustain any injury. Henceforth, till I deliver it up to my master, no hand but my own shall touch it lest any harm should happen to it.

Strange story has that cup. Born to life in the cell of a captive torn from his artist home beyond the sea, to enhance the splendour of a feast by his labour-seen at work by spies, and traced and followed till a chance-cruel chance for him-gave him into the hands of the emissaries of my master. He too, poor moth, fluttered about the flame: the name of freedom spurred him on to exertion till he wore away his life. The beauty of that cup was dearly bought for him. Many a man would forget his captivity whilst he worked at such a piece of loveliness; but he appeared to have some sorrow at his heart, some sorrow so great that it quenched his pride.

How he used to rave at first! How he used to rush about his chamber, and then climb into the embrasure of his window, and gaze out away over the sea! Poor captive! perhaps over the sea some one waited for his coming who was dearer to him than many cups, even many cups as beautiful as this, if such could be on earth. . . . Well, well, we must all die soon or late, and who dies first escapes the more sorrow, perhaps, who knows? How, when he had commenced the cup, he used to sing all day long, from the moment the sun shot its first fiery arrow into the retreating hosts of night-clouds, till the shades of evening advancing drove the lingering sunbeams into the west-and always the same song!

How he used to sing, all alone! Yet sometimes I could almost imagine I heard not one voice from his chamber, but two. . . . No more will it echo again from the wall of a dungeon, or from a hillside in free air. No more will his eyes behold the beauty of his crystal cup.

It was well he lived to finish it. Often and often have I trembled to think of his death, as I saw him day by day grow weaker as he worked at the unfinished vase. Must his eyes never more behold the beauty that was born of his soul? Oh, never more! Oh Death, grim King of

Terrors, how mighty is thy sceptre! All-powerful is the wave of thy hand that summons us in turn to thy kingdom away beyond the poles!

Would that thou, poor captive, hadst lived to behold thy triumph, for victory will be thine at the Feast of Beauty such as man never before achieved. Then thou mightst have heard the shout that hails the victor in the contest, and the plaudits that greet him as he passes out, a free man, through the palace gates. But now thy cup will come to light amid the smiles of beauty and rank and power, whilst thou liest there in thy lonely chamber, cold as the marble of its walls.

And, after all, the feast will be imperfect, since the victors cannot all be crowned. I must ask my master's direction as to how a blank place of a competitor, should he prove a victor, is to be filled up. So late? I must see him ere the noontide hour of rest be past.

***

Great Spirit! how I trembled as my master answered my question!

I found him in his chamber, as usual in the noontide. He was lying on his couch disrobed, half-sleeping; and the drowsy zephyr, scented with rich odours from the garden, wafted through the windows at either side by the fans, lulled him to complete repose. The darkened chamber was cool and silent. From the vestibule came the murmuring of many fountains, and the pleasant splash of falling waters. 'Oh, happy,' said I, in my heart, 'oh, happy great King, that has such pleasures to enjoy!' The breeze from the fans swept over the strings of the AEolian harps, and a sweet, confused, happy melody arose like the murmuring of children's voices singing afar off in the valleys, and floating on the wind.

As I entered the chamber softly, with muffled foot-fall and pent-in breath, I felt a kind of awe stealing over me. To me who was born and have dwelt all my life within the precincts of the court-to me who talk daily with my royal master, and take his minutest directions as to the coming feast-to me who had all my life looked up to my king as to a spirit, and had venerated him as more than mortal-came a feeling of almost horror; for my master looked then, in his quiet chamber, half-sleeping amid the drowsy music of the harps and fountains, more like a common man than a God. As the thought came to me I shuddered in affright, for it seemed to me that I had been guilty of sacrilege. So much had my veneration for my royal master become a part of my nature, that but to think of him as another man seemed like the anarchy of my own soul.

I came beside the couch, and watched him in silence. He seemed to be half-listening to the fitful music; and as the melody swelled and died away his chest rose and fell as he breathed in unison with the sound.

After a moment or two he appeared to become conscious of the presence of some one in the room, although by no motion of his face could I see that he heard any sound, and his eyes were shut. He opened his eyes, and, seeing me, asked, 'Was all right about the Feast of Beauty?' for that is the subject ever nearest to his thoughts. I answered that all was well, but that I had come to ask his royal pleasure as to how a vacant place amongst the competitors was to be filled up. He asked, 'How vacant?' and on my telling him, 'from death,' he asked again, quickly, 'Was the work finished?' When I told him that it was, he lay back again on his couch with a sigh of relief, for he had half arisen in his anxiety as he asked the question. Then he said, after a minute, 'All the competitors must be present at the feast.' 'All?' said I. 'All,' he answered again, 'alive or dead; for the old custom must be preserved, and the victors crowned.' He stayed still for a minute more, and then said, slowly, 'Victors or martyrs.' And I could see that the kingly spirit was coming back to him.

Again he went on. 'This will be my last Feast of Beauty; and all the captives shall be set free. Too much sorrow has sprung already from my ambition. Too much injustice has soiled the name of king.'

He said no more, but lay still and closed his eyes. I could see by the working of his hands and the heaving of his chest that some violent emotion troubled him, and the thought arose, 'He is a man, but he is yet a king; and, though a king as he is, still happiness is not for him.

Great Spirit of Justice! thou metest out his pleasures and his woes to man, to king and slave alike! Thou lovest best to whom thou givest peace!'

Gradually my master grew more calm, and at length sunk into a gentle slumber; but even in his sleep he breathed in unison with the swelling murmur of the harps.

'To each is given,' said I gently, 'something in common with the world of actual things. Thy life, oh King, is bound by chains of sympathy to the voice of Truth, which is Music! Tremble, lest in the presence of a master-strain thou shouldst feel thy littleness, and die!' and I softly left the room.

III. The Story of the Moonbeam

Slowly I creep along the bosom of the waters.

Sometimes I look back as I rise upon a billow, and see behind me many of my kin sitting each upon a wave-summit as upon a throne.

So I go on for long, a power that I wist not forcing me onward, without will or purpose of mine.

At length, as I rise upon a mimic wave, I see afar a hazy light that springs from a vast palace, through whose countless windows flame lamps and torches. But at the first view, as if my coming had been the signal, the lights disappear in an instant.

Impatiently I await what may happen; and as I rise with each heart-beat of the sea, I look forward to where the torches had gleamed. Can it be a deed of darkness that shuns the light?

***

The time has come when I can behold the palace without waiting to mount upon the waves. It is built of white marble, and rises steep from the brine. Its sea-front is glorious with columns and statues; and from the portals the marble steps sweep down, broad and wide to the waters, and below them, down as deep as I can see.

No sound is heard, no light is seen. A solemn silence abounds, a perfect calm.

Slowly I climb the palace walls, my brethren following as soldiers up a breach. I slide along the roofs, and as I look behind me walls and roofs are glistening as with silver. At length I meet with something smooth and hard and translucent; but through it I pass and enter a vast hall, where for an instant I hang in mid-air and wonder.

My coming has been the signal for such a burst of harmony as brings back to my memory the music of the spheres as they rush through space; and in the full-swelling anthem of welcome I feel that I am indeed a sun-spirit, a child of light, and that this is homage to my master.

I look upon the face of a great monarch, who sits at the head of a banquet-table. He has turned his head upwards and backwards, and looks as if he had been awaiting my approach. He rises and fronts me with the ringing out of the welcome-song, and all the others in the great hall turn towards me as well. I can see their eyes gleaming. Down along the immense table, laden with plate and glass and flowers, they stand holding each a cup of ruby wine, with which they pledge the monarch when the song is ended, as they drink success to him and to the 'Feast of Beauty.'

I survey the hall. An immense chamber, with marble walls covered with bas-reliefs and frescoes and sculptured figures, and panelled by great columns that rise along the surface and support a dome-ceiling painted wondrously; in its centre the glass lantern by which I entered.

On the walls are hung pictures of various forms and sizes, and down the centre of the table stretches a raised platform on which are placed works of art of various kinds.

At one side of the hall is a dais on which sit persons of both sexes with noble faces and lordly brows, but all wearing the same expression-care tempered by hope. All these hold scrolls in their hands.

At the other side of the hall is a similar dais, on which sit others fairer to earthly view, less spiritual and more marked by surface-passion. They hold music-scores. All these look more joyous than those on the other platform, all save one, a woman, who sits with downcast face and dejected mien, as of one without hope. As my light falls at her feet she looks up, and I feel happy. The sympathy between us has called a faint gleam of hope to cheer that poor pale face.

Many are the forms of art that rise above the banquet-table, and all are lovely to behold. I look on all with pleasure one by one, till I see the last of them at the end of the table away from the monarch, and then all the others seem as nothing to me. What is this that makes other forms of beauty seem as nought when compared with it, when brought within the radius of its lustre? A crystal cup, wrought with such wondrous skill that light seems to lose its individual glory as it shines upon it and is merged in its beauty. 'Oh Universal Mother, let me enter there.

Let my life be merged in its beauty, and no more will I regret my sun-strength hidden deep in the chasms of my moon-mother. Let me live there and perish there, and I will be joyous whilst it lasts, and content to pass into the great vortex of nothingness to be born again when the glory of the cup has fled.'

Can it be that my wish is granted, that I have entered the cup and become a part of its beauty? 'Great Mother, I thank thee.'

Has the cup life? or is it merely its wondrous perfectness that makes it tremble, like a beating heart, in unison with the ebb and flow, the great wave-pulse of nature? To me it feels as if it had life.

I look through the crystal walls and see at the end of the table, isolated from all others, the figure of a man seated. Are those cords that bind his limbs? How suits that crown of laurel those wide, dim eyes, and that pallid hue? It is passing strange. This Feast of Beauty holds some dread secrets, and sees some wondrous sights.

I hear a voice of strange, rich sweetness, yet wavering-the voice of one almost a king by nature. He is standing up; I see him through my palace-wall. He calls a name and sits down again.

Again I hear a voice from the platform of scrolls, the Throne of Brows; and again I look and behold a man who stands trembling yet flushed, as though the morning light shone bright upon his soul. He reads in cadenced measure a song in praise of my moon-mother, the Feast of Beauty, and the king. As he speaks, he trembles no more, but seems inspired, and his voice rises to a tone of power and grandeur, and rings back from walls and dome. I hear his words distinctly, though saddened in tone, in the echo from my crystal home. He concludes and sits down, half-fainting, amid a whirlwind of applause, every note, every beat of which is echoed as the words had been.

Again the monarch rises and calls 'Aurora,' that she may sing for freedom. The name echoes in the cup with a sweet, sad sound. So sad, so despairing seems the echo, that the hall seems to darken and the scene to grow dim.

'Can a sun-spirit mourn, or a crystal vessel weep?'

She, the dejected one, rises from her seat on the Throne of Sound, and all eyes turn upon her save those of the pale one, laurel-crowned. Thrice she essays to begin, and thrice nought comes from her lips but a dry, husky sigh, till an old man who has been moving round the hall settling all things, cries out, in fear lest she should fail, 'Freedom!'

The word is re-echoed from the cup. She hears the sound, turns towards it and begins.

Oh, the melody of that voice! And yet it is not perfect alone; for after the first note comes an echo from the cup that swells in unison with the voice, and the two sounds together, seem as if one strain came ringing sweet from the lips of the All-Father himself. So sweet it is, that all throughout the hall sit spell-bound, and scarcely dare to breathe.

In the pause after the first verses of the song, I hear the voice of the old man speaking to a comrade, but his words are unheard by any other, 'Look at the king. His spirit seems lost in a trance of melody. Ah! I fear me some evil: the nearer the music approaches to perfection the more rapt he becomes. I dread lest a perfect note shall prove his death-call.' His voice dies away as the singer commences the last verse.

Sad and plaintive is the song; full of feeling and tender love, but love overshadowed by grief and despair. As it goes on the voice of the singer grows sweeter and more thrilling, more real; and the cup, my crystal time-home, vibrates more and more as it gives back the echo. The monarch looks like one entranced, and no movement is within the hall. . . . The song dies away in a wild wail that seems to tear the heart of the singer in twain; and the cup vibrates still more as it gives back the echo. As the note, long-swelling, reaches its highest, the cup, the Crystal Cup, my wondrous home, the gift of the All-Father, shivers into millions of atoms, and passes away.

Ere I am lost in the great vortex I see the singer throw up her arms and fall, freed at last, and the King sitting, glory-faced, but pallid with the hue of Death.

Buried Treasures

Chapter I - The Old Wreck

Mr. Stedman spoke.

"I do not wish to be too hard on you; but I will not, I cannot consent to Ellen's marrying you till you have sufficient means to keep her in comfort. I know too well what poverty is. I saw her poor mother droop and pine away till she died, and all from poverty. No, no, Ellen must be spared that sorrow at all events."

"But, sir, we are young. You say you have always earned your living. I can do the same and I thought" - this with a flush - "I thought that if I might be so happy as to win Ellen's love that you might help us."

"And so I would, my dear boy; but what help could I give? I find it hard to keep the pot boiling as it is, and there is only Ellen and myself to feed. No, no, I must have some certainty for Ellen before I let her leave me. Just suppose anything should happen to me" -

"Then, sir, what could be better than to have some one to look after Ellen - some one with a heart to love her as she should be loved, and a pair of hands to be worked to the bone for her sake."

"True, boy; true. But still it cannot be. I must be certain of Ellen's future before I trust her out of my own care. Come now, let me see you with a hundred pounds of your own, and I shall not refuse to let you speak to her. But mind, I shall trust to your honour not to forestall that time."

"It is cruel, sir, although you mean it in kindness. I could as easily learn to fly as raise a hundred pounds with my present opportunities. Just think of my circumstances, sir. If my poor father had lived all would have been different; but you know that sad story."

"No, I do not. Tell it to me."

"He left the Gold Coast after spending half his life there toiling for my poor mother and me. We knew from his letter that he was about to start for home, and that he was coming in a small sailing vessel, taking all his savings with him. But from that time to this he has never been heard of."

"Did you make inquiries?"

"We tried every means, or rather poor mother did, for I was too young, and we could find out nothing."

"Poor boy. From my heart I pity you; still I cannot change my opinion. I have always hoped that Ellen would marry happily. I have worked for her, early and late, since she was born, and it would be mistaken kindness to let her marry without sufficient provisions for her welfare."

Robert Hamilton left Mr. Stedman's cottage in great dejection. He had entered it with much misgiving, but with a hope so strong that it brightened the prospect of success. He went slowly along the streets till he got to his office, and when once there he had so much work to do that little time was left him for reflection until his work for the day was over. That night he lay awake, trying with all the intentness of his nature to conceive some plan by which he might make the necessary sum to entitle him to seek the hand of Ellen Stedman: but all in vain. Scheme after scheme rose up before him, but each one, though born of hope, quickly perished in succession. Gradually his imagination grew in force as the real world seemed to fade away; he built bright castles in the air and installed Ellen as their queen. He thought of all the vast sums of money made each year by chances, of old treasures found after centuries, new treasures dug from mines, and turned from mills and commerce. But all these required capital - except the old treasures - and this source of wealth being a possibility, to it his thoughts clung as a man lost in mid-ocean clings to a spar - clung as he often conceived that his poor father had clung when lost with all his treasure far at sea.

"Vigo Bay, the Schelde, already giving up their long-buried spoil," so thought he. "All round our coasts lie millions lost, hidden but for a time. Other men have benefited by them - why should not I have a chance also?" And then, as he sunk to sleep the possibility seemed to become reality, and as he slept he found treasure after treasure, and all was real to him, for he knew not that he dreamt.

He had many dreams. Most of them connected with the finding of treasures, and in all of them Ellen took a prominent place. He seemed in his dreams to renew his first acquaintance with the girl he loved, and when he thought of the accident that brought them together, it might be expected that the seashore was the scene of many of his dreams. The meeting was in this wise: One holiday, some three years before, he had been walking on the flat shore of the 'Bull,' when he noticed at some distance off a very beautiful young girl, and set to longing for some means of making her acquaintance. The means came even as he wished. The wind was blowing freely, and the girl's hat blew off and hurried seawards over the flat shore. He ran after it and brought it back: and from that hour the two had, after their casual acquaintance had been sanctioned by her father, became fast friends.

Most of his dreams of the night had faded against morning, but one he remembered.

He seemed to be in a wide stretch of sand near the hulk of a great vessel. Beside him lay a large iron-bound box of great weight, which he tried in vain to lift. He had by a lever just forced it through a hole in the side of the ship, and it had fallen on the sand and was sinking. Despite all he could do, it still continued to go down into the sand, but by slow degrees. The mist was getting round him, shutting out the moonlight, and from far he could hear a dull echoing roar muffled by the fog, and the air seemed laden with the clang of distant bells. Then the air became instinct with the forms of life, and amid them floated the form of Ellen, and with her presence the gloom and fog and darkness were dispelled, and the sun rose brightly on the instant, and all was fair and happy.

Next day was Sunday, and so after prayers he went for a walk with his friend, Tom Harrison.

They directed their steps towards Dollymount, and passing across the bridge, over Crab Lake, found themselves on the North Bull. The tide was "black" out, and when they crossed the line of low bent-covered sand-hills, or dunnes, as they are called in Holland, a wide stretch of sand intersected with shallow tidal streams lay before them, out towards the mouth of the bay. As they looked, Robert's dream of the night before flashed into his memory, and he expected to see before him the hulk of the old ship.

Presently Tom remarked:

"I do not think I ever saw the tide so far out before. What an immense stretch of sand there is. It is a wonder there is no rock or anything of the kind all along this shore."

"There is one," said Robert, pointing to where, on the very edge of the water, rose a little mound, seemingly a couple of feet at most, over the level of the sand.

"Let us go out to it," said Tom, and accordingly they both took off their boots and stockings, and walked over the wet sand, and forded the shallow streams till they got within a hundred yards of the mound. Suddenly Tom called out: "It is not a rock at all; it is a ship, bottom upwards, with the end towards us, and sunk in the sand."

Robert's heart stood still for an instant.

What if this should be a treasure-ship, and his dream prove prophetic? In an instant more he shook aside the fancy and hurried on.

They found that Tom had not been mistaken. There lay the hulk of an old ship, with just its bottom over the sand. Close round it the ebb and flow of the tide had worn a hole like the moat round an old castle; and in this pool small fishes darted about, and lazy crabs sidled into the sand.

Tom jumped the narrow moat, and stood balanced on the keel, and a hard task he had to keep his footing on the slippery seaweed. He tapped the timbers with his stick, and they gave back a hollow sound. "The inside is not yet choked up," he remarked.

Robert joined him, and walked all over the bottom of the ship, noticing how some of the planks, half rotten with long exposure, were sinking inwards.

After a few minutes Tom spoke -

"I say, Bob, suppose that this old ship was full of money, and that you and I could get it out."

"I have just been thinking the same."

"Suppose we try," said Tom, and he commenced to endeavour to prize up the end of a broken timber with his stick. Robert watched him for some minutes, and when he had given up the attempt in despair, spoke -

"Suppose we do try, Tom. I have a very strange idea. I had a curious dream last night, and this old ship reminds me of it."

Tom asked Robert to tell the dream. He did so, and when he had finished, and had also confided his difficulty about the hundred pounds, Tom remarked -

"We'll try the hulk, at any rate. Let us come some night and cut a hole in her and look. It might be worth our while; it will be a lark at any rate."

He seemed so interested in the matter that Robert asked him the reason.

"Well, I will tell you," he said. "You know Tomlinson. Well, he told me the other day that he was going to ask Miss Stedman to marry him. He is well off - comparatively, and unless you get your chance soon you may be too late. Don't be offended at me for telling you. I wanted to get an opportunity."

"Thanks, old boy," was Robert's answer, as he squeezed his hand. No more was spoken for a time. Both men examined the hulk carefully, and then came away, and sat again on a sand hill.

Presently a coastguard came along, with his telescope under his arm. Tom entered into conversation with him about the wreck.

"Well, sir," he said, "that was afore my time here. I've been here only about a year, and that's there a matter o' fifteen year or thereabouts. She came ashore here in the great storm when the

'Mallard' was lost in the Scillies. I've heerd tell" -

Robert interrupted him to ask -

"Did anyone ever try what was in her?"

"Well, sir, there I'm out. By rights there should, but I've bin told that about then there was a lawsuit on as to who the shore belonged to. The ship lay in the line between the Ballast Board ground and the Manor ground, or whatever it is, and so nothin' could be done till the suit was ended, and when it was there weren't much use lookin' for anything, for she was settled nigh as low as she is now, and if there ever was anything worth havin' in her the salt water had ruined it long ago."

"Then she was never examined?" said Tom.

"Most like not, sir; they don't never examine little ships like her - if she was a big one we might," and the coastguard departed.

When he was gone Tom said, "By Jove, he forgot to say on whose ground she is," and he ran after him to ask the question. When he came back he said, "It's all right; it belongs to Sir Arthur Forres."

After watching for some time in silence Robert said, "Tom, I have very strange thoughts about this. Let us get leave from Sir Arthur - he is, I believe, a very generous man - and regularly explore."

"Done," said Tom, and, it being now late, they returned to town.

Chapter II - Wind and Tide

Robert and Tom next day wrote a letter to Sir Arthur Forres asking him to let them explore the ship, and by return of post got a kind answer, not only granting the required permission, but making over the whole ship to them to do what they pleased with. Accordingly they held a consultation as to the best means of proceeding, and agreed to commence operations as soon as possible, as it was now well on in December, and every advance of winter would throw new obstacles in their way. Next day they bought some tools, and brought them home in great glee. It often occurred to both of them that they were setting out on the wildest of wild-goose chases, but the novelty and excitement of the whole affair always overcame their scruples. The first moonlight night that came they took their tools, and sallied out to Dollymount to make the first effort on their treasure ship. So intent were they on their object that their immediate surroundings did not excite their attention. It was not, therefore, till they arrived at the summit of the sand hill, from which they had first seen the hulk, that they discovered that the tide was coming in, and had advanced about half way. The knowledge was like a cold bath to each of them, for here were all their hopes dashed to the ground, for an indefinite time at least. It might be far into the winter time - perhaps months - before they could get a union of tide, moonlight, and fair weather, such as alone could make their scheme practicable. They had already tried to get leave from office, but so great was the press of business that their employer told them that unless they had special business, which they could name, he could not dispense with their services. To name their object would be to excite ridicule, and as the whole affair was but based on a chimera they were of course silent.

They went home sadder than they had left it, and next day, by a careful study of the almanac, made out a list of the nights which might suit their purpose - if moon and weather proved favourable. From the fact of their living in their employer's house their time was further curtailed, for it was an inflexible rule that by twelve o'clock everyone should be home. Therefore, the only nights which could suit were those from the 11th to the 15th December, on which there would be low water between the hours of seven and eleven. This would give them on each night about one hour in which to work, for that length of time only was the wreck exposed between the ebbing and flowing tides.

They waited in anxiety for the 11th December, the weather continued beautifully fine, and nearly every night the two friends walked to view the scene of their future operations. Robert was debarred from visiting Ellen by her father's direction, and so was glad to have some object of interest to occupy his thoughts whilst away from her.

As the time wore on, the weather began to change, and Robert and Tom grew anxious. The wind began to blow in short sharp gusts, which whirled the sodden dead leaves angrily about exposed corners, and on the seaboard sent the waves shorewards topped with angry crests. Misty clouds came drifting hurriedly over the sea, and at times the fog became so thick that it was hardly possible to see more than a few yards ahead, still the young men continued to visit their treasure every night. At first, the coastguards had a watchful eye on them, noticing which they unfolded their purpose and showed Sir Arthur's letter making the ship over to their hands.

The sailors treated the whole affair as a good joke, but still promised to do what they could to help them, in the good-humoured way which is their special charm. A certain fear had for some time haunted the two friends - a fear which neither of them had ever spoken out. From brooding so much as they did on their adventure, they came to think, or rather to feel, that the ship which for fifteen years had been unnoticed and untouched in the sand, had suddenly acquired as great an interest in the eyes of all the world as of themselves. Accordingly, they thought that some evil-designing person might try to cut them out of their adventure by forestalling them in searching the wreck. Their fear was dispelled by the kindly promise of the coastguards not to let anyone meddle with the vessel without their permission. As the weather continued to get more and more broken, the very disappointment of their hopes, which the break threatened served to enlarge those hopes, and when on the night of the tenth they heard a wild storm howling round the chimneys, as they lay in bed, each was assured in his secret heart that the old wreck contained such a treasure as the world had seldom seen.

Seven o'clock next night saw them on the shore of the Bull looking out into the pitchy darkness. The wind was blowing so strongly inshore that the waves were driven high beyond their accustomed line at the same state of the tide, and the channels were running like mill-dams. As each wave came down over the flat shore it was broke up into a mass of foam and spray, and the wind swept away the spume until on shore it fell like rain. Far along the sandy shore was heard the roaring of the waves, hoarsely bellowing, so that hearing the sound we could well imagine how the district got its quaint name.

On such a night it would have been impossible to have worked at the wreck, even could the treasure-seekers have reached it, or could they have even found it in the pitchy darkness. They waited some time, but seeing that it was in vain, they sadly departed homeward, hoping fondly that the next evening would prove more propitious.

Vain were their hopes. The storm continued for two whole days, for not one moment of which, except between the pauses of the rushing or receding waves, was the wreck exposed. Seven o'clock each night saw the two young men looking over the sand-hills, waiting in the vain hope of a chance of visiting the vessel, hoping against hope that a sudden calm would give the opportunity they wished. When the storm began to abate their hopes were proportionally raised, and on the morning of the 14th when they awoke and could not hear the wind whistling through the chimneys next their attic, they grew again sanguine of success. That night they went to the Bull in hope, and came home filled with despair. Although the storm had ceased, the sea was still rough. Great, heavy, sullen waves, sprayless, but crested ominously, from ridges of foam, came rolling into the bay, swelling onward with great speed and resistless force, and bursting over the shallow waste of sand so violently that even any attempt to reach the wreck was out of the question. As Robert and Tom hurried homeward - they had waited to the latest moment on the Bull, and feared being late - they felt spiritless and dejected. But one more evening remained on which they might possibly visit the wreck, and they feared that even should wind and tide be suitable one hour would not do to explore it. However, youth is never without hope, and next morning they both had that sanguine feeling which is the outcome of despair - the feeling that the tide of fortune must sometime turn, and that the loser as well as the winner has his time. As they neared the Bull that night their hearts beat so loud that they could almost hear them. They felt that there was ground for hope. All the way from town they could see the great flats opposite Clontarf lying black in the moonlight, and they thought that over the sands the same calm must surely rest. But, alas, they did not allow for the fact that two great breakwaters protect the harbour, but that the sands of the Bull are open to all the storms that blow - that the great Atlantic billows, broken up on the northern and southern coasts, yet still strong enough to be feared, sweep up and down the Channel, and beat with every tide into the harbours and bays along the coast. Accordingly, on reaching the sand-hills, they saw what dashed their hopes at once.

The moon rose straight before them beyond the Bailey Lighthouse, and the broad belt of light which stretched from it passed over the treasure-ship. The waves, now black, save where the light caught the sloping sides, lay blank, but ever and anon as they passed on far over their usual range, the black hull rose among the gleams of light. There was not a chance that the wreck could be attempted, and so they went sadly home - remembering the fact that the night of the 24th December was the earliest time at which they could again renew their effort.

Chapter III - The Iron Chest

The days that intervened were long to both men.

To Robert they were endless; even the nepenthe of continued hard work could not quiet his mind. Distracted on one side by his forbidden love for Ellen, and on the other by the expected fortune by which he might win her, he could hardly sleep at night. When he did sleep he always dreamed, and in his dreams Ellen and the wreck were always associated. At one time his dream would be of unqualified good fortune - a vast treasure found and shared with his love; at another, all would be gloom, and in the search for the treasure he would endanger his life, or, what was far greater pain, forfeit her love.

However, it is one consolation, that, whatever else may happen in the world, time wears on without ceasing, and the day longest expected comes at last.

On the evening of the 24th December, Tom and Robert took their way to Dollymount in breathless excitement.

As they passed through town, and saw the vast concourse of people all intent on one common object - the preparation for the greatest of all Christian festivals - the greatest festival, which is kept all over the world, wherever the True Light has fallen, they could not but feel a certain regret that they, too, could not join in the throng. Robert's temper was somewhat ruffled by seeing Ellen leaning on the arm of Tomlinson, looking into a brilliantly-lighted shop window, so intently, that she did not notice him passing. When they had left the town, and the crowds, and the overflowing stalls, and brilliant holly-decked shops, they did not so much mind, but hurried on.

So long as they were within city bounds, and even whilst there were brightly-lit shop windows, all seemed light enough. When, however, they were so far from town as to lose the glamour of the lamplight in the sky overhead, they began to fear that the night would indeed be too dark for work.

They were prepared for such an emergency, and when they stood on the slope of sand, below the dunnes, they lit a dark lantern and prepared to cross the sands. After a few moments they found that the lantern was a mistake. They saw the ground immediately before them so far as the sharp triangle of light, whose apex was the bulls-eye, extended, but beyond this the darkness rose like a solid black wall. They closed the lantern, but this was even worse, for after leaving the light, small though it was, their eyes were useless in the complete darkness. It took them nearly an hour to reach the wreck.

At last they got to work, and with hammer and chisel and saw commenced to open the treasure ship.

The want of light told sorely against them, and their work progressed slowly despite their exertions. All things have an end, however, and in time they had removed several planks so as to form a hole some four feet wide, by six long - one of the timbers crossed this; but as it was not in the middle, and left a hole large enough to descend by, it did not matter.

It was with beating hearts that the two young men slanted the lantern so as to turn the light in through the aperture. All within was black, and not four feet below them was a calm glassy pool of water that seemed like ink. Even as they looked this began slowly to rise, and they saw that the tide had turned, and that but a few minutes more remained. They reached down as far as they could, plunging their arms up to their shoulders in the water, but could find nothing. Robert stood up and began to undress.

"What are you going to do?" said Tom.

"Going to dive - it is the only chance we have."

Tom did not hinder him, but got the piece of rope they had brought with them and fastened it under Robert's shoulders and grasped the other end firmly. Robert arranged the lamp so as to throw the light as much downwards as possible, and then, with a silent prayer, let himself down through the aperture and hung on by the beam. The water was deadly cold - so cold, that, despite the fever heat to which he was brought through excitement, he felt chilled. Nevertheless he did not hesitate, but, letting go the beam, dropped into the black water.

"For Ellen," he said, as he disappeared.

In a quarter of a minute he appeared again, gasping, and with a convulsive effort climbed the short rope, and stood beside his friend.

"Well?" asked Tom, excitedly.

"Oh-h-h-h! good heavens, I am chilled to the heart. I went down about six feet, and then touched a hard substance. I felt round it, and so far as I can tell it is a barrel. Next to it was a square corner of a box, and further still something square made of iron."

"How do you know it is iron?"

"By the rust. Hold the rope again, there is no time to lose; the tide is rising every minute, and we will soon have to go."

Again he went into the black water and this time stayed longer. Tom began to be frightened at the delay, and shook the rope for him to ascend. The instant after he appeared with face almost black with suffused blood. Tom hauled at the rope, and once more he stood on the bottom of the vessel. This time he did not complain of the cold. He seemed quivering with a great excitement that overcame the cold. When he had recovered his breath he almost shouted out –

"There's something there. I know it – I feel it."

"Anything strange?" asked Tom, in fierce excitement.

"Yes, the iron box is heavy – so heavy that I could not stir it. I could easily lift the end of the cask, and two or three other boxes, but I could not stir it."

Whilst he was speaking, both heard a queer kind of hissing noise, and looking down in alarm saw the water running into the pool around the vessel. A few minutes more and they would be cut off from shore by some of the tidal streams. Tom cried out:

"Quick, quick! or we shall be late. We must put down the beams before the tide rises or it will wash the hold full of sand."

Without waiting even to dress, Robert assisted him and they placed the planks on their original position and secured them with a few strong nails. Then they rushed away for shore. When they had reached the sand-hill, Robert, despite his exertions, was so chilled that he was unable to put on his clothes.

To bathe and stay naked for half an hour on a December night is no joke.

Tom drew his clothes on him as well as he could, and after adding his overcoat and giving him a pull from the flask, he was something better. They hurried away, and what with exercise, excitement, and hope were glowing when they reached home.

Before going to bed they held a consultation as to what was best to be done. Both wished to renew their attempt as they could begin at half-past seven o'clock; for although the morrow was Christmas Day, they knew that any attempt to rescue goods from the wreck should be made at once. There were now two dangers to be avoided – rough weather and the drifting of the sand – and so they decided that not a moment was to be lost.

At the daybreak they were up, and the first moment that saw the wreck approachable found them wading out towards it. This time they were prepared for wet and cold. They had left their clothes on the beach and put on old ones, which, even if wet, would still keep off the wind, for a strong, fitful breeze was now blowing in eddies, and the waves were beginning to rise ominously. With beating hearts they examined the closed-up gap; and, as they looked, their hopes fell. One of the timbers had been lifted off by the tide, and from the deposit of sand in the crevices, they feared that much must have found its way in. They had brought several strong pieces of rope with them, for their effort to-day was to be to lift out the iron chest, which both fancied contained a treasure.

Robert prepared himself to descend again. He tied one rope round his waist, as before, and took the other in his hands. Tom waited breathlessly till he returned. He was a long time coming up, and rose with his teeth chattering, but had the rope no longer with him. He told Tom that he had succeeded in putting it under the chest. Then he went down again with the other rope, and when he rose the second time, said that he had put it under also, but crossing the first. He was so chilled that he was unable to go down a third time. Indeed, he was hardly able to stand so cold did he seem; and it was with much shrinking of spirit that his friend prepared to descend to make the ropes fast, for he knew that should anything happen to him Robert could not help him up.

This did not lighten his task or serve to cheer his spirits as he went down for the first time into the black water. He took two pieces of rope; his intention being to tie Robert's ropes round the chest, and then bring the spare ends up. When he rose he told Robert that he had tied one of the ropes round the box, but had not time to tie the others. He was so chilled that he could not venture to go down again, and so both men hurriedly closed the gap as well as they could, and went on shore to change their clothes. When they had dressed, and got tolerably warm, the tide had begun to turn, and so they went home, longing for the evening to come, when they might make the final effort.

Chapter IV - Lost and Found

Tom was to dine with some relatives where he was living. When he was leaving Robert he said to him, "Well, Bob, seven o'clock, sharp."

"Tom, do not forget or be late. Mind, I trust you."

"Never fear, old boy. Nothing short of death shall keep me away; but if I should happen not to turn up do not wait for me. I will be with you in spirit if I cannot be in the flesh."

"Tom, don't talk that way. I don't know what I should do if you didn't come. It may be all a phantom we're after, but I do not like to think so. It seems so much to me."

"All right, old man," said Tom, cheerily, "I shan't fail - seven o'clock," and he was gone.

Robert was in a fever all day. He went to the church where he knew he would see Ellen, and get a smile from her in passing. He did get a smile, and a glance from her lovely dark eyes which said as plainly as if she had spoken the words with her sweet lips, "How long you have been away; you never come to see me now." This set Robert's heart bounding, but it increased his fever. "How would it be," he thought, "if the wreck turned out a failure, and the iron box a deception? If I cannot get £100 those dark eyes will have to look sweet things to some other man; that beautiful mouth to whisper in the ears of some one who would not - could not - love her half so well as I do."

He could not bear to meet her, so when service was over he hurried away. When she came out her eyes were beaming, for she expected to see Robert waiting for her. She looked anxiously, but could only see Mr. Tomlinson, who did not rise in her favour for appearing just then.

Robert had to force himself to eat his dinner. Every morsel almost choked him, but he knew that strength was necessary for his undertaking, and so compelled himself to eat. As the hour of seven approached he began to get fidgety. He went often to the window, but could see no sign of Tom. Seven o'clock struck, but no Tom came. He began to be alarmed. Tom's words seemed to ring in his ears, "nothing short of death shall keep me away." He waited a little while in terrible anxiety, but then bethought him of his companion's other words, "if I should not happen to turn up do not wait for me," and knowing that whether he waited or no the tide would still come in all the same, and his chance of getting out the box would pass away, determined to set out alone.

His determination was strengthened by the fact that the gusty wind of the morning had much increased, and sometimes swept along laden with heavy clinging mist that bespoke a great fog bank somewhere behind the wind.

Till he had reached the very shore of the "Bull" he did not give up hopes of Tom, for he thought it just possible that he might have been delayed, and instead of increasing the delay by going home, had come on straight to the scene of operation.

There was, however, no help for it; as Tom had not come he should work alone. With misgivings he prepared himself. He left his clothes on the top of a sand-hill, put on the old ones he had brought with him, took his tools, ropes, and lantern, and set out. There was cause for alarm. The wind was rising, and it whistled in his ears as the gusts swept past. Far away in the darkness the sea was beginning to roar on the edge of the flats, and the mist came driving inland in sheets like the spume from a cataract. The water in the tidal streams as he waded across them beat against his legs and seemed cold as ice. Although now experienced in the road, he had some difficulty in finding the wreck, but at length reached it and commenced operations.

He had taken the precaution of bringing with him a second suit of old clothes and an oilskin coat. His first care was to fix the lamp where the wind could not harm it; his second, to raise the planks, and expose the interior of the wreck. Then he prepared his ropes, and, having undressed once again, went beneath the water to fasten the second rope. This he accomplished safely, and let the knot of it be on the opposite side to where the first rope was tied. He then ascended and dressed himself in all his clothes to keep him warm. He then cut off a portion in another plank, so as to expose a second one of the ship's timbers. Round this he tied one of the ropes, keeping it as taut as he could. He took a turn of the other rope round the other beam and commenced to pull. Little by little he raised the great chest from its position, and when he had raised it all he could he made that rope fast and went to the other.

By attacking the ropes alternately he raised the chest, so that he could feel from its situation that it hung suspended in the water. Then he began to shake the ropes till the chest swung like a pendulum. He held firmly both ropes, having a turn of each round its beam, and each time the weight swung he gained a little rope. So he worked on little by little, till at last, to his infinite joy, he saw the top of the box rise above the water. His excitement then changed to frenzy. His strength redoubled, and, as faster and faster the box swung, he gained more and more rope, and raised it higher and higher, till at last it ceased to rise, and he found he had reached the maximum height attainable by this means. As, however, it was now nearly up he detached a long timber, and using it as a lever, slowly, after repeated failures, prized up the chest through the gap till it reached the bottom of the ship, and then, toppling over, fell with a dull thud upon the sand.

With a cry of joy Robert jumped down after it, but in jumping lit on the edge of it and wrenched his ankle so severely that when he rose up and attempted to stand on it it gave way under him, and he fell again. He managed, however, to crawl out of the hulk, and reached his lantern. The wind by this time was blowing louder and louder, and the mist was gathering in white masses, and sweeping by, mingled with sleet. In endeavouring to guard the lantern from the wind he slipped once more on the wet timbers, and fell down, striking his leg against the sharp edge of the chest. So severe was the pain that for a few moments he became almost insensible, and when he recovered his senses found he was quite unable to stir.

The lantern had fallen in a pool of water, and had of course gone out. It was a terrible situation, and Robert's heart sank within him, as well it might, as he thought of what was to come. The wind was rapidly rising to a storm, and swept by him, laden with the deadly mist in fierce gusts. The roaring of the tide grew nearer and nearer, and louder and louder. Overhead was a pall of darkness, save when in the leaden winter sky some white pillar of mist swept onward like an embodied spirit of the storm. All the past began to crowd Robert's memory, and more especially the recent past. He thought of his friend's words - "Nothing short of death shall keep me away," and so full of dismal shadows, and forms of horror was all the air, that he could well fancy that Tom was dead, and that his spirit was circling round him, wailing through the night. Then again, arose the memory of his dream, and his very heart stood still, as he thought of how awfully it had been fulfilled. There he now lay; not in a dream, but in reality, beside a ship on a waste of desert sand. Beside him lay a chest such as he had seen in his dreams, and, as before, death seemed flapping his giant wings over his head. Strange horrors seemed to gather round him, borne on the wings of the blast. His father, whom he had never seen, he felt to be now beside him. All the dead that he had ever known circled round him in a weird dance. As the stormy gusts swept by, he heard amid their screams the lugubrious tolling of bells; bells seemed to be all around him; whichever way he turned he heard his knell. All forms were gathered there, as in his dreams - all save Ellen. But hark! even as the thought flashed across his brain; his ears seemed to hear her voice as one hears in a dream. He tried to cry out, but was so overcome by cold, that he could barely hear his own voice. He tried to rise, but in vain, and then, overcome by pain and excitement, and disappointed hope, he became insensible.

Was his treasure-hunting to end thus?

As Mr. Stedman and Ellen was sitting down to tea that evening, Arthur Tomlinson being the only other guest, a hurried knock came to the cottage door. The little servant came into the room a moment after, looking quite scared, and holding a letter in her hand. She came over to Ellen and faltered out, "Oh, please, miss, there's a man from the hospital, and he says as how you're to open the letter and to come at once; it's a matter of life and death."

Ellen grew white as a sheet, and stood up quickly, trembling as she opened the letter. Mr. Stedman rose up, too. Arthur Tomlinson sat still, and glared at the young servant till, thinking she had done something wrong, she began to cry. The letter was from the doctor of the hospital, written for Tom, and praying her to come at once, as the latter had something to tell her of the greatest import to one for whom he was sure she would do much. She immediately ran and put on her cloak, and asked her father to come with her.

"Surely you won't go?" said Tomlinson.

"What else should I do?" she asked, scornfully; "I must apologise for leaving you, unless you will come with us."

"No, thank you; I am not a philanthropist."

In half an hour they had reached the hospital, and had heard Tom's story. Poor fellow, when hurrying home to Robert, he had been knocked down by a car and had his leg broken. As soon as he could he had sent word to Ellen, for he feared for Robert being out alone at the wreck, knowing how chilled he had been on the previous night, and he thought that if any one would send him aid Ellen would.

No sooner had the story been told, and Ellen had understood the danger Robert was in, than with her father she hurried off to the "Bull."

They got a car with some difficulty, and drove as fast as the horse could go, and arriving at the "Bull," called to the coastguard-station. None of the coastguards had seen Robert that evening, but on learning of his possible danger all that were in the station at once turned out. They wrapped Ellen and her father in oilskins, and, taking lanterns and ropes, set out for the wreck. They all knew its position, and went as straight for it as they could, and, as they crossed the sandhills, found Robert's clothes. At this they grew very grave. They wanted to leave Ellen on the shore, but she refused point blank. By this time the storm was blowing wildly, and the roaring of the sea being borne on the storm was frightful to hear. The tidal streams were running deeper than usual, and there was some difficulty in crossing to the wreck.

In the mist the men lost their way a little, and could not tell exactly how far to go. They shouted as loudly as they could, but there was no reply. Ellen's terror grew into despair. She too, shouted, although fearing that to shout in the teeth of such a wind her woman's voice would be of no avail. However, her clear soprano rang out louder than the hoarse shouts of the sturdy sailors, and cleft the storm like a wedge. Twice or thrice she cried, "Robert, Robert, Robert," but still there was no reply. Suddenly she stopped, and, bending her head, cried joyfully, "He is there, he is there; I hear his voice," and commenced running as fast as she could through the darkness towards the raging sea. The coastguards called out to her to mind where she was going, and followed her with the lanterns as fast as they could run.

When they came up with her they found her sitting on an iron chest close to the wreck, with Robert resting on her knees, and his head pillowed on her breast. He had opened his eyes, and was faintly whispering, "Ellen, my love, my love. It was to win you I risked my life."

She bent and kissed him, even there among rough sailors, and then, amid the storm, she whispered softly, "It was not risked in vain."

The Chain of Destiny

I. A Warning

It was so late in the evening when I arrived at Scarp that I had but little opportunity of observing the external appearance of the house; but, as far as I could judge in the dim twilight, it was a very stately edifice of seemingly great age, built of white stone. When I passed the porch, however, I could observe its internal beauties much more closely, for a large wood fire burned in the hall and all the rooms and passages were lighted. The hall was almost baronial in its size, and opened on to a staircase of dark oak so wide and so generous in its slope that a carriage might almost have been driven up it. The rooms were large and lofty, with their walls, like those of the staircase, panelled with oak black from age. This sombre material would have made the house intensely gloomy but for the enormous width and height of both rooms and passages. As it was, the effect was a homely combination of size and warmth. The windows were set in deep embrasures, and, on the ground story, reached from quite level with the floor to almost the ceiling. The fireplaces were quite in the old style, large and surrounded with massive oak carvings, representing on each some scene from Biblical history, and at the side of each fireplace rose a pair of massive carved iron fire-dogs. It was altogether just such a house as would have delighted the heart of Washington Irving or Nathaniel Hawthorne.

The house had been lately restored; but in effecting the restoration comfort had not been forgotten, and any modern improvement which tended to increase the homelike appearance of the rooms had been added. The old diamond-paned casements, which had remained probably from the Elizabethan age, had given place to more useful plate glass; and, in like manner, many other changes had taken place. But so judiciously had every change been effected that nothing of the new clashed with the old, but the harmony of all the parts seemed complete.

I thought it no wonder that Mrs. Trevor had fallen in love with Scarp the first time she had seen it. Mrs. Trevor's liking the place was tantamount to her husband's buying it, for he was so wealthy that he could get almost anything money could purchase. He was himself a man of good taste, but still he felt his inferiority to his wife in this respect so much that he never dreamt of differing in opinion from her on any matter of choice or judgment. Mrs. Trevor had, without exception, the best taste of any one whom I ever knew, and, strange to say, her taste was not confined to any branch of art. She did not write, or paint, or sing; but still her judgment in writing, painting, or music, was unquestioned by her friends. It seemed as if nature had denied to her the power of execution in any separate branch of art, in order to make her perfect in her appreciation of what was beautiful and true in all. She was perfect in the art of harmonising-the art of every-day life. Her husband used to say, with a far-fetched joke, that her star must have been in the House of Libra, because everything which she said and did showed such a nicety of balance.

Mr. and Mrs. Trevor were the most model couple I ever knew-they really seemed not twain, but one. They appeared to have adopted something of the French idea of man and wife-that they should not be the less like friends because they were linked together by indissoluble bonds-that they should share their pleasures as well as their sorrows. The former outbalanced the latter, for both husband and wife were of that happy temperament which can take pleasure from everything, and find consolation even in the chastening rod of affliction.

Still, through their web of peaceful happiness ran a thread of care. One that cropped up in strange places, and disappeared again, but which left a quiet tone over the whole fabric-they had no child.

> "They had their share of sorrow, for when time was ripe
> The still affection of the heart became an outward breathing type,
> That into stillness passed again,
> But left a want unknown before."

There was something simple and holy in their patient endurance of their lonely life-for lonely a house must ever be without children to those who love truly. Theirs was not the eager, disappointed longing of those whose union had proved fruitless. It was the simple, patient, hopeless resignation of those who find that a common sorrow draws them more closely together than many common joys. I myself could note the warmth of their hearts and their strong philoprogenitive feeling in their manner towards me.

From the time when I lay sick in college when Mrs. Trevor appeared to my fever-dimmed eyes like an angel of mercy, I felt myself growing in their hearts. Who can imagine my gratitude to the lady who, merely because she heard of my sickness and desolation from a college friend, came and nursed me night and day till the fever left me. When I was sufficiently strong to be moved she had me brought away to the country, where good air, care, and attention soon made me stronger than ever. From that time I became a constant visitor at the Trevors' house; and as month after month rolled by I felt that I was growing in their affections. For four summers I spent my long vacation in their house, and each year I could feel Mr. Trevor's shake of the hand grow heartier, and his wife's kiss on my forehead-for so she always saluted me-grow more tender and motherly.

Their liking for me had now grown so much that in their heart of hearts-and it was a sanctum common to them both-they secretly loved me as a son. Their love was returned manifold by the lonely boy, whose devotion to the kindest friends of his youth and his trouble had increased with his growth into manhood. Even in my own heart I was ashamed to confess how I loved them both-how I worshipped Mrs. Trevor as I adored the mother whom I had lost so young, and whose eyes shone sometimes even then upon me, like stars, in my sleep.

It is strange how timorous we are when our affections are concerned. Merely because I had never told her how I loved her as a mother, because she had never told me how she loved me as a son, I used sometimes to think of her with a sort of lurking suspicion that I was trusting too much to my imagination. Sometimes even I would try to avoid thinking of her altogether, till my yearning would grow too strong to be repelled, and then I would think of her long and silently, and would love her more and more. My life was so lonely that I clung to her as the only thing I had to love. Of course I loved her husband, too, but I never thought about him in the same way; for men are less demonstrative about their affections to each other, and even acknowledge them to themselves less.

Mrs. Trevor was an excellent hostess. She always let her guests see that they were welcome, and, unless in the case of casual visitors, that they were expected. She was, as may be imagined, very popular with all classes; but what is more rare, she was equally popular with both sexes. To be popular with her own sex is the touchstone of a woman's worth. To the houses of the peasantry she came, they said, like an angel, and brought comfort wherever she came. She knew the proper way to deal with the poor; she always helped them materially, but never offended their feelings in so doing. Young people all adored her.

My curiosity had been aroused as to the sort of place Scarp was; for, in order to give me a surprise, they would not tell me anything about it, but said that I must wait and judge it for myself. I had looked forward to my visit with both expectation and curiosity.

When I entered the hall, Mrs. Trevor came out to welcome me and kissed me on the forehead, after her usual manner. Several of the old servants came near, smiling and bowing, and wishing welcome to "Master Frank." I shook hands with several of them, whilst their mistress looked on with a pleased smile.

As we went into a snug parlour, where a table was laid out with the materials for a comfortable supper, Mrs. Trevor said to me:

"I am glad you came so soon, Frank. We have no one here at present, so you will be quite alone with us for a few days; and you will be quite alone with me this evening, for Charley is gone to a dinner-party at Westholm."

I told her that I was glad that there was no one else at Scarp, for that I would rather be with her and her husband than any one else in the world. She smiled as she said:

"Frank, if any one else said that, I would put it down as a mere compliment; but I know you always speak the truth. It is all very well to be alone with an old couple like Charley and me for two or three days; but just you wait till Thursday, and you will look on the intervening days as quite wasted."

"Why?" I inquired.

"Because, Frank, there is a girl coming to stay with me then, with whom I intend you to fall in love."

I answered jocosely:

"Oh, thank you, Mrs. Trevor, very much for your kind intentions-but suppose for a moment that they should be impracticable. 'One man may lead a horse to the pond's brink.' 'The best laid schemes o' mice an' men.' Eh?"

"Frank, don't be silly. I do not want to make you fall in love against your inclination; but I hope and I believe that you will."

"Well, I'm sure I hope you won't be disappointed; but I never yet heard a person praised that I did not experience a disappointment when I came to know him or her."

"Frank, did I praise any one?"

"Well, I am vain enough to think that your saying that you knew I would fall in love with her was a sort of indirect praise."

"Dear, me, Frank, how modest you have grown. 'A sort of indirect praise!' Your humility is quite touching."

"May I ask who the lady is, as I am supposed to be an interested party?"

"I do not know that I ought to tell you on account of your having expressed any doubt as to her merits. Besides, I might weaken the effect of the introduction. If I stimulate your curiosity it will be a point in my favour."

"Oh, very well; I suppose I must only wait?"

"Ah, well, Frank, I will tell you. It is not fair to keep you waiting. She is a Miss Fothering."

"Fothering? Fothering? I think I know that name. I remember hearing it somewhere, a long time ago, if I do not mistake. Where does she come from?"

"Her father is a clergyman in Norfolk, but he belongs to the Warwickshire family. I met her at Winthrop, Sir Harry Blount's place, a few months ago, and took a great liking for her, which she returned, and so we became fast friends. I made her promise to pay me a visit this summer, so she and her sister are coming here on Thursday to stay for some time."

"And, may I be bold enough to inquire what she is like?"

"You may inquire if you like, Frank; but you won't get an answer. I shall not try to describe her. You must wait and judge for yourself."

"Wait," said I, "three whole days? How can I do that? Do, tell me."

She remained firm to her determination. I tried several times in the course of the evening to find out something more about Miss Fothering, for my curiosity was roused; but all the answer I could get on the subject was-"Wait, Frank; wait, and judge for yourself."

When I was bidding her g'ood night, Mrs. Trevor said to me-

"By-the-bye, Frank, you will have to give up the room which you will sleep in to-night, after to-morrow. I will have such a full house that I cannot let you have a doubled-bedded room all to yourself; so I will give that room to the Miss Fotherings, and move you up to the second floor. I just want you to see the room, as it has a romantic look about it, and has all the old furniture that was in it when we came here. There are several pictures in it worth looking at."

My bedroom was a large chamber-immense for a bedroom-with two windows opening level with the floor, like those of the parlours and drawingrooms. The furniture was old-fashioned, but not old enough to be curious, and on the walls hung many pictures-portraits-the house was full of portraits-and landscapes. I just glanced at these, intending to examine them in the morning, and went to bed. There was a fire in the room, and I lay awake for some time looking dreamily at the shadows of the furniture flitting over the walls and ceiling as the flames of the wood fire leaped and fell, and the red embers dropped whitening on the hearth. I tried to give the rein to my thoughts, but they kept constantly to the one subject-the mysterious Miss Fothering, with whom I was to fall in love. I was sure that I had heard her name somewhere, and I had at times lazy recollections of a child's face. At such times I would start awake from my growing drowsiness, but before I could collect my scattered thoughts the idea had eluded me. I could remember neither when nor where I had heard the name, nor could I recall even the expression of the child's face. It must have been long, long ago, when I was young. When I was young my mother was alive. My mother-mother-mother. I found myself half awakening, and repeating the word over and over again. At last I fell asleep.

I thought that I awoke suddenly to that peculiar feeling which we sometimes have on starting from sleep, as if some one had been speaking in the room, and the voice is still echoing through it. All was quite silent, and the fire had gone out. I looked out of the window that lay straight opposite the foot of the bed, and observed a light outside, which gradually grew brighter till the room was almost as light as by day. The window looked like a picture in the framework formed by the cornice over the foot of the bed, and the massive pillars shrouded in curtains which supported it.

With the new accession of light I looked round the room, but nothing was changed. All was as before, except that some of the objects of furniture and ornament were shown in stronger relief than hitherto. Amongst these, those most in relief were the other bed, which was placed across the room, and an old picture that hung on the wall at its foot. As the bed was merely the counterpart of the one in which I lay, my attention became fixed on the picture. I observed it closely and with great interest. It seemed old, and was the portrait of a young girl, whose face, though kindly and merry, bore signs of thought and a capacity for deep feeling-almost for passion. At some moments, as I looked at it, it called up before my mind a vision of Shakespeare's Beatrice, and once I thought of Beatrice Cenci. But this was probably caused by the association of ideas suggested by the similarity of names.

The light in the room continued to grow even brighter, so I looked again out of the window to seek its source, and saw there a lovely sight. It seemed as if there were grouped without the window three lovely children, who seemed to float in mid-air. The light seemed to spring from a point far behind them, and by their side was something dark and shadowy, which served to set off their radiance.

The children seemed to be smiling in upon something in the room, and, following their glances, I saw that their eyes rested upon the other bed. There, strange to say, the head which I had lately seen in the picture rested upon the pillow. I looked at the wall, but the frame was empty, the picture was gone. Then I looked at the bed again, and saw the young girl asleep, with the expression of her face constantly changing, as though she were dreaming.

As I was observing her, a sudden look of terror spread over her face, and she sat up like a sleep-walker, with her eyes wide open, staring out of the window.

Again turning to the window, my gaze became fixed, for a great and weird change had taken place. The figures were still there, but their features and expressions had become woefully different. Instead of the happy innocent look of childhood was one of malignity. With the change the children had grown old, and now three hags, decrepit and deformed, like typical witches, were before me.

But a thousand times worse than this transformation was the change in the dark mass that was near them. From a cloud, misty and undefined, it became a sort of shadow with a form. This gradually, as I looked, grew darker and fuller, till at length it made me shudder. There stood before me the phantom of the Fiend.

There was a long period of dead silence, in which I could hear the beating of my heart; but at length the phantom spoke to the others. His words seemed to issue from his lips mechanically, and without expression-"To-morrow, and to-morrow, and to-morrow. The fairest and the best." He looked so awful that the question arose in my mind-"Would I dare to face him without the window-would any one dare to go amongst those fiends?" A harsh, strident, diabolical laugh from without seemed to answer my unasked question in the negative.

But as well as the laugh I heard another sound-the tones of a sweet sad voice in despair coming across the room.

"Oh, alone, alone! is there no human thing near me? No hope-no hope. I shall go mad-or die."

The last words were spoken with a gasp.

I tried to jump out of bed, but could not stir, my limbs were bound in sleep. The young girl's head fell suddenly back upon the pillow, and the limp-hanging jaw and wide-open, purposeless mouth spoke but too plainly of what had happened.

Again I heard from without the fierce, diabolical laughter, which swelled louder and louder, till at last it grew so strong that in very horror I shook aside my sleep and sat up in bed. listened and heard a knocking at the door, but in another moment I became more awake, and knew that the sound came from the hall. It was, no doubt, Mr. Trevor returning from his party.

The hall-door was opened and shut, and then came a subdued sound of tramping and voices, but this soon died away, and there was silence throughout the house.

I lay awake for long thinking, and looking across the room at the picture and at the empty bed; for the moon now shone brightly, and the night was rendered still brighter by occasional flashes of summer lightning. At times the silence was broken by an owl screeching outside.

As I lay awake, pondering, I was very much troubled by what I had seen; but at length, putting several things together, I came to the conclusion that I had had a dream of a kind that might have been expected. The lightning, the knocking at the hall-door, the screeching of the owl, the empty bed, and the face in the picture, when grouped together, supplied materials for the main facts of the vision. The rest was, of course, the offspring of pure fancy, and the natural consequence of the component elements mentioned acting with each other in the mind.

I got up and looked out of the window, but saw nothing but the broad belt of moonlight glittering on the bosom of the lake, which extended miles and miles away, till its farther shore was lost in the night haze, and the green sward, dotted with shrubs and tall grasses, which lay between the lake and the house.

The vision had utterly faded. However, the dream-for so, I suppose, I should call it-was very powerful, and I slept no more till the sunlight was streaming broadly in at the window, and then I fell into a doze.

II. More Links

Late in the morning I was awakened by Parks, Mr. Trevor's man, who always used to attend on me when I visited my friends. He brought me hot water and the local news; and, chatting with him, I forgot for a time my alarm of the night.

Parks was staid and elderly, and a type of a class now rapidly disappearing-the class of old family servants who are as proud of their hereditary loyalty to their masters, as those masters are of name and rank. Like all old servants he had a great loving for all sorts of traditions. He believed them, and feared them, and had the most profound reverence for anything which had a story.

I asked him if he knew anything of the legendary history of Scarp. He answered with an air of doubt and hesitation, as of one carefully delivering an opinion which was still incomplete.

"Well, you see, Master Frank, that Scarp is so old that it must have any number of legends; but it is so long since it was inhabited that no one in the village remembers them. The place seems to have become in a kind of way forgotten, and died out of people's thoughts, and so I am very much afraid, sir, that all the genuine history is lost."

"What do you mean by the genuine history?" I inquired.

"Well, sir, I mean the true tradition, and not the inventions of the village folk. I heard the sexton tell some stories, but I am quite sure that they were not true, for I could see, Master Frank, that he did not believe them himself, but was only trying to frighten us."

"And could you not hear of any story that appeared to you to be true?"

"No, sir, and I tried very hard. You see, Master Frank, that there is a sort of club held every week in the tavern down in the village, composed of very respectable men, sir-very respectable men, indeed-and they asked me to be their chairman. I spoke to the master about it, and he gave me leave to accept their proposal. I accepted it as they made a point of it; and from my position I have of course a fine opportunity of making inquiries. It was at the club, sir, that I was, last night, so that I was not here to attend on you, which I hope that you will excuse."

Parks's air of mingled pride and condescension, as he made the announcement of the club, was very fine, and the effect was heightened by the confiding frankness with which he spoke. I asked him if he could find no clue to any of the legends which must have existed about such an old place. He answered with a very slight reluctance-

"Well, sir, there was one woman in the village who was awfully old and doting, and she evidently knew something about Scarp, for when she heard the name she mumbled out something about 'awful stories,' and 'times of horror,' and such like things, but I couldn't make her understand what it was I wanted to know, or keep her up to the point."

"And have you tried often, Parks? Why do you not try again?"

"She is dead, sir!"

I had felt inclined to laugh at Parks when he was telling me of the old woman. The way in which he gloated over the words "awful stories," and "times of horror," was beyond the power of description; it should have been heard and seen to have been properly appreciated. His voice became deep and mysterious, and he almost smacked his lips at the thought of so much pabulum for nightmares. But when he calmly told me that the woman was dead, a sense of blankness, mingled with awe, came upon me. Here, the last link between myself and the mysterious past was broken, never to be mended. All the rich stores of legend and tradition that had arisen from strange conjunctures of circumstances, and from the belief and imagination of long lines of villagers, loyal to their suzerain lord, were lost forever. I felt quite sad and disappointed; and no attempt was made either by Parks or myself to continue the conversation. Mr. Trevor came presently into my room, and having greeted each other warmly we went together to breakfast.

At breakfast Mrs. Trevor asked me what I thought of the girl's portrait in my bedroom. We had often had discussions as to characters in faces for we were both physiognomists, and she asked the question as if she were really curious to hear my opinion. I told her that I had only seen it for a short time, and so would rather not attempt to give a final opinion without a more careful study; but from what I had seen of it I had been favourably impressed.

"Well, Frank, after breakfast go and look at it again carefully, and then tell me exactly what you think about it."

After breakfast I did as directed and returned to the breakfast room, where Mrs. Trevor was still sitting.

"Well, Frank, what is your opinion-mind, correctly. I want it for a particular reason."

I told her what I thought of the girl's character; which, if there be any truth in physiognomy, must have been a very fine one.

"Then you like the face?"

I answered-

"It is a great pity that we have none such now-a-days. They seem to have died out with Sir Joshua and Greuze. If I could meet such a girl as I believe the prototype of that portrait to have been I would never be happy till I had made her my wife."

To my intense astonishment my hostess jumped up and clapped her hands. I asked her why she did it, and she laughed as she replied in a mocking tone imitating my own voice-

"But suppose for a moment that your kind intentions should be frustrated. 'One man may lead a horse to the pond's brink.' 'The best laid schemes o' mice an' men.' Eh?"

"Well," said I, "there may be some point in the observation. I suppose there must be since you have made it. But for my part I don't see it."

"Oh, I forgot to tell you, Frank, that that portrait might have been painted for Diana Fothering."

I felt a blush stealing over my face. She observed it and took my hand between hers as we sat down on the sofa, and said to me tenderly-

"Frank, my dear boy, I intend to jest with you no more on the subject. I have a conviction that you will like Diana, which has been strengthened by your admiration for her portrait, and from what I know of human nature I am sure that she will like you. Charley and I both wish to see you married, and we would not think of a wife for you who was not in every way eligible. I have never in my life met a girl like Di; and if you and she fancy each other it will be Charley's pleasure and my own to enable you to marry-as far as means are concerned. Now, don't speak. You must know perfectly well how much we both love you. We have always regarded you as our son, and we intend to treat you as our only child when it pleases God to separate us. There now, think the matter over, after you have seen Diana. But, mind me, unless you love each other well and truly, we would far rather not see you married. At all events, whatever may happen you have our best wishes and prayers for your happiness. God bless you, Frank, my dear, dear boy."

There were tears in her eyes as she spoke. When she had finished she leaned over, drew down my head and kissed my forehead very, very tenderly, and then got up softly and left the room. I felt inclined to cry myself. Her words to me were tender, and sensible, and womanly, but I cannot attempt to describe the infinite tenderness and gentleness of her voice and manner. I prayed for every blessing on her in my secret heart, and the swelling of my throat did not prevent my prayers finding voice. There may have been women in the world like Mrs. Trevor, but if there had been I had never met any of them, except herself.

As may be imagined, I was most anxious to see Miss Fothering, and or the remainder of the day she was constantly in my thoughts. That evening a letter came from the younger Miss Fothering apologising for her not being able to keep her promise with reference to her visit, on account of the unexpected arrival of her aunt, with whom she was obliged to go to Paris for some months. That night I slept in my new room, and had neither dream nor vision. I awoke in the morning half ashamed of having ever paid any attention to such a silly circumstance as a strange dream in my first night in an old house.

After breakfast next morning, as I was going along the corridor, I saw the door of my old bedroom open, and went in to have another look at the portrait. Whilst I was looking at it I began to wonder how it could be that it was so like Miss Fothering as Mrs. Trevor said it was.

The more I thought of this the more it puzzled me, till suddenly the dream came back-the face in the picture, and the figure in the bed, the phantoms out in the night, and the ominous words-"The fairest and the best." As I thought of these things all the possibilities of the lost legends of the old house thronged so quickly into my mind that I began to feel a buzzing in my ears and my head began to swim, so that I was obliged to sit down.

"Could it be possible," I asked myself, "that some old curse hangs over the race that once dwelt within these walls, and can she be of that race? Such things have been before now!"

The idea was a terrible one for me, for it made to me a reality that which I had come to look upon as merely the dream of a distempered imagination. If the thought had come to me in the darkness and stillness of the night it would have been awful. How happy I was that it had come by daylight, when the sun was shining brightly, and the air was cheerful with the trilling of the song birds, and the lively, strident cawing from the old rookery.

I stayed in the room for some little time longer, thinking over the scene, and, as is natural, when I had got over the remnants of my fear, my reason began to question the genuineness-vraisemblance of the dream. I began to look for the internal evidence of the untruth to facts; but, after thinking earnestly for some time the only fact that seemed to me of any importance was the confirmatory one of the younger Miss Fothering's apology. In the dream the frightened girl had been alone, and the mere fact of two girls coming on a visit had seemed a sort of disproof of its truth. But, just as if things were conspiring to force on the truth of the dream, one of the sisters was not to come, and the other was she who resembled the portrait whose prototype I had seen sleeping in a vision. I could hardly imagine that I had only dreamt.

I determined to ask Mrs. Trevor if she could explain in any way Miss Fothering's resemblance to the portrait, and so went at once to seek her.

I found her in the large drawingroom alone, and, after a few casual remarks, I broached the subject on which I had come to seek for information. She had not said anything further to me about marrying since our conversation on the previous day, but when I mentioned Miss Fothering's name I could see a glad look on her face which gave me great pleasure. She made none of those vulgar commonplace remarks which many women find it necessary to make when talking to a man about a girl for whom he is supposed to have an affection, but by her manner she put me entirely at my ease, as I sat fidgeting on the sofa, pulling purposelessly the woolly tufts of an antimacassar, painfully conscious that my cheeks were red, and my voice slightly forced and unnatural.

She merely said, "Of course, Frank, I am ready if you want to talk about Miss Fothering, or any other subject." She then put a marker in her book and laid it aside, and, folding her arms, looked at me with a grave, kind, expectant smile.

I asked her if she knew anything about the family history of Miss Fothering. She answered-

"Not further than I have already told you. Her father's is a fine old family, although reduced in circumstances."

"Has it ever been connected with any family in this county? With the former owners of Scarp, for instance?"

"Not that I know of. Why do you ask?"

"I want to find out how she comes to be so like that portrait."

"I never thought of that. It may be that there was some remote connection between her family and the Kirks who formerly owned Scarp. I will ask her when she comes. Or stay. Let us go and look if there is any old book or tree in the library that will throw a light upon the subject. We have rather a good library now, Frank, for we have all our own books, and all those which belonged to the Scarp library also. They are in great disorder, for we have been waiting till you came to arrange them, for we knew that you delighted in such work."

"There is nothing I should enjoy more than arranging all these splendid books. What a magnificent library. It is almost a pity to keep it in a private house."

We proceeded to look for some of those old books of family history which are occasionally to be found in old county houses. The library of Scarp, I saw, was very valuable, and as we prosecuted our search I came across many splendid and rare volumes which I determined to examine at my leisure, for I had come to Scarp for a long visit.

We searched first in the old folio shelves, and, after some few disappointments, found at length a large volume, magnificently printed and bound, which contained views and plans of the house, illuminations of the armorial bearings of the family of Kirk, and all the families with whom it was connected, and having the history of all these families carefully set forth. It was called on the title-page "The Book of Kirk," and was full of anecdotes and legends, and contained a large stock of family tradition. As this was exactly the book which we required, we searched no further, but, having carefully dusted the volume, bore it to Mrs. Trevor's boudoir where we could look over it quite undisturbed.

On looking in the index, we found the name of Fothering mentioned, and on turning to the page specified, found the arms of Kirk quartered on those of Fothering. From the text we learned that one of the daughters of Kirk had, in the year 1573, married the brother of Fothering against the united wills of her father and brother, and that after a bitter feud of some ten or twelve years, the latter, then master of Scarp, had met the brother of Fothering in a duel and had killed him. Upon receiving the news Fothering had sworn a great oath to revenge his brother, invoking the most fearful curses upon himself and his race if he should fail to cut off the hand that had slain his brother, and to nail it over the gate of Fothering. The feud then became so bitter that Kirk seems to have gone quite mad on the subject. When he heard of Fothering's oath he knew that he had but little chance of escape, since his enemy was his master at every weapon; so he determined upon a mode of revenge which, although costing him his own life, he fondly hoped would accomplish the eternal destruction of his brother-in-law through his violated oath. He sent Fothering a letter cursing him and his race, and praying for the consummation of his own curse invoked in case of failure. He concluded his missive by a prayer for the complete destruction, soul, mind, and body, of the first Fothering who should enter the gate of Scarp, who he hoped would be the fairest and best of the race. Having despatched this letter he cut off his right hand and threw it into the centre of a roaring fire, which he had made for the purpose. When it was entirely consumed he threw himself upon his sword, and so died.

A cold shiver went through me when I read the words "fairest and best." All my dream came back in a moment, and I seemed to hear in my ears again the echo of the fiendish laughter. I looked up at Mrs. Trevor, and saw that she had become very grave. Her face had a half-frightened look, as if some wild thought had struck her. I was more frightened than ever, for nothing increases our alarms so much as the sympathy of others with regard to them; however, I tried to conceal my fear. We sat silent for some minutes, and then Mrs. Trevor rose up saying:

"Come with me, and let us look at the portrait."

I remember her saying the and not that portrait, as if some concealed thought of it had been occupying her mind. The same dread had assailed her from a coincidence as had grown in me from a vision. Surely-surely I had good grounds for fear!

We went to the bedroom and stood before the picture, which seemed to gaze upon us with an expression which reflected our own fears. My companion said to me in slightly excited tones: "Frank, lift down the picture till we see its back." I did so, and we found written in strange old writing on the grimy canvas a name and a date, which, after a great deal of trouble, we made out to be "Margaret Kirk, 1572." It was the name of the lady in the book.

Mrs. Trevor turned round and faced me slowly, with a look of horror on her face.

"Frank, I don't like this at all. There is something very strange here."

I had it on my tongue to tell her my dream, but was ashamed to do so. Besides, I feared that it might frighten her too much, as she was already alarmed.

I continued to look at the picture as a relief from my embarrassment, and was struck with the excessive griminess of the back in comparison to the freshness of the front. I mentioned my difficulty to my companion, who thought for a moment, and then suddenly said-

"I see how it is. It has been turned with its face to the wall."

I said no word but hung up the picture again; and we went back to the boudoir.

On the way I began to think that my fears were too wildly improbable to bear to be spoken about. It was so hard to believe in the horrors of darkness when the sunlight was falling brightly around me. The same idea seemed to have struck Mrs. Trevor, for she said, when we entered the room:

"Frank, it strikes me that we are both rather silly to let our imaginations carry us away so. The story is merely a tradition, and we know how report distorts even the most innocent facts. It is true that the Fothering family was formerly connected with the Kirks, and that the picture is that of the Miss Kirk who married against her father's will; it is likely that he quarrelled with her for so doing, and had her picture turned to the wall-a common trick of angry fathers at all times-but that is all. There can be nothing beyond that. Let us not think any more upon the subject, as it is one likely to lead us into absurdities. However, the picture is a really beautiful one-independent of its being such a likeness of Diana, and I will have it placed in the dining-room."

The change was effected that afternoon, but she did not again allude to the subject. She appeared, when talking to me, to be a little constrained in manner-a very unusual thing with her, and seemed to fear that I would renew the forbidden topic. I think that she did not wish to let her imagination lead her astray, and was distrustful of herself. However, the feeling of constraint wore off before night-but she did not renew the subject.

I slept well that night, without dreams of any kind; and next morning-the third to-morrow promised in the dream-when I came down to breakfast, I was told that I would see Miss Fothering before that evening.

I could not help blushing, and stammered out some commonplace remark, and then glancing up, feeling very sheepish, I saw my hostess looking at me with her kindly smile intensified. She said:

"Do you know, Frank, I felt quite frightened yesterday when we were looking at the picture; but I have been thinking the matter over since, and have come to the conclusion that my folly was perfectly unfounded. I am sure you agree with me. In fact, I look now upon our fright as a good joke, and will tell it to Diana when she arrives."

Once again I was about to tell my dream; but again was restrained by shame. I knew, of course, that Mrs. Trevor would not laugh at me or even think little of me for my fears, for she was too well-bred, and kind-hearted, and sympathetic to do anything of the kind, and, besides, the fear was one which we had shared in common.

But how could I confess my fright at what might appear to others to be a ridiculous dream, when she had conquered the fear that had been common to us both, and which had arisen from a really strange conjuncture of facts. She appeared to look on the matter so lightly that I could not do otherwise. And I did it honestly for the time.

III. The Third To-morrow

In the afternoon I was out in the garden lying in the shadow of an immense beech, when I saw Mrs. Trevor approaching. I had been reading Shelley's "Stanzas Written in Dejection," and my heart was full of melancholy and a vague yearning after human sympathy. I had thought of Mrs. Trevor's love for me, but even that did not seem sufficient. I wanted the love of some one more nearly of my own level, some equal spirit, for I looked on her, of course, as I would have regarded my mother. Somehow my thoughts kept returning to Miss Fothering till I could almost see her before me in my memory of the portrait. I had begun to ask myself the question: "Are you in love?" when I heard the voice of my hostess as she drew near.

"Ha! Frank, I thought I would find you here. I want you to come to my boudoir."

"What for?" I inquired, as I rose from the grass and picked up my volume of Shelley.

"Di has come ever so long ago; and I want to introduce you and have a chat before dinner," said she, as we went towards the house.

"But won't you let me change my dress? I am not in correct costume for the afternoon."

I felt somewhat afraid of the unknown beauty when the introduction was imminent. Perhaps it was because I had come to believe too firmly in Mrs. Trevor's prediction.

"Nonsense, Frank, just as if any woman worth thinking about cares how a man is dressed."

We entered the boudoir and found a young lady seated by a window that overlooked the croquet-ground. She turned round as we came in, so Mrs. Trevor introduced us, and we were soon engaged in a lively conversation. I observed her, as may be supposed, with more than curiosity, and shortly found that she was worth looking at. She was very beautiful, and her beauty lay not only in her features but in her expression. At first her appearance did not seem to me so perfect as it afterwards did, on account of her wonderful resemblance to the portrait with whose beauty I was already acquainted. But it was not long before I came to experience the difference between the portrait and the reality. No matter how well it may be painted a picture falls far short of its prototype. There is something in a real face which cannot exist on canvas-some difference far greater than that contained in the contrast between the one expression, however beautiful of the picture, and the moving features and varying expression of the reality. There is something living and lovable in a real face that no art can represent.

When we had been talking for a while in the usual conventional style, Mrs. Trevor said, "Di, my love, I want to tell you of a discovery Frank and I have made. You must know that I always call Mr. Stanford, Frank-he is more like my own son than my friend, and that I am very fond of him."

She then put her arms round Miss Fothering's waist, as they sat on the sofa together, and kissed her, and then, turning towards me, said, "I don't approve of kissing girls in the presence of gentlemen, but you know that Frank is not supposed to be here. This is my sanctum, and who invades it must take the consequences. But I must tell you about the discovery."

She then proceeded to tell the legend, and about her finding the name of Margaret Kirk on the back of the picture.

Miss Fothering laughed gleefully as she heard the story, and then said, suddenly,

"Oh, I had forgotten to tell you, dear Mrs. Trevor, that I had such a fright the other day. I thought I was going to be prevented coming here. Aunt Deborah came to us last week for a few days, and when she heard that I was about to go on a visit to Scarp she seemed quite frightened, and went straight off to papa and asked him to forbid me to go. Papa asked her why she made the request, so she told a long family legend about any of us coming to Scarp-just the same story that you have been telling me. She said she was sure that some misfortune would happen if I came; so you see that the tradition exists in our branch of the family too. Oh, you can't fancy the scene there was between papa and Aunt Deborah. I must laugh whenever I think of it, although I did not laugh then, for I was greatly afraid that aunty would prevent me coming. Papa got very grave, and aunty thought she had carried her point when he said, in his dear, old, pompous manner,

"'Deborah, Diana has promised to pay Mrs. Trevor, of Scarp, a visit, and, of course, must keep her engagement. And if it were for no other reason than the one you have just alleged, I would strain a point of convenience to have her go to Scarp. I have always educated my children in such a manner that they ought not to be influenced by such vain superstitions; and with my will their practice shall never be at variance with the precepts which I have instilled into them.'

"Poor aunty was quite overcome. She seemed almost speechless for a time at the thought that her wishes had been neglected, for you know that Aunt Deborah's wishes are commands to all our family."

Mrs. Trevor said-

"I hope Mrs. Howard was not offended?"

"Oh, no. Papa talked to her seriously, and at length-with a great deal of difficulty I must say-succeeded in convincing her that her fears were groundless-at least, he forced her to confess that such things as she was afraid of could not be."

I thought of the couplet-

>"A man convinced against his will

>Is of the same opinion still,"

but said nothing.

Miss Fothering finished her story by saying-

"Aunty ended by hoping that I might enjoy myself, which I am sure, my dear Mrs. Trevor, that I will do."

"I hope you will, my love."

I had been struck during the above conversation by the mention of Mrs. Howard. I was trying to think of where I had heard the name, Deborah Howard, when suddenly it all came back to me. Mrs. Howard had been Miss Fothering, and was an old friend of my mother's. It was thus that I had been accustomed to her name when I was a child. I remembered now that once she had brought a nice little girl, almost a baby, with her to visit. The child was her niece, and it was thus that I now accounted for my half-recollection of the name and the circumstance on the first night of my arrival at Scarp. The thought of my dream here recalled me to Mrs. Trevor's object in bringing Miss Fothering to her boudoir, so I said to the latter-

"Do you believe these legends?"

"Indeed I do not, Mr. Stanford; I do not believe in anything half so silly."

"Then you do not believe in ghosts or visions?"

"Most certainly not."

How could I tell my dream to a girl who had such profound disbelief? And yet I felt something whispering to me that I ought to tell it to her. It was, no doubt, foolish of me to have this fear of a dream, but I could not help it. I was just going to risk being laughed at, and unburden my mind, when Mrs. Trevor started up, after looking at her watch, saying-

"Dear me, I never thought it was so late. I must go and see if any others have come. It will not do for me to neglect my guests."

We all left the boudoir, and as we did so the gong sounded for dressing for dinner, and so we each sought our rooms.

When I came down to the drawingroom I found assembled a number of persons who had arrived during the course of the afternoon. I was introduced to them all, and chatted with them till dinner was announced. I was given Miss Fothering to take into dinner, and when it was over I found that we had improved our acquaintance very much.

She was a delightful girl, and as I looked at her I thought with a glow of pleasure of Mrs. Trevor's prediction. Occasionally I saw our hostess observing us, and as she saw us chatting pleasantly together as though we enjoyed it a more than happy look came into her face. It was one of her most fascinating points that in the midst of gaiety, while she never neglected anyone, she specially remembered her particular friends. No matter what position she might be placed in she would still remember that there were some persons who would treasure up her recognition at such moments.

After dinner, as I did not feel inclined to enter the drawingroom with the other gentlemen, I strolled out into the garden by myself, and thought over things in general, and Miss Fothering in particular. The subject was such a pleasant one that I quite lost myself in it, and strayed off farther than I had intended. Suddenly I remembered myself and looked around. I was far away from the house, and in the midst of a dark, gloomy walk between old yew trees. I could not see through them on either side on account of their thickness, and as the walk was curved I could see but a short distance either before or behind me. I looked up and saw a yellowish, luminous sky with heavy clouds passing sluggishly across it. The moon had not yet risen, and the general gloom reminded me forcibly of some of the weird pictures which William Blake so loved to paint. There was a sort of vague melancholy and ghostliness in the place that made me shiver, and I hurried on.

At length the walk opened and I came out on a large sloping lawn, dotted here and there with yew trees and tufts of pampass grass of immense height, whose stalks were crowned with large flowers. To the right lay the house, grim and gigantic in the gloom, and to the left the lake which stretched away so far that it was lost in the evening shadow. The lawn sloped from the terrace round the house down to the water's edge, and was only broken by the walk which continued to run on round the house in a wide sweep.

As I came near the house a light appeared in one of the windows which lay before me, and as I looked into the room I saw that it was the chamber of my dream.

Unconsciously I approached nearer and ascended the terrace from the top of which I could see across the deep trench which surrounded the house, and looked earnestly into the room. I shivered as I looked. My spirits had been damped by the gloom and desolation of the yew walk, and now the dream and all the subsequent revelations came before my mind with such vividness that the horror of the thing again seized me, but more forcibly than before. I looked at the sleeping arrangements, and groaned as I saw that the bed where the dying woman had seemed to lie was alone prepared, while the other bed, that in which I had slept, had its curtains drawn all round. This was but another link in the chain of doom. Whilst I stood looking, the servant who was in the room came and pulled down one of the blinds, but, as she was about to do the same with the other, Miss Fothering entered the room, and, seeing what she was about, evidently gave her contrary directions, for she let go the window string, and then went and pulled up again the blind which she had let down. Having done so she followed her mistress out of the room. So wrapped up was I in all that took place with reference to that chamber, that it never even struck me that I was guilty of any impropriety in watching what took place.

I stayed there for some little time longer purposeless and terrified. The horror grew so great to me as I thought of the events of the last few days, that I determined to tell Miss Fothering of my dream, in order that she might not be frightened in case she should see anything like it, or at least that she might be prepared for anything that might happen. As soon as I had come to this determination the inevitable question "when?" presented itself. The means of making the communication was a subject most disagreeable to contemplate, but as I had made up my mind to do it, I thought that there was no time like the present. Accordingly I was determined to seek the drawingroom, where I knew I should find Miss Fothering and Mrs. Trevor, for, of course, I had determined to take the latter into our confidence. As I was really afraid to go through the awful yew walk again, I completed the half circle of the house and entered the backdoor, from which I easily found my way to the drawingroom.

When I entered Mrs. Trevor, who was sitting near the door, said to me, "Good gracious, Frank, where have you been to make you look so pale? One would think you had seen a ghost!"

I answered that I had been strolling in the garden, but made no other remark, as I did not wish to say anything about my dream before the persons to whom she was talking, as they were strangers to me. I waited for some time for an opportunity of speaking to her alone, but her duties, as hostess, kept her so constantly occupied that I waited in vain. Accordingly I determined to tell Miss Fothering at all events, at once, and then to tell Mrs. Trevor as soon as an opportunity for doing so presented itself.

With a good deal of difficulty-for I did not wish to do anything marked-I succeeded in getting Miss Fothering away from the persons by whom she was surrounded, and took her to one of the embrasures, under the pretence of looking out at the night view. Here we were quite removed from observation, as the heavy window curtains completely covered the recess, and almost isolated us from the rest of the company as perfectly as if we were in a separate chamber. I proceeded at once to broach the subject for which I had sought the interview; for I feared lest contact with the lively company of the drawingroom would do away with my present fears, and so breakdown the only barrier that stood between her and Fate.

"Miss Fothering, do you ever dream?"

"Oh, yes, often. But I generally find that my dreams are most

ridiculous."

"How so?"

"Well, you see, that no matter whether they are good or bad they appear real and coherent whilst I am dreaming them; but when I wake I find them unreal and incoherent, when I remember them at all. They are, in fact, mere disconnected nonsense."

"Are you fond of dreams?"

"Of course I am. I delight in them, for whether they are sense or gibberish when you wake, they are real whilst you are asleep."

"Do you believe in dreams?"

"Indeed, Mr. Stanford, I do not."

"Do you like hearing them told?"

"I do, very much, when they are worth telling. Have you been dreaming anything? If you have, do tell it to me."

"I will be glad to do so. It is about a dream which I had that concerns you, that I came here to tell you."

"About me. Oh, how nice. Do, go on."

I told her all my dream, after calling her attention to our conversation in the boudoir as a means of introducing the subject.

I did not attempt to heighten the effect in any way or to draw any inferences. I tried to suppress my own emotion and merely to let the facts speak for themselves. She listened with great eagerness, but, as far as I could see, without a particle of either fear or belief in the dream as a warning. When I had finished she laughed a quiet, soft laugh, and said-

"That is delicious. And was I really the girl that you saw afraid of ghosts? If papa heard of such a thing as that even in a dream what a lecture he would give me! I wish I could dream anything like that."

"Take care," said I, "you might find it too awful. It might indeed prove the fulfilling of the ban which we saw in the legend in the old book, and which you heard from your aunt."

She laughed musically again, and shook her head at me wisely and warningly.

"Oh, pray do not talk nonsense and try to frighten me-for I warn you that you will not succeed."

"I assure you on my honour, Miss Fothering, that I was never more in earnest in my whole life."

"Do you not think that we had better go into the room?" said she, after a few moment's pause.

"Stay just a moment, I entreat you," said I. "What I say is true. I am really in earnest."

"Oh, pray forgive me if what I said led you to believe that I doubted your word. It was merely your inference which I disagreed with. I thought you had been jesting to try and frighten me."

"Miss Fothering, I would not presume to take such a liberty.

But I am glad that you trust me. May I venture to ask you a favour?

Will you promise me one thing?"

Her answer was characteristic-

"No. What is it?"

"That you will not be frightened at anything which may take place to-night?"

She laughed softly again.

"I do not intend to be. But is that all?"

"Yes, Miss Fothering, that is all; but I want to be assured that you will not be alarmed-that you will be prepared for anything which may happen. I have a horrid foreboding of evil-some evil that I dread to think of-and it will be a great comfort to me if you will do one thing."

"Oh, nonsense. Oh, well, if you really wish it I will tell you if I will do it when I hear what it is."

Her levity was all gone when she saw how terribly in earnest I was. She looked at me boldly and fearlessly, but with a tender, half-pitying glance as if conscious of the possession of strength superior to mine. Her fearlessness was in her free, independent attitude, but her pity was in her eyes. I went on-

"Miss Fothering, the worst part of my dream was seeing the look of agony on the face of the girl when she looked round and found herself alone. Will you take some token and keep it with you till morning to remind you, in case anything should happen, that you are not alone-that there is one thinking of you, and one human intelligence awake for you, though all the rest of the world should be asleep or dead?"

In my excitement I spoke with fervour, for the possibility of her enduring the horror which had assailed me seemed to be growing more and more each instant. At times since that awful night I had disbelieved the existence of the warning, but when I thought of it by night I could not but believe, for the very air in the darkness seemed to be peopled by phantoms to my fevered imagination. My belief had been perfected to-night by the horror of the yew walk, and all the sombre, ghostly thoughts that had arisen amid its gloom.

There was a short pause. Miss Fothering leaned on the edge of the window, looking out at the dark, moonless sky. At length she turned and said to me, with some hesitation, "But really, Mr.

Stanford, I do not like doing anything from fear of supernatural things, or from a belief in them. What you want me to do is so simple a thing in itself that I would not hesitate a moment to do it, but that papa has always taught me to believe that such occurrences as you seem to dread are quite impossible, and I know that he would be very much displeased if any act of mine showed a belief in them."

"Miss Fothering, I honestly think that there is not a man living who would wish less than I would to see you or anyone else disobeying a father either in word or spirit, and more particularly when that father is a clergyman; but I entreat you to gratify me on this one point. It cannot do you any harm; and I assure you that if you do not I will be inexpressibly miserable. I have endured the greatest tortures of suspense for the last three days, and to-night I feel a nervous horror of which words can give you no conception. I know that I have not the smallest right to make the request, and no reason for doing it except that I was fortunate, or unfortunate, enough to get the warning. I apologise most sincerely for the great liberty which I have taken, but believe me that I act with the best intentions."

My excitement was so great that my knees were trembling, and the large drops of perspiration rolling down my face.

There was a long pause, and I had almost made up my mind for a refusal of my request when my companion spoke again.

"Mr. Stanford, on that plea alone I will grant your request. I can see that for some reason which I cannot quite comprehend you are deeply moved; and that I may be the means of saving pain to any one, I will do what you ask. Just please to state what you wish me to do."

I thought from her manner that she was offended with me; however I explained my purpose:

"I want you to keep about you, when you go to bed, some token which will remind you in an instant of what has passed between us, so that you may not feel lonely or frightened-no matter what may happen."

"I will do it. What shall I take?"

She had her handkerchief in her hand as she spoke. So I put my hand upon it and blessed it in the name of the Father, Son, and Holy Ghost. I did this to fix its existence in her memory by awing her slightly about it. "This," said I, "shall be a token that you are not alone." My object in blessing the handkerchief was fully achieved, for she did seem somewhat awed, but still she thanked me with a sweet smile. "I feel that you act from your heart," said she, "and my heart thanks you." She gave me her hand as she spoke, in an honest, straightforward manner, with more the independence of a man than the timorousness of a woman. As I grasped it I felt the blood rushing to my face, but before I let it go an impulse seized me and I bent down and touched it with my lips. She drew it quickly away, and said more coldly than she had yet spoken: "I did not mean you to do that."

"Believe me I did not mean to take a liberty-it was merely the natural expression of my gratitude. I feel as if you had done me some great personal service. You do not know how much lighter my heart is now than it was an hour ago, or you would forgive me for having so offended."

As I made my apologetic excuse, I looked at her wistfully. She returned my glance fearlessly, but with a bright, forgiving smile.

She then shook her head slightly, as if to banish the subject.

There was a short pause, and then she said:

"I am glad to be of any service to you; but if there be any possibility of what you fear happening it is I who will be benefited. But mind, I will depend upon you not to say a word of this to anybody. I am afraid that we are both very foolish."

"No, no, Miss Fothering. I may be foolish, but you are acting nobly in doing what seems to you to be foolish in order that you may save me from pain. But may I not even tell Mrs. Trevor?"

"No, not even her. I should be ashamed of myself if I thought that anyone except ourselves knew about it."

"You may depend upon me. I will keep it secret if you wish."

"Do so, until morning at all events. Mind, if I laugh at you then I will expect you to join in my laugh."

"I will," said I. "I will be only too glad to be able to laugh at it." And we joined the rest of the company.

When I retired to my bedroom that night I was too much excited to sleep-even had my promise not forbidden me to do so. I paced up and down the room for some time, thinking and doubting. I could not believe completely in what I expected to happen, and yet my heart was filled with a vague dread. I thought over the events of the evening-particularly my stroll after dinner through that awful yew walk and my looking into the bedroom where I had dreamed. From these my thoughts wandered to the deep embrasure of the window where I had given Miss Fothering the token. I could hardly realise that whole interview as a fact. I knew that it had taken place, but that was all. It was so strange to recall a scene that, now that it was enacted, seemed half comedy and half tragedy, and to remember that it was played in this practical nineteenth century, in secret, within earshot of a room full of people, and only hidden from them by a curtain, I felt myself blushing, half from excitement, half from shame, when I thought of it. But then my thoughts turned to the way in which Miss Fothering had acceded to my request, strange as it was; and as I thought of her my blundering shame changed to a deeper glow of hope. I remembered Mrs. Trevor's prediction-"from what I know of human nature I think that she will like you"-and as I did so I felt how dear to me Miss Fothering was already becoming. But my joy was turned to anger on thinking what she might be called on to endure; and the thought of her suffering pain or fright caused me greater distress than any suffered myself. Again my thoughts flew back to the time of my own fright and my dream, with all the subsequent revelations concerning it, rushed across my mind. I felt again the feeling of extreme terror-as if something was about to happen-as if the tragedy was approaching its climax. Naturally I thought of the time of night and so I looked at my watch. It was within a few minutes of one o'clock. I remembered that the clock had struck twelve after Mr. Trevor had come home on the night of my dream. There was a large clock at Scarp which tolled the hours so loudly that for a long way round the estate the country people all regulated their affairs by it. The next few minutes passed so slowly that each moment seemed an age.

I was standing, with my watch in my hand, counting the moments when suddenly a light came into the room that made the candle on the table appear quite dim, and my shadow was reflected on the wall by some brilliant light which streamed in through the window. My heart for an instant ceased to beat, and then the blood rushed so violently to my temples that my eyes grew dim and my brain began to reel. However, I shortly became more composed, and then went to the window expecting to see my dream again repeated.

The light was there as formerly, but there were no figures of children, or witches, or fiends. The moon had just risen, and I could see its reflection upon the far end of the lake. I turned my head in trembling expectation to the ground below where I had seen the children and the hags, but saw merely the dark yew trees and tall crested pampass tufts gently moving in the night wind. The light caught the edges of the flowers of the grass, and made them most conspicuous.

As I looked a sudden thought flashed like a flame of fire through my brain. I saw in one second of time all the folly of my wild fancies. The moonlight and its reflection on the water shining into the room was the light of my dream, or phantasm as I now understood it to be. Those three tufts of pampass grass clumped together were in turn the fair young children and the withered leaves and the dark foliage of the yew beside them gave substance to the semblance of the fiend. For the rest, the empty bed and the face of the picture, my half recollection of the name of Fothering, and the long-forgotten legend of the curse. Oh, fool! fool that I had been! How I had been the victim of circumstances, and of my own wild imagination! Then came the bitter reflection of the agony of mind which Miss Fothering might be compelled to suffer. Might not the recital of my dream, and my strange request regarding the token, combined with the natural causes of night and scene, produce the very effect which I so dreaded? It was only at that bitter, bitter moment that I realised how foolish I had been. But what was my anguish of mind to hers? For an instant I conceived the idea of rousing Mrs. Trevor and telling her all the facts of the case so that she might go to Miss Fothering and tell her not to be alarmed. But I had no time to act upon my thought. As I was hastening to the door the clock struck one and a moment later I heard from the room below me a sharp scream-a cry of surprise rather than fear. Miss Fothering had no doubt been awakened by the striking of the clock, and had seen outside the window the very figures which I had described to her.

I rushed madly down the stairs and arrived at the door of her bedroom, which was directly under the one which I now occupied.

As I was about to rush in I was instinctively restrained from so doing by the thoughts of propriety; and so for a few moments I stood silent, trembling, with my hand upon the door-handle.

Within I heard a voice-her voice-exclaiming, in tones of stupefied surprise-

"Has it come then? Am I alone?" She then continued joyously, "No, I am not alone. His token! Oh, thank God for that. Thank God for that."

Through my heart at her words came a rush of wild delight. I felt my bosom swell and the tears of gladness spring to my eyes. In that moment I knew that I had strength and courage to face the world, alone, for her sake. But before my hopes had well time to manifest themselves they were destroyed, for again the voice came wailing from the room of blank despair that made me cold from head to foot.

"Ah-h-h! still there? Oh! God, preserve my reason. Oh! for some human thing near me." Then her voice changed slightly to a tone of entreaty: "You will not leave me alone? Your token. Remember your token. Help me. Help me now." Then her voice became more wild, and rose to an inarticulate, wailing scream of horror.

As I heard that agonised cry, I realised the idea that it was madness to delay-that I had hesitated too long already-I must cast aside the shackles of conventionality if I wished to repair my fatal error. Nothing could save her from some serious injury-perhaps madness-perhaps death; save a shock which would break the spell which was over her from fear and her excited imagination. I flung open the door and rushed in, shouting loudly:

"Courage, courage. You are not alone. I am here. Remember the token."

She grasped the handkerchief instinctively, but she hardly comprehended my words, and did not seem to heed my presence.

She was sitting up in bed, her face being distorted with terror, and was gazing out upon the scene. I heard from without the hooting of an owl as it flew across the border of the lake. She heard it also, and screamed-

"The laugh, too! Oh, there is no hope. Even he will not dare to go amongst them."

Then she gave vent to a scream, so wild, so appalling that, as I heard it, I trembled, and the hair on the back of my head bristled up. Throughout the house I could hear screams of affright, and the ringing of bells, and the banging of doors, and the rush of hurried feet; but the poor sufferer comprehended not these sounds; she still continued gazing out of the window awaiting the consummation of the dream.

I saw that the time for action and self-sacrifice was come. There was but one way now to repair my fatal error. To burst through the window and try by the shock to wake her from her trance of fear.

I said no word but rushed across the room and hurled myself, back foremost, against the massive plate glass. As I turned I saw Mrs. Trevor rushing into the room, her face wild with excitement. She was calling out-

"Diana, Diana, what is it?"

The glass crashed and shivered into a thousand pieces, and I could feel its sharp edges cutting me like so many knives. But I heeded not the pain, for above the rushing of feet and crashing of glass and the shouting both within and without the room I heard her voice ring forth in a joyous, fervent cry, "Saved. He has dared," as she sank down in the arms of Mrs. Trevor, who had thrown herself upon the bed.

Then I felt a mighty shock, and all the universe seemed filled with sparks of fire that whirled around me with lightning speed, till I seemed to be in the centre of a world of flame, and then came in my ears the rushing of a mighty wind, swelling ever louder, and then came a blackness over all things and a deadness of sound as if all the earth had passed away, and I remembered no more.

IV. Afterwards

When I next became conscious I was lying in bed in a dark room. I wondered what this was for, and tried to look around me, but could hardly stir my head. I attempted to speak, but my voice was without power–it was like a whisper from another world. The effort to speak made me feel faint, and again I felt a darkness gathering round me.

***

I became gradually conscious of something cool on my forehead. I wondered what it was. All sorts of things I conjectured, but could not fix my mind on any of them. I lay thus for some time, and at length opened my eyes and saw my mother bending over me–it was her hand which was so deliciously cool on my brow. I felt amazed somehow. I expected to see her; and yet I was surprised, for I had not seen her for a long time–a long, long time. I knew that she was dead–could I be dead, too? I looked at her again more carefully, and as I looked, the old features died away, but the expression remained the same. And then the dear, well-known face of Mrs. Trevor grew slowly before me. She smiled as she saw the look of recognition in my eyes, and, bending down, kissed me very tenderly. As she drew back her head something warm fell on my face.

I wondered what this could be, and after thinking for a long time, to do which I closed my eyes, I came to the conclusion that it was a tear. After some more thinking I opened my eyes to see why she was crying; but she was gone, and I could see that although the window-blinds were pulled up the room was almost dark. I felt much more awake and much stronger than I had been before, and tried to call Mrs. Trevor. A woman got up from a chair behind the bed-curtains and went to the door, said something, and came back and settled my pillows.

"Where is Mrs. Trevor?" I asked, feebly. "She was here just now."

The woman smiled at me cheerfully, and answered:

"She will be here in a moment. Dear heart! but she will be glad to see you so strong and sensible."

After a few minutes she came into the room, and, bending over me, asked me how I felt. I said that I was all right–and then a thought struck me, so I asked,

"What was the matter with me?"

I was told that I had been ill, very ill, but that I was now much better. Something, I know not what, suddenly recalled to my memory all the scene of the bedroom, and the fright which my folly had caused, and I grew quite dizzy with the rush of blood to my head. But Mrs. Trevor's arm supported me, and after a time the faintness passed away, and my memory was completely restored. I started violently from the arm that held me up, and called out:

"Is she all right? I heard her say, 'saved.' Is she all right?"

"Hush, dear boy, hush–she is all right. Do not excite yourself."

"Are you deceiving me?" I inquired. "Tell me all–I can bear it. Is she well or no?"

"She has been very ill, but she is now getting strong and well, thank God."

I began to cry, half from weakness and half from joy, and Mrs. Trevor seeing this, and knowing with the sweet instinct of womanhood that I would rather be alone, quickly left the room, after making a sign to the nurse, who sank again to her old place behind the bed-curtain.

I thought for long; and all the time from my first coming to Scarp to the moment of unconsciousness after I sprung through the window came back to me as in a dream. Gradually the room became darker and darker, and my thoughts began to give semblance to the objects around me, till at length the visible world passed away from my wearied eyes, and in my dreams I continued to think of all that had been. I have a hazy recollection of taking some food and then relapsing into sleep; but remember no more distinctly until I woke fully in the morning and found Mrs. Trevor again in the room. She came over to my bedside, and sitting down said gaily–

"Ah, Frank, you look bright and strong this morning, dear boy. You will soon be well now I trust."

Her cool deft fingers settled my pillow and brushed back the hair from my forehead. I took her hand and kissed it, and the doing so made me very happy. By-and-by I asked her how was Miss Fothering.

"Better, much better this morning. She has been asking after you ever since she has been able; and to-day when I told her how much better you were she brightened up at once."

I felt a flush painfully strong rushing over my face as she spoke, but she went on-

"She has asked me to let her see you as soon as both of you are able. She wants to thank you for your conduct on that awful night.

But there, I won't tell any more tales-let her tell you what she likes herself."

"To thank me-me-for what? For having brought her to the verge of madness or perhaps death through my silly fears and imagination. Oh, Mrs. Trevor, I know that you never mock anyone-but to me that sounds like mockery."

She leaned over me as she sat on my bedside and said, oh, so sweetly, yet so firmly that a sense of the truth of her words came at once upon me-

"If I had a son I would wish him to think as you have thought, and to act as you have acted. I would pray for it night and day and if he suffered as you have done, I would lean over him as I lean over you now and feel glad, as I feel now, that he had thought and acted as a true-hearted man should think and act. I would rejoice that God had given me such a son; and if he should die-as I feared at first that you should-I would be a prouder and happier woman kneeling by his dead body than I would in clasping a different son, living, in my arms.

Oh, how my weak fluttering heart did beat as she spoke. With pity for her blighted maternal instincts, with gladness that a true-hearted woman had approved of my conduct toward a woman whom I loved, and with joy for the deep love for myself. There was no mistaking the honesty of her words-her face was perfectly radiant as she spoke them.

I put up my arms-it took all my strength to do it-round her neck, and whispered softly in her ear one word, "mother."

She did not expect it, for it seemed to startle her; but her arms tightened around me convulsively. I could feel a perfect rain of tears falling on my upturned face as I looked into her eyes, full of love and long-sought joy. As I looked I felt stronger and better; my sympathy for her joy did much to restore my strength.

For some little time she was silent, and then she spoke as if to herself-"God has given me a son at last. I thank thee, O Father; forgive me if I have at any time repined. The son I prayed for might have been different from what I would wish. Thou doest best in all things."

For some time after this she stayed quite silent, still supporting me in her arms. I felt inexpressibly happy. There was an atmosphere of love around me, for which I had longed all my life. The love of a mother, for which I had pined since my orphan childhood, I had got at last, and the love of a woman to become far dearer to me than a mother I felt was close at hand.

At length I began to feel tired, and Mrs. Trevor laid me back on my pillow. It pleased me inexpressibly to observe her kind motherly manner with me now. The ice between us had at last been broken, we had declared our mutual love, and the white-haired woman was as happy in the declaration as the young man.

The next day I felt a shade stronger, and a similar improvement was manifested on the next. Mrs. Trevor always attended me herself, and her good reports of Miss Fothering's progress helped to cheer me not a little. And so the days wore on, and many passed away before I was allowed to rise from bed.

One day Mrs. Trevor came into the room in a state of suppressed delight. By this time I had been allowed to sit up a little while each day, and was beginning to get strong, or rather less weak, for I was still very helpless.

"Frank, the doctor says that you may be moved into another room to-morrow for a change, and that you may see Di."

As may be supposed I was anxious to see Miss Fothering. Whilst I had been able to think during my illness, I had thought about her all day long, and sometimes all night long. I had been in love with her even before that fatal night. My heart told me that secret whilst I was waiting to hear the clock strike, and saw all my folly about the dream; but now I not only loved the woman but I almost worshipped my own bright ideal which was merged in her. The constant series of kind messages that passed between us tended not a little to increase my attachment, and now I eagerly looked forward to a meeting with her face to face.

I awoke earlier than usual next morning, and grew rather feverish as the time for our interview approached. However, I soon cooled down upon a vague threat being held out, that if I did not become more composed I must defer my visit.

The expected time at length arrived, and I was wheeled in my chair into Mrs. Trevor's boudoir. As I entered the door I looked eagerly round and saw, seated in another chair near one of the windows, a girl, who, turning her head round languidly, disclosed the features of Miss Fothering. She was very pale and ethereal looking, and seemed extremely delicate; but in my opinion this only heightened her natural beauty. As she caught sight of me a beautiful blush rushed over her poor, pale face, and even tinged her alabaster forehead. This passed quickly, and she became calm again, and paler than before. My chair was wheeled over to her, and Mrs. Trevor said, as she bent over and kissed her, after soothing the pillow in her chair-

"Di, my love, I have brought Frank to see you. You may talk together for a little while; but, mind, the doctor's orders are very strict, and if either of you excite yourselves about anything I must forbid you to meet again until you are both much stronger."

She said the last words as she was leaving the room.

I felt red and pale, hot and cold by turns. I looked at Miss Fothering and faltered. However, in a moment or two I summoned up courage to address her.

"Miss Fothering, I hope you forgive me for the pain and danger I caused you by that foolish fear of mine. I assure you that nothing I ever did"-

Here she interrupted me.

"Mr. Stanford, I beg you will not talk like that. I must thank you for the care you thought me worthy of. I will not say how proud I feel of it, and for the generous courage and wisdom you displayed in rescuing me from the terror of that awful scene."

She grew pale, even paler than she had been before, as she spoke the last words, and trembled all over. I feared for her, and said as cheerfully as I could:

"Don't be alarmed. Do calm yourself. That is all over now and past. Don't let its horror disturb you ever again."

My speaking, although it calmed her somewhat, was not sufficient to banish her fear, and, seeing that she was really excited, I called to Mrs. Trevor, who came in from the next room and talked to us for a little while. She gradually did away with Miss Fothering's fear by her pleasant cheery conversation. She, poor girl, had received a sad shock, and the thought that I had been the cause of it gave me great anguish. After a little quiet chat, however, I grew more cheerful, but presently feeling faintish, was wheeled back to my own room and put to bed.

For many long days I continued very weak, and hardly made any advance. I saw Miss Fothering every day, and each day I loved her more and more. She got stronger as the days advanced, and after a few weeks was comparatively in good health, but still I continued weak. Her illness had been merely the result of the fright she had sustained on that unhappy night; but mine was the nervous prostration consequent on the long period of anxiety between the dream and its seeming fulfilment, united with the physical weakness resulting from my wounds caused by jumping through the window. During all this time of weakness Mrs. Trevor was, indeed, a mother to me. She watched me day and night, and as far as a woman could, made my life a dream of happiness. But the crowning glory of that time was the thought that sometimes forced itself upon me-that Diana cared for me. She continued to remain at Scarp by Mrs. Trevor's request, as her father had gone to the Continent for the winter, and with my adopted mother she shared the attendance on me. Day after day her care for my every want grew greater, till I came to fancy her like a guardian angel keeping watch over me. With the peculiar delicate sense that accompanies extreme physical prostration I could see that the growth of her pity kept pace with the growth of her strength. My love kept pace with both. I often wondered if it could be sympathy and not pity that so forestalled my wants and wishes; or if it could be love that answered in her heart when mine beat for her. She only showed pity and tenderness in her acts and words, but still I hoped and longed for something more.

Those days of my long-continued weakness were to me sweet, sweet days. I used to watch her for hours as she sat opposite to me reading or working, and my eyes would fill with tears as I thought how hard it would be to die and leave her behind me. So strong was the flame of my love that I believed, in spite of my religious teaching, that, should I die, I would leave the better part of my being behind me. I used to think in a vague imaginative way, that was no less powerful because it was undefined, of what speeches I would make to her-if I were well. How I would talk to her in nobler language than that in which I would now allow my thoughts to mould themselves. How, as I talked, my passion, and honesty, and purity would make me so eloquent that she would love to hear me speak. How I would wander with her through the sunny-gladed woods that stretched away before me through the open window, and sit by her feet on a mossy bank beside some purling brook that rippled gaily over the stones, gazing into the depths of her eyes, where my future life was pictured in one long sheen of light. How I would whisper in her ear sweet words that would make me tremble to speak them, and her tremble to hear. How she would bend to me and show me her love by letting me tell her mine without reproof. And then would come, like the shadow of a sudden rain-cloud over an April landscape, the bitter, bitter thought that all this longing was but a dream, and that when the time had come when such things might have been, I would, most likely, be sleeping under the green turf. And she might, perhaps, be weeping in the silence of her chamber sad, sad tears for her blighted love and for me. Then my thoughts would become less selfish, and I would try to imagine the bitter blow of my death-if she loved me-for I knew that a woman loves not by the value of what she loves, but by the strength of her affection and admiration for her own ideal, which she thinks she sees bodied forth in some man. But these thoughts had always the proviso that the dreams of happiness were prophetic. Alas! I had altogether lost faith in dreams. Still, I could not but feel that even if I had never frightened Miss Fothering by telling my vision, she might, nevertheless, have been terrified by the effect of the moonlight upon the flowers of the pampass tufts, and that, under Providence, I was the instrument of saving her from a shock even greater than that which she did experience, for help might not have come to her so soon. This thought always gave me hope. Whenever I thought of her sorrow for my death, I would find my eyes filled with a sudden rush of tears which would shut out from my waking vision the object of my thoughts and fears. Then she would come over to me and place her cool hand on my forehead, and whisper sweet words of comfort and hope in my ears. As I would feel her warm breath upon my cheek and wafting my hair from my brow, I would lose all sense of pain and sorrow and care, and live only in the brightness of the present. At such times I would cry silently from very happiness, for I was sadly weak, and even trifling things touched me deeply. Many a stray memory of some tender word heard or some gentle deed done, or of some sorrow or distress, would set me thinking for hours and stir all the tender feelings of my nature.

Slowly-very slowly-I began to get stronger, but for many days more I was almost completely helpless. With returning strength came the strengthening of my passion-for passion my love for Diana had become. She had been so woven into my thoughts that my love for her was a part of my being, and I felt that away from her my future life would be but a bare existence and no more. But strange to say, with increasing strength and passion came increasing diffidence. I felt in her presence so bashful and timorous that I hardly dared to look at her, and could not speak save to answer an occasional question. I had ceased to dream entirely, for such day-dreams as I used to have seemed now wild and almost sacrilegious to my sur-excited imagination. But when she was not looking at me I would be happy in merely seeing her or hearing her speak. I could tell the moment she left the house or entered it, and her footfall was the music sweetest to my ears-except her voice. Sometimes she would catch sight of my bashful looks at her, and then, at my conscious blushing, a bright smile would flit over her face. It was sweet and womanly, but sometimes I would think that it was no more than her pity finding expression. She was always in my thoughts and these doubts and fears constantly assailed me, so that I could feel that the brooding over the subject-a matter which I was powerless to prevent-was doing me an injury; perhaps seriously retarding my recovery.

One day I felt very sad. There had a bitter sense of loneliness come over me which was unusual. It was a good sign of returning health, for it was like the waking from a dream to a world of fact, with all its troubles and cares. There was a sense of coldness and loneliness in the world, and I felt that I had lost something without gaining anything in return-I had, in fact, lost somewhat of my sense of dependence, which is a consequence of prostration, but had not yet regained my strength. I sat opposite a window itself in shade, but looking over a garden that in the summer had been bright with flowers, and sweet with their odours, but which, now, was lit up only in patches by the quiet mellow gleams of the autumn sun, and brightened by a few stray flowers that had survived the first frosts.

As I sat I could not help thinking of what my future would be. I felt that I was getting strong, and the possibilities of my life seemed very real to me. How I longed for courage to ask Diana to be my wife! Any certainty would be better than the suspense I now constantly endured. I had but little hope that she would accept me, for she seemed to care less for me now than in the early days of my illness. As I grew stronger she seemed to hold somewhat aloof from me; and as my fears and doubts grew more and more, I could hardly bear to think of my joy should she accept me, or of my despair should she refuse. Either emotion seemed too great to be borne.

To-day when she entered the room my fears were vastly increased. She seemed much stronger than usual, for a glow, as of health, ruddied her cheeks, and she seemed so lovely that I could not conceive that such a woman would ever condescend to be my wife. There was an unusual constraint in her manner as she came and spoke to me, and flitted round me, doing in her own graceful way all the thousand little offices that only a woman's hand can do for an invalid. She turned to me two or three times, as if she was about to speak; but turned away again, each time silent, and with a blush. I could see that her heart was beating violently. At length she spoke.

"Frank."

Oh! what a wild throb went through me as I heard my name from her lips for the first time. The blood rushed to my head, so that for a moment I was quite faint. Her cool hand on my forehead revived me.

"Frank, will you let me speak to you for a few minutes as honestly as I would wish to speak, and as freely?"

"Go on."

"You will promise me not to think me unwomanly or forward, for indeed I act from the best motives-promise me?"

This was said slowly with much hesitation, and a convulsive heaving of the chest.

"I promise."

"We can see that you are not getting as strong as you ought, and the doctor says that there is some idea too much in your mind-that you brood over it, and that it is retarding your recovery. Mrs.

Trevor and I have been talking about it. We have been comparing notes, and I think we have found out what your idea is. Now, Frank, you must not pale and red like that, or I will have to leave off."

"I will be calm-indeed, I will. Go on."

"We both thought that it might do you good to talk to you freely, and we want to know if our idea is correct. Mrs. Trevor thought it better that I should speak to you than she should."

"What is the idea?"

Hitherto, although she had manifested considerable emotion, her voice had been full and clear, but she answered this last question very faintly, and with much hesitation.

"You are attached to me, and you are afraid I-I don't love you."

Here her voice was checked by a rush of tears, and she turned her head away.

"Diana," said I, "dear Diana," and I held out my arms with what strength I had.

The colour rushed over her face and neck, and then she turned, and with a convulsive sigh laid her head upon my shoulder. One weak arm fell round her waist, and my other hand rested on her head. I said nothing. I could not speak, but I felt the beating of her heart against mine, and thought that if I died then I must be happy for ever, if there be memory in the other world.

For a long, long, blissful time she kept her place, and gradually our hearts ceased to beat so violently, and we became calm.

Such was the confession of our love. No plighted faith, no passionate vows, but the silence and the thrill of sympathy through our hearts were sweeter than words could be.

Diana raised her head and looked fearlessly but appealingly into my eyes as she asked me-

"Oh, Frank, did I do right to speak? Could it have been better if I had waited?"

She saw my wishes in my eyes, and bent down her head to me. I kissed her on the forehead and fervently prayed, "Thank God that all was as it has been. May He bless my own darling wife for ever and ever."

"Amen," said a sweet, tender voice.

We both looked up without shame, for we knew the tones of my second mother. Her face, streaming with tears of joy, was lit up by a sudden ray of sunlight through the casement.

Our New House

We spoke of it as our New House simply because we thought of it as such and not from any claim to the title, for it was just about as old and as ricketty as a house supposed to be habitable could well be. It was only new to us. Indeed with the exception of the house there was nothing new about us. Neither my wife nor myself was, in any sense of the word, old, and we were still, comparatively speaking, new to each other.

It had been my habit, for the few years I had been in Somerset House, to take my holidays at Littlehampton, partly because I liked the place, and partly - and chiefly, because it was cheap. I used to have lodgings in the house of a widow, Mrs. Compton, in a quiet street off the sea frontage. I had this year, on my summer holiday, met there my fate in the person of Mrs. Compton's daughter Mary, just home from school. I returned to London engaged. There was no reason why we should wait, for I had few friends and no near relatives living, and Mary had the consent of her mother. I was told that her father, who was a merchant captain, had gone to sea shortly after her birth, but had never been heard of since, and had consequently been long ago reckoned as "with the majority." I never met any of my new relatives; indeed, there was not the family opportunity afforded by marriage under conventional social conditions. We were married in the early morning at the church at Littlehampton, and, without any formal wedding breakfast, came straight away in the train. As I had to attend to my duties at Somerset House, the preliminaries were all arranged by Mrs. Compton at Littlehampton, and Mary gave the required notice of residency. We were all in a hurry to be off, as we feared missing the train; indeed, whilst Mary was signing the registry I was settling the fees and tipping the verger.

When we began to look about for a house, we settled on one which was vacant in a small street near Sloane Square. There was absolutely nothing to recommend the place except the smallness of the rent - but this was everything to us. The landlord, Mr. Gradder, was the very hardest man I ever came across. He did not even go through the form of civility in his dealing.

"There is the house," he said, "and you can either take it or leave it. I have painted the outside, and you must paint the inside. Or, if you like it as it is, you can have it so; only you must paint and paper it before you give it up to me again - be it in one year or more."

I was pretty much of a handy man, and felt equal to doing the work myself; so, having looked over the place carefully, we determined to take it. It was, however, in such a terribly neglected condition that I could not help asking my ironclad lessor as to who had been the former tenant, and what kind of person he had been to have been content with such a dwelling.

His answer was vague. "Who he was I don't know. I never knew more than his name. He was a regular oddity. Had this house and another of mine near here, and used to live in them both, and all by himself. Think he was afraid of being murdered or robbed. Never knew which he was in. Dead lately. Had to bury him - worse luck. Expenses swallowed up value of all he'd got."

We signed an agreement to take out a lease, and when, in a few days, I had put in order two rooms and a kitchen, my wife and I moved in. I worked hard every morning before I went to my office, and every evening after I got home, so I got the place in a couple of weeks in a state of comparative order. We had, in fact, arrived so far on our way to perfection that we had seriously begun to consider dispensing with the services of our charwoman and getting a regular servant.

One evening my landlord called on me. It was about nine o'clock, and, as our temporary servant had gone home, I opened the door myself. I was somewhat astonished at recognising my visitor, and not a little alarmed, for he was so brutally simple in dealing with me that I rather dreaded any kind of interview. To my astonishment he began to speak in what he evidently meant for a hearty manner.

"Well, how are you getting on with your touching up?"

"Pretty well," I answered, "but 'touching up' is rather a queer name for it. Why, the place was like an old ash heap. The very walls seemed pulled about."

"Indeed !" he said quickly.

I went on, "It is getting into something like order, however. There is only one more room to do, and then we shall be all right."

"Do you know," he said, "that I have been thinking it is hardly fair that you should have to do all this yourself."

I must say that I was astonished as well as pleased, and found myself forming a resolution not to condemn ever again anyone for hardness until I had come to know something about his real nature. I felt somewhat guilty as I answered, "You are very kind, Mr. Gradder. I shall let you know what it all costs me, and then you can repay me a part as you think fair."

"Oh, I don't mean that at all." This was said very quickly.

"Then what do you mean," I asked.

"That I should do some of it in my own way, at my own cost."

I did not feel at all inclined to have either Mr. Gradder or strange workmen in the house. Moreover, my pride rebelled at the thought that I should be seen by real workmen doing labourers' work - I suppose there is something of the spirit of snobbery in all of us. So I told him I could not think of such a thing; that all was going on very well; and more to the same effect. He seemed more irritated than the occasion warranted. Indeed, it struck me as odd that a man should be annoyed at his generous impulse being thwarted. He tried, with a struggle for calmness, to persuade me, but I did not like the controversy, and stood to my refusal of assistance. He went away in a positive fury of suppressed rage.

The next evening he called in to see me. Mary had, after he had gone, asked me not to allow him to assist, as she did not like him; so when he came in I refused again with what urbanity I could. Mary kept nudging me to be firm, and he could not help noticing it. He said: "Of course, if your wife objects" - and stopped. He spoke the words very rudely, and Mary spoke out:

"She does object, Mr. Gradder. We are all right, thank you, and do not want help from any one."

For reply Mr. Gradder put on his hat, knocked it down on his head firmly and viciously, and walked out, banging the door behind him.

"There is a nice specimen of a philanthropist," said Mary, and we both laughed.

The next day, while I was in my office, Mr. Gradder called to see me. He was in a very amiable mood, and commenced by apologising for what he called "his unruly exit." "I am afraid you must have thought me rude," he said.

As the nearest approach to mendacity I could allow myself, was the suppressio veri, I was silent.

"You see," he went on, "your wife dislikes me, and that annoys me; so I just called to see you alone, and try if we could arrange this matter - we men alone."

"What matter?" I asked.

"You know - about the doing up those rooms."

I began to get annoyed myself, for there was evidently some underlying motive of advantage to himself in his persistence. Any shadowy belief I had ever entertained as to a benevolent idea had long ago vanished and left not a wrack behind. I told him promptly and briefly that I would not do as he desired, and that I did not care to enter any further upon the matter. He again made an "unruly exit." This time he nearly swept away in his violence a young man who was entering through the swing door, to get some papers stamped. The youth remonstrated with that satirical force which is characteristic of the lawyer's clerk. Mr. Gradder was too enraged to stop to listen, and the young man entered the room grumbling and looking back at him.

"Old brute!" he said. "I know him. Next time I see him I'll advise him to buy some manners with his new fortune."

"His new fortune?" I asked, naturally interested about him. "How do you mean, Wigley?"

"Lucky old brute! I wish I had a share of it. I heard all about it at Doctors Commons yesterday."

"Why, is it anything strange?"

"Strange! Why, it's no name for it. What do you think of an old flint like that having a miser for a tenant who goes and dies and leaves him all he's got - £40,000 or £50,000 - in a will, providing a child of his own doesn't turn up to claim it.

"He died recently, then?"

"About three or four weeks ago. Old Gradder only found the will a few days since. He had been finding pots of gold and bundles of notes all over the house, and it was like drawing a tooth from him to make an inventory, as he had to do under a clause of the will. The old thief would have pocketed all the coin without a word, only for the will, and he was afraid he'd risk everything if he did not do it legally.

"You know all about it," I remarked, wishing to hear more.

"I should think I did. I asked Cripps, of Bogg and Snagleys, about it this morning. They're working for him, and Cripps says that if they had not threatened him with the Public Prosecutor, he would not have given even a list of the money he found."

I began now to understand the motive of Mr. Gradder's anxiety to aid in working at my house. I said to Wigley:

"This is very interesting. Do you know that he is my landlord?"

"Your landlord! Well, I wish you joy of him. I must be off now. I have to go down to Doctors Commons before one o'clock. Would you mind getting these stamped for me, and keeping them till I come back?"

"With pleasure," I said, "and look here! Would you mind looking out that will of Gradder's, and make a mem. of it for me, if it isn't too long? I'll go a shilling on it." And I handed him the coin.

Later in the day he came hack and handed me a paper.

"It isn't long," he said. "We might put up the shutters if men made wills like that. That is an exact copy. It is duly witnessed, and all regular."

I took the paper and put it in my pocket, for I was very busy at the time.

After supper that evening I got a note from Gradder, saying that he had got an offer from another person who had been in treaty with him before I had taken the, house, wanting to have it, and offering to pay a premium. "He is an old friend," wrote Gradder, "and I would like to oblige him; so if you choose I will take back the lease and hand you over what he offers to pay." This was £25, altered from £20.

I then told Mary of his having called on me at the office, and of the subsequent revelation of the will. She was much impressed.

"Oh, Bob," she said, "it is a real romance."

With a woman's quickness of perception, she guessed at once our landlord's reason for wishing to help us.

"Why, he thinks the old miser has hidden money here, and wants to look for it. Bob," this excitedly, "this house may be full of money; the walls round us may hold a fortune. Let us begin to look at once!"

I was as much excited as she was, but I felt that someone must keep cool, so I said:

"Mary, dear, there may be nothing; but even if there is, it does not belong to us."

"Why not?" she asked.

"Because it is all arranged in the will," I answered; "and, by the bye, I have a mem. of it here," and I took from my pocket the paper which Wigley had given me.

With intense interest we read it together, Mary holding me tightly by the arm. It certainly was short. It ran as follows:

"7, Little Butler Street, S.W., London. - I hereby leave to my child or children, if I have any living, all I own, and in default of such everything is to go to John Gradder, my landlord, who is to make an inventory of all he can find in the two houses occupied by me, this house and 2, Lampeter Street, S.W. London, and to lodge all money and securities in Coutts's Bank. If my children or any of them do not claim in writing by an application before a Justice of the

Peace within one calendar month from my decease, they are to forfeit all rights. Ignorance of my death or their relationship to be no reason for noncompliance. Lest there be any doubt of my intentions, I hereby declare that I wish in such default of my natural heirs John Gradder aforesaid to have my property, because he is the hardest-hearted man I ever knew, and will not fool it away in charities or otherwise, but keep it together. If any fooling is to be done, it will be by my own.

(Signed) GILES ARMER, Master Mariner,

Formerly of Whitby."

When I came near the end, Mary, who had been looking down the paper in advance of my reading, cried out; "Giles Armer! Why, that was my father!"

"Good God!" I cried out, as I jumped to my feet.

"Yes," she said, excitedly; "didn't you see me sign Mary Armer at the registry? We never spoke of the name because he had a quarrel with mother and deserted her, and after seven years she married my step-father, and I was always called by his name."

"And was he from Whitby?" I asked. I was nearly wild with excitement.

"Yes," said Mary. "Mother was married there, and I was born there."

I was reading over the will again. My hands were trembling so that I could hardly read. An awful thought struck me. What day did he die? Perhaps it was too late - it was now the thirtieth of October. However, we were determined to be on the safe side, and then and there Mary and I put on our hats and wraps and went to the nearest police-station.

There we learned the address of a magistrate, after we had explained to the inspector the urgency of the case.

We went to the address given, and after some delay were admitted to an interview.

The Magistrate was at first somewhat crusty at being disturbed at such an hour, for by this time it was pretty late in the evening. However, when we had explained matters to him he was greatly interested, and we went through the necessary formalities. When it was done he ordered in cake and wine, and wished us both luck. "But remember," he said to Mary, "that as yet your possible fortune is a long way off. There may be more Giles Armers than one, and moreover there may be some difficulty in proving legally that the dead man was the same person as your father. Then you will also have to prove, in a formal way, your mother's marriage and your own birth. This will probably involve heavy expenses, for lawyers fight hard when they are well paid. However, I do not wish to discourage you, but only to prevent false hopes; at any rate, you have done well in making your Declaration at once. So far you are on the high road to success." So he sent us away filled with hopes as well as fears.

When we got home we set to work to look for hidden treasures in the unfinished room. I knew too well that there was nothing hidden in the rooms which were finished, for I had done the work myself, and had even stripped the walls and uncovered the floors.

It took us a couple of hours to make an accurate search, but there was absolutely no result. The late Master Mariner had made his treasury in the other house.

Next morning I went to find out from the parish registry the date of the death of Giles Armer, and to my intense relief and joy learned that it had occurred on the 30th of September, so that by our prompt action in going at once to the magistrate's, we had, if not secured a fortune, at least, not forfeited our rights or allowed them to lapse.

The incident was a sort of good omen, and cheered us up; and we needed a little cheering, for, despite the possible good fortune, we feared we might have to contest a lawsuit, a luxury which we could not afford.

We determined to keep our own counsel for a little, and did not mention the matter to a soul.

That evening Mr. Gradder called again, and renewed his offer of taking the house off my hands. I still refused, for I did not wish him to see any difference in my demeanour. He evidently came determined to effect a surrender of the lease, and kept bidding higher and higher, till at last I thought it best to let him have his way; and so we agreed for no less a sum than a hundred pounds that I should give him immediate possession and cancel the agreement. I told him we would clear out within one hour after the money was handed to me.

Next morning at half-past nine o'clock he came with the money. I had all our effects - they were not many - packed up and taken to a new lodging, and before ten o'clock Mr. Gradder was in possession of the premises.

Whilst he was tearing down my new wall papers, and pulling out the grates, and sticking his head up the chimneys and down the water tanks in the search for more treasures, Mary and I were consulting the eminent solicitor, Mr. George, as to our method of procedure. He said he would not lose an hour, but go by the first train to Littlehampton himself to examine Mrs. Compton as to dates and places.

Mary and I went with him. In the course of the next twenty-four hours he had, by various documents and the recollections of my mother-in-law, made out a clear case, the details of which only wanted formal verification.

We all came back to London jubilant, and were engaged on a high tea when there came a loud knocking at the door. There was a noise and scuffle in the passage, and into the room rushed Mr. Gradder, covered with soot and lime dust, with hair dishevelled and eyes wild with anger, and haggard with want of sleep. He burst out at me in a torrent of invective.

"Give me back my money, you thief! You ransacked the house yourself, and have taken it all away! My money, do you hear? my money!" He grew positively speechless with rage, and almost foamed at the mouth.

I took Mary by the hand and led her up to him.

"Mr. Gradder," I said, "let us both thank you. Only for your hurry and persistency we might have let the time lapse, and have omitted the declaration which, on the evening before last, we, or rather, she, made.

He started as though struck.

"What declaration? What do you mean?"

"The declaration made by my wife, only daughter of Giles Armer, Master Mariner, late of Whitby."

The Man from Shorrox'

Throth, yer 'ann'rs, I'll tell ye wid pleasure; though, trooth to tell, it's only poor wurrk telling the same shtory over an' over agin. But I niver object to tell it to rale gintlemin, like yer 'ann'rs, what don't forget that a poor man has a mouth on to him as much as Creeshus himself has.

The place was a market town in Kilkenny-or maybe King's County or Queen's County. At all evints, it was wan of them counties what Cromwell-bad cess to him! —gev his name to. An' the house was called after him that was the Lord Liftinint an' invinted the polis-God forgive him! It was kep' be a man iv the name iv Misther Mickey Byrne an' his good lady-at laste it was till wan dark night whin the bhoys mistuk him for another gindeman, an unknown man, what had bought a contagious property-mind ye the impidence iv him. Mickey was comin' back from the Curragh Races wid his skin that tight wid the full of the whiskey inside of him that he couldn't open his eyes to see what was goin' on, or his mouth to set the bhoys right afther he had got the first tap on the head wid wan of the blackthorns what they done such jobs wid. The poor bhoys was that full of sorra for their mishap whin they brung him home to his widdy that the crather hadn't the hearrt to be too sevare on thim. At the first iv course she was wroth, bein' only a woman afther all, an' weemun not bein' gave to rayson like nun is. Millia murdher! but for a bit she was like a madwoman, and was nigh to have cut the heads from affav thim wid the mate chopper, till, seein' thim so white and quite, she all at wance flung down the chopper an' knelt down be the corp.

'Lave me to me dead,' she sez. 'Oh mm! it's no use more people nor is needful bein' made unhappy over this night's terrible wurrk. Mick Byrne would have no man worse for him whin he was living, and he'll have harm to none for his death! Now go; an', oh bhoys, be dacent and quite, an' don't thry a poor widdied sowl too hard!'

Well, afther that she made no change in things ginerally, but kep' on the hotel jist the same; an' whin some iv her friends wanted her to get help, she only sez: 'Mick an' me run this house well enough; an' whin I'm thinkin' of takun' help I'll tell yez. I'll go on be meself, as I mane to, till Mick an' me comes together agun.'

An', sure enough, the ould place wint on jist the same, though, more betoken, there wasn't Mick wid his shillelagh to kape the pace whin things got pretty hot on fair nights, an' in the gran' ould election times, when heads was bruk like eggs-glory be to God!

My! but she was the fine woman, was the Widdy Byrne! A gran' crathur intirely: a fine upshtandin' woman, nigh as tall as a modheratesized man, wid a forrm on her that'd warrm yer hearrt to look at, it sthood out that way in the right places. She had shkin like satin, wid a warrm flush in it, like the sun shinun' on a crock iv yesterday's crame; an' her cheeks an' her neck was that firrm that ye couldn't take a pinch iv thim-though sorra wan iver dar'd to thry, the worse luck! But her hair! Begor, that was the finishing touch that set all the min crazy. It was jist wan mass iv red, like the heart iv a burnun' furze-bush whin the smoke goes from aff iv it. Musha! but it'd make the blood come up in yer eyes to see the glint iv that hair wid the light shunun' on it. There was niver a man, what was a man at all at all, iver kem in be the door that he didn't want to put his two arrms round the widdy an' giv' her a hug immadiate. They was fine min too, some iv thim-and warrm men-big graziers from Kildare, and the like, that counted their cattle be scores, an' used to come ridin' in to market on huntin' horses what they'd refuse hundlireds iv pounds for from officers in the Curragh an' the quality. Begor, but some iv thim an' the dhrovers was rare miii in a fight. More nor wance I seen them, forty, maybe half a hundred, strong, clear the market-place at Banagher or Athy. Well do I remimber the way the down'd come the springy ground-ash saplins what they carried for switches. The whole lot iv thim wanted to come coortun' the widdy; but sorra wan iv her'd look at thim. She'd flirt an' be coy an' taze thim and make thim mad for love iv her, as weemin likes to do. Thank God for the same! for mayhap we min wouldn't love thim as we do only for their thricky ways; an' thin what'd become iv the counthry wid nothin' in it at all except single min an' ould maids jist dyin', and growin' crabbed for want iv chuidher to kiss an' tache an' shpank an' make love to? Shure, yer 'ann'rs, 'tis childher as makes the hearrt iv man green, jist as it is fresh wather that makes the grass grow. Divil a shtep nearer would the widdy iver let mortial man come. 'No,' she'd say; 'whin I see a man fit to fill Mick's place, I'll let yez know iv it; thank ye kindly'; an' wid that she'd shake her head till the beautiful red hair iv it'd be like shparks iv fire-an' the mm more mad for her nor iver.

But, mind ye, she wasn't no shpoil-shport; Mick's wife knew more nor that, an' his widdy didn't forgit the thrick iv it. She'd lade the laugh herself if 'twas anything a dacent woman could shmile at; an' if it wasn't, she'd send the girrls aff to their beds, an' tell the min they might go on talkin' that way, for there was only herself to be insulted; an' that'd shut thim up pretty quick I'm tellin' yez. But av any iv thim'd thry to git affectionate, as min do whin they've had all they can carry, well, thin she had a playful way iv dalin' wid thim what'd always turn the laugh agin' thim. She used to say that she lamed the beginnun' iv it at the school an' the rest iv it from Mick. She always kep by her on the counther iv the bar wan iv thim rattan canes wid the curly ends, what the soldiers carries whin they can't barry a whip, an' are goin' out wid their cap on three hairs, an' thim new oiled, to scorch the girrls. An' thin whin any iv the shuitors'd get too affectionate she'd lift the cane an' swish them wid it, her laughin' out iv her like mad all the time. At first wan or two iv the min'd say that a kiss at the widdy was worth a clip iv a cane; an' wan iv thim, a warrm horse-fanner from Poul-a-Phoka, said he'd complate the job av she was to cut him into ribbons. But she was a handy woman wid the cane-which was shtrange enough, for she had no childer to be practisin' on-an' whin she threw what was left iv him back over the bar, wid his face like a gridiron, the other min what was laughin' along wid her tuk the lesson to hearrt. Whiniver afther that she laid her hand on the cane, no matther how quietly, there'd be no more talk iv thryin' for kissin' in that quarther.

Well, at the time I'm comm' to there was great divarshuns intirely goin' on in the town. The fair was on the morra, an' there was a power iv people in the town; an' cattle, an' geese, an' turkeys, an' butther, an' pigs, an' vegetables, an' all kinds iv divilment, includin' a berryin' —the same bein' an ould attorney-man, savin' yer prisince; a lone man widout friends, lyin' out there in the gran' room iv the hotel what they call the 'Queen's Room'. Well, I needn't tell yer 'ann'rs that the place was pretty full that night. Musha, but it's the fleas thimselves what had the bad time iv it, wid thim crowded out on the outside, an' shakin', an' thrimblin' wid the cowld. The widdy, av coorse, was in the bar passin' the time iv the day wid all that kem in, an' keepin' her eyes afore an' ahint her to hould the girrls up to their wurrk an' not to be thriflin' wid the mm. My! but there was a power iv min at the bar that night; warrm farmers from four counties, an' graziers wid their ground-ash plants an' big frieze coats, an' plinty iv commercials, too. In the middle iv it all, up the shtreet at a hand gallop comes an Athy carriage wid two horses, an' pulls up at the door wid the horses shmokin'. An' begor', the man in it was smokin' too, a big cygar nigh ~s long as yer arrm. He jumps out an' walks up as bould as brass to the bar, jist as if there was niver a livin' sowl but himself in the place. He chucks the widdy undher the chin at wanst, an', taking aff his hat, sez: 'I want the best room in the house. I travel for Shorrox', the greatest long-cotton firrm in the whole worrld, an' I want to open up a new line here! The best is what I want, an' that's not good enough for me!'

Well, gintlemun, ivery wan in the place was spacheless at his impidence; an', begor! that was the only time in her life I'm tould whin the widdy was tuk back. But, glory be, it didn't take long for her to recover herself, an' sez she quitely: 'I don't doubt ye, sur! The best can't be too good for a gintleman what makes himself so aisy at home!' an' she shmiled at him till her teeth shone like jools.

God knows, gintlemin, what does be in weemin's minds whin they're dalin' wid a man! Maybe it was that Widdy Byrne only wanted to kape the pace wid all thim min crowdin' roun' her, an' thim clutchin' on tight to their shticks an' aiger for a fight wid any man on her account. Or maybe it was that she forgive him his impidence; for well I know that it's not the most modest man, nor him what kapes his distance, that the girrls, much less the widdies, like the best. But anyhow she spake out iv her to the man from Manchesther: 'I'm sorry, sur, that I can't give ye the best room-what we call the best-for it is engaged already.'

'Then turn him out!' sez he.

'I can't,' she says —'at laste not till tomorra; an' ye can have the room thin iv ye like.'

There was a kind iv a sort iv a shnicker among some iv the min, thim knowin' iv the corp, an' the Manchesther man tuk it that they was laughin' at him; so he sez: 'I'll shleep in that room tonight; the other gintleman can put up wid me iv I can wid him. Unless,' sez he, oglin' the widdy, 'I can have the place iv the masther iv the house, if there's a priest or a parson handy in this town-an' sober,' sez he.

Well, tho' the widdy got as red as a Claddagh cloak, she jist laughed an' turned aside, sayin': 'Throth, sur, but it's poor Mick's place ye might have, an' welkim, this night.'

'An' where might that be now, ma'am?' sez he, lanin' over the bar; an' him would have chucked her under the chin agun, only that she moved her head away that quick.

'In the churchyard!' she sez. 'Ye might take Mick's place there, av ye like, an' I'll not be wan to say ye no.'

At that the min round all laughed, an' the man from Manchesther got mad, an' shpoke out, rough enough too it seemed: 'Oh, he's all right where he is. I daresay he's quiter times where he is than whin he had my luk out. Him an' the Devil can toss for choice in bein' lonely or bein' quite.'

Wid that the widdy blazes up all iv a suddunt, like a live sod shtuck in the thatch, an' sez she: 'Who are ye that dares to shpake ill iv the dead, an' to couple his name wid the Divil, an' to his widdy's very face? It's aisy seen that poor Mick is gone!' an' wid that she threw her apron over her head an' sot down an' rocked herself to and fro, as widdies do whin the fit is on thim iv missin' the dead.

There was more nor wan man there what'd like to have shtud opposite the Manchesther man wid a bit iv a blackthorn in his hand; but they knew the widdy too well to dar to intherfere till they were let. At length wan iv thim-Mr Hogan, from nigh Portarlington, a warrm man, that'd put down a thousand pounds iv dhry money any day in the week-kem over to the bar an' tuk aff his hat, an' sez he: 'Mrs Byrne, ma'am, as a friend of poor dear ould Mick, I'd be glad to take his quarrel on meself on his account, an' more than proud to take it on his widdy's, if, ma'am, ye'll only honour me be saying the wurrd.'

Wid that she tuk down the apron from aff iv her head an' wiped away the tears in her jools iv eyes wid the corner iv it.

'Thank ye kindly,' sez she; 'but, guntlemin, Mick an' me run this hotel long together, an' I've run it alone since thin, an' I mane to go on running' it be meself, even if new min from Manchesther itself does be bringin' us new ways. As to you, sur,' sez she, turnin' to him, 'it's powerful afraid I am that there isn't accommodation here for a guntlemin what's so requireful. An' so I think I'll be askin' ye to find convanience in some other hotel in the town.'

Wid that he turned on her an' sez, 'I'm here now, an' I offer to pay me charges. Be the law ye can't refuse to resave me or refuse me lodgmint, especially whin I'm on the primises.'

So the Widdy Byrne drewed herself up, an' sez she, 'Sur, ye ask yer legal rights; ye shall have them. Tell me what it is ye require.'

Sez he sthraight out: 'I want the best room.'

'I've tould you already,' sez she, 'there's a gintleman in it.'

'Well,' sez he, 'what other room have ye vacant?'

'Sorra wan at all,' sez she. 'Every room in the house is tuk. Perhaps, sur, ye don't think or remimber that there's a fair on tomorra.'

She shpoke so polite that ivery man in the place knew there was somethin' comin' —later on. The Manchesther man felt that the laugh was on him; but he didn't want for impidence, so he up, an' sez he: 'Thin, if I have to share wid another, I'll share wid the best! It's the Queen's Room I'll be shleepin' in this night.'

Well, the min shtandin' by wasn't too well plazed wid what was going on; for the man from Manchesther he was plumin' himself for all the world like a cock on a dunghill. He laned agin over the bar an' began makin' love to the widdy hot an' fast. He was a fine, shtout-made man, wid a bull neck on to him an' short hair, like wan iv thim 'two-to-wan-bar-wans' what I've seen at Punchestown an' Fairy House an' the Galway races. But he seemed to have no manners at all in his coortin', but done it as quick an' business-like as takun' his commercial ordhers. It was like this: 'I want to make love; you want to be made love to, bein' a woman. Hould up yer head!'

We all could see the widdy was boilin' mad; but, to do him fair, the man from Manchesther didn't seem to care what any wan thought. But we all seen what he didn't see at first, that the widdy began widout thinkin' to handle the rattan cane on the bar. Well, prisintly he began agun to ask about his room, an' what kind iv a man it was that was to share it wid him.

So sez the widdy, 'A man wid less wickedness in him nor you have, an' less impidence.'

'I hope he's a quite man,' sez he.

So the widdy began to laugh, an' sez she: 'I'll warrant he's quite enough.'

'Does he shnore? I hate a man-or a woman ayther-what shnores.'

'Throth,' sez she, 'there's no shnore in him'; an' she laughed agin.

Some iv the min round what knew iv the ould attorney-man —saving yer prisince-began to laugh too; and this made the Manchesther man suspicious. When the likes iv him gets suspicious he gets rale nasty; so he sez, wid a shneer: 'You seem to be pretty well up in his habits, ma'am!'

The widdy looked round at the graziers, what was clutchin' their ash plants hard, an' there was a laughin' divil in her eye that kep' thim quite; an' thin she turned round to the man, and sez she: 'Oh, I know that much, anyhow, wid wan thing an' another, begor!' But she looked more enticin' nor iver at that moment. For sure the man from Manchesther thought so, for he laned nigh his whole body over the counther, an' whispered somethin' at her, puttin' out his hand as he did so, an' layin' it on her neck to dhraw her to him. The widdy seemed to know what was comm', an' had her hand on the rattan; so whin he was draggin' her to him an' puttin' out his lips to kiss her-an' her first as red as a turkey-cock an' thin as pale as a sheet-she ups wid the cane and gev him wan skelp across the face wid it, shpringin' back as she done so. Oh jool! but that was a skelp! A big wale iv blood riz up as quick as the blow was shtruck, jist as I've seen on the pigs' backs whin they do be prayin' aloud not to be tuk where they're wanted.

'Hands off, Misther Impidence!' sez she. The man from Manchesther was that mad that he ups wid the tumbler formnst him an' was goin' to throw it at her, whin there kem an odd sound from the graziers —a sort of 'Ach!' as whin a man is workin' a sledge, an' I seen the ground-ash plants an' the big fists what held thim, and the big hairy wrists go up in the air. Begor, but polis thimselves wid bayonets wouldn't care to face thim like that! In the half of two twos the man from Manchesther would have been cut in ribbons, but there came a cry from the widdy what made the glasses ring: 'Shtop! I'm not goin' to have any fightin' here; an' besides, there's bounds to the bad manners iv even a man from Shorrox'. He wouldn't dar to shtrike me-though I have no head! Maybe I hit a thought too hard; but I had rayson to remimber that somethin' was due on Mick's account too. I'm sorry, sur,' sez she to the man, quite polite, 'that I had to defind meself; but whin a gintleman claims the law to come into a house, an' thin assaults th' owner iv it, though she has no head, it's more restrainful he should be intirely!'

'Hear, hear!' cried some iv the mm, an' wan iv thim sez 'Amen', sez he, an' they all begin to laugh. The Manchesther man he didn't know what to do; for begor he didn't like the look of thim ash plants up in the air, an' yit he was not wan to like the laugh agin' him or to take it aisy. So he turns to the widdy an' he lifts his hat an' sez he wid mock politeness: 'I must complimint ye, ma'am, upon the shtrength iv yer arrm, as upon the mildness iv yer disposition. Throth, an' I'm thinkin' that it's misther Mick that has the best iv it, wid his body lyin' paceful in the churchyard, anyhow; though the poor sowl doesn't seem to have much good in changin' wan devil for another!' An' he looked at her rale spiteful.

Well, for a minit her eyes blazed, but thin she shmiled at him, an' made a low curtsey, an' sez she-oh! mind ye, she was a gran' woman at givin' back as good as she got —'Thank ye kindly, sur, for yer polite remarks about me arrm. Sure me poor dear Mick often said the same; only he said more an' wid shuparior knowledge! "Molly", sez he —"I'd mislike the shtrength iv yer arrm whin ye shtrike, only that I forgive ye for it whin it comes to the huggin'!" But as to poor Mick's prisint condition I'm not goin' to argue wid ye, though I can't say that I forgive ye for the way you've shpoke iv him that's gone. Bedad, it's fond iv the dead y'are, for ye seem onable to kape thim out iv yer mouth. Maybe ye'll be more respectful to thim before ye die!'

'I don't want no sarmons!' sez he, wery savage. 'Am I to have me room tonight, or am I not?'

'Did I undherstand ye to say,' sez she, 'that ye wanted a share iv the Queen's Room?'

'I did! an' I demand it.'

'Very well, sur,' sez she very quitely, 'ye shall have it!' Jist thin the supper war ready, and most iv the mm at the bar thronged into the coffee-room, an' among thim the man from Manchesther, what wint bang up to the top iv the table an sot down as though he owned the place, an' him niver in the house before.

A few iv the bhoys shtayed a minit to say another word to the widdy, an' as soon as they was alone Misther Hogan up, an' sez he: 'Oh, darlint! but it's a jool iv a woman y' are! Do ye raly mane to put him in the room wid the corp?'

'He said he insisted on being in that room!' she says, quite sarious; an' thin givin' a look undher her lashes at the bhoys as made thim lep, sez she: 'Oh! min, an ye love me give him his shkin that full that he'll tumble into his bed this night wid his sinses obscurifled. Dhrink toasts till he misremimbers where he is! Whist! Go, quick, so that he won't suspect nothin'!'

That was a warrm night, I'm telling ye! The man from Shorrox' had wine galore wid his mate; an' afther, whin the plates an' dishes was tuk away an' the nuts was brought in, Hogan got up an' proposed his health, an' wished him prosperity in his new line. Iv coorse he had to dhrink that; an' thin others got up, an' there was more toasts dhrunk than there was min in the room, till the man, him not bein' used to whiskey-punch, began to git onsartin in his shpache. So they gev him more toasts — 'Ireland as a nation', an' 'Home Rule', an' 'The ruimory iv Dan O'Connell', an' 'Bad luck to Boney', an' 'God save the Queen', an' 'More power to Manchesther', an' other things what they thought would plaze him, him bein' English. Long hours before it was time for the house to shut, he was as dhrunk as a whole row of fiddlers, an' kep shakin' hands wid ivery man an' promisin' thim to open a new line in Home Rule, an' sich nonsinse. So they tuk him up to the door iv the Queen's Room an' left him there.

He managed to undhress himself all except his hat, and got into bed wid the corp iv th' ould attorney-man, an' thin an' there fell asleep widout noticin' him.

Well, prisintly he woke wid a cowld feelin' all over him. He had lit no candle, an' there was only the light from the passage comm' in through the glass over the door. He felt himself nigh fallin' out iv the bed wid him almost on the edge, an' the cowld shtrange gindeman lyin' shlap on the broad iv his back in the middle. He had enough iv the dhrink in him to be quarrelsome.

'I'll throuble ye,' sez he, 'to kape over yer own side iv the bed-or I'll soon let ye know the rayson why.' An' wid that he give him a shove. But iv coorse the ould attorney-man tuk no notice whatsumiver.

'Y'are not that warrm that one'd like to lie contagious to ye,' sez he. 'Move over, I say, to yer own side!' But divil a shtir iv the corp.

Well, thin he began to get fightin' angry, an' to kick an' shove the corp; but not gittin' any answer at all, he turned round an' hit him a clip on the side iv the head.

'Gitup,' he sez, 'iv ye're a man at all, an' put up yer dooks.'

Then he got more madder shrill, for the dhrink was shtirrin' in him, an' he kicked an' shoved an' grabbed him be the leg an' the arrm to move him.

'Begor!' sez he, 'but ye're the cowldest chap I iver kem anigh iv. Musha! but yer hairs is like icicles.'

Thin he tuk him be the head, an' shuk him an' brung him to the bedside, an' kicked him clane out on to the flure on the far side iv the bed.

'Lie there,' he sez, 'ye ould blast furnace! Ye can warrm yerself up on the flure till tomorra.'

Be this time the power iv the dhrink he had tuk got ahoult iv him agin, an' he fell back in the middle iv the bed, wid his head on the pilla an' his toes up, an' wint aff ashleep, like a cat in the frost.

By-an'-by, whin the house was about shuttin' up, the watcher from th' undhertaker's kem to sit be the corp till the mornin', an' th' attorney him bein' a Protestan' there was no candles. Whin the house was quite, wan iv the girris, what was coortin' wid the watcher, shtole into the room.

'Are ye there, Michael?' sez she.

'Yis, me darlint!' he sez, comm' to her; an' there they shtood be the door, wid the lamp in the passage shinin' on the red heads iv the two iv thim.

'I've come,' sez Katty, 'to kape ye company for a bit, Michael; for it's crool lonesome worrk sittin' there alone all night. But I mustn't shtay long, for they're all goin' to bed soon, when the dishes is washed up.'

'Give us a kiss,' sez Michael.

'Oh, Michael!' sez she: 'kissin' in the prisince iv a corp! It's ashamed iv ye I am.'

'Sorra cause, Katty. Sure, it's more respectful than any other way. Isn't it next to kissin' in the chapel? — an' ye do that whin ye're bein' married. If ye kiss me now, begor but I don't know as it's mortial nigh a weddin' it is! Anyhow, give us a kiss, an' we'll talk iv the rights an' wrongs iv it aftherwards.'

Well, somehow, yer 'ann'rs, that kiss was bern' gave-an' a kiss in the prisince iv a corp is a sarious thing an' takes a long time. Thim two was payin' such attintion to what was going on betune thim that 0they didn't heed nothin', whin suddint Katty stops, and sez: 'Whist! what is that?'

Michael felt creepy too, for there was a quare sound comm' from the bed. So they grabbed one another as they shtud in the doorway an looked at the bed almost afraid to breathe till the hair on both iv thim began to shtand up in horror; for the corp rose up in the bed, an' they seen it pointin' at thim, an' heard a hoarse voice say, 'It's in hell I am —Divils around me! Don't I see thim burnin' wid their heads like flames? an' it's burnin' lam too-burnin', burnin', burnin'! Me throat is on fire, an' me face is burnin'! Wather! wather! Give me wather, if only a dhrop on me tongue's tip!'

Well, thin Katty let one screetch out iv her, like to wake the dead, an' tore down the passage till she kem to the shtairs, and tuk a flyin' lep down an' fell in a dead faint on the mat below; and Michael yelled 'murdher' wid all his might.

0It wasn't long till there was a crowd in that room, I tell ye; an' a mighty shtrange thing it was that sorra wan iv the graziers had even tuk his coat from aff iv him to go to bed, or laid by his shtick. An' the widdy too, she was as nate an' tidy as iver, though seemin' surprised out iv a sound shleep, an' her clothes onto her, all savin' a white bedgown, an' a candle in her hand. There was some others what had been in bed, min an' wimin wid their bare feet an' slippers on to some iv thim, wid their bracers down their backs, an' their petticoats flung on anyhow. An' some iv thim in big nightcaps, an' some wid their hair all screwed up in knots wid little wisps iv paper, like farden screws iv Limerick twist or Lundy Foot snuff. Musha! but it was the ould weemin what was afraid iv things what didn't alarrm the young wans at all. Divil resave me! but the sole thing they seemed to dhread was the min-dead or alive it was all wan to thim-an' 'twas ghosts an' corpses an' mayhap divils that the rest was afeard iv.

Well, whin the Manchesther man seen thim all come tumblin' into the room he began to git his wits about him; for the dhrink was wearin' aff, an' he was thryin' to remimber where he was. So whin he seen the widdy he put his hand up to his face where the red welt was, an' at wance seemed to undhershtand, for he got mad agin an' roared out: 'What does this mane? Why this invasion iv me chamber? Clear out the whole kit, or I'll let yez know!'

Wid that he was goin' to jump out of bed, but the moment they seen his toes the ould weemin let a screech out iv thim, an' clung to the mm an' implored thim to save thim from murdher-an' worse. An' there was the Widdy Byrne laughin' like mad; an' Misther Hogan shtepped out, an' sez he: 'Do jump out, Misther Shorrox! The boys has their switches, an' it's a mighty handy costume ye're in for a 00leatherin'!'

So wid that he jumped back into bed an' covered the clothes over him.

'In the name of God,' sez he, 'what does it all mane?'

'It manes this,' sez Hogan, goin' round the bed an' draggin' up the corp an' layin' it on the bed beside him. 'Begorra! but it's cantankerous kind iv a scut y'are. First nothin' will do ye but sharin' a room wid a corp; an' thin ye want the whole place to yerself.'

'Take it away! Take it away,' he yells out.

'Begorra,' sez Mister Hogan, 'I'll do no such thing. The gintleman ordhered the room first, an' it's he has the right to ordher you to be brung out!'

'Did he shnore much, sur?' says the widdy; an' wid that she burst out laughin' an' cryin' all at wanst. 'That'll tache ye to shpake ill iv the dead agin!' An' she flung her petticoat over her head an' run out iv the room.

Well, we turned the min all back to their own rooms; for the most part iv thim had plenty iv dhrink on board, an' we feared for a row. Now that the fun was over, we didn't want any unplisintness to follow. So two iv the graziers wint into wan bed, an' we put the man from Manchesther in th' other room, an' gev him a screechin' tumbler iv punch to put the hearrt in him agin.

I thought the widdy had gone to her bed; but whin I wint to put out the lights I seen one in the little room behind the bar, an' I shtepped quite, not to dishturb her, and peeped in. There she was on a low shtool rockin' herself to an' fro, an' goin' on wid her laughin' an' cryin' both together, while she tapped wid her fut on the flume. She was talkin' to herselfin a kind iv a whisper, an' I heerd her say: 'Oh, but it's the crool woman I am to have such a thing done in me house-an' that poor sowl, wid none to weep for him, knocked about that a way for shport iv dhrunken min while me poor dear darlin' himself is in the cowid clay! —But oh! Mick, Mick, if ye were only here! Wouldn't it be you-you wid the fun iv ye an' yer merry hearrt-that'd be plazed wid the doin's iv this night!'

A Yellow Duster

When my old friend Stanhope came unexpectedly, late in life, into a huge fortune he went traveling round the world for a whole year with his wife before settling down. We had been friends in college days, but I had seen little of him during his busy professional life. Now, however, in our declining years, chance threw us together again, and our old intimacy became renewed. I often stayed with him, both at Stanhope Towers and in his beautiful house in St. James's-square; and I noticed that wherever he was, certain of his curios went with him. He had always been a collector in a small way, and I have no doubt that in his hard-working time, though he had not the means to gratify his exquisite taste, the little he could do served as a relief to the worry and tedium of daily toil. His great-uncle, from whom he inherited, had a wonderful collection of interesting things; and Stanhope kept them much in the same way as he had found them - not grouped or classified in any way, but placed in juxtaposition as taste or pleasure prompted. There was one glass-covered table which stood always in the small drawing room, or rather sitting room, which Mr. and Mrs. Stanhope held as their own particular sanctum. In it was a small but very wonderful collection of precious and beautiful things; an enormous gold scarib with graven pictures on its natural panels, such a scarib as is not to be found even amongst the wonderful collection at Leyden; a carved star ruby from Persia, a New Zealand chieftain's head wrought in greenstone, a jade amulet from Central India, a enamelled watch with an exquisitely-painted miniature of Madame du Barri, a perfect Queen Anne farthing laid in a contemporary pounce-box of gold and enamel, a Borgia ring, a coiled serpent with emerald eyes, a miniature of Peg Woffington by Gainsborough, in a quaint frame of aqua marines, a tiny Elzivir Bible in cover of lapis lazuli mounted in red gold, a chain of wrought iron as delicate as hair, and many other such things, which were not only rare and costly as well as beautiful, but each of which seemed to have some personal association.

And yet in the very middle of the case was placed a common cotton duster, carefully folded. It was not only coarse and common in its texture, but it was of such crude and vulgar colours that it looked startlingly out of place in such a congeries of beautiful treasures. It was so manifestly a personal relic that for a long time I felt some diffidence in alluding to it; though I always looked at that particular table, for as Mrs. Stanhope was good enough to share her husband's liking for me, I was always treated as one of themselves and admitted to their special sitting-room.

One day when Stanhope and I were bending over the case, I remarked:-

"I see one treasure there which must be supreme, for it has not the same intrinsic claim as the others!" He smiled as he said:-

"Oh, that! You are right; that is one of the best treasures I have got. Only for it all the rest might be of no avail!"

This piqued my curiosity, so I said:-

"May an old friend hear the story? Of course, it is evident by its being there that it is not a subject to be shunned."

"Right again!" he answered, and opening the case he took out the duster and held it in his hand lovingly. I could see that it was not even clean; it was one that had manifestly done service.

"You ask the missis," he said: "and if she doesn't mind I'll tell you with pleasure."

At tea that afternoon, when we were alone, I asked Mrs. Stanhope if I might hear the story. Her reply was quick and hearty:-

"Indeed you may! Moreover, I hope I may hear it, too!"

"Do you mean to tell me," I said, "that you don't know why it is there?" She smiled as she replied:-

"I have often wondered; but Frank never told me, and I never asked. It is a long, long time since he kept it. It used to be in the safe of his study till he came into Stanhope Towers; and then he put it where it is now. He keeps the key of the table himself, and no one touches the things in it but him. You noticed, I suppose, that every thing in it is fastened down for traveling?"

When I told Stanhope that his wife permitted him to tell me the story, I added her own hope that she, too, might hear it. He said:

"Very well! To-night after dinner - we are alone this evening - we will come in here and I shall tell you."

When we were alone in the room and the coffee cups had been removed he began:

"Of all the possessions I have, which come under the designation of real or personal estate, that old, dirty, flaring, common duster is the most precious. It is, and has been, a secret pleasure to me for all these years to surround it with the most pretty and costly of my treasures; for so it has a symbolical effect to me. I was once near a grave misunderstanding with my wife - indeed it had begun. This was not long into the second year of our marriage, when the bloom of young wedlock had worn off, and we had begun to settle down to the grim realities of working life. You know my wife is a good many years younger than I am, and when we married I had just about come to that time of life when a man begins to distrust himself as important in the eyes of a beautiful young woman. Lily was always so sweet to me, however, that out of her very sweetness I began to distrust her somewhat. It seemed almost unreasonable that she should be always willing to yield her wishes to mine. At first this distrust was on a very shadowy and unreal basis; but as we grew into the realities of life on small means, it was not always possible for her to forego her wishes in the same way. I had my work to do; and she had her own life to lead, and her own plans to make. I daresay I was pretty unreasonable at times. A man gets worried about his work, and if he tries to keep the worry to himself he sometimes overlooks the fact that his wife, not knowing the facts, cannot understand the almost vital importance of small arrangements which he has to make. So she unconsciously thwarts him."

Here Mrs. Stanhope came over and sat on a stool beside him, and put her hand in his. He stroked it gently and went on:-

"I was especially anxious not to worry her about this time, for there was a hope that our wishes for a child were to be realised, and in my very anxiety to save her from trouble I created the very thing I dreaded. Some little question arose between us; a matter in itself of so small importance that I have quite forgotten it, though the issues then bearing on it were big enough to be remembered. For the purpose of my work things had to be settled in my way, but I could not explain to her without letting her share the worry, and, in addition, I feared that as we were at two, my having held back anything from her might be construed into a want of confidence. Thus it was that her opposition to me became far graver than the occasion itself warranted; and in my blind helplessness, with no one to confide in, I began to fancy that the reason of her opposition was that she did not love me. Let me tell you, old friend - you cannot know, since you were never married - that when once you raise this spirit it is hard to exorcise it. It grows, and grows, and grows, like the genius in the 'Arabian Nights,' until it fills the universe. With this fatal suspicion in my mind every little act of petulance or self-will, everything done or undone, said or unsaid, became 'proof as strong as Holy Writ' that she did not love me; until I grew morbid on the subject. Like the people of old, I wanted a sign.

"One day the strain of silence became too great for me to bear. I broke my resolution of reticence, and taxed her that she did not love me. At first she laughed; for she felt, as she told me afterwards, that the idea was ridiculous. Anyhow, I did not wait to understand, or to weigh her feeling. Her laughter maddened me, and I spoke out some bitter things. 'Oh, yes, my dear, I did!' [This in response to a pressure from the hand that held his, and a warning finger of the other raised.] She tried to bear with me bravely for a while; but at length her feelings mastered her, and the tears rose in her eyes and trickled down her cheeks. But even then I was obdurate. The suspicion of weeks, and all the bitterness of it which had kept me awake so many nights, could not be allayed in a moment. I began to doubt even her very tears. They might, I thought, have come from annoyance at having to explain, from chagrin, from vexation, from anything except the real cause, true womanly and wifely feeling. Again I wanted a sign. And I got it."

His wife's hand closed harder on his; I could see the answering pressure of his hand as he went on:

"She had been dusting the little knick-knacks in the drawing-room, using for the purpose a duster of a peculiarly aggressive pattern. It was one of a set put aside for this special purpose, and therefore chosen of a colour not to be confused with the rest of the domestic appliances. She still held this in her hand; and whilst I stood looking at her with something like rage in my heart, and with my brain a seething mass of doubt as to her half-hysterical sobbing, she raised the duster unconsciously to her face and began to wipe her tears away with it.

"That settled me! Here was a sign that not even a jealous idiot could mistake! Had the thing been less gaudily hideous, had it even been clean, I might still have wallowed in my doubt; but now the conviction of the genuineness of her grief swept me like a great burst of sunshine through fog, and cleared it away for ever. I took her in my arms and tried to comfort her; and from that hour to this there has never been - I thank God for it with all my heart - a doubt between us. Nothing but love and trust and affection! I noticed where she placed the duster, and in the night I came and took it and put it safely away. Do you wonder now, old friend, why I value that rag; why it has a sacred value in my eyes?"

By this time Mrs. Stanhope was shading her face, and I could see the tears roll down her cheeks. "Frank, dear," she said, "let me have your key a moment?" He handed the bunch to her without a word. She selected the key, opened the table top, and took out the duster, which she kissed. Then turning to her husband, as she dried her eyes, she said, Frank, dear, this is the second time you have made me cry in my long, happy life; but, ho, how different!" Stanhope spoke: "Lily, dear, the first time you used that duster I noticed the glaring contrast of its colour to your black hair, and now it holds its own against the coming grey," and he took her in his arms and kissed her. She turned to me and said: "I think the story was worth the telling - and the hearing - don't you? I have allowed this poor, dear old rag to remain in its place of honour all these years because my husband wished it so; but now it shall hold its place in my heart as well as his. God does not always speak in thunder; there are softer notes in the expression of His love and tenderness. Oh, Frank!"

What more she said I know not; for by this time I had stolen quietly away, leaving them alone together.

The 'Eroes of the Thames

When Peter Jimpson, the professional swimmer, had won all the prizes to be had in the towns of Southern England, he thought that the time had come when he should attempt the possibilities of London. He was the more encouraged in the idea because his young son, whom he had brought up to his own calling, had developed quite a genius for his work. Not only could he swim so fast and stay so well that his father looked upon him as a future champion, but he had manifested a decided ability as an aquatic actor.

His tricks were always amusing, and, whether in the humours of a duck chase or exhibiting possibilities of the disasters which may happen to the imperfect swimmer, he showed undoubted power. Peter, therefore, determined to turn young Peter's gift to advantage. He had long known that to win the attention of magnificent, rich, indifferent London, some sort of coup is necessary; there are so many workers of all kinds in the vast metropolis that merely to work is only to be one of many.

So all the early summer the two Peters rehearsed a little aquatic scena-that of a drowning boy rescued by a brave passing stranger. Many a time and oft, and always in secret-for the elder Peter impressed on his son the absolute necessity for silence-they went through every detail, till at last Peter junior could simulate the entire dangers and possibilities of an immersion.

He would fall into the water in the most natural way in the world; would struggle violently with his hands above water and his mouth open, after the manner of the ignorant; he would sink and rise again with strange portions of his anatomy appearing first above water, as though forced up by an irresistible current; he would gasp and choke and go down again; rise again with only his hands above water, and clutch at the empty air with writhing fingers in a manner which was positively heartrending to witness. Then the proud father knew that in his son were all the elements of success.

Wherefore they took their way to London. Having surveyed the various bridges they fixed on London Bridge as the scene of their exploit, and the hour when the afternoon throng was greatest as the time. They had several consultations, for it was necessary to be circumspect; the bridge was always well-furnished with police, and on two occasions they had noticed that different men had eyed them curiously, as though they were suspicious characters.

However, they fixed on every detail of their plan, leaving nothing to chance. As the construction of London Bridge does not allow of a small boy who is simply passing along to fall off by accident, and as to climb the parapet is at least a suspicious act, they arranged that Peter, having ascertained that neither passing barge nor steamer made a special source of danger, was to throw his son right over the parapet, and immediately jump after him.

They felt that in the excitement of the rescue-which they knew so well how to play-the crowd would instantly line the parapet, and would lose sight of the seemingly lethal act. They anticipated a rich harvest of praise, and possibly of a more tangible kind of reward; in any case, their fame as swimmers would be noised abroad.

Next day at the appointed time, when London Bridge was almost a solid mass of vehicles, horsemen, and pedestrians, they made their enterprise. Having seen that no barge or steamer was close, they moved to the pathway over the very centre arch of the bridge on the down-river side as the current was running up.

There Peter, suddenly seizing the boy, hurled him with a mighty effort over the parapet into the water, and the instant after began to climb after him. But just as he was gaining a footing a man rushed forward and caught him by the ankles, and dragged him back upon the pavement. Peter turned on him furiously, and saw that his captor was one of the very men whom he had seen watching him on a previous occasion.

"Let me go!" he cried, "let me go! I must save my boy!" and he struggled frantically.

"A new way to save him, to throw him over the bridge!" said the man, who held him in a grip of iron.

"My boy! my boy! I must save my boy!" cried Peter appealingly to the crowd.

"Your boy will be saved if the bravest fellow in England can do it. Look there!" came the answer, and the crowd began to cheer; for just at the moment another man leapt upon the parapet, and, throwing off his coat, dived into the river. Some of the crowd helped to hold Peter, who struggled wildly, none the less that he had recognised in the man who jumped from the bridge another of the men whom he had seen watching him.

The tide was running so strongly up stream that young Peter was in a second or two after his immersion carried under the shadow of the arch, and close behind him his rescuer also disappeared from view. There was an instant rush across the bridge, and in a moment the up-river parapet was black with people, all looking eagerly for their coming through the arch.

The seconds seemed ages; but at length those exactly over it saw the body of the little boy drifting along just under the water, and turning round as it came. As soon as the bridge was cleared, and the sunlight reached the water above him, there was a violent struggle, a kicking about of the little chap's arms and legs in seemingly a death-struggle. And then the horrified spectators saw two little hands rise above the water, clutch violently at the air, and sink again. Then the angle of refraction became too great, and even those on the centre arch could see no more.

There was a deep groan from the crowd; which, however, turned to a cheer as a man swimming overhand with a powerful stroke swept through the arch in the wake of the missing boy. A thousand hands pointed to where the child had gone down, and a thousand voices roared a thousand different directions. But the swimmer seemed to know instinctively the right spot, and making for it, turned head foremost and went down into the deep water to search for him.

There must have been some strange currents running round the piers of London Bridge that tide, for suddenly the crowd seemed to realise all at once that the boy's body had risen out of the water not directly in the track of the stream, but at a spot some dozen or more yards on the Surrey side. In the moments that had elapsed the little chap had had time to draw his breath, and in the stillness around-for the roar of the traffic had ceased for the moment-the crowd hearth his faint cry:

"Oh, father! father!"

There was an instant shiver through the crowd, such as is seen when a sudden breeze sweeps over a cornfield, for instinctively everyone had turned his head backward to look at the guilty father. The fierce howl that swept from the mass of people showed that it was just as well that a strong force of police now surrounded the prisoner, or his life might have been in danger.

In the meantime, the man had risen from his dive and the boy had again sunk; again the crowd roared and pointed, and the man had with a few powerful strokes gained the place. This time, however, he did not dive, for he knew that he must be ready to seize the body when it rose again, for it would be the last chance.

The crowd and the man alike waited in fearful suspense. The swimmer was a keen-eyed, powerful fellow; he raised his head well above the water, and kept looking all around him. It was well that he did so, for by another effort of those strange currents round the piers the boy's body rose down the river this time, having travelled against the current, and being still close to London Bridge, where the great crowd could plainly see.

The swimmer seemed to jump forward in the water, and with half-a-dozen mighty overhand strokes came close and seized the boy by the back of the neck, and raised his head out of the water. The boy could not see him from the position in which he was held, but he again shouted, "Father! father!" but this time in ringing, joyous tones, which reached the crowd from Surrey to Middlesex.

By this time boats were coming up and down the river to the rescue, and it appeared to be well that they were at hand, for it seemed to be no easy task to rescue a child. The man who had appeared to swim so powerfully when alone seemed, now that he was hampered with the boy, to be hardly able to support himself.

Boy and man struggled together in a little maelstrom of their own creation, and more than once went under water, leaving only a mass of froth to show where they went down. Once, though, after such a disappearance, the boy rose first, and appeared to be making frantic efforts to get away; but the instant after appeared the man, who, with seemingly renewed vigour, followed him up and again caught him by the nape of the neck, and then never let him go-over water or under it-till the two were taken into the police boat, the man gasping, and the child seemingly senseless.

Then a mighty roar arose from the watching crowd. Handkerchiefs and hats were waved, and the rescuer looked proud as he waved his hand in recognition, sitting in the stern of the boat, and holding on his knees the little chap, who had now opened his eyes, and only struggled faintly as though by instinct. Then the boat took its way to the river police-station, and the crowd went about its business, all except two sections, one of which followed the boy and his gallant rescuer, and the other the father, under arrest for attempted murder.

At the police-court the magistrate was sitting and when Peter Jimpson was brought into the station he was told with policeman pleasantry how nice it would be that he would not have long to wait for his committal. Somehow, he did not seem to see the joke-it is wonderful what a difference in point of view there is between the inside and the outside of the dock-especially in matters of humour.

However, he began to think, with the result that when he was brought before the magistrate he found himself prepared to make a clean breast of his ill-starred effort to achieve notoriety. A policeman who had been on duty on London Bridge had from a little distance seen him throw the boy into the water, and the man who had first laid hands on him, John Polter, testified to the same; the charge was therefore simple enough, and no time was lost.

When in the court the charge was entered upon, Peter Jimpson made his explanation, saying that all that had been done was with his son's consent and connivance, simply in order to bring their names as swimmers before the public. To which the magistrate drily replied that such a course was apt to be attended with misapprehension, and was not devoid even of serious risk, as doubtless the grand jury would let him know later on.

Whilst the proceedings were at this stage a great cheering was heard outside, and very soon the rescued boy and his rescuer entered the court. Young Peter, with every appearance of regret, corroborated his father's statement as to his having been a consenting party to his immersion; whereupon the rescuer indignantly said:

"And do you mean to say, you little wretch, that you tried to deceive the public by a base pretence of danger? Oh, boy! boy! I feel a certain love for you since your life is due to my own valour; but I trust that such an acted lie shall never again be due to you-even in part!"

The boy covered his eyes with his hands, and his voice was broken as he answered:

"Oh, your worship, I ain't agoin' on such a racket never no more. This brave, kind gentleman has taught me a lesson which I'll never forget!" And he took the man's big hand in his two small ones, and bent over it and kissed it, whilst there was scarcely a dry eye in the court, even the magistrate being visibly affected. Peter Jimpson was about to say something angrily, but the clerk of the court motioned him to be silent. Then the rescuer, who gave his name as Tom Bolter, spoke:

"May I ask your worship to dismiss the case. I wouldn't go for to take the liberty of speaking only as how it was me what saved the boy at the risk of my life; and mayhap on that account you'll let me say what I feels. These here two professionals has been trying to rig up a bit of biz, but the chance was against them, and they got queerer. No doubt but it'll be a lesson to them not to play tricks again with the feelins of the public! It's a harrowin' up tenderness; that's what it is, and I am sure that if your worship will let them off this time they will never go for to do it again. Isn't that so, mateys?"

Both the Peters pronounced eager acquiescence; so after some deliberation the genial, bald-headed magistrate said:

"Peter Jimpson, and you, too, Peter Jimpson junior, I trust that the severe lesson which you have this day learnt may not be thrown away upon you. You must always remember that any form of fraud is obnoxious to the law; and this was distinctly a fraud on your part. Perhaps-indeed, I am satisfied, that you thought it an innocent proceeding enough; but let me tell you that there was manifest throughout the mens rea, which the law holds to be a necessary part of ill-doing-the intent to deceive. I am convinced that you, Peter Jimpson, fully intended to follow your son into the water, or otherwise I should have by this time committed you for trial on the serious charge of attempted murder, and for this reason I shall dismiss the charge; but I trust that as you lay your head on your pillow to-night you will breathe a warm and earnest prayer for that most gallant fellow, Thomas Bolter-that most excellent swimmer and master of the art of life-saving, to whom you owe so much!"

There was great applause in court, and a voice in the back of the crowd said, "Good old Bolter!" but the crier instantly called, "Silence in the court."

Then Tom Bolter stood forward, and pulling his forelock respectfully, said:

"Your worship, what I done I done for the dear child's good; but I thank your worship all the same for the kind and useful-and I hope I may say true-words which you have spoke of me. I'm only a unknown man in London as yet; but I am sure that before long you'll hear of me in connection with saving life from drowning. When that time comes I 'ope as you, your worship, and all these 'ere ladies and gents as has done me so proud to-day concernin' my gallant act'll remember the name of Tom Bolter, and come and see me, even if you have to plank down your money for it. My service to you, your worship, and you ladies and gents all!" and Tom Bolter retired from the court amid a murmur of applause, the court emptying after him in a stream.

Outside there was soon a buzz and hum of many persons speaking, for each of the chief actors in the river episode was surrounded by a group of sympathisers or admirers.

One little group of sporting-looking young men stood apart listening to a betting man, whose calling was writ large on every square inch of his face and clothing.

"Well, blow me tight!" they heard him say, "if that ain't the very cheekiest thing I ever see done; and, mind you, I've seen a few."

"How do you mean, Sam?" came the chorus of questions.

" 'Ow do I mean? Why, this, that the bally court and the 'ole bloomin' lot of yer is took in! They've been playin' yer for suckers, the 'ole bloomin' lot of yer."

"Who has, Sam?"

"Why, them two Northern chaps, Polter and Bolter, the champion swimmers of the Tyne. They've come to London to give an exhibition of life savin' at the Hippodrome, an' I've seen their printin' lyin' ready till their chance come. 'Polter and Bolter, the 'Eroes of the Thames,' is wot they're down as, and I've seen them the 'ole of last week prowlin' round the bridge lookin' out for a chanst. My stars! but they done it fine; but the kiddy is the daisy of them all!"

In the meantime, in the group round the two Peters, the boy's voice was heard above the babel:

"I tell you he's the bravest chap and the finest swimmer in all the world! I ought to know since he took me out of the jaws of death! God bless him!"

Here Peter the elder whispered to him fiercely:

"Stow all that and keep yer 'ead shut! Don't crack him up; keep that for ourselves!" to which the dutiful boy answered aloud;

"No, father, I cannot hold my tongue! I must speak up for the brave and true!" Then he added in a whisper:

"Keep it up, dad! I've settled with them as we came up to the court. They're goin' to open in the Hippodrome and they're to give you and me twenty quid a week to play up to them! You go on swimmin', father, and be quicker in your jumps; but leave the business of the firm to me!"

The Way of Peace

I knew both Michael Hennessey and his wife Katty, though under the local pronunciation of the surname-Hinnessey. I had often gone into the little farmhouse to smoke a pipe with the old man, and to have, before I came away, a glass of milk from the old woman's clean, cool dairy. I had always understood that they were looked upon as a model couple; and it was within my knowledge that a little more than a year ago they had celebrated their golden wedding. But when old Lord Killendell - "The Lard" as they called him locally - suggested that I should ask old Michael how it was that they had lived such a happy life, there was something in his tone and the quiet laugh which followed it, which made me take the advice to heart. More especially when Lady Killendell, who had always been most kind to me, added with an approving smile -

"Do! You are a young man and a bachelor; you will learn something which may be of some service to you later on in your life."

The next time I was near Hennessey's farm the advice occurred to me, and I went in. The two old folk were alone in the house. Their work for the day - the strenuous work - was done, and they were beginning the long evening of rest, which is the farmer's reward for patient toil. We three sat round the hearth enjoying the glowing fire, and the aromatic smell of the burning turf, which is the only fuel used in that part of Ireland.

I gradually led conversation round to the point of happy marriages by way of the Golden Wedding, which was not yet so far off as to have lost interest to the old folk.

"They tell me," I said presently, "that you two are the happiest couple in the Country. I hope that is so? You look it anyway; and every time I have seen you the idea has been with me."

"That's true, God be thanked!" said Michael, after a pause.

"Amin!" joined in Katty, as she crossed herself.

"I wish you'd tell me how you do it?" I asked. Michael smiled this time, and his wife laughed.

"Why do ye want to know, acushla?" she said in reply. This put me in a little personal difficulty. As a matter of fact, I was engaged to be married, but I had been enjoined not to say anything about it - as yet. So I had to put my request on general grounds, which is never so appealing as when such information is asked for personal reasons.

"Well, you see, Mrs. Hennessey," I said, stumbling along as well as I could, "a man would always like to know a secret like that. It is one which might - at some time in his life - be - be useful to him. He - "

"Begob it might, yer 'ann'r," broke in Michael. "Divil recave me if a young man beginnin' life wid a knowledge like that mightn't have all the young women iv a township follyin' round afther him like a flock iv geese afther a ghander." He was interrupted in turn by Katty -

"Ay, or th' ould wans too!" Then she turned to me -

"An' so ye're goin' to be married, yer 'ann'r. More power to ye; an' as many childher as there's days in the month."

"Hold hard there, ma'am!" I retorted. "That would be an embarras de richesse." She winced at the foreign phrase, so I translated it - "too much of a good thing - as the French say. But why do you think I'm going to be married?"

"Ah, go on out iv that wid ye! For what would a young man like yer 'ann'r want to know how marrid people does get on wid wan another, unless he's ceasin' to be a bhoy himself!" (In Ireland a man is a "bhoy" so long as he remains a bachelor. I have myself known a "bhoy" over ninety.) Her inductive ratiocination was too much for me; I remained silent.

"Begob, surr, Katty was wan too many for ye there!" chuckled the old man.

"Quite right, Michael, so she was!" I said. "But now that she has found me out, mayn't I have the price of the discovery? Won't you tell me how you have lived together so happily for so many years?"

"Ay, surr, there hasn't been a harrd wurrd betune us since the day afther we was married."

"The day after you were married?" I commented. "I wonder you didn't begin on the wedding-day itself!"

"Now that's all right, surr, an' mayhap so we would if we was beginnin' life out iv a book. Mayhap it was that we found out the way for ourselves, bekase we wasn't lookin' for it on any particular road. I'm thinkin' that that's the usual way for threasures bein' found 'Tisn't always - aye or mostly - the people that goes about shtickin' rods into places or knockin' chunks wid hammers from off iv other people's property that finds hidden money. Sure 'tis thim that goes about mindin' their own business that comes across it whin they're laste expectin' it." This was a long speech for Michael; and Katty, with her instinctive wish to please, expressed herself in subtle flattery given in an overt aside -

"Mind ye, the wisdom iv him. It does come bubblin' up, like a spring out iv a big book full iv writin' what no man can undhershtand!" Then I joined in myself -

"That is a good idea, Michael. The knowledge that can make two people happy is indeed a treasure. Won't you tell me how to find it? The finding, of course, a man must do for himself. But where there is a road, it is wise to know something about it before you start on a journey."

"Thrue for ye, surr. But I'm misdoubtin' meself if there's a road at all - a high-road iv coorse, I mane. But mind ye, 'tisn't on the high-roads that happiness walks. 'Tis the boreens in a man's own houldin' - nigh to his own home - an' his own heart!" This time Katty's comment was made directly to her husband -

"Begob, Mike, but it's a pote ye're becomin' in yer ould age. Boreens in yer heart! indade! An' here have I been thrampin' for half a century up an' down our own boreen; an' sorra wance have I seen happiness walkin' there more than on the mail-road itself."

This new philosophy was taking us away from the subject, so I led them back to it - "

"Well, even if there isn't a high-road - a road for all - won't you tell me what road you and Katty took? Then I may be able - some day - to find a road like it." The old man winked at me and chuckled; taking the pipe from his lips he jerked the mouth-piece backward over his shoulder.

"Ask her, surr. 'Tis she that can tell you - av she plases."

"Won't you tell me, Katty?" I asked.

"Wid all the plisure in life, yer 'ann'r. 'Tis not much to tell for sure - an' mayhap not worth the tellin'; but av ye wish ye shall hear.

"As that ould man there says, it began the mornin' afther he was married on to me. Mind ye, at the beginnin' - I don't want ye to decave yerself about that bekase that's part iv the shtory - we was mighty fond of aich other. My! but he was the fine bhoy! Tall an' big an' shtrong an' mastherful; an' 'tis the proud girrl I was whin he ixprissed himself to me. I was that proud that I kem home leppin' so that me mother noticed it an' said: 'Katty, has that impident villin Mike Hinnessey been tellin' ye that ye're a good-lookin' girleen?' - for mind ye I wasn't thin grown up but only a shtep afther a skeuneuch. 'H'm'!' sez I. ' 'Tis more than that; he has asked me no less than to be married on to me.' That fetched her up, I can tell ye. 'Glory be,' sez she. 'What is the childher comin' to at all at all? You to be marrid that has no more to yer feet nor yer back than a flapper duck on the bog; an' him that can't bring a thing to the fair that he can't carry. Him that has but only yistherday left his father's cabin an' got one for himself; widout a shtick in it but the thruckle he lies on, an' the creel he ates aff.' "

Instinctively I looked round the fine farm-kitchen in which we sat, with its good, solid, oak furniture, its plentitude of glass and crockery all daintily clean and bright. Michael noticed my look and said, gravely nodding his head as he spoke -

"That's all her doin', surr. That's Katty's!"

"Don't mind him, surr! 'Tis the kind good heart iv him that says it. But it's not my doin'. That's Michael's own work. Surely I only was careful wid the money that he arn'd!" Here I harked back to the main subject with a hint -

"And you said to your mother - ?"

"Well, yer 'ann'r, I shtood right up to her - wasn't Michael worth it? - an' sez I: 'Michael is the bist man nor iver I see; an' I'm for him an' for no one else. He's poor I know, an' so am I. But plaze God he'll not be poor always; an' I'll wait for him if 'tis all me life!' Well, me mother was a good woman, an' she seen the tears in me eyes an' knew I was in arnest. She kem an' put her arms round me an' sez she: 'That's right, me child. That's the way to love; an' it's worth all the rist iv the wurrld. He's a good bhoy is Michael; an' 'tis right sure I am that he loves ye. An' whin the both iv ye think the time has come 'tis not me nor yer poor dead father that'll shtand betune ye.' I knew - faix only too well - what a harrd time me poor mother had, for the times was bad. That was the year of the potato-rot, an' throughout the counthry min an' weemin - an' worse still, the poor childhers - was dyin' be shcores. An' Michael knew too; an' ere long he sez to me: 'Katty, come wid me soon. Sure, acushla, if 'tis nothin' else 'twill be wan mouth less for yer poor mother to feed.' When Michael shpoke like that I wasn't the wan to say him nay."

Both were silent and I waited a while, till, seeing that they considered the tale as told, I ventured to recall them once again -

"But you haven't told me about the road yet."

"Oh, that, surr," said Katty with a laugh - "that was simple enough - may I tell him, Michael?"

"Go an, woman! Go an!" he answered with a growl.

"As Michael tould ye, surr, it began the day afther our weddin'. Ye know, surr, people like us didn't go off on honeymoons in thim days - not like they do now, poor or rich. Whin a woman kem into her husband's home she took life as 'twas to be foreninst her. I cooked Michael's supper an' me own on our weddin' night, just as I've done iver since. I knew that the fair at Killen was on the nixt day an' that Michael was lookin' to goin' to it; an' I made up me mind that he'd not go that day. So in the mornin' whin I done me hair - for a coorse I got up first to get the breakfast - I hid the rack. . . ."

"The rack? Pardon my interrupting, but I don't understand." She was not offended but proceeded to explain -

"The rack-comb, surr. The thing ye brush yer hair wid. Wid poor folk it's all the brush-an'-comb they have. It was not thin like it is now whin ivery wan in a house has their own. Why, me son from Ameriky when he kem to shtay wid us had what he called a 'dressin'-bag' wid brushes an' combs enough to clane the heads iv all the parish. But in thim times if the house had wan that was all that was needed. When I looked back Michael was up an' was shavin' himself.

" 'Gettin' ready for the fair?' sez I to him.

" 'Yiz!' sez he, not sayin' much for the lip iv him was that twitched up to get smooth for the razor.

" 'Ye're not!' sez I.

" 'I am!' sez he.

" 'Ye're not!' sez I again.

"I don't suppose ye undhershtand, surr, the feelin' iv a young wife when she knows that her man is her own. I had only been marrid on the yistherday, an' whin I knew how Michael loved me I thought I was him as well as meself too. When a woman is marrid she thinks - an' never more than the day afther - that what she wishes is fixed an' done. She manes so well be her man - an' for all her life, mind ye - that she has no thought that everything isn't right. She has to larn! She has to larn; an' the sooner that she larns the betther for herself an' ivery wan else! Whin Michael had wiped his razor he put his hand on the windy-sill to take up the rack where it always lay. Not findin' it, he sez to me -

" 'Katty, where's the rack?'

" 'I won't tell ye,' sez I. I was up in meself afther me wan day iv a wife.

" 'I want the rack, Katty,' he sez quite quiet.

" 'Ye'll not get it,' sez I. . . . 'Ye're not goin' to the fair today!'

" 'I'm goin' to the fair to-day, an' ivery day I like!' he sez quieter nor iver, 'an' I want the rack.'

" 'Ye'll not get it,' sez I. Wid that he took me face in his hands an' kissed me on the mouth. An' thin whin I let him go afther I had giv it back, he fetched me a shlap on the side iv me head that made me think that the house was full iv bells all clattherin' away at wanst, as sez he -

" 'Katty, bring me the rack!'

She stopped and sat down, resuming her knitting as though she had said all she intended.

"And then?" I ventured to hint. She looked up at me and then over at Michael and said -

"Well, I wint acoorse an' brung him the rack. An' from that day to this we niver had a harrd wurrd wan for th'other." Michael chuckled.

"That's the road, surr. Some wan must be masther iv th' house. That time it had got to be me. An' I was - an' I am!" Here he stood up and bent over and kissed the old lady heartily. "An', surr, take it to mind that there's been no happier woman in Ireland - no, nor out of it - nor Katty."

It didn't seem quite a sufficient charting of the Road, so I ventured to appeal to Mrs. Hennessey again: -

"Did he go to the fair?" She had evidently been thinking, for she began almost at my first word. Since then, in trying to find a motive for her interruption, I have concluded that she thought her words might put Michael in a bad light; as one who was more or less of a bully.

"He combed his hair an' his moustache, an' he put on his coat wid the tails, an' shtuck his pipe in the front iv his caubeen, an' tuk his blackthorn. Thin he kissed me an' wint out. I looked out iv the door afther him, an' saw him turn the comer; an' then I kem in an' began to tidy up the house.

"Thin the door darkened, an' in kem Michael. He flung his caubeen an' his blackthorn in the corner, an' tuk me in his arrms, an' sez he -

" 'Katty, alana-ma-chree, I'm not goin' to the fair this day. Bekase ye don't wish it, me darlin', not bekase ye merely want to kape me from it. Shure I love you alone, an' I wouldn't do nothin' to hurt ye. But always remimber that I'm a man an' used to man's ways; an' a man doesn't like bein' ordhered about be any wan - even be a wife that he loves an' that loves him.' " Her eyes were soft and shiny, and she looked affectionately at the sturdy old man. Then she turned to me and went on -

"An' that's the sort iv man that I've kep the peace wid for all these years. An' isn't he worth it? An' doesn't he desarve it - a man like that? I tell ye, surr, that's the way to thrate a woman; an' that's the way that a woman ought to be thrated. Sure, afther all, they're but childher iv a bigger kind. An' what's the way to thrate childher? 'Tisn't all done be shmiles an' pettin', an' be bread an' sugar. They want to get the hard hand now and again, an' they does the same whin they're grown into min and weemin. 'Tis the hand iv the mother that's the most tindher. Thin, whin that's not enough, the father has to give thim a clip on the ear if it's a girrl, or a cut wid a switch if it's a bhoy.

"An', mind ye, that's the aisiest punishment they iver gits. Whin they don't larn things from them 'tis harder they git it whin they come to larn from the warld!"

Greater Love

We was just standin' here at about eleven in the evenin', an' the moon was beginnin' to rise. We could see the little patch of light growin' bigger an' bigger, just as it is now, an' we knew that before many moments the light would be up over the sea. My back was to the sea, an' Bill was leanin' agin' the handrail, just like you now.

It ain't much, sir, after all; leastwise to you; but it was, aye, an' it is, a deal to me, for it has all my life in it, such as it is. There's a deal of poetry an' story-tellin' in books; but, Lor' bless ye, if ye could see the heart right through of even such men as me, you'd have no need o' books when you wanted poetry and romance. I often think that them chaps in them don't feel a bit more nor we do when things is happenin'; it's only when they're written down that they become heroes an' martyrs, an' suchlike. Why, Bill was as big a hero as any of them. I often wished as how I could write, that I might tell all about him.

Howsumdever, if I can't write, I can talk, an' if you're not in a hurry, an'll wait till I tell you all, I'll be proud. It does me good to talk about Bill.

Well, when I turned round an' faced Bill I see his eyes with the light in 'em, an' they was glistenin'. Bill gives a big gulp, an' says to me:

"Joe, the world's a big place, big enough for you an' me to live in without quarrelin'. An', mayhap, the same God as made one woman would make another, an' we might both live an' be happy. You an' me has been comrades for long, an' God knows that, next to Mary, I'd be sad to see you die, so whatever comes, we won't quarrel or think hard of one another, sure we won't, Joe."

He put out his hand, an' I took it sudden. We held hands for a long time. I thought he was in low spirits, and I wished to cheer him, so I says:

"Why, Bill, who talks o' dyin' that's as hearty as we?"

He shook his head sadly, an' says he:

"Joe, I don't vally my life at a pin's head, an' I ain't afraid to die. For her sake or for yours - aye, even for her pleasure - I'd - No matter. Just see if I turn coward if I ever get the chance to do her a service."

Well, we stood there for a long time. Neither of us said a word, for I didn't like to speak, although I would several times have liked to ask him a question. An' then I gave up wishin' to speak, an' began to think, like him.

I thought of all the time Bill an' me had been friends an' comrades, an' how fond we were both of Mary, an' she of us. Ye see, when we was all children, the little thing took such a fancy for both of us that we couldn't help likin' her for it, and so we became, in course of time, like big brothers to her. She would come down on the shore with Bill an' me an' sit quiet all the day an' never say a word or do anything to annoy us or put us out Sometimes we'd go out sailin', an' then she would come an' sit beside whoever was steerin' till he'd ask her to come up an' sit on his knee. Then she'd put up her little arms round his neck an' kiss him, an' would stay as quiet as a mouse till she'd have to change her place. That was the way, sir, that we both came to be so fond of her.

An', sure enough, when she began to grow up, Bill an' me wanted none other but her. An' the more she grew, the prouder we were of her, till at last we found out that we were both of us in love with her. But we never told her so, or let her see it; an' she had grown up so amongst us that she never suspected it. She said so long after.

Then Bill an' me held a kind of council about what was to be done, an' so we came to be talkin' on the bridge that night. Mary was growin' into a young woman, an' we feared that some other chap might take her fancy, if one of us didn't get her at once. Bill was very serious, far more serious than me, for I had somehow got the idea into my head as how Mary cared for me, an' as long as I felt that I couldn't feel either unhappy or downhearted.

All at once Bill's face grew brighter, an' there was a soft look in his eyes.

"Joe," he says, "whatever happens, Mary must never hang her head. The lass is tender-hearted, and she likes both of us, we know; an' as she can only love one of us, it might pain her to think that when she was marryin' one man she was leavin' a hole in the life of his comrade. So she must never know as how we both love her, if we can prevent it."

When we got that far, I began to grow uneasy. I began to distrust Bill - God forgive me for it - an' to think that maybe he was fixin' some plan for to cut me out. I must have been jealous, that was it. But I was punished for my distrust when he went on:

"Joe, old lad, we both love her an' we love each other; an' God knows I'd go away, an' willin', an' leave her to you, but who knows that mayhap she'd like me better of the two. Women is queer creatures in lettin' a fellow see their hearts till they see his first."

Then he stayed quiet, an' so I says to him:

"How are we to manage to do that, Bill? If we tell her, won't she know that we both love her? An' you said you wouldn't like her to do that."

"That's just what I was thinkin' of," he says. "An' I see how we may do it. One of us must go to her an' find out if she loves him, an' if she does, the other will say nothin'."

I felt feared, so I asked him:

"Who is to go, Bill?"

He came over an' took me by the shoulder, an' says he:

"Joe, so far as I can see, the lass cares for you the most; you must go first an' find out."

I tried not to appear joyful, an' I says:

"Bill, that isn't fair; whoever goes first has the best chance. Why won't you go, or why not draw lots?" I've had a many hard tussles in my time, both with men an' things, but I never had such a struggle as I had to say them words.

"Joe," says Bill, "you must do all you can to win her yourself, an' don't let any thoughts of me hinder you. I'll be best pleased by seein' her an' you happy, if so be she loves you." Then he stood up from leaning on the rail, an' says he:

"Joe, give me your hand before we go, an' mind, I charge you on your honor as a man, never while I'm livin', to let Mary know as how I loved her, in case she chooses you." So I promised. I felt Bill's hand grip like a vice, an' then we turned an' walked away home an' never spoke another word that night, either of us.

I didn't sleep much that night, and when it began to get to mornin' I got up an' went down to the sea an' had a swim, an' that freshened me up somewhat. I wasn't much of a swimmer myself, but I could manage to keep myself up pretty well. That was the point where I envied Bill most of all. He was the finest swimmer I ever see. He did a many things well, an' no lad in this county could come near him in anything he chose to do; but in swimmin' none could come anigh him at all. An' many's the time it stood to others as well as himself.

Well, when I had had my bathe, I went up toward Mary's home, an' found myself goin' in to ask her straight off to marry me. Then I began to think it was too early for Mary to be up; so I stole away on tiptoe, an' walked round the house. Then I thought I'd go an' look up Bill, an' came anigh his house. But when I came to the door, as I didn't like to knock, I thought I'd speer in, an' see if he was asleep. So I stole to the window an' looked in.

I never shall forget to my dyin' day what I saw then. I wasn't a bad fellow, thank God, at any time, but I couldn't be a bad fellow or do anything I thought very wrong after that. There was Bill, just as I had left him the night before. He had never changed his clothes, an' the candle was flickerin' down in the socket, unheeded. He was kneelin' down by the bed, with his arms stretched out before him, an' his face down on the quilt. That was thirty-seven year ago, but it seems like yesterday. I thought at first he was sleepin', but I saw from a movement he made that he was awake. So I stole away, guilty-like, an' went down an' stood beside the sea. I took off my hat, an' let the wind blow about my forehead, for somehow it felt burnin', an' I looked out over the sea for long. Somehow my heart beat like as if it was lead, an' I felt half choked. I dunno how long I would have stayed there only for Bill. He came behind me, and put his hand on my shoulder and said, sudden:

"Why, Joe, what are you doin' here?"

I turned, startled, an' saw that he was smilin'. I was so thunderstruck at seein' the change, that for a moment I said nothin'. He says to me again:

"Joe, I thought you'd have more to do than think of eatin' this mornin', an' it's bad to court on an empty stomach! So come up to my place; I've got breakfast for the both of us."

I couldn't realize that this hearty chap was the man I saw prayin' after the long night. I looked at him keenly, but could see no sign of his actin' a part in his face. He was gayer an' livelier than ever, an' in such good spirits that he made me gay, too. I couldn't forget how I'd seen him a short while since; but I laid the thought by, an' didn't let it trouble me. I went up to his place. It was clean an' tidy as ever, an' the breakfast was ready. He made me eat some, an' when I was done, he brushed me up an' tidied me, an' says he:

"Go in an' win, old lad. God bless ye!" I went away toward Mary's house; but before I lost sight of Bill, I turned, an' he waved his hand to me with a kind smile an' went in an' shut the door.

I went on toward Mary's; but the farther I went the slower I got. An' when I got to the garden gate I stopped altogether. I stayed moonin' about there for a while, till at last Mary sees me an' comes out. I don't know how to tell you what took place then. I ain't more bashfuller than a man of my years ought to be, but somehow it comes rough on a man to tell this kind of ting. Oh, no; it ain't that I don't remember it all; for I do, well. But, ye see - ye won't laugh at me? I know'd ye wouldn't; I ax yer pardon. Well, to prove it to ye, I'll say what I never said yet to mortal, except Mary - an' that only once.

Mary comes out to me, runnin' like a little girl, with her face all dimplin' over with pleasure, an' she says:

"Why, Joe, what brings you here at this hour? Come in, Joe! Mother, here's Joe! Have you had your breakfast, Joe? Come in!"

I felt that I would never have courage to speak out before her mother if I went into the cottage, so I stayed beside the gate an' let her talk on. As I looked at her then, I could hardly believe what I was come for; it seemed like doin' something wrong to try to change her from what she was. She looked so lovely an' so bright that it seemed a pity ever to wish her to be aught else - even my own wife. An', beside, the thought came an' hit me hard, that mayhap she wouldn't have me, after all. I tried to think on that; but, Lor' bless ye, I couldn't. It seemed somethin' so terrible that I couldn't think it. However, I stood still, sayin' nothin', till she began to notice. I wasn't used to be sheepish before Mary or any one else; so when she had done her talkin' she looked at me sudden, an' then her eyes fell, an', after a moment, she blushed up to the roots of her hair an' says:

"Joe, what's the matter with you? You don't look as usual."

I blurted out all in a moment:

"No, Mary; nor I ain't the same as usual, for I'm in trouble."

She came close to me before I could say any more - she wasn't lookin' down or blushin' then - an' she says:

"Oh, Joe, I'm sorry for that." An' she put her arm on my shoulder. Then she went on, in a kind o' tender voice:

"Did you tell Bill?"

"Yes," I says.

"And what did he say?"

"He told me to come to you!"

"To me, Joe?" she says, an' looked puzzled.

"Yes," I says, in despair like. "I'm in trouble, Mary, for I want you to marry me."

"Oh, Joe!" she says, an' drew away a little. Then she says to me, with a queer look on her face:

"Joe, run an' tell Bill I want to see him - to come as soon as he can."

Well, them words went through me like so many knives, an' if ever I could have hated Bill, it would have been then. What could she want Bill for, I thinks to myself, but to find out if he loves her, too - an' to have him? I thinks how mad a woman would be to have me when she could get a man like Bill. I was afraid to say anything, so I set off smart for him, for I feared I wouldn't be able to tell him if I didn't go at once. I tried not to think while I was goin' down the road; but I couldn't get her words out of my head. They seemed to keep time with my feet, an' I heard them over an' over again:

"Tell - Bill - I - want - to - see - him! Tell - Bill - I - want - to - see - him!"

At last I got to the house, an' found Bill inside, mendin' a net that hung agin' the wall. He turned round quickly when I came in, an' his heart began to beat so hard that I could see it thumpin' inside his guernsey. He saw I wasn't lookin' pleased, so he came near an' put his two hands on my shoulders an' looked me in the face.

"What cheer, Joe?" he says, an' I could see that he was tryin' to control himself. When I told him the message, he began tremblin' all over, an' got as white as a sheet. Then he says to me in a thick kind o' voice:

"Joe, how did she look when she said it?"

I tried to tell him, an' asked him to hurry on.

"In a minute," says he, an' went into the other room.

When he came back I turned round, expectin' to see him got up a bit; but there he was just as he went in, in his old workin' clothes. But he was quiet lookin', an' had a smile on his face.

"Bill, old lad," I says, "aren't ye goin' to tidy up a bit? Mayhap Mary'd like to see ye neat."

"No," he says; "I'll go as I am. If it be as it may be, she won't like me none the worse for comin' quick; an' if it don't be - Come on, Joe, an' don't keep her waitin'.'"

Well, we walked up the road without sayin' a word. When we came in sight of Mary's cottage it seemed darker to me than it had been.

Mary came out of the gate to meet us, an' when she spoke to Bill I dropped behind. They two went into the arbor that we had built for her. They sat talkin' for a few minutes - I could see them through the hedge - an' at last I saw Bill bend down his head an' kiss her. She put her arms round his neck an' kissed him. An' at that the whole of the light seemed to go out of the sky, an' I wished I was dead.

I would have gone away, but I could hardly stir. I leaned up against the hedge, an' didn't mind any more till I heard Bill's voice callin' me. I came in at the gate, puttin' on as good a face as I could, an' came into the arbor.

Bill an' Mary was standin' up, an' Bill's face looked beamin', while Mary's was red as a rose.

Bill beckoned me over, an' when I came near, he says:

"Well, Mary, shall I tell him now?"

"Yes, Bill," she says, in a kind of a whisper; so he says to me:

"Joe, I give her to you! She wouldn't let none do it but me; for she says she loves me like as a brother. Take her, Joe, an' love her well, an' God bless ye both!"

He put her in my arms, an' she clung to me.

I was bewildered, an' could hardly see; but when I came to look about there was Mary in my arms, with her face buried in my breast, an' her arms round my neck.

Bill was makin' down the road, upright an' steady as ever. Even then, for a moment, I couldn't think of Mary, for my thoughts went back to when I saw Bill kneelin' beside his bed, with his arms stretched out, an' I felt - if you'll believe me - more sorrow than joy. I know now that Bill had wrestled with the devil that night, an' threw him, if ever a man did. Poor Bill! Poor Bill!

I suppose I needn't tell you what Mary an' me said? It wouldn't sound much, at any rate, altho' it pleased us. When I felt that she loved me I forgot even Bill, an' we was happier than tongue could tell.

Well, the time went on for a month or two, an' we was thinkin' of gettin' married soon. I was gettin' my cottage ready an' spendin' some of the money I had saved to make it bright for Mary. Bill worked with me early an' late, but it wasn't only his time that he gave to me. He would often go into the town to buy the things I wanted, an' I'm sure he never got them for what he told me. I said nothin', for I knew that it would only hurt him, an' it was little enough that I could do for Bill to let him help if he chose. I used to watch him to see if he wasn't unhappy, but I never seed a sign of sorrow on him. He always looked happy an' bright, an' he worked harder than ever, an' was kinder to all around him. I knew he didn't forget - for how could he forget Mary? - an' I feared at times lest he might fret in secret. But I never seed him grieve. I could hardly imagine, when I would think on it, how Mary came to take me or love me when Bill was nigh her.

Well, the time wasn't long goin' by, for we was happy, an' had all our lives before us, an', at length, the day came round before we was to be married. It was Easter Sunday we was to be married on, an' all the people as knew Mary an' me - an' that was all the village - was goin' to have a grand holiday. We was to go an' have a feast out on the island, an' we was gettin' the boats cleaned an' nice an' smart for the occasion. In coorse, everybody had to bring their own dinners; but we was to join them all together an' make a grand feast. We had got a cask o' beer, an' we was to have great doin's an' a dance on the grass. There's the finest sod for dancin' in the countryside out yonder on the island, an' we'd got Mike Wheeler to bring his fiddle, with an extra set of strings. We weren't to come home till evenin' when the tide turned, an' then we would have a race home.

Well, Bill an' me, we both took tea at Mary's house that evenin', an' when we came home Bill asked me to go into his house for awhile an' have a quiet talk. We lit our pipes, drew up our chairs, an' sat down by the fire an' puffed away, without sayin' a word for some time, an' then Bill says to me:

"Well, Joe, there won't be a man in the church to-morrow that won't envy you - except myself."

I thought of him kneelin' down by the bedside that mornin' when he says that, so I thought to tell him. I put down my pipe an' came an' put my arms on his shoulder, as I used to do when we was boys together, an' told him all I knew. He just shook hands with me, an' says he:

"Joe, it was a hard fight, but, thank God, I won. I've crushed out all the old love now. Why, lad, to-morrow she'll be your wife, an' I'll care for her no more than any other woman - as a sweetheart, I mean, for I'm a brother to her now as long as we live - an' to you, Joe. It ain't that I think less of her, for I'd walk into the fire for her this minute, but - I can't explain it, Joe. You know what I mean."

"Bill," I says, "you've been a true friend to me an' Mary, an' I hope we'll always be able to show how much we both love you. May God judge me hard when I die if ever I have a hard thought of you as long as I live!"

We said no more after that. I went out, but came back in a minute to tell Bill to be sure to come an' wake me if he was up first; but when I was passin' the window I see him hangin' a coat up over it. It wasn't that he thought I'd spy on him again that he did that. I saw that in his face; but he feared I might see him again somehow, and that it might pain me.

Well, I woke in the mornin' as soon as it was daylight, an' went down an' had a swim, an' then came home an' brushed my new clothes an' laid out the shirt that Mary had worked for me herself, an' washed as white as snow. Then Bill came down to me. He was to take his breakfast with me that mornin', an' he came all dressed for the weddin' in a new suit of clothes. He was a real handsome, fine fellow at any time, but he looked like a gentleman that mornin'. Then I thought that Mary must have done right to choose a laborin' man like me rather than a chap like Bill, that was above all of us, except in his heart.

We went off to the church an' waited till Mary an' her mother came. All the people was there outside the porch, an' some of the gentlefolks was inside. The squire's family was in their pew, for, ye see, Mary was a favorite with them all, an' they came early to church to see her married. I felt very solemn then, but I could hardly feel as how Mary was goin' to marry me. There she was, as lovely as an angel, an' blushin' like a rose. I said my "I will" in a low voice, for it seemed awkward to me to say it loud; but Mary said hers out in a clear, sweet voice, an' then the parson blessed us, an' spoke to us so solemn that we both cried, an' Mary nestled up close to me. When it came to kiss the bride, Bill was first, an' claimed the kiss, so the other lads had to give up. Bill bent down an' took her pretty face between his two hands an' kissed her on the forehead.

Agin the weddin' was over, it was time for service, so we all went to our seats – an' I never felt solemner in my life than I did then; nor did Mary, either.

When the service was over we all came out; an' the people stood by on both sides to let Mary an' me walk down the churchyard together an' go first out of the gate.

We all went down to the beach, where the boats was ready on the shore. Some of them was freshly painted, an' a couple had bright ribbons tied about them. Bill's boat was the one that Mary an' me was to go in, an' Bill himself was to pull stroke oar in her. He had got for a crew three of the young fellows we knew best, an' who was the cracks at rowin', an' we was determined to race all the other boats to the island. The lads had all run on before us, an' when we came down to the beach the boats was all ready, an' the baskets with the dinner put in them, so we all got on board, an' off we started.

Mary an' me, we held the rudder together, an' Bill an' his lads bent to their oars, an' away we flew, an' in a quarter of an hour came to the island, leading the others by a hundred yards. We all got out, an' the lads carried up the baskets to the slope up yonder, where you see the moonlight shine on the island, where there was a fine, level place on the edge of the cliff.

The grass there was short an' as smooth as a table; an' when you stood on the edge of the cliff the water was straight below you, for the rock went sheer some forty feet. Mary an' me stood there on the edge while the lads an' the girls got ready the feast, for they wouldn't let us put hand to anything; an' we looked at the water hurryin' by under us. The tide had turned, an' the water was runnin' like a mill race down away past the island, an' runnin' straight away for the head off there as far as you can see. The currents is very contrary here, so you'd better not get caught in them when you're sailin' or swimmin'.

We all sat down, an' if we didn't enjoy our dinner, all of us, it was a queer thing; an' after dinner was over the girls insisted on havin' a dance. We got the things all cleared off an' danced away for some time, an' then some one proposed blind man's buff. One young fellow was blinded, an' we all stood round; an' then the fun began. The young chap – Mark Somers by name – used to make wild rushes to try an' get some one, an' then the girls yelled out, an' they all scurried away as quick as they could, an' the fun grew greater an' greater. At last he made a dive over to the place where Mary was standin' near the brink of the cliff. We all yelled to her to take care where she was goin'; but I suppose she thought it was merely our fun, for she laughed an' screamed out like the others – an' stepped backward. Before any one could stop her, she went over the edge of the cliff an' disappeared. I was sittin' up on a rock, an' when I saw her fall over the edge I gave a cry that you might have heard a mile away an' jumped down an' ran across the grass.

But a better man than me was there before me. Bill had pulled off his jacket an' kicked off his shoes, an' was at the edge before me. Before he jumped, he cried out:

"Joe, run for the boats, quick! I'll keep her up till you come. I can swim stronger nor you."

I didn't wait a second, but ran down to where the boats was drawn up on the beach. Some of the chaps came with me as hard as they could run, an' we shoved down the nearest boat. But in spite of all our efforts – an' we was so mad with excitement that not one of us but had the strength of ten – it took us a couple of minutes to get out fair on the water.

Well, when we was fair started I pulled so hard that I broke my oar, an' we had to stop to get another; an' then we had to row all the way round the spur of the rocks out there before we could even see whereabout Mary an' Bill should be. The men an' women on the rocks screamed out to us an' pointed in their direction, an' the boat flew along at every stroke. But the current was mortal strong, an' they had been for nigh five minutes in the water before we caught sight of them. An' it seemed to me to be years before we came anigh them at all. Mary was weighed down with her clothes, an' Bill with his; an', in spite of what a swimmer I knew Bill was, I feared lest we should come too late.

At last we began to close on them. I could see over my shoulder as we rowed. I could only see Mary's face, but that was beacon enough for me. I called to one of the men to slip into my place an' row, an' he did, an' I got out into the bows. There was Mary with her face all white an' her eyes closed, as if she was dead; her hair was all draggin' in the water, an' as the current rolled her along, her dress moved as if it was some strange fish under the water. I could see nothin' of Bill; but I hadn't need to think, for I knew that where Mary was there was Bill somewhere anigh to her. When we came nearer I saw where Bill was.

Look here, he was down under the water, an' with his last breath he was keepin' her afloat till we came. I saw his two hands rise up out of the water, holdin' her up by the hair; but that was all. Many's the time since then that, in spite of all I loved Mary, I was tempted to be cross with her – for we laborin' men is only rough folk, after all, an' we have a deal o' hardship to bear at times. But whenever I was tempted to say a hard word, or even to think hard of her, them two hands of Bill's seemed to rise up between me an' her, and I could no more think or say a hard word than I could stand quiet an' see another man strike her. An' I wouldn't be like for to do that!

Well, we took them into the boat an' came home. Mary recovered, for she had only had the shock of her fall; but when we took in Bill, it was only –

He kept his word that he spoke to me that night; he gave up his life for hers! You'll see that on his tomb in the churchyard that we all put up to him:

"Greater Love Hath No Man Than This: That a Man Shall Give Up His Life For His Friend."

There's no more left like Bill. An' Mary thinks it, too, as well as me.

Lord Castleton Explains

Lord Francis Onslow lifted his cap. The action was an instinctive one, for he was face to face with a lady; but he was half dazed with the unexpected meeting, and could not collect his thoughts. He only remembered that when he had last seen his wife she was opening the door of her chamber to De Murger. For weeks he had been schooling himself for such a meeting, for he knew that on his return such might at any time occur; but now, when the moment had come, and unexpectedly, the old pain of his shame overwhelmed him anew. His face grew white-white till it seemed to Fenella that it was of the pallor of death. She knew that she had been so far guilty of what had happened that the murder had been the outcome of her previous acts. She knew also that her husband was ignorant of his part in the deed-and her horror of the man, blood-guilty in such a way, was fined down by the sense of her own partial guilt. The trial, with all its consequent pain to a proud and sensitive woman, had softened her, and she grasped at any hope. The sight of Frank, his gaunt cheeks, which told their tale of suffering, and now the deadly pallor, awoke all the protective feeling which is a part of a woman's love. It was with her whole soul in her voice that she said again:

"Frank!" His voice was stern as well as sad as he answered her:

"What is it?" Her heart went cold, but she persevered.

"Frank, I must have a word with you-I must. For God's sake, for Ronny's sake, do not deny me." She did not know that as yet Frank Onslow was in ignorance of De Murger's death; and when his answer came it seemed more hard than even he intended:

"Do you wish to speak of that night?" In a faint voice she answered:

"I do." Then looking in his eyes and seeing the hard look becoming harder still-for a man is seldom generous with a woman where his honour is concerned, she added:

"O Heaven! Frank! You do not think me guilty! No, no, not you! not you! That would be too cruel!"

Frank Onslow paused and said:

"Fenella, God help me! but I do," and he turned away his head. His wife, of course, thought that he alluded to the murder, and not to her sin against him as he saw it, and with a low moan she turned away and hid her face in her hands. Then with an effort she drew herself up, and without a word or a single movement to show that she even recognized his presence, she passed on up the street.

Frank Onslow stood for a few moments watching her retreating figure, and then went across the street and turned the next corner on his way to the post-office, for which he had been inquiring when he met his wife. At the door he was stopped by a cheery voice and an out-stretched hand:

"Onslow!"

"Castleton! The two men shook hands warmly.

"I see you did not get my telegram," said Lord Castleton. "It is waiting for you at the post-office."

"What telegram?"

"To tell you that I was on my way here from London. I went in your interest, old fellow. I thought you would like full particulars-the newspapers are so vague."

"What papers? My interest? Tell me all. I am ignorant of all that has passed for the last six weeks." A vague, shadowy fear began to creep over his spirits. Castleton's voice was full of sympathy as he answered:

"Then you have not heard of-but stay. It is a long story. Come back to the yacht. I was just going to join you there. We shall be all alone, and I can tell you all. I have the newspapers here for you." He motioned to a roll under his arm.

The two went down to the harbour, and finding the sailor waiting with the boat at the steps, were rowed to the yacht and got on board. Here the two men were all alone. Then, with a preliminary clearing of his voice, Castleton began his story:

"Frank Onslow-better get the worst over at once-just after you went away from Harrogate your wife was tried for murder and acquitted."

"My God! Fenella tried for murder? Whose murder?"

"That scoundrel De Murger. It seems he went into her room in the night and attempted violence, so she stabbed him-"

Castleton stopped in amazement, for a look of radiance came over Frank Onslow's face, as he murmured "Thank God!" Recalled to himself by Castleton's silence, for he was too amazed to go on, Frank said. "I have a reason, old fellow; I shall tell it to you later, but go on. Tell me all the facts, or let me read the papers. Remember I am as yet quite ignorant of it all and I am full of anxiety!"

Without a word Castleton handed him the papers, and, lighting a fresh cigar, sat down with his back to him, and presently yielded to the sun and fresh air and fell into a doze.

Frank Onslow took the papers, and read carefully from end to end the account of the trial of his wife for the murder of De Murger. When he had finished he sat with the folded paper in his hand, and his eyes had the same far-away look in them which they had had on that fatal night. The hypnotic trance was on him again.

Presently he rose, and with stealthy steps approached his sleeping friend. Murmuring "Why did I not kill him?" he struck with the folded paper, as though with a dagger, the form before him. Castleton, who had sunk into a pleasant sleep and whose fat face was wreathed with a smile, was annoyed at the rude awakening. "What the devil!" he began angrily, and then stopped as his eyes met the face of his friend and he realized that he was in some sort of trance. He grew very pale as he saw Frank Onslow stab, and stab, and stab again. There was a certain grotesqueness in the affair-the man in such terrible earnest, in his mind committing murder, while his real weapon was but a folded paper. As he stabbed he hissed, "Why did I not kill him? Why did I not kill him?" Then he went through a series of movements as though he were softly pulling an imaginary door shut behind him, and so back to his own chair, where he sat down hiding his face in his hands.

Castleton sat looking at him in amazement, and then murmured to himself:

"They thought it was someone stronger than Fenella whose grasp made those marks on the dead man's throat." He suddenly looked round to see that no one but himself had observed what had happened, and then, being satisfied on this point, murmured again:

"A noble woman, by Jove! A noble woman!" He called out:

"Frank-Frank Onslow! Wake up, man." Onslow raised his head as a man does when suddenly awakened, and smiled as he said:

"What is it, old man? Have I been asleep?" It was quite evident that he had no recollection of what had just passed. Castleton came and sat down beside him, and his kindly face was grave as he asked:

"You have read the papers?"

"I have."

"Now tell me-you offered to do so-why you said 'Thank God!' when I told you that your wife had killed De Murger?"

Frank Onslow paused. Although the memory of what he had thought to be his shame had been with him daily and nightly until he had become familiarized with it, it was another thing to speak of it, even to such a friend as Castleton. Even now, when it was apparent from the issue of the trial that his wife had avenged so dreadfully the attempt upon her honour, he felt it hard to speak on the subject. Castleton saw the doubt and struggle in his mind which was reflected in his face, and said earnestly, as he laid his hand upon his shoulder:

"Do not hesitate to tell me, Frank. I do not ask out of mere curiosity. I am perhaps a better friend than you think in helping to clear up a certain doubt which I see before me. I think you know I am a friend."

"One of the best a man ever had!" said Frank impulsively, as he took the other's hand. Then turning away his head, he said slowly:

"You were surprised because I was glad Fenella killed that scoundrel. I can tell you, Castleton, but I would not tell anyone else. It was because I saw him enter her room, and, God forgive me! I thought at the time that it was by her wish. That is why I came away from Harrogate that night. That is what kept me away. How could I go back and face my friends with such a shame fresh upon me? It was your lending me your yacht, old man, that made life possible. When I was by myself through the wildness of the Bay of Biscay and among the great billows of the Atlantic I began to be able to bear. I had steeled myself, I thought, and when I heard that so far from my wife being guilty of such a shame, she actually killed the man that attempted her honour, is it any wonder that I felt joyful?"

After a pause Castleton asked:

"How did you come to see-to see it. Why did you take no step to prevent it? Forgive me, old fellow, but I want to understand."

Frank Onslow went to the rail, and leaned over. When he came back Castleton saw that his eyes were wet. With what cheerfulness he could assume, he answered:

"On that very night I had made up my mind to try to win back my wife's love. I wrote a letter to her, a letter in which I poured out my whole soul, and I left my room to put it under her door, so that she would get it in the morning. But"-here he paused, and then said, slowly, "but when in the corridor, I saw her door open, and at the same moment De Murger appeared."

"Did she seem surprised?"

"Not at first. But a moment after a look of amazement crossed her face, and she stepped back into the room, he following her." As he said this he put his head between his hands and groaned.

"And then?" added his friend.

"And then I hardly know what happened. My mind seems full of a dim memory of a blank existence, and then a series of wild whirling thoughts, something like that last moment after death in Wiertz's picture. I think I must have slept, for it was two o'clock when I saw Fenella, and the clock was striking five when I crossed the bridge after I had left the hotel.

"And the letter? What became of it?"

Frank started. "The letter? I never thought of it. Stay! I must have left it on the table in my room. I remember seeing it there a little while before I came away."

"How was it addressed? Do not think me inquisitive, but I cannot help thinking that that letter may yet be of some great importance."

Frank smiled, a sad smile enough, as he answered: "By the pet name I had for Fenella-Mrs Right. I used to chaff her because she always defended her position when we argued, and so, when I wanted to tease her, I called her Mrs Right."

"Was it written on hotel paper?"

"No. I was going to write on some, but I thought it would be better to use the sort we had when-when we were first married. There were a few sheets in my writing case, so I took one."

"That was headed somewhere in Surrey, was it not?"

"Yes; Chiddingford, near Haslemere. It was a pretty place, too, called The Grange. Fenella fell in love with it, and made me buy it right away."

"Is anyone living there now?"

"It is let to someone. I don't think that I heard the name. The agent knows. When the trouble came I told him to do what he could with it, and not to bother me with it any more. After a while he wrote and asked if I would mind it being let to a foreigner? I told him he might let it to a devil so long as he did not worry me."

Lord Castleton paused awhile, and asked the next question in a hesitating way. He felt embarrassed, and showed it:

"Tell me one thing more, old fellow-if-if you don't mind."

"My dear Castleton, I'll tell you anything you like."

"How did you sign the letter?" Onslow's face looked sad as he answered:

"I signed it by another old pet name we both understood. We had pet names-people always have when they are first married," he added with embarrassment.

"Of course," murmured the sympathetic Castleton.

"One such name lasted a long time. An old friend of my father's came to see us, and in a playful moment he said I was a 'sad dog'. Fenella took it up and used to call me 'Doggie,' and I often signed myself 'Frank Doggie'-as men usually do."

"Of course," again murmured Castleton, as if such a signature was a customary thing. Then he added, "And on this occasion?"

"On this occasion I used the name that seemed full of happiest memories. 'Frank Doggie' may seem idiotic to an outsider, but to Fenella and myself it might mean much."

The two men sat silent awhile, and then Castleton asked softly:

"I suppose it may be taken for granted that Lady Francis never got the letter?"

"I take it, it is so; but it is no matter now, I refused to speak with her just before I met you. I did not know then what I know now-and she will never speak to me again." He sighed as he spoke, and turned away. Then he went to the rail of the yacht and leaned over with his head down, looking into the still blue water beneath him.

"Poor old Frank!" said Castleton to himself. "I can't but think that this matter may come right yet. I must find out what became of that letter, in case Lady Francis never got it. It would prove to her that Frank-"

His train of thought suddenly stopped. A new idea seemed to strike him so forcibly that it quite upset him. Onslow, who had come over from the rail, noticed it. "I say, Castleton, what is wrong with you? You have got quite white about the gills."

"Nothing-nothing," he answered hastily, "I am subject to it. They call it heart. Pardon me for a bit, I'll go to my bunk and lie down," and he went below.

In truth, he was overwhelmed by the thought which had just struck him. If his surmise were true, that Onslow, in a hypnotic trance, as he had almost proved by its recurrence, had killed De Murger, where, then, was Fenella's heroism after all? True that she had taken the blame on herself; but might it not have been that she was morally guilty all the same? Why, then, had she taken the blame? Was it not because she feared that her husband might have refused to screen her shame; or because she feared that if any less heroic aspect of the tragedy was presented to the public, her own fair fame might suffer in greater degree? Could it indeed be that Fenella Onslow was not a heroine, but only a calculating woman of exceeding smartness? Then, again, if Frank Onslow believed that his wife had avenged her honour, was it wise to disturb such belief? He might think, if once the suggestion were made to him, that his honour was preserved only by his own unconscious act.

Was it then wise to disturb existing relations between the husband and wife, sad though they were? Did they come together again, they might in mutual confidence arrive at a real knowledge of the facts, and then-and then, what would be the result? And besides, might there not be some danger in any suggestion made as to his suspicion of who struck the blow? It was true that Lady Francis had been acquitted of the crime, although she confessed to the killing; but her husband might still be tried-and if tried? What then would be the result of the discovery of the missing letter on which he had been building such hopes?

The problem was too much for Lord Castleton. His life had been too sunny and easy-going to allow of familiarity with great emotions, and such a problem as this was to him overwhelming. The issue was too big for him; and revolving in his own mind all that belonged to it, he glided into sleep.

The Seer

CHAPTER I
Second Sight

I HAD just arrived at Cruden Bay on my annual visit, and after a late breakfast was sitting on the low wall which was a continuation of the escarpment of the bridge over the Water of Cruden. Opposite to me, across the road and standing under the only little clump of trees in the place was a tall, gaunt old woman, who kept looking at me intently. As I sat, a little group, consisting of a man and two women, went by. I found my eyes follow them, for it seemed to me after they had passed me that the two women walked together and the man alone in front carrying on his shoulder a little black box —a coffin. I shuddered as I thought, but a moment later I saw all three abreast just as they had been. The old woman was now looking at me with eyes that blazed. She came across the road and said to me without preface:

"What saw ye then, that yer e'en looked so awed?" I did not like to tell her so I did not answer. Her great eyes were fixed keenly upon me, seeming to look me through and through. I felt that I grew quite red, whereupon she said, apparently to herself: "I thocht so! Even I did not see that which he saw."

"How do you mean?" I queried. She answered ambiguously:

"Wait! Ye shall perhaps know before this hour to-morrow!"

Her answer interested me and I tried to get her to say more; but she would not. She moved away with a grand stately movement that seemed to become her great gaunt form.

After dinner whilst I was sitting in front of the hotel, there was a great commotion in the village; much running to and fro of men and women with sad mien. On questioning them I found that a child had been drowned in the little harbour below. Just then a woman and a man, the same that had passed the bridge earlier in the day, ran by with wild looks. One of the bystanders looked after them pityingly as he said:

"Puir souls. It's a sad home-comin' for them the nicht."

"Who are they?" I asked. The man took off his cap reverently as he answered:

"The father and mother of the child that was drowned!" As he spoke I looked round as though some one had called me.

There stood the gaunt woman with a look of triumph on her face.

* * * * * *

The curved shore of Cruden Bay, Aberdeenshire, is backed by a waste of sandhills in whose hollows seagrass and moss and wild violets, together with the pretty "grass of Parnassus" form a green carpet. The surface of the hills is held together by bent-grass and is eternally shifting as the wind takes the fine sand and drifts it to and fro. All behind is green, from the meadows that mark the southern edge of the bay to the swelling uplands that stretch away and away far in the distance, till the blue mist of the mountains at Braemar sets a kind of barrier. In the centre of the bay the highest point of the land that runs downward to the sea looks like a miniature hill known as the Hawklaw; from this point onward to the extreme south, the land runs high with a gentle trend downwards.

Cruden sands are wide and firm and the sea runs out a considerable distance. When there is a storm with the wind on shore the whole bay is a mass of leaping waves and broken water that threatens every instant to annihilate the stake-nets which stretch out here and there along the shore. More than a few vessels have been lost on these wide stretching sands, and it was perhaps the roaring of the shallow seas and the terror which they inspired which sent the crews to the spirit room and the bodies of those of them which came to shore later on, to the churchyard on the hill.

If Cruden Bay is to be taken figuratively as a mouth, with the sand hills for soft palate, and the green Hawklaw as the tongue, the rocks which work the extremities are its teeth. To the north the rocks of red granite rise jagged and broken. To the south, a mile and a half away as the crow flies, Nature seems to have manifested its wildest forces. It is here, where the little promontory called Whinnyfold juts out, that the two great geological features of the Aberdeen coast meet. The red sienite of the north joins the black gneiss of the south. That union must have been originally a wild one; there are evidences of an upheaval which must have shaken the earth to its centre. Here and there are great masses of either species of rock hurled upwards in every conceivable variety of form, sometimes fused or pressed together so that it is impossible to say exactly where gneiss ends or sienite begins; but broadly speaking here is an irregular line of separation. This line runs seawards to the east and its strength is shown in its outcrop. For half a mile or more the rocks rise through the sea singly or in broken masses ending in a dangerous cluster known as "The Skares" and which has had for centuries its full toll of wreck and disaster. Did the sea hold its dead where they fell, its floor around the Skares would be whitened with their bones, and new islands could build themselves with the piling wreckage. At times one may see here the ocean in her fiercest mood; for it is when the tempest drives from the southeast that the sea is fretted amongst the rugged rocks and sends its spume landwards. The rocks that at calmer times rise dark from the briny deep are lost to sight for moments in the grand onrush of the waves. The seagulls which usually whiten them, now flutter around screaming, and the sound of their shrieks comes in on the gale almost in a continuous note, for the single cries are merged in the multitudinous roar of sea and air.

The village, squatted beside the emboucher of the Water of Cruden at the northern side of the bay is simple enough; a few rows of fishermen's cottages, two or three great red-tiled drying-sheds nestled in the sand-heap behind the fishers' houses. For the rest of the place as it was when first I saw it, a little lookout beside a tall flagstaff on the northern cliff, a few scattered farms over the inland prospect, one little hotel down on the western bank of the Water of Cruden with a fringe of willows protecting its sunk garden which was always lull of fruits and flowers.

From the most southern part of the beach of Cruden Bay to Whinnyfold village the distance is but a few hundred yards; first a steep pull up the face of the rock; and then an even way, beside part of which runs a tiny stream. To the left of this path, going towards Whinnyfold, the ground rises in a bold slope and then falls again all round, forming a sort of wide miniature hill of some eighteen or twenty acres. Of this the southern side is sheer, the black rock dipping into the waters of the little bay of Whinnyfold, in the centre of which is a picturesque island of rock shelving steeply from the water on the northern side, as is the tendency of all the gneiss and granite in this part. But to east and north there are irregular bays or openings, so that the furthest points of the promontory stretch out like fingers. At the tips of these are reefs of sunken rock falling down to deep water and whose existence can only be suspected in bad weather when the rush of the current beneath sends up swirling eddies or curling masses of foam. These little bays are mostly curved and are green where falling earth or drifting sand have hidden the outmost side of the rocks and given a foothold to the seagrass and clover. Here have been at some time or other great caves, now either fallen in or silted up with sand, or obliterated with the earth brought down in the rush of surface-water in times of long rain. In one of these bays, Broad Haven, facing right out to the Skares, stands an isolated pillar of rock called locally the "Puir mon" through whose base, time and weather have worn a hole through which one may walk dryshod.

Through the masses of rocks that run down to the sea from the sides and shores of all these bays are here and there natural channels with straight edges as though cut on purpose for the taking in of the cobbles belonging to the fisher folk of Whinnyfold.

When first I saw the place I fell in love with it. Had it been possible I should have spent my summer there, in a house of my own, but the want of any place in which to live forbade such an opportunity. So I stayed in the little hotel, the Kilmarnock Arms.

The next year I came again, and the next, and the next. And then I arranged to take a feu at Whinnyfold and to build a house overlooking the Skares for myself. The details of this kept me constantly going to Whinnyfold, and my house to be was always in my thoughts.

Hitherto my life had been an uneventful one. At school I was, though secretly ambitious, dull as to results. At College I was better off, for my big body and athletic powers gave me a certain position in which I had to overcome my natural shyness. When I was about eight and twenty I found myself nominally a barrister, with no knowledge whatever of the practice of law and but little less of the theory, and with a commission in the Devil's Own-the irreverent name given to the Inns of Court Volunteers. I had few relatives, but a comfortable, though not great, fortune; and I had been round the world, dilettante fashion.

CHAPTER II
Gormala

ALL that night I thought of the dead child and of the peculiar vision which had come to me. Sleeping or waking it was all the same; my mind could not leave the parents in procession as seen in imagination, or their distracted mien in reality. Mingled with them was the great-eyed, aquiline-featured, gaunt old woman who had taken such an interest in the affair, and in my part of it. I asked the landlord if he knew her, since, from his position as postmaster he knew almost everyone for miles around. He told me that she was a stranger to the place. Then he added:

"I can't imagine what brings her here. She has come over from Peterhead two or three times lately; but she doesn't seem to have anything at all to do. She has nothing to sell and she buys nothing. She's not a tripper, and she's not a beggar, and she's not a thief, and she's not a worker of any sort. She's a queer-looking lot anyhow. I fancy from her speech that she's from the west; probably from some of the far-out islands. I can tell that she has the Gaelic from the way she speaks."

Later on in the day, when I was walking on the shore near the Hawklaw, she came up to speak to me. The shore was quite lonely, for in those days it was rare to see anyone on the beach except when the salmon fishers drew their nets at the ebbing tide. I was walking towards Whinnyfold when she came upon me silently from behind. She must have been hidden among the bent-grass of the sandhills for had she been anywhere in view I must have seen her on that desolate shore. She was evidently a most imperious person; she at once addressed me in a tone and manner which made me feel as though I were in some way an inferior, and in somehow to blame:

"What for did ye no tell me what ye saw yesterday?" Instinctively I answered:

"I don't know why. Perhaps because it seemed so ridiculous." Her stern features hardened into scorn as she replied:

"Are Death and the Doom then so redeekulous that they pleasure ye intil silence?" I somehow felt that this was a little too much and was about to make a sharp answer, when suddenly it struck me as a remarkable thing that she knew already. Filled with surprise I straightway asked her:

"Why, how on earth do you know? I told no one." I stopped for I felt all at sea; there was some mystery here which I could not fathom. She seemed to read my mind like an open book, for she went on looking at me as she spoke, searchingly and with an odd smile.

"Eh! laddie, do ye no ken that ye hae een that can see? Do ye no understand that ye hae een that can speak? Is it that one with the Gift o' Second Sight has no an understandin' o' it. Why, yer face when ye saw the mark o' the Doom, was like a printed book to een like mine." "Do you mean to tell me" I asked "that you could tell what I saw, simply by looking at my face?"

"Na! na! laddie. Not all that, though a Seer am I; but I knew that you had seen the Doom! It's no that varied that there need be any mistake. After all Death is only one, in whatever way we may speak!" After a pause of thought I asked her:

"If you have the power of Second Sight why did you not see the vision, or whatever it was, yourself?"

"Eh! laddie" she answered, shaking her head "'Tis little ye ken o' the wark o' the Fates! Learn ye then that the Voice speaks only as it listeth into chosen ears, and the Vision comes only to chosen een. None can will to hear or to see, to pleasure themselves."

"Then" I said, and I felt that there was a measure of triumph in my tone "if to none but the chosen is given to know, how comes it that you, who seem not to have been chosen on this occasion at all events, know all the same?" She answered with a touch of impatience:

"Do ye ken, young sir, that even mortal een have power to see much, if there be behind them the thocht, an' the knowledge and the experience to guide them aright. How, think ye, is it that some can see much, and learn much as they gang; while others go blind as the mowdiwart, at the end o' the journey as before it?"

"Then perhaps you will tell me how much you saw, and how you saw it?"

"Ah! to them that have seen the Doom there needs but sma' guidance to their thochts. Too lang, an' too often hae I mysen seen the death-sark an' the watch-candle an' the dead-hole, not to know when they are seen tae ither een. Na, na! laddie, what I kent o' yer seein' was no by the Gift but only by the use o' my proper een. I kent not the muckle o' what ye saw. Not whether it was ane or ither o' the garnishins o' the dead; but weel I kent that it was o' death."

"Then," I said interrogatively "Second Sight is altogether a matter of chance?"

"Chance! chance!" she repeated with scorn. "Na! young sir; when the Voice has spoken there is no more chance than that the nicht will follow the day."

"You mistake me," I said, feeling somewhat superior now that I had caught her in an error, "I did not for a moment mean that the Doom-whatever it is-is not a true forerunner. What I meant was that it seems to be a matter of chance in whose ear the Voice-whatever it is-speaks; when once it has been ordained that it is to sound in the ear of some one." Again she answered with scorn:

"Na, na! there is no chance o' ocht aboot the Doom. Them that send forth the Voice and the Seein' know well to whom it is sent and why. Can ye no comprehend that it is for no bairn-play that such goes forth. When the Voice speaks, it is mainly followed by tears an' woe an' lamentation! Nae! nor is it only one bit manifestation that stands by its lanes, remote and isolate from all ither. Truly 'tis but a pairt o' the great scheme o' things; an' be sure that whoso is chosen to see or to hear is chosen weel, an' must hae their pairt in what is to be, on to the verra end"

"Am I to take it" I asked, "that Second Sight is but a little bit of some great purpose which has to be wrought out by means of many kinds; and that whoso sees the Vision or hears the Voice is but the blind unconscious instrument of Fate?"

"Aye! laddie. Weel eneuch the Fates know their wishes an' their wark, no to need the help or the thocht of any human-blind or seein', sane or silly, conscious or unconscious."

All through her speaking I had been struck by the old woman's use of the word 'Fate,' and more especially when she used it in the plural. It was evident that, Christian though she might be-and in the West they are generally devout observants of the duties of their creed-her belief in this respect came from some of the old pagan mythologies. I should have liked to question her on this point; but I feared to shut her lips against me. Instead I asked her:

"Tell me, will you, if you don't mind, of some case you have known yourself of Second Sight?"

"'Tis no for them to brag or boast to whom has been given to see the wark o' the hand o' Fate. But sine ye are yerself a Seer an' would learn, then I may speak. I hae seen the sea ruffle wi'oot cause in the verra spot where later a boat was to gang doon, I hae heard on a lone moor the hammerin' o' the coffin-wright when one passed me who was soon to dee. I hae seen the death-sark fold round the speerit o' a drowned one, in baith ma sleepin' an' ma wakin' dreams. I hae heard the settin' doom o' the Spaiks, an' I hae seen the Weepers on a' the crood that walked. Aye, an' in mony anither way hae I seen an' heard the Coming o' the Doom."

"But did all the seeings and hearings come true?" I asked. "Did it ever happen that you heard queer sounds or saw strange sights and that yet nothing came of them? I gather that you do not always know to whom something is going to happen; but only that death is coming to some one!" She was not displeased at my questioning but replied at once:

"Na doot! but there are times when what is seen or heard has no manifest following. But think ye, young sir, how mony a corp, still waited for, lies in the depths o' the sea; how mony lie oot on the hillsides, or are fallen in deep places where their bones whiten unkent. Nay! more, to how many has Death come in a way that men think the wark o' nature when his hastening has come frae the hand of man, untold." This was a difficult matter to answer so I changed or rather varied the subject.

"How long must elapse before the warning comes true?"

"Ye know yersel', for but yestreen ye hae seen, how the Death can follow hard upon the Doom; but there be times, nay mostly are they so, when days or weeks pass away ere the Doom is fulfilled."

"Is this so?" I asked "when you know the person regarding whom the Doom is spoken." She answered with an air of certainty which somehow carried conviction, secretly, with it.

"Even so! I know one who walks the airth now in all the pride o' his strength. But the Doom has been spoken of him. I saw him with these verra een lie prone on rocks, wi' the water rinnin' down from his hair. An' again I heard the minute bells as he went by me on a road where is no bell for a score o' miles. Aye, an' yet again I saw him in the kirk itsel' wi' corbies flyin' round him, an' mair gatherin' from afar!"

Here was indeed a case where Second Sight might be tested; so I asked her at once, though to do so I had to overcome a strange sort of repugnance:

"Could this be proved? Would it not be a splendid case to make known; so that if the death happened it would prove beyond all doubt the existence of such a thing as Second Sight." My suggestion was not well received. She answered with slow scorn:

"Beyon' all doot! Doot! Wha is there that doots the bein' o' the Doom? Learn ye too, young sir, that the Doom an' all thereby is no for traffickin' wi' them that only cares for curiosity and publeecity. The Voice and the Vision o' the Seer is no for fine madams and idle gentles to while away their time in play-toy make-believe!" I climbed down at once.

"Pardon me!" I said "I spoke without thinking. I should not have said so-to you at any rate." She accepted my apology with a sort of regal inclination; but the moment after she showed by her words she was after all but a woman!

"I will tell ye; that so in the full time ye may hae no doot yersel'. For ye are a Seer and as Them that has the power hae gien ye the Gift it is no for the like o' me to cumber the road o' their doin'. Know ye then, and remember weel, how it was told ye by Gormala MacNiel that Lauchlane Macleod o' the Outer Isles hae been Called; tho' as yet the Voice has no sounded in his ears but only in mine. But ye will see the time————"

She stopped suddenly as though some thought had struck her, and then went on impressively:

"When I saw him lie prone on the rocks there was ane that bent ower him that I kent not in the nicht wha it was, though the licht o' the moon was around him. We shall see! We shall see!"

Without a word more she turned and left me. She would not listen to my calling after her; but with long strides passed up the beach and was lost among the sandhills.

Midnight Tales

(A Widower's Grief)

The other story was of the funeral in Dublin of a young married woman. The undertaker, after the wont of his craft, was arranging the whole affair according to the completest local rules of mortuary etiquette. He bustled up to the widower saying:

"You, sir, will of course go in the carriage with the mother of the deceased."

"What! Me go in the carriage with me mother-in-law! Not likely!"

"Oh, sir, but I assure you it is necessary. The rule is an inviolable one, established by precedents beyond all cavil!" expostulated the horrified undertaker. But the widower was obdurate.

"I won't go. That's flat!"

"Oh, but my good sir. Remember the gravity of the occasion--the publicity--the--the--possibility--scandal." His voice faded into a gasp. The widower stuck to his resolution and so the undertaker laid the matter before some of his intimate friends who were waiting instructions. These surrounded the chief mourner and began to remonstrate with him:

"You really must, old chap; it is necessary."

"I'll not! Go with me mother-in-law! Rot!"

"But look here, old chap--"

"I'll not I tell ye--I'll go in any other carriage that ye wish; but not in that."

"Oh, of course, if ye won't, ye won't. But remember it beforehand that afterwards when it'll be thrown up against ye, that it'll be construed into an affront on the poor girl that's gone. Ye loved her Jack, we all know, an' ye wouldn't like that!"

This argument prevailed. He signed to the undertaker and began to pull on his black gloves. As he began to move towards the carriage he turned to his friends and said in a low voice:

"I'm doin' it because ye say I ought to, and for the poor girl that's gone. But ye'll spoil me day!"

The Shakespeare Mystery

"In a hotel 'out West' a lot of men in the barroom were discussing the Shakespeare and Bacon question. They got greatly excited and presently a lot of them had their guns out. Some one interfered and suggested that the matter should be left to arbitration. The arbitrator selected was an Irishman, who had all the time sat quiet smoking and not saying a word--which circumstance probably suggested his suitability for the office. When he had heard the arguments on both sides formally stated, he gave his decision:

" 'Well, Gintlemin, me decision is this: Thim plays was not wrote be Shakespeare! But they was wrote be a man iv the saame naame!' "

A Deal With the Devil

Another story was of a little boy, one of a large family. This little chap on one occasion asked to be allowed to go to bed at the children's tea time, a circumstance so unique as to puzzle the domestic authorities. The mother refused, but the child whimpered and persevered--and succeeded. The father was presently in his study at the back of the house looking out on the garden when he saw the child in his little night-shirt come secretly down the steps and steal to a corner of the garden behind some shrubs. He had a garden fork in his hand. After a lapse of some minutes he came out again and stole quietly upstairs. The father's curiosity was aroused, and he too went behind the shrubs to see what had happened. He found some freshly turned earth, and began to investigate. Some few inches down was a closed envelope which the child had buried. On opening it he found a lucifer match and a slip of paper on which was written in pencil in a sprawling hand:

"DEAR DEVIL,–Please take away Aunt Julia."